PENGUIN BOOKS

TRIAL BY SILENCE

Perumal Murugan is the star of contemporary Tamil literature. An award-winning writer, poet and scholar, he has garnered both critical acclaim and commercial success for his vast array of work. Some of his novels have been translated into English to immense acclaim, including *Seasons of the Palm*, which was shortlisted for the Kiriyama Prize in 2005, and *One Part Woman*, his best-known work, which was shortlisted for the Crossword Award and won the prestigious ILF Samanvay Bhasha Samman in 2015.

Aniruddhan Vasudevan is a performer, writer, translator and PhD student in anthropology at the University of Texas, Austin. His much-lauded translation of Perumal Murugan's *One Part Woman* has become an award-winning bestseller.

A Lonely Harvest and *Trial by Silence*

'In both the books, Perumal, the consummate storyteller, is in top form and makes the reader come face to face with questions of morality, fairness, faithfulness, family, grief and hope time and again. He has the ability to speak of intimacy, lust and love with equal sincerity and ease. A generous and free writer, he shares his uncanny understanding of human nature'—*The News Minute*

Pyre

'Powerful and compelling'—International Booker Prize Committee

'*Pyre* is beautifully done, with flashbacks to the lovers' meeting in a soda shop, second thoughts as Saroja finds herself thinking fondly of the confinement of her old home and a further elopement to evade what prejudice threatens to bring down on them. The title promises a dramatic conclusion, and the book delivers'—*Guardian*

'A book marked with the same quality of luminous integrity and beauty seen in *Maadhorubaagan* (*One Part Woman*). What a world of hidden treasure is being unveiled by this writer and his sensitive translator . . . In reading someone like Murugan, there is always a sense of wonderment and mourning at the resonances lost in not reading in Tamil, but Aniruddhan translates with a fine ear that beautifully preserves the music of the original . . . I have yet to read an Indian author who writes of love as beautifully as Murugan does . . . the love between man and wife glows with a sweet, strong passion that draws you into its folds like the drowsy buzzing of bees on a heady summer afternoon . . . the tenderness pours off the pages like golden honey . . . This is Murugan's rich Kongu land, which he has mined so deeply and well. It's a barren, sun-scorched and unforgiving land but it comes blazingly alive in the writer's eloquent voice . . . To classify Perumal Murugan's books as *vattaara ilakkiyam* or sub-regional literature would be tragic, because he succeeds in universalising Kongu Nadu to such a degree that place and person fall away and all that remains is a hard and glittering gem of a story'—*The Hindu*

'Murugan's *Pyre* is haunted by its title—a word that appears nowhere in the novel, but contributes to the growing sense of dread and desperation that shadows it . . . [A] very readable English version by Vasudevan . . . In addition to drawing the reader into Murugan's Tamil-language environment, Vasudevan also signals the subtle differences in dialect, distinguishing Saroja's speech from Kumaresan's. The translation succeeds in reminding the reader of the work's non-Western, multilingual setting, without compromising the fluency of the narrative'—*New York Times Book Review*

'A novel with a title like *Pyre* is unlikely to have a happy ending. Nevertheless, the journey towards this inevitable outcome delivers a disturbing insight into human bigotry and brutality whose application extends far beyond the novel's treatment of inter-caste marriage in contemporary Tamil Nadu . . . The translation from the original Tamil relies on simple English and the occasional American idiom yet comprehensively captures the claustrophobic atmosphere in which the lovers exist'—*The Asian Review of Books*

'The prose is deceptively simple and sparse. And yet it has the effect of hitting you hard like the blazing sun, the parched land, the rock and the thorny karuvelum shrubs . . . Perumal Murugan, a poet and a scholar, knows how to handle masterful imagery and human emotions. Especially when he delves into the emotional space of his women characters, be it a coarse, unloving mother-in-law or the soft, sparrow-like, bewildered new bride . . . It is a sensitive translation done with great care. There is not a single word that jars, and the narrative is more tightly woven . . . It will haunt the reader for a long time'—*Indian Express*

'Murugan gives us a tight narrative, a memorable love story, and a truly unforgettable ending'—*Chicago Review of Books*

'An acclaimed writer in his native India, Murugan skilfully contrasts the young couple's innocence with the increasingly caustic attacks on their marital union. His spare prose mesmerizes, and Vasudevan's translation of the original Tamil conveys both meaning and needed context for Western English readers. India's casteism is on full display, but what makes this novel so powerful is how Murugan shows that intolerance, cruelty and bigotry are universal traits of humankind, even while tailored to the peculiarity of each society. Universal too, are the love, kindness and familial bonds that exist between individuals who have the sensitivity to look beyond societal custom and coercion . . . A haunting story of forbidden love set in southern India that illustrates the cruel consequences of societal intolerance'—Kirkus Reviews (starred review)

'Murugan delivers a powerful fable of star-crossed lovers and societal intolerance . . . Murugan describes rural life in piercing detail, making the everyday toil and inner lives of humble people the backdrop to the unfolding drama of escalating threats from Kumaresan's relatives and neighbours. The simple, elegant prose of Vasudevan's translation ranges from poetic to suspenseful as the hopeful innocence of young love bristles against tradition and Saroja faces increasing danger from the villagers . . . Murugan deserves worldwide recognition'— Publishers Weekly (starred review)

'It is one of those books that will forever haunt one, especially the dramatically chilling end. It is seminal reading. It is stories that like this that bring out the rich diversity of Indian literature.'—Jaya Bhattacharji Rose

'[A] sensitive, richly textured translation . . . Murugan writes with cinematic power, and the final images of *Pyre* will sear your heart'— *Business Standard*

One Part Woman

'Murugan's unsurpassed ability to capture Tamil speech lays bare the complex organism of the society he adeptly portrays . . .'—Meena Kandasamy, *Guardian*

'The life of an innocent couple, who are led to believe that the expectations of the system define their pursuit of happiness forms Perumal Murugan's captivating story of love and desire. With his brilliant artistry, he captures the ups and downs of their lives. Works such as these have the power to subject contemporary value systems to intense introspection, it is for the same reason they are met with resistance. This work of art by Perumal Murugan can be acclaimed as modern mythology for its unusual access to cultural memories of the land and language, and the extraordinary courage with which it is dealt'—Vivek Shanbhag, author of *Ghachar Ghochar*

'It is rare to come across a writer who enjoys such intimacy with a land and those who live in close contact with it. *One Part Woman* is so rooted in the soil of tradition that its rebellion against it is all the more unexpected and moving'—Amitava Kumar, author of *Immigrant, Montana*

'Perumal Murugan's Tamil is vivid and terse, an instrument he uses with great care and precision to cut through the dense meshes of rural Tamil social life. The result, in this novel, is a brutally elegant examination of caste, family and sex in South India'—Anuk Arudpragasam, author of *The Story of a Brief Marriage*

'It's poignant, funny and painful and will expose readers of English to a region and class they likely haven't seen represented in literature . . . Murugan has an ear for the gentle absurdities of marriage as well as sympathy for his characters' woes'—Kirkus Reviews

'Murugan works his themes with a light hand; they always emanate from his characters, who are endowed with enough contradiction and mystery to keep from devolving into mouthpieces . . . I'm hoping for a whole shelf of books from this writer'—*New York Times*

'Beautiful . . . Plunges readers into Tamil culture through a story of love within a caste system undergoing British colonization in the early nineteenth century . . . Murugan's touching, harrowing love story captures the toll that infertility has on a marriage in a world where having a child is the greatest measure of one's worth'—*Publishers Weekly* (starred review)

'Perumal Murugan brings a playful, fable-like quality to his tale of traditional values and their subversion'—*Vanity Fair*

'Intimate and affecting . . . Throughout the novel, Murugan pits the individual against the group. How far you willing to go, he asks, in order to belong? . . . The true pleasure of this book lies in his adept explorations of male and female relationships, and in his unmistakable affection for people who find themselves pitted against the world'—*New York Times Book Review*

'Translated by Aniruddhan Vasudevan, this novel from the globally bestselling Murugan will give fans of South Asian fiction a new perspective and fans of excellent historical fiction a new read'—*Literary Hub*

'Perumal Murugan's *One Part Woman* contains the sweetest, most substantial portrait of an Indian marriage in recent fiction. A touching and original novel'—Karan Mahajan, author of *The Association of Small Bombs*

'A superb book in which tenderness, love and desire kindle each other into a conflagration of sexual rapture'—Bapsi Sidhwa, author of *Water*

'Perumal Murugan opens up the layers of desire, longing, loss and fulfilment in a relationship with extraordinary sensitivity and surgical precision'—Ambai, author of *In a Forest, A Deer*

'Perumal Murugan turns an intimate and crystalline gaze on a married couple in interior Tamil Nadu. It is a gaze that lays bare the intricacies of their story, culminating in a heart-wrenching denouement that allows no room for apathy . . . *One Part Woman* is a powerful and insightful rendering of an entire milieu which is certainly still in existence. [Murugan] handles myriad complexities with an enviable sophistication, creating an evocative, even haunting, work . . . Murugan's writing is taut and suspenseful . . . Aniruddhan Vasudevan's translation deserves mention—the language is crisp, retaining local flavour without jarring, and often lyrical'—*The Hindu Business Line*

'This is a novel of many layers; of richly textured relationships; of raw and resonant dialogues and characters . . . Perumal Murugan's voice is distinct; it is the voice of writing in the Indian languages rich in characters, dialogues and locales that are unerringly drawn and intensely evocative. As the novel moves towards its inevitable climax, tragic yet redemptive, the reader shares in the anguish of the characters caught in a fate beyond their control. It is because a superb writer has drawn us adroitly into the lives of those far removed from our acquaintance'—*Indian Express*

'Murugan imbues the simple story of a young couple, deeply in love and anxious to have a child, with the complexities of convention, obligation and, ultimately, conviction . . . An engaging story'—*Time Out* (India)

Resolve

'*Resolve* is an extended meditation on the politics of marriage in India'—Scroll.in

'Translated with an elegance that reflects Murugan's deep understanding of the unbreakable links between farmers and their land, Resolve is a searing indictment of the skewed gender equations in India'—*Financial Express*

'*Resolve* is a typical Perumal Murugan story that beautifully brings out typical problems faced by rural societies. Translated from the original *Kanganam*, Aniruddhan Vasudevan's translation works beautifully . . .'—*The Hindu Business Line*

'Replete with marriage brokers, horoscopes and rejections as is signature to the tradition of Indian arranged marriages, this seemingly comical book is a treasure waiting to be discovered by a reader'—*The Telegraph*

Current Show

'*Current Show* will force you to pause and ponder on the impermanence of our experiences. It will make you involuntarily sending up a prayer in gratefulness. Pick up this book on a day when you feel that you've been dealt a bad hand'—Anjana Balakrishnan, *The News Minute*

Seasons of the Palm

The writing is filled with grace and compassion and bears a fable-like quality'—The Quint

Rising Heat

'With news about the climate crisis and environment taking centre stage in the last few years, this moving book is still as relevant today as it was when it first released in 1991. Through this novel, Murugan makes the readers question the human cost and true value of never-ending development in the name of progress and urbanisation'—Times of India

trial by silence

PERUMAL MURUGAN

Translated from the Tamil by
Aniruddhan Vasudevan

PENGUIN BOOKS

An imprint of Penguin Random House

PENGUIN BOOKS

USA | Canada | UK | Ireland | Australia
New Zealand | India | South Africa | China | Singapore

Penguin Books is part of the Penguin Random House group of companies
whose addresses can be found at global.penguinrandomhouse.com

Published by Penguin Random House India Pvt. Ltd
4th Floor, Capital Tower 1, MG Road,
Gurugram 122 002, Haryana, India

First published in Tamil as *Ardhanaari* by Kalachuvadu Publications Pvt. Ltd,
Nagercoil 2014
First published in English in Penguin Books by Penguin Random House India 2018

Copyright © Perumal Murugan 2018
English translation copyright © Aniruddhan Vasudevan 2018

ISBN 9780143428336

Typeset in Adobe Caslon Pro by Manipal Digital Systems, Manipal

Printed at Manipal Technologies Limited, India

www.penguin.co.in

This is a legitimate digitally printed version of the book and therefore might not
have certain extra finishing on the cover.

CONTENTS

AUTHOR'S PREFACE TO THE
TAMIL EDITION
Let Him Live

Several readers of *One Part Woman* (*Madhorubagan*) wondered what would happen to Kali at the end of the novel. Eager to see if I could respond to their queries, I wrote two sequels.

Releasing everyone from the uncertainty of whether Kali survives or not, I let him live in *Ardhanaari* (*Trial by Silence*). Kali is a common man. And the world of common folk has very narrow boundaries. Much like Kali's barn. I tried to bring him out of this confined world and let him wander away a bit. But he was not capable of all that. He returned to the barn and confined himself to it. All right, let him live.

When I wrote this novel, I experienced a great freedom of mind. My mind and hands worked together with much ease. You can see the effects of that freedom in this novel. But now I wonder if so much freedom of mind is appropriate for these times. I don't think I will ever again experience that state of mind. Therefore, my mind celebrates this novel as one that emerged from the rarest of rare moments in life.

This is the second edition of this novel. I have made some changes in the text of the first edition. I request you to understand that this is a novel and, hence, fiction. That is, I want to emphasize that it is entirely a product of my imagination. In particular, I want to point out that the names that occur in the novel do not refer to any specific persons or places. In this novel, I have used various folk tales, descriptions of events, expressions and words. These were necessary for the world I was creating through words. Please read them with that understanding. If any of this turns out to be intolerable to you, I request you to kindly avoid reading the novel. Thank you.

Namakkal

26 November 2016

Perumal Murugan

TRANSLATOR'S NOTE

It has been my pleasure and privilege to translate Perumal Murugan's sequels to his celebrated Tamil novel *Madhorubagan*, which I translated to English some years ago. *One Part Woman* portrays the agrarian life of a loving young couple, Ponna and Kali, who are unable to conceive a child. The social expectations around marriage and childbirth and the couple's own intense longing for a child weigh heavily on them. Towards the end of the novel, we see Ponna going to a temple festival where, on one particular night, consensual union between any man and woman is sanctioned. She meets a man who—because custom accords him the status of a god for that one night—might help her get pregnant. The Tamil sequels *Aalavaayan* and *Ardhanaari* imagine two possible, alternative futures for Ponna—one as a widow after Kali's suicide, and the other a life with Kali, bearing his judgement, rejection and eloquent silence.

In *A Lonely Harvest* (*Aalavaayan*), we see Murugan detailing Ponna's life after Kali succeeds in committing suicide, unable to bear the thought that Ponna could have consented to being with another man, even if only for a night, even if only for the sake of a child and even if in a way sanctioned by custom. In this novel, we encounter Ponna's grief and confusion as well as the amazing ways in which solidarity, friendship and care operate among women. Her mother and mother-in-law close ranks around Ponna and do all they can to support her and protect her from the judgements of the world.

In *Trial by Silence* (*Ardhanaari*), Murugan imagines a different future, where Kali survives his suicide attempt but is unable to forgive Ponna or any of the others he holds responsible for ruining his marriage and life. Ponna is faced with Kali's incredible silence and withdrawal, his inability to even inhabit the same space as her. This novel, then, is a portrayal of the attempts at forgiveness, reconciliation and reclaiming of happiness and love.

I could not take 'Madhorubagan' simply to be the name of a deity and translate it as 'The Half-Female God', because the novel and its title are not about the deity in any significant sense. Despite its discussion of human attachments to divine forms, worship and practices, the novel is about the relationship between Kali and Ponna and their intense love for each other. It is about Kali's understanding that Ponna is an inseparable part of him—he is unable to imagine himself without her. And hence the intensity of his suffering when he sees her decision to go to the festival as a great betrayal of that oneness. Hence the poignance of his torment. Similarly, though at a superficially cultural level, the words 'Aalavaayan' and 'Ardhanaari' could be read as names of different forms of a deity, the novels have little to do with them. Translating them as such would have been misleading.

As someone who grew up in Tamil Nadu, and with caste and class backgrounds different from the one Murugan details in these novels, I am forever fascinated by both the familiar and the unfamiliar I find in his descriptions of people, land, food, customs, practices, animals, plants and so on. I have attempted to keep some balance of familiarity and distance alive in the translation. We find in these novels an agrarian world of a particular region in a not-so-distant past, with its social structures, relationships, values, possibilities and constraints. My focus has been on the tone, texture and feelings that rise up to meet us as we follow these richly imagined characters navigating their world.

It is not necessary to read *One Part Woman* in order to understand the sequels. Perumal Murugan's narrative beautifully catches you up with key aspects of the earlier novel's plot that animate and give force to these sequels and their imagination of alternative futures for the main characters.

I can only hope I am getting, at least, a little better at this work with every act of translation. And I hope you enjoy reading these novels.

Austin, Texas   Aniruddhan Vasudevan
19 September 2018

ONE

Kali stared ceaselessly at the stump on the portia tree where the branch had been cut down.

It looked very much like the sort of small stump that would stick out of the shoulder if an arm were severed from a body. He could still see the desiccated cuts left by the sickle on the bark. They looked like fish scales. It was he who had cut down the branch, having grown tired of his mother's insistence to get it done. That particular branch of the tree had been a favourite of his. He used to see it as the tree kindly lowering an arm towards him, lovingly asking him to climb on to it. In moments of excitement, he would jump up and grab hold of that branch. And he would swing from it until he couldn't bear the pain in his hands. At that point, he would heave himself to make a wide leap and land five or six feet away. The cow and oxen tethered in the tree's shade would look at him in amazement.

Once, when his uncle's children had come over for some festival, he set a swing on this very branch for them to play on. It took just a push for them to swing a great arc with nothing to hinder their movement. The branch held itself tight, much like the sturdy arms of a wrestler. No matter how hard the children swung from it, they never had to worry that the branch might break and fall. Kali was very sad that he eventually had to chop that branch off. But he had to—his mother was absolutely firm about that. In fact, she had wanted the entire tree to be felled. But since he had put up much resistance to that idea, she conceded to just severing that one branch.

When he looked at that branch in his beleaguered state that day, he felt as though it was calling out to him. He had already reached a point where he was considering death as the only way he could move past the impasse in his life. What an extraordinary situation it was. So many people had conspired to fool one man. His mother, mother-in-law, father-in-law, brother-in-law, Ponna. All the others might have consented to that plan. But how could Ponna? Surely, she wouldn't have agreed to the plan if she hadn't secretly desired to sleep with another man? In his blinding rage, his first impulse was to hack her down with the sickle, severing her head from her body. But if he did that, she would shudder and suffer for just a little while, and then die. And Kali would have had to bear the lifelong stigma of having murdered his wife. No, that wouldn't do. She needed to suffer for the rest of her life, agonizing constantly about what she had done. And he concluded that his death would be that perfect punishment for her.

He also thought that dying would put an end to his own torment. 'You should suffer for the rest of your life,' he said out loud, thinking of Ponna. He kept chanting this like a mantra for a little while. As he gritted his teeth and repeated the incantation again and again, he felt invigorated. He looked at the length of rope he had unravelled from the bundle of maize sheaths. It was an old rope, but it had several strong twining strands and it would never break. He picked up that rope and flung it over the branch, where it dangled like a snake. He pulled the other end and formed a noose. Then, realizing that he would need some object to stand on—if he were to carry out his grim plan—Kali looked around for something suitable. He spotted the big upturned basket in which they enclosed the chickens. When he picked it up, the chickens scattered in all directions, clucking in panic.

The day had not fully dawned yet. The light was so dim it seemed as though you were looking at things through a sieve. The chickens continued to run around in the darkness. Kali dropped the basket under the dangling rope. The chickens clucked even louder. At this hour, his mother, Seerayi, was headed towards the barnyard from her house in the village. She thought she would take care of all the cleaning work in the cattle shed since Kali was away. She had woken up very early, as soon as she heard the crows cawing from the tamarind trees in the village. Now as she neared the barnyard, she heard the ruckus of the chicken clucking about. Assuming it was some wildcat trying to hunt the chickens, she ran towards the enclosure, making noises to chase away the intruder. Then she saw that the gate was wide open. 'It must be a thief,' she thought, and was annoyed with herself for not staying overnight in the barnyard and keeping an eye on things. As she ran in, she saw Kali. She could tell it was him even though everything was cloaked in shadow. And the moment she saw the basket and the rope, she understood.

She ran to him, beating herself on the chest, crying, 'My god! My precious boy!' and flung herself on the ground, firmly holding on to his legs to keep him from proceeding. Her grip was like iron shackles. Kali could not move even an inch. Angry that she had come at just that precise moment, he tried to kick himself free of her, shouting, 'Let go of me!' But she did not loosen her grip. He was amazed that a scrawny woman like her possessed so much strength. He felt like a rat caught in a trap. He calmed down a bit and again said, 'Let go of me.'

'I have kept myself alive all these years just for your sake!' Seerayi shouted. 'Hang me on that rope! Witness me shudder and die before you decide to kill yourself. This tree has plenty of branches to hang from!'

Her desperate plea brought him to his senses. 'All right, Amma,' he said. 'I won't do anything to myself. Don't worry. Let go of me.' He was still trying to extricate himself from her hold.

'Promise me you won't,' she said. 'On my life.'

'On your life. I promise,' he said.

'Promise me, with the goddess Koolithaayi as witness.'

'I promise, with the goddess Koolithaayi as witness. Let go of me.' By now, he was also concerned that if anyone were to witness this scene it would be a source of much embarrassment.

Seerayi let go of him immediately and pushed away the basket, before falling flat on the ground. Kali finally found his bearings. He realized that if his mother had not come at the right time, he wouldn't be witnessing the new, red dawn.

Kali walked to the pot of water kept near the cattle shed, only to discover that it was less than half-full. He had to reach in deep before his hand could scoop up any water. Had he stayed in the barnyard the night before, he would have replenished the various pots and tubs by now. He picked up the little piece of soap kept nearby and washed his face. He also drank some water and sat down right there, panting.

Meanwhile, Seerayi had sat up and started beating her chest, singing:

> *When even ripe and old palmyra leaves are shining and*
> *thriving here*
> *The fresh new leaf wants to take leave*
> *When even dead trees are blossoming forth*
> *The fresh young tree wants to uproot itself*
> *When old fronds are holding firm*
> *The fresh new frond wants to fall*

When withered trees are standing tall
The healthy tree here insists on dying

By this time, Kali had been completely shaken out of the desire to die. He was fully aware of the world around him. He looked over the fence. If anyone walking along the path, taking their cattle out, were to hear this song of lament, they might come in to inquire what was going on. And if they saw the rope, they would go and tell the entire village that Kali had tried to hang himself. After that, he would have to explain his actions to everyone. In just one second, his fate had changed. And his mind, which had just moments ago been filled with rage, was now a tumult of embarrassment and shame. He shouted at Seerayi, 'I am still alive, aren't I? Why are you singing this dirge now? Think of the shame if anyone hears it.'

She rose quickly from where she was sitting and rushed to him. Holding his head in her hands, she said, 'What went so wrong in your life that you had to consider killing yourself? You are talking about shame and honour now? If I had come even a second late, you would have dishonoured me for the rest of my life!'

Kali started sobbing. 'All of you have conspired to dishonour *me*! Why do I need to live? How can I claim to be a man in this world ever again?' He walked away and sat down on the cot.

She went closer, gently caressed his head, and said, 'My little god, please don't think of it that way. We did it for your own good. You are still a child, you don't know what is good and what is bad for you. It is my job to do the right thing. And that's what I did.'

She went closer, gently caressed his head, and said, 'My little boy, please don't think of it that way. We did it for your own good. You are still a child, you don't know what is good and what is bad for you. It is my job to do the right thing. And that's what I did.'

TWO

'My dear boy,' pleaded Seerayi, 'whatever it is, let us talk about it. Don't even think about killing yourself.' And she looked at the portia tree and the rope hanging from it. 'We cannot have this tree here any more. It has become Yaman to the very person who planted and nurtured it. Bring me the axe, let's chop it down right away!' She stood up in a rage. 'This tree has asked for a sacrifice. Let us sacrifice the tree itself.'

Kali stopped sobbing. 'We humans do all sorts of things. How can the poor tree be blamed for that? Besides, although it wouldn't take long to chop down this tree, just think about how many years it takes to grow one.'

'So you have one sense of fairness for trees and another for people? This earth and the time I have spent on it—both have borne witness to all that I have endured as a single mother raising you. But here you were, trying to end that life I nurtured, and you would have done it in a matter of minutes. Tell me, if you die today, will you be able to replace yourself? Bring me a little boy to raise?' Seerayi spoke in anger, but even as she said these words, she realized this was perhaps not the best time to reason with him. So she said, 'All right. We don't have to cut down the entire tree, but let us at least chop off this branch. Come.' She pulled him by the hand. He fetched the sickle, climbed the tree a bit unsteadily and started chopping down the branch. It was quite a robust one. He thought he might use it to fashion a bow or to make a picotah. But he was also surprised that even at such a moment his mind dwelled on matters of land and farming.

Seerayi untied the cows and oxen from the shade of the tree and took them out, all the while checking if people were up and about. She could see that there were a few people already walking along the common path outside, but she knew that no visitors would come by so early in the morning. The big branch fell down with a loud noise. The place from where it had been chopped off looked like a wide wailing mouth. Kali threw down the sickle and calmly climbed down the tree. At any other time, he might have just jumped down, but right then he was not in the frame of mind to do that. As he sat down on the cot, he felt overwhelmed by a sudden exhaustion and the need to sleep. His body ached and demanded that he lay right there and sleep for several hours.

Meanwhile, no one had cleared the cattle floor of all the dung. The chickens were now scattering the dung all over the place, looking for food to peck on. Seerayi made some sounds, attracting their attention. They all came to her. She was ready with some corn to feed them. As the chickens came closer, she dropped some corn in the gap between her feet. The roosters beat the others to it—they came running and started to peck at the seeds of corn. Then all the rest joined in and soon it was a large crowd of chickens around Seerayi. When they least expected it, Seerayi swiftly reached down and grabbed a rooster firmly with both her hands.

The rooster struggled to set itself free. The other chickens scattered away at this commotion but soon they were cautiously inching back towards the corn. The rooster persisted in its struggle with Seerayi. It was part of a big brood of chickens. A young rooster. Seerayi reached for a small rope from the ground and tied it around the rooster's legs. Then she tied the other end of the rope to a pole on the side of the hut. The rooster was still trying to free itself and reach for its food.

Seerayi then picked up the pot she had filled with water just a little while ago. The water was cold. She called out to Kali just as he was getting ready to lie down on the cot. He walked up to her when, without warning, she poured all the water from the pot over his head. 'What is this, Amma!' Kali muttered. Then he removed his veshti and stood in his loincloth. That one pot of water didn't feel enough for him. He picked up the wide-mouthed pot that was nearby and emptied that water over himself too. Meanwhile, Seerayi brought a dry loincloth for him to change into. He changed into it and wiped himself with the towel she gave him. With the same towel, he also dried his hair, which had come undone and now fell over his upper back.

Whether it was from last night's drinking or from sheer exhaustion, he couldn't tell, but he felt sleep overtaking him. Seerayi, however, did not let him fall asleep. There was one thing she still needed him to do. She asked him to untie the rooster and make an offering of it under the tree. She held the rooster's head firmly to make sure it didn't scream while he chopped off the head.

'All right,' she then said. 'You go and sleep well. Don't start thinking about anything. I will wake you up once I have finished cooking. I will take care of the cattle.'

Kali's hair was still wet. So he let it stay untied and lay down on the cot inside the hut. He thought, 'It looks like that small creature had to die so that a big creature could live. Who knows when the lord of death comes for whom?' He then fell into a deep sleep.

Even though Seerayi could not fully guess what might have transpired during Kali's trip out of town the day before, she was certain of one thing: Kali now knew everything. She felt that it was goddess Koolithaayi who had sent her to the barnyard at just the right moment. Seerayi let all the blood from the rooster drain out under the portia tree. She spoke to the tree: 'Is this enough blood for you? Did we let you grow and thrive here all these years so that you can take one of our lives? You must end it all with this offering, all right?' Then she carried the rooster's body and head and put them in a basket. Covering the basket with palm fronds, she placed it inside the shed. She looked at Kali sleeping peacefully on the cot, and was overcome with great sadness. 'You might have been dead and lying on the bier by now,' she said. She felt that it might comfort her to cry and sing out loud. But she stopped herself because she knew this was not the right time. She just mumbled to herself, 'This is the time for you to lie on cots that have legs. It is not yet time for you to lie on a legless bier.'

She then walked to a corner of the barnyard. Gathering five or six palm fronds drying there, she placed them together. She then tried to untie the rope from the felled branch. The knot had hardened. It made all her sadness well up again. She cried, mumbling, 'There is the field, there is the hearth, and there is the woman you married. What reason do you have to tie a rope and make a noose?' She fetched the sickle and cut at the knot, tugging it free of the branch at last. As she held one end of it, it hung straight down from her hand, with the noose dangling at the other end. For a second, she felt as though her own neck had been caught in that noose. She shook her head to get that image out of her mind.

Then she dropped the rope on the fronds she had laid down together on the ground. She worked in an agitated manner, consumed in the frenzy and excitement that came with the realization that she had just managed to stop someone from dying. She then tried to drag the branch away, but it was large and expansive, covering the ground in a wide arc. She was unable move it. But she didn't want to leave it lying there. When she looked out towards the fields, she saw the oxen tethered there. She fetched them and tied the branch to the ropes on their necks in such a way that it lay between them. Then as she raised her voice to make them move, the oxen walked ahead, dragging the branch along.

The end of that thick and long branch was covered in leaves and stalks. It looked like there might be some difficulty getting it through the barnyard's gate, but the oxen had no difficulty at all; they dragged it away with great ease. Once they had taken it away to the stretch of wasteland away from the fields and the barnyard, she brought the oxen back and secured them in their place again. Then she picked up the basket in which she had placed the rooster's body and head and walked to the fields. There was a hoe hanging from a branch of the palai tree near the well. With that, she dug a pit about three feet deep right next to the tree, and buried the rooster in it. She then ran back to the barnyard. Kali was still sleeping soundly.

Seerayi still had a lot of work to finish. She remembered all the tasks. Cow dung lay scattered about on the floor of the cattle enclosure. The sheep were bleating. There was no water in the large earthen pot. But first she fed the chickens again and caught another fowl. A nice robust hen, heavy and firm. It too was destined to die today. Holding it by its feet, she slammed its head against the slab in front of the shed. The hen died with just one croak. Seerayi then carried it to the spot where she had laid the palm fronds and the rope. She started plucking the chicken. Its body was still warm. That—as well as the fact that the hen was tender because it was poised to lay eggs soon—made it easier for her to pluck off the feathers. She only tore away the big feathers. The small ones would be consumed by the fire. She then set fire to the fronds. They caught fire first, and then the rope too. She held the chicken in the fire. The rope didn't burn easily. It smoked, resisted the flame. She made sure the fronds burnt well. And when the fire grew stronger, that rope which might have taken away Kali's life caught fire at last and burnt, hissing and sizzling like a raging snake.

THREE

As Seerayi went about completing all the chores in the barnyard, she kept an eye on Kali. He slumbered like he had not done so in ages. Her plan was to cook the chicken and some saaru before waking him up. All the ingredients she needed for cooking were in the shed—right there in the barnyard. They had cooked there in the past. There was also an old, large grinding stone she could use. This was good, because she did not want to leave Kali alone and go all the way to her house in the village quarters to do the cooking. She had not even imagined that he would go to the extent of wanting to kill himself. She had thought that he might be a little difficult initially but would eventually calm down. Seerayi had been instrumental in sending Ponna to the big temple festival.

The Karattur festival lasted three months. People would start preparing for it as soon as the month of Maasi began. All the shops and entertainments that sprang up around the festival would stay on till Panguni or even Chithirai.

But the actual festival lasted only for twenty-two days. And for most people, the twenty-third day would be the day of feasting and meat-eating. The most important days were the day the deity came down from the hillock and the day the deity was taken back up. An incredible crowd gathered to get a glimpse of the deity. The night the deity returned to the hillock was the most significant event of the festival.

People usually started coming in on the morning of that day, on foot and on bullock carts from various villages and towns—it would look like an army marching. En route to the place were small makeshift stalls providing free drinking water for everyone. All the fields surrounding the village lay fallow and unused during that period. Even if there had been some rains, the farmers would stop with some superficial ploughing and let the fields be. All the bullock carts that came to the village for the festival were parked in these fields. On that one day, no one squabbled over ownership or encroachment of land. In fact, there were so many bullocks in the fields that one would wonder if this was a fair selling oxen. Visitors brought large parcels of food with them. But even if they didn't, there were stalls in the festival grounds they could eat from. Some people brought hens and roosters with them to make an offering for another deity, Poochisaami, the next day. They would complete the offering, cook and eat the fowl, and only then lock their bullocks back to their carts. Several cultural performances and entertainments were staged in all the eight streets of the village. Flaming torches and lanterns would transform the festival grounds, as though brightening the night into day. The usually untrodden, dusty streets would come alive with the pattering feet of the passing crowds. There were four ponds in the village. The women of the village would fetch water from these ponds and sprinkle them on the streets to keep the ground cool and the dust settled.

This was a time for people to come together and rejoice. Toddy and arrack were sold in the outskirts of the festival area. Shops selling puttu and various snacks enticed people with their fragrances. Policemen constantly patrolled the streets. Despite that, at the pinnacle of the celebrations, all rules and norms were shattered when the torches were dimmed. Only the night bore witness to itself. Darkness fell like a veil over all faces. Only the full moon did its best to cast some light, show some support. It was during these nocturnal celebrations that the primal urges in all men would surface.

At first, Kali was under pressure to marry and bring home a second wife. The fact that he and Ponna hadn't had a child for twelve years was a source of much grief. But since Kali refused to marry again, it was Seerayi who spoke to him about this festival and suggested they send Ponna there. He did not, however, consent to that either. His heart simply could not accept it. The mere broaching of this topic had been enough to shatter Kali's peace of mind. He constantly thought about it and felt conflicted. He was not willing to send Ponna to the festival. Besides, he was not sure he could accept as his own a child given by some unknown man. He thought that if such a thing were to ever happen, Ponna was sure to lose all respect for him. He was also afraid that everyone would take that as confirmation of Kali's impotence. He tormented himself, agonizing over all these questions. Things dragged on in this way for two years. But finally this year they had decided to send Ponna to the festival without Kali's knowledge. His brother-in-law took him to a grove far away, where he got him drunk on toddy and arrack. And they tricked Ponna into thinking she had Kali's permission to go to the festival. But when Kali found out about it later that night, he rushed back to the barnyard, feeling betrayed by everyone.

He could not bring himself to accept that Ponna had been with another man that night. Their lives were entwined inextricably. He could not bear the idea of another man leaving his smell over Ponna's body. Her body was linked to his forever. It had taken his fragrances upon itself for twelve years. No one could prise their two bodies apart. He felt that every inch of her body belonged to him. It would be a blemish if her body were to be stained by the scent of any other man. And Kali said to himself firmly that once that body was tainted, he wouldn't touch it. If it was true that all men were gods on that night, then let that god enter Kali's body too. If it was a true god, it ought to help Ponna conceive through Kali. Why was the deity refusing to inhabit him?

He had heard before that several of the children in the village had been born this way. But he didn't believe any of that. It was possible that people did these things in the olden days. But that didn't mean they had to continue doing those things, did it? There must have been a time when a younger brother had access to his older brother's wife, or an older brother thought of his younger brother's wife as his. But would people accept such a thing today? When Nallayyan Uncle was claiming his share of inheritance—which his brothers coveted—he had offered, 'Let my sisters-in-law supply me with milk. I will give them my share of the property.' But did they accept the proposal? In the olden days, people lived in large families. Not any more. These days, families were together until the last son got married. After that, they went their own separate ways, chased off just like a crow sends away its chicks to fend for themselves. Certain things might have been acceptable in those days. But that did not mean they had to be acceptable now. Times had changed.

At weddings, there is a ritual in which the bride's maternal uncle carries her on his shoulder and brings her to the wedding altar. But recently, at a wedding that took place in Kullur, the bridegroom had said, 'I cannot bear the sight of some other man touching and lifting my wife. Let us not do that.' Apparently, the maternal uncle went away in a huff. Well, let him! Was the wedding important or the uncle? Kali too felt similarly about Ponna, that she was his alone. So he felt utterly let-down that Ponna had gone to the festival despite his objection. In a bid to punish her for the rest of her life, he had thrown a rope on the portia tree and made a noose.

That night, neither Kali nor Ponna got any sleep. Even Seerayi could not sleep. She had stayed in the barnyard until the full moon was overhead. Then she fed the cows and oxen again and, thinking that it would now be safe to leave the barnyard unattended, went to her house in the village to catch a wink.

Seerayi's lips had kept muttering all night long, 'Devaatha, please show my daughter-in-law a way out of this misery.' She lay down on the cot in her house, but she did not sleep; she only kept tossing and turning. It had occurred to her that she might as well have stayed in the barnyard. She was concerned about her daughter-in-law that night, but she failed to think of her son. Perhaps that was what was unacceptable to god. She had no idea that Kali had returned to the barnyard. Thinking that he was still away at his father-in-law's, Seerayi woke up very early the next morning and walked back to the barnyard. She had to feed the cattle and clear out all the dung. If Kali was in town, she wouldn't have to do any of these chores. But it was only when she walked into the barnyard that she saw Kali preparing to hang himself from the portia tree.

Today, as she kept going about her chores, her mind was always on Kali. She had managed to stop him from suicide once. For some people, that put an end to that line of thought. But there are others whose will to die grows stronger and stronger—and that suicidal impulse would seek out another such opportunity. That was why she kept a close watch over Kali. Looking at him sleep now no one would guess such a thing had transpired only that morning. She had finished boiling rice and cooking some chicken in a thick gravy, and now sat wondering if he would wake up anytime soon. Earlier, when she went to fetch the cattle from the pasture, she ran into Kaaraan. She sent a message with him to Ponna's family in Adaiyur—that Kali was back, and that since he had to take care of the cows and oxen here, he would stay put and that they would offer a chicken and make their own feast here in the barnyard, and that Ponna could stay at her parents' home for a few days more and not rush back. When she offered him eight annas for this job, he took the money and set about happily. He anticipated that when he conveyed the news at Ponna's parents' home, they might give him eight annas more or even a rupee. Also, even though he would get to eat lamb at his own house, he might still get to eat chicken at Ponna's.

Seerayi knew that if she did not inform them that Kali was back, someone from there might come looking for him—and that would complicate matters immeasurably, given Kali's current state of mind. There would be loud arguments and accusations, and the entire village would come to know of the situation. But if she could find a way to avoid all of that for a few days, it was likely that Kali's anger would subside. By then, she thought, she might even be able to get him to see things in perspective. After all, Kali never talked back at her. He mostly agreed with her. His mother had raised him single-handedly, enduring many difficulties. And he was always one to make sure he never hurt her in any way. If he did not agree with something she said, he usually just kept quiet. He would later express his disagreement very gently. Seerayi was aware of all this, and now she set about strategizing the ways in which she would handle him.

Kali was very fond of the chicken dish she made. Ponna took much care with cooking this particular dish, but he always told her that it did not match the one his mother made. 'I am doing it exactly like your mother does,' Ponna would insist. 'It is the same chillies. It is the same castor oil. I grind it all in the same stone. Then how come it does not taste the same?' And he would reply, 'You need something else too—some deftness of hand.' But she'd disagree, laughing. 'No, no. Nothing of that sort. Your mother does not add water when she grinds the paste. She just spits into it twice. That's why it stinks so badly.' But that never made him angry. He would just say, 'All right then. Why don't you spit into it next time? Let's see how that tastes. It might even intoxicate like Muniyannan's arrack.' She would blush at this remark, and say, 'Then why do you go there to get drunk? I can spit in your food every day.'

The chicken Seerayi had chosen to cook was young and fresh. It might have even started laying its very first eggs in four or five days. She had carefully removed the little, newly forming eggs—more like egg blossoms, she thought—and had fried it separately in the ladle in which she crackled seasoning. Kali was particularly fond of that. If she were to feed him all this lovingly prepared food, and then speak to him carefully about things, he would certainly listen to her. In her mind, she rehearsed how that conversation would go.

FOUR

It was midday and Kali was still sleeping. Seerayi went near the cot to take a closer look. He had not spread even a thin piece of cloth over the cot before lying down. The coir weave had pressed into his skin, leaving its impression. The loincloth was all he was wearing. His abdomen looked like a wilted plantain leaf. 'There is nothing in there,' she thought. He had not eaten anything. He must be very hungry. Kali's legs stretched out beyond the edge of the cot. The hair on his head was thick and long, like women's tresses. It looked like he had applied castor oil on it the day before, since he was travelling out of town. Now it glistened with a dark oiliness, and as it lay spread out over the cot, it looked like a dam containing him. He had a broad face, like two palms held together side by side. He has shaved his beard and trimmed his moustache. And he had a wide chest. It occurred to Seerayi that Kali was a bigger and healthier-looking man than his father had ever been.

Several years ago, when Kali told her that he wanted to marry Ponna, Seerayi's first thought was whether Ponna would be a physical match to his strong, stone-idol-like body. She had not responded right away, but after a few minutes she asked, 'Is she a good match for you?' He had not quite understood what she meant. Thinking that she was asking about Ponna's character, he said, 'Yes, yes, she is a girl of very good character.' Then Seerayi had to ask more explicitly. 'Not that, you idiot! Here you are, built like a big black tree. What if she is built like a mouse! That's what I meant.' He had laughed. And Seerayi felt bad that her remark had amounted to casting an evil eye on her own son. As they say, the proud gaze of parents causes more damage than the jealous and evil eye cast by townspeople, relatives, the deformed and the widowed. So on that day, she used some chillies to perform a little ritual to ward off any evil eye she might have inadvertently cast on him. Now when she thought about how Kali might have reduced this strong, living body into a dead one that morning, she was reminded of her husband.

Kali's father too had been hale and hearty before he died suddenly. It was the month of Aadi. In all the fields across the village, the ragi crop had grown well and stood proud and lush. But that was also the time rats attacked the crops. So the farmers formed groups to hunt and kill the rats. They would set the traps on one side of a field and chase the rats into those traps from the other side. Kali's father was among the people engaged in the hunt. He had accidentally stepped on a trap as he tried to avoid tripping over an old, petrified rat on the way. He died even before they brought him home. Had he been alive, Seerayi's life would have been much easier. He had loved her just the way Kali loved Ponna.

Kali now looked a lot like his father. Seerayi touched him gently, trying to wake him up. But he didn't budge. So she shook him more vigorously. Usually he would waken at the gentlest touch. In fact, if the cows mooed even once, his eyes would open right away. It made her fearful now that Kali was not waking up. She even wondered if he might have mixed some poison in the arrack he drank before he tried to hang himself. She couldn't even count the number of people who died by mixing ground arali seeds into their toddy or arrack. Growing agitated at these thoughts, Seerayi now slapped his cheek and called out, 'Kaliyappa . . . Kaliyappa!'

He opened his eyes to be greeted by his mother's face right in front of him. It took him a while to find his bearings. Then she asked him to eat.

'I don't want anything,' he said and turned over.

Upset, she said, 'Look here, I have cooked chicken gravy. I have not eaten either. I have been waiting for you to wake up. If you are not eating, I am not eating anything either. There!'

He sat up, irritated. 'Why are you acting like this, Amma?' he snapped, and stepped outside. He had never experienced daylight so intensely before. It disoriented him. Holding a hand over his eyes, he walked over to the pot and splashed some water over his face. Only then did he feel even a little steady, and slowly came to his senses. He looked up to know the time. It was a little past midday. The sun had passed overhead and had started its descent on the other side.

'Did you eat anything at all this morning?' he asked as he stepped inside the hut.

By then, Seerayi had placed food ready on two plates. She gave one to him, saying, 'What do you think? Considering what you were about to do this morning, do you think I was capable of swallowing food?'

He took the plate from her and sat down on the cot to eat. Slowly, he mixed the curry with the rice. His mind was now light and blank. She had put a lot of meat over the rice. He now moved the pieces of meat aside and just ate a mouthful of the rice mixed with the thick gravy. She kept looking at him as he ate. He ate the first mouthful without showing any interest in the food, but after that he slowly seemed to register the taste. So when he started eating patiently and with some relish, she was relieved. She ate a little too. She paid attention to his plate and served him more meat. Even though her mind was clear, she still found herself sighing frequently.

He ate to his heart's content and lay down again on the cot. Seerayi did not comment on that; she let him sleep as much as he wanted. She took charge of all the things that needed to be done that day. Kali woke up at dusk and stepped outside and sat down on a rock. He could see his mother doing all the chores, but he did not feel the urge to do anything himself. He just sat there for a while. Then he ate his dinner, and he ate well. After that, he set the cot right outside the hut and lay there, awake. This was the first time he was experiencing such an emptiness of mind for so many hours. He found it pleasant. Seerayi came and sat down on the rock nearby and started talking to him.

'Kaliyappa . . . look here. You have promised me, so you should not do anything like that ever again, all right? If you die, what is there for me to live for? I will grab hold of your feet and just follow you where you go. But then what would Ponna do on her own? Don't you know how much she loves you? Even I might hesitate for a moment to give up my life after you. But she—she would follow you right away. Did I endure all those hardships only to see our family ruined? What's the point in dying? If we die today, the world still carries on tomorrow. The point is to live well and show that to the world. Do you know how much I have had to endure? The difficulties I had to overcome until you grew up and became a responsible man . . .'

He was listening to her.

'Do you know how the men in this village behaved?' she went on. 'As soon as night fell, they would knock on my door, throw stones at the house, shout out my name . . . No matter how much they persisted, I never opened the door. Our Nallayyan. You know him. Don't judge him too kindly. He said to me, "Sister-in-law, live with me. I will bequeath my property to your son." I said to him, "Get lost. All your wealth isn't worth even a single strand of hair on my leg." I was only thinking of you all the time—the one person I could call mine, the one person I needed to protect from any suffering. That was why I stayed strong.'

He was still listening to her.

'When there is a child in your life, it is a whole other matter. That is when you feel you have a hold on life. You have been yearning for a child, and you have shut yourself up in this barnyard. And there in the house Ponna lies staring at the ceiling. I could not bear to see the two of you suffer so much. That was why I made that suggestion. I could have taken her there myself without saying a word about it to you. But she wouldn't have agreed to it without your permission. That was why I spoke about it to you first. Even now Ponna thinks you consented to it. Would she have gone otherwise?'

He continued to listen to her.

'We have not done anything that other people in this world don't do, have we? You know the old man in Madakkaadu, don't you? Do you know his name? It's Maacchaami. In those days, people revered him for being a god-given child. He was born after his father and mother had been childless for ten years. Aren't they living well? What have they lost because of this? Why—do you know how many women go to another man even when they have their own husbands? Did I recommend that? This festival has been happening for ages. We pray and promise various kinds of offerings to god. This too is such an appeal. We say to god, "You give me a child. I will name the child after you . . ."'

And he listened.

'Do you think I was unaware of all the times *you* went to this festival? You used to look so radiant on those occasions. I did not want to stop you. I did not want to come in the way of your enjoyment. If Ponna accuses you of having been with another woman, what would you say to her? Or is it one sense of justice for you and a different one for her? Tell me. Look here, this was entirely my idea. You should not blame anyone else for this. Your parents-in-law, or your brother-in-law, Muthu—everyone acted according to my plan. If anyone is at fault here, it is me. Accuse me any which way you want. Hit me and kill me, if that's what you want to do. This portia tree has so many more branches left. If you hang me on one of these, I will die happily. But please don't blame Ponna or her family for this.'

He kept listening.

'I am responsible for this. I did this so that my son can be sociable again—meet people without hesitation, go anywhere he wants to, do things, be happy. I want my family line to continue. When I die, I want at least a grandson or granddaughter to be there to hold the torch to light my pyre. That's why I did this. I did not think I was doing anything wrong. I thought of this as a prayer. If you insist that it was wrong, you please decide the appropriate punishment for me. Blame me. It is all on me. No one else is to blame . . .'

He just kept listening.

* * *

Well into their marriage, one day when Kali and Ponna were intimate, he told her about the time his mother had asked him if Ponna was an adequate match for him.

Ponna said, 'That's so inappropriate of your mother. How could she ask a thing like that!'

'Why not?' he replied. 'Listen, you see the various sizes of pestles we have in the house? Why do you think that is? We use one with a big ferrule to separate ragi from the husk. Then we use a pestle with a small ferrule to pound the ragi. If we need just half a cup of flour, we only need a small mortar. But if we need to pound flour for four or five people, we need a mortar that is deep, and a pestle that is big. There are so many such details. This too is just like that.'

'Well,' she said, 'the man's parents think about all this. But do the woman's parents worry about such things? No. As soon as they find a man, they marry their daughter off to him.'

'No, no,' he responded. 'Don't say that. A girl's parents worry a lot more about such things. Let me tell you a story . . .'

Kali had a lot of stories. These were bawdy stories that circulated only among men. Once in a while, he entertained

Ponna with such a story. She would say, 'How can you talk so freely about such things? Aren't you ashamed?' But she eagerly listened to them nevertheless.

So there was this man in this town. He had just one daughter. It had been five or six years since she came of age, but she was still not married. Both she and her mother were quite worried about this. But the actual reason for her not getting married was her father. He was very fond of his daughter. She was his only child. He had seen her naked when she was a child. At that time, he thought to himself that his daughter's reproductive organ was very small, like a doodlebug's nest. So he decided that since hers was a small hole and would only be able to take something as big as a little finger, he was determined to find a man who had a small penis. He was concerned that if the man who married his daughter had a large one, she would suffer.

And so he came up with a plan. Whenever prospective bridegrooms came over to take a look at the girl, he would give them a lot of water and buttermilk to drink. After drinking all that, the fellow would start squirming in his seat because he would have to pee. Just then, the girl's father would find some excuse to take the young man out into the fields. There, he would keep talking non-stop to the fellow until he simply had to undo his loincloth to pee or shit. And when the fellow sat down to do his business, our man would also quietly sit down next to him and sneak a peek at his penis. He was looking for a fellow with one as small as a little finger. But none of the men had such a small penis. And he was worried how his daughter would manage if her husband had a big penis. So he would find some excuse to reject all the men.

Since her father kept turning away the men she actually liked, the daughter was curious to know why. She asked her mother to find out the reason. So the mother spoke to her husband one day. And that's when he explained to her his views on the matter. Apparently, the wife yelled at him, 'I have not met a stupider man in my life!' But still he did not relent. That was how much he cared for his daughter. So the mother reported all this to her daughter and said, 'I don't think you are going to get married anytime soon.' The daughter had to find a way out of this. She already knew a little about penises. So the next time a man came to see her and explore the possibilities of marrying her, she was ready with a plan. When the young man came to the backyard to wash his hands, she explained the situation to him. Then she suggested that when he went to the outfields he carry a pitcher of water with him and splash some water from it on his penis a few times. As expected, the father took the young man to the outfields. And as instructed, the young man carried a pitcher of water with him and, when the father was not looking, he splashed some cool water on his own penis. When he squatted down to pee, the older man too sat next to him and looked. He could not even see the fellow's penis clearly; it was so small. So he decided right away that this man would be his son-in-law. Thus the wedding happened. And the daughter lived happily.

When he finished the story, Ponna was overcome with embarrassment.

'Actually there is more to the story,' said Kali. 'Want to hear?'

'No need!' she said, blushing further.

'All right,' he said. 'Some other time then.' He found it very hard that day to coax her out of her shyness and embarrassment.

FIVE

Muthu was very restless for a couple of days. He had wanted to visit Kali, but was not sure if it would be a good idea. Kali had come to his in-laws' home in Adaiyur on the day of the big festival. But since they had planned to take Ponna to Karattur to the festival grounds that night without Kali's knowledge, it was Muthu's task to provide a distraction for Kali. And so he led Kali far away to drink arrack. They went to Mandayan's house, located in a coconut grove, where they all drank the arrack made from coconut toddy. Muthu went to sleep right there. But Kali decided to return to his in-laws' place because he was really missing Ponna and wanted to be with her. That's when he found out that Ponna was not at home and had, in fact, gone to the festival. Unable to bear the shock of this news, he rushed to his barnyard and decided to hang himself on the portia tree.

Muthu had known nothing about the things that had happened after he had got drunk and dozed off in Mandayan's cottage. He had woken up late and chided himself for failing to keep an eye on Kali. Neither Mandayan nor Kathayi were able to tell him precisely at what time Kali had left. He was not sure if Kali had gone back to Adaiyur to his in-laws' home or to his own barnyard in Aattur. In case he had gone to Adaiyur, would Ponna have returned by then? On the other hand, he might have gone to his barnyard. Kali found it hard to be away from there for even a single day. His mind was constantly preoccupied by the sounds of his sheep and cattle. Even if a small rat had newly made the barnyard fence its home, Kali would somehow notice it first thing in the morning. Muthu often teased Kali, 'How many lizards live in the barnyard fence?' Kali would only smile in response.

It had been some years since Kali had started confining himself to the barnyard. He never socialized with anyone. Only those who happened to traverse the pathway that ran by his barnyard got to talk to him. Since everyone seemed to ask him constantly about his childlessness, he had decided to avoid everyone's company. When they were younger, Muthu and Kali had roamed these parts. Since Muthu was very fond of Kali, he let him marry his sister and made him his brother-in-law. Muthu had only got involved in this new plan of Seerayi's because he was concerned that being childless was making Kali a recluse.

Muthu had left from Mandayan's place when the day's heat began to sting him, making it difficult to lounge about any more. When he reached his place, his father had already killed a chicken and was roasting it. Muthu realized that Kali had not come there. As he walked to the cattle enclosure, wondering if he should go to Kali's barnyard and check if he had reached there safely, Kaaraan arrived with news from Seerayi. That brought him some relief, but something kept niggling at him. When Ponna asked him why Kali had left, he said to her, 'Apparently, your husband cannot stay away from the barnyard for even a single night. He has asked you to stay here for a few days and return at leisure.' The only thing he asked his mother was if everything went to plan at the festival. She nodded.

There was an excitement in Ponna's face. It looked as though the deity had definitely blessed Ponna. Muthu prayed that this should lead to a pregnancy—and a child. He was confident that Kali could be managed later. But he needed to know if Kali had found out about the plan. Not knowing that for sure made him very restless.

So he set out one afternoon to Kali's. As soon as he stepped inside Kali's fields, he realized something had changed. The brinjal patch Kali used to tend to very carefully now lay dry. It had not been watered. Kali would never leave things this way. Seerayi was sitting in the shade of the palai tree by the well, looking at the sheep. As soon as she saw Muthu, she came running to him. 'Dear boy,' she exclaimed. 'Don't even ask! That morning he came over here and hung a noose on the portia tree. Somehow the goddess Kooliyatha made sure I arrived here at just the right moment. I managed to save him. What do I tell you? What can I tell you? I can manage one or two difficulties, but when so many of them pile on at the same time, I will break. He has not done any work since then. He doesn't eat well either. He just lies on the cot and stares at the ceiling. I have been talking to him, trying to get him to say something. He hasn't budged. If he was a little boy, I'd slap him and tell him off . . . So I have been staying here. I was hoping his anger would subside in four or five days, and then I could send for Ponna. You go and try talking to him. Please get your dear friend back to normal!'

Muthu was now scared to even enter the barnyard. He didn't know how he would face Kali. He removed his headcloth and draped it over his shoulder. From behind him, he could hear Seerayi singing . . .

> *He used to wear a white veshti, he'd fold it up in style*
> *He'd walk with a swagger on the streets*
> *And people would salute, people would make way for him*
> *Now he wears no white dhoti, doesn't care for style*
> *There is no swagger in his walk, he walks on no street*
> *And he lies in a corner, staring at the ceiling . . .*

Seerayi alone could launch into a dirge on the spot. Her voice sent shivers down his spine.

How could he even look at Kali's face? What would he say to him? How would he begin? So Kali had been so hurt that he had gone to the extent of preparing to hang himself? How terrible it would have been had Kali succeeded in his morbid plan! Muthu shuddered even at the thought. If that had happened, how would Muthu have broken it to Ponna? He walked towards the barnyard. It was very quiet there. Kali might be lying down in the shade of the portia tree or inside the hut. Muthu approached hesitantly. He also tried to comfort himself—after all, Kali had been saved from dying. What could he do now that could be worse? Would Kali attack him and kill him? Muthu had done it all solely for Kali's good. Kali may or may not understand that. Muthu just had to face things as they came.

Muthu opened the thatched gate flap a little loudly to announce his arrival. The dog came running to him, wagging his tail in welcome. Muthu spoke to the dog in a loud voice. It looked like Kali was inside the hut. Muthu wondered if he was asleep. He decided that he would wake him up even if he was sleeping. 'Mapillai, Mapillai!' he called out as he walked inside. There was no response from Kali. He continued to stare at a distant point, unaware that Muthu was addressing him. Even when Muthu went and stood right next to him, Kali did not register his friend's presence. He seemed oblivious to all noise and movement around him. It was as though he was lost in some other world. Muthu gathered some courage and touched Kali on the shoulder and said, 'Dey, Mapillai!'

Kali suddenly jerked awake and shook himself free to Muthu's touch. Then he lifted his head and looked at Muthu. 'Come!' he said. 'Are you here for my final rites? But I was saved, you see. My mother, that wretched widow, that whore who has raised me and is responsible for the state I am in, she held my feet firmly and refused to let me die. Otherwise, right now that dog we have here would be peeing on the spot where they would have cremated me.'

Muthu shivered on the inside. He saw tears pouring down Kali's face. 'Please don't dwell on it, Mapillai,' he said. 'Only good things will come to us. Why do you have die for this?' But his lips went dry and his tongue parched even with these few words.

'Right!' said Kali 'So it is a good thing to send one's wife to another man? You plied me with arrack the other day, didn't you? You could have mixed some poison in it and killed me, and perhaps then sent your sister to another man. Why didn't you?'

'Please don't say that,' said Muthu gently. 'There are so many people in the village who have done this and been blessed by the deity. We are only doing what others have done.'

'Do you know if all those men who agreed to send their wives to the festival did so wholeheartedly?' said Kali, weeping. 'How would you know if those other men too had all these thoughts I am holding in my heart? When they play with the child that comes from this, how could they not remember that it was some other man's child? And the women who went there once—won't they be tempted to go again? You have turned my home into a whorehouse!'

'We are all here with you,' reassured Muthu. 'Nothing bad will happen. Please don't cry.'

'What do you mean nothing bad will happen?' snapped Kali. 'She went and slept with some other man, that whore! And now she is spending time happily at your place? Let me see how she manages to come here and look me in the eye.'

'Please don't call Ponna that,' pleaded Muthu, his voice trembling. 'We tricked her into believing she had your permission. Please don't blame her for this!'

'So she would go just because you told her I said yes?' Kali spat out. 'Even if I had said that to her myself, if she really had any love for me, would she have gone? The truth is that she was horny. One man was not enough for her any more. *That's* why she went!' He then proceeded to aim more expletives at Ponna.

Muthu could not bear to listen to any of this. He said in a pleading voice, 'Please don't say such things about her. Don't you know how much she loves you?'

But Kali suddenly grabbed Muthu by the piece of cloth draped over his shoulders. 'Look at him! A brother who pimped his own sister! And he has come to advise me! Go away. Get out!' And with that, Kali pushed Muthu out of the hut.

Muthu was taken aback. 'Mapillai . . .' he managed to say.

'Who is Mapillai?' shouted Kali. 'We have no relationship any more. If you come here again, I will break your legs. Go away, you dog!'

Muthu tried to say something placatory, and walked back towards the hut, but Kali came running, punched him in the back and pushed him away. Muthu fell on the ground. Kali attacked him without restraint. He held Muthu by his head-knot and slapped him repeatedly on his face. He kicked Muthu's feet. Noticing a long stalk from the portia tree lying on the ground nearby, he picked it up and, eyes closed, whipped Muthu with it. Muthu tried to shield himself from the blows using his hands. But when that proved to be ineffective, he tossed and turned and writhed on the ground, trying to evade Kali's assault.

Seerayi came running. 'You wretched motherfucker!' she screamed. 'How can you hit your friend like this? Didn't I tell you that it was all my idea, that I am responsible for everything? Then why are you hitting him? Here, hit me. If your rage has not subsided, hit me. Here, punch me. I will die of heartbreak. Come, hit me on these breasts that suckled you!' The words poured out of Seerayi as she knelt down in front of Kali, looking up at him.

Kali spat on Muthu and went back into the hut and lay down on the cot. He was still enraged, and his angry gasps sounded like the noise the portia tree made when it swayed in the wind.

Seerayi gave Muthu a hand and lifted him up. He was covered in soil and he bled from the cuts caused by the tree stalk. Rising from the ground, Muthu looked around for the towel he usually wore around his neck; when he found it, he wiped himself with it, and said, 'Dey, Kali, I am not upset at all that you hit me. If you are still not satisfied, come back out and hit me some more. If you want to kill me, do that too, come. But please don't blame Ponna and call her names. She is a good girl. She considers you her life. I will tell you just one thing. I only wanted to do you good. You may not see that now, but you will at some point. You will always be my friend, Kali.'

Muthu then slowly walked out of the barnyard. Seerayi walked after him without saying anything, without knowing what to say. Outside, she stood watching as he walked past the fields, over the common path, and until his figure vanished in the distance.

SIX

Poovayi waited for Muthu until the sun climbed over the hillock, hoping he would return home at least for the morning meal. But he did not show up. He had been gone since the day before. And he had not eaten anything since lunch. They lived in Thottakkaadu. Five or six farmsteads beyond that was Mettukkaadu, the elevated fields. That was where they had built the enclosure for cattle and sheep since they could use the animal refuse for manure in these fields. Muthu spent all his time in Mettukkaadu. Toddy tapping from the palmyra trees was well under way. This was almost the end of the toddy season. What they tap now would be the final batch of toddy for the year. It was particularly potent. Poovayi wondered if Muthu had drunk a lot of this toddy and was lying somewhere in those elevated fields.

She gave voice to her frustration. 'Even a dog would come running back to be fed if you call out to it. But who can keep track of where this man goes and when he comes back? This has become a constant nuisance!' The night before, she had sent food for Muthu with the farmhand. When she asked him later, he said he couldn't find Muthu and had hung the food carrier on a pole near the cattle shed. She then asked him if he had looked inside the enclosure. To that, the farmhand replied that there was no one in the enclosure and that he had shut the sheep in and latched the gate on the outside before he left. Usually, Muthu went to the enclosure to sleep only after the eight o'clock siren was sounded at the local municipal building.

Muthu's mother too was annoyed at his behaviour: 'Can't a man return home at the appropriate hour? Look at that poor little boy. He is staring at the path eagerly waiting for his father. Can't he come back to at least look at the kid's face before he sets off again? He has really become uncontrollable.'

But Poovayi retorted, 'Well, you will say all this now, but when you see him, you go quiet.'

Ponna found all of this rather amusing. Their father, on the other hand, said, 'Where can he go? He must be sleeping in some hideout of his. He will wake up and return home. Stop worrying.'

But when Muthu did not return home in the morning, Poovayi went to Mettukkaadu herself to look for him. The makeshift latch the farmhand had put on the outer side of the gate was still intact. No one had cleared the cow dung in the enclosure. When they saw her, the sheep started bleating non-stop. The dog had not been tied up inside, and was roaming all over the fields. 'Even this dog is more responsible than this man,' Poovayi ranted. 'How could he stay away leaving all these sheep uncared for? Anyone could come and just herd the entire flock away. That is definitely going to happen one day, and that's when he will mend his ways.'

Poovayi emptied the previous night's food from the carrier into the dog's bowl. The dog came running to her and stood by, wagging its tail. They only fed the dog once a day: at night. Otherwise, it fended for itself, hunting rats in the fields. Days like this, when it got to eat leftovers, were lucky days for the dog. 'From now on, I should just tie him up like a dog and feed him,' she vented as she walked back home. But her ranting did not stop; it only got worse as the day progressed. Ponna was really irritated. In her view, everyone knew what her brother was like. He would wander around here and there and would return for sure. Where else would he go? She spent her time playing with her brother's son, Murugesan. Kali had not sent her to her parents' home for two years. Somehow this year he agreed not only to visit this place but to go to the festival as well. Now he had even sent word to her asking her to stay here for a week. All of this made her very happy. She believed that the deity had definitely granted her wish. But she was discomfited thinking about how she would tell Kali about the night at the festival and how she would look him in the face. So she welcomed the prospect of spending another week here.

Ponna and her sister-in-law Poovayi had stopped talking to each other four or five years ago. It had happened during one of Ponna's visits. Murugesan must have been a year or a year and a half old then. Muthu had got married two and a half years after Ponna, but he and Poovayi already had a child, a boy, while Ponna was still praying and appealing to various deities for a similar blessing. During that visit, she had been playing with the dog as she always used to do in those days. She chased around little lambs. She was like an excited little girl who could not stay put even for a little while. But that was how Ponna always was whenever she came to her mother's house. She was full of excitement and she did not do any household work. Even her mother would scold her, 'She falls sick as soon as we ask her to do any work.' But nothing bothered Ponna.

Poovayi, who was then handling an infant, was annoyed at Ponna's behaviour. She said in the course of some exchange, 'If you'd had children at the right time after your marriage, you would by now have one holding your hand and one on your hip. You wouldn't have had the time to be goofing around like this.'

Ponna replied, laughing, 'Even if that was the case, I would still be just the same when I come to my mother's.'

And Poovayi said sharply, 'Only if that mentality changes will you be able to conceive, let me tell you.'

Ponna was deeply offended by this remark. 'You are being nasty to me because you were able to conceive? Why do you worry? I am quite happy that I don't have to clean piss and shit all the time.'

They had stopped talking to each other on that day. They did not even look directly at each other. Even now Ponna found Poovayi's words and behaviour very annoying.

Their father went to Mettukkaadu looking for Muthu. When he peeped into the sheep enclosure, he saw that Muthu's slippers were lying there, trampled by the sheep. When he walked inside, he found Muthu lying on the cot. He woke him up and brought him back home. Muthu quietly followed him. His eyes were bloodshot. Thinking that he was intoxicated, his father scolded him all the way home. Muthu said nothing in response.

But as soon as she looked at her brother, Ponna realized it was not drunkenness. He had not slept all night. His eyes were swollen. She sensed that something was wrong. He sat down on the cot laid in the shade of the portia tree. She sat next to him and asked, 'What happened, Anna?'

He did not lift his head. She saw the wounds on his body.

'You are swollen all over,' she exclaimed. 'Whom did you fight with? Who beat you up?'

His father had not noticed the swellings. So he was saying, 'He must have been lying about on the ground or on the rocks, this dog! Who is going to beat up this spineless creature?'

But Poovayi came running to Muthu and gently ran her hand over his body. 'This is swollen so badly!' she said and ran back into the house. When he saw everyone fussing

48

over him and getting agitated, he started crying. He could not control himself.

Ponna shook him by the shoulder and said, 'What happened, Anna? Tell me!'

He said, crying, 'Your husband now knows everything, Ponna.'

Ponna was shocked. 'Does that mean he did not know anything until now?' she shouted.

Muthu remained silent. Ponna ran to her mother and asked the same thing. She too hesitated to reply, but she tried to manage the situation: 'It was all your mother-in-law's idea. She told us she had told him and there was no problem.'

Ponna could see it all very clearly now. Kali had not consented to this plan. When he had sat in the shade of the tree, eating snacks, her mother had not let her have a quiet moment with Kali. She had kept calling Ponna to do this and that. Ponna had not got to speak to him that day. She had been too embarrassed to ask directly, 'Can I go?' And she had thought he was also too embarrassed to tell her directly that she could go. When he had said to her, 'Go. We can manage,' he had only referred to her going to her mother's home. But she had taken his 'We can manage' to be his indirect way of agreeing to the plan. Her brother had also said to her, 'I explained to Kali that this was a religious matter and I got him to agree.' It had all been a lie.

Now Ponna was frantic, wondering what might have transpired once Kali found out. She shook Muthu and said, 'Tell me! Did you go there to hit him?'

Muthu replied, still in tears and whimpering, 'It was he who hit me.' And then he told her everything, from Kali leaving from the coconut grove late that night, Muthu discovering that only the next morning, Kali finding out everything and then going to his barnyard and trying to hang himself, Muthu paying Kali a visit the day before, Kali hitting him—everything.

'My husband tried to hang himself!' Ponna cried. 'You wretched people! You all have led me to this place. You have betrayed me! Couldn't you have told me that he did not consent to this idea? For how long have you been scheming to ruin my life? I knew my husband well, but I believed you. How was I such a fool! Ayyo! How he must have suffered! What all must have gone through his mind!' Ponna wept, beating her chest.

Then she turned on Muthu, screaming, 'You motherfucker! You told me you explained to him that this was a religious matter and secured his permission. How could you lie to me like that! Did you hope that if both of us died you can take over our lands, you wretched motherfucker?' She hit him on his face with both her hands.

Muthu lowered his face and submitted to the blows on his head. Poovayi strove to prise Muthu and Ponna apart, saying, 'He is a man, you can't hit him like this! We have suffered enough ever since you got married.'

But Muthu said, 'Let her hit me. I deserve this and more. You hit me, girl, go ahead.'

Suddenly, Ponna spoke as though she had entered a trance. 'If you are capable of tricking me and betraying me this way, you are also capable of poisoning me to death because you have an eye on my inheritance. From now on, I have no father or mother, no sibling, nothing to call my maternal home. I will not drink even a drop a water from this house ever again. None of you should visit even if I die. If anyone dies here, you should not send for me. I say this with goddess Kooliyatha as my witness. None of you should visit me ever—not even to catch a glimpse of my face. I cast you all away like spit from my mouth. I shall never take you back!'

Then she spat on the ground forcefully. Her mother screamed, 'Ponna! What are you doing?'

But Ponna gathered some soil from under the portia tree in both her hands and flung it in the direction of the house. Without another word she turned and raced along the narrow path that led away from the house.

SEVEN

Ponna ran quite a distance, slowing down only when she was on the elevated mud road. Now she thought she only had herself to blame. How could I have allowed myself to be fooled by my mother-in-law, my mother, my brother? There was no way Kali could have given his permission in so many words. That was out of the question. But, in that case, she could at least have asked him directly. On the other hand, she had not expected everyone to conspire in this manner. If he was the kind of man who would agree to such an idea, he would have done that much sooner. He wouldn't have taken two years. Her mother-in-law and mother had suggested it two years ago. But Kali did not speak to Ponna about it right away. He took his time in broaching the subject with her. During an intimate moment he had asked, 'Will you go to the festival like they are suggesting?' Considering their emotional state in those days, she had said, 'I will go if you want me to.'

Kali had not been able to digest that response from her. She had had to console him with all kinds of explanations. After that, he went silent every time the topic came up. And she wanted to be careful, because if she brought it up too often he might construe that she indeed desired to go to the festival. Eventually she stopped talking about it. In fact, she avoided even mentioning visiting her parents' village, fearing it would somehow lead to the dreaded topic of the festival. However, this year, Muthu had visited them and insisted that they go to her parents' home—but even then she had no idea that they had all been planning everything on the sly. Later, she assumed that Kali may have softened his resistance to the idea over the past two years and thus might have eventually agreed to the plan. After all, not a day went by without the question of their childlessness coming up in conversations. Kali might have shut himself up in the barnyard to avoid seeing people, but people were not going to leave him in peace.

In fact, it had happened two months ago on this very road she was now walking on. Kali had herded the sheep up the path and was standing about when Vavuthupaattar came along. Vavuthupaattar had been taking his cows back from grazing, and he stopped to chat with Kali, rubbing his belly as he spoke. Usually, Kali would find some way to wriggle out of a conversation if anyone stopped to chat with him. But it was dusk and the sheep were still grazing about lazily. They always grazed happily until it grew pitch-dark, and Kali did not want to spoil their meal by leaving right away. So he stayed put and gave clipped responses to the old man's questions. The other man's cows too settled down to graze alongside the road. He loosened the rope he held in his hands, allowing them a bit of leeway. The conversation somehow turned to the man's groundnut crop not having done well the year before.

'What can I do, Kaliyappa?' he said. 'The seed looks fine, but it doesn't seem to sprout. You know the man from Selloor whom I hired to plough the fields? His plough was a rather small one, so he ended up doing some shallow ploughing. So all the seeds stayed close to the surface and dried up in the heat. That was why nothing grew. What could I do? This is just like your situation. You and Ponna are both perfectly healthy. You look as robust as a strong palmyra tree. But nothing seems to work out for you two. Don't get disheartened if your plough is too small. Just plough hard and sow it deep. Let's see if that works.' And he walked away, chuckling to himself.

That night, Kali had narrated this incident to Ponna. She had said, 'We are trying to distance ourselves from all these despicable people. But they somehow seek us out and torment us.' They had endured several such insults. So Ponna had thought these experiences had perhaps changed Kali's mind and he had eventually agreed to the plan.

Ponna was amazed at how much Kali could keep to himself. He had tried to hang himself! What would have happened to her if he had indeed succeeded in his attempt?

She was entirely dependent on him, but he seemed to have not spared her a thought. And that was a sign of how angry he was. When Seerayi had said to him once, 'No one else will know about it. Just the four of us,' he had retorted, 'That might be true, but you see, my heart knows. It will keep asking me about it. What do I tell my heart?' That was his approach to things. He always wanted to keep Ponna right beside him. Whenever she went to her mother's place, he followed her within a day. Or he would send for her, saying there was a lot of work for her to do in the barnyard.

Her mother, Vallayi, had once remarked, 'I have never seen a husband like him! Imagine how much more he would pamper you if you give him a child or two!' To which Ponna had said, laughing, 'That's where you are wrong. If I had given him children, he would have directed all his love towards them. It is just as well that we don't have any.' He was so devoted to her.

As soon as she arrived at the farmstead, she would fall at his feet, she said to herself. Would he believe her if she told him that she too had been tricked, that she had not been privy to the plan? He was not a cruel man, was he? The mud road was quite smooth at this point. On either side, trees and shrubs grew and thrived. She could hear little rustlings here and there but she did not pause to linger. The people she passed by on the road were either herding sheep or taking their cows and oxen back home. She did not stop to chat with anyone, but those who saw her rushing down the road talked among themselves: 'Wonder why Ponna is in such a hurry. She is coming back from her village, but she hasn't even combed her hair. And she is wearing an old, faded sari, and she seems to be in a tearing rush.'

Seerayi spotted Ponna when she turned from the road and walked into the fields. She called out to Ponna, but Ponna ignored her and ran towards the barnyard. Seerayi discerned that Muthu must have informed Ponna of everything. She was now terrified. Kali had beaten Muthu to a pulp. What would he do with Ponna? The day before, after Muthu had left, Seerayi had said to Kali, 'He loves you. How many people are lucky enough to get such a brother-in-law? He comes rushing here as soon as we send for him. He wishes you well. And you hit him like that! Have you gone mad?' But Kali did not respond. Seerayi was also scared that if she said too much, his wrath might fall upon her. So she didn't say anything further. At night, she called him for dinner, and he ate. No conversation. In the morning, he did some chores. He cleared out the dung, but he took a lot longer than usual. She even wondered if he was playing with the balls of dung. But she was happy that at least he was engaging himself in some work.

Seerayi ran after Ponna. The barnyard gate was open. Ponna ran in, calling out, 'Maama . . .' She noticed the severed branch of the portia tree lying outside and the vacant spot on the tree where the branch should have been. She quickly guessed how things must have unfolded. She also realized that had Seerayi not been in the barnyard at the right time, Kali would be dead now. At first, she could not find him anywhere, but then she spotted him standing in the northern corner, brushing his teeth with a twig and staring at some crows cawing at a distance. She ran to him and held his feet in her hands. He did not respond to Ponna's endearments. 'Maama!' she cried. 'I did not know. They told me you had agreed to it. I did not know how to ask you myself. I did fear that they might lie to me. And they did! They lied to me. They have ruined my marriage. I am definitely in the wrong. Kill me. Punish me however you want. Why should you die? What were you about to do?'

A crow cawed non-stop. But through that ruckus she thought she heard him say, 'Yes, innocent little whore.'

She calmed down and looked at his face. It was absolutely impassive. He was staring somewhere into the distance, completely disengaged from the situation at hand. 'Maama, please say something,' she pleaded. 'Please hit me if you want.'

He casually released himself from her hold. Walking over to the corner, he split the twig into two and started cleaning his tongue. Then he coughed up his phlegm and spat it out. After that, he gargled and rinsed his mouth with some water from the pot. Seerayi stood in the shade of the portia tree. Ponna walked closer to him and said, 'Please don't be like this, Maama. Why did you try to hang yourself? Please don't even think that way again. You used to be so sociable and happy. But you confined yourself to the barnyard. I thought I could remedy that. That's why I went. But I would not have gone if I had known you did not agree to it, would I? They have fooled you, and they have fooled me too.'

When he finished gargling, he turned around. And Ponna thought she heard him say something.

She did not hear it clearly, but reading this lips, she inferred what he had said: 'Whore.' He had called her a whore. She knew that when his mind spoke, his lips moved without making the sounds. Often, by reading his lips, she could tell what was going on in his mind. She was quite certain of what he had just said. He had called her that. It was definitely that word. She walked after him, saying, 'What did you say? You called me that, didn't you? Say it to my face. Your lips moved, you said that word, I heard it. You called me that. How could you?' And she grabbed him by the shoulder and demanded a reply. He tried to release himself from her hold, gently at first. But she held his shoulder firmly. So he used all his strength and pushed her away. It sent her staggering to a side and she fell down.

Seerayi came running to her, lifted her up, and asked, 'What did he say?'

'Your son called me a whore,' said Ponna. 'Tell me, am I a whore? All of you have managed to get me a new title. Damn you!' And sobbing, she began beating herself hard on her forehead.

EIGHT

Now things were such that it fell to Seerayi to take care of both Kali and Ponna. She could never have anticipated that her plan would lead to such a situation. She had thought that Kali would be angry for a few days and then calm down. She also found herself being very active suddenly. Until now, she had lived a rather relaxed and uninteresting life—going to work in other people's fields when needed, cooking Kali's favourite dishes, gossiping and chatting with people, cooking a little something for herself every day. But now, suddenly, she had taken on a lot of responsibility. She believed, however, that this was temporary, that both Kali and Ponna would soon be all right.

Kali had simply stopped speaking. She teased him once, 'Did I give birth to a mute son?' He did not respond to that. As for Ponna, whenever Seerayi tried to talk to her, she would start weeping. Seerayi was shocked when she found out that Ponna had ritually severed all ties with her family. On Thursday, when she went to the market, she paid a visit to Ponna's parents in Adaiyur. All of them looked really miserable. In fact, they even hesitated to give her a glass of water. That's when she found out that Ponna had sworn, with the goddess Kooli as witness, to cut off ties with her family—even throwing a handful of earth at the house to solemnize the oath. After hearing that, Seerayi did not even drink water there.

'I can't even give a glass of water to you!' cried Vallayi.

Seerayi did not know how to comfort Muthu. How badly Kali had hit him the other day! In this peasant community, when things got physical between brothers-in-law, it sometimes ended in murder. But here was Muthu, bearing it all silently. And Ponna had broken her ties with such a family? Seerayi had a hard time digesting that.

Ponna's family were pretty much the only relatives Seerayi had. She relied on them. Kali's father too had been an only son to his parents. If he had had brothers and sisters, Kali would have had uncles and aunts and all those relatives. But for three generations, his side of the family had just one son. So they did not have a lot of relatives. There were some close kinsmen in the village, but they were only bound by their clan identity. Some seventeen or eighteen families. She had to reach out to them for anything and everything. And they showed up out of a sense of duty, not love.

As for Seerayi's side of the family, she was not really in touch with anyone any more. Things soured when Kali married Ponna. Those relatives had expected Kali to marry a girl from one of their families, and they did not like that Kali married from outside the clan. Before Ponna entered this family, Kali's uncles on Seerayi's side of the family would visit them at least once a month with their wives and children. They would cook and eat chicken and spend at least two days with them. In fact, this continued for a while even after Kali married Ponna. Once, Seerayi's younger brother had come for a visit. He was sporting large gold ear studs, and he wore his hair in a bun-like knot just above his nape like women usually do. He had brought his third daughter with him. Ponna took a deep dislike to that man. He stayed in the barnyard and ordered them about. They had to kill a chicken, cook chicken kuzhambu and paddy rice for him. And when they left, they took a rooster with them.

And just fifteen days after that, Seerayi's other brother and his two sons landed up. That brother constantly stared at Ponna. She found his relentless gaze very troubling, but she knew that if she shared that observation with Kali, he would not take her seriously. He would flippantly reply that that was how men looked at women. They had to cook chicken and rice for these guests as well. And then they left, they too took a chicken with them. Ponna remarked, as if addressing the chicken that was hanging from one of the boys' hands, 'Look at its thieving gaze. It happily ate a whole measure of rice and still looks greedy. I feel like burning its eyes with a firebrand.' Seerayi's brother rushed away, looking sheepish. He never visited them again. It bothered Ponna that they never brought any gifts when they visited. They knew that their sister Seerayi was a widow who had raised her son all by herself. They could have helped her out if they'd wanted to. But no. They just visited whenever they felt like it, stuffed themselves happily, and left.

What did they need such relatives for? When Ponna had brought this up with Seerayi, the old woman said, 'Brothers will always visit their sisters. And when they do, we can't send them away empty-handed.' To this Ponna had replied, 'Why not? They don't seem to care about coming empty-handed to their elder sister's house, do they?' Seerayi brushed it aside, saying, 'We don't depend on their largesse, do we? They have children. Let them enjoy the gifts we give them.' In Ponna's view Kali was generous to a fault. 'How can we not be gracious to our guests?' he would say. Ponna did not mind their visiting, but she could not tolerate how they ordered everyone about, and demanded that a chicken be caught and cooked. Although Ponna was irritated by all this, she let it be, waiting for a chance to do something about it someday soon.

Sometime later, the uncle with the head-knot came by again, this time with one of his sons. Ponna was alone in the barnyard that day. Seerayi was in her house in the village. Kali was away on the mud path, herding sheep. Ponna just said, 'Come,' and carried on with her chores in the cattle enclosure. The uncle lay down on the cot in the shade of the portia tree. His son was around fourteen or fifteen then. He said to Ponna, 'Father wants us to catch a nice, young chicken, one that hasn't laid eggs yet.'

That sent Ponna into a rage. 'Father and son have arrived here empty-handed. He is coming to see his elder sister, isn't he? Can't he bring a chicken and five measures of rice? Do you think we are growing rice in our fields here? Are we doing wetland farming here? All right, you two, father and son, just lie about in the shade of the tree. And let us wait for it to rain, so that the well fills up, so that we can plough the fields, irrigate them, plant the saplings and harvest a rice crop. Be patient until then and go lie there in the shade of the tree!' She added, 'These people come once a month without fail to eat rice and chicken.' And then she spat. 'Thoo!'

By the time she finished cleaning the sheep enclosure, the visitors were gone. Ponna did not tell Seerayi and Kali about this visit. When the uncle's wife ran into Seerayi in the market one day, she said, 'Why is your daughter-in-law so arrogant?' But she did not explain further. She only called Ponna names. When Seerayi returned home, she asked Ponna, 'Did the first thambi visit?' referring to the older of her two brothers. Ponna said, 'First thambi who?' When Seerayi replied, 'My first thambi. Who else?' Ponna said, 'How would I know?' She never told Seerayi about the visit and what had happened. She counted on the fact that the visitors couldn't really tell people what Ponna had said to them. It would be a disgrace to them. Besides, people might say Ponna was right in saying what she had. But

Seerayi was confused. Ponna just said, 'They might have dreamed that they visited here. What did they say I told them in their dream?' And Kali had laughed.

But the visits stopped. Kali then said to her one day, 'You have performed some trick and have put an end to my uncles' visits.' Ponna knew that Kali too was not happy about their just dropping by to stuff themselves. She said to him, 'I asked why they couldn't bring a chicken with them. Then I asked them to wait till I grow some rice in our fields for them to eat.' Kali burst out laughing. Those relationships pretty much ended at that point. Seerayi was quite unhappy about that at first, but she soon came to feel that it was good in a way that those visits had stopped.

And now, Ponna had thrown a handful of earth at her own father's house and broken her ties with them. Would she change her mind and reunite with her family? Besides, once the severing was done in this way, with god as witness, it was not easy to take it back. Since Ponna had invoked the goddess Kooli, both families would have to go together to the temple, offer pongal and arrange for a ritual wash for the deity. Only then would the curse end. Until that came to pass, the families could not accept even a glass of water from each other's houses. And they were not supposed to even talk to one another.

Seerayi said to Ponna's parents, 'She did this in anger. Let us not stop talking to one another. Kooli is our goddess. She won't harm us. All right, we shall let it be for a little while. Things will change. Time heals. We can resume our relations. We don't have any other relatives besides you. Let us refrain from exchanges and visits for now. You were only trying to implement my idea. You had their well-being at heart. But those two asses don't understand that now. Though they will, one day. Then she will have to come to you. It will happen. It is not like there are a thousand relatives vying with each other to invite these two to their homes. They only have you. They will have to come around. Don't worry. We all acted together. Now let us hope things go well and a new life forms in Ponna's womb. Everything will become all right then.'

Seerayi did not ask Ponna about her decision. But she told Kali about it. She said to him, 'They are her own family. Her own father's home. She has cast them all away and has ritually severed her ties with them. If she was guilty in this matter, would she have done that?'

But he said nothing in reply.

'I might as well speak to rocks and sand and trees. What is the point in telling you anything? If you had any siblings, you would know what a painful situation this is. But you were born a singleton, you grew up alone, you live alone!' And she started a lament:

I don't have a son
I don't have a daughter
I have no one to call my own
When I die, when I die
I have no one to carry my body

Wanting to express his irritation at this dirge, Kali picked up a club and hit the ox brutally on its back. He had never hit the animal before. The beast was utterly taken aback by this attack and ran around the cattle shed in fear. This sight brought to Seerayi's mind the way Kali had beaten up Muthu. She stopped singing her dirge and numbly sat as Kali continued to hit the ox.

NINE

Ponna felt like everything sort of came undone the moment Kali called her a 'whore'. She had nothing more to say to him. How could he call her that? 'We have been married for twelve years. How can you not understand someone with whom you have spent so many years?'

But Kali had used the word against her once before. In the early days of their marriage, Kali came to the house in the village for his dinner every night. And there he would spend some time with Ponna. Later in the night, he would wake up and return to the barnyard. Before leaving, he would wake Ponna up, so that she could latch the door. But this didn't last long. He started spending his nights in the barnyard. And so Ponna would carry dinner for him there. On some nights, he asked her to stay over. At other times, he walked back to the house in the middle of the night and knocked on the door.

Ponna now surmised that even on that night, the night of the festival, when he went out to drink with Muthu, he must have woken up in the middle of the night, thinking of her. In fact, she remembered that earlier that day, all his looks and comments had been very lustful. Had they been in their own barnyard, he would have taken her into the hut. There was no way of knowing when he would want her. On days when he got drunk, he definitely needed to be with her. It could be at any stage of intoxication. Sometimes he dozed off when he was drunk, but he woke up suddenly and came looking for her. No matter what hour of the night and how drunk he was, she never said no to him. He knew the days she was menstruating, because those were days of great sadness for them. On those days, she carried her clothes to the barnyard to wash. He looked at these clothes with much sorrow and yearning. It was hard to tell if he was sad because her menstruating meant she was not pregnant or because it meant he could not have sex with her. He had to sleep with her at least twice every week. Based on his actions and the slant of his talk during the day, Ponna would guess whether he would come to her that particular night. But there were also times when she was not able to guess right. He was very loving towards her, and he also treated her with importance, with great kindness.

One day he asked her, 'How come you never take the initiative and come to me first?'

She said, 'Women cannot do that, can they?'

He replied, 'But women too must need it, don't they? You are not a piece of wood. I can tell by the way you are embracing me now how much you want me.'

Later one night, he was lying on the cot after eating his dinner in the barnyard. She picked up the food carrier. 'So I will get going then . . .' she said meaningfully, dragging the end of her sentence.

'All right, go,' he said, and looked at her.

She walked closer and sat down on the cot. Then she held his lips firmly in her hand and kissed him deeply. He embraced her and said, 'Ah! You mean "get going" in this sense!' That night, she had taken charge. At the end when she lay exhausted and happy, he embraced her tightly and whispered in her ear, 'Where were you hiding all this desire all these days, you whore!'

When she heard that word, she pushed him away. She was upset. He had tried his best to console her. 'You can't take these things literally. I said it endearingly, in a moment of passion.'

'Still. How can you call me that?' she said, and wept.

He said, cajoling her, 'When a husband and wife fight in the village, you know the sort of things they say. The husband calls his wife a whore who sleeps around. And the wife tells the husband he is the one who goes to prostitutes. But the very next day they are going about laughing and talking with each other. They said all those things just the day before, and the entire village heard that. But none of it matters the next day. I called you that with affection. Please don't be so upset by it.'

But she was not placated by his words. 'All that is fine,' she said. 'But you called me that on the one day I initiated things.'

He said, 'You know how my grandmother affectionately addressed young women? "Ey, whore!" But it was said with love. And this was meant the same way.'

But Ponna would not relent. 'Old women say all sorts of things. We can't go by that.'

Then he found a better way to argue his case. 'One day you said to me, "You motherfucker! Nothing will satisfy you. You need a body like a rock!" The other day you called me an ox that greedily munched its fodder from its basket. You have called me all sorts of things. Have I ever been upset with you for any of that?' This consoled her a little. Then he said to her, 'From now on, I won't go to you until you call me.' Ponna thought he might not be able to keep to his words for too long. She thought he would come to her at night and knock on the door. But he didn't. That month when she washed and hung a piece of her sanitary cloth to dry, he asked sadly, 'So it happened this month too?'

And she replied, laughing, 'Of course. It won't come only if you come to me!'

After that, she had to make the first move. He was very adamant, but he was also careful not to use that word again. Abashed, she was never again as forward and forceful as she had been that night. But there was a big difference between his use of that word on that night and his use of that word now. The first time he called her that, he was affectionate and commending her for expressing her desire. But when he called her that now, it was a slur. And he didn't even have to say it out loud. He managed to communicate it to her with just the movement of his lips. No. He was saying it in his mind, but unbeknownst to himself, his lips betrayed his thought.

Ponna would wonder: 'Did I stand in the streets of Karattur, soliciting clients? Did I wave to men and invite them to sleep with me? Or did I go looking for other men at nights, like some women in the village secretly do? Have I ever gone anywhere without his knowledge? They all came up with the plan, they told me he had agreed to it, and they sent me there.'

Even there, all faces appeared to her like Kali's. She could not keep his face away from her mind and look afresh at the crowd. That was how strongly Kali's face was imprinted in her mind. No other man's face would stick in her mind. When she had once found out that Kali had been to this same festival night with Muthu sometime before she married him, he was able to console her. And that was because of the strength of her love for him. When we love someone, we become blind to their faults. Even if we do notice those faults, even if they are really big faults, we brush those aside easily, as if we are pushing aside our hair when it falls over our foreheads. How is it that Kali did not love her in that same way?

Perhaps Kali wanted to brand her a whore so that he could now marry another woman? But if that was the case, why did he try to hang himself? He wanted Ponna to experience no one's touch but his. She had realized that two years ago, the first time the topic of the temple festival came up. And it had been a frightening experience. It made her realize that it was easy to make Kali jealous and suspicious and that she had to be very careful with him. She was always able to tell his arrival at the house in the night by the sound of his footsteps. She could tell the sound of his footsteps apart from the sound of other people's footsteps. He always placed both his feet firmly on the ground and distributed his weight equally between the two. Not everyone walked like that.

Some nights she thought she heard his footsteps. And she was ready to hear his knock on the door. But nothing would happen. Then she would hear the sound of receding footsteps. She'd come running and open the door. But he wasn't there. At other times, she wanted to quickly open the door when the footsteps stopped right outside the door. But what if it was not him? What if it was some other man who knew that her mother-in-law slept next door and Ponna was alone in this room? Someone who knew how to imitate the sound of Kali's footsteps? She grew very confused.

She even asked him once. 'Maama, last night I thought I heard the sound of your footsteps. I thought of opening the door to check, but I was also scared. Then I told myself that it was perhaps a dream, and then I dozed off.'

He laughed, saying, 'It is your imagination.'

'Don't lie to me,' she said. 'I know the sound of your footsteps. You stopped right outside the door and went away.'

'Are you mad? Why would I go all the way home and then just turn around? Was I going to some other woman's house that I had to worry about her husband being home? If I had come to the door, I would've certainly knocked and spent time with you. You are imagining things. Maybe we should go to the temple and smear some holy ash on your forehead.'

But her suspicions never went away. And all of this happened only after the topic of going to the temple festival was broached. She knew that he wanted her to be his and his alone, but still she ended up thinking that the desire for a child might have thawed his earlier reluctance. He too wanted a child very badly. It was true that the world around them was putting pressure on them, but independent of all that he too yearned for a child of his own. Whenever he saw children playing, he'd stop and watch, mesmerized. And Ponna believed that that yearning must have eventually made him agree to Seerayi's plan. But she was wrong. What could she do now? How could she make him not see her as a whore?

TEN

He did not even touch the food Ponna cooked for him. She found that out only two days later.

In the morning, she usually took some pap or ragi meal for him in a carrier. At night too she cooked pap or ragi meal but with some gravy. This was their long-standing pattern. On the rare occasion when she could make some special gravy dish, she cooked rice. On those days, she sent some food for her mother-in-law as well. But now, for some days since her return, Ponna did not cook anything.

Seerayi scolded her. 'If you two just hang about doing nothing, how can I manage anything? I am not young any more, am I? I cannot take on everything. I am really exhausted. That dog! He does not respond to anything, he has gone all mute on us, as if he has swallowed a crowbar or something! I don't know what has come over him. But if you are going to be the same way, I cannot manage. Get up and light the stove. I cannot cook for three people on top of doing all the other chores.'

74

In this manner, Seerayi compelled Ponna to get up and do things. And so Ponna cooked. She carried some food for Kali to the barnyard. But when she went there, she never made any effort to see if he was around. She just left the carrier in the usual spot inside the hut. The next day, however, she saw that he had not eaten the food she had left for him the previous day. She assumed that he might have got drunk the previous night and forgotten to eat, so she decided to empty the food into the wide-mouthed waste pot kept for these purposes. As she dropped the food into the pot, she realized that the pot was not empty. Reaching in to check what was there, she discovered two more balls of food in addition to the ones she had just put in. This was the food she had left for him the morning of the previous day. She did not say anything about this for two days, hoping things would change. But they remained the same. Finally, she said to Seerayi, 'It looks like your son won't eat food cooked by a whore. He just empties everything into the waste pot or into the dog's bowl. From now on, you do the cooking and take the food to him. Let him eat out of his chaste mother's hands.'

Seerayi asked her, 'Then what did he eat for two days?'

Annoyed, Ponna replied, 'Who knows? He must have eaten the crap lying around on the road.'

That day, Seerayi carried food for Kali. She placed the carrier in the hut, and said, 'Listen, apparently you did not eat the food she made, so she has said she is not cooking any more. I made this food. So please don't stay hungry.

Eat this and do at least a little work in the cattle enclosure. I have been doing back-breaking work here.' Kali resumed eating that day. Gradually, Seerayi asked Ponna to do the cooking; but it was Seerayi who continued to take the food to Kali.

Ponna, however, warned her: 'This is a man who tried to hang himself because he thought everyone had fooled him. Now if he finds out I am the one cooking, he might accuse me again of cheating him. Then we might have to chop down another branch of the portia tree.'

Seerayi said, 'He won't say that. And if he does, we will worry about it then. Let him open his mouth and say something in the first place.' Then she added, 'If you set right the brinjal patch, we can get a few vegetables. Then we can draw some water from the well and irrigate that patch. Can you do that, please?' She hoped that if she slowly got Ponna and Kali engaged in these activities, they might move past their current predicament. As per Seerayi's request, Ponna went to the fields to see about the brinjal patch. She was shocked at the state of the fields. She had been coming to the barnyard regularly, but she had not really stopped to linger at the fields. Everyone else's fields were all lush and fertile, with ragi and groundnuts thriving on them. But theirs were lying uncared for—and this left her shaken. If Kali just lay about in the barn, nothing would get done. Once the month of Aadi began and they got the first bout of rains, they should at least sow maize.

The brinjal patch was right next to the well. Just a single row. Two years ago, when Kali took one of the cows to Pazhaiyur for mating, he saw people planting brinjal in a field there. He brought some thirteen saplings back with him. They were not very hopeful about two or three of these which were really tiny. He had planted them right next to the well, since that way it would be easier to water them even in summer. It was a wide patch. While planting them, he had asked Ponna to leave a large gap between the plants. When she asked why, he only said, 'Just do it the way I tell you to.' Only later, when the plants grew big, did she realize why he had said that. This particular type of brinjal was called 'cat's head' brinjal. Each vegetable was as big as a cat's head. If she cooked just one brinjal, it was enough for all of them to eat. And it was really fresh and fragrant. So Ponna cooked it in various ways. She also shared the brinjals with people who visited them. Their brinjals became quite famous throughout the village, and many people started showing up just to get some.

There were also people who decided to help themselves to the vegetable without asking. So Ponna decided to sell them for one kaasu each. But no one felt like paying for it. 'One kaasu for a brinjal?' they would exclaim. 'Ponna is greedy!' Since people stopped coming for the brinjals, there was a lot left on the plants one week. Ponna harvested them and carried them in a basket to the Thursday market. And since she was selling them only for one kaasu per vegetable, they were all sold out quickly. She got a total of eight annas from that sale, which she spent happily at the same market. After that, Ponna became known in the village as the woman who sold brinjals in the market. That was because, until then, most houses had just one or two brinjal plants near their drains. Whatever grew on these plants, they used for their domestic consumption. Sometimes they might grow brinjal alongside water channels. But until then no one had allotted an entire bed for brinjals and grown so many.

For a few weeks, Ponna went to the market carrying her basketful of brinjals. Seeing her do that, some people tried to grow their own brinjals, but none of them could tend to the plants the way Kali did. Kali took great care to make sure worms didn't attack the plants. He would carefully make sure the aphid did not take over the leaves. To prevent that from happening, Kali took some ashes from the stove and sprinkled them on the leaves of the brinjal plants. He made sure the ashes also coated the underside of the leaves. Those plants produced fruits last year and this year as well. They were still healthy and strong. He had done another thing last year. He had used two vegetables from these plants to extract seeds. To do this, he had left those two brinjals on the plant until they ripened and shrivelled. Then he plucked and dried them and extracted the seeds. This year, his plan was to plant an entire square measure of brinjals. If they had indeed done that, they might have made enough money to cover all their purchases at the Thursday market.

Had he been in a good frame of mind, Kali would not have left the plants unattended. He would have tended to them and made them thrive. Now Ponna could not bear to look at the state of those plants. Even Kali would be shocked if he looked at them now. How could she make him see? It didn't look like she would be able to accomplish that anytime soon.

Ponna worked on the brinjal bed for two days. She removed all the stalks that had dried up on top and just left the main stem and the healthy branches intact. She then plucked away all the leaves. The plants were now reduced to just the stem and stalks. She turned the soil near the roots by poking with a spade, and also mixed some dried dung manure in the soil. On the third day, she drew water from the well and irrigated the brinjal patch. It took nearly ten pots of water. Since she watered it late in the evening, the water did not evaporate soon but stayed stagnant in the water channel. After that, she just used two pots of water every day and made sure the bed was always moist. Within a week, the main stems started turning green again and even sprouted a few shoots. This work on the brinjal plants now set a routine for Ponna to go and work in the fields every day. She used the rest of her time there to do some weeding. After that, the fields looked like they were ready for action.

Despite all this, she still felt odd and unwelcome at the barnyard. Somehow she came to feel that she no longer had any relationship with that place. Everything there was his. If she touched anything there, he might get upset. He might not say anything, but he would glower at her. And she felt that his scowls had the power to reduce her to ashes. Besides, she did not carry food for him any more either. So she did not have much to do in the barnyard. She went straight to the part of the fields where the well was. If she needed to take a break, she would sit in the shade of the palai tree there. She had weeded out about ten bales of kolunji plants and set them on the rock. Someone had told her that there were people in Veyyur who would buy them for a price. But she was not sure she had the strength to take them all the way to Veyyur. Seerayi gave her an idea. They could ask Kaaraan's daughter-in-law Vengayi to do the job, and they could give her half the profits.

From under the shade of the palai tree, she had a good view of the barnyard. She could see the entrance to the hut and the tops of bales stacked up outside. And from there the portia tree looked like a demoness. In the alley on the other side of the fence, she could sense the movement of the cows grazing. The sheep enclosure was inside the barn. In this season, it would be a better idea to place it outside, especially since one would then no longer have the additional job of clearing out the refuse. Besides, sheep droppings made for good manure. Whenever this train of thought led Ponna to wonder if those happy days in the barnyard would ever return, she grew sad and started crying.

Kali liked to set his cot in the vacant spot on the north side of the hut. Visitors to the barnyard could not spot him easily there. Walking in past the gate, one would first see the portia tree. If one walked past the cattle floor and the bales of produce stacked in the shade of the tree, one would reach the hut. Beyond that was the concealed spot where Kali liked to lie on the cot. On moonlit nights, Kali used to feel particularly aroused and lust after his wife. He wouldn't let her out of his sight for even a minute. Lying on the cot, he would hold her in his embrace, huddling close to her as if he were a child. And he would go to sleep in that position. Even a slight movement from her would wake him up. Then he would pull her even closer. Ponna too loved embracing him that way. When she asked him, 'What do you do on nights when I am not here?' he replied, 'I go to sleep thinking of you. I imagine that you are here on this cot with me. That is all I need.'

Will this barnyard turn into just a place of memories for her?

ELEVEN

Even though Kali could not bring himself to look at Ponna's face, his mind kept conjuring it involuntarily. But along with that came another face, a face he could not recognize. It did not look like any of the faces he was familiar with. And this face didn't just show up in his mind and go away. It did things. It rubbed itself against Ponna's face. It bit her lips. It pulled away and looked at her naked body. At that point, he could not bear it any more, and slapped himself hard on his cheeks. It produced in him a rage to destroy the face that had usurped his rightful place. He also could not gather the courage to imagine the look on Ponna's face when he destroyed that other face. Would she look happy and relieved? Or would her face be twisted in disgust?

Kali was intimately familiar with every inch of Ponna's body. He did not even know his own body that well. There was one little lash on Ponna's eyelids that was thick and slanting away from the other eyelashes. He sometimes held it between his lips and tugged at it. She once said to him, 'Let me know if you want me to remove it.'

But he replied, 'It is my most favourite piece of hair, let me tell you.' He also liked to play with her tongue by keeping his finger on it. She would pull it in at his touch, and he would ask her to bring it out again. 'It feels soft, like touching a snail,' he said once.

'See, now the snail is going into its shell!' she said, and closed her mouth.

He loved the fine lines on her lips. He once counted them and said, 'Fourteen.'

She said, 'You are crazy.'

And he agreed. 'Yes, indeed I am.'

Now he wondered if the other face might have enjoyed biting those lips, or if it might have tasted the mild sweetness of her saliva.

Whenever such thoughts took over, he felt the urge to hang himself on the portia tree again. At such moments, it took a while for the rage to subside. He reminded himself of his mother's words to help contain his anger. Sometimes he felt it would be a lot better if he could just forget Ponna's face. Yes, that would help. It would give him a lot of peace. But how? Could he simply command his mind to do that? Would it listen to him? There was no greater enemy than one's own mind. It pretended to listen and understand, but then it went ahead and did just the opposite. If he asked it to forget her face, it said yes. But the next moment it presented to him an enlarged version

Muthu had once taken Kali to Chinnapallam to drink some good arrack. As they sat around drinking, a man there said, 'They live nearby. We just need to send a word. Someone will come. The kind you want. Let me know, I can make arrangements.'

Muthu was very keen. He asked Kali, 'What do you say? Do you want to try poratta here today?' Muthu was, in fact, alluding to a previous conversation he had had with Kali in which he had once said, 'I am tired of eating home-cooked food. My tongue has gone numb. I hear there is a new dish in the shops now. They call it poratta. Do you want to go try it?' At the time Kali had replied. 'What? Puraa kari? You mean pigeon meat?' And Muthu had said, 'No, no, poratta.' They never did try that new dish. But they kept alluding to it in subsequent conversations.

Kali declined the offer. He said, 'Ponna is enough for me. I don't need to go anywhere else,' and returned home. Muthu ran after him, feeling happy. He said, 'Well, we have clearly married off Ponna to a good man.' That made Kali wonder if Muthu had been testing him.

Once he married Ponna, no other woman's body tempted him. That was the truth. Then what was the point in his mother bringing up his earlier visits to the festival night? Didn't she know how faithful he had been to Ponna? And they thought he didn't know it was Ponna's food he was still eating. It was true that he did not want to eat anything she cooked. Only if you like a person will you also like the things they do. Initially he had resolved to himself that he wouldn't eat food cooked by her. He stayed hungry for a few days and only drank toddy. Then his mother started bringing over the food she made. But gradually he noticed a change in the taste of the food. He had tasted his mother's cooking since he was a child. Wouldn't he be able to tell the difference? Besides, he was observing Ponna carefully tending to the brinjal plants. He may not have stepped outside the barn, but he still knew she was working on the brinjal patch. And soon he was served all these brinjal dishes. He knew it was all Ponna's excellent cooking.

Ponna knew how to cook brinjals with coconut. Even his mother could not do it so well. No one could. One day she made brinjal with dried fish. It was incredibly tasty. It went very well with the pap she served. He licked it all clean. In the past two years, Ponna had got Kali hooked to the taste of brinjal. Now he wondered if she was using brinjal as a sort of message of peace. He was putting up with all this only for his mother's sake. She was working so hard. She was at that age where she should just do a few chores and spend her time chatting and relaxing. He did not want to make her life even harder. Otherwise he would have flung that brinjal dish away.

He was thinking of leaving the fields fallow indefinitely. And also about selling off the cattle and just shutting himself up in the barn. But his mother wouldn't let him do that. His mother and wife were working together now. Though there was a time when they were like snake and mongoose.

Sometime ago, when Ponna's behaviour had put an end to visits from Kali's uncles and their families, Seerayi came to hate Ponna. 'She behaves as if she has brought a ton of wealth,' she complained to Kali. 'We have got a few chickens here. So what if my brothers come and eat them? What do we lose? I can always raise more chickens.'

But now the two women were close. He could see it all from the barn. They sometimes sat in the shade of the palai tree by the well, chatting away. Seerayi kept nagging him: 'Sow maize. If you sell the sheep and cattle, what will you do for a living? You haven't planted ragi, you have not sown kambu. Now we have to buy everything. She has broken all ties with her family, so we cannot ask them for provisions either. The three of us have to survive. Everyone in the village is asking why you have not planted anything. I don't know what to tell them. They want to know what the problem is between you and Ponna. They even seem to know we have broken relations with your in-laws. I don't know how these people find out everything.'

And so he relented and sowed maize. It had been two months since he had done anything. He stepped out to the fields. He did two rounds of ploughing and planted white maize in all the fields. They had now started to grow.

TWELVE

Every night, Ponna hoped Kali would come to her. During the day, she sometimes took a nap in the shade of the palai tree. That afternoon nap sometimes made it difficult for her to fall asleep at night. Porasa's children from next door often came by to play at Seerayi's place. They were quite noisy, climbing over the raised porch, jumping from there on to the ground, and running out. Everyone in the village retired to bed once the seven o'clock siren sounded at the Karattur factory. Also, this was the season to work in the fields. People had a lot to do during the day: weeding, cutting grass, taking sheep and cattle to the pastures for grazing, and so on. The maize had been sown in Kali's fields by now. For their meals every day, Ponna had to wake up early and pound kambu millets. Or she needed to crush ragi grains and make a pap. And since nakkiri greens were abundantly available in this season, they also cooked those.

The village grew very quiet early in the night. The crows went to roost on the trees lining the streets. Ponna could hear women calling out to their husbands and children for dinner. She could also hear people calling out to their dogs to come and eat the food they kept in bowls. Then the whimpering sounds of the infants would slowly fade. Finally, the barking of the dogs would come to an end. After that, there was only the buzzing of night insects. But that too would diminish soon. Then she would hear the hooting of hungry owls from the wild palmyra trees on the outskirts of the village. And then even those sounds would slowly end. But Ponna's mind alone could never settle in peace at night. It listened keenly to all sounds. In particular, her ears were expectant for the sound of footsteps. Her mind and ears worked together, alert for the faintest noise. And even though her body was tired, her eyes were wide awake.

Ponna constantly chided herself for her pathetic state. He called you a whore, but here you are, yearning for him. Do you have even an ounce of pride or self-respect or shame? Sometimes she even said these things out loud to herself. That house had a large room, a veranda with a sloping roof, a raised platform out front and a small inner yard. In that spacious room were a lot of cooking pots, Ponna's cot and a vessel to cook rice. This was Ponna's space. Seerayi was right on the other side of the wall, in the veranda area. Kali had made this arrangement at a time in the past when the two women couldn't get along. But when this new situation arose, Seerayi moved her cot into the large room and kept Ponna company at night. But she could not fall asleep there. She was far too accustomed to her spot on the veranda. Earlier, Seerayi was able to fall asleep anywhere, but now she was not able to sleep even in the barn. She could catch a wink only in that one spot she had grown used to. As for Ponna, she fell asleep only in the early hours of the morning. So she slept very little.

Ponna said, 'Atthai, why are you troubling yourself, trying to keep an eye on me? I am not stupid like your son. The way I think about it is that somehow I have been born as this particular person. I have to live this life. So I won't do anything to myself. Don't worry. You go back to the veranda and sleep peacefully.'

That gave Seerayi some comfort and she went back to her usual spot. But sometimes in the night, she would hear Ponna scolding herself. In those moments, she would call out, 'What happened, Ponna?' And Ponna would reply, 'Nothing. I heard a rat.' Rats did show up no matter how well you maintained the house. They would scamper around, running and making noises. Sometimes, in their ruckus, little roof tiles would shift and crumble. Ponna thought her mind too was as noisy as that.

How could she expect him to come to her? Would he step inside a whorehouse? After having called her that, how would he look her in the eye? But she continued to yearn for him. And she did not know what to think of her fickle mind which continued to seek him out despite everything. Perhaps her mind hoped he would come and apologize for calling her that? Ponna even knew how his knock would sound on the door. If he came at the early part of the night when people might have just fallen asleep, he would tread softly like a cat. And he would gently rap on the door—like a rat gnawing at a piece of coconut. But if he came later, in the middle of the night, he knocked twice. It was the sound of a single knuckle tapping on the door. If he arrived early in the morning, he would use his entire palm on the door.

In these various ways, she had mapped him out as sounds in the night. Even now, she awaited his arrival. He knew that the dogs in the village would bark if he walked through the main streets. So he took a circuitous route home. That meant he would have to walk past two or three fields. He somehow managed not to alert any of the dogs on the farms on the way and slip in through the gate in the backyard fence. On those nights, she'd say to him, 'There might be dangerous insects about in the fields. Don't go now. Eat something and spend the night here.' But he would reply, 'I like it this way. I come whenever I think of you. It makes me happy.' And she would angrily respond, 'Does that mean you are not thinking of me all the time?' He would laugh at this, saying, 'I think of you all the time. But I feel this need only now and then.' Did that mean he did not feel that need for her over the past two months? Had he forgotten her? What if he never came to her again? Was her life with him over? These anxieties kept her awake well into the night. And she did not know when she fell asleep.

He did come that night—well past midnight. She had dozed off, but she heard his footsteps. She woke up hurriedly and listened carefully. Those were definitely his footsteps—two feet planting themselves with equal force on the ground. The sound grew louder. He was climbing up the stairs out front. Then he came to a stop at the porch. And the sounds died.

He had stopped right outside, and she heard very clearly the sound of his knuckle on the door. She rose from the cot in a rush. She usually put out the lamp before going to bed and only kept a window open. But the matchbox was right next to the lamp. She lit it quickly. Then she heard the knock on the door again. It was definitely him. It was a single large door with a wooden latch. She had to press the door away from her and slowly remove the latch. Otherwise, it would make a loud noise which could awaken everyone. She could see that he was pulling the door towards him on the outside to make the task easy for her. She released the latch.

From the darkness outside, he stepped into the light. She stood with her head lowered, indicating that she did not want to look at him. He closed the door quietly. He then came closer to her right away and gathered her in an embrace. She tried to wiggle away, refusing to be contained in his embrace. 'Come on,' he said, and held her tighter. She stopped resisting him. He gently lifted her face up with his hand. Her tears glittered in the light from the lamp. 'Are you angry with me?' he said. 'It was a mistake. I don't know how that word came to my lips. But you sensed it right away. I will never ever call you that again.'

And she said, crying, 'But you did say it once. What about that?'

'For that, hit me with your own hand,' he said, and took her hand in his and struck himself with it across his face. Feeling sorry for him, she pulled back her hand. But he held on tight and hit himself on his mouth with her hand, saying, 'Please hit me until your anger subsides. Hit this mouth for using that word.' His lips reddened. Scared, she pulled her hand away. Then she placed her lips on his, in an attempt to soothe them. That one touch conveyed all her yearning and suffering. He moved her to the cot.

It was a large cot made with coir ropes. Once their wedding was fixed, he had the carpenter in Anjoor make it according to the specific measurements he had given. The cot's four legs were made of neem wood, the frame from portia wood. It was spacious enough for two people to lie down comfortably. In fact, when he got it made, Kali was too embarrassed to let anyone in the village see it. He was afraid they would tease him. So he brought it in his bullock cart one night from the carpenter's to his barnyard. Another night, he brought it here to the house in the village. Even Seerayi teased him: 'Why do you need such a big cot!' But Ponna was very fond of that cot. Kali had wanted aloe coir ropes for the cot, because they were gentle on the body.

They lay down on the cot. She turned to look at him. There were tears in his eyes. She wiped them away immediately. 'Please don't cry, Maama,' she said.

'I have tormented you way too much, haven't I?' he said, sadly.

Weeping, she said, 'You call me anything you want. You have the right. But please don't abandon me. I can't bear it.'

He pinched her cheek, saying, 'I will never leave you alone for even a single day, my dear. And I won't blame you for anything.'

Then she found herself trapped under him. He nuzzled his face against hers. Now she took him in fully. He was in no hurry. He gradually entered every cell of her body. And she felt him enter her.

THIRTEEN

Ponna slept in the next morning. She did not know a new day had dawned.

Seerayi, on the other hand, woke up early and left for the fields. Her presence in the farmstead served as an incentive for Kali to engage himself in farming activities. Otherwise, he simply sat on his cot, staring at the ceiling. So she took off very early from the house, when it was still quite dark. She did not wake Ponna up. Her idea was to spend a little time in the barnyard and then return home to pick up some food for Kali. Ponna would be up and about by then and she would have also made some food. Porasa, who lived next door and was struggling to handle her children, was quite jealous of Ponna. Once she even said out loud that Ponna was living an enviable life. After all, Ponna didn't have to do any work. She just had to do some cooking, eat it, and go sit in the fields for a little while. 'What a lucky life,' thought Porasa.

She expressed her envy to Seerayi, who happened to walk by her house that morning. 'Are we all lucky enough to sleep well past daybreak? We have given birth to little children and so we have to run after them. But some people are still sleeping!' Saying this, she subtly pointed towards Ponna's house. Seerayi smiled but kept on walking. She was scared of Ponna's sharp tongue. If she said anything in response to Porasa's remark now, she knew it was likely to reach Ponna's ears soon. Porasa, however, was hoping Ponna would step out soon and she could make some sarcastic remark about the day just dawning for Ponna. But Ponna did not give her that satisfaction. So Porasa had to leave for the fields, her wish unfulfilled.

It was late in the morning when Seerayi returned home. The night before, Ponna had cooked some pap with nakkiri greens. She wondered if Ponna was going to offer her the leftovers with curd or if she had cooked something fresh. But she found Ponna's door closed, and she panicked, thinking Ponna might have done something to herself. None of the neighbours were around; they had all left for the day's work in the fields. Seerayi banged on Ponna's door with great urgency and panic, calling out, 'Ponna! Ponna!'

Ponna heard that voice as though it was part of her dream. Kali has come to me after so long. Why is this old hag bothering us now? She might wake Kali up. Ponna was annoyed, and she reached over to the other side of the bed, addressing Kali, 'Maama.' But he was not there. When did he leave? She did not remember waking up to lock the door behind him. If it was not locked, Seerayi wouldn't be knocking now. Even though all these thoughts raced through her mind, she still couldn't open her eyes. She just mumbled 'Mmm' in response.

Seerayi was relieved to hear that. She then called out more forcefully, 'Ponna!'

That made Ponna sit up with a jolt. She rubbed her eyes and opened them a little. At first, she thought it was still dark. Then, as she opened her eyes some more, she saw daylight streaming through the gaps between the roof tiles. Seerayi was still knocking at the door. Ponna responded, 'I am coming, Atthai.' So Seerayi stopped knocking and waited for Ponna to open the door. Inside, Ponna stood up, holding on to the cot for balance. Did Kali suck away all her energy the night before? Her sari was not even a little out of place, but she did not remember tying it back up in the night. Did Kali really come to her? She felt dizzy. She thought she would collapse even if she dared to take just one step forward. She continued to hold on to the cot and extended her arms to brace herself against the wall. Then she walked forward, one hand on the wall for support. She could see that daylight had now spread all over the house. How did Kali leave and manage to latch the door on the inside? The latch looked like it had not been disturbed at all. She opened it with much effort.

When she opened the door, the brightness of the day hit her with a force that unsettled her. She held on to the door to keep her bearings. Seerayi rushed in, saying, 'Ponna! What happened?' She helped Ponna stand up. But Ponna was not able to express how she was feeling. She just wanted to go and lie down again. So she walked back to the cot with Seerayi's help and lay down on it. Seerayi placed her hand on Ponna's forehead to see if she had a fever. But no.

Ponna asked her in a soft voice, 'Where is your son?'

Seerayi said, 'Where else? He is in the barnyard, he has become one of the cattle.'

Ponna asked hesitantly, 'So he didn't come here?'

Seerayi said, 'Why would he come here? Wait. Let me heat up some water for you. Looks like you are not well.' And she went to light up the stove. Ponna was feeling better now that she was lying down with her eyes closed.

Kali had come to her for sure. Otherwise, why would she feel this massive physical exhaustion and body ache? He had come and released two months of pent-up desire on her. He had been with her in the night. Why else would her body feel this way? Kali expressed his passion in various ways. He had once explained, 'One day, it is the toddy from aamaram tree. It goes straight to the head. Another day, it is toddy from the pommaram tree. It is sweet and it takes its time to hit you. If it is toddy tapped from the tender spathe, it has absolutely no effect. But if it is from the mature spathe, all you need to drink is one glass.' Sometimes, when he was like the toddy from aamaram tree, he was so overcome with desire that he had no control over himself. He would even forget that it was a body he was dealing with, a body with bones and muscles. He would treat her body like the folded veshti he wore on his waist. He would do as he pleased with it. He'd fold her, roll her, unfold her. He wouldn't listen to her protests. It was not easy to deal with his rough and strong hands.

Seerayi woke Ponna up again once the hot water was ready. Ponna walked outside with Seerayi, holding her for support. She then sat down and rinsed out her mouth with some warm water. She felt a bitterness coating her tongue, as though a lot of phlegm had got caught in her throat. When she took some more water in her mouth to gargle, she retched intensely. Since it caught her by surprise, she could not control herself and she lurched forward and spat it out. It fell a good distance away. And the retching did not stop. Her stomach was empty but she felt the urge to keep trying to spit something out. It was all so forceful that she felt her intestines would come out. Seerayi, who was holding her head, said, 'Ponna! This is it for sure!' and smiled. Ponna did not understand. She was tired and annoyed and looked up at Seerayi, who then said softly, 'Our prayers have been answered. The deity has come into your womb now!' Seerayi could not contain her excitement. She rushed into the house, brought some ash from the stove and, thinking of it as holy ash, made a mark with it on Ponna's head.

Ponna was both surprised and shocked. Seerayi kept talking, 'It has been two months since you had your menses. In fact, this is the third month. Remember? I have been keeping track of it. You have not washed and hung the sanitary cloths anywhere here or in the barnyard. I did wonder if you were drying them somewhere else out of my sight. But considering how you two have been, I was too scared to ask. But I was expecting this!' Ponna started crying. She was not sure she wanted this. 'Why are you crying?' said Seerayi. 'Everything will be all right. Don't cry thinking of him, that dog! A child will melt even the hardest of hearts. Once you have a child, all his anger will go away, all worry and sorrow will vanish.' Seerayi cast her gaze outside to see if any people were about. But there was no one. Then she found a piece of dried ginger she had put inside the spice box long ago and made some dried ginger concoction for Ponna to drink. It only took her a few minutes to make it.

Seerayi was overcome with excitement at this development. She said to Ponna, 'It will be difficult for a little while with all this retching and sickness. You just have to be patient.' She caressed Ponna's head with great affection.

Ponna began to feel better once she started drinking the hot ginger concoction. 'God did not give me this,' she found the strength to say. 'My husband gave me this. He was with me last night. He told me all sorts of things. It is he who has given me this.' Her eyes brightened with joy.

'All right,' said Seerayi. 'Your husband gave you this. He is such a paragon of generosity. He came flying to you to give you this. I won't contradict that. We have suffered so much. But we have it now. Feel happy, don't cry. Your maama will act funny in the beginning, but you should not let that upset you. That's not good for the child growing inside you, all right?' And she wiped away Ponna's tears. She had never spoken such comforting words to Ponna before. Ponna wondered and hoped Seerayi's words would come true, that things would change for the better, and she gently rubbed her belly.

FOURTEEN

Seerayi was like a headless chicken that day. At first, she did not know what to focus on, what to put off for later. Eventually she decided that attending to Ponna was her first priority, so she soaked some rice for lunch. She could cook rice and lentils. Ponna would like that. But she should not crackle mustard seeds in oil for seasoning. That fragrance might be too much for Ponna right now. She decided to make some rasam as well, using a mixture of spices. She soaked some lentils in water, and then left for the barnyard, taking two balls of pudding in a carrier for Kali.

It looked as though Kali was hungry. He was pacing about, looking constantly towards the path. Did he really go to Ponna the night before? Seerayi couldn't be sure. Did she sleep so soundly that she didn't hear anything? She gave him the food she had brought and waited till he diluted and drank his meal.

As he mixed the curd with the pudding, he was reminded of Ponna. He could tell that this was Ponna's cooking. He lifted the vessel and poured it directly into his mouth. Usually, when people drank water-soaked leftovers, they liked to crunch on raw onions or green chillies. Seerayi also made lemon pickle when the season was right. And just a piece of that pickle would make the meal go down smoothly. But Kali did not need any of that. Curd was all he needed. Whether it was pap or kambu meal, he would empty the curd on top of it. He already required half a can of curd just for himself. Then he would mix and liquefy the meal. The meal and the curd had to mix really well. After that, he could drink it all in one gulp.

Ponna used to say, 'I don't know how you drink that without adding even salt.'

He would respond, 'If I add salt, I cannot taste the meal. The grain has its own taste. The curd too. And when they come together, they bring about a new taste. You have to experience that. It is a cultivated taste, it grows on you. After that, you need no salt in it. Or pickle on the side.'

She would also tease him. 'I know how you drink it all in one gulp. It is all the practice you have had drinking toddy.'

He'd respond, 'That stuff is pure nectar of the gods. Does anyone drink nectar in small, measured portions? Do you think we can resist its taste?'

'Yes, indeed, as though you have tasted the nectar of the gods,' she said, making a face at him.

'Oh yes, I have definitely tasted the divine nectar. I can get it in two places.'

'You mean palmyra toddy and coconut toddy? Or toddy and arrack?'

'Nonsense. You seem to know nothing. Shall I tell you where? I find it in your lips and your nipples. You have the nectar right with you, but you don't seem to know!' And he winked.

She replied, sighing, 'Well, I have been waiting for a child to taste that from my breasts, but it looks like I am not fortunate enough for that. If you drink it all, nothing will be left, only your own saliva.'

No matter how often he resolved not to think about her, she somehow surfaced in his mind. She was there in everything. He sighed deeply, drank the rest of the meal and wiped his mouth.

Seerayi went closer to him as if she were about to tell him a secret, and whispered, 'All our troubles of all these years have come to an end. You have to make sure you set your mind right about things. We found out just today. Ponna is pregnant.' Kali had been looking at her as she spoke to him, but then he lowered his head. 'When I tell her this is a god-given child, she starts crying. She says, "My maama came to me last night. This child has been given to me by my husband." Perhaps she dreamed of you coming to her in the night. Before last night, she wasn't sleeping well. She would pace about like a rat. Perhaps she dreamt of you. She keeps saying you went to her last night. Did you come?'

He did not say anything in reply, but just sat there with his head resting on his hands.

'It does not matter if it is god's child or your child,' went on Seerayi. 'From now on, it is our child. How we have struggled! How many insults and indignities we have endured! How many people have been rude to us! This child has brought an end to all of that. Think about that. There are childless folk who adopt one from their relatives. But this child is ours. That Devaatha has decided to give us her blessings. So you should not do anything to ruin things now. Both my heart and my eyes had gone dry and hopeless for a long time. But today both my heart and my eyes feel like a field of lush green harvest. Let me spend the rest of my life playing with a grandchild. Please don't spoil that.'

He continued to sit with his head lowered. She got hold of his head-knot and pulled up his head. He closed his eyes, but tears flowed from them. A beard now covered his cheeks and jaw. He had been refusing to shave. He also had thick eyebrows. His face looked like it was completely covered in hair. She couldn't bear to look at his sad, unkempt visage. She gently tapped his cheek with her hand. 'What's wrong now? She says it is your child. And what a mother says about her child is the truth. It is the mother who has the final word about who the father of her child is. Ponna says it was you who gave her this child . . .

Let me ask you, how do you know for sure who your father is? I tell you, "This man is your father," and you accept it. That is all. Can anyone contradict a mother's statement on that?' He sat there, unable to free himself from her grip.

'You have grown into a big man,' she said, 'but you are not very smart. It was all my mistake, I am a stupid widow, I let you do whatever you wanted. I should have been stricter, I should have hit you more, been clearer about right and wrong. You are still a child to me. You are the only child I have. Please listen to your mother and act properly. What have I really had in my life that I could call my own? Do I have any close relatives? Do I get to attend auspicious occasions? Wherever I go, I stay with other widows, lumped to a side. Would anyone let me take the lead in a family function? Why, do you know how much I worry even about coming here from the village early in the morning? There are people who consider the sight of a widow very unlucky as they set out for the day.' She began to weep inconsolably. Then she said, almost in the tune of a lament, 'When you narrate a widow's story, even a rock would melt, even a crow would cry. If you narrate this Seerayi's story, even this earth would dissolve, trees would weep.' She sat down, and then continued, 'There are people who said I was not doing the farming work properly. You set up this barn. Could I have done something like this on my own? Could I have come and stayed alone like you do? Men would roam around here like dogs. Would it have been a safe prospect for me, tell me? You know how men looked at your wife when they knew you were childless. Then imagine how they would look at a widow.'

He went back to sitting huddled.

'You know what will happen if I leave the house in the morning and come here to the fields?' Seerayi ranted. 'That is when people would be setting out of their houses, walking this way to their various tasks. If I show up in front of them, they will make a face wondering why a widow is crossing their path. That is why I often stay put in the house in the morning and set out late. And once I arrive here, I stay in. Do you think this has been easy? The point of human life is to go to places where people throng, to meet people, to talk to people, to do our work in a way others can witness it. Have I been fortunate enough to have any of that? Tell me. Not a day has gone by when I have not cried thinking of my life. Wherever I go, I stand to a side, away from the action, and just make sure I go and mark my presence, that's all.'

When he heard her voice breaking, he looked up at her. She was staring into a distance, sighing. Then she started speaking again. 'Do you know how eager I was for you to grow up and turn my life around? What else do I have in this life? Just you. When you grew into a man, I thought you could henceforth represent me, go everywhere on my behalf, receive respect from people. But I was not lucky enough to experience that. Wherever I went, everyone only wanted to know if my daughter-in-law had conceived or not. What could I tell them? You two could not happily go anywhere either.'

He let out a deep sigh and got up. He washed his hands with some water from the large earthen pot.

She spoke louder now. 'Wherever you two went, you either came back crying or feeling angry. You have told me so many stories of people being rude to you, insulting you. But it looks like things are meant to change for the better for me, at least in what is left of my life. Now both you and Ponna can mingle with people fearlessly, you can go to events and occasions. No one will dare say anything about you. And I can go with you too. Or I can feel happy listening to the stories you bring back with you. I think my life is really beginning only now. Please don't ruin it.'

It looked as though Kali was unable to understand what she was saying.

'I do know what is going on in your mind,' she continued. 'You are wondering how you would bring yourself to find joy in a child that is not yours. But when it comes to children, what is the point of such distinctions? Try spending time with the baby. You will know the pleasure of parenthood then. All children are given by god. It is only we humans who discriminate between ours and others'. You will change some day. And you will act according to my words. But until then, do what you can, and be good.'

Kali kept staring at her.

'Yes,' she said, without a pause. 'Now we have to take care of her. We have to take good care of her and make sure the birth goes well. She has come to us, severing her relations with her parents. They can't come here. And we cannot do anything about that when she is pregnant. So I will have to take care of everything. In the middle of all this, if you are uncooperative and you pull in a different direction, how will I manage? Tell me. I am sure that you will change your mind about things. And that both of you will go back to how you used to be—chatting and laughing and enjoying each other's company. That day will come. Until then, engage yourself in a few tasks. There are a thousand things to do in the fields. When you are engaged in work, you won't feel the force of your other problems. Only the person who sits in a corner, dejected, feels everything acutely. So please do the work. Don't make a mess of things now.'

For a little while, they both sat silently. Then she washed the lunch carrier and got ready to go back home. 'Good days have begun for us,' she said. 'All our hurdles are over. Everything will be all right from now. Please be smart and try to live well, my dear.' She gently caressed his head before leaving. He sat looking at her receding figure, amazed at her speech. What clarity and force. Was this the same mother who used to be tired and listless all the time? How often had he judged her in his own mind for her lack of interest in anything? This was not the mother he knew. And when it occurred to him that until then he had never really thought about her properly, he was overcome with sadness, and he sat there on that rock for quite a while.

FIFTEEN

When Seerayi turned away from the mud road and entered the path that led to the village quarters, she ran into Periyaan.

'Periyaan, are you on your way to work?' she asked him.

'No, saami. I have a buffalo calf. I am going to get some grass to feed it.'

Seerayi said, 'All right. I need someone to go to Adaiyur to inform our in-laws that Ponna is pregnant. Can you go? For such good news, they will reward you very well.'

'I am happy that god has finally opened his eyes,' he said. 'I will go right away. What could be more important than this? Also, your in-laws are always very generous, saami.'

Seerayi immediately added, 'On your way, if you see the midwife Thangamma on the other side of the village, can you please ask her to pay us a visit? Ponna is retching for sure. But I would feel better if the midwife comes and confirms the news.'

Periyaan said, 'I will do that too. As for going to Adaiyur, do I wait till the midwife checks on Ponna and confirms it? What shall I do?'

'No, no,' said Seerayi. 'I am very certain. You go, give them the news. And come and see me tomorrow.' She then continued on her way home.

The door was unlocked, and Ponna was lying inside, her eyes closed. She was perhaps asleep, but it also looked like she might just be dizzy and tired. So Seerayi decided not to wake her up, and went straight to see about the cooking.

She set the rice on one stove and the lentils on the other. She wanted to get the cooking done fast, so that Ponna could eat soon. Ponna would definitely feel better as the day progressed, but she would feel stronger once she ate something. Seerayi kept feeling that everything would become all right soon. If Ponna had not impulsively severed her ties with her family, they would have rushed here in a bullock cart as soon as they got the news. But that was not possible now, but never mind. Once the child was born, the first thing they would do was go to the Kooli temple, offer pongal and revoke the ritual separation. Then things would be restored to normal. But, until then, her parents could not come here carrying parcels of food and take her to their place for the birth. Everything would have to be done right here. Seerayi realized it was all going to be a lot of responsibility for her.

Ponna's retching would last another month or month and a half. Basically, they needed to be careful until the fifth month. Things would become smooth after that. Seerayi was recollecting the days of her own pregnancy, things she thought she had long forgotten. As she was cooking, Thangamma, the midwife, arrived. And along with her came a few old women from the village. Thangamma said, 'Aaya, so finally god has blessed our little landlady?' It did not seem as though there was any insinuation in what she said, but Seerayi decided to respond cautiously anyway. 'Yes, Thangamma, she has conceived only after appealing to the goddess Kooli. But you please feel her pulse and let us know for sure.'

Pacchakizhavi and the other elderly women sat down on the raised porch. Seerayi addressed them in general, and said, 'Come!' Pacchakizhavi was called that—the green old woman—because of the green tattoos she had all over her. She said, 'It was Periyaan who informed us. I had just settled down to rest after fetching some greens for the lamb to eat. But when I heard this news, I decided to pay a visit. The girl has conceived after so many years. All your bad time has now come to an end. You have seen so much suffering in your life. May it be good times at least from now on.' All the other paattis too spoke words of blessings and wishes.

Thangamma went into the house and felt Ponna's pulse. When the midwife's cold hand touched hers, Ponna woke up, startled. 'Don't be scared. It is just me— Thanga. When you are in this state, you feel even little things very intensely. The way you shuddered awake at

113

my touch. It is definitely that. And your pulse confirms that. A boy or a girl? What do you want? You are all landowners. You'd always want a boy.' Saying this, the midwife laughed.

Ponna smiled and said, 'Let it be a girl.'

Thangamma called out to Seerayi, who was sitting outside. 'Seerayi, lady, do you want a grandson or a granddaughter?'

Seerayi replied, 'Either is fine by me. Why worry about it? It could even be both!'

Now the paattis went into the house to see Ponna. Pacchakizhavi started singing as soon as she saw Ponna:

> *Look at her face, look at the face*
> *of the pregnant woman*
> *Look at her face, look at her face*
> *that looks like the earth cooled by rain*
> *The seed sown has borne its crop*
> *Look at her face, look at her face*

As she sang, she swayed her body in a kind of dance, and walked towards Ponna. She touched her face and cracked her knuckles in a gesture of warding off the evil eye. The other women blessed her, 'May you give birth and live well.' Thangamma said, 'Look at the old hags dancing!'

Pacchakizhavi said, 'Why not! If our girl Ponna is happy, so are we.' Then she added, 'Don't we know the dancing you do with your husband?'

To which Thangamma replied, 'Yes, indeed. We are newly-weds, you see. That's why I am so excited.'

'Oh, why do you say that? Has the milking stopped?'

'Mhmm! What is the point in trying to milk an old cow? No matter how hard you keep pulling at the teats, you will get nothing. Only the udder keeps growing longer.'

'You should try feeding it some fresh green grass.'

'Where do I go for fresh grass? All I find are dried-up fields.'

'All right, then, find a young heifer. The old one will start milking as soon the young one touches it.'

Thangamma interrupted. 'You all might have got old, but you still talk like this!'

'Oh! Look at what she says. So you are an innocent girl? Don't you talk like this too?'

Thangamma made a face, and said, 'When you grow old, that is all you can do anyway—just talk.' She then said to Ponna, 'Ponnu, you will continue to feel this way for one or two months. Just be patient. Later I will bring you some medicine. Just swallow that. It will help you a little.'

Seerayi brought some food on a plate and gave it to Ponna. Ponna felt that even her fingers were weak. She ate a few morsels. But more visitors arrived by then. All the people who had been on their way to the fields to cut grass and to leave the cattle out for grazing had heard the news and came over to see Ponna. Even some men stopped by to confirm the news with Seerayi. Their neighbour Porasa returned home from the fields quite late. When she saw women sitting outside her house and on her porch, she came running in panic, wondering if something untoward had occurred. When she heard the news, she rushed to Ponna and said happily, 'Ponna! This morning you slept quite late. I kept looking towards your door. There were no sounds. I thought to myself—Ponna is lucky, she can sleep late, I can't. And I went to the fields. If I had known this was the case, I would have come to you sooner. But I am the last one to find out, and I live next door to you!'

As people kept dropping by for a visit, the entire house brimmed with excitement. All the paattis left for their homes, but they returned later in the day and stretched themselves comfortably on the porch and spent their time chatting and gossiping. 'Ponna!' exclaimed one of the women. 'Is it true that you have cut off ties with your parents? Why did you do that? Who else does a woman have besides her own parents? We are not like men, are we? We can't go looking for toddy and wander around here and there. We take care of the house and these dry lands. Our father's house is our only refuge.'

Seerayi told them that it was a simple misunderstanding that had led to Ponna flinging a handful of earth at her parents' house, breaking her ties with them. 'Apparently, her mother said in the course of an argument, "You would understand if you had your own child." And that made Ponna angry and she acted in that way. But this is good in a way. She has conceived after so many years of marriage.

If everything was well, the evil eye might fall on her. Once the child is born, we can reunite with them.'

Ponna lay listening to everything. Everyone from the village had appeared on the scene, but the man whose child it was did not come. She did not even mind the fact that no one from her family had come to visit. In a way, it was good they did not come now. If they came, it might lead to some argument with Kali and things would get worse.

But Ponna had expected Kali to come. He might not want to talk to her, but couldn't he at least come to see her? All these years, how much they had struggled for this moment! Hadn't this news given him at least a little happiness? What would he say? He might think that the whore was carrying another man's child. He would say he wouldn't touch a whore's child. It was Kali who had come to her the night before, wasn't it? She refused to believe that it was not him. She clearly remembered that he had arrived, she remembered the things they had talked about. If it was a dream, how could she remember everything so vividly? She had felt him entering her womb. So he was definitely the reason for her state this morning. But would he accept that?

This might be the third month, but Ponna remembered that on the night her brother Muthu had come to invite them home at the time of the festival, Kali had come to her late. Ponna had scolded him, 'My brother is visiting you! How could you leave him in the barnyard and come to me stealthily?'

'What do I care what your brother thinks?' he had said. 'I was thinking of you, so I decided to come here and give you one.'

'All right, give it to me and leave soon,' she had consented, and showed him her cheek. He gave her one on her cheek, and then he proceeded to her lips. And on that night, he gave it to her fully. That *must* be the cause. It was definitely him. He had been able to do it after so many years. Why did he not understand that?

It would have made her very happy if Kali had come to see her. Perhaps he would come to her at night the way he had done the night before?

SIXTEEN

Kali set out very early in the morning, when it was still quite dark, taking the cow with him. It had been bellowing endlessly for two days. It needed a bull. It cried so loudly in the night that Kali was afraid it might wake up the entire village. It had also not been eating even a mouthful of food. It didn't want to eat oil cake and bran. It just smelt the food once and moved away. The cow was clearly making a point. All it did was walk around the cattle shed restlessly. Whenever a calf or a sheep happened to pass nearby, the cow started trying to mount them. Why, it even tried to lift its front legs over Kali. He had never seen the cow so badly in heat before.

Kali was very good at recognizing when a cow started to cry for a bull. He'd know in the very first cry. When a cow made noises out of hunger or thirst, it was not quite so intense. That was the call of the stomach. But this was the sound of its yearning for the company of a beast of its own kind. It was the sound of its entire body. When that happened, Kali would make sure the cow got to mate with a bull right away. He would never let them suffer. He now remembered that this cow had bellowed in heat even two months ago. He should have taken care of it then, but Kali had not been in the right frame of mind to do all that. If he had done it then, the cow would be two months pregnant by now.

In fact, Kali was still not in the frame of mind to do anything about it. But he could not tolerate the cow's antics. Since it had not eaten for two days and had been bellowing non-stop, the volume of milk it produced had diminished. If the rope tether had been an old and frayed one, the cow would have definitely torn itself away. He hit it with a stick, saying, 'You are so horny, huh? I think I have pampered you too much, given you too much food. That's why you are demanding a bull now.' It ran around the cattle shed to avoid the blows, but it never stopped bellowing.

And Seerayi too nagged him. 'Why can't you take it for mating? If you can't do that, what is the point in us having cattle? What do we do for the curd we need to mix with our pap?' But Kali did not budge.

Finally, she said, 'All right then, I will take the cow tomorrow for mating. The problem is, if it has to be me, it will have to be later in the day. I have a pregnant woman at home. I need to cook some food for her to eat. But the day would be well on its way by then. If we go early, they would let our cow be the first one to mate with the bull. Usually, the first two or three cows get the best semen, and those cows get pregnant quite soon. If the bull has already mated with four or five cows, the semen will be diluted, and we can't be sure the cow will get pregnant. Then we might have to do this all over again. I hear that they are now charging one rupee per cow. How many times can we spend that kind of money?' Then she added, 'Instead of giving birth to him, I could have given birth to a grinding stone. That would have been useful for grinding and pounding things. What do I do with him?'

Kali did not want to put her through all that trouble, so he took the cow and set out very early in the morning. He had to walk quite a distance, three villages away. The bull was in Tharanur. And that was the preferred bull in the entire region. It was a lot of work raising and taking care of bulls meant for mating purposes. You had to attend to the bull all morning. There was no way you could rush away to the fields. And it was no easy task pulling and dragging and tethering those bulls. It required a very strong man for the job. This was why no one wanted to raise a bull. If they got a good bull calf, they had it castrated before it started mounting cows, and turned it into an ox. The cow was now trotting ahead of him, and he had to restrain it by pulling at the rope. This was the same cow he had to drag out to the pastures every day.

It had been two months since Ponna had seen Kali. She stayed put in the house. Seerayi brought him news of her. Ponna's retching continued. She woke up late in the mornings. And since no food really stayed in her stomach for too long, she had grown thin and pale. She cried now and then. Seerayi told him that Ponna looked like a frayed old sari. Each day, she would try to persuade Kali to visit Ponna: 'She will feel better if you come and see her just once. You have stopped talking, we know that. I will just tell myself that I gave birth to a mute son. So you don't have to talk. Come and look at her from a distance. It will give her strength. The child is going to take your name. It will be Kaliyappan's son or daughter. I am saying it is going to be a boy, but she says she wants a girl. She says, it has been just one boy each for the last three generations in this family, so let it be a girl this time. We should not let her suffer when she is in this condition, da. Come and see her once. If you don't want to do this for her, do it for me.'

Despite these daily entreaties, he could not bring himself to go. When Ponna used to come to the fields to work, he could at least see her from a distance. Even though he was angry at her, he felt good that he was still able to see her. But now he did not want to actively seek her out. No matter what she said about it, she now carried a faceless stranger's child. And Kali was the father just for name's sake. She needed Kali to give the child a father's name. That was all. It didn't matter whether it was going to be a boy or a girl. It would be Ponna's child. It was another man's child. Kali had nothing to do with it. He was still not able to get rid of that image of some other man's body lying over Ponna's, occupying every inch of her body. It crept up on him frequently and tormented him. He was confused about what he should do. He wondered if he could just spend the rest of his life confined to the barnyard, or if he could go away somewhere. He could not decide on anything. And he performed all his tasks disinterestedly.

It was all lush and green in the fields. This would be a good time to cut some grass and bundle it up in bales, so that the cows would have something to munch on in the summer. He could also find leaves and shoots for the sheep. But Kali wasn't even taking the cattle out to graze on the sides of the maize fields. He just wanted to lie about and do nothing. However, since he wanted to be considerate to his mother, he forced himself to carry out a few tasks. Even though he did not respond to anything she said, she continued chatting with him tirelessly. Sometimes he did not want to listen to her, so he went and stood in a corner of the barn. Even then she followed him there and sustained her chatter. He wondered if she could ever shut up, but his mind did compose answers for all her questions. It was not an easy task to make the mind accept things.

His mother told him that the people in the village were beginning to say that there were troubles in Kali and Ponna's marriage. There were even people who came all the way to the barnyard to talk to him. He found it very tiring even to respond to them in a word or two and send them on their way. He was able to manage only because he already had a reputation for being a man of few words. Seerayi had told everyone that he visited Ponna at night. All these complications would end if Ponna resumed her visits to the fields. Kali was beginning to feel restless in the barnyard; he did not want to be there. He wanted to run away. But where could he go? What could he do?

When he reached his destination with the cow, he realized that they were the first to arrive that morning. The bull sniffed out the cow even from a distance, and it started bellowing and pulling at its rope. The wind had evidently carried the cow's fragrance all the way to the beast. The wind had a way of spreading the scent of lust everywhere. The man of that house was called the Bullman. Since they had been in that business for over two or three generations, even their house was referred to as the Bullmen's house. He had a labourer who took care of the bull and handled the mating. But the owner was also always present on these occasions. Very soon after Kali arrived there with his cow, another man got there with his cow in tow. He asked that his cow be the first one to mate. He said the cow had not got pregnant even after mating with a bull two or three times. Kali wondered if the owner of the bull would let the man mate his cow out of turn. But the owner was clear. He said it would be done in the order in which people arrived.

Kali's cow stood welcoming and ready. No wonder, since it had been leaking from its vagina for two days, bellowing and struggling. When the bull came near the cow, it smelt its rear. The cow lifted its tail and urinated. The bull pulled its upper lip over its teeth and, displaying its teeth, drank the cow's urine. When the flow of urine stopped, it suddenly leapt on to the cow. On just a single mounting, the cow hunched and cowered. The owner immediately asked him to move the cow away from the bull. When Kali hesitated, he said, 'She got the first one. Once is enough.'

The other customer was upset that his cow had not been the first one to mate. He said to the owner, 'What happened to the other bull you had?'

The owner replied, 'We have tied it up in the field. That bull's semen is not strong. This bull, on the other hand, has semen that looks thick like curd from buffalo milk. The other one's is very watery. Cows that mated with it aren't getting pregnant. That is why I have changed the bulls.'

The customer said, 'But you are not selling the other bull?'

The owner replied, 'Well, everyone has asked me to sell it, but it is a good bull, good breed. It is not easy to come by such bulls. So I have kept it for other tasks. And since it had mounted several cows, I took pity on it and did not castrate it. Once or twice a week, we get people who want their cows to be mated twice. For those cows, I bring out the other bull for the second mating. Shall we do that for your cow?'

The man said, 'Sure. I just want the cow to get pregnant.'

The owner said, 'Let's do that. If the cow's body cools down, it will definitely get pregnant. That other bull will cool down any cow in just one push.' And he laughed.

He then brought the other bull for the second round of mating. It was wonderful to simply look at that bull walking towards them. It had a steady hump, like a temple's tower, that did not move at all as the bull walked. Kali kept staring at that majestic animal. It mounted the cow as soon as it arrived on the spot, but it did not mate right away. Kali was enjoying the lovely sight of the bull mounting the cow. Then he asked for his cow too to be mated with that bull. And his cow was delighted at the idea of mating with two bulls. At first, the bull's penis did not enter the cow's vagina easily. Then the owner had to intercede, holding the bull's penis and placing it in the cow's vagina. After that, this bull too mated with the same force as the other one. The cow shrank and cowered. The owner made the bull dismount right away. He told them that there were cows that completely collapsed. Kali paid the man for the job. He splashed some water on his cow's back and rubbed it gently. Then he held it by the rope and started walking away. Now the cow was absolutely quiet as it had finally calmed down.

Even after he returned to the barnyard, Kali kept thinking of that bull he had seen earlier that day. So many thoughts crowded his mind. What a gorgeous bull it was. The hair on its head was perfectly curled—the sign of a high-quality animal. It was amazing to see it lifting its tail and protruding its penis. He had taken cows for mating several times before, but this was the first time he saw it all properly. The owner told them that the semen of that particular bull was not very good. How could he have found out? Sometimes a bull's organ did not penetrate the

126

cow's vagina properly and the semen ended up spilling outside. Perhaps the owner had noticed some such thing happening with the animal. He also told them the other bull's semen was thick like the curd made from buffalo milk. How did he know? Did he touch it and feel the texture? Or was he able to tell that the quality of semen was not very good for a particular bull because it was not successful in impregnating a cow in one attempt and people had to keep bringing their cows back for mating? Kali continued to think along these lines.

It was afternoon when Seerayi went home. After she left, Kali tied the thatched gate to the barnyard tightly. Then he lay down on the cot inside the hut. He removed his loincloth and held his cock in his hand. He was over thirty years old, but his cock still rose up like a snake. Whom should he think of now? He could not think of anyone other than Ponna. Her? He paused. Her lovely, smiling lips. Then she turned her head a little. The little hair on her earlobes that moved when his breath brushed past them. She closed her eyes. She always closed her eyes. No matter how many times he asked her to open her eyes, she wouldn't. If they were having sex at night, she would open her eyes perhaps once. But if it was in the day, she would shut her eyes and not open them at all. That image of her was set firmly in his mind.

It had been years since he stopped masturbating. He used to do it a lot before he got married. The rope cot was a convenient place for that. It was Muthu who had told him about that. Muthu knew all sorts of things. When Kali asked him how he knew these things, he said, 'I just know somehow.' Since Kali had not masturbated in a long time, it did not take him too long to ejaculate. He held his semen in his hand and looked at it. Was it thick or watery? It had the bitter fragrance of neem leaves. It lay in his hand, sticky like phlegm. He touched it and thought about it for quite a while. But he could not come to any conclusion. Was it like thick curd? Should it be thicker? Was it diluted and watery?

He was reminded of that bull that was said to have watery semen. There was so much self-assurance in its gait, in the way it held its hump, in the arrogance in its eyes. It was a very attractive animal. But although it was a strong animal that made the cow buckle and cower under it, it could not impregnate it successfully. Kali compared himself to that animal, and sighed deeply. Kesan, a man in the village, once said about Kali, 'He is great to look at, but not good at the task.' Was he right then? But Kali did not think he was bad at the task. It was his semen that was the problem. He could only ask about it to the god who made it. But where could he find god so that he could ask him about it? If Kali had managed to die, perhaps he could have gone to heaven, caught hold of god—by wrapping his towel around god's neck—before asking that question. But that had not worked out.

He suddenly felt an increased sense of respect for the bull's owner. Not only had the man not castrated the bull, he was also giving the bull a chance now and then. Would Ponna too accept Kali out of pity from now on? Why did she close her eyes when they made love? The compassion in her eyes would perhaps betray the fact that she was only being charitable to a poor, useless creature.

SEVENTEEN

It was the month of Margazhi. Even before dusk, mist started falling like a smoke screen. Kali had braved worse mists and fogs in his youth. But he was not able to do that any more. Even the sheep and cattle were sniffling and had runny noses. It looked like being under the portia tree was not enough shelter from the weather for the cows and oxen. As for the sheep, even though they had their thatched roof in the enclosure, they were still affected by the mist. It also grew dark very quickly these days, and it settled like a dense honeycomb.

Ponna had started coming to the fields during the day. She walked around a bit. Kali was able to see her from the barn. He saw her belly had started growing and she walked pushing it a little to the front. The brinjal plants she had tended to were still bearing fruits, but not like before. Now the leaves ripened and fell. When Kali happened to see them in that state once, he took pity on them and tended to them a little. He sprinkled some ash on the leaves. And he also made a shelter for them from the mist with palmyra and coconut fronds. When Ponna saw that, it made her very happy.

Ponna was so amazed at the way he was caring for the brinjals that she could not stop talking about it to Seerayi. Kali had asked his mother not to walk all the way to the barnyard in that weather, carrying lunch for him. Instead, he went to the house to eat every day. Since Kali had not gone to the house at all for the past three or four months, their neighbour Porasa had made a note of it and shared it with the entire village. When people asked Seerayi about it, she said, 'He only comes at night. He is a nocturnal creature. They both stay up talking into the night. I don't know at what time he leaves.'

It had started raining in the month of Purattaasi, and by Aippasi and Karthikai, the rains were quite heavy. In those months, people were in the habit of returning home and closing the doors early. So they were able to reply to Porasa when she brought up Kali's absence: 'Apparently he comes at night like an owl. But you shut your door early and sleep. Then how would you know?'

Besides, since this was the season when everyone had a lot of work to do, no one had the time for idle gossip. Seerayi once picked up an argument with Porasa: 'Why is it any of your business? I hear you are telling everyone that Kali does not come home? How do you know? For all three meals he eats the food my daughter-in-law makes. And when she goes to the fields, they talk to each other. Then he comes here at that time of the day when you shut your door and sleep like a corpse. If you don't believe me, go to the barnyard and check with him yourself. Why do you care so much about other people's shit? Mind your own!'

Porasa always addressed Seerayi as 'Atthai'. She said, 'Atthai, why would I talk to people about it? They are not innocent. They try to gossip, extract information from me. Then they tell people I told them things. A couple of them asked me on their own if Kali was coming to the house. I told them I did not get to see him myself but he came at night. They are now decorating that statement and spreading it around. I have a lot of work to do these days. My children spend a little time every day playing pallankuzhi with Ponna. That is why I am able to do my work in peace. Why would I speak ill of Ponna? I am only happy that Ponna has conceived a child after so many years of marriage. But do you think people mind their own business? There are people who even say Ponna got the child by going to the temple festival. Tongues are wagging in all directions.'

Seerayi was not going to let that remark go. 'Who has the standing and right to talk about my family? Don't I know which women in the village are going to which men? I can break it down into details if they want. These bitches, they walk out of the house as if they are going to pee, but they go elsewhere and hitch up their saris. And they talk about *us*? In all these years, did anyone say anything bad about us? That is because they all thought this was heirless property they could scramble to fight over later. Now since they know that cannot happen, they are speaking ill of us. These women have to keep their mouths shut. Otherwise, I will expose all of them and humiliate them in front of the entire village. Tell them not to mess with me!'

It was a quiet night, and Seerayi had spoken very loudly. Everyone in the village must have heard it. Some elderly women came by and asked, 'What happened, Seera?' Porasa went into her house and closed the door.

Seerayi appealed to the paattis' sense of fairness. They said, 'Oh, don't worry about it. People always need something to talk about. Why do you even take them seriously? Go and focus on important things.'

Ponna said to her, 'Don't respond to them, Atthai. If they know we care, they will keep talking. Why are you shouting at this time of the night?'

The old women then said, 'See, even your daughter-in-law agrees. So drop the subject. People will say whatever they want. We don't need to take it seriously.'

Seerayi was somewhat assuaged by all their remarks.

Then one of the paattis said, 'Do you know the things people in this village said about me long ago? Do you know how much I struggled to recover from all their gossips and rumours?' And she began to tell her story. So everyone settled down on the porch to listen and chat. They ended up sleeping right there on the porch that night, and dispersed only in the morning.

These days, Kali came during the day to eat. He sat and ate on the porch, while Ponna stayed inside the house. They still did not look directly at each other. Sometimes, Ponna would be sitting on the porch when she would hear the sound of Kali's footsteps. She would get up immediately and rush indoors. She really wanted to see him and embrace him. This was the first time in their marriage they had been apart for so long. In fact, they had never not spoken to each other for more than a day. Even on those occasions, it was Ponna who would turn her face away and go silent, especially if she was angry. He was never able to be angry with her. And he was also good at soothing her anger and coaxing her out of her silence.

It was quite easy for him. He would pinch her waist when she wasn't expecting it, and run away before she could react. But she would still run after him. He'd run out into the fields. She would pick up stones and hardened mud and fling them at him. He'd deftly avoid all her attacks, but she would eventually catch hold of him. He'd bravely withstand her punches on his face and chest. 'Oh, it feels like a shower of flowers on my chest!' He'd laugh. She on the other hand would grow tired and get caught in his tight embrace. Not that she wanted to escape from it. Sometimes he'd make as if he was letting her go from his embrace. She'd get annoyed and hit him on the chest again. And he'd pull her back into his embrace.

The first time she saw them at this sport, Seerayi was terrified. She scolded Ponna. 'You can't hit a man!' she said. 'You are throwing stones at him. What if it gets him in the head?' But they didn't pay any attention to her. Once

Seerayi realized what this game was all about, she stood by, watching quietly. It made her happy. But she was anxious to ward off any evil eye that people might cast on the happy couple. She would say, 'See, this is why a new life is not being born here. There are husbands and wives who can't get along with each other, but they are able to produce children.'

Ponna had not been able to bear that one thing he called her. If she happened to look him in the eye now, who knows what else he might say?

Besides, Kali was now coming home to eat. Whenever Ponna brought brinjal from the fields, Seerayi said loudly, 'Please cook them yourself. Your husband only likes them the way you make it. He says yours is full of ghee and mine is full of shit!'

Ponna said, annoyed, 'Why do you talk like this, Atthai?'

'Oh, don't worry about it. I wanted to make sure our neighbours hear what I said.'

And Seerayi was right. Porasa next door asked cheerfully, 'What is this talk of ghee and shit?' For some reason, Porasa was always tickled when Seerayi scolded Ponna. Seerayi said, again loudly, 'Well, I called ghee ghee, shit shit. What else can we do? We have to let things know what they are and where they belong, don't we?'

Porasa did not say anything in response.

After Kali started tending to the brinjal patch again, the plants started bearing vegetables. He found out that it was the mist that most affected the plants. So he hung some thatched panels on the sides of the shelter he had already made for them. He let them down like a screen at the end of the day. Then in the morning when it was quite sunny and warm, he lifted the screen. He realized that just like humans needed blankets and scarves to protect themselves from the cold, plants too needed protection. And the well-protected plants expressed their gratitude by bearing brinjals. While there weren't enough brinjals to sell, they still got more than what they needed.

Ponna cooked them in various ways. She made a poriyal with brinjals and coconut. It was a bright green dish that went with hot rice. Kali especially loved that slightly thick gravy that was left at the bottom of this dish. She also mashed brinjals to eat with pap. As for the ragi meal, any brinjal recipe would go with it, but the best side dish for that was brinjal cooked in a thickened gravy that she made. She was delighted to hear the sounds of him smacking his lips tasting the brinjal she cooked with black-eyed peas. One day she cooked brinjals with lentils, but without using any tamarind. Seerayi always used tamarind in that recipe. She asked Ponna, 'How do you get this taste without tamarind?' Kali too loved that dish. Earlier he had wondered if Ponna was deploying her cooking as a way of communicating with him. Now he was sure of it.

While Kali had not completely changed his mind in her favour, his reserve had certainly thawed a little. But something in him kept telling him that he should not let her come close to him. And he was not able to reason it out. As he sat on the porch eating his lunch, sometimes people from the village quarters stopped by to chat with him. It was usually about farming, sheep and cattle. If anyone mentioned that they had run into Muthu, Kali said nothing in response. Ponna always listened eagerly to these conversations he had with others. But she could tell that there was no excitement in his voice. He weighed each word carefully. Did the voice become cautious when the mind became secretive? Seerayi too could hear Kali's voice only when he spoke to others. And one day, when Kali got ready to return to the barnyard, she said sarcastically, 'So it is fine to talk to the useless people from the village. Only we lowly folks at home don't deserve that kindness?'

He understood the import of her remark, but he still did not say a word in response.

EIGHTEEN

Margazhi was the eighth month of her pregnancy. The midwife had told them that the delivery was likely to be at the end of Thaii. These days, Ponna was able to feel the child kicking inside her. Whenever that happened, Ponna had to stand hunched. It was uneasy at first, but once she started closing her eyes and enjoying it, she found that it made her happy. Sometimes she wondered if the baby was swimming inside her, paddling with an arm, quickly turning around. And these days, Ponna never felt lonely. Even the fact that Kali did not come to her or talk to her became a piece of stale news. She shared everything with the child growing inside her.

She sometimes scolded Kali in her mind and then said to the child, 'Are you upset that I am scolding your father?' She shared whatever came to her mind with the foetus. And it listened. She narrated her story to it. The baby was lulled into sadness, and stopped moving. That scared her. She chided herself for bothering the baby with all that stuff. Why did it need to hear these stories of suffering even before it came into this world? There were times when she did not feel its movement for two whole days. She grew quite fearful on those occasions. She patted her stomach to try and wake up the baby. She thought it was in a deep sleep. She worried that the baby might not have liked something she had said. So she apologized, 'I won't talk like that again.'

But soon she would be talking to the unborn child again: 'Do you know what your father called me? He called me a whore. I never said no to him. When he asked me to go to him in the barnyard, I did. He'd ask me to go to bed. He would ask me to lie in the shade of the portia tree with him. He wanted to sleep outside in the moonlight. He'd insist I drank toddy. He has even made me drink arrack. It burnt my throat. But when I said, "This tastes like donkey piss," he asked me when I had tasted donkey piss. One night he even made me lie down on the flat slab of stone he has laid there. No matter what time of the day it was, or where it was, I undressed for him whenever he wanted me to. That's why he has called me a whore. I should have been like those women who keep themselves covered and only show a little at a time, like the way the priests in the temples offer you holy water. But I was a fool. I went along with him. And that has made him think I want it badly. It has made him think, "She came wherever I asked her to, so she must be willing to go with anyone."'

Then she sighed deeply before continuing.

'You have to demand an explanation from him one day. "How could you call my mother that? Is your heart made of stone?" you should ask him. Will you? You should do that for me. You are my only companion from now on. Who else do I have? I have pushed away my parents, and I don't know if we can ever reunite. How could they lie to me and trick me the way they did? How can I bring myself to reach out to them now? It will forever be an unhealed wound in my heart. I have no father, mother or brother. But then, you see, had they not done what they did, I won't have you now. Perhaps this is what they mean when they say even bad things have some good within them. Now my husband does not talk to me. I have to be content with seeing him from a distance. My mother-in-law has always talked constantly about raising her son all by herself. I used to think, she talks as if no one else has ever raised a son, as if she is the only one who has done it. But she is the one who takes care of this entire family now. She has saved not one life but three. You have to take care of her in the last years of her life. Tell me, are you a boy or a girl? I can hear you laughing.'

There were days when the baby kicked her a lot. 'What happened? Did I eat something that is bothering you now? Are you not able to sleep? There are days you stay absolutely quiet, just like your father. And on other days, you trouble me just like he used to on days he got drunk. Look here, once you are born, it is possible that he might pick you up and play with you. That does not mean you can abandon me and shift your loyalties to him. You should ask him, "How come you paid no attention to me before I was born? You did not speak to me even once. Your voice is not familiar to me at all." Will you ask him that? Or will you take his side and abuse me? You might. He is capable of seducing anyone.' And she laughed.

There were so many words available for scolding someone. One could do the scolding differently depending on the context. You could even praise someone in the guise of scolding them. You could use scolding as an expression of endearment. You could scold to tease. There are various motivations for scolding. Ponna scolded Kali in these ways, because that was her way of thinking of him. Her words could only fall like flowers on him. Some flowers had the appearance of stones. But when they fall on their target, they will reveal themselves for what they truly are. The baby surely understood all this, didn't it? She couldn't be sure. So she added, 'Listen, just because I scold him, don't you think poorly of him.'

Kali did give her some reason to feel happy about him. It was the month of Karthikai, the seventh month. That was usually the month when the woman's parents came over for a visit, cooked a lot of food and took their daughter home for the birth. Once the child was born, both families would discuss and agree on when the woman and the child would return to her marital home. Usually, when the baby was seven months old, the woman's family would buy silver anklets and a waist chain for the baby and send them both to the husband's home. If they were better off, they might even buy a gold chain and bangles for the baby. Even if they were poor people, they did one thing for sure. In the seventh month of the pregnancy, they all arrived at their daughter's husband's home and hosted a feast. Since this was the seventh month for Ponna, people were sure to ask Seerayi when the feast was going to be. What would she tell them? She might say, 'She has severed her ties. They do want to come and host a feast, but how can they come now?' Then the news of Ponna's severed ties with her family would spread everywhere.

Whenever Seerayi ran into Vallayi in the market, she lamented, 'We have just one daughter, and she is pregnant after twelve years of marriage. But we are not lucky enough to pamper her at this time. We can't even see her.' Apparently, Muthu had come over a couple of times and, from the mud path, caught a glimpse of Ponna in the fields. How could they simply not have the feast?

Ponna said, 'There is no need for all that.' If they came over to host the feast and Kali refused to partake of it, that would be a great insult. It was better not to do anything. But people came over from Seerayi's family. Kali's uncles arrived at the barnyard one day to speak to him and Seerayi.

They said, 'She is an innocent girl. She did not mean the things she said to us. We can't stay away on account of that. She has conceived after all these years. We have to celebrate that. Even her parents cannot come and offer a feast here. But you are our elder sister. You are now getting a grandchild,

142

and how can we, your brothers, not do anything to mark the occasion? People will fault us for failing in our duties. So we will do what we can. Please don't refuse.' Seerayi was very happy to hear that. Kali had nothing to say. He kept quiet. But his uncles insisted, 'Ponna will not object. If Kali says yes, some ten of us will come one day, make food for the day and take her with us. If she can stay with us until the baby is born, that is fine with us too. People should not say you have no relatives to care for you. People are already asking us. What do you say, Kali?'

Seerayi did not say anything. She wanted the response to come from Kali. He suspected that his mother was behind this arrangement. But even though Seerayi did consider such a plan, she had not acted on it. Ponna had been responsible for the rift in her relationship with her brother's families. So she was not sure they would be eager to do anything for her now. Besides, even if they agreed, Ponna might not. But now Seerayi's brothers had made the offer on their own, and this made Seerayi very happy. And since both brothers had cornered Kali with their insistence, he could not refuse. So they left after agreeing on a date. Then Seerayi used Kali's acceptance to make Ponna agree to this arrangement. 'He might have agreed under duress, but he will definitely come to the feast, he will eat and he will talk to everyone. Please don't look for reasons to say no to this.'

It made Ponna happy to know that Kali, who had been uninterested in everything, had actually opened his mouth and said yes to this. She spoke to the baby in her womb that day, 'I hear your father has said yes to the feast. I thought he was scared pearls would drop from his mouth if he opened it to talk. How come he said yes to this?'

Ponna had a suspicion. She found it hard to believe that Kali's miserly uncles from Thalaiyur were going to spend money on this feast. She wondered if Kali had actually given them the money and asked them to do it. Ponna knew that they wouldn't completely abandon her, but she was still amazed that they were offering to do this despite her insults in the past. She thought it was quite magnanimous of them. They all arrived the following Friday. Not too many people. Just the two uncles' families. Here, they had invited just a few neighbours to the feast. The uncles' wives were very friendly towards Ponna that day.

There were three kinds of rice dishes: tamarind rice, tomato rice and curd rice. Also kachayam sweet and karavadai snack. They did all the cooking. They had also brought a silk sari for Ponna. Both uncles went to the barnyard to talk to Kali. Then Kali came along with them for the midday feast. They had Ponna wear the new silk sari and made her sit on a wooden seat in the porch. They asked Kali to stand next to her. He stood right behind her. It had been seven months since they had stood so close to each other. But he did not bend forward to look at her. He could see the sari and the top of her head. It was a bright red sari. When he walked up the porch stairs and later walked back down, Ponna stole a quick glance at him. It occurred to her that he had lost weight, and his face was covered in a beard. Everyone thought he was growing a beard for ritual reasons, and that he would shave it off once the baby was born. Kali used to have a strong and firm body, much like a field that had hardened after a period of lying fallow. But now it was loose, like soil that had been ploughed a few times. Thinking of him made Ponna tear up.

The visitors remarked, 'She is feeling bad her parents cannot be here. It must be hard for her.' The midwife and her husband came for the feast and they also participated in the ritual to ward off evil eyes from Ponna. The rituals included a gesture marking Ponna's journey to her mother's house. They did this by taking Ponna next door to Porasa's, making her sit down on the porch there and drink some water. Then they brought her back home. Kali seemed to be chatting happily with his uncles. Looking at Kali's face, she thought that he was drunk. He drank a lot these days. That was why his body has lost its form. She glanced in his direction whenever she could. She hoped that he might look towards her too, and their eyes might meet. But it did not seem as though he looked at her at all.

NINETEEN

Kali tied the thatched gate to the barnyard tight, and lay curled up on the cot. It had become even colder once the month of Thaii began. Even the ground under one's feet seemed frozen. He completed all his tasks earlier than usual. The tapper had given him toddy in a dried-up gourd-skin bowl. Kali had drunk most of it well before dark, and he was not hungry. He was more intoxicated than usual. All he wanted to do was lie down. But if he did not go home for dinner, his mother would come to the barnyard, a jute bag draped over her head. There was much demand for jute bags in this season. He wondered if his mother had some bags of this kind in her house, or if she had left all of them here in the barn. If she could not find any in the house, she would just drape her sari over her head. But that was no protection from the cold weather.

She'd wait for him in the house only till the seven o'clock siren sounded before setting off. Then she would start talking as soon as she arrived here: 'How can you be so drunk all the time? The sheep and cattle are in the shed. People in the market were talking about all the burglary that's been going on. We cannot afford to buy things if we lose them. Do you know how much prices have gone up these days? Gold is now at seventy-five rupees. That is equal to the price of two cows. How can we survive if you get drunk and just lie about like this?'

But despite having drunk so much, Kali was not able to sleep. He lay tossing and turning. Then, in the middle of the night, he'd get up and even drink up the leftover toddy. It was not before dawn that he was finally able to fall asleep. And he woke up only when the sun's rays fell on him, piercing through the gaps in the fence.

Since he did not want to upset his mother, Kali went to the house and brought some food in a carrier. There were some leftovers from lunch, which he diluted and fed to the dog. But he did not even bother to open the carrier he had brought from home. He hung it in its place in the hut and went and lay down on the cot. He felt quite dizzy, but he still could not fall asleep. He just lay awake, eyes closed. And he could not avoid wondering how lovely it would be to have Ponna with him there on such cold nights. At the feast, he had managed to catch a glimpse of her when she was not looking. She had gone quite thin, and one could begin to discern the shapes of her bones through her skin. Only her stomach was big. There was no freshness or sparkle in her face. In fact, she was pale as a white-washed wall. She had always been a little fair-skinned, but now she seemed to have lost all colour. Seeing her up close like that after so long, he had started imagining her body next to his every night. No matter how much he tried to keep her away from his thoughts, she climbed right back into his heart. And it got worse in the winter. The cot's frame seemed to crack under the additional weight.

In the past, he always asked Ponna to stay in the barn for the entire winter season. She'd say, 'I cannot do it every day, Maama. My entire body goes sore.' And he would say, 'Just come and lie next to me.' If she insisted on going back home for the night, he'd say, 'I have a good story for you tonight. I will tell you if you stay. It is up to you. Go if you want.' But she could not resist a story. 'All right, tell me,' she'd say, and settle down to listen. But he wouldn't get to the story so quickly. He had different stories for different seasons. He had a particular story for winter. Even though she had heard that story from him several times, she still liked listening to it.

Kali now got drunk precisely to avoid thinking about her. Every time he sensed the intoxication wearing off, he drank more. He now worried that he would soon come to take pity on her. These days, that other face he used to picture being intimate with Ponna had not been bothering him much. Now he laboured hard to bring it to his mind. He deliberately visualized that face going close to Ponna's face. Earlier, that face sneaked up on him on its own and terrorized him. But now he wanted to summon it himself. Otherwise, he was afraid that he might end up making peace with Ponna.

What could be going on in her mind? He had been having sex with her for so many years, but he could not give her a child. The other man had accomplished it in just one day. Clearly, she would compare them both. Whom would she prefer? Whose face would have made the deeper impression on her? He might have spent many years with her, but why would she hold in her heart the face of a useless man? It must definitely be the other face which had managed to alleviate her troubles. She wouldn't be able to dispel it from her mind. Wouldn't she recollect that other face even if Kali went near her? She wouldn't be able to think of Kali without also thinking of the other man. She would superimpose that other face on Kali's. Kali would certainly not have any place in her mind any more. Only that stranger would. Only he could make Ponna happy now.

What did that man look like? Was he bigger than Kali in physical appearance? Tall or short? Dark or fair-skinned? Did he have a mane of hair that sprang from his head and rolled down all the way to his waist? Did he have bushy eyebrows? Was he a man of few words too? Ponna always wanted Kali to talk more. Did that mean she had sought out a man who talked a lot? Did he regale her with stories all night? Would he have also known the kind of stories Kali knew? Ponna used to find great joy in tickling Kali on his waist. Would she have done the same thing to that other man? And if she had, did Kali come to her mind at the time? What did she do then? Did she chase him away?

He could not give her a child no matter what he did. She would not even consider him a man any more.

The other man who had taken possession of her that night—no matter how he looked, no matter what his background, no matter where he was from—he was the one who now had a place in her mind. She would definitely have found out his name and his village. She might even go meet him sometime. She had had a taste of him, so she wouldn't let him go, would she? Why, when Kali found toddy from a new tree, he went back for more and more. The same way, she too wouldn't forget the new toddy she had experienced. She would even go looking for it. Kali rose from the cot and drank what was left of the toddy.

* * *

There was a story that Kali once told Ponna in the winter.

There was this man who had been married for four or five months. One winter, he and his wife went to his mother-in-law's place for some occasion. His wife warned him in advance. 'You should not keep pestering me there. You should control yourself, all right?' He nodded his head like an obedient child. There was only one room in his mother-in-law's house. And since she had two or three daughters, who had children of their own, all the womenfolk slept inside the house in that room. He had a cot out on the porch. They gave him two blankets, but he still felt quite cold. He tried wrapping them tightly around himself, but they were simply not enough—the chill of the night

150

assaulted him like needles. He could not fall asleep. Earlier that night, since the son-in-law was visiting, they had soaked rice and ulundhu lentils, ground them into a batter and made dosais for him. Nice big dosais. He had eaten nearly ten dosais, and that overindulgence now kept him awake.

It was a moonlit night. The moonbeams leapt into the mist and created an intoxicating ambience. The man was waiting for his wife to step out of the house to go pee. And quite a while later, she did, just as he had anticipated. He pulled her close and made her lie down next to him on the cot. She warned him again, 'We are just going to lie down here.' He agreed, but he could not control himself for too long. He started feeling her up. Perhaps because he had been horny for so many hours, he could not control himself at all. He finished with the deed quickly and went to the backyard.

The man sleeping on the porch in the house across the street was also having a hard time falling asleep. The cold was tormenting him too. So he lay awake and watched the action that went on here. He saw that the husband had stepped away, but the wife was still lying on the cot. He took this as a cue, and decided to try his luck. She lay with her eyes closed. He lay on top of her and completed the job. She went back into the house. The husband was still cleaning himself in the backyard. Then he stood about, chewing tobacco and looking at the moon. When he felt he was ready to have another go, he returned to the porch. But she had already gone back in. So he thought perhaps that was all for the night, and went to sleep.

Having seen her son-in-law gobble down ten dosais the night before, the mother-in-law understood he was very fond

151

of dosais. So she had arranged for more dosais to be made the next morning. His wife made the dosais for him. He asked his wife in code, 'So how was the dosai last night?' She said, 'The first one was not good, but the second one was great.' He was utterly confused. 'The second one?' he asked. She said, 'Yes, the second dosai.' But, he wondered, when he had been ready to make the second 'dosai' the night before, she had already gone back into the house. How then? The man from across the street was listening to this exchange between husband and wife. He was standing outside, brushing his teeth with a twig. He now decided to participate in the conversation, and said, 'Oh, don't worry about it. The pan was still hot, so I decided to make a dosai for myself. That was the second dosai. Shall we make some dosais tonight as well?'

Kali had another version of this story too.

When the husband was expecting the wife to step outside the house, his mother-in-law emerged instead. He dragged her to the cot without realizing his mistake. And since she did not want to refuse her son-in-law, she obliged. That was a different experience for him. She was loose on top and tight down there. But he did not brood on it at that hour and in the dark. It comforted him on that cold night. So he indulged himself. The next day, they discussed it over dosai. He asked his wife, 'Last night, the first dosai was a bit loose and raggedy, perhaps because it was made with batter from the top. But the one made with batter from below was firm. How come?' She had no idea what he was talking about. 'You ate ten dosais last night. Then why are you complaining about loose top ones and tight bottom ones now?' He said, 'I mean the dosai we made later on a different pan.' Even then she failed to understand.

The mother-in-law, who was listening to this conversation, now intervened, 'Yes, my son-in-law ended up making his dosai in the wrong pan last night. The batter was all right. The pan was the problem. It was an old pan, that's why the first dosai fell apart. But even though it was an old pan, it was still used to the job, and that's why the dosai was firm at the bottom.'

TWENTY

His uncle Nallayyan arrived at the barnyard on Maattu Pongal, the day of the harvest festival when the focus is on the cattle. He was Kali's uncle on his father's side of the family. He had never married. He did a little farming in the land he had got as part of his inheritance, but he also frequently dropped everything and went abroad for most of the year. Sometimes he brought along a woman and kept her with him for a little while. He had his own way of doing things and never cared for what others said. Kali and he were quite close. He was sort of a distant paternal uncle to Kali. If Nallayyan happened to be in town, he always came over to the barnyard to spend some time chatting with Kali. He often also stayed there for a few days. Kali was very glad that Nallayyan Uncle landed up on that day in particular. He was in no mood to celebrate Pongal, but Seerayi had told him strictly that he just had to. They had never missed celebrating a single Pongal ever since Kali started doing his own farming.

When things were going well for them, when the barnyard was thriving with animals, why stop the tradition of offering pongal? 'You anyway wash the animals every day,' said Seerayi. 'So there is no extra work for you in this. Cooking pongal is women's task. We have a pregnant woman in the house, so we have to offer pongal and do the right thing.' Kali was apprehensive about Ponna's visit to the barnyard that day. He never asked her to stop coming there. The day she had read his lips and realized he had called her a whore, she ran out of there and had never set foot in the place since. She did come to the fields, however, and did some work there and also spent time just sitting and resting. Why couldn't she do the sitting inside the barn? She acted as if he had deliberately kept her away. Maybe she was afraid that if she entered the barn, she might hear the word 'whore' again. He wondered if she would step inside today, and thought about how he might react if she did. But, thankfully, Nallayyan Uncle showed up at the right time. He didn't know what Seerayi might have said to Ponna to convince her to come.

For Maattu Pongal, they always started the cooking only after dark. Ponna arrived after Seerayi had started things. She walked in slowly, dispelling the dark. Kali was minding his chores, feeding the cattle. He had let them graze to their heart's content that day. 'We cannot allow our suffering to reflect on how we treat these animals,' he thought. The two women busied themselves with preparing the pongal. Right when his mother called out to him to

155

start making the offering to the deities, they heard a voice saying, 'You have one more person to eat the pongal.' And Nallayyan Uncle walked in, bearing two sugar canes.

Seerayi welcomed him and said incredulously, 'People in the village have been saying you went abroad and were killed in a road accident. But you are alive!'

'Come, Uncle,' said Ponna softly.

Kali smiled at him quietly, but Nallayyan could not see that. He said, 'How come our son here does not say anything?'

'I did smile at you. You didn't see it,' replied Kali.

Nallayyan Uncle teased him: 'When you smile in the dark, even you can't be sure if you are smiling. That is as good as saying the cat is smiling in the backyard! Who'd know? Besides, do you think you are so fair-complexioned that your teeth are sparkling white, that your smile would glow in the dark?'

Before they began the prayers and the pongal offering, Kali stepped aside to swathe the animals in frankincense smoke. He took some glowing hot coals in a spatula and added a little frankincense powder on it to produce some smoke. The fragrance spread everywhere. It was an iron spatula. He held the end with the piece of cloth draped over his shoulder so that it wouldn't burn his hand. Seerayi took some pongal out of the cooking pot and set it down on a plate for offering to the deities, and she said to Uncle, 'Where did you go? It must have been six months since we saw you last, right?' They all knew that Nallayyan liked to narrate stories of his travels in detail. Both Ponna and Kali were now eager to listen to some of his stories.

'Six months?' he exclaimed. 'It has been eight months. I hated this place and never wanted to return. But now my daughter-in-law here is pregnant. So I came back to see you all happy. Once the child is born, these two cannot be with each other like they used to. He would want her, but she should say, "Wait, the baby is crying." She won't even let him pull her by the hand. She'd use the baby as an excuse. He too would be hesitant to do much in front of the baby. I tell everyone not to have children. But who listens? Never mind. If this is what makes you happy, so be it.'

'Who wouldn't want children?' countered Seerayi. 'You are a strange fellow. You want nothing. But we have families and fields to take care of. How would we survive without children?'

'Yes, indeed. It is children who are responsible for my running away from the village. Both my younger brothers have shat out so many children! When I look at them, I feel very old. It feels like it was only yesterday when they were all tiny. But now they are all ready to get married. I had gone out of town once, and by the time I returned, the older of my two brothers had married off one daughter. Now the other one is ready too. And his son is so burly, he looks taller than me. The other brother too is looking for brides for his two sons. His daughter is very young. But those two boys, they look like rocks. And these dogs covet my share of the inheritance. All they want to do is breed.

Someone else must earn and give them their wealth! Now they have an eye on my property. They say I am quite old. Seera, I am younger than you. You married my brother, so I call you a sister or a sister-in-law. I must be, what, fifty-five years old? Kali must be over thirty now. When he was born, I must have been twenty-five or something.'

Seerayi kept everything ready for the prayers and the offering. Kali returned to the spot after walking around with frankincense smoke among the cattle and sheep. She said, 'In the month of Maasi, Kali will complete thirty-three and enter thirty-four. All right, come, let's pray.' Kali touched and circled the water in a little vessel with his fingers. He then lit a piece of camphor and made the offering. Ponna quickly touched the camphor flame and placed those fingers over her eyelids. Then she took some holy ash from the plate he was holding up, put some on her forehead, and moved away, all the while keeping her head down. When she moved closer to him, he'd fixed his gaze on the portia tree. Seerayi then picked up the pot of the offering and handed it over to Kali. He walked away with it to feed the cattle first. The two oxen relished such food. He fed them and gave a little to the calf.

Seerayi resumed the conversation. 'So then, why are you talking about age now?'

He said, 'Let me tell you why. There is a woman in Sellur they are asking me to marry. The thing is, she was married before, but her husband died just five months after the wedding. They say someone beat him to death. The girl has a large family. She has five brothers. And they are all determined to get her married again. One of them in particular is a member in that progressive political party. Its leader advocates widow remarriage, doesn't he? She is only twenty-five. I am thinking of marrying her.'

Seerayi said, 'But why do you want to marry a widow?'

'Why not? There are so many communities in which widows can marry again. Why should we care? The brothers say they are unable to look at their sister wearing white. I'd readily marry her, but I am not sure if running a family and all that suits me. I know one of the brothers. He says, "You go and come as you please. My sister will take care of the fields. Besides, we are all here too, so we will help." All this makes me want to say yes. I am thinking about it. A man can go to a thousand women. But she married and lived with one man. There is nothing wrong with her.'

Kali said, 'Sure, sure. If the brothers themselves are asking you to marry her, do it happily. You will also be giving a new life to the woman. And you will get a family too. If all five brothers-in-law help out, you can live a luxurious life. Then you won't even think of going abroad.'

'See! Even you think this is a good idea. Then who are my brothers to object? If I marry her, I will have five brothers-in-law to come running if I am ever in any trouble. So my brothers can threaten me as much as they want. I will just live quietly to a side. What more do I need in this old age?'

Seerayi said, 'Don't you know how hard the life of a widow is? They must be lucky to get her married to someone like you. I will come to the wedding!'

Kali said, 'Uncle, but if you find a woman with a child, you won't have to worry about getting her pregnant.'

'You know nothing about the world, Kali,' said Nallayyan. 'You are like a frog in a well. Do you know what is happening in the world around? That bespectacled old man is negotiating with the white man. They are saying the white man is going to give back the country to us and leave in a year's time. Do you know all this? Even the lizard crawling on your barnyard's fence knows more than you do.'

Seerayi handed them each a plate of food. 'Eat as you talk,' she said. The pongal tasted very good with the green gram gravy. Then, turning to Nallayyan, she added, 'I hoped my son would travel and know the world. I didn't expect him to shut himself up here. Do give him some advice.'

'My brothers now say, "If you bring a woman, we will hack you to death and bury you in the ragi fields." They both have no scruples whatsoever. They want my share of the inheritance so badly that they are willing to send their wives to me. The two women come to me and bare their breasts. And they are fighting with each other over this! Both their breasts are so saggy that they look like their waist pouches. They brought those breasts and rubbed them on my face. I chased them away like dogs. They are all in this together—the husbands, the sons, the daughters. They think that if they show me their breasts, I will bequeath my property to them. That became a big argument between us, and I left town to get away from all that. Now I have made some arrangements to deal with all this. I found a lawyer and got my will written.'

Seerayi said, 'You carry on. It is late for us. I have to take Ponna back to the village.'

Nallayyan Uncle teased Ponna, 'It looks like the pregnant girl has lost her power of speech. She has not spoken a word. The wife has become just like her husband.' Then he said to Kali, 'You go with them for company. I can be alone here for a little while.'

Kali did not know what to say to that, but Seerayi had been waiting for such a moment. She said to him, 'Can you come with us?' And since he did not want Nallayyan Uncle to get upset with him, Kali set off with Seerayi and Ponna.

TWENTY-ONE

While Kali accompanied the women to the house in the village, Nallayyan Uncle chopped up the sugar cane, fed the sheath to the cows and chewed on the juicy pieces. Kali walked in front, carrying the pot of pongal on his head. Ponna walked right behind him. Seerayi was at the end, talking non-stop about Nallayyan. Kali and Ponna did not speak a word.

'He has been with several women,' prattled Seerayi. 'He has absolutely no sense of discernment when it comes to women. He will go with just about anyone. But I have to applaud this plan of his to marry a widow now. How many men are willing to do something like that? There are men who doubt their wives even if they see them speaking to other men. He is definitely large-hearted to consider this. I wish him well. He should marry her, bring her here, and live well in this village . . .'

Kali felt that her speech was for his benefit. This had become a routine. No matter what she talked about, Kali

162

had come to see it as indirectly intended for him—it was her way of giving him advice. And that was true in a way. Those were, indeed, Seerayi's intentions most of the time.

'Did you hear what he said?' she continued. 'He said, "She was married to one man. In what way is she inferior to men who have gone to a thousand women?" That's where he revealed his character. His brothers are sending their wives to him! What kind of men they must be! They might even eat shit if that assured them the property. But let me tell you, no matter how prosperously they live, they are not equal even to the dust under his feet.'

Kali could not help but feel that she was trying to make a point to him. He thought about all that on his way back to the barnyard, where he found that Nallayyan Uncle had already chewed and spat four or five pieces of sugar cane. Kali sat down next to him and picked up a piece for himself.

'Are you really going to marry that woman, Uncle?'

Nallayyan replied, 'I am considering it. I cannot live peacefully in this village any longer. My brothers won't let me. They will constantly find ways to make my life miserable. They will do anything for money. If they hack me to death at night, bury me in the fields, do some ploughing and plant something on the field the very next day, will anyone come to find out what happened to me? People like you might just think that I was out on my travels. Then a little later, they will tell you all that I died in a faraway land and perform some kind of death ritual and divvy up my share of inheritance among themselves.

Why should I let that happen? Besides, I am not young any more. I don't have the same energy. All these years, I have wandered everywhere and encountered all kinds of people. From now on, I just want to stay in one place . . . Let's say I live for another twenty years. I can spend those years as happily as I have spent these past years. It is true that there are still women who could come to me if I just call them. But I won't have the energy for all this in the future. My brothers won't leave me in peace. They'd constantly harass me. You should see how my brothers' sons look at me. With so much hatred. As if I had somehow appropriated the wealth that ought to have gone to them.'

Kali had a difficult time believing this change in his uncle. He said, 'Are you really going to get married at this advanced age? Or is this one of those stories you entertain us with?' He was both amazed at and unsure of his uncle's decision.

But Nallayyan said, 'Kaliyappa, do you think of the stuff I tell you as mere stories? It is all true. I told you all that my brothers' wives came to me and bared their breasts, didn't I? In fact, I did not reveal everything. I didn't want to be indelicate since your mother and wife were present. Let me tell you what really happened. One of the wives came to me at night and lay down on the cot with me. She said, "I will do whatever you want. Let us go and transfer the property to my sons' names first thing in the morning." Do you believe that? I admit that I am a womanizer, but have I ever forced any woman to be with me, have I ever used force? I go with them if they say yes. If they say no, I go my way. I only bring and keep with me women who are like me, who are on their own and have no families. All this does not mean those brothers of mine can send their wives to me as a means to take away *my* inheritance. I have seen all sorts of things in the world, but this was the first time I was seeing husbands and sons pimping together. That's when I left town. I have been roaming around from village to village. In the meantime, they have divided my land among themselves and have sowed maize. When I asked them about it, they said they did not want to let the land lie waste. If I spent the night in my own house, they will definitely kill me. That's why I have been looking for someone to marry and have finally found this woman. One of her brothers knows me very well. He says to me, "Just say yes to marrying her. I will help you deal with anyone, no matter how powerful he is." So I have decided to marry her. But I need your help.'

'Me?' said Kali. 'How can I help you? I am overwhelmed by my own problems here.'

'You don't have to do anything. Just stand by me, let the village know you are on my side. Then the woman's brothers will handle everything else. I can marry her and bring her here in just two days.'

'But if we do that, they will call a meeting in the village and excommunicate you. They will do that to me too.'

'Let me see who dares to do that in the village. The woman's brothers are not only worldly-wise, they are also quite influential. They can even speak to the revenue authority and arrange for their enemies to be locked up in jail. We can even make sure no village council meeting happens on this matter. Who will demand a meeting? Only my brothers. Let me marry her and bring her here. Her brothers will stay here for a month or two after that. And if my brothers protest, we could set these fellows upon them. Then who will dare to talk? Do you know this man called Rangan in Karattur? He controls a lot of rowdies. This woman's brothers can even send for some of those thugs. They can break legs and arms, and they can also kill. They can do everything. Don't you worry about anything. If you love me and if you are bold enough, come with me and stand by me. If you are a coward, stay here in the barnyard. I won't say anything further.'

Kali was quiet. He felt that his uncle had put him in a tight spot. Kali had never got involved in such matters before. These were usually part of Muthu's repertoire, but things were such that Kali could not seek Muthu's help now—even though Muthu would have had the best advice on such matters. Kali bit into the bitter edge of the sugar cane by mistake, and its sharp taste now spread in his mouth. How long could Kali stay silent? Nallayyan Uncle was planning to get married. He was considering becoming a family man. No one else would come forward to offer their girl in marriage to a man of his age. He could only marry the kind of woman he had now found. And he was worried his brothers might kill him. His plan sounded fair to Kali. What could go wrong in lending Uncle his support?

'What are you thinking about, Kali? I knew you would turn out to be useless. You will think about things endlessly and just huddle up inside yourself. You have no idea how the world works. There is a woman to whom I want to transfer all my wealth if only she would say yes. Then I don't have to worry about marriage and all that. But she has declined. Do you know where I have been these past three or four months?'

Kali set aside his thoughts, and said, 'Where were you, Uncle?'

'I lived with a family that herds pigs. They are foragers. Raising and herding pigs is their occupation. They would take their pigs to a certain place, and raise them there for a while. Then they would move on. Just the way we herd sheep. If they find a place that had a lake or a pond, they'd set up a hut and stay there a little longer. I lived with such a family. It is a great life, you know. We are not lucky enough to experience such a life. I knew the husband from before. I had met him in the market when he sold pig's meat there. His wife fried the meat right there. For a price, she made excellent fried meat. You can eat it with rice or just as it is. She cooks it so well. But how will you know? You never go anywhere. The Thursday market is not only about the official market. There are stalls in the various streets and gullies outside the market area. Do you know there is a particular spot where they only sell pork? Every week, they have some twenty stalls. I have run into this family in various markets. I always bought some meat from them. I don't know how it happened, but one day he said to me in the market, "Saami . . . do you want to come to my house?" I wondered what it was about. He said, "I have five children. I am not able to have sex with my wife like I used to. Poor thing, she is struggling. I thought I could find the right man and take him to her. I have been observing you for some time now. You seem to be a good man. Come and stay with us for ten days." I was completely taken aback!'

'Uncle, my ears have already been pierced! You can't sell that story to me.'

'Ey! If you think I am lying, come with me. They have their stall right now in Sennaankuttai. They have ten pigs and some thirty or forty piglets. I will take you there, and you can verify the story yourself. Even you will desire her once you see her. But she won't go with men like you, let me tell you. She liked me. I went there with the idea of spending just ten days with them, but I ended up staying for four or five months. I liked her so much. He'd leave us inside the hut and quietly sit by himself outside. One day I asked him, "Doesn't it bother you seeing your wife with another man?" And he said, "What do you mean? Why should it upset me?" I said, "You pig of a man! When I am sleeping with your wife inside the hut, what goes on in your mind?" He said, "I think she should be happy." I wanted to write my property over to her. I said, "Keep the property. Your entire family can come and live there.

I have a house and some fields. You can herd your pigs there. Or we can do some farming. All I need is some food to eat." But she refused: "What do I need property for? The pigs are enough for me. We are used to wandering from town to town, relying on the kindness of others for our food. We are not supposed to stay put in one place." But one thing came out of this. I learnt to herd pigs. If you call out "bababa . . . baba" they come running to you faster than little lambs. They are such affectionate creatures, pigs. Once I get married, I plan to raise five or six pigs on my farm.'

Kali was utterly confused by all this. He did not know if he should believe any of it.

TWENTY-TWO

Kali had always had his doubts about Nallayyan Uncle's narratives. He suspected more than half of them to be lies. He had always thought things couldn't quite be the way his uncle portrayed them, that he was just trying to paint himself as more adventurous than he really was. But if the world was indeed the way Nallayyan described it, were things right or wrong? When he asked his uncle about it once, Nallayyan said, 'Who are we to decide right and wrong? Something that seemed right to your father now seems wrong to you. And what seems right to you now will seem wrong to your son in the future. These are all big questions. You just do your thing and keep moving.'

On that night too, his uncle had warmed up and was eager to tell more stories. 'Do you know of the big landlord in Semmur?' Nallayyan asked. Kali replied that he had heard of the man. He had never been to Semmur himself, but he had heard that the family owned a palatial house and lots of land. He had also heard that they owned several horses. Fixing Kali with his gaze, Nallayyan Uncle pointedly asked, 'Did you know that one of our children is growing up in that family?' He could not see Kali's face clearly, but he was hoping this piece of news would shock and scandalize him.

The feudal lord from Semmur owned several villages. In each village, he appointed his relatives and their families to oversee the management of these lands. One such family lived in Vellur. The man of the house was a cousin to the feudal lord, on his father's side. He was in charge of five or six villages. He was immensely wealthy and was a bit of a show-off. He travelled everywhere in a horse-drawn cart. And he got off the cart wherever he felt like and wandered around on foot wherever he pleased. People who recognized him would rise and pay their respects as soon as they saw him, but he would keep walking as though he did not notice them at all. One could even spot him in the markets and streets. Sometimes he'd sit down and chat with the astrologers who had parrots pick the cards. He even sat with the man who played the small double-drum and sang folk tunes, and sold songbooks. He ate both pork and beef.

Once, Nallayyan Uncle was staying at the Mondichattiram rest house that was near Mollur. This man, the Vellur landlord, arrived there and stayed for a night. Nallayyan Uncle recognized the man, but neither the staff at the rest house nor the other guests knew who he was. When Nallayyan had got up and bowed to the landlord, the man told him firmly that his identity must not be revealed to anyone there. At night, they both lay on the rest-house porch and chatted about this and that. Then they strolled on the road in the moonlight. The man said, 'Everyone wants the white man to leave. But look here—without the white man, we wouldn't have this road. He has also given us trains to go from anywhere to anywhere. They say there are even ships that traverse the skies. If the white man weren't here, our people would fight among themselves and die.'

Nallayyan Uncle did not want to argue with him, so he just said, 'That's true, sir.'

Then the man said, 'I really like walking like this in the moonlight. Also, not even heaven can compare to the rest-house porch, let me tell you.'

Nallayyan Uncle nodded in agreement to that too. But he asked the man, 'You have all the comfort you need at home. Then why do you come out here and suffer through this?'

The man replied, 'There is so much more to this world than we know. If we think that the world is just the place where we live and the people we know, we are fools. I don't want to be a fool, and I want to see as much of the world as I can. That's why I travel.'

Nallayyan Uncle then asked him, 'People say that you even eat beef . . .'

'Why not?' the man replied. 'The white man eats both beef and pork, and we get up and salute him whenever we

see him. But we object when our own people eat them. The people who eat beef are human beings too.'

Nallayyan Uncle got to chat a lot with the man that night. He learnt that this landlord was the first man in his house to cut off his head-knot. And he did not wear ear studs either. 'There are thieves looking just for ear studs to steal,' the man told Nallayyan. 'Can anyone travel in peace wearing them? Without them, I can fearlessly go anywhere, stay anywhere. That's why I don't wear them.' The man took a strong liking to Nallayyan Uncle when he found out that he too constantly wandered from town to town. He asked about all these various places, and Nallayyan obliged. The next day, he said to Nallayyan, 'Come with me. Stay at my place for a few days.' And Nallayyan accepted the invitation.

The landlord's house had every conceivable comfort. Seeing all that, Nallayyan grew suspicious about the man's habit of wandering away from all that luxury. Nallayyan had originally intended to stay in that house for four days, but he ended up staying there for a whole month. He grew familiar with the man's family. One night, the man took Uncle to a room he had not shown him before. It was designed to host white officials and for them to drink alcohol in comfort. Nallayyan refused to drink anything. He might have had all sorts of questionable habits, but drinking was not one of them.

A long time ago, when Nallayyan was a little boy, his father had asked him to drink some alcohol. When

Nallayyan took the cup close to his mouth, he inhaled its pungent odour and felt like throwing up. So he flung the alcohol away—along with the cup. His father got very angry at that and asked Nallayyan to pick up the empty cup, after which he poured some toddy into it. But the cup had cracked under the impact of being flung aside, so the toddy kept leaking. 'You broke the cup!' his father shouted and hit him on the head. Then he asked someone to fetch a different cup and filled it with toddy for Nallayyan to drink. However, the boy flung that one away as well. In this manner, he threw away four or five cups of toddy. His father was enraged. 'I am asking you to drink, and you won't? You are so disobedient!' And he dragged the boy close, trapped him between his legs and, holding his face in a tight grip, pressed his own cup of alcohol to Nallayyan's lips. But the boy kept his mouth firmly closed.

No matter how hard the father tried, he could not get even a drop of toddy into his son's mouth. 'Are you really a peasant's son? You are a peasant only if you drink. I am not asking you to drink an old woman's piss, am I? This is palmyra toddy. Who knows whom your mother slept with to give birth to you?' Scolding the boy in this manner, he hit him hard with a stick. That was the first time Nallayyan ran away from the village. And, ever since, his anger at his father made him detest the idea of drinking alcohol. So from that day in his childhood, Nallayyan had not drunk even a drop of alcohol. The landlord was amazed at this

fact. He said to Nallayyan, 'I have some old white woman's piss. Want to taste it?'

Nallayyan declined the offer, saying, 'I cannot even bear the smell.'

The man did not force him any further. But he freely spoke his mind to Nallayyan that day. He said to him that while he might have had the freedom to wander around and see the world, there was still a big sense of lack in his life. He was childless. 'No matter how rich you are,' said the man, 'it is a child who brings that special sparkle to a house. That's the one thing lacking in this house. I have even married twice, but nothing has worked. We have also tried all sorts of medicines and prayers and rituals and magic—with no results whatsoever. That's why I have come up with this new idea.' Having said this, the man stopped.

Nallayyan Uncle too paused the story at this point. Kali fetched the gourd-skin pitcher from inside the hut and poured some toddy into a cup. Nallayyan Uncle said, 'Even a toddy tapper wouldn't have such a steady supply at his place! How did you get used to drinking this stinking nonsense?' Kali just laughed. Nallayyan Uncle sat watching him drink, and resumed his story.

The landlord had then said to him, 'What do we do when a cow does not get pregnant? We try mating it with a bull a few times. Then we change the bull and try again. So why not do the same with humans? What's wrong with that? You are the new bull to have come to this house now. You have no bad habits. Just stay here for another month, and let us try doing this—mating the cow with the new bull.' Nallayyan was stunned and didn't know how to respond to that. The man nonetheless tried to convince him in various ways: 'It is all just skin, this body. It is tight and firm today, but will it stay this way after ten years? It will shrink and become useless. Why worry about this body? If I did not have this landlord status and all this prestige that goes with it, I'd send them to get pregnant by anyone. But this status weighs like a heavy burden.'

Recalling that incident, Nallayyan Uncle now said, 'I did not know how to say no to such an important man. So I did stay there for a month. Then the landlord had children. Not one, but two. One each for both wives. Now the children have grown and they travel in horse-drawn coaches.' And thus did Nallayyan Uncle end the story.

Kali burped loudly. Nallayyan Uncle could not see his face in the dark. He whispered, 'Don't share this with anyone else. If it becomes known, those people will have me killed. Not just me, they will kill you too.' Kali said nothing in response. He wondered if Nallayyan Uncle had a particular motive behind telling him this story. He sighed, and said, 'Tell me when you want to have the wedding. We can also involve my brother-in-law Muthu in this. If he is with us, I will feel a bit more confident too.'

'But didn't you say your ties with them are severed for now?' Nallayyan Uncle asked.

'So what?' said Kali. 'That's between us. He can still come to your wedding. Ponna acted impulsively and cut her ties with them.'

'All right, then. Next week, I plan to go to the Manchaami temple in Mangoor with a group of pilgrims. I have never gone there by foot before. Do you know why my parents named me Nallayyan? Nallayyan is the clan deity for my father's family. And Nallayyan is no one but Manchaami in Mangoor. So I want to go there and put in a good word. We can have the wedding after that.'

Kali then asked him, 'Can I go on the pilgrimage with you, Uncle?'

TWENTY-THREE

Ponna was not happy that Kali was setting out on this pilgrimage at a time when there was a lot of work to do in the fields. But she knew she would not be able to make him change his plans. Besides, Seerayi was actually keen that Kali went on this trip. 'He needs to travel and see places and meet people,' she said. 'He can't just be shut up in the barnyard, drinking toddy all the time. He doesn't even know how to converse with people, does he? You were the only one who was so besotted with him. No one else seems to care for him. He needs to understand that what we get depends on what we give. So let him go. We can handle the work in the fields. I know it will be difficult for a month, but I still have some strength in this body. So we will take care of it.'

Ponna knew this was a big step for Seerayi.

'Have a safe journey, my dear,' said Seerayi to her son. 'Pray to Manchaami that he should bless you with right thinking.' And then to Nallayyan, she said, 'I have never let him go anywhere like this. He has only roamed around the Karattur area for ten or fifteen years, but even then he was with his group of friends. Once he got married, he hasn't gone anywhere, and this is the first time he is doing something like this. I am letting him go only because I know you are with him. Please don't abandon him along the way and wander off on your own. Let him interact with people.'

Nallayyan Uncle laughed. 'I understand, sister-in-law. You are setting your child down on my hip. Don't worry. I will feed him milk at the right time, take good care of him and return him safely to you.'

Until Kali was around, neither Seerayi nor Ponna had to worry about the fields. In the wake of the temple festival, Kali had at first stopped working in the fields and would just lie on his cot and stare listlessly at the ceiling. But after Seerayi spoke to him about it several times, he had slowly resumed his tasks. Now it was winter. They couldn't start the work early in the morning. Also, they had to finish all the work even earlier and return home before dusk. The big question was how to keep watch over the barnyard. Kali had simply said, 'Amma, you sleep in the barn at night.' But how could Seerayi leave Ponna alone in the house in the village? Ponna was in her final trimester, and she found it hard even to sit down and get back up. Her belly had grown quite big. The midwife had told them, looking at the size of Ponna's belly, that it would be a boy. Ponna tried to keep herself as active as she could, so she walked around a bit and also did some cooking.

But how could Seerayi leave her alone at home in the night? Perhaps they could ask Porasa to send one of her children to keep Ponna company at night. But they were all quite young, and would fall asleep promptly at night and wake up very late in the morning. So they wouldn't be of much use to Ponna. If she had not cut off her ties with her family, by now her parents from Adaiyur would have landed up to take care of her. They would even have brought one of their farmhands to watch over the barnyard here in Kali's absence and taken Ponna back home with them. Whenever Seerayi ran into Vallayi in the market, they both became teary-eyed thinking about their situation. 'She did it unthinkingly,' mourned Vallayi. 'Now we cannot even go and see our own daughter.'

'The rules of separation do not apply to the farmhand,' Seerayi once tried to persuade Ponna. 'Shall I send for him?'

But Ponna vehemently refused. 'The shoes we remove outside the house should stay right there,' she insisted. 'We don't have to bring them into the house.'

Eventually Seerayi decided to go by Ponna's plans, and they both moved to the barn for the time being. All they needed to take with themselves were a few pots and pans. They already had some cooking utensils in the barn, since they had cooked there in the past. There was also a spice box there. Ponna felt that they should now stay in one place and not shuttle back and forth between the house and the barnyard. She at least wanted to give it a try.

Her optimism lasted a day. It was very cold in the barnyard. The cold weather felt like needles pricking them all over their bodies. The hut was decently warm at first. But since Kali had trimmed the thatched panels on the inside to keep termites away, and because the hut did not have a wall but only thatched panels, the cold entered through the gaps. The next day, they blocked these gaps with all the palm fronds and thatched panels they could find lying about. Ponna spread two blankets on the cot and used two more blankets to cover herself on top. She also found some jute bags. She spread some of these on the cot, and also inserted her feet into one when she went to bed. Despite the chilly weather, Seerayi rose early in the morning and, wearing a jute bag over her head for protection, attended to the tasks in the cattle shed. She told Ponna not to step out of the house until it was sufficiently warm during the day. At night, they made sure they finished all the tasks before going to bed, so that they did not have to step out in the middle of the night. But despite all these preparations, Ponna was not sure how long they would last there.

She wouldn't worry if it was just the cooking work and the chores in the cattle shed. But there were other things to do. Maize had grown tall in the fields. Kali had done the sowing late, out of step with all the other fields growing maize. So the crop was ready, with ears of corn shooting erect. They had to harvest them and bring them in safely. Seerayi was worried about this. But Kaaraan's daughter-in-law Vengayi arrived there at just the right time. Ponna knew Vengayi from before. She must have been Ponna's age, but she was struggling to take care of her three children. Harvest work was over in all the other fields, so Vengayi had come to see if there was any work here. The timing turned out to be perfect for Ponna.

If they employed a lot of people for the harvest, it would become difficult to oversee the work. But she could manage things with Vengayi. So she told Vengayi to come every day to work for a month. She had to start work in the fields in the morning. Then at midday, she could drink some water-soaked leftovers right there and keep working. And she could leave before sunset. One rupee a day was what she was paid. Ponna became confident that she could get the work done with Vengayi's help. She first decided to streamline things in the barnyard. She asked Vengayi to carry two pots and two large-mouthed earthen pots and place them close to the well where they draw and release water. This way, they could fill them up with water right there. She also set aside a pot for Vengayi's use. Seerayi would draw water from the well and pour it into Vengayi's pot. Vengayi would carry it to the larger pots and tubs and fill them up. The oxen and the cows grazed in the pastures out by the fields. They could bring them to the well for water. In this manner, Ponna simplified the task of carrying several pots of water and walking the length and breadth of the barnyard. These tasks were easier for Kali. Every day, they needed at least twenty pots of water. How many could Seerayi carry?

Ponna made one more useful change. She asked for the cattle to be tied up in the vacant field. This way they only had to clear out the dung they had dropped on the floor of the cattle shed at night. It had been quite a while since the two oxen had been put to work, but Kali really pampered them. He did not pay much attention to the cows. It had been seven or eight months since he had used the oxen to operate the picotah, or even the bullock cart. The last time they were put to work was when he ploughed the fields to sow maize. They just lay about lazily in the shade of the portia tree, chewing the cud. Ponna took them out in the morning and tied them up on the mud road in an elevated corner. They were very gentle creatures; even a child could drag them along by the rope. They grazed all day, and at night she fed them ragi sheaths. The oxen were not very fond of the latter; they chewed the husks and left the stem untouched.

Kali could have planted ragi that year, but he had lost interest in everything then. No kambu millets either. Maize is all they had managed to sow. And only the white kind. All this meant that they had to buy provisions for their domestic use.

Ponna also moved the sheep enclosure outside. She wondered why Kali had kept everything right inside the barn. As she went about doing these things in his absence, she found herself brimming with ideas. He had organized things to suit his convenience, but that wouldn't be convenient for the womenfolk. Ponna moved the sheep enclosure out to a spot she could keep an eye on from the barn, and also tied up the dog out there. If anyone happened to walk nearby, the dog would bark. She also placed the sickle, the spear and some thick clubs in various strategic spots. This way, they could be ready for a snake as well as any intruder.

Soon Ponna got really engrossed in making further changes in and around the barn. So far Kali had done most things himself. And the women carried out the tasks he had set for them. But now everything appeared in a new light to Ponna. While Seerayi was happy at Ponna's initiatives, she also warned her, 'Kali might not like all these changes, Ponna.'

Ponna said, 'We are not changing too much. If he does not like any of this, he can always change them back to his way. But the fact remains that for this one month we have to do all the work here.'

The only fields that were unused were the two beside the well. Together, they were about an acre. The only thing growing in one of them were the brinjal plants. The fields had been left vacant for planting ragi or chillies. In fact, as soon as they walked outside, opening the thatched gate to the barnyard, they set foot right on one of these vacant fields. The well was in the adjacent plot. Why did Kali set up the barn at the very edge of the fields? Ponna felt that things would have been easier had he set it up right next to the well.

When a person takes over someone else's tasks, it is natural for them to reorganize things and even to feel the previous person had not been doing things right. She told herself that she shouldn't criticize his work. He had organized things the way they worked for him. That was the right way for him. And this was the right way for Seerayi and herself. The empty plots were useful to keep the cattle tied up and to house the sheep enclosure. The rest of the three acres were lush with maize. Ponna wanted to make sure they got the best of that maize crop. She asked Vengayi to harvest the maize ears that they could see in the fields adjacent to the vacant plots. The job took only a day to complete. The next day she asked Vengayi to cut the maize stalks from the same fields. Seerayi too joined Vengayi that day. As she cut the maize stalks, she said to Vengayi, 'Her way of doing this is just like Kali's. She never tells you what is in her mind. Only when you complete a task do you get to see what she had been planning.'

TWENTY-FOUR

The women harvested the maize from the two fields, tied it up in bundles and dropped them all in the unused plot of land to dry.

Ponna then sent for Vengayi's husband, Chinnaan, to set the picotah and draw water the next day. There was plenty of water in the well. Had Kali planted ragi and used the water for the crop, there wouldn't be so much water left in it. But he hadn't, so all the water was stored up in there. Now, for one week, they'd need to irrigate the fields from which they had harvested maize stalks. It would make the crop shoot up again from the root. And since there was also the winter's moisture in the air, both fields would see a good crop. The oxen cooperated with Chinnaan and made it easier for him to use the picotah and irrigate the channels. In addition to watering the fields, they also irrigated the brinjal patch and the coconut trees. They even quickly filled up all the vats and tubs with water.

Even though Ponna did not do any of the work herself, everything happened according to her plans. In an unguarded moment, it occurred to Seerayi, 'Even if he had died, Ponna would have managed the farm work well.' But she stopped and chastised herself right away for that thought. The womenfolk might be able to do the farming, but was that enough? Kali's presence in the fields was like the deity Karunchaami himself guarding them. There is a saying: 'Even if the woman is as strong as an elephant, she still needs a husband, even if he is meek as a cat.' There was some truth to it, wasn't there?

The night they watered the two fields, Ponna said, 'Atthai, let us build a hut with a wall right here in the barnyard. Perhaps we can just live here from now on?' The thought had occurred to Seerayi as well, but she wasn't sure how it would all work out.

Ponna said, 'I think we should get used to living here in the barnyard, Atthai. Maama will soon get used to travelling a lot. Then you and I will have to run back and forth between the house and here. Why struggle? We can do all the cooking here. We can store all the dried grains in the village house. When Maama is here, you can sleep in the house. He is not going to kill me if I stay here. I no longer care if he talks to me or not. Let him do as he pleases. I will live right here.'

'How will you both live here, not even looking at each other's faces? He refuses even to speak to us. How will you handle him?'

'I don't know if my husband will come and see the child once it is born. I don't know if he will pick up the child in his arms. I don't know if he will think of himself as the father and play and talk to the baby. I don't know if my child is blessed with the chance to sit on its father's shoulder. This child is coming very late into our lives. Perhaps it has to rely entirely on its mother. If I stayed in the village, people will ask why my husband hasn't come to see the baby. What will I tell them? We are already racking our brains to come up with plausible excuses and explanations. But if I moved here, we won't have to say anything to anyone. I can be at peace. If anyone wants to know what is going on between us, he can tackle them himself. That's why I want to move here.' Ponna's voice cracked as she made her case.

Seerayi teared up, listening to this. 'Don't worry, Ponna. Your child is blessed. All the curses that are on this family are coming to an end, you will see. When Kali tried to hang himself, I thought that was the end of this family. But he lived. And I understood from that. Only good things for us from now on. Be strong. We can move to the barnyard like you say. I don't know why women in the village are itching to find out what is happening in our family. They are so restless, as if some lizard has wriggled into their saris. If we live in the village house, we will have to respond to all their queries. Yours is a good idea. Let us consult him once he returns and build a wall for this hut?'

But Ponna had a clear idea of what she wanted to do. 'No, Atthai. Let us build a new cottage here before he comes back. There is a lot of space in the northern corner. We can build one there. If we consult him, he might even say no. But if we build it now, what can he do after he comes back? Will he tear it apart? Or will he chase us away with a club? And so what if he does? There are plenty of branches on the portia tree.'

'Look here!' said Seerayi fiercely. 'That's the kind of talk I don't want to hear. You have been seeing my struggle for the past eight months. Things are now taking a turn for the better. Please don't do anything to ruin them. I am too old to raise a baby on my own. We have to go on living somehow. Nothing will happen to Kali. His uncle will speak to him and give him some perspective. Just watch him when he gets back from this pilgrimage. Do you think that deity Manchaami will let him return the way he went there? If he did, what's the point in his sitting there as a deity? All right. About the cottage . . . That will be a lot of work. How can we women manage all that?'

Ponna stayed silent for a little while. Then she replied, 'Send my brother a message. He needn't come himself. He can send one of his men with four cartloads of sand, two loads of stones and all that. We have our own cart here, so we can send that. My brother will arrange for sacks of sand to be sent. As for dried palmyra husks, there is plenty of it right under the bales of kambu stalks. For the central beam, we can use that portia branch that was cut down.'

'Oh, dear girl,' said Seerayi happily. 'I am glad you are talking about your family. I worried that you had completely forgotten about them. The other day you referred to them as slippers. They are the only relatives we really have, and I was anxious we will lose them too. I wonder how poor Muthu is. He got beaten up so badly by Kali, but never complained about it to anyone. Like a mute man with a dream to tell, Muthu kept it all to himself. I just have to send him a message today, he will send the person tomorrow.'

'We can't just leave the slippers outside the house forever, can we?' said Ponna. 'We have to put them back on when needed.'

Seerayi said, 'All right! But listen, there is one thing I don't like about your idea. Let us get rid of that cut-up branch of the portia tree. Let's not use it for the cottage. There is a dried palm tree by the roadside. We can cut that up for the roof frame. Or, we can use the portia branch as firewood to heat water this winter.'

'Why waste such a big branch?' replied Ponna with a flash of resentment. 'If we use it for the cottage, every time he looks up at it, will remember that that's the branch he tried to hang himself on.'

Seerayi said, 'Don't talk like that, Ponna. Everyone makes mistakes. If you ask Uncle Nallayyan, he will say there is nothing inherently wrong. When one looks up the ceiling, they must be able to have good thoughts. You might even get back together soon. Then when you look up at this branch, it will hurt your feelings. It will constantly remind you of what you wish to forget. So let us not do that.'

Ponna remained silent. Seerayi was determined not to let them use that wood for the cottage. The very next day Seerayi sent word with Kaaraan and asked Muthu to meet her at the banyan tree on the mud road. She and Vengayi were working in the fields that day, plucking ears of corn, when Kaaraan returned with Muthu's response. She carried a basket of corn and spread them on the rock in the field. She then walked up the mud road. Walking past four or five fields, she came to the large banyan tree. Muthu was sitting underneath the tree. Plenty of birds were roosting on it, creating a ruckus. Muthu was listening to their cacophony, thinking about how the birds must have set out very early, even when it was still dark, to look for food, and they must have returned before the day grew hot, and were now happily singing and chatting among themselves.

What else but happiness could these birds experience? Well, it is possible that they fell sick sometimes. They might even be sad that they didn't find food. But none of that was a hurdle to happiness. He was delighted to see them chirping and playing intimately with each other. He started looking closely at the kinds of birds that were on that tree. He could see crows and cuckoos right away. Cuckoos sense immediately that they are being observed, and so they hide. Then he spotted mynahs, sparrows, pigeons, and he also saw some birds he was not familiar with. When he hunted birds in the woods sometimes, he would think that he knew all the various kinds of birds. But now he saw that there were some he did not recognize. There was a certain delight in encountering the unfamiliar. Muthu felt like climbing up the tree and sitting there on a branch with those birds. But would they accept him?

He was brought back from his thoughts by Seerayi's voice calling out, 'Muthayya!' He had gone very thin. He was more upset about Kali's treatment of him than about Ponna breaking off her ties with them. Muthu constantly thought about what he could say to Kali that would wash away his anger, make him understand. Would Kali accept Ponna and the child? Muthu got drunk every day. He did not listen to anyone's advice. Seerayi was shocked to see Muthu in that state. Was this the same Muthu who used to take delight in talking to people? She stared at him, distressed.

'Muthayya, what has happened to you?' she said. 'Our family problems have shaken you to the core. So many people have had to suffer on account of us. You gave your sister in marriage to him. You wanted them to be happy. All those good wishes have not gone to waste, I assure you. All is going to be well. Ponna herself said to me, "Speak to my brother." Kali too will come around. You are the only friend he has. One of these days, he will fall at your feet and ask for your forgiveness, I know. Please don't lose heart. The well-being of both families depends on your well-being. Once the child is born, we will have you, the maternal uncle, hold the child on your lap when they pierce its earlobes. You need to be there on that day, the proud maternal uncle to the child. How can you let yourself go like this? Kali, that dog! He has also been drinking a lot. But we make sure he eats on time. Here in the barnyard, neither he nor the dog has much work to do. So he will eat promptly. I hear you get drunk and lie about here and there. Please don't do that, dear boy. Please take care of your health. Your sister says to me, "Just talk to my brother about it. He will get it done." And very soon Kali too will seek you out. We should never lose heart. If I had given up on things and lost hope, would I have survived?'

She then explained what she wanted to see him about. Listening to her, happiness spread over Muthu's face. Right then, some sparrow shit fell on his head. He touched his head and took it to be a good omen.

TWENTY-FIVE

It usually took pilgrims ten days to get to Mangoor. Then they spent one full day there in addition to the day of their arrival. And then it was another ten full days to return. But it might take even longer if the itinerary included other temples nearby.

Kali had no difficulty walking the distance, but Nallayyan Uncle did. So Kali slowed himself down for his uncle. There were lots of pilgrims along the way, walking in groups—men, women and children, all in various kinds of groups. But there was such happiness on all their faces. They halted in the shade of tamarind trees, brought out their pots and pans and did their cooking. There were wells by the roadside, and people gathered around them to have a wash. And the farmers who owned these wells did not complain or turn people away and instead just went about their business of drawing water and irrigating their fields. Each village en route had shelters on the roadside offering free drinking water to travellers, and these shelters were constructed with thatched palm fronds that still retained their fresh, green fragrance. And water collected in large pots, with people standing by, offering cups of water to the pilgrims. These shelters also had bamboo pipes on one side, and some travellers drank water from these pipes by receiving it in the cupped palms of their hands. In some villages, people had got together and were offering free food to the pilgrims. In addition to all this, there were also separate spots where the big landowners were offering food to the travellers. Sweet panagam and diluted buttermilk were also available in various places. Kali walked along the path, amazed at all these sights and the sounds of people's constant chatter that felt like the cawing of crows.

Until then, Kali had only heard that some people undertook this walk holding aloft a kavadi, a decorated arch stretched over a pole that devotees carried on their shoulders. He had not known that it was such an important promise and offering. In each group, there was at least one person carrying a kavadi. Wherever there were temples on the way, the crowds stopped for a while, and some ritual dancing ensued. Some villages in the area had their own Manchaami shrines. And there were groups from these places, with pilgrims carrying kavadis, that travelled with their own drummers. At regular intervals, these groups launched into dances, accompanied by the drums. Kali and Nallayyan Uncle had joined the group from Semmoor. There were thirty-two people in it. Since they walked at different speeds, they had arranged to gather together every few days in one or another of the rest houses along the way. They'd spend the night in these places. Some preferred to sleep outside under the trees.

While some carried large sacks, some, like Kali, carried small bags. All he had in his bag were two blankets. Nallayyan Uncle had told him that that was all they would need. Nallayyan was used to travelling light. 'The whole point of travelling is not to carry burdens. If we insist on carrying everything, we might as well stay put. Our people have the desire to travel, but they don't know how. Come with me. I will show you all sorts of people.'

Pointing to a man who walked with a large bundle on his head and two other bundles on his shoulders, he said, 'He is like a load-bearing rock. We can place as much weight as we want on him. It will stay rock solid, but it will be very difficult to move it.' Then he pointed to a man who carried a large bundle on his back, and said, 'He is a donkey. He can carry things, but he knows nothing else. A donkey is happy as long as it finds a place where it can be by itself.' Then he directed Kali's attention to a man who carried a lot of pots and pans and was walking with his family. About him, Nallayyan said, 'Look at him carefully. He is basically carrying his entire household on his head. No matter where he goes, he can never set that burden down. I cannot show you worse idiocy than this.' Kali laughed at all these remarks.

Nallayyan Uncle sometimes chatted up fellow travellers. He approached a man who was clad in a dhoti that covered his entire legs, a shawl that draped his torso and a large kerchief tied over his head, and asked him, 'Where are you headed? To the fancy hospital of the white man?' And the man replied, laughing, 'Well, I do want to go there, but my body does not cooperate.' Nallayyan Uncle said, 'True. You might desire it, but you can't. You are getting old, aren't you?' Everyone laughed at this exchange.

Since Kali and Nallayyan were new to this pilgrimage, they found it easy to talk and chat with everyone. But Nallayyan happened to know a lot of people there. Even people from other villages approached him and chatted him up. One elder teased him with great liberty, 'What a surprise! The dog who'd sleep and eat and hang about anywhere has now set out on a pilgrimage to see Manchaami!'

Nallayyan did not mind. He said, 'Thatha, you old man, the sheep can roam around anywhere they want during the day, but they have to return to the fold at nightfall, don't they? And the dog too must return home at that time if it wants to eat, mustn't it? Otherwise, it'd have to go hungry the entire day. So now it is time to feed the dog and tie it up in the sheep enclosure. That's the reason.'

Nallayyan walked very slowly. It took immense patience on Kali's part to slow himself down on his uncle's account. But there were times when they speeded up a little. In another place, they saw a man walking with his little daughter. He carried her on his shoulders for a while.

She was around six or seven years old. How far could he carry her on his shoulders? So he'd set her down to walk with him every now and then, distracting her with stories. But the moment the story was finished, she demanded to be lifted up and carried on his shoulders again. Kali felt bad looking at them, but he was also moved at how lovingly the father spoke to his child, using many endearments. 'Muthaayi! My little piece of gold. Chellayi! Muruvaayi!'

Kali asked him, 'What have you named her?'

The man smiled as he replied, 'Manjaatha.' Kali said, 'But you never called her that even once!' And the man explained, 'She was born to us after appealing to Manchaami. Seven years ago, her mother conceived her when she went to the midday rituals at the temple. It is the deity himself who is born to us in the form of this child. We can call that god by various names. How lovely it is that we can do that! There might be one god, but the names are many. As for us, this little one is our goddess. That's why I call her by all these names of deities.'

Kali did not know how to respond to that. His uncle came closer to him and explained, 'See, she was born after praying to the deity.' Kali lifted the little girl and carried her on his shoulders. Her father now walked beside Kali, saying, 'Her mother too always walked this route with us every year. But now she is unwell. She was wounded by a thorn in her feet and now has her feet bandaged. She said to me, "This year, Manchaami does not want to see me. You take the girl and show her to him." So here I am. We need to show Manchaami that we are taking good care of the child he gave us, don't we?'

Nallayyan was walking a little ahead of them. So Kali now asked the man directly, 'Don't you feel bad that this is a child born through those prayers?'

The man said, 'Who are we to discriminate between god's creatures? Who does not have a lack in their lives? Everyone does. For some it is something physical—some physical suffering you can directly witness. But there are some others that you can't. I mean, if someone has a limp, you can see it. If someone is deaf, you find that out by talking to them. But if someone has ulcers, how would you know? If someone has a problem in their arse, how would you even know? You'd know if you lived with them. Likewise, point out to me one person who is without worries. Everyone has their own form of suffering. But what the gods offer are ways to remove these sufferings. They tell us, "Do this and be rid of your suffering." If the gods themselves have given us these ways, why should we humans have a problem with that? I have no worries and concerns now. The deity has given me the joy of carrying and playing with this child. My only concern is that I need to take good care of what god has given me.'

Kali walked quite a distance carrying that little girl on his shoulders. The father said, 'Please set her down. She can walk a little way.'

And the child said, 'I will walk only if you tell me a story.'

199

Her father said, 'All right, I will,' and started a story. It was the one about the new bridegroom who ate sesame flour.

Kali walked alongside, listening to the story. Once the story ended, he walked a little faster and joined his uncle. When he told him that he had been listening to that story, his uncle said, 'Do you know that there is more to that story?' and started telling him the rest of the story. The others who were walking close by listened to this story too.

* * *

Thus went the story the father told his little girl:

There was this man in this village. He got married and went to his mother-in-law's house. He was a little shy, because, after all, he was a new mapillai, a new son-in-law. In the course of her cooking, his mother-in-law pounded some sesame seeds. He found the smell very appetizing and he wanted to eat some of that flour, but he was too shy to ask. When she finished pounding, the mother-in-law asked him, 'Mapillai, would you like to eat some sesame flour?' But he was still quite shy, so he said, 'No, no, thank you.' They offered it to him repeatedly. His father-in-law asked him if he would like to eat some sesame flour. He declined. His two brothers-in-law offered it to him. He declined again. His sister-in-law asked him. He still said no. Then his wife too invited him to partake of some sesame flour. He said no to her too. He said no to all of them. But late that night, he still kept thinking about that sesame flour. The smell still wafting from the stone grinder did not help matters. He didn't know what to do. He waited for everyone to go to bed. His cot was on the porch. Once everyone had gone to bed, he walked over to the grinding stone, put his head into the stone's pit and licked it. The fragrance and the sweetness enchanted him and he kept licking. He put his head in further and continued licking away. And then his head got caught in the pit of the grinding stone! No matter how hard he tried, he could not extricate himself. Thankfully, his mother-in-law stepped out of the house to relieve herself in the backyard. She saw him in his ordeal, called for help and pulled his head out safely. Then she brought him a ball of sesame flour to eat, and he ate it with much gusto.

And this is what Uncle Nallayyan added to the tale:

One version goes thus. After they had managed to safely extricate his head from the pit of the grinding stone, the mother-in-law brought him a ball of sesame flour, and said, 'I offered it to you so many times earlier, and you said no. You could have eaten a little then, couldn't you?' But the son-in-law declined even then. He protested, 'I don't really like sesame flour, Atthai. I just did not want all that flour in the grinding stone to go to waste. That's why I wanted to lick it clean.'

But there is another version too. The son-in-law had his head caught in the grinding stone, and was struggling to pull himself out. A little calf happened to be nearby, tied to a pole. The man was not wearing a loincloth inside this veshti. So when he wriggled himself to set his head free, his penis swayed in full view. When the calf saw that, it mistook the penis for a cow's udder and started sucking on it. The penis grew hard and big. It was at that precise moment that the man's mother-in-law happened to step outside. She too became excited at the sight of the penis. She moved the calf away and tied it up at a distance. Then she started sucking her son-in-law's penis and did not let go until she milked it dry.

TWENTY-SIX

Everybody laughed when Uncle finished telling the story. But one man said, 'We shouldn't be telling such stories when we are on our way to a temple, should we?' The others too now looked as if they agreed with the man. Kali felt the same way too.

'All right,' said Nallayyan Uncle. 'I won't talk like that. It has been three days since we set out on this journey. We are all walking barefoot over dust and grime, enduring many difficulties. We shiver in the cold at night. Now tell me, does none of you wonder how lovely it would be to sleep cuddling your wife or some other woman?'

No one responded. Everyone walked in silence.

For the past two nights, Ponna had been slipping into Kali's blanket at night. Even when he sent her away, saying, 'Didn't I make it clear that I do not want you? Go away,' the cold weather kept bringing her back into his blanket. And he was able to fall asleep only when he stopped resisting, and embraced her. But Kali was not sure what he thought of his uncle speaking so frankly to everyone. One or two people moved away, disgusted. But Nallayyan Uncle just said, 'Naïve fellows! They wouldn't even know where their mouths need to go. They are like newborns who haven't even opened their eyes!' Perhaps those men shared Nallayyan Uncle's story and remarks with others walking ahead, because now more men walked over and joined this group. 'There will always be a crowd for this kind of banter. They'd pretend to dislike it, but see how they are coming to us now,' Uncle whispered in Kali's ears.

Nallayyan Uncle then asked everyone loudly, 'How many wives does Mangoor Manchaami have?'

Some people replied in unison, 'Three.'

When he asked, 'Who is the first wife?' some said, 'Vangi,' a few said, 'Thembi,' and yet others said, 'Thiruni.' Kali was familiar with all three names, but he did not know which one of them was the deity's first wife.

Nallayyan Uncle explained. 'Thembi was the first one. Her parents, who are gods themselves, married her to Manchaami. But do you know who Thembi is? She is the daughter of Ravanasura, the king of the entire demon world. She was such a fine bride for Manchaami. But Thembi and he could not have children even after several years of marriage. What is a hundred years for us is a single day for the gods. They waited a hundred years, hoping a child would be born. But nothing happened. Then, having decided to find a wife for Manchaami from a more modest background, Manchaami's family approached a fisher family and found Vangi as the second wife for him. They too waited for a hundred years, but were unable to produce a child. Then he decided to marry for a third time, and found Thiruni. This time, too, they waited a hundred years, but to no avail. He had married three women but he still could not have a child. He wondered what he could do. Then he thought of consulting his father, the god who fed and took care of the entire world. His father laughed, and said, "So it took you so long to come to me?"

'He said, "Manchaya, try to remember. There was something you did when you were a little boy. You went to the woods one day for a hunt. There, you heard the sounds of someone slurping water from a stream. You assumed it was some kind of a beast. You are skilled at marking a perfect aim with your lance just by hearing your prey; you don't even have to see it. So you threw your lance in that direction. But it was not a wild animal, it was a mother who had been feeding her little child some water. Your lance pierced that little child's heart. And that mother had to witness the painful death of her own child. You quickly revealed yourself in your divine form to her. But although she realized you were a god, she still cursed you, saying that you shall never have a child of your own. She then pulled out the lance from her child's body and killed herself by plunging it into her own heart. You did not take her curse seriously, because you thought a mere human's curse could not affect a god. Then you forgot all about it.

"'But we know that the curse laid by someone at the moment of their death will always come true. So your mother ran to the woman right away and begged that you had done this unknowingly and that you needed to be protected from this curse. To which, the woman said before she died, 'You are the people who protect those like us. Your son Manchaami lives on a hillock. The day he blesses people from a thousand hillocks, the curse will lift and he will be able to have a child.'" Then the father god said to Manchaami, "Go and dwell on a thousand hillocks. Then you will be able to have children." Since then, Manchaami has been climbing one hillock after another, blessing people. But he has not managed to climb a thousand of them yet. That's why he is still childless.'

People who heard this story from Nallayyan Uncle remarked, 'We have been going to the temple for all these years, but we did not know this story.'

Kali said to his uncle, 'Chithappa, you just made up this story, didn't you?'

To which his uncle replied, 'You are such an ignorant fellow. All this is written in our sacred texts. Let me know if you would like to read it for yourself. I will bring you a copy.'

Kali said, 'But I can't read.'

'Nor can I,' said Nallayyan Uncle. 'But I have heard these stories from the elders.'

As they walked past Odaiyur, they only encountered vacant fields. They weren't even sure if many of the villages were inhabited at all. But the lands were all fenced up, just the way Kali had maintained a fence around his barnyard.

Even a small piece of land in this place had its own fence. Some fields showed signs of past harvests. Sheep were grazing here and there. After this point, there were fewer villages closer to the road. But those who had walked this path several times were able to tell everyone where water and food could be found next. So they had to plan their walk accordingly thereon. No one walked alone in these parts. They walked together in a group.

Kali and Nallayyan Uncle walked with the old man from Semmur for an entire day. It seemed as though Nallayyan was not his usual braggart self when in the elder man's company.

'How many years have you been undertaking this pilgrimage, Thathayyan?' Kali asked the old man.

'Do you see that man carrying his little daughter over his shoulder?' began the old man. 'I have sat like that on my father's shoulders and travelled this path. Since then, I have gone every single year. Sometimes my sons join me. But whether anyone joins me or not, I set off on the journey at this time of the year. One year, my wife gave birth around the same time, but I still went on this pilgrimage and saw my child only upon my return. And one year my mother died when I was away on this visit to the temple. I visited her grave only ten days after her death. She died on a full moon day, and I took it as Manchaami taking her back to himself. Somehow this journey always makes me happy. I have come to know so many people because of this. They all invite me to visit them. And I do. Most of my time goes by in these visits.'

The elderly man had a very feeble voice. Kali had to walk very close to him to be able to hear him. A blanket and a bowl were all he carried. 'Wherever I go, I receive food in this bowl. That way, I will have a little food to eat later even if I have to spend a night alone somewhere.'

Kali asked him, 'Is Thathayyan your name?'

The man laughed, and said, 'My name is Manchaami. For many years now, people have been calling me Thathayyan.'

That night they stayed in a village beyond Veerur. They lay down under a tamarind tree, but they could not sleep. It was a very cold night. Then they lit a bonfire to keep warm. Along that path, as far as their eyes could see, they spotted several bonfires. As they settled around the fire, someone mentioned the story that Nallayyan Uncle had told them earlier. The old man laughed hearing this and said to Kali, 'Your uncle always had some such story to tell.'

One of the men then narrated Nallayyan's version of the story of the son-in-law eating the sesame flower, and remarked, 'How could somebody tell such a story, Thathayyan?'

Nallayyan defended himself right away. 'All stories have such a version, let me tell you. I know so many of them. Why don't you tell me a story? I will tell you a bawdy version of your story too.'

The man got angry at this, and said in a challenging tone, 'Why don't you try that with the kozhukattai story?'

'You mean the Atthiribaccha dumpling story, right?' said Nallayyan, launching into his tale.

'There was once a man who did not even know how a kozhukattai looked. He had travelled to some place, and there, someone served him a kozhukattai. He loved it. He asked them what the dish was called and decided that he would ask his wife to make it for him as soon as he returned home. But since it was a completely new name to him, he kept repeating to himself, "Kozhukattai, kozhukattai . . ." all the way back. On the way, he had to cross a small canal by leaping across it. While leaping, he exclaimed, "Ayy! Atthiribaccha!" and landed on the other side. But now he forgot the word "kozhukattai". He tried his best to recollect it, but he couldn't. Once he reached home, he said to his wife, "They had cooked that dish there. I ate it. It was very good. You make it for me too. I want to eat it." But his wife had no clue what "it" was. So she asked him. He thought he was beginning to recollect the name of the dish, but he got it wrong. So he said, "That one, monnachi—make it for me." The word he had used meant "the stupid one". For a moment, the wife wondered if her husband was insulting her. Just to be sure, she asked him to repeat the word. He said, "Make monnachi for me. That's what they called it there." She asked all her neighbours, but they only laughed at the name. They had no idea how to make monnachi. But everyone from the village dropped by just to hear him say that word. He kept saying "monnachi", and they all laughed at him. He beat his wife for making him the laughing stock of the entire village. He hit her so badly that her bruised body swelled up all over. An old woman from the village took a look at the wife's swellings, and scolded him, "You monnaya! You idiot! How could you hit her like this? Her body has swollen up like a kozhukattai!" Hearing that, he started jumping up and down, and said, "That's the one! What you just said!" The old woman laughed. "You mean when I called you 'monnaya,' the limp one?" But the wife understood what he meant. "You mean kozhukattai?" she asked. He said, "Yes, yes!" and jumped in joy. From then on, he became known as "the limp one" in the village.'

Everyone laughed. The man who had challenged Nallayyan for another version of the story was now speechless. Then people started mentioning the stories they knew and asked if those stories too had similarly vulgar renditions.

'Every story does,' said Nallayyan. 'I can tell you one for each of your stories.'

Thathayyan, the elder, said, 'Whatever we consider the right way, there will always be something that is the direct opposite of that. Like Nallayyan said, every story has its counter. Young men used to tell these stories. But this is how it is generally. If we set a norm, there will always be a way to violate it. The norm is what looks clear and bright to us. The violation is hidden and hushed.'

Kali sat pondering those words for quite a while that night.

TWENTY-SEVEN

When Kali returned from his pilgrimage, everything in the barnyard appeared new and unfamiliar to him. He was not sure if this newness was in the place itself or simply in the way he was now looking at it.

It was daytime when they arrived from the trip. Nallayyan Uncle left for his house, but he told Kali that he would come right back to the barnyard. He was too afraid to spend the night at his own house. He had planned to set out in a day or two, go to his prospective bride's house and get the wedding fixed for sometime in the month of Vaigasi. The pilgrimage had kindled a state of happiness in Kali. His mind was filled with memories of bathing in the Vinnaga river and shouting 'Manchaami!' at the temple. There were many other memories too. He had spent pretty much an entire month like a wandering mendicant. He had been relieved to find that he could expel everything else from his mind for a while and just go on a pilgrimage like that. And he had already made up his mind to speak to Ponna as soon as he returned.

There were all kinds of people inhabiting this world. What had Ponna done that was so terrible? Why should he make her suffer so much? Next year, if possible, he should take her on the pilgrimage. But if Ponna went with him on the journey, who would take care of the child? He remembered the man who carried his six-year-old daughter over his shoulders. The man said, 'Every word my child speaks is a wonder to me.' That father also addressed his child so lovingly in so many different ways. He had no frustrations, no tiredness, no complaints. And Kali had also met an elderly man who had been undertaking that pilgrimage for seventy years but who said each year's journey was new, that it was never boring or repetitive. How many kinds of people Kali had met on that journey! Even his uncle, Nallayyan Chithappa, was like a whole other person during that trip. Once he was with a crowd, he became a member of that crowd.

At first, Kali was tense at the prospect of talking to strangers. But Nallayyan Uncle had said, 'They are people too, my boy!' and jumped right in. When Kali asked his uncle, 'How do you move so freely among unfamiliar people?' he had said, 'How else do you make unfamiliar people familiar?' Nallayyan Uncle was met with warmth wherever he went.

The hillock in Mangoor was smaller than the one in Karattur. So it was quite easy to scale. But the crowd was massive. The throngs kept pushing others forward in the temple. There was going to be a long wait before they could see the deity dressed as a demon. Some people said, 'If we see the deity naked save for the loincloth, that's how our life will turn out too. Let us wait and see him in demon's attire.' But Nallayyan Uncle said, 'We are already in that state, in our loincloths. How could it get worse? Perhaps we will be stripped of even this? So what?' And he took Kali to see the deity right away.

Manchaami was beautiful no matter when and how they looked at him. It felt like both his lips and his heart smiled together. But Kali was not contented with that vision of the deity. He waited for the deity to be adorned in demon's attire. Nallayyan Uncle said, 'The deity is right in front of us. If we say to him, "I will look at you only if you come to me wearing different clothes, would that god come to you again?"' But Kali was not bothered. He made his uncle go with him to see the deity attired as a demon.

A majority of the devotees got their heads tonsured. Kali did too. He had thick, long hair. He had heard from his mother that they had had his head tonsured once when he was a child. But after that, she had told him, seeing his hair grow thick and dark, she did not promise hair as an offering to any deity. After all those years, this was the first time he was getting a tonsure. It felt like a huge burden had been removed from his head.

His uncle asked him, smiling, 'Have you set down your burdens?'

Kali replied, also smiling, 'All of it.'

'Don't wear your hair in a tuft from now on. Get a shorter cut,' his uncle said to him.

Kali too wanted that. But the barber in the village wouldn't know how to crop his hair properly. Kali would have to go to the shop in the market.

Nallayyan Uncle said, 'Go to the riverside in Karattur. There are barbers who have set shop there all along the road. They sit there, with a rock for a chair for the customer, and they call out, "Shave! Crop! Tonsure!" It will only cost you eight annas, and they will do it the way you want it. These days, the fashion is Bhagavathar crop—to get it cut like a musician. I get mine cut very close. That's what keeps my head from itching. But you are a young man, you should get the musician cut.'

On their return journey, they stopped briefly at some of the temples on the way. The entire trip gave Kali a major sense of accomplishment.

The fields he had come back to now weren't the ones he had left behind. When he had left, the fields were covered with white corn ears. Now all he could find there were just a few stray sheaths carried by the wind. The fields welcomed him like a vast, free expanse. Two of the plots looked green and lush with some crop coming up after the first round of harvesting. He walked closer, happily, to take a look. He could see that someone had dug water channels to those fields and had irrigated them. They had also fenced the plots with thorny karuvela twigs, perhaps to protect this second harvest from the sheep. He could see a few large pots of water next to the well. So he walked there to see the changes. Pots and tubs. And signs of cattle having been tethered nearby. How did these fields get renewed? He had left here thinking that the ears of corn would have to wait for him to return. He had worried that they might stay out in the fields a little too long and the corn might start to peel. But he had consoled himself that he could always do a better and timely job the year after. As for the brinjal patch, the shelter he had made was still intact and the plants were doing very well.

Now he grew disconcerted looking at these changes. He trotted towards the barn, wondering what changes would have occurred there. On his way, he saw that the sheep enclosure was now outside. The sheep had been herded back in after grazing. The sheep that had been pregnant when he had set out on his trip had now yielded a lamb. He saw the dog's chain outside the sheepfold. In the barnyard, he spotted two new piles of corn bales. Why were they laid out this way? What had happened to the bales of kambu? As he walked further into the barnyard, he grew tense and even more agitated. Looking at these changes, Kali felt like he was increasingly becoming old and irrelevant. Several questions ran through his mind—Why have they done this? Why have they changed this? Who gave them permission to make these changes? Seerayi, who had been lying on a cot in the shade of the portia tree, rose when she heard him approaching.

He felt irritated at the sight of her sprawled on the cot, her slightly greying hair open and spread out. She got up and tied her hair, saying, 'Come, Kaliyappa! Did you just arrive? You have gone so thin!' She then laughed. 'With that tonsured head, you look like a newborn crow chick that is yet to grow wings!' He handed her the packet of prasadam, the consecrated food offerings from the temple, without saying a word. He could see the new cottage that been built in his absence. The mud wall was quite high; it had been plastered on the outside. He understood that the women had moved to the barnyard. Clearly, Ponna slept luxuriously in the new cottage, while her mother-in-law had the shade of the portia tree for herself. Both cottages now had their roofs secured with kambu stalks. All the bales he had gathered and piled up over the course of four years were now on the roofs of the cottages. His anger grew uncontrollable at this point. Someone had also separated the corn harvest into two neat and equal piles. Who had done all this? He wanted to pick a fight with them.

He couldn't see the oxen. The calf was freely bounding about inside the barnyard, running from one end to another. The mother cow was nowhere to be seen. Kali caught hold of the calf and tied it up. That made him feel a little calmer. 'Where are the oxen? Did you sell them?' he asked Seerayi, without looking at her.

'We have left them grazing on the mud road. Shall I fetch them?' she replied calmly. She knew he had a special affection for the oxen, and perhaps that was why he was asking after them now.

He said, 'No. I will go,' and stepped outdoors. It was quite sunny outside, but he thought he felt better there in the open rather than inside.

'Wait,' said Seerayi, and went to the new cottage to wake Ponna up.

There was a wall erected in the middle of the cottage to separate the area into two rooms. They could use the other room to cook and to store pots and pans. The front portion was for the cot and to keep their clothes. It was quite a spacious cottage. All of this had been built according to Muthu's plans. He had given clear instructions to the man who brought the sand needed for the construction. And he personally supervised everything, from making sure the workers brought the proper kind of soil for the plastering work to making sure they got the right quantity of wood.

Ponna handled all the finances. She had enough to cover all the expenses, and she was absolutely keen to make sure Muthu did not spend anything out of his own pocket. She had also communicated that very clearly to him through Seerayi. 'Until the ritual separation is lifted, we should not accept even a penny from them, Atthai,' she had said several times.

Ponna's face was expressionless now. These days she struggled even to sit and walk. The child's kicks had grown stronger—and Ponna had grown impatient and kept saying she couldn't wait for the child to be born.

On waking her up, Seerayi did not say too much to Ponna. Laughing, she just said, 'The officer is here. You should see his tonsured head and his tone of authority!' Ponna wanted to see Kali with his hairless head. She rose from the cot slowly and stepped outside the cottage. But, to her disappointment, Kali had gone out. He had been an away for a month—how lovely it would have been if he had come to her and said, 'Ponna, how are you?' She might have felt better even if he had come into the cottage and yelled at her. Ponna let out a deep sigh and went back to lie down on the cot. She felt exhausted.

By the time Seerayi ran out through the gate to see where Kali was, he had already walked into the fields. She trotted after him, and said, 'Did everything go well on the journey?'

He just murmured, 'Mmm.'

'We were very confused as to what we should do until you returned, my boy,' Seerayi said, walking alongside him as she launched into an explanation. 'People say that farming is a man's job, don't they? We did not know whom to find to keep a watch over the barnyard at night. So we did that ourselves for two nights. Our teeth shuddered in the cold. That's when we thought the best thing to do would be to move here, and we got the cottage done. Ponna protested, "How can we do all this without asking him?" It was I who convinced her that I'd talk to you myself. Things are better now. Even after the child is born, we can continue to live right here. If we lived in the village, people will talk. Why put ourselves through all that? Then, I also hired Vengayi for a month. She and I cut the maize stalks, picked the corn ears and did all of that work together. Here, look at my hand. The stalks have cut my hand in so many places. Not a day went by when I did not think of how my son usually protects me from such hardship. I prayed to god to make sure you returned to us safely. Having Vengayi's help made the tasks a little easier. I even managed to separate the bales of corn into two piles. All the kambu stalks were just lying around for so long. The cows were not eating it. I thought they were of better use on the roof. As for the corn stalks, I made sure they were made into smaller bundles. Otherwise, it becomes difficult to pull out stalks from larger bundles. This way, I can still pull out stalks for the cattle to eat even when you are away.'

Seerayi did not fault Ponna in any of this. She only said, 'She is a pregnant woman. She finds it hard even to walk, carrying her large belly. Poor thing, she is so frail.'

Kali walked on to the mud road and looked the oxen grazing. As soon as they saw him, they lifted their heads and mooed. He had been worried that the oxen might have gone thin. After all, who would take care of them the way he used to? But they looked healthy and fine. One of them even had a new rope. Kali had nothing to say. His mother's voice carried on prattling. But Kali said to her, 'You go in. I'll be back soon.'

She hesitated, but then moved away from the mud road. And he walked further along the road, looking for the toddy tapper.

TWENTY-EIGHT

On the morning of the last Thursday of the month of Thaii, Ponna gave birth to a baby boy.

Everyone was convinced that the baby was the spitting image of Kali. All the relatives who came by to see the child said he looked just like Kali. But for a month after childbirth, all Ponna did was cry. She herself could not understand what made her cry so much—whether it was the fact that the child was a boy and not a girl as she had hoped, or if it was because Kali never came by to see the child. In that month, Ponna did not regain any strength. How could she, if all she did was cry? Was it good for the baby? No matter what Seerayi said, Ponna could not bring herself to act differently.

Every day, Seerayi asked Ponna to go to bed even before it grew properly dark. And she did all the work herself—carrying the baby, bathing him, rubbing oil on his tiny body. She also cooked various things for Ponna to eat in a bid to recover her strength. 'A god is born here, but the chariot refuses to carry him,' she said, directing her sarcasm at Kali. Whenever she carried the child to him, he walked away. Once she even said to him directly, 'It is a newborn baby. What did it do to you to deserve this treatment? Wait for it to grow up a little, to run around and play, and climb up on you and pee and shit on you. You won't be able to resist him then.' But Kali did not appear to pay any attention.

It had been a very painful labour and delivery for Ponna. Earlier, when she had asked Vengayi how difficult labour could be, Vengayi had said, smiling, 'Well, it will be a little difficult for sure.' But that was not the case. It was immensely difficult. She'd started having a light pain the morning before, but she did not realize it was labour pain. She had often had a sharp pain in her hip and lower abdomen in the mornings, but it usually waned as the day progressed. But this pain just kept increasing. By midday, when she felt she could not bear it any longer, she told Seerayi about it. Seerayi asked her to describe the pain, and at the end of it said with absolute certainty that it was indeed labour pain. As the pain kept mounting, Ponna grew terrified. She sent Vengayi to fetch the midwife. Seerayi asked the worker in the adjacent farm to make a trip to Adaiyur.

By the time the midwife, Thangamma, prepared and packed everything and arrived there, it was well past dusk. Until then, Ponna kept asking every few minutes when the midwife would come. It was as if she believed that once she arrived, the midwife would simply take over and miraculously absorb all of Ponna's pain herself. But Thangamma came unhurriedly, felt Ponna's abdomen with the palm of her hand and told them that the baby would be born by the morning. Ponna was deeply disappointed at that. She had assumed that the delivery would happen as soon as Thangamma arrived on the scene. Now she had to endure this awful pain all night?

Vengayi left for her home. Seerayi went to secure the sheep and the cattle in their places. And Thangamma said, 'Ponnu, don't be afraid. The pain is always a bit more during the first delivery. Try to bear it patiently. You were able to bear all the insults people directed at you. What can this pain do to you? This is the good kind of pain. It leads to good things.' She asked Ponna not to eat anything more that night, and she also asked her to try and shit right away. The midwife then gave her a concoction made of karupatti to drink. She had brought all sorts of medicines in a box, but she did not take anything out. Then she too left.

After that, only Seerayi and Ponna remained. Kali had been walking around the barnyard until a little while ago, but he too suddenly disappeared. Perhaps he did not think he could bear Ponna's suffering. Or perhaps he wondered, 'Is this my child? What will I do if they expect me to go see the child once it is born?' Ponna felt like everyone had abandoned her. When she went to the outfields to relieve herself, she looked in the direction of the Karattur hillock and temple and said a prayer. She couldn't pray at leisure, but she stood holding her hip, and said, 'This is your child, isn't it? Please make sure things go well.' She could not say anything more.

She drank more of the karupatti concoction and lay down on the cot. But she could not stay lying down for even a second. She rose again and then lay down on her side, though that didn't seem to help either. So she got up and stepped outside. She sat on the rock and wept. Looking at her crying, Seerayi said, in an attempt to be jocular, 'You can cry all you want, but you, and only you, will still have to go through with giving birth!' She laughed.

'I am crying here,' hissed Ponna angrily, 'and you find it funny?'

'If you can't bear even this pain,' said Seerayi, 'how are you going to deal with what's to come? You will have contractions first. Once you start having those, the birth will happen soon. And that will feel like your entire hip is breaking apart. You will have to endure all that agony.'

Slowly, one by one, a crowd gathered there. The entire barnyard was eventually full. Once the midwife returned, she boiled another concoction and gave it to Ponna in a little cup. Ponna drank it in one gulp, hoping that the bitter and pungent medicine would alleviate her pain or perhaps increase it and hasten the birthing process. But nothing of that sort happened. After a while, people began to leave, muttering among themselves, 'It will happen only in the morning.' Those who stayed behind sat chatting, laughing and enjoying themselves. Some stretched themselves and went to sleep right there. Kali too returned and lay down on the cot under the portia tree. Ponna was irritated by all this. The midwife would check up on Ponna every now and then. Then she too lay down to catch a wink.

Ponna did not know how long she had slept. And she was also not sure if she had managed to get some sleep at all. Early in the morning, Thangamma gave her another round of the medicinal concoction. At dawn, when the blackbirds on the palmyra trees started their chatter, Ponna's pain suddenly intensified. Unable to bear it, she shouted, 'Ayyo! Ayyo!'

'Don't yell that,' the midwife cautioned. 'Call out god's name.'

Ponna could see that Kali was awake and was taking care of things in the cattle shed. She could also hear him responding to the visitors.

When the contractions began and Ponna's waters broke, the midwife made her lie down and asked her to push. Ponna held her breath, and heaved. Thangamma pressed down on Ponna's belly with her hand and rubbed it fastidiously. But nothing worked. Then Thangamma sent for some ropes, and once they were brought, she asked for the ropes to be suspended from the central beam in the inner roof. They needed Kali for this job. Seeing him pulling and tying the rope properly, Ponna could not help but think: he had experience hanging ropes, didn't he? Once he finished the task, he walked away without even a glance at her. Two or three women lifted Ponna from the cot, brought her close to the rope hanging from the ceiling, and asked her to grab hold of it. Ponna kept her feet apart, knelt down and got hold of the rope. It felt like the rope was hanging from the portia tree.

She had closed her eyes, held on to the rope, and pushed. Just one push. She had then felt her stomach loosening—and she fainted before she could properly hear someone say, 'It's a boy!' When she came to, she saw everyone happy and excited. She heard Seerayi saying, 'The baby boy is pitch-dark just like his father, Ponna!' Ponna did not have the strength to wail, so she whimpered. Did Kali see the child? Seerayi told her later that he had come to see the baby in front of everyone. She also told Ponna that when she tried to give him the child to hold, he declined, saying he had never handled infants before. Ponna had not taken a good look at the baby until then. And she could not do so afterwards either.

For an entire month, it was Seerayi who took care of the baby. Slowly, Ponna started eating proper food. Gradually she was able to walk to the outfields without anyone's assistance.

Seerayi told her it was a month since the child was born. 'We need to show a lamp flame to the child,' she said, and busied herself in preparing for that ritual. They had some castor oil made from their own castor seeds. Kali had taken them to the oil press and got the oil made. The very day he brought the new oil from the press, Seerayi went to the village temple and lit some lamps there using that oil.

There were a lot of preparations leading up to the ritual. On the seventh day after the child was born, the potter family had come by with three large earthen lamps and accepted kambu millets in exchange for them. Seerayi now poured castor oil into one of those three new lamps. She then put in a thick wick and set the lamp on its plank. Ponna was sitting on the cot, and the baby had been laid on the other end of the cot. Seerayi placed the lamp in such a way that it was on the same side of the cot as the baby's head. She then lit the lamp. As the wick slowly caught the flame, a yellow glow spread all over the cottage. It reminded Ponna of the way lamps illuminated the inside of the temple. Seerayi gently patted the baby's cheeks to make him open his eyes, saying, 'Look here, darling.' The baby woke up, whimpering, twisting and wringing his infant body. He shut and opened his eyes, trying to adjust to the glow of light in the room. Then he looked in amazement at the flame.

That was the first wonder the child was witnessing in this world. Seerayi cooed and played with the baby and then stepped outside to bring the things she needed to ward off the evil eye.

Ponna observed the movements of the flame and of the baby's eyes. She felt a sudden desire to look at the baby properly, so she moved closer. The baby's gaze then alternated between her face and the flame. She happily ran her hand over its unkempt hair and its dark body. She was suddenly overcome with the care and affection she had not felt until then. She gently massaged the baby's legs. She unfurled his little fingers and placed his hands on her face. She looked at the baby's penis. It looked like another little finger. 'Chinna kunjaan! Little penis!' she said affectionately, touching it gently with her fingers and then bringing those fingers to her lips for a kiss. The baby flung his legs about and made some sounds.

She was lost in enjoying her little baby. 'Mottukutti!' she said, and touched his little belly. 'Chinna muthu! My little pearl!' she said and brought her face close to the baby's. The baby looked wide-eyed and wonderstruck at the way her face at first grew bigger and brighter as it came closer and then smaller when she pulled herself away. After she repeated this playful movement a few times, the baby laughed. He opened its mouth wide and let out a happy gurgle. Ponna was delighted. As she brought her hand close to the baby's lips, she suddenly heard a voice saying, 'What's my name?'

Did the baby just speak? When she looked closely at the baby's face right then, she was reminded of that voice and that mouth. That face she had encountered at the festival. That face which had asked her, 'What's my name?'

TWENTY-NINE

He had spotted Ponna standing alone in the middle of that festival crowd. Then she too recognized him. He called her 'Selvi'. But she did not feel the need to call him by any name. Massive crowds had gathered to have a glimpse of the deity on that festival day. Cultural events and performances were being staged all along the streets.

Some people whistled at them both. 'Oy!' they shouted and teased. 'Mapillai! So you found someone, huh?' they called out to him. Ponna was irritated. She walked, head down. He held her hand with much liberty, and said, 'This is how festival crowds are.' Then he quickly managed to take her past these crowds.

They walked around the hillock in the moonlight that had draped itself over things. Now he was holding her close with an arm around her waist. She felt that that embrace was meant to dispel her fears. She huddled close to him. In his physique and appearance, he looked a lot like Kali. She even wondered if it was in fact Kali in disguise. He was wearing a veshti around his waist. Even though the dhoti came all the way down to his ankles, he walked with ease, without tripping. A piece of cloth was draped around this neck, falling over his bare chest. On his head he wore a large handkerchief like a bandana. Ponna thought this must be his way of concealing his identity.

Kali too always wore his dhoti folded and two-layered whenever he went out of the house. He also wore a piece of cloth over his shoulders, which he sometimes tied around his head. And whenever she huddled close to him, Kali's body too felt firm like granite, just like this man's did now. She shook her head to avoid seeing Kali in her mind. But this was indeed Kali. The Kali who was in her mind was superimposed perfectly on this man. This was definitely Kali. This was Kali who had come to take her somewhere. Ponna hesitantly placed her hand on his waist. He pulled her hand close and placed it more firmly around him. Where was he taking her? She was unable to recognize the road. There were a few people walking about, but it was mostly deserted with only the moonlight providing illumination. Suddenly, Kali turned and walked towards the hillock. Or at least that's what she thought he was doing. She did not think there could be a path down there. It was only rocks. But he still led her along.

Kali climbed the rock deftly like a goat. He let her walk for small stretches and at other times he lifted her gently and carried her over the rocks. They seemed to have climbed a quarter of the way up the hillock. There was a large rock at that point, and right behind it was a flat, floor-like surface. Nothing other than the moon could know that spot. He removed the kerchief from his head. It was neither the size of a towel nor a dhoti. More like a shawl, a dupatta. He spread it on the ground. Then he sat down and invited her to sit down with him. She did. He pulled her closer to his chest. She wanted to embrace Kali, entwining her hands over his back.

He held her hands and gently draped them around himself. The moon was spreading its sweetness all over the world. There was not a spot of cloud in the sky. The moon had no obstacle in reaching across the vast heavens. The earth, drunk on the nectar of moonbeams, lay in a stupor. An intoxicated expanse.

Then he asked her, 'Did you come seeking a child?'

She did not say anything in reply, and placed her face on his chest.

He said, 'You will have one.' He touched her lips gently. 'Won't you talk to me?'

It was only her hands that communicated.

'Will you name your child after me?' he asked.

She softly whispered, 'Mm,' in his ears.

'Do you know my name?' he asked.

'Mhmm,' she murmured.

'. . .' he said. 'Call the child by my name whether it is a boy or a girl. That way you won't forget me.' He waited for her murmured response. But he could sense her nodding in agreement against his chest. 'So, what's my name?' he asked her.

She did not respond.

'Tell me what my name is,' he asked her again.

She whispered in his ears, 'Kali.'

'What did you say?' he said. She was momentarily confused about what name she had uttered. But he said, laughing, 'I couldn't hear it properly. But it felt like the moonlight had entered my ears.'

He then lifted her face with his hands and held it right in front of his own, and said, 'I have another name too.' Then he added, 'See, in this darkness, there is neither you nor me. It is only us, we are the same. Tell me what my name is.'

She felt very shy. He was clearly talking about Maachaami, who took whatever form you wanted him to. Was that his name? He sensed that she was smiling.

'So you got it?' he said. 'Maachaami. That's my name. I want to forget myself and get together with you. I never want to let go of you.' And he took her into a tight embrace.

She couldn't breathe properly, but she did not want that embrace to end. For some reason, she felt like laughing.

'Are you laughing?' he said. 'Do you know what I plan to do with that mouth that is laughing?' He drew her face closer. The moonlight cooled her.

'Do you know where I am from?' he then asked.

She put her hand over his mouth and shook her head to indicate that she did not want to know.

'Don't worry. I am from right here, this hillock. All you need to do is come to any part of this hillock, and call out, "Maachaami!" I will show up right away.'

She nodded to let him know she understood.

'You should come next year too. And you should bring the child. I'll be expecting you. Will you? You will. I know. You won't forget me. I won't forget you, even if you do. Tell me, do you want to go away with me? I will take you right away. I like you a lot. Come with me!' And he kept saying sweet nothings to her. She drowned in his entreaties, and found it hard to resurface.

THIRTY

Ponna had put her baby to sleep and was sitting on the stone slab outside the hut. Seerayi had gone to the house in the village to fetch more kambu millets. She was gone for quite a while. Seerayi had lived in that village house for several years. She knew all her neighbours there. The houses were all set quite close to each other, and people could just shout out to call each other. If anyone got hold of Seerayi for a chat, they would certainly not let her go easily. It was even possible that Seerayi might stay over in the house for the night. She had done that twice already since the child was born. It was her way of seeing if it was her presence in the barnyard that prevented Ponna and Kali from reconnecting. Ponna was constantly amazed at the various schemes Seerayi came up with.

Seerayi's schemes were to blame for all the present troubles. It was she who had lied and arranged for Ponna to go to the temple festival that day. She got everyone involved in that plan. It had led to Kali almost killing himself. And after that Kali and Ponna even stopped talking to each other. Then came Ponna's breaking of ties with her family. The long years of friendship between Kali and Muthu were over. Ponna's family couldn't even visit to see the child. Muthu became an alcoholic. Ponna had thought that the pilgrimage Kali had undertaken would change him for the better. But, in fact, he was now drinking more than ever before.

At least, earlier, he did all the drinking right there in the barnyard. But now since Ponna and the baby were there, he did not want to have to face them, so he drank elsewhere and wandered about. Sometimes it looked like he sat and drank under one of the palmyra trees. There were also times when she spotted his head under the palai tree out in the fields. But at other times, she could not find him anywhere nearby. He returned late at night, coughing and spitting. The sheep and the cattle had grown weary and dull in the heat of the month of Chithirai. But Kali did not seem to pay them any attention. He was not even making sure they were grazing or seeing to whether they had enough water to drink. Seerayi took care of the baby's needs in the morning and then set out to do the other chores. Ponna had still not got the hang of doing everything for the baby. She was too scared to do it on her own.

The only good thing to come out of all of Seerayi's scheming was the baby. His face was the only thing that gave Ponna some happiness. But there were times when she felt angry at the child, wondering why he was born, feeling that he was responsible for all her troubles. It was three months and one week since childbirth. Kali had still not come to look at the baby properly. He gave vent to his anger by hitting the oxen, chasing the sheep and throwing stones at the dog. Seeing all this made Ponna want to leave the barnyard to his care and move back to the house in the village quarters. Let him take care of the sheep, the cattle, the bales of harvest and the cottage. Let him have so much free space that he could hang a swing on the portia tree and freely swing about from one end to the other. Or else, let him hang himself from one of the other branches.

If she went away with the child, she could always find some work in the fields in some other village, couldn't she? She could make enough to feed the baby. Here she felt like an unwanted orphan. If she went away to her parents' home, they would definitely feed her at least some leftovers they kept for the dog, wouldn't they? Why was she struggling here? All right, if he felt that his wife had become a prostitute, he could call for a village meeting, make it public and annul their marriage. Then he could always bring a chaste woman and start a new family here. Instead he was tormenting her without speaking a word to her. What kind of torture was this?

The man she had met on the festival night said to her several times, 'Come with me.' She did not even look at his face properly. She only saw Kali's face superimposed on it. On that moonlit night, he had appeared to her like Kali. But so what? If she went to the festival this year, he'd certainly be there. And he'd look for her. She was familiar with his touch. How sweetly he spoke to her! He said to her, 'Why don't you just stay with me forever?' Was it all just said in the heat of passion? But he said it with such care, it had felt honest. What did it matter which village he was from, and which community? If she went to the festival this year and asked him to take her with him, he would. He would also lift the child and play with it.

The twelve years of togetherness and affection with Kali had come to nothing. It had paled, lost its sheen. In contrast, how loving was that man who had spent just a day—in fact, just one night—with her. She remembered every word he spoke that night. But despite all that, for a while, she only saw Kali in the baby's face. Not any more, though. She didn't see Kali. She saw Maachaami. It was not Kali's child. What was the point in insisting it was Kali's child when he himself said it was not his and did not even want to look at the baby? No, this is not your child. This is his child. It will take his name.

The man was not married when she met him. He had his very new moustache and beard. He had not even had his first shave. He might still be single. But so what if he had married by now. If she said to him, 'My child and I will not bother you. We will quietly live to a side,' he wouldn't object, would he? Would he say, 'If I have to take care of children conceived at the festival, do you know how many kids I'd have to fend for?' He had not wanted to let her go that night. He had told her she was one half of him. He had wanted to just stay together forever. It was she who had left in a hurry, anxious that it was already quite late.

He had made space for her in his heart. He wouldn't turn her away. But he'd have family and relatives for sure. Would they chase her away? Would he abide by their words? What if he too said to her, 'You are a whore! You don't even know with whom you conceived this child.' On one side, she had Kali who did not want her. And on the other, she had Maachaami who also would not want her. Where would Ponna go? She could drown herself and the baby in the Kaveri river. Death by drowning would be the kindest way to take the child. She should not leave the baby behind. If she did, he'd tell everyone that it was a whore's child. When the child grew bigger, Kali might even ask, 'You were not born to me, were you?' Why should the child suffer such lifelong ignominy?

Seerayi wanted a grandchild to take care of her final rites, didn't she? Perhaps Ponna could drop the baby on her lap and go far away—perhaps even outside the region. Why could only men travel abroad? And not women? Nallayyan Uncle brought all these women from elsewhere, didn't he? Like those women, Ponna could go with some man. Going with a man once had made her a whore. So what difference would it make now if she went with nine other men? There were ways to survive in this world, weren't there?

She thought she heard the baby whimper, so she walked into the cottage to check. It looked like the baby was dreaming. It kept its mouth pouted and was smiling slightly like a blossoming bud. Ponna kept gazing at that smile. The baby then went back to sleep. Perhaps god spoke to the baby in its dream. God spoke only to babies, but the babies never revealed the content of that conversation to anyone. This was god's child, so the deity must have spoken a lot to this child. Why can't that god speak to me too? Why can't he show me a way out of this situation? God, you gave me a way to bring this child into the world. Can't you also show me a way to raise this child? If you are indeed this powerful god that everyone bows to, please show me a way. Whose child is this? Kali's, or Maachaami's, or yours? Was it you who entered me that night? Tell me!

The child whimpered again, so she ran back into the cottage. The lamp was going dry, so she poured some oil into it. The baby laughed, kicking its arms and feet in the air. You are so delightful when you laugh. I wonder where you father's gone. Is he your father? You are my child. I carried you for nine months. Only the hen that lays eggs knows the hardship of childbirth. Why should I care who looks at you and who doesn't? You are *my* child. Why did I not think of that before? Why should I worry about that man and this? If they want, let them come and claim you as their child. Seerayi has no qualms accepting you as her grandson. What more do I need? Why worry about these useless dogs? He has so much pride, but he could not give me a child! He acts as if there are some ten or fifteen children here in the barnyard climbing on his shoulders and calling him their father and this is the only child that is not his. Considering that he couldn't do the job, why the pride?

She heard the dog barking outside in the sheepfold. Kali did not like the fact that they had moved the sheepfold outside and built this new cottage inside. He want to be the only one who lives and pees and shits here. How long can he live like this? When he is old and frail, who will come and clean his piss and shit? He is such a loner.

Ponna looked outside to see if Kali or Seerayi were coming back. She heard some voices, but she could not hear them clearly over the dog's loud barking. They were clearly some new folk. Otherwise, the dog wouldn't bark so much. Was it perhaps Uncle Nallayyan? Who was he talking to? It was so dark in that corner of the barnyard that she could not see anything clearly. And she was also too scared to leave the baby sleeping and go and check who was coming.

She was angry with Seerayi for leaving her alone with the baby here. Couldn't the old hag go and come back quickly? She must be gossiping with people there, talking about who slept with whom. Ponna felt a sudden rush of rage. If it was Seerayi who was coming back to the barnyard, she'd say to her, 'You wretched old widow! Here's your grandson. Take care of him, play with him! Leave me alone!'

The thatched gate to the barnyard had not been tied up. Someone was now pushing it open. The dog was still barking. Who could it be? Ponna took a quick look at the sleeping baby and then ventured forth to check.

THIRTY-ONE

'Who is there?' she called out.

Through the dog's incessant barking, she heard a voice reply loud and clear, 'It is only us, saami.' She thought she heard the baby crying, so she rushed inside to attend to him. The baby stirred in his sleep, somewhat disturbed, but he did not waken. She did not want to leave the baby indoors and bolt the door from outside. Nor did she want to walk away leaving the door wide open. So she kept pacing in and out, not knowing what to do. By then, the voices came closer. Two men were holding Kali up by his arms. His head fell to a side.

Ponna was agitated looking at him like this. 'What happened?' she asked.

'Please don't be scared,' said one of the men. 'We found him drunk and lying on the mud road. Let him sleep inside.'

Ponna saw that it was Chinnaan, Vengayi's husband, along with a young man she did not recognize. For a second, she wondered if she should ask them to lay Kali down on the cot under the portia tree, but she changed her mind quickly. The men might think she was heartless to make a man sleep outside in such a condition. They carried Kali right up to the doorstep of the cottage, and she guided him further to the cot, her arm over his shoulder in a tentative embrace. This was the first time she was touching him in nearly a year. She lay him down on Seerayi's cot which was across the room from the cot on which the baby was sleeping. Then she stepped outside. The men were getting ready to leave.

'This is my brother-in-law,' said Chinnaan. 'He happened to be visiting. So I took him out to drink some toddy. On the way back, as we walked past the banyan tree on the mud road, we spotted someone lying on the ground. When we went closer, we saw it was him. It was so dark, I had to light a matchstick to identify him. He never steps outside the barnyard. Perhaps he wanted to go out and drink and celebrate his new son. It looks like he has drunk arrack on top of toddy. That's what has caused so much intoxication. Otherwise, he is not the kind to lose his bearings easily. Please make him eat something. That will help him.'

'Chinnaan,' Ponna requested, as the men prepared to leave, 'please don't tell anyone about this. I'll make sure he does not collapse this way again.'

'Why would I tell anyone about this?' he said. 'Don't worry. He will be well soon and he will do all the ploughing himself. If there is any work in the fields, do send for us. Vengayi too will come and help.'

And then they left. She waited for the sound of the gate being shut and then for the dog to stop barking before she went back into the cottage.

She recollected the way it felt when she touched him. Had he been conscious, he'd not have allowed that to happen. She looked at him lying like a child on the cot, sand and dust all over him. The veshti he had worn around his waist over the loincloth had come undone. She brought an old sari of hers and used it to wipe his body clean. She wondered how long he had been lying on the road. He was not used to drinking to the point of losing consciousness. She knew he had been drinking way too much alcohol of late, but how could she say anything to him? They had not been speaking to each other for a year. The last they spoke was the day he called her a whore. That wound had healed. Once the baby was born, it had lost whatever residual sting it had had earlier. 'Let him call me whatever he wants,' was her attitude. 'I could not have given birth to this lovely baby boy otherwise.' But the slur had nonetheless left its scar.

What if he said something even more hurtful if she attempted to speak to him now? Besides, she had not got much of a chance to look at his face directly for so long. She now drank in the sight of him lying on the cot. Hair had started sprouting on his tonsured head, and it now looked like a week-old crop in the fields. His face had lost its lustre, and now exuded a deep sadness. His body had lost its muscle tone. He had not been eating properly. His mother had been trying to keep him well fed, but he did not eat enough. Seerayi too was not able to attend to him the way she used to when he was younger. She was also upset about how unrelenting and adamant he was even after the baby was born. She was angry because she had thought that everything would become all right the moment he became all right. But that had not happened. Ponna touched his arm. It felt like touching a bony stick. Were these really Kali's cheeks? She could not control herself, and she bent down and kissed him on his cheek. Then she sat there looking at him. In a while, unbeknownst to herself, she started talking to him.

'Maama, this is indeed your child. The child born to me is also born to you, isn't it? I went to the festival because I thought you had given me permission. Do you know who I was with there? I knew god would come to me in your image. It was with you that I spent that night. Whose face do I know but yours? Do you think I could even think of a face other than yours? I have been with you all these years. How come you have not understood me at all? Even if I were in the wrong, how could you abandon me like this? Do you think I will leave you if you do something wrong?

'How much I have suffered in this past year! I was also witnessing your suffering. But our struggles are not the same. I was carrying a child in my womb, I was trying to deal with your rejection, and I had also pushed away my parents and my brother. Do you know how hard all of this was? You were getting drunk and lying flat on your back. You went on a pilgrimage. Where could I go? My only options were to drown myself in a pond or lake. No matter how much you pushed me away, I kept trying to reach out to you. You didn't want to look at my face. You didn't want to talk to me. You didn't want to be with me. Where could I go and survive on my own? This world has set its limits on how far a woman can go. How could I cross that line? Where could I go? What could I do?

'That's why I have come to this decision. Listen to me. You don't have to suffer any more. I won't live any longer. It is better to die than to live like this. The noose you tried to put around your neck will also fit mine, won't it? I have waited a year for you to talk to me. I even thought it was your love for me that made you so upset with me. But there has to be a limit to anger. If you can be so angry for an entire year, there is little hope it will go away anytime soon. I have tried to think of a way out of this predicament, but nothing seems to work out. You be happy. I have given you a baby boy. Keep him if you like. Or feed him to the birds. I cannot suffer any more. Nor can I watch your suffering. Please don't torment yourself over me and spoil your health. Make this barnyard a safe haven for yourself again—safe as a mother's womb.'

Ponna couldn't tell how long she sat there speaking to him. Then, calmly, she picked out a sari. It was the same sandal-hued one she had worn to the festival. She climbed on to the cot on which Kali was lying, reached up and draped the sari over the central beam on the ceiling, and pulled the other end down. She climbed down from the cot, walked to the other cot and kissed her child. She pressed her face close to the infant's, and blessed the little one with all her heart, 'Darling Maachaami, may you live well.' The baby whimpered and wriggled his tiny body. She gently patted his soft chest, and soon he went back to sleep.

She sighed, looking at the baby, and then walked towards the hanging sari. In that instant, she felt a hand pulling her away. Kali.

GLOSSARY

atthai: a kinship term; used to refer to and address paternal aunts and mothers-in-law

dey: a friendly and familiar way to address men, particular used among young men

kaasu: an old currency unit; one kaasu was one-twelfth of an anna, which was one-sixteenth of a rupee

paatti: grandmother; used to address or refer to any elderly woman

panagam: a cooling sweet drink made with jaggery

BHISHAM SAHNI

Mansion

Translated from the Hindi by Shveta Sarda

PENGUIN BOOKS

An imprint of Penguin Random House

PENGUIN BOOKS

USA | Canada | UK | Ireland | Australia
New Zealand | India | South Africa | China | Singapore

Penguin Books is part of the Penguin Random House group of companies
whose addresses can be found at global.penguinrandomhouse.com

Published by Penguin Random House India Pvt. Ltd
4th Floor, Capital Tower 1, MG Road,
Gurugram 122 002, Haryana, India

Penguin
Random House
India

First published in Hindi as *Mayyadas Ki Marhi* by Rajkamal Prakashan 1988
Published by Penguin Books India 2016

ISBN 9780143419822

Typeset in Adobe Caslon Pro by Manipal Digital Systems, Manipal

Printed at Repro India Limited

www.penguin.co.in

MIX
Paper from
responsible sources
FSC® C047271

This is a legitimate digitally printed version of the book and therefore might not
have certain extra finishing on the cover.

To my dearest, departed parents

BOOK ONE

1

The lord of the mansion, Diwan Dhanpat Rai, sat on the terrace to the left of the mansion's arched gateway, his feet tucked under him on an easy chair, puffing leisurely at a handheld hookah. The long-time priest of the community stood before him in the lane, obsequiously uttering after everything the Diwan said, 'What you say is true; you are absolutely right, my lord.'

'This is now your responsibility, Ramdas. Don't say later that you forgot.'

'What you say is true; with Lord Ram's blessings, all will be well,' the purohit repeated deferentially.

How far could the purohit be trusted? From beneath thick, bushy eyebrows, Diwan Dhanpat Rai's small, keen eyes scanned the old man's face. He felt blocked by the haze that the purohit had created with his 'What you say is true; you are absolutely right, my lord'. Both men had lived long enough to know how much of a person his face betrays. Diwan Dhanpat was unable to gauge if the purohit was playing him, or if he was being sincere.

It was early morning. Only a few people were about town at this hour. Some were returning from the river after a bath, some were on their way to open their shops. Young lads emerged from akharas after bouts of wrestling and exercise. There was a nip in the air.

Diwan Dhanpat took another long puff from his hookah, his fingers wrapped around it, his head tilted to one side and cloaked by the smoke, a picture of one submerged in thought.

He believed his manner of sitting was a statement of his eminence. Eccentricity wasn't something he'd acquired with age. He'd been named 'Eccentric Diwan' a long time ago. He was the only Diwan who still wore a yellow *angrakha* and saffron turban, unmindful that this manner of collared, tunic-styled kurta had gone out of fashion since the time the British began to rule, or that the saffron turban was now worn only for wedding ceremonies.

'Chacha', 'Mad Diwan', 'Trim-Tail Diwan'—these were just a few of the epithets he'd been awarded over the years. There was a time when no one shied from jeering at him or cracking a joke at his expense. For there was a time when he was a Diwan only in name: he owned no property nor land to administer over; and yet, he would don a yellow angrakha, highlight his eyes with eyeliner, wear rings in his ears and roam the lanes of the town on his sickly mule, as if touring his principality. Today he was a Diwan for real; the mansion he was sitting in front of was *his*. It was the same mansion that, once upon a time, he'd been unceremoniously thrown out of, bag and baggage. Dhanpat Rai had reached where he was today after persevering for years on the crooked paths of life. And so it was that today he could sit on an easy chair, with his legs tucked under him, puffing at his hookah, a picture of a content man—a man who doesn't care what others think of him and so can do as he pleases.

He could, now, every week or so, apply henna on his beard and moustache and sit where he was sitting today, and passers-by in the street would still bend in respect and greet him with 'Jai Ramji' and 'My humble respect to you, Diwanji'. He could, now, stroll up and down this same terrace, popping almonds and pistachios into his mouth at will. He could, now, take to the lanes when he liked, in a bedecked palanquin and dressed with the aplomb befitting a Diwan—not just a yellow angrakha and saffron turban, but also with strings of pearls around his neck. And he could, now, whenever he went to meet the deputy commissioner, replace the pearls with a tie. Four palanquin bearers would carry his palanquin on their shoulders, each man with—and could this be attributed to the Diwan's eccentricity or was it a natural expression of his stature?—bells tied around his forehead and ankles.

Whenever the palanquin threaded its way through the narrow streets of the town, people knew from the approaching sounds of the bells that Diwanji was on his way. The palanquin would pass, followed by a fifth man with a low wicker stool in his hands—in the event that the Diwan wished to alight at any point and came to be in need of a seat.

Diwan Dhanpat narrowed his eyes to a slit and spoke in his deep, thick voice, 'So tell me news from around town, Purohit. You'd know if there was something to know; you're quite the cat that peeps into every home.'

The old purohit joined his hands in deference, 'What's hidden from you, Diwanji? You know everything.' But then he thought it was better not to disappoint the Diwan, and said, 'I've heard Lekhraj is coming back into town.'

The Diwan opened his eyes.

'Who told you that?'

'It's something I've heard, Maharaj. No one knows for sure.'

'What have you heard?'

'Malik Sundardas's elder brother returned just yesterday. He was saying that someone saw Lekhraj in Huzoorpur. And it was he who said to me that Lekhraj would be back in town soon.'

A small, mysterious smile danced on the Diwan's lips. How did it matter any more whether or not Lekhraj returned? What could he possibly do even if he came back? He'd just knock about town and leave empty-handed. The Diwan shifted his weight to his other leg and relaxed.

'And? What else have you heard? What news of the commissioning agent Mansaram?'

'He's rolling in wealth, Maharaj! Receiving with both hands. A steady inflow of merchandise, and a constant outflow through sales. I've heard he's engaged Ramjawaya as his agent. It's as if the railway line was laid only to bring him riches.'

The Diwan watched the purohit. *The purohit too is becoming old*, he mused. *And yet, his worn and wrinkled face remains indiscernible; there's always more to him than meets the eye.* He scanned the purohit's face with his astute eyes, but it gave away no more than what the purohit volunteered. Finally, he smiled and let it go with, 'Let me know if you hear anything further, Ramdas.'

'Of course I will, Generous One. But please, what I've told you is only from rumours I've heard.'

'And who's better than you at spotting and ensnaring a bird that others would let get away? Nothing's difficult for you, Purohit.'

The words 'Generous One' escaped the purohit's lips again, before he continued, muttering, 'May you live long, Maharaj. May you be blessed with boundless property.'

As the purohit turned to leave, an elderly man with a small brass pot passed by. He was returning from his morning bath in the river, a short, thin waistcloth wrapped around him, the sacred thread hanging over his ear.

'My respects to you, Diwanji; Ram Ram, Purohit,' he said as he walked slowly past the two men.

The purohit watched him with alert eyes.

'What is it, Ramdas?' Diwan Dhanpat asked. 'Why are you staring at the old man?'

'It's nothing, Maharaj.'

'There must be something that's making you stare like that.'

'Maharaj, that's Maniram. One of your subjects. He lives close by, just where the street turns.'

'I'm aware of that,' the Diwan nodded his head.

The purohit remained silent for some time, then muttered, 'His time has come, Generous One.'

'What do you mean?'

'His life's thread was only this long. His end is here.'

'Don't say inauspicious things, Purohit! And that too this early in the morning! He looks perfectly well to me.'

'No, Maharaj. His time is up.'

'You've become senile, Purohit. There's nothing wrong with Maniram. He's just taken a bath in the river, walked half a mile, and you're saying his time's up!' But Diwan Dhanpat's eyes didn't leave the purohit's face for even a second. The purohit wouldn't have uttered such a thing without reason.

Maniram had reached the bend in the street; he disappeared from view.

'It's a different matter if you just cast an evil spell on him. There's no knowing what you can do.'

'His time has come, Maharaj,' the purohit muttered, almost inaudibly.

The Diwan's heart filled with revulsion for the purohit; a shiver ran down his spine. He watched the purohit's withered, slippery face, frayed by the lines of time, into which the purohit's eyes had sunk. Dhanpat felt he was looking not at a face but at a ruin.

'Have you made some astrological calculations?'

'No, Generous One, I needn't make astrological calculations for this.'

Besides being the community priest, Ramdas also dabbled in astrology. Whenever someone asked him to make a prediction, he would make calculations about the position of planets on his fingers. If the prediction bode well, he'd mutter, 'God will be kind.' If it bode something untoward, he would mutter, 'The constellation is under a cloud,' shut his eyes tight and shake his head.

Diwan Dhanpat's eyes were still trained on the purohit's face. It seemed to him that the purohit's tiny eyes were looking out at the world from inside a deep, dark cave. His teeth had almost entirely eroded over the years; they were mere stumps covered over by thin lips. The purohit was a short man; his clothes always the worse for wear. Oh, how the Diwan's heart recoiled at the sight of this man. Diwan Dhanpat had heard one shouldn't look too keenly at a purohit's face; shadows—both auspicious and inauspicious—hover over the faces of purohits at all times.

The purohit was still muttering to himself when wails began to emerge from the direction in which Maniram had gone. A boy appeared from around the bend; he was running.

The purohit's words had proven true.

'Chacha has departed!' the boy shouted out as he ran past them and into a narrow lane. Diwan Dhanpat was shaken to his roots. *Who is to know if this isn't the result of a spell the purohit cast on Maniram?* The purohit was silent, he hadn't moved; the expression on his face was unchanged—detached, unmoved. He seemed neither satisfied at the accuracy of his own prediction nor saddened by the occurrence of death.

'Ramdas,' the Diwan's voice was agitated, 'how did you know Maniram's time had come?'

'The spool of thread that was his life was only this long,' the purohit repeated himself.

'But how did you know that?'

'Maharaj, he was carrying his life in the small brass pot that was in his hand.'

'But how did you know that?' The purohit's reply only deepened the mystery for Dhanpat. He felt even more certain that Maniram was a victim of the purohit's evil eye.

'Generous One, what's so special about knowing how I knew?' the purohit spoke patiently. 'Did you observe the sandalwood mark on his forehead?'

Dhanpat didn't reply; he just watched the purohit incredulously.

'He had walked half a mile and yet the mark on his forehead hadn't dried. It was still moist. Generous One, for sandalwood paste to not dry after that much time can only mean one thing: the body has turned cold from inside. Maniram was being carried forward by the momentum of the brass pot in his hand.'

Dhanpat watched the purohit silently.

'I'll take your leave now, Maharaj,' the purohit said and turned once more to leave, his fingers dancing in a secret conversation with each other. 'May you live long!' he mumbled.

'Don't forget to do what I've asked. And bring me good news soon.'

'It'll be as you say, Maharaj. God will be kind,' the purohit replied.

And with that, the short purohit, his customary plaid cloth towel on his shoulder, dragged his feet slowly along the street that led right from the mansion.

The street narrowed between the high wall of the mansion and a few old houses. The purohit knew the story of each of these houses. One among them had once belonged to the first cousin of a man named Diwan Ram Labhaya. The doors of this century-old house were still intact. Large iron locks secured the chains guarding the doors, but the links of the chain were broken. The wooden doors were finely carved in the old style, but the wood had turned black. And the house itself, which lay behind them, was a heap of rubble.

Many years ago, as Ramdas was passing by this house, something made him stop in front of it. Its walls were still sturdy then, and its balcony was painted a beautiful green. Three brothers and their families lived in it. Ramdas had sensed the presence of an owl on the roof of the house. No, he was certain there was an owl—a brown owl with large eyes—that had come visiting the house in broad daylight. He saw it perched on the parapet of the room on the roof that overlooked the street. Ramdas saw it, or he intuited its presence, whether anyone else did or didn't. And sure enough, in a matter of days, the most acrimonious discord erupted between the brothers. Soon, the brothers divided the property between them. But even that didn't calm the waters and, one by one, each brother auctioned off his share of the property and the three families moved out and went their separate ways. The entire neighbourhood saw the walls of the house crumble and turn to rubble. A full and vibrant house turned into a skeleton in front of everyone's eyes.

Maybe the purohit was clairvoyant. Perhaps he could look precisely into the future. Who knows, maybe he had the power of casting spells. But without doubt, his gaze was evil. Before it, anything—however strong—could turn to debris. This awareness settled heavily in every heart; it made the purohit indispensable. People sought him for counsel on which days were auspicious for them, on which days they should avoid doing something important, on how to mellow the fury of a planet that was affecting the course of their lives. Even one bitten by a snake or stung by a scorpion sought the purohit out before any other help. And then there were the usual festivals, betrothals, weddings and rituals for newborns and young boys, for which a priest was always needed. Purohit Ramdas became important not only in the fraternity he was the priest of, but for every caste in the entire town.

Something quite peculiar had happened in relation to the widow Goma's death as well. The purohit was passing by the widow's house when he felt she had died. He sensed her dead body inside the house, that no one had yet laid her on the ground nor lit incense by her head, nor put drops of the holy waters of the Ganga in her mouth. Purohit Ramdas stood outside Goma's house, unmoving. After some time, he pushed the door open and peeped inside—and sure enough, Goma lay there, dead. Ramdas then went from house to house to inform people; he was the one who took care of the cremation and performed all the necessary rituals. He even sat by Goma's side reciting prayers the entire time. And yet, when the dug-up hole behind the stove was discovered, it was assumed that must have been where Goma had hidden the vessel in which she safekept her life's savings. It was gone, and it was the purohit that everyone doubted. 'The rascal Brahmin,' people said, 'he sits there chanting prayers! Isn't he the one who's swallowed up her pot of jewels?' But though they spoke ill of him in this way behind his back, no one ever said anything to his face. For who knew what spell he would cast upon those who angered him?

Being married to the purohit had already sent three women to the other world one after the other, and now his current—that is, fourth—wife too looked as though blood was draining out of her body. Her name was Parmeshwari. She was twenty-eight years old; her husband had crossed sixty. She was tall and fair, and had a slender body, but she was growing weak and her teeth had started protruding from beneath her lips. Every morning while her husband roamed about being purohit, she would go from door to door, a basket on her head, collecting food set aside by every household to feed the priest: *handa*. Even though he had married four times, the purohit didn't have any children; a small portion of the handa was sufficient for the husband and wife. They would dry the rest and sell it as cattle feed, but not before setting some aside for the adorable little cow that they owned, which the purohit was devoted to.

The room that Ramdas lived in was small and dingy, and at the far end of the neighbourhood. Besides the cow, his possessions included a few utensils, some old, worn-out clothes and, of course, his wife. The brass utensils shone in the dark; the clothes remained hanging on a string tied across the room; the wife withered in silence. If he had some wealth hidden away, buried in the ground in his house, then that was between him and his god.

Ramdas had walked only a small distance along the high wall of the mansion when Mausi Bhagsuddhi emerged from a narrow lane on the left. She was a tall woman; her body blocked the purohit's path.

'Why, Brahmin, which unfortunate soul's future have you foretold this morning?'

The purohit produced a crack of a smile on his wrinkle-crossed face and replied guardedly, 'I was just at the Diwan's, that's all.'

'I hope for your sake that you haven't been up to some mischief again, you sinful man. You don't want to end up in hell and have worms feasting on your flesh.'

The purohit's deceptive eyes didn't look directly at Bhagsuddhi. No one would have been able to tell from his face whether Bhagsuddhi's words had irked or surprised him. He simply looked as if he was ready to be on his way again.

'Snakes rule your head, Brahmin,' Bhagsuddhi continued, and then lowered her voice. 'Give good counsel even to the people in the mansion; don't send them on the wrong path. You've lived a long life, Brahmin; you've nothing to gain any more from misguiding people.'

Then Mausi Bhagsuddhi stepped aside and squeezed her body past the purohit, careful not to let even her clothes brush his, lest she get tarnished by bad luck.

The mansion was built on a square floor plan; its boundary walls were endless and each had a gate. All the gates were massive, but none was as big as the one on the Sadar side—the side with the terrace. The purohit had walked from the Sadar gate into this lane, still moving along the mansion wall, and was about to reach the second gate.

As he neared it, he stopped. Two cots had been set up parallel to each other in the middle of the lane right next to the gate, and a few young lads sat on them, chatting. The purohit recognized them; they were friends of the Diwan's sons. The purohit's first impulse was to retrace his steps. A mistake to have come this way, he thought to himself. The lads looked like they were in one of those moods where they wouldn't think twice before overstepping boundaries with their words. Plus, it was plain to see that something had in fact happened but moments ago: a hawker's basket lay upside down near the cots, and the hawker was gathering up his things that lay scattered on the ground; he was crouching, and his turban had come unfurled and hung loosely around his neck. Evidently, and not for the first time either, the insolent boys had taken eats from the hawker, and beaten him up and overturned his basket when he asked them to pay.

Nevertheless, the purohit didn't turn away. He walked slowly on, keeping his gaze away from the cots and fixed to the ground, hoping to slink past. But he'd barely crossed the cots when he heard a voice from behind him: 'Purohit, how come your wife hasn't done her rounds today?'

Unruly laughter followed.

'Yes, young Diwanji, she hasn't yet,' he replied evenly and, his fingers dancing, the purohit walked on without stopping, continuing his undecipherable mumbling under his breath. But he sneaked a look in the direction of the hawker. He was a young boy, no more than fifteen years old, and his cheek was crimson, clearly smarting from the slap he had received.

'So, did you read the Diwan's future in the lines on his palm today?'

The purohit didn't reply and kept walking. The Diwan's middle son got up and blocked his path.

'First answer our question. What were you at the mansion for?'

One of the others chimed in, 'Tell us the truth, Purohit; we implore you in your wife's name.'

The lads roared with laughter at this. The purohit, cunning as he was, didn't lose his cool, but smiled gently and muttered genially, 'Oh, young Diwanji . . .' and tried once more to walk away.

'Where are you going? Come sit here.'

Dhanpat's son had walked back to the cot, and now he pulled the purohit's sleeve to make him sit.

'Now how will you escape?' The unruly gathering was laughing again.

'So why hasn't your lady purohit come by today?'

One of the lads proffered an answer: 'Because she's expecting.'

'Oh my! Is that true, Purohit?'

The purohit forced a smile and, his eyes blinking rapidly, only said, 'Oh, young Diwan, how you joke. Good, good.'

Now one of the other lads spoke. 'Show the purohit your palm, Manjhle. Let him read it.'

Being the middle or *manjhla* son, the lad was called Manjhle. He immediately held out his hand in front of the purohit.

'Go on, Purohit, read his palm and tell us when he's going to get married.'

The purohit smiled, 'Oh, Diwanji, very good Diwanji, how you joke with me . . .'

'Go on, read the lines.'

'And if you don't read them properly, I'll carry your wife away from your house.'

'Oh Diwanji, oh Diwanji, ha ha . . .'

'Go on, what do the lines tell?'

The purohit craned his head over the lines criss-crossing Manjhle's palm, made some calculations on his fingers, muttered under his breath for some moments, then said, 'God will be kind. May you live a happy life, young Diwanji; God will be kind.'

'What do they foretell, Purohit? When will my darling boy be married?' asked a plump lad, stroking Manjhle's head.

'Soon, Diwanji; God will be kind.'

'Will the girl be fair or dark?' asked another.

'Tall or short?' another piped in.

'Sweet or salty?'

This prompted a round of guffawing. The purohit made yet another attempt at escaping.

'Keep sitting. Sit down!'

One of Manjhle's friends snatched the purohit's cloth towel off his shoulder and called out to a young man who was sitting to one side, on a wicker stool on the porch, 'Come here, Kalle, and get your fortune read as well. Come on, come here.' Kalle was the eldest of the Diwan's three sons. The youngest one, Hukumat Rai, had been sent abroad, just a few months back, to study law. The British deputy commissioner had been most helpful.

When the lad shook his head, someone got up, took him by his wrist and dragged him to the purohit. Kalle seemed unwell; he was staggering as he walked.

'Show the purohit your hand.' He shoved the lad's hand towards the purohit. 'Come on, read, Purohit.'

Ramdas muttered under his breath again. He tried to bring a smile to his face while running his thumb up and down his fingers, making calculations. Then, his fingers still dancing, he said, 'God will be kind. Everything will turn out well; God will be kind.'

At this the purohit heard the same chorus: 'Will our sister-in-law be fair or dark?'

'Fat or slim?'

'Sweet or salty?'

The plump one slapped Kalle on his back and said, 'This calls for another round of samosas for everyone.' He turned around and called out to the hawker, who had by now straightened up the basket and was retying the turban back on his head. His cheek still seemed to be smarting.

With everyone now distracted by snacks, the purohit got up quietly, picked up his cloth towel, and slunk away.

On reaching the end of the lane, he decided to head towards Oil Pressers' Neighbourhood, and started to weave his way through its labyrinthine streets as a spider weaves its way through its web.

ॐ

Before heading back home, the purohit decided to go meet Harnarayan, and turned towards Goldsmiths' Street. Harnarayan lived in an ancestral house that could be reached through Goldsmiths' Street, like most other lanes in this part of town, and then turning right into a narrower lane. Goldsmiths' Street, which also led to the lone market of the neighbourhood, was always buzzing with activity; this narrow lane, on the other hand, was always quiet, and could be covered in a few steps. It ended in a high, arched gate, which must have been an entrance into a haveli at some point. Harnarayan's house was a few steps away. Well, it could hardly be called a 'house'. Land so little—it seemed barely larger than the span of a hand—had been organized into two rooms behind a raised platform. Another room had been built on the first floor. Harnarayan, his widowed daughter and granddaughter lived here.

The morning sun had only just reached this lane, and Harnarayan was sitting on a wicker stool that he had placed in a small patch of sun on the raised platform, hoping to warm up his shivering body. He looked up to find the purohit standing in front of him.

'Welcome, Ramdas. What brings you here this early in the morning?'

Supporting his knees with his hands, the purohit lowered himself slowly on to the platform. 'Hope all is well with you, Diwanji?'

Harnarayan nodded and searched the purohit's wrinkled face and deceptive eyes for clues about why he had come visiting.

'I was on my way to Grain Market and thought I'd come by. Things are going well, I hope.'

'God is kind. Grain Market this early in the morning?'

'There's a shortage this time. Diwanji has asked me to see how things are faring in the market; grain might need to be bought.'

'But the Diwan's store is always filled. Why would he need to buy from the market?'

'There's talk of marriage, and more might be needed. State officials are picking up grain directly from the villages, right after it is being harvested. The flow to the market is broken.'

'Who's getting married?' Harnarayan became alert and lowered his legs from the stool.

'There's talk of the Diwan's son's engagement with Malik Mansaram's daughter.'

This intrigued Harnarayan somewhat.

'Really? Well, big people bring big surprises. Did you make this match, Purohit?'

'No, Maharaj, matches are all made in God's divine court.'

'But you must have matched their horoscopes?'

The purohit's face lit up with a slight smile. 'That I did, indeed. But it's all talk right now.'

Harnarayan's daughter, Veeranwali, came out, wiping her hands with her dupatta.

'But it's decided that they'll be engaged, isn't it?'

'It will be. The alignment of stars is favourable.'

'For when is it being planned?'

'Soon. It's just a question of formalities now. The month of Baisakh is auspicious and bodes well.'

'The wedding's going to be grand, I'm sure,' Veeranwali said, 'Both families will try to go one up on the other.' Then she smiled. 'But who cares about old rivalries any more? What happened is all in the past now.'

As she turned back into the house, she stopped to ask, 'Parmeshwari didn't come by today? Will you take the handa, Purohit?'

'No, no, Parmeshwari will be here. I just wanted to meet the Diwan, that's all.'

Veeranwali—a lean woman of about forty, her head covered with a colourless, old dupatta, like widows wore—went back into the room.

'I've heard Lekhraj is coming back?' The purohit turned once more to Harnarayan.

'Really?' Harnarayan asked, intrigued. 'Is that true? Who told you?'

The note of excitement in his voice was unmistakable and hadn't been heard for a long time now.

'It's just a rumour I heard. Who can really know what Lekhraj is going to do! We've been hearing of his return for years now.'

'Where is he at the moment?'

'In Huzoorpur, I hear.'

Harnarayan nodded. Images from boyhood days flashed through his mind, when he and Lekhraj used to walk around the neighbourhood, arm in arm. These memories contained other people, too, who were now no more.

'You've brought me very good news, Ramdas,' he said, but then reined in his enthusiasm. It isn't wise to show too much eagerness for something, for then fate doesn't favour it.

Years ago, when Diwan Dhanpat had received land from the British, he'd begun searching for a man he could trust—one who could be relied on to collect rent on the land and also supervise work on the fields. He chose his distant relative, Harnarayan. Besides being honest, Harnarayan would be grateful for the opportunity. His daughter had been recently widowed, and he had brought her, and her infant girl, to live with him in his broken-down ancestral home. But things didn't work out. Harnarayan proved to be an able bookkeeper, but an incapable supervisor. He was too kind for that; he would give in every time someone begged him to forgo his rent. It was clear soon enough that he was too self-effacing and God-fearing to be a rent collector. Some tenant-workers used his sympathetic nature to evade paying rent. It took Diwan Dhanpat Rai all of two years to dismiss him. This did unsettle Harnarayan—after all, his household was running on his income—but he made peace with this turn of events and let his life be shaped by it. A kind of stoic reclusion took hold of his mind. Land and material wealth, he concluded, were the quagmire of life, a temptation. It's God who feeds us, he now believed; a human is a mere instrument.

Harnarayan owned a small plot of land that had come to him through inheritance, and which brought him three to four sacks of grain every harvest season. Content with this much, he immersed himself in God and had faith that if this supply of grain stopped, God would find another way for him. And while he was aware that there was a chance that the small house he owned too could be further divided up—since one Diwan or another could stake a claim to a portion of it, and properties had after all been divided over generations by erecting walls within houses—he would no doubt be able to manage in just one room. As time went by, Harnarayan was able to rein in any remaining and residual desires. He made peace with life. That which hadn't come to him, that which couldn't possibly become his, was not worth longing for. Harnarayan would bathe in the river each morning, and read the Gita Sahasranama on returning home. He would sit outside the house for some time, and when the sun became too hot, he would saunter off to the humpbacked sweet seller's shop and sit awhile on the raised platform that fronted it. And although, on account of his lineage, he thought it didn't befit him to play the game of dice with those who gathered there every day, he saw no harm in watching. Besides, it was one of the ways of keeping contact with others. And for that, he also attended the thirteen-day mourning period following anyone's death, and stayed the entire evening through the reading from the Bhagavad Gita or Garud Purana, often eating there. Harnarayan moulded himself into a man content with what and how much he had: an unassertive man who wanted nothing more than to live within his means and be sympathetic to others.

'The elder Diwan was asking after you,' the purohit said.

Harnarayan looked at the purohit and nodded his head, but didn't say anything.

'He too was very surprised to hear about Lekhraj. It got him wondering about how you were.'

Harnarayan continued to nod silently.

'He was talking about sending a few sacks of grain.'

'To whom?' It was as if Harnarayan had snapped out of his somnolence.

'To you, Diwanji. There's a shortage this year. He was worried about you. I told him: "You are well aware Harnarayan wouldn't spread his hands before anyone; but no one is unaware of his condition." At this he scolded me for not having told him you might be in need. Whatever one says, Diwanji, it is the same blood that courses through his veins and yours.'

Just then Harnarayan's granddaughter, Rukmini, came rushing in from the street. Startled to see the purohit, she looked away and dashed into the house, to her mother.

'The little girl has grown. She's shy even of me now,' the purohit observed.

'She's not shy,' Veeranwali replied from inside, 'She's still scared of you.' Then she laughed and added, 'Don't you remember how, when she was little, she'd always hide under the cot whenever you arrived? She thought you were a "baba", that you would carry her off in your sack.'

The purohit spoke in his muffled priest-voice, 'May you live long; may you have a happy life.'

Then he turned his deceptive eyes towards Harnarayan and continued in the same voice, 'When will you get the girl married? Rukmo is no longer a child; she's grown up now.'

True to his nature, Harnarayan replied like a recluse: 'She will get married when God wills it.'

'Have you approached anyone yet? You are, after all, the one who has to take her boat to shore.'

Harnarayan smiled. 'Why should I be worried as long as the community has a priest?'

'What you say is true. But you are the helmsman of her life's boat.'

'The God above is the true helmsman, Purohit.'

But Harnarayan was pleased by the purohit's concern for the girl.

'Why don't you take charge, Purohit, and lighten our burden?'

'A burden it certainly is, Diwanji. Girls are always a concern. You are a braveheart for having her under your roof even now. She must be twelve or thirteen now?'

'She's in her thirteenth year.'

Veeranwali's attention was glued to this conversation. Rukmo had been a source of anxiety ever since she'd turned twelve. She did not have much faith in her father about her daughter's marriage. The purohit would at least broach the subject in a few houses.

'Why do you want to strain yourself thinking about the girl's marriage, Diwan? Hand her over to me.' The purohit smiled.

Veeranwali was taken aback for a second, but then she smiled. The purohit was right; her father would never be able to get Rukmo married. Earlier it was just his heart that had been defeated, but now he was physically weak as well. He would never be able to gather up a dowry for Rukmo. Even if they were to sell this house, it wouldn't fetch them enough to manage a half-decent wedding feast.

This was Purohit Ramdas's gift: he always knew where and how to strike. He knew how to offer something that one could neither accept nor decline. He always managed to strike the right balance between a certain amount of veiled respect and an adequate measure of disdain—just enough praise and a tolerable amount of scorn. The recipient of his words would be filled with doubt and hope simultaneously. The purohit's words had bluntly summed up for them the precariousness of their situation: a widowed daughter, an ageing father, a dilapidated two-room house, a few meagre sacks of grain every year and no guarantees. Veeranwali felt a stab in her heart. And yet, at the same time, she felt hopeful. The purohit would no doubt pave the way for her daughter's future. *May God bless his soul*, her aching heart sang, *he is taking on the responsibility of my daughter's marriage.*

'You've earned much goodwill and the grace of God is upon you, Diwanji.'

Harnarayan liked what he heard. He felt the purohit's words were plucking him out of the dark pit of self-remorse in which he often found himself, immersed in the feeling that he'd achieved nothing in life, fulfilled none of his obligations, accepted defeat too early in his youth. *There's at least one person*, he thought, *who has noticed my good deeds, who sees how hard I pray, who holds in regard the simplicity of my way of living. For this is my achievement: I have salvaged my soul from the illusions and enchantments of this world.*

'The child is yours, Ramdas. You are the community's priest. You've seen generations grow up in front of you. Who will know better than you what's best for this child?'

The purohit smiled. His small, deceptive eyes didn't leave Harnarayan's face for a second.

Sitting inside the house, Veeranwali's heart worked away at trying to figure out what the purohit was starting. *Does he already have someone in mind, or is Rukmo's marriage something that came to him when he saw her?* Veeranwali had spent too many years as a widow to let her heart become too hopeful with something for long.

But then, she thought, *everyone's fate is preordained. Even if the purohit doesn't manage something good for Rukmo, at least his doing something can't harm her. And if he does bring a proposal, we'll think it through; the decision will be ours.*

It did seem, though, that the purohit had brought up Rukmo's wedding only in passing, because he wasn't pursuing it any further, and when Harnarayan asked him if he had someone in mind, he merely shook his head and said, 'Things will be as the lord wills them. The girl is blessed. She will bring good fortune to the house she marries into.'

After that he started about other things. He'd heard the goldsmith Narsinghdas had disinherited his son. He'd heard a priest had arrived from across the Jhelum and was going to construct a church here; that he distributes sugar cakes among children. The two men talked in subdued voices about the neighbourhood for a long time, and came to the conclusion that good was dwindling from the world, Kalyug had commenced, and things were no longer the way they used to be.

After some time, promising Harnarayan that he'd have two sacks of grain delivered to his house, the purohit got up. Mumbling 'May God bless you' even as his fingers danced, he took his leave and walked away into the lane.

The wedding procession should have arrived soon after sunset, but there was still no sign of it. In fact, it was well into the night now and the procession hadn't even left its starting point. The *maanji* had begun to grow tired with the wait; a few had even slipped away without letting Mansaram know. No one wanted to sit around and wait all night. The drums accompanying the *baraat* would let them know when it was near, and they could always come back then. The cooks, stationed behind the wedding pandal, yawned. All their preparations had turned cold. Firewood had been pulled out; stoves could be lit again once the drums were heard.

Malik Mansaram sat with a long face, surrounded by his friends and relatives. *If the arrival of the baraat was this delayed, how long would the ceremonies take? When will the baraat eat, when will the fire ceremony be performed?* The auspicious hour was upon them, and would pass soon. Two elders of the Malik family, Lakhmidas and Lachhmidas, their turbans in their laps, were going over the situation.

'Why in the world did they choose to assemble the baraat on the hillock? Why couldn't everyone just gather at the mansion and start from there?' Lala Lakhmidas said.

'Let's send someone to ask them to hurry; the maanji are getting restless and slipping away.'

'Enthusiasm is dipping,' the other elder, Lala Lachhmidas, turned to the bride's father and said.

Malik Mansaram replied irritably, 'I've sent my man to them thrice already. He's come back with the same reply every time: they're about to leave any minute now.'

Malik Mansaram's patience was withering.

Lala Lakhmidas raised his arm and gestured to Ramjawaya. He walked towards Lala Lakhmidas, scratching his stomach.

'What are your orders, Lalaji?'

'We have to find out how long the baraat is going to take. Stop standing around scratching your stomach.'

'What should I do?'

'Send someone to find out where the baraat is, and when it's reaching. Are they going to make us sit here waiting for them all night?'

'I sent the purohit, but he's gone and joined the procession, it seems.'

Malik Mansaram flared up again at this. 'If they arrive so late, the greeting ceremony will turn into nonsense.'

'Speak well, Mansaram. Delays are to be expected. Everything will work itself out. There's no need to worry,' Lakhmidas said.

Mansaram's wife had been standing outside the pandal, near where the cooks were. She heard Mansaram and came in immediately. 'Don't send anyone! You're not supposed to hurry the groom's side. What's a little while longer when we've waited this long already? It's not like the baraat is going to run off somewhere; they'll come when they come.'

'You go look after the things you're supposed to look after. The auspicious hour is passing, the maanji are leaving. Ramjawaya isn't about to go pick a fight with them. He's only going to beg them to hurry.'

'Please, there's no need for that. Don't send anyone. It's the baraat of the Diwans; they know what has to be done.'

Ishradeyi had only uttered these words when they heard a firecracker burst in the night sky. With that sound it was as if the entire atmosphere stirred back to life. Just as the sound of the azan makes everyone rise to break their fast during Ramzaan, everyone stood up all at once as a wave of excitement swept through the pandal. Ishradeyi's face lit up, and she joined her hands to express her gratitude to God. The courtyard filled with children's laughter. And inside the house, everyone resumed attending to whatever they were in charge of. The cooks woke up from their slumber. The atmosphere returned to one expected of a wedding. Lachhmidas and Lakhmidas put their turbans back on their heads.

The pandal had been set up in the sprawling grounds of Gajmandi, Grain Market, where Malik Mansaram had just finished making a new two-storeyed house. The house was so new, in fact, that the talisman warding off the evil eye hadn't been taken off it yet. The open ground had been festooned with multicoloured paper flags; the entrance gate had been covered with broad, green banana leaves. Right above the gate, wreathed in flowers, was a bright 'Welcome' sign. The ground underneath the entire pandal was covered with rugs and carpets.

The pandal had begun to fill up once more. The entire neighbourhood had been eager to witness this wedding. Diwan Dhanpat's son was getting married to Malik Mansaram's daughter, after all. The grandest families of the neighbourhood were about to tie the knot. While this in itself was an event worthy of interest, the curiosity was compounded by the fact that the two families had not been on the best terms in the past.

On descending from the hillock, the baraat turned right instead of heading straight for Grain Market, or even the neighbourhood via Kabuli Darwaza. They headed instead for Oil Pressers' Neighbourhood, choosing to take a circuitous route, one that would give them more opportunity to show their splendour in town than if they had taken a shorter, more direct route to the market. The saffron turbans that everyone was wearing shone brightly under the flaming torches that accompanied the baraat. The music being played by the band drew all the women in the neighbourhood out from their houses, and they gathered on their roofs. All along the lane, men—old and young—lads and boys gathered, waiting to see the procession pass by.

Heading the procession was the son of the town's ballad singer. He'd tied a vivid wooden horse to his waist, so it looked like he was riding a horse. Children raced up to him to see him from close, and were thrilled by his performance—he jumped and skipped and trotted, just like a rider on a horse. They cheered and clapped and followed him.

Behind the wooden horse and rider was the music band—with drums, cymbals and three British trumpets, a novelty. The puffed-up cheeks of the men blowing the trumpets in sync with each other were a sight to behold. They were followed by the baraat—all the men sported saffron turbans, as was customary when there was a wedding in any of the Diwan's families, and some of them wore matching angrakhas. Others wore angrakhas with exquisite Kashmiri embroidery. The angrakhas had gone out of fashion ever since the administration had changed, but they were always pulled out of old trunks for weddings. The manner of all those part of the wedding procession gave it an air of a military unit on its way to conquer a fort. The style of walking, the stiffness of moustaches, heavily lined eyes, glittering earrings and protruding stomachs—these were all in accordance with the status of the Diwans. But this show of ostentation was only for weddings. Once a wedding was over, the clothes would return into trunks, prickly beards would begin to grow back on clean-shaven cheeks. There was even a joke about these beards—like ants crawling on white bread. Everyone would return to wearing what they usually wore—a dirty pyjamas and clean shirt, or a dirty shirt and clean pyjamas. But for now, the glory of the procession was unmatched.

The word 'Diwan' evoked stature. At one time, it was the title for the minister of a king. Some members of this tribe of Diwans too had held important positions during the Sikh rule—Diwan Mohakchand, Diwan Motiram, Diwan Gangaram and others. But now they were all called Diwans either because they were direct descendants of those Diwans, or because they belonged to the fraternity. The Diwans also traced their lineage back to the time of King Porus and Alexander the Great. They believed they were descendants of Porus. Not only that, they also believed Alexander was so impressed by the valour of King Porus that he took five young Diwans back with him, and appointed them commanders in his army. There were others who traced their lineage to the warrior sage Parashuram.

The aura of the past enveloped everyone in this town. Some people, as a result, were called Diwan, while others were called Malik, and yet others Raizada. These titles were tokens from the past, and found full expression in moments such as this wedding procession where everybody's gait seemed to say, 'Don't you know who we are? We are the Diwans!'

The wedding procession was headed by Diwan Kundanlal, appointed *mukhtaar* by Diwan Dhanpat Rai—the overseer of his estate. The tall, well-built Diwan Kundanlal, a customary saffron turban adorning his head, wearing a long coat that came until his knees after the latest fashion of the time, carried himself with great aplomb. His small eyes always looked alert and agile, and when he looked at someone from his immense height, it was as if a hawk was locking his gaze on to its prey. He had served as a revenue officer in the administration, and became known for touring villages on his horse. He so terrified the villagers that the government had to relieve him of his post. That's when the Diwan appointed him as his mukhtaar. A small bag in his hand, he was walking up and down the marriage procession and directing its movement as if he was commanding a battalion of soldiers.

Banshi—the lone man in the neighbourhood who knew how to perform tricks with cards—was in the procession too. He had spent his entire life playing the dice by the humpbacked sweet seller's shop with his friends. In his youth he'd been at the forefront of those who publicly rebuked and made fun of the Diwan. But with advancing years, he had started working for the Diwan, who employed him to collect rent on his behalf. A man with a heavy, sluggish body, he was proud to have been invited by the Diwan as a guest and to be part of the baraat.

There were a number of professional *baraati*s here as well. They were a special crop of this town; weddings were their mainstay. Their days were usually spent outside sundry shops, sunning themselves, playing dice, smoking hookahs and gossiping to while away time. They always stayed abreast of news about weddings in town, and knew all about the preparations that were afoot. In the eyes of others they were slackers, but their self-image was of the Diwans. They were woman-like in their keenness for learning about what was going on in different households, and in their openness to demand their share when sweets were sent from house to house announcing a wedding. 'Why, my share this time is more than a quintal; I will accept nothing less than a quintal and a half. Sukhanlal, last time you . . .' they could be heard arguing and, more often than not, winning. Two or three weddings and one infant's tonsure, or one wedding, one infant's tonsure and one death of an old man per conjunction of stars could ensure many months' supply of sweets and eatables for their household—usually until the next wedding season.

Also part of the wedding procession were a number of men holding high positions in the administration—well-to-do and wealthy men. They were landlords and moneylenders, higher-ups from Grain Market and jewellers. Diwan Dhanpat's palanquin preceded the horses these men of means rode in the baraat; this was the first baraat in the history of the town where the groom's father was in a palanquin. He wore a yellow, silk angrakha, a saffron turban and a white wrap over his shoulders. He puffed continuously at his brass-tipped hookah. And even though his bushy eyebrows shaded them, one could tell that his tiny eyes were alert and darting this way and that, taking everything in. Whether it was because of his hot-headedness and eccentricity, or because he was always smoking tobacco, the veins in his eyes stood out and his eyes were always streaked.

The groom rode a white mare, atop a red-and-gold saddlecloth. He too wore a saffron turban, and strings of jasmine flowers hung from it, over his face. His gang of friends accompanied him—teasing and joking with one another, creating their own racket. The groom's spindly elder brother rode right behind him. He kept tumbling off his horse, and one or the other always saved him from falling, helping him regain his balance. He was unwell; prone to epileptic attacks. He also had a lisp, and people were of the opinion he was a little touched in the head.

The baraat had slowed down considerably in the narrow lanes it was moving through. It was abundantly clear now that, instead of by sunset, this baraat would reach its destination just before midnight. But it was custom—a baraat shouldn't arrive on time. And if it was a baraat of a Diwan, then never!

This town was witnessing a baraat this grand after a very long time. Standing on the roofs of their houses, women—young and old—watched this slow-moving flood of saffron turbans aglow with the light from the flaming torches that accompanied them, mesmerized. Exaggerated shadows of dancing bodies flickered on walls, and from time to time, other images jumped out from behind them—a crack along the length of this wall, exquisite carving on that wooden door that went back a couple of centuries, a pile of rubble here, bright faces peeping out from behind the broken wall of that roof. The grand procession of the Diwans, led by the son of the town's ballad singer 'on' a wooden horse, crawled its way through the delicate weave of time embedded in the lanes of the neighbourhood.

Sethi Street was a crossroads—if the procession turned right here, they would take Chandok Street, a shorter route to Grain Market, and if they turned left, they would take a long, winding route and enter Grain Market through Kabuli Darwaza. The ballad singer's son stopped. Taking his cue, the flame-torchbearers and the music band stopped as well.

It was Diwan Kundanlal who would decide which direction to continue in.

He walked up to the head of the procession and elected to enter Grain Market via Kabuli Darwaza. The baraat was on its way again.

Kundanlal saw Bhagsuddhi sitting on a cot laid out on the terrace in front of her house. She couldn't see well any more because of cataract in both her eyes, but she too had stepped out of her house to witness the marriage procession of Diwan Dhanpat Rai's son.

'My respects to you, Mausi,' Kundanlal greeted her and touched her feet.

Bhagsuddhi moved her fingers along the contours of his face in an attempt to recognize who this was, though she had more or less identified him by his voice, and said, 'You're taking your time with the baraat, Kundanlal. Are you planning to humiliate the bride's side?'

Mausi Bhagsuddhi was known across town for saying things as she saw fit. She knew right from wrong, and wasn't afraid to say it. She always seemed to know things that were going on in every house. Living in penury had not translated into her reining in her outspokenness. And yet, Diwan Kundanlal was taken aback.

'It sure looks like your plan is to humiliate the girl's side, Kundanlal. You had agreed to bring forty guests, and here you are with an entire battalion! What's to be gained from humiliating them? Daughters are like children of the entire town.'

Kundanlal was at a loss for words, but found his footing soon enough. 'Our fraternity is very big, Mausi,' he said. 'You won't understand how difficult it is to decide whom to invite and whom to leave out.'

'So this immense baraat is going for a wedding feast, which you have managed to delay until midnight?'

'The bride's side is better off than us, Mausi. They won't even notice if we take three hundred instead of a hundred and fifty guests.'

Mausi Bhagsuddhi became quiet for a few seconds, but then released her arrow again, 'Every home has daughters, Kundanlal; every father must get his daughter married.'

'Everyone manages, Mausi. No one's daughter stays unmarried.' Then he adopted a superior tone and said, 'Keep your humbug to yourself, Mausi. At least on certain occasions.' Then, hanging his bag properly on his shoulder again, he walked away.

Word had reached Malik Mansaram that there were at least a hundred and fifty people in the baraat. The elders of the family once again put their heads together to think and find a solution to this new problem. Fifty, even sixty guests would have been manageable, but how were a hundred and fifty people to be fed?

'Get some lentil soup made. It cooks quickly,' a young man suggested. Lala Lachhmidas replied curtly, 'That's a good plan to get us humiliated. Who in the world feeds lentils to a baraat?'

'Then get a lot more halwa made. With dollops of clarified butter. Serve it before the meal, even twice over. At least it will douse everyone's hunger a little bit.'

'Nothing will lessen their hunger. It's nearly midnight. They'll attack food like hungry wolves.'

'Get lots of curd then. Make a lot of buttermilk. Thin it down with water so there can be a whole lot of it. Guests always want buttermilk. At least there'll be enough buttermilk for them all.'

'And where do you suppose we can get curd from at this hour?'

The situation was tricky indeed. Diwan Dhanpat was an unpredictable man. Panicked, the bride's relatives ran helter-skelter in search of any resource available. Provisions were dipped into; sacks of grains were opened. The baraat was approaching; it had already reached the courtyard of Kohlis' Neighbourhood—the large, open courtyard made of bricks. Diwan Dhanpat stuck his head out of the palanquin to turn and look at the baraat he had brought with him. The procession was spilling out from the narrow lane and filling up the courtyard. Ah, to his eyes, the baraat really was an army, and the flaming torches added to its mood. What magnificence this baraat emitted; how majestic it would look when it gathered at the entrance of the bride's house! Diwan Dhanpat felt immensely satisfied with the image.

Having stopped in the open courtyard, the music band now started playing a popular love song with a peppy dance beat:

> *Your teeth are like a diamond necklace*
> *Oh my girl, Jamalo*

Kundanlal walked up behind the groom, drew out a fistful of coins from the bag he was carrying, circled them around the groom's head, and threw them into the air. The coins fell to the ground, and hearing their clinks against the brick floor the children who had been following the wooden horse raced each other to reach them and gather them up. Diwan Kundanlal's bag was filled with coins of different denominations—cowries, pies, paise and half annas. The paise and half annas were a first at a wedding; usually it was just cowries and pies.

The baraat resumed its onward journey, and reached the entrance of the wedding pavilion after just two more turns. It stopped here, and Diwan Dhanpat emerged from his palanquin to take his place at the head of his relatives outside the gate. Malik Mansaram stood on the other side of the gate with his relatives, each one holding a garland. It had already been planned and decided who would garland whom, and how much money he would then slip into the garlanded relative's hands. Purohit Ramdas quickly stationed himself at the threshold, between the two parties. His movements were brisk and precise; he wore a saffron turban, a long, flowing gown, and had a white scarf wrapped around his neck.

The excitement this wedding had caused in the neighbourhood wasn't only on account of how grand the marriage procession was, or even because two of the wealthiest families—one the lord of the lands, the other an established trader—were going to get related through marriage, but because there had been a bitter feud between Dhanpat and Mansaram many years ago, when the land adjoining the mansion had been auctioned. But that had been a time when both families had seen ascension and a certain rivalry was therefore building between them. This marriage suggested that both families had moved past this rivalry.

The baraat continued its revelries at the gate for some time. The band played on, at full steam, and the groom's friends danced and shouted with joy. But then they quietened down. The old purohit began chanting mantras, and Malik Mansaram and Diwan Dhanpat started walking with slow footsteps towards one another.

Mansaram garlanded Dhanpat. The two men embraced each other. Wide smiles adorned their faces. Malik Mansaram joined his hands before Diwan Dhanpat as a show of respect, then extended his arm and put five gold ashrafis in his hand. After this, other relatives from the bride's side took turns to similarly greet the relatives from the groom's side—the girl's chacha greeted the boy's chacha, the girl's mama greeted the boy's mama. The importance of the relative dictated whether he was given one or two ashrafis.

But things became tense when Diwan Kundanlal started insisting that more and more of the groom's relatives be similarly greeted—even those who were as much as three generations removed. He even went as far as insisting that distant relatives, and those who were no more than acquaintances of the family, also be honoured with an ashrafi each.

When the bride's mother heard about this, she sent word to Malik Mansaram and urged him, 'Don't hold back. Don't refuse the baraat what they want. It doesn't matter if we have to empty our house today; these are our *samdhi*s and our daughter has to spend the rest of her life in their house.'

Though Malik Mansaram was angered by this behaviour of the Diwans, he kept his temper in check, and let all his relatives know that they must keep giving the Diwans what they wanted.

But when this went on endlessly, with no sign of ending, even the purohit saw the strangeness of the situation and decided to intervene. He increased the pitch at which he was uttering his chants, raised his arms and took the lead in inviting the baraat into the marriage pavilion.

The baraat now broke up into smaller groups. The bride's friends, who had come out to witness the arrival of the baraat, ran back to the house, where the groom would be ceremoniously welcomed shortly. The groom's friends left him and walked into the pavilion. The purohit headed towards the specially created and decorated platform on which the fire ceremony for the wedding was going to be performed. Some of the guests settled down on the carpets. Others went into the area where food would be served. While some of the girl's relatives had by now taken their places behind the pavilion to oversee the preparation of the food, some of them stayed inside it to keep the boy's relatives company, and to look after their needs.

But things took a bad turn after that, and then went ricocheting out of control.

By the time the groom sat down to eat, two groups from the baraat had already finished eating. Forty men ate in the first round. They sat in two rows, and the bride's relatives positioned themselves along these rows, at short intervals all the way from where the cooks were. Food was served with great agility. First the plates were brought and set up before all the guests, then the tumblers. Those who were in charge of serving water filled all the tumblers. Piping hot, sweet halwa was served next, then fluffy puris and vegetables. Everything was done efficiently, and not once did anyone need any prompting. Guests who should be given special attention had been identified beforehand by the maanjis, and they were served lavishly. Two fresh, hot puris would be served on any plate that had just one remaining. Not a single guest would have got up from his meal displeased. When they finished eating, each person was gifted a silk scarf.

The maanjis didn't have a moment's rest. But they were confident the second group could be served with just as much agility. What did it matter if there was no food left after the guests finished eating—maanjis would never eat at the girl's house anyway. In this moment, Malik Mansaram's honour was at stake; and Malik Mansaram's honour was the honour of the entire fraternity.

There were about forty people in the second round as well. The maanjis served them with dedication. Yes, it is true that some of the guests made a face to say they were not entirely pleased. One, for instance, ran his forefinger along the rim of the tumbler to show it hadn't been washed properly. But before he could say anything, one of the maanjis replaced his tumbler with another, and the matter ended there. When a couple of guests complained the puris were cold, the alert maanjis immediately served them straight out of the frying pan. The guests ate heartily.

The third round of guests included the groom and his friends, and they sat scattered across the two rows. Food began to be served. It's possible that after serving two rounds of guests, the maanjis had become overconfident that nothing could go wrong, or maybe their interest had somewhat waned. Because soon enough, guests started calling out for things—one would call from one row, another from the other row. It seemed curry wasn't being served properly. Then it seemed vegetables weren't being served properly. But then it also seemed buttermilk wasn't being served properly. The maanjis leapt from corner to corner, making valiant attempts to keep everyone happy. But then suddenly, the groom raised his right arm and screamed: 'Papad! Pa . . . aa . . . pad!' He had screamed so loudly that it stunned everybody. There was pin-drop silence in the pavilion.

The maanjis leapt into action. Three of them ran towards the groom, calling out to the maanji who was serving papadams.

Roshanlal, a friend of the groom, was sitting right beside the groom. He seemed to be smiling to himself. This was his doing, in fact. He had been inciting the groom for a long time now, saying that no one was paying attention to him even though he was the groom. It had so happened that when the bride's mama had been serving papadams, he didn't stop in front of the groom specially and insist that he have another one. Once before that, he hadn't even bothered to slow down as he walked past the groom and his friends. It didn't matter now that every time he had done his rounds to serve papadams, he'd seen that nobody had eaten them yet. The meal was about to end, and he had assumed that no one wanted papadams any more.

'Didn't you get a papad? Wow, that's great! They aren't even feeding you properly here. If they aren't asking after the groom, whom are they going to care about here? Can you imagine, they didn't even ask you!'

When the groom merely smiled in response, Roshanlal had said agitatedly, 'I've noticed no one pays you any attention here. You're just sitting here like some orphan. The man who had come to serve papad didn't even lift his eyes to look at you.'

The groom looked crestfallen; his laughter grew embarrassed. And then, all of a sudden, he burst his fuse. 'Papad! Pa . . . aa . . . pad!' He was screaming.

Diwan Kundanlal thought this behaviour very unbecoming of the groom. He got up immediately to tell him to calm down and not behave in a way that would embarrass the Diwans. But hell-bent on proving he was the groom and therefore it was wrong to insult him by not serving him papadams, the boy was already on his feet, yelling, 'Papad! Pa . . . aa . . . pad!' He was surrounded by maanjis, and three papadams had been placed on his plate.

Diwan Dhanpat was beside himself. He couldn't bear to see his son like this. 'What's this, Malikji?' He turned to Malik Mansaram, who was standing next to him. 'Did you invite us to your home to insult us?'

Malik Mansaram swallowed his pride, joined his hands politely before the Diwan, and said, 'It's nothing, Maharaj. The kids are teasing each other, playing pranks. The dear lad asked for papad and an entire basket has been promptly presented before him.'

While all this was going on, one of the groom's friends, sitting in the other row and quite a distance from the groom, called out, '*Chhaachh!*' He raised the tumbler that the buttermilk was supposed to be in, held it above his head and inverted it, showing everybody how utterly empty it was. Some others laughed at this. Then, one of them quickly gulped down all the buttermilk in his tumbler, raised it in the air, inverted it and yelled, 'Chhaachh!' Now a few more of the lads followed their friends' lead and started screaming, 'Chhaachh!' The maanjis were running helter-skelter, trying to replenish everyone's tumblers. But the groom's friends lapped up the buttermilk the moment it was poured into their tumblers, so they could ask for more by screaming, 'Chhaachh!'

Things, however, took a turn for the worse when a spat broke out between one of the baraatis and one of the maanjis. 'What are you crying yourself hoarse for buttermilk for?' the maanji asked, irritated. 'Haven't any of you ever had any buttermilk before today?'

'No,' the baraati replied. 'We're all having it for the very first time today in your house.'

The maanjis had had an exhausting day. To them it seemed the baraatis had planned and come prepared to misbehave. 'What the hell do they think of themselves?' They were beside themselves, 'Do they think we can't show them . . .' When the groom's friends heard this, they got up from their seats, ready to join the fray.

The baraati who had been arguing with the maanji now spoke again. 'It's only out of respect for Diwanji that we're quiet,' he said. 'Otherwise there's absolutely nothing stopping us from beating you to pulp.'

'I'm holding back,' the maanji retorted, 'only because this is a wedding. Or I would have slapped you so hard that all your teeth would have fallen out.'

This only made the baraati leap up at him and hold his neck. 'Slap me. Go on, slap me. I dare you, if you've drunk your mother's milk, slap me!'

All hell broke loose. There was pandemonium. Some people ran into the lane to escape. Many maanjis had jumped into the fray by now. Voices were raised. The baraatis got up and left their plates just as they were.

Malik Mansaram's rage knew no bounds, but he understood how delicate the situation was. 'Diwanji, you are my elder, more senior than I am,' he joined his hands and pleaded with Diwan Dhanpat. 'A terrible mistake has been made; we are at fault. Please let it go. Please forgive us. Please let this end here.'

But Diwan Dhanpat pressed his lips around his hookah and turned away without uttering a word.

Purohit Ramdas rushed towards the gathering and urged everyone to start moving towards the arbour for the wedding ritual. He was worried the auspicious hour would pass if there were any more delays. Hearing this, the close relatives of the bride and the groom, realizing that there was no time to drag the matter any further, left whatever they were doing and started moving in the direction of the platform that stood in readiness for the fire ceremony.

The baraat had left. The bride had been sent with it, in a palanquin.

Ishradeyi felt emptiness in the house. The air was heavy with smells—of withered flowers, of leftover sweetmeats, of a combination of henna and the essence from rose and *kevra* flowers, of scents from clothes and odours from the bodies of women. The smells were turning stale, the air oppressive. Tormented, Ishradeyi walked from room to room, putting things back in their place, settling things—just as she wished she could her heart. A lot had already been, and a lot had yet to be, taken care of. Tears welled up in her eyes, unexpectedly, repeatedly. Why did she feel so empty inside? Nothing could hold her attention long enough to distract her. She had embraced her daughter and bid her farewell; her daughter was gone, but it seemed her innocence and the warmth of her body still lingered here. Ishradeyi sat down. She tried to wipe her eyes dry; she joined her hands, silently praying. She wasn't able to hold back her tears.

Outside, in the courtyard, the cooks' helpers washed the utensils from last night, unmindful of the dogs not so far from them. It seemed dogs from the entire neighbourhood had sniffed out the leftovers and arrived to lick them off the leaf-plates. On the other side of the courtyard, a crowd of people waited for leftovers to be distributed. There was a smaller gathering at the door as well—barbers, cobblers, landless peasants. The eunuchs too had arrived, dancing, singing, clapping, making a rumpus.

The bride's friends had stood in the balconies of their houses, dupattas with golden borders covering their heads, bangles jingling, enveloped in their fineries, and watched her palanquin, the palanquin bearers, the groom and the baraatis disappear from view.

Outside the house, near where the fire ceremony had been performed, men of the household were in a deep, heated discussion. The two elders, Lachhmidas and Lakhmidas, without whose advice no step was ever taken, sat at the centre of the gathering, their turbans on their laps.

Ishradeyi's brother, the bride's mama, was still fuming.

'If it weren't for the regard I have for Malikji, I would have thrown that Roshanlal out.'

'That's quite enough! Don't let your tongue run loose like this,' Malik Mansaram's younger brother, the girl's chacha, tried to calm him down.

The youngsters were still agitated.

'They insulted us in our own house. Are we supposed to sit quiet? That Meghraj was misbehaving with Malikji. I wanted to give him one hard slap across his face. That would've fixed his brain.'

This encouraged another young lad. 'Chachaji was bowing before all their demands, asking for forgiveness, when it was the baraatis who were misbehaving. Such arrogance! They got up without finishing their meal. The more we bent, the more they hit us,' he said.

Ishradeyi stepped out of the house on some work. 'This entire mischief was pre-planned. It was all done to insult us, humiliate us,' she heard someone say.

'But why couldn't you control yourself? Why did you have to answer back? Why couldn't you just keep quiet and listen and let it go? Who argues with the baraat?' She saw the bride's chacha was trying, quite unsuccessfully, to reason with everyone.

'What's this? What's going on?' Ishradeyi turned to the gathering. 'For God's sake, don't do something that turns the mole hill from last night into a mountain. Our daughter's just been sent off to her in-laws'.' Her eyes welled up.

'Go back inside, Mausi. We don't need your intervention here.'

'Please, my good fellows, your words strike terror in my heart. I beg you, don't do anything stupid. We're here, safe in our home; it's my daughter who's in their house. Let her settle down. Baraatis always misbehave. Everyone knows this. The bride's side has to stay strong. I'm begging you.'

'So we should let go of the fact that we were insulted? They humiliated us in front of the entire town. Everyone's laughing at us.'

'Oh, stop it! Don't take this any further. What's happened is past. We're not supposed to assert equality with the groom's side. Stop all this and pray to God the girl lives a happy life.'

'All right, Mausi, that's quite enough. Go back inside.'

Ishradeyi didn't leave before urging them a few more times to calm down. When she reached the door, she turned around and said, 'If you do something, you'll see my dead body.'

But things didn't end there. Yes, everyone was quiet for a few minutes after Ishradeyi left, but then the girl's mama,

Ishradeyi's brother, said, 'If we let this kind of misbehaviour go, if we don't answer back, it'll only signal to the boy's side that they can do what they want. They can dance on our heads if they like.'

'It's their money talking. The Diwan's head has been swollen ever since he got that land endowment from the government.'

'Stop now. What's happened has happened. Let it go,' the girl's father now spoke. 'Forget that anything happened.'

'How can you expect us to forget, Chachaji . . . ?'

Everyone was agitated and unhappy, but no one had any idea what they could do. To let the misbehaviour of the baraat pass without comment would mean the town condoned such behaviour, and it would keep repeating itself.

Lachhmidas shook his head for a long time, then said, 'There's nothing to be gained from doing anything now. But let's resolve that no girl from this family is ever going to be married into the Diwans'. Everything else can continue as it is; nothing need be changed. Only, we won't marry any of our girls into the Diwans', that's all. That should set them right.'

Everyone considered this suggestion silently, though it meant there would be no tit for tat for now.

Casting a sideways glance at Lachhmidas, his hands firmly on his turban, the other elder, Lakhmidas, said, 'Suggest things that can actually be followed through, Lachhmidas.'

'Once the fraternity takes a decision, everyone will respect and follow it. They'll have to; everyone has daughters to marry off after all. We're all proud people,' the girl's mama said.

'We'll stand by the fraternity's decision,' a man who was related to the family through marriage said.

Lala Lakhmidas kept looking at Lala Lachhmidas. Realizing this was a conversation that must be led by the two elders, everyone else was quiet. 'So then, does everyone agree?' Lala Lachhmidas asked.

Everyone exchanged glances. Something this important shouldn't be agreed to lightly. But the baraatis' misbehaviour must be contended with; it wouldn't be right to let it pass. If Malik Mansaram had been insulted today, it could be one of them tomorrow.

'Don't speak without understanding how delicate the situation is, Lachhmidas,' Lala Lakhmidas started gently, but grew agitated as he spoke. 'Don't think you have wisdom just because the hair on your head has turned grey. Do you think just because you wear a turban and wrap a scarf around your neck, that you are wise?'

Some of the younger people in the gathering tittered at this. The two old men were always shooting barbs and poking fun at each other. It was possible that right now the Lala had adopted this tone deliberately. Evidently, the discussion was going to end here; the tension in the air eased.

But everyone had underestimated how agitated the girl's mama was. 'Lalaji is right, something must be done,' he said. 'Otherwise the baraatis will feel more emboldened. They won't think twice before asking us to drink water from their shoes!'

'That's quite enough,' Lala Lachhmidas retorted. 'And there's no need to make declarations either. Everyone make a mental note that they won't marry their daughters into that fraternity—so our boys can marry their girls, but not the other way round. That will teach those Diwans a lesson.'

'Has everyone forgotten there are a hundred things to be done?' It was Ishradeyi again, addressing her husband and brother. 'Get up and attend to things. Sweets have to be sent; organize that. Get up. By the good grace of God, our girl has left for her home. May she stay happy, and may God grant peace and joy to every household. Now get up.'

But she stopped short when she saw how silent everyone was. 'You're all behaving as if something unprecedented has happened. Baraatis are always up to something or the other. One has to bear with that. One shouldn't make the mistake of thinking of asserting equality in such contexts.' Then she turned to the purohit and said, 'Get up, Brahminji, the dowry has to be sent. I've readied the trunk and baskets. Come with me and get the sweets weighed. Tell me how much has to be sent to whom. Come on, hurry up.'

But seeing no response from anyone, Ishradeyi knew something wasn't right. 'Seeing you like this terrifies me. You men are always stubborn, and there's no knowing what you might do. Listen to me; pray to God that our daughters live with dignity in their homes. We don't need anything more. Get up now, my good people, get up and help me with things.'

She turned around and went into the house.

It was nearly midday; the baraat was still on the hillock. Ideally, it should have headed straight for the mansion—the women were expecting the bride's arrival. But it wasn't unusual for a baraat to halt at the hillock before heading home.

The hillock was right outside the town, close to Grain Market, near Orchard of the Sheikhs. This was usually where an out-of-town baraat assembled before heading towards the bride's house. It was also where a newly wed bride's palanquin would be brought when such a baraat returned home after a wedding ceremony, for the performance of rituals before seeing the bride off. Innumerable sages used this hillock as their temporary abode, and for meditation. Caravans halted here, to rest before carrying on with their journeys—though this changed after the trains started. The hillock was also the assembling point before the start of any pilgrimage.

Some of the lads were in the mood for fun; a little gaiety and games, they thought, before reaching the mansion. They were over the moon when the Diwan agreed. Rugs were spread in a clearing on the hillock. A seat was prepared for the Diwan in the shade of an old tree with spread out branches, on a raised platform that skirted the tree. From where he sat, puffing at his hookah, it looked as if the Diwan was presiding over the gathering, that the gathering was his flock and was under his protection. That was usually the case, for the Diwan was an elder of the fraternity, and commanded an awe-inspiring presence. As elder, he spoke for the ancestors, of whom he was an incarnation. His blessing, which is to say his permission, was a must for anything important, and whenever there was a crisis, his commanding, authoritative voice would pronounce decisions and show the way. He seldom interfered in daily life, though, and kept to himself for the most part.

The groom's friends sat a good distance from him, recounting their mischief from the night before, laughing with the retelling.

'I thought to myself, to hell with them, let's ask for papad.' Roshanlal was the centre of attention. 'It was incredible when our dear friend, the groom, got up and started yelling for papad!'

'The girl's mama's face was a sight! He looked as if he was being beaten with shoes!'

The lads were in splits.

'The best was when all of us started yelling for buttermilk, all at once. That really stunned the life out of them, didn't it?'

'That got three people running around like crazy with jars of buttermilk. Including the bride's chacha. Did you see how his belly was bouncing?' The laughter grew louder.

'Speak a bit softer,' someone said. 'Our new sister-in-law must be listening.'

The bride was in a closed palanquin that had been set down on the raised platform that skirted around the banyan tree. She could hear their voices, but couldn't really follow what they were talking about. Still in her wedding clothes, draped with a dupatta that was decorated with gold lace, her forearms covered with a newly wedded bride's bangles and more jewellery than she had ever worn in her life, she felt uncomfortable. She had no idea why they'd stopped, and she sat quietly in the palanquin, hugging her knees. Her head felt heavy, and she was fighting to keep herself awake. In the days preceding the wedding, her mother had underlined she was not a child now, who could sleep wherever she was and whenever she wanted. She didn't want her in-laws to find her napping on the way to their house. She took the tumbler of sherbet every time an arm that had red thread tied around its wrist came through the curtains of the palanquin. She guessed it must be her husband's arm, but neither that thought nor the arm stirred any particular emotion in her. Instead, whenever the curtains parted, it was an opportunity to catch a glimpse of the greenery outside and breathe in a draft of fresh air. It was spring and the air outside was laden with the scent of wild flowers, fresh grass and mulberries. Her mind travelled to how often, and until so recently, her friends and she had come to this hillock to collect shells. She sat quietly, counting the bangles on her forearms to spend time and keep herself from falling asleep. The thought did come to her once, to peep out and gather a few pebbles to play with them. But her mother's voice in her head said to her, 'You're not a child now. You are the daughter-in-law of the Diwans. Act accordingly.' Surely, her mother wouldn't approve of her playing five stones inside the palanquin.

The sun was high up in the sky now, and the day was becoming warmer. On Diwan Dhanpat's orders, two men were dispatched with mules to the nearest village for water. They returned with pitchers of cool water from the village well, and two bottles of sandalwood sherbet. Handheld wicker fans had been brought out and palanquin bearers had spread themselves out amidst the baraatis and were fanning them. Someone spotted a row of labourers bearing baskets and a trunk, led by the purohit, climbing up the hillock— they were bringing the dowry. The girl's mama was walking alongside the purohit, and there were some other relatives of the girl's with them as well. When they reached the gathering, the dowry began to be set up by the tree on the platform. One glance at it, and the Diwan had assessed the value of the dowry.

Having supervised the setting down of the dowry, the girl's relatives sat down near the Diwan. The purohit placed a small case of jewellery in front of the Diwan, separate from the rest of the dowry. The Diwan kept his lips pursed tightly on the mouth of the hookah and nodded, but didn't reach out for the case.

'The girl must have done some good deeds in her past life to be married into your household in this life,' the girl's mama said. The Diwan glanced in his direction, then looked away.

'The kids created such a lively atmosphere last night,' the girl's mama said through the lads' laughter that reached them from nearby. The lads were still busy with each other. 'Such mischief befits their age. We were all like them when we were young. It's mischief that makes a wedding a wedding.'

The Diwan cast a sideways glance at him. Everyone was still for a few seconds. The Diwan puffed at his hookah and broke the silence: 'Is that why you people have decided never to marry your daughters into our family?'

How in the world had the Diwan come to know! Blood drained from the girl's mama's body. He was speechless. The girl's chacha took over: 'The lads—yours and ours—got a bit worked up. That's all.' But he wasn't quite at his articulate best either. 'Boys will be boys. It was nothing.'

'But this decision has been pronounced by the elders, not the lads.'

The girl's mama mumbled incoherently. The purohit shifted in his seat. There was deathly silence. 'Purohit,' the Diwan finally spoke. 'You arranged this match. These are the in-laws you found us, who think nothing of the fact that we agreed to marry their daughter into our family?'

The Diwan's eyes were redder than usual. He took a small puff at his hookah before continuing, 'Our in-laws no longer consider us worthy. Isn't that what Lachhmidas said?'

The girl's mama realized this was the moment to act, or things would go horribly wrong. The Diwan was known not only to be a vain man, but also a vindictive one. He could let a thing brew in his heart for years before striking his blow. The girl's mama folded his hands and adopted his most pleading tone, 'Please forgive us if we have made a mistake, Diwanji. It's not what you think. How can we stop anyone from speaking? Lala Lachhmidas felt rebuked by one of the lads, and he lashed out with this strange pronouncement. But Lala Lachhmidas is not the elder of the family, and anyway,

Lala Lakhmidas has already reprimanded him for saying such a thing. Someone has misinformed you. It is not what you think.' Then, forcing a smile on his face, he respectfully touched the Diwan's knee and said, 'Matches are made in the divine court of God, Diwanji. We merely follow what's already ordained. We do what God . . .'

He stopped mid-sentence. The Diwan was looking directly at him and it was clear from his eyes that he'd already made up his mind about something. When the Diwan spoke next, he wasn't addressing the girl's relatives, but the purohit. 'Take the girl back to her parents' house, Purohit. The palanquin bearers are all here. They'll carry her palanquin.'

It was as if the Diwan had struck the girl's relatives with a bolt of lightning. 'What are you saying, Diwanji?' Beads of perspiration gathered on the girl's chacha's forehead. 'This can't be; such a thing has never happened before.'

'The bride hasn't set foot in our house yet. She becomes ours only after she reaches our house. Take her back.'

'But the marriage has been consecrated with the fire ceremony. How can you be saying what you're saying?'

'Yes, I'm aware the fire ceremony has been performed. I never said it hadn't been.'

This couldn't be happening. This was worse than anyone could have ever imagined. The girl's mama felt his legs turn into jelly. How would he face his sister and her family? What should he do now? Maybe he could fall at the Diwan's feet and beg his forgiveness? But he couldn't muster up the strength to do even that. Fear paralysed him. 'Mistakes happen; tempers flare,' he somehow managed to say. 'These things are known to happen during weddings,' he kept his hands joined together, and didn't leave the posture of someone begging before one more powerful than him for even a second. 'You are the wiser one, the elder. We are nothing compared to you. Your heart is an ocean; please forgive us. With this wedding, our lives are tied together for not just this lifetime, but for all others that will follow. We are a family now.'

The Diwan trained his eyes on the girl's mama. He had shown him his proper place, taught him a lesson for making the mistake of thinking the two families were equal in stature. How audaciously he had been speaking last night!

'Call Kundanlal,' he sent for his right-hand man.

Kundanlal was going over the articles that had been sent as dowry, and joined the gathering as soon as he received the summons.

'The in-laws are apologizing. They claim we have been misinformed,' the Diwan said to him.

Kundanlal studied the Diwan's face to gauge what response was expected of him, then said, 'Do they think the matter can end just by their saying they are sorry?' Kundanlal was an astute man who kept himself ingratiated with the Diwan by agreeing with him on everything. He had sensed the Diwan wasn't pleased with his in-laws' apology. 'Do they think they can insult our name and then brush it under the carpet with an apology?' He watched the Diwan's face to see if his response had been deemed appropriate.

'Kundanlal,' the Diwan said, 'I've told the purohit to take the girl back to her parents' house.'

'What?' Even the astute Kundanlal couldn't keep his surprise in check.

'Listen,' the Diwan continued. 'The purohit will accompany the palanquin back. He should convey to the girl's family that we accept her mama's apology. We forgive them, and agree to let bygones be bygones. But we're sending the girl back.'

The Diwan was using his loud, declamatory voice; the lads realized something serious was going on and slowly gathered around. The Diwan continued, addressing the purohit directly, 'Tell our in-laws that their daughter can set foot in our house only if another girl from their fraternity marries one of our boys, and today. If they agree, we will bring a baraat in the evening. Two weddings in the same auspicious period can only be a good thing. Both brides will be welcomed into our home. If they don't agree, though, they can keep their daughter, and we our son.'

The Diwan's lips parted with a slight smile as he said this. He had made his pronouncement with an air of victory.

Kundanlal was looking at the Diwan, bewildered. But while he was somewhat stunned by his harshness, he was also impressed. He respected how the elders never went back on something once they stated it. It was as if the moment their pronouncements left their mouths, they got etched in stone. That's what gave these people their stature.

The lads weren't certain whether they understood fully the implication of what had just happened. But they sensed that Diwanji had said something that the in-laws would find insulting, and that he had dared them to defy him. To them, this seemed right. They stood quietly, studying everyone's faces and trying to figure out if they had missed the import somewhat.

'Have you understood, Brahmin?' The Diwan adopted a superior tone. 'Stick to what I have said; don't go there and talk nonsense. Tell them clearly that we are ready to come with the baraat this evening. Tell them that if they haven't taken the decision that we've heard they have, then there shouldn't be a problem—all they have to do is marry another girl into our house. That's all. Understood? We'll wait for their reply until late afternoon. Now call the palanquin bearers and be on your way.'

There was pin-drop silence. The lads felt a strange twinge of excitement. Two weddings on the same day with the same baraat! It was unheard of. Surely, the Diwan had thought this up to teach the in-laws a lesson for what had happened yesterday.

'Your word is my command,' the purohit spoke very softly. 'I'll take your message to your in-laws.' He got up.

'And let me know what happens. The baraat will be readied only after we get a reply from them. If they refuse, however, then they may as well think no wedding took place yesterday either.'

No one stirred. This irritated the Diwan. 'What are you staring at me for? Go now and take the palanquin with you. We'll know soon enough where my in-laws stand.' With that, the Diwan turned his face away from the purohit and the girl's relatives, and started stirring the coals in his hookah with a tiny, narrow stick.

The bride was oblivious of these goings-on. She was sitting in her palanquin, getting more and more tired and bored by the second. She had only just mustered enough courage to part the curtains slightly and stick out her hand to gather pebbles, when her palanquin was lifted off the ground.

The lads stood silently on the hillock, watching the palanquin's descent down the hillock with the purohit at the helm. He was wearing the same clothes that he had on the night before, which was fitting, as last night's wedding rituals had not yet concluded. The bride's mama and chacha, their heads lowered, followed the palanquin. The small procession was out of sight in some time, but the lads lingered where they were and looked on pensively. While it seemed to them it was good that something was being done to dent the in-laws' conceit, uncertainty about how things would unfold from this point on troubled their young hearts.

∽

The village at the base of the hillock had narrow, winding lanes and dilapidated houses. The in-laws' house, decked out with strings of vibrant flags, could be glimpsed beyond them. Kabuli Darwaza, worn with time, stood towards the hillock. A broad street led into town through it. This was the street that slowly branched into narrow lanes through town, one of which would lead to the bride's house. The groom and his friends stood on the hillock, waiting for the palanquin to appear in the street.

From where they were standing, the town seemed busy with its routine. Women slapped cow-dung cakes on the outer walls of their houses, to dry them. Others walked about the lanes with baskets on their heads, selling vegetables. Bullock carts laden with cattle feed drew into Grain Market. Nearer the hillock, before the town started with Kabuli Darwaza, bullocks lazed about in the rain-fed, perennial pond. Children sat on the backs of some of these bullocks, splashing water at each other. The afternoon sun cast long shadows everywhere. Seen from the hillock, the town seemed to have slowed down, as if in an afternoon siesta.

The lads spotted the palanquin as it emerged near the pond. The purohit walked ahead of it, like Hanuman leading a Ramlila procession. The bride's mama and chacha followed the palanquin. The small party walked along the edge of the pond and entered the town through Kabuli Darwaza and disappeared from view.

'Now that's called taking action,' Roshanlal slapped the groom on his back and said, 'I'm impressed. Our elders have spines. Your in-laws have been brought to their knees in a day!' Then he teased, 'Don't weep; your bride will be back. Look at you! You haven't even seen your bride's face and already you look so sad. You shouldn't have demanded papad if your heart was this weak!' This got the lads laughing. Their tension eased and they returned to the rugs in the clearing, to resume where they had left off.

'If not this bride, you'll have another. There's no shortage.'

The joking and leg-pulling started again.

'Take her by the wrist and squeeze tightly so a few of her bangles break,' Balmukund, who'd been married six months, advised the groom. 'And she'll be under your thumb the rest of your life.'

For no apparent reason, Roshanlal raised his arms and screamed, 'Let's kill a sheep!'

Balmukund expressed his disagreement, 'But that's a custom of the Mohyals, not ours.'

'So what! It's a wedding custom and that's enough.'

The lads needed something to pass time. Everyone agreed in a blink.

Kundanlal was standing before the Diwan. 'The boys want to kill a sheep. I tried to reason with them, but they're not listening.'

The Diwan stopped puffing at his hookah and looked up at Kundanlal. 'Have the Mohyals got it written in some charter that they have an exclusive right to this custom?' he said irritably. 'Why should the boys be stopped from having some fun? They have my permission.'

The lads were so elated at this decision, they lifted the groom and his brother Kalle over their shoulders and ran around the clearing once, cheering loudly.

Shortly afterwards, the boys watched Kundanlal drag a sheep from the hamlet on the other side of the hillock. The sheep wasn't big, but it was muscular.

'It's going to be no joke, killing this sheep,' Balmukund mumbled.

'Killing a sheep is no child's play. The sheep fights back; it aims straight for the chest.'

The groom and his friends, Beera, Balmukund, Roshanlal, Lachhman, Chamanlal, got ready—they rolled up their sleeves and sat in a circle.

'Let's get Kalle as well. He shouldn't miss out,' Balmukund joked.

'Yes, let's call him. Let him observe the custom as well,' Roshanlal added.

'Call him; call him.'

'Let Kalle be,' the groom interjected, hoping to curb everyone's enthusiasm. 'He's not cut out for this. Imagine what will happen if the sheep attacks him!' Kalle was older than the groom, but his epilepsy made him weaker. Sure, like all the others, he had dressed up for the wedding in a flowing, embroidered kurta, crisp salwar and *joote* embroidered with gold thread on his feet, and participated enthusiastically in the baraat. But while he had danced with gusto in the marriage procession, waving the cane he was carrying with him in the air, right now he was sitting quietly under a tree, with his cane beside him, resting against the tree trunk.

Balmukund went and brought Kalle.

'He'll start.'

'Bring the sheep.'

The sheep was brought and stood at the centre of the circle. The lads became alert and contemplated its small horns, and the sheep seemed to be contemplating them in return, its eyes shining. None of the lads except Balmukund, who was a Mohyal, had participated in this custom before. But everyone knew that even though the sheep seemed quiet right now, it could spring at them any moment and ram its horns into someone's chest or, at least, make it impossible for them to approach it by stomping its hooves wildly on the ground. The risk in the ritual was substantial. Kundanlal deputed one of the palanquin bearers near the lads, a big stick in his hands, with instructions to strike the sheep if things went out of control. The rest of the baraatis—except Diwan Dhanpat, who sat on his seat puffing at his hookah—gathered around to watch.

'Untie the rope.'

'What if it runs away?'

'Why? What are all of us standing here for?' Balmukund rolled up his sleeves; everyone followed his lead. They were still sitting.

The palanquin bearer freed the sheep from its rope. The sheep lowered its head and ran. It would have escaped had the palanquin bearer not chased it and brought it back.

'Close the circle,' Balmukund shouted. 'Don't let the sheep out of the circle.' He turned towards Kalle. 'Kalle will kick things off.' He bent down, looped his arms around the sheep's belly, from below, and lifted it off the ground. 'Kalle, come on, strike it hard with your fist.'

Kalle stared incredulously at Balmukund. Something set him off laughing like a madman; as usual, no one knew what. His bare, pale chest filled up with laughter and his ribs stuck out. He didn't stop laughing even when saliva started dribbling down the corners of his lips.

'Strike it; strike it with your fist.'

Kalle laughed.

'Forget about him. He won't do it.'

'Yes, he will. He will start. His will be the first blow.'

Kalle raised his arm. He was still laughing. Then he lowered his hand on the sheep and gently stroked its back.

'He's mad. He's always been, and he'll always be. Why did you have to bring him into this?' Roshanlal screeched, irritated. He turned to Kalle and said, 'The sheep's been brought here to be killed, not loved.'

'OK, he's touched it and that's all that custom requires. Now get him out of the way.'

Kalle was still laughing and stroking the sheep.

'It's the groom's turn. Come on, Manjhle,' Roshanlal said.

The groom rolled up his right sleeve, knelt down and made a fist with his hand. He aimed for the sheep's neck and struck his blow. But he missed. His fist hit the sheep near its ear, where the sheep's horn started; Manjhle's hand smarted with pain. The sheep jerked its head and took a step forward.

'You're amateurs,' Balmukund mocked. He struck the sheep's chest. The blow was dealt with force and it hit its mark. It stunned the sheep.

This was a make-or-break moment. The sheep would definitely have attacked, but Chamanlal struck its chest—not by design, but only because Manjhle had failed and Balmukund had chided them. A tremor ran through the sheep's body. It lowered its head and took a step forward, towards Roshanlal. The air thickened with tension. Emboldened by his nearness to Balmukund, Lachhman struck the sheep from the left. The palanquin bearer inched closer, stick raised in the air, alert and ready to strike. Sheep are unpredictable; this one could attack suddenly. As if their bodies relayed fear to each other because they were next to one another, Bishnu and Beera struck the sheep simultaneously. Beera's blow landed on the sheep's back, and Bishnu's landed on the sheep's neck.

'One by one,' Balmukund said immediately. 'Those are the rules.'

The sheep charged at Lachhman. Three lads struck it at once. The sheep tottered and stopped in its track. The brightness of its eyes had dimmed a notch. But then, without warning, it charged towards the groom. Chamanlal struck it on its back. Balmukund struck it on its ribs. The sheep turned into a statue; Balmukund was clearly adept at this ritual and knew a sheep's anatomy well. Within a few moments, the sheep's body was overcome with tremors, and its leg buckled; it struggled to keep standing.

After this, Roshanlal struck the sheep, and then, one by one, so did each of the other boys—there was no urgency in their movements, neither any uncertainty. The sheep had surrendered to the ritual and to the certainty of its death.

'You've brought us a kid. Just two strong blows and it's done in,' Balmukund boasted. 'It would have been so much more fun if it had been a full-grown sheep.'

The lads had indeed beaten the sheep senseless—it was absolutely still, except for the tremors in its body. But though it had stopped moving, it was still alive and killing it with bare hands wasn't going to be an easy thing. The lads were throwing punches at it, by turn. They were laughing. In front of everyone's eyes, the sheep turned from a kid into an old, lifeless thing. Suddenly, it shat.

'Oh hell, what's this!' the groom squealed.

'*Chhi chhi!* Pooh pooh! What have you brought, Chachaji?'

'You should have made sure it had done its business before bringing him here!' Chamanlal joked before striking the sheep in its belly.

'Not much longer now,' Balmukund spoke slowly, like one with experience.

'Who will strike the last blow?' Roshanlal asked.

'The groom, of course! Come on, groom, let's see you be a man.'

Kalle threw up.

'Oh goodness, what's Kalle doing?'

'Someone take him away from here. Lalaji will get very angry.'

Kundanlal held Kalle's hand and led him away.

The groom got on his knees beside the sheep and struck it in its chest with all the force he could muster.

The sheep's hind legs gave in; the tremors that had racked its body stopped. It remained standing for a few moments like a wooden doll, its eyes open wide. Then, like a wall crumbles to the ground, it fell on its side. The groom had succeeded; he had given everyone proof of his masculinity. The sheep's mouth was wide open, its teeth bared. Its chest stopped heaving. Its legs stiffened for a second before turning limp.

'We've done it! The ritual has been completed!' everyone yelled all at once.

'The duckling's actually a swan!' Balmukund patted the groom's back. 'You are a real man. You'll have no problem controlling your wife.'

The groom's friends surrounded him, threw their arms up in the air and broke into a victory dance. Everyone patted him on his back; the groom swelled with pride. He had struck the first blow and the last; surely, both had been equally decisive in taking the sheep down.

Kundanlal spotted the purohit in the distance. Following his gaze, everyone's attention shifted from the sheep. The palanquin bearer dragged the sheep's carcass away from the clearing, towards the bushes behind the platform.

∽

Torches were lit. It was evening. The decked-up mare stood near the platform around the tree. Two people from the crematorium had been called to carry the sheep carcass—a gift from the Diwans. The stars bode well; the baraat readied itself for its new conquest, saffron turbans adorned every head, trumpets rolled. The elders sat around the elder Diwan. They had proved their authority; the youngsters were impressed.

Word spread, and children from the village at the base of the hillock ran up to the clearing to witness the preparation of the baraat and watch its second descent into town. Another page in the history of the town was on the brink of being turned.

Ishradeyi flitted from room to room. Putting the house in order and getting the dowry readied had occupied her until early evening. But now she was full of worries—*Did our in-laws receive my daughter well? What was her welcoming ceremony like?*

She was still lost in her thoughts when Ramjawaya arrived for his share of sweets. His unabashed entitlement irritated her. Last night he'd accompanied the baraat, and today he'd come here for 'his share' of sweets as if he belonged to the bride's side. He was a distant relative of both families—and not just these two, but of a number of families in the neighbourhood. That's how he came to present himself from both the groom and the bride's side in almost every other wedding. 'Good-for-nothing,' Ishradeyi cursed silently. 'Doesn't lift a finger and lives off weddings year after year.' Ramjawaya had a knack for conjuring up some relationship between himself and any family in which someone was getting wedded. And once he arrived, he never left until he had gathered up twice what was due to him.

'*Bhabhi*,' he said the moment he walked in through the door. 'Such a rush to send the dowry! You should at least have waited until your daughter reached her in-laws' house.'

Ishradeyi was preparing a basket of *shakarpaara*s; her hands stopped midway.

'What do you mean? Is the baraat still on the hillock?'

'That's right.'

Ramjawaya was quick to gauge that Ishradeyi hadn't been told. He cast a sidelong glance at her and repeated, 'You should have waited until your daughter reached her new house.'

'Say auspicious things, Ramjawaya! Don't be such a loudmouth.' Ishradeyi's irritation increased. 'I saw how quiet you were just yesterday! Not a squeak from you when the baraatis were misbehaving. Weren't you one of the baraatis yesterday?'

'What was there for me to do? The lads had already planned their mischief before they got here.'

Ishradeyi couldn't believe her ears.

'What do you mean "planned"? What plan? Why are you saying such things?'

'Of course that was all part of a larger plan. Just wait and see how things unfold.'

'Don't say such untoward things, Ramjawaya! I beg you. Good or bad, please tell me the truth. Sweets I'll give you as much as you want. Not one, take three quintals if you like.'

Ishradeyi heard a slight din on the roof. Children and young girls had been playing there. They seemed excited about something. Just then, a young girl came running into the room, 'Chachi, chachi, the palanquin's arriving.'

'Whose palanquin?' Ishradeyi couldn't understand. Her heart pounded.

'Chachi, it's the palanquin, and the purohit is also with it.' This young girl was Rukmini, Harnarayan's granddaughter. She was still draped in the green dupatta from last night, and her mouth was stuffed with paan. She had been the darling of the baraat throughout the wedding ceremony, when she had kept everyone entertained with her childish pranks.

'Did you look carefully, Rukmo, my child? Or have you come running to me just like that?' Ishradeyi was sitting on the edge of the bed. 'Is the groom accompanying the palanquin?'

'I didn't see him. It's coming from the direction of the hillock.'

'Then it must be empty. They must have reached the mansion by now.'

Ramjawaya picked up the parcel of sweets Ishradeyi had prepared for him and stood up, 'Rukmo is right, Bhabhi. Your in-laws have sent back the palanquin.'

Ishradeyi stared at him with unblinking eyes. His words struck her like a thunderbolt. 'Why didn't you say anything? You've been standing in front of me all this time, and you never said anything?' Ishradeyi ran out of the room, towards the main entrance of the house.

'I begged you people not to start a spat with the in-laws.' She ran out of the house. 'It's my daughter's life that's at stake; I begged you . . .'

We register some scenes so vividly they mark us forever. The ground before her, like wreckage that rolled out into the distance; a futile log of wood on her left; two distant, towering shisham trees, like a gateway through which her daughter's palanquin was returning—life was marking Ishradeyi. It was the palanquin she had seen her daughter off in and the same bearers who had been entrusted to take her daughter to her new home were carrying it back. She spotted the Diwan's purohit at the helm of this unfortunate procession. The intimidating shadows of dusk deepened the gloom. How lonely the palanquin looked; how she wished the Diwans had thought of letting a few baraatis accompany it. Trembling, and barefoot, she quickened her pace towards her daughter. All she wanted now was to hold her. She was running by the time she reached the palanquin. She halted the palanquin bearers at the gate and parted the curtains.

The bride, who had been sitting hugging her knees, rolled up into a tiny bundle, was startled to see her mother. She threw out her arms and hugged her.

'How come you're here, Ma? What are you doing here?' Still clinging to her mother, she surveyed her surroundings. 'Where am I?'

She disentangled herself from her mother's arms. 'Ma, where am I? How come I'm back home?' Filled with hope, her large eyes dancing on her mother's face, she murmured, 'Here I was thinking . . .' She let out a deep sigh. She couldn't believe her luck. She perked up, sprang out of the palanquin and rushed towards her house to meet her friends.

～

The elders of the Malik household gathered once more to deliberate on the crisis that had befallen them. This time Ishradeyi made sure to be among them from the beginning. Malik Mansaram was present too, but his anger made him withdraw into himself, and he mentally replayed the insult that had been meted out to him. His blood boiled, but the delicacy of the situation rendered him helpless. Diwan Dhanpat had humiliated him before the entire town and he no longer had years ahead of him in which to rebuild that which had been destroyed.

Lakhmidas and Lachhmidas sat side by side, their turbans on their heads. Everyone was annoyed with Lachhmidas; it was his reckless suggestion that had brought them to this abyss.

'I cautioned you, Lachhmidas, that you must speak as the situation warrants. I warned you that we mustn't rub the in-laws the wrong way.'

'Who rubbed them the wrong way?' Lachhmidas retorted angrily. 'They came here hell-bent on humiliating us. How much is one supposed to bear?'

'Who's the base-born informer in our midst? Speak up!' he asked heatedly.

At exactly this moment, the purohit came walking down the street. He crossed the street and headed towards the wedding pavilion, where everyone was gathered. He was still in the same get-up as the night before—his clothes embellished with lace, a bag in his hand, a cloth towel thrown over his shoulder. He looked ordinary and dirty, like every other ordinary and dirty person in the neighbourhood. For all one knew, underneath his fancy attire and the saffron turban of the Diwans that he had on his head, he was still wearing his dirty, everyday clothes.

Mansaram's temper shot through the roof the moment he saw him.

'Here, Purohit, come here, right in front of me,' Mansaram said, struggling to rein in his anger.

The purohit stood before him with his hands joined.

'Who told the in-laws we've discussed we won't marry our daughters into their family? Speak truthfully, or your death will be merciless; you will spend your afterlife in hell.'

The Brahmin wasn't perturbed. He knew that however the townsfolk might sometimes speak with him, no one was audacious enough to raise a hand to him. He was aware that everyone knew that anyone who hits a Brahmin ends up in hell himself.

'What's happened is most unfortunate, Generous One!' he said calmly, his hands still joined.

'Who told on us?' Malik Mansaram screamed. A stark silence descended.

Trying to restore some gravity to the situation, Lakhmidas said, 'How does it matter to you, Mansaram, if a crow cawed the information as it flew, or if a dark thief told them? It doesn't matter any more.'

'I'm going to pull your tongue out, Pandit, if I learn that it was you.'

But even this didn't affect the purohit in the least. He just stood there, blinking.

'It was a conversation in the family; how did it get out and reach them?' Malik Mansaram's younger brother asked.

Mansaram darted his eyes at the purohit as he pronounced, 'Purohit, go and sit outside. You'll be sent for when you're needed.'

'What you say is right, Malikji!' said the purohit, and he lifted his bag and walked out as he was told to, chanting softly under his breath.

'It has to be him. Who else?' Mansaram was agitated.

At this the turbaned Lakhmidas spoke in a placating voice, 'That's not the way of the world, Mansaram! Your temper always gets the better of you!'

Mansaram lost all composure. 'Should I stay silent while they insult me? Let them do what they will, then. My daughter can stay here, in her own house. I'll tell myself she's been widowed.'

'Oh God, oh God! Why are you uttering such curses?' Ishradeyi became restless. It distressed her to see her husband so unhappy.

'Let Diwan Dhanpat do what he will. If I'm my father's son, I'll take my revenge. Let him do his . . .'

Mansaram's voice choked with emotion.

'Talk sensibly, Mansaram! Your daughter has to spend her life in that house. Let's not sow thorns for our children to reap.'

'I'll tell myself my daughter has died.' Mansaram's lips trembled with anguish.

'Say auspicious things, Mansaram. Talk sensibly. Don't panic like this.'

But Mansaram was inconsolable.

The rudeness of the baraatis had already ensured that last night had been sleepless for Mansaram. Stress lines had taken over his forehead; his back was tired. He was exhausted. No one can remain unmoved on seeing an elder break down.

Ishradeyi stepped in. She too was worn out, but the situation demanded that she hold back her pain. Their daughter had been sent back home; it was time to act.

'Good fellows, call that cursed purohit in,' she said. 'Let's hear what the in-laws are saying. Call him here.' She held her husband's hand and said, 'Be strong. Have faith. A difficult moment has come upon us. Come what may, we have to prevail over it.'

But the waves of restlessness wouldn't leave her. She cursed, 'May those who have insulted my daughter die a painful death.' She covered her mouth with her dupatta and sobbed.

The girl's maternal uncle stepped out and brought the purohit back with him. The purohit glided in slyly and stood humbly, his hands joined.

'Tell us, Purohit, what have the in-laws said?' Ishradeyi asked calmly. 'Tell us what they want, and we'll follow their wishes.'

The purohit, his fingers engaged in their usual dance, said, 'Respected madam, they have asked that a second wedding be performed in today's auspicious moment itself.'

Ishradeyi said with patience, 'What else?'

'Diwanji says, marry another daughter from your house or your clan into ours, and we will take both the brides with full honour and pride to our house.'

'Certainly. Purohitji, go and tell Diwanji that we accept. They can come with the baraat,' said Ishradeyi, with folded hands.

The purohit stood there, stunned for a moment. Then he left.

Ishradeyi had overcome her restlessness, and she said patiently to her husband, 'All they are asking for is another girl, nothing else. They're not returning my daughter. If one girl can go to their house, so can another.'

'Here the in-laws are bent upon smearing our faces with dirt, and you agreed to their demands!'

'What else will you do? Will you make your daughter sit at home? You people have created this mess yourselves. You go around making decisions on your own. Is there any sense in saying we won't marry any daughter into the Diwan's house? Who the hell are we to make such rules? When it's come back to bite you, you're squirming.'

She continued calmly, 'I would say, find a girl from the clan and get her married. What's wrong in this? Another girl will find a home with the Diwans. Nothing is ruined yet. Our in-laws have played with us. They haven't returned our daughter. With the blessing of our Guru, everything will sort itself out.'

Mansaram's cousin intervened, 'But the world is laughing at us, the entire town is mocking us.' No one joined him. Everyone had understood the situation needed deft handling.

'The in-laws haven't said the second girl has to be from our house. She can be anyone's daughter, as long as it's from the clan.'

'What did Dhanpat say?' Mansaram asked his wife's elder brother, as he was the one who had accompanied the dowry to the Diwan. But he had been so stumped by the turn of events that the Diwan's words and conditions had blurred in his mind.

'He didn't say anything clearly. He only said that we'll take the bride home only when you give another girl in marriage to us.'

'What is that supposed to mean?'

At this Lakhmidas said in a steady voice, 'The meaning is simple—another girl from the clan. After all, our decision had been to not marry another girl from the clan into that family.'

This calmed Mansaram. To marry a second daughter into that family would have meant total surrender.

Since dignity was no longer the pivot around which the situation was evolving, the thought arose in the minds of the various Maliks gathered there that the girl will, after all, be married into the Diwans. *If Mansaram's daughter can go there, so can someone else's. Why not take advantage of the situation and get my daughter married? The situation is ripe; my daughter will find a home, and at no cost.*

But everyone kept quiet. No one expressed agreement. It wouldn't be right to be seen jumping at the situation.

In the intervening silence, Mansaram's cousin had a thought, 'But who is the groom? To whose house is the girl going to be married? Whom is the Diwan bringing as the groom?'

This startled everyone. No one had considered this aspect of the problem.

'Dhanpat's elder son is unwell. What if the Diwan brings him as the groom?' Turning to his sister-in-law, he said, 'Bhabhi, you agreed in haste. What if they bring their ill son as the groom?'

Ishradeyi shuddered. She had thought that if no one agrees to marry his daughter into the Diwan's house, then she would have no choice but to marry her younger daughter as well into that house. But she hadn't anticipated this. What if this had been the Diwan's plan all along!

'What is his illness?' Ishradeyi asked weakly. She saw darkness ahead. *What will we do if he's seeking our second daughter for his ill son in order to further insult my husband? Will we then have our first daughter sit at home, or throw our second daughter down an abyss? What have I done?*

'He has epileptic fits,' someone said.

The situation was becoming clearer. None of the Maliks wanted to risk marrying his daughter to an ill person. And no one was under any compulsion to do so either. Mansaram would have to face this critical moment alone. Hadn't he, after all, compounded the situation? But for now, he should be given courage.

'Epilepsy isn't a serious disease. If the body is strong, it goes away. In any case, a seizure can be calmed by smelling a shoe.'

The girl's mama spoke again, 'Diwan Dhanpat has neither said that the groom will be from his house nor that the bride has to be from this very family.'

Lala Lakhmidas had been nodding silently. Now he said, 'It could be the case, or not. Let's not speculate. Let's come to the point.' He looked around and addressed everyone, 'Speak up, who is willing?'

Someone added, 'It's been said that the Diwan's son is under treatment. He's being treated by a hakim from Lahore.'

This riled Mansaram, 'To hell with the hakim.'

'Let us hear it, Malikji. If the boy is getting cured, it changes things.'

Women would never have agreed to consider getting their daughters married to someone who was ill. But some of the men were in a dilemma. Epilepsy isn't such a serious illness after all. And here it has become known before the wedding—often one doesn't come to know until much later. Marriages don't stop because of such things.

A man sitting next to Lala Lakhmidas whispered in his ear, 'Consider a poor man's daughter for this. She'll find a home. It'll be good for her.'

'But we need to know who the groom is.'

'What's to be gained from knowing?'

Silence descended. Then someone said, 'Epilepsy isn't all that bad an illness. It's not tuberculosis. And it's being said that he's much healthier now than before.'

Everyone listened keenly.

'Think about it, even those without an arm or a leg get married, and this one is able-bodied. The girl will go to a well-off family and have a happy life.'

Confusion returned to the minds of many. *What if a golden opportunity to get my daughter married into a good house was getting frittered away? After all, the Diwan can't possibly harbour such ill will. And the Diwan has also said that he will take the second bride home with pride and honour. The Diwan's intentions must not be doubted.*

Arguments raged; no solutions emerged. Whenever a suggestion surfaced, it quickly dissipated in arguments.

Arjundas almost came to a decision to have his daughter be the one, but he didn't utter it; the risk seemed too grave.

Suddenly, the sound of firecrackers filled the air. The groom's procession had set off from the hillock. Everyone became alert. Ishradeyi screamed, 'Oh well-wishers, nobody is for anyone here. I'll give my own daughter. Whoever the groom may be, my other daughter it will be . . . !'

And she burst into tears.

ಲ

The scatter of the previous night had to be attended to. The decorations had come undone; the ropes were hanging loose and needed to be tied back. The mats needed straightening. Leftovers from the feast and unwashed utensils lay accumulated. The will to clean up had been lost; desolation had taken over. But the commotion of the second marriage procession stirred things up. There was a sudden flurry of activity, but without any excitement. It was as if a horse faint with exertion had jolted back into action on been whipped. Ishradeyi wiped her tears and dove into this atmosphere heavy with her relatives' anxiety, doubt, humiliation, disbelief and irritation, demonstrating even more agility and alacrity than she had for the first wedding.

Malik Mansaram's agitation refused to quieten down. He sat limply on a wicker stool, cursing the moment when he had taken the decision to marry his daughter into Dhanpat's house. He felt defeated and as if he couldn't care less how things might unfold from this point.

Cooks were summoned back. Haste was made to gather up provisions for another feast. Torchbearers took their positions again. On the surface, the hustle and bustle of a wedding had resumed. Women gathered in the house; the house filled with festive percussions of the dholak. Ishradeyi chatted with everyone. She readied her younger daughter. Having bathed her and dressed her in red, silk finery, she applied henna on her hands. Then she lit an oil lamp and sat her down by it, just like she had done with her older daughter the night before. The older daughter sat in the neighbouring room, still in her bridal finery, puzzled by this turn of events. The younger one watched the flame of the oil lamp like a doe caught in crossfire. Ishradeyi flitted between the rooms, comforting her daughters, stroking one daughter's back one moment, and the other's the next.

'This is what God has willed for me. No one can change that. But if I have acted virtuously in the world, then both my daughters will live happily,' she told herself silently, over and over again.

'So dark, how black this night is,' her restlessness deepened with the night. But she kept her anxious heart from sinking by cursing and cajoling it by turn.

The atmosphere in the house remained tense. Women spoke about this and that with Ishradeyi, but they whispered among themselves, exaggerated for each other the stories they had heard about the Diwan's older son, curled their lips and made their own estimates. Ishradeyi wasn't unaware. 'Whatever has befallen me is mine to bear,' she kept repeating to herself.

Outside, children laughed and played under the temporary canopy. Men rushed about taking care of things for the wedding, but hearts were heavy. It was Malik Mansaram's daughter who was going to be married, but the entire Malik clan had been insulted. And yet, the clan had failed to stand by him at the crucial moment. Not one Malik had shown the courage to go and reason with Diwan Dhanpat. They had all left Malik Mansaram alone to fend for himself. Now they hesitated to meet his eye. Whether egged on by guilt, solidarity, habit or custom, the men went about organizing the wedding carefully and earnestly.

Word came that someone from the Diwan's side had arrived. It wasn't just anyone who walked in, but Diwan Kundanlal himself. He looked around and made an assessment of the arrangement, then stood with his hands folded in front of Malik Mansaram. This gesture of respect from an ill-tempered man like Kundanlal surprised everyone even more than his uninvited appearance.

'Maharaj,' he said, 'Diwanji sends word that he respectfully accepts the dowry you sent already. No more need be sent. He has also said that the baraat will comprise some forty men, and has requested that no elaborate preparations need be made for them. We have already been feasting on the hillock all day, and whatever you serve will be like nectar to us. We are coming here only to take the bride. She is no less than Goddess Lakshmi to us, and her arrival in our home will bestow prosperity upon us. He also humbly requests that no gifts need be given to us during the greeting ceremony . . .'

In response, Malik Mansaram joined his hands together. But he didn't say anything; he didn't even get up from the wicker stool. It seemed Diwan Dhanpat had recognized the error in what he had done. This was no small thing. Some of the Maliks felt a pang of regret that it wasn't their daughter getting married that evening. Not only would she be settled, each father thought, but Malik Mansaram's hurt would also be somewhat reduced. It no longer mattered to anyone who the boy was.

But this wedding procession turned out to be similar to the previous one in at least one respect—it arrived late. It was way past midnight by the time the sound of drums that accompanied the procession were heard from Grain Market. The bride's side was exhausted. When they heard the drums, they did spur into action, and everyone took their respective positions, but all that everyone wanted now was for this ordeal to end.

The baraat arrived with aplomb, just like it had the night before. Once again, it looked majestic—there was loud music, everyone was dressed up, and the young men were dancing. Once more, people peeped out of their windows and stood on the roofs of houses and watched—though this time their curiosity was laced with an expectation of yet another drama.

Some things were different, though. This procession was smaller compared to the last one. And unlike the previous night, there were two palanquins tonight. One carried Diwan Dhanpat—dressed in his traditional turban and angrakha, looking about proudly with his sharp eyes, his hookah set up by his side like before. But the other palanquin, it seemed, carried the groom! It had to be the groom—the fine silk robe he was wearing, and the groom's mantle that hung from his turban over his face, were evidence that it was. The mantle was so elaborate that a thick veil of silver strings covered the groom's face; it was impossible to tell who he was. This, together with the oddness of the groom arriving in a palanquin for his wedding, confirmed for the onlookers that the groom was none other than the Diwan's ill son. The Malik household knew this by now—word that it was on the Diwan's older son's head that the groom's mantle had been tied on the hillock had reached them long before. And the town, in its long existence, had seen wedding processions of grooms of all sorts sing and dance their way through its lanes. So even though eyes had only now acknowledged that which had already become common knowledge, there was nothing here to cause naive shock or disbelief.

Diwan Kundanlal headed this wedding procession as well, and showered coins from his bag each time the procession entered a new lane. As before, children jostled to gather up the coins. The procession turned into Bhagsuddhi's lane. Kundanlal saw her sitting on her cot, but this time he didn't go near her to pay his respects. Bhagsuddhi's ageing eyes wouldn't be able to see him anyway. But she heard someone say Diwan Dhanpat's palanquin was approaching. 'Well done, Dhanpat,' she called out loudly. 'Your deeds are great indeed. They're sure to add lustre to the title of the Diwans. You will be remembered forever, Dhanpat. Have you no shame at all?'

Who was to say if Bhagsuddhi's words had reached the Diwan? He didn't bat an eyelid, didn't shift in his seat.

The procession had barely stopped in front of the wedding pavilion, the music band was still beating out a tune and the Diwan hadn't even stepped out of the palanquin when the purohit rushed to him, 'Generous One, you are late. The auspicious hour is waning. We only have time for the fire ceremony now. The greeting ceremony can wait. Generous One, I urge you.'

The bride's relatives were waiting at the gate with garlands. Malik Mansaram, his face pale and hands trembling, stood in the centre. Beads of perspiration gathered on his forehead.

The Diwan got out of the palanquin and headed straight towards Malik Mansaram, garlanded him, and said, 'When the Maliks honour us, we honour them back. Each man's daughter is the daughter of the entire community. Our families are now related through marriage. Our lives are tied together, forever.' Diwan Dhanpat's voice was sweet as saccharine. He embraced Malik Mansaram for a long moment, as if they were long-lost relatives, united at last.

Eyes soaking in this scene were filled with reverence for Diwan Dhanpat. People were moved by this expression of nobility from the Diwan. He was right to be angry about what had happened, after all. It was wrong for the Maliks to say they won't marry their daughters into the Diwans. They didn't do right by the Diwans, inviting them to their house and insulting them the way they did. Baraats in which young people don't create a scene are unheard of, after all.

The relatives and guests of both sides began gathering at the gate. The purohit, who had taken on the role of the manager of ceremonies, stood amidst them and pressed on yet again, 'We won't be able to perform the ceremony if the auspicious hour passes. Generous Ones, please don't delay things. The guests are welcome to proceed for the wedding feast, but close relatives must make their way at once to where the fire ceremony will be performed.'

Paying heed, some of the guests went ahead to eat while others followed the Diwan for the ceremony. Malik Mansaram still looked crestfallen, but he quietly followed the Diwan, as did his relatives.

The purohit started to quickly ready the receptacle that would hold the fire, lit incense sticks around it and set up the materials with which all those present would participate in the ritual. 'Please send for the groom; it's getting late,' he urged.

'Let your blessings be with her, oh Guru,' Ishradeyi prayed under her breath as she went up to her daughter to take her for the ceremony. 'Please be merciful.' The young girl, a veil covering her face all the way to her chest, let herself be helped up. She was trembling. Ishradeyi sensed her daughter's unexpressed doubts, her foreboding and unnamed fears. She held her tighter and led her towards the door. *What if she knows whom she is about to be married to?* Ishradeyi covered her lips with her dupatta in dismay.

As they crossed the threshold of the house, Ishradeyi felt a deep unhappiness surge up within her. Yesterday, the groom had come to the threshold. That custom hadn't been followed today. The threshold wasn't alive with the laughter of the bride's friends as they surrounded the groom and teased him, asking him to recite couplets. Yesterday, the bride and the groom had even played a little game in which the groom had to prise open his bride's fist. He'd found a gold ring inside for him.

The groom, accompanied by his friends and his brother, had already reached the pedestal on which the fire would be lit. Strings of fragrant flowers hung from his neck. His friends helped him sit down, and Balmukund sat down right behind him, close to him, so he could support his back through the long ceremony.

The purohit was troubled by the slow pace of things. He'd been rushing through the preparations himself. 'There should be no further delay now,' he said. 'Please bring the bride.'

All heads turned towards the house, expecting to see the bride emerge any moment now with her mother and friends. Instead, they heard screams. The wedding pavilion was thrown into disarray as everyone stood up. Ramjawaya and Ishradeyi's brother ran towards the house.

Ishradeyi had felt faint and lost her balance. She'd hit her forehead against the frame of the door. There was a lot of blood.

Some more people ran towards the house. Ishradeyi's daughters—the two brides—were sitting on either side of her and crying.

'The auspicious hour is passing. Oh Generous Ones, the auspicious hour is passing! This wedding can't be performed once the auspicious star sets,' the purohit started to yell.

Then he turned towards Malik Mansaram and pleaded with folded hands, 'Maharaj, think of something; if the auspicious hour passes, everything will be ruined. If the auspicious star sets, the wedding won't be possible.'

Seeing that things weren't moving at all, Purohit Ramdas got up from his seat. A group of young girls had been standing nearby, watching the proceedings. The purohit walked towards them with long strides, held one of them by her arm, brought her with him, sat her down by the groom and started reciting the wedding mantras.

Bewildered, all those gathered around waiting for the wedding ceremony to be performed strained their eyes to make out who the girl was. Before anyone could even make sense of what was going on, the purohit had completed the ceremony.

And that is how Diwan Dhanpat's ill son came to be married to Rukmini, the not-yet-thirteen-year-old daughter of Harnarayan's widowed daughter, Veeranwali. It was a wedding that the people of the town wouldn't be able to stop talking about for years and years to come.

The town responded strangely to the wedding. People discussed it everywhere. The lanes and markets were filled with talk about it. Men and women didn't seem to tire of going over what had happened. Everyone mostly saw the incident as a tug of war between the two families.

'That was an impressive sleight of hand by the Diwan,' Banshi said over a game of dice. 'With one move, he got his crackbrained son settled, and also showed Malik Mansaram his place.'

'What settled? And as for humiliating the Maliks, it's not as if he managed to take Mansaram's other daughter as the bride. Instead, all he got was the poverty-stricken Harnarayan's granddaughter. What's to be gained in that?'

'Oh, but it's no small thing that he sent Malik Mansaram's daughter back. He humbled Malik Mansaram before the entire town.'

'One should be wary of Diwan Dhanpat. You can survive the bite of a poisonous snake, but not if you're stung by Dhanpat.'

'It's Mansaram's own fault. What got into him? Why go about saying we won't marry our daughters into the Diwans? Wasn't that an insult to the Diwans?'

'He must have been so enraged by what the Maliks were saying. He was bound to make Malik Mansaram bite the dust. The Diwans aren't lacking in guts.'

'Dhanpat is no Diwan.'

'Well, he's at least a half Diwan. His father was a Diwan, after all.'

'The Diwan is a noble man. He showed Malik Mansaram his place, but then he didn't ask for any dowry, didn't ask the guests to be loaded with gifts. He took both the brides back honourably. No one in this entire town has as much gumption as the Diwan.'

'What nonsense! First he created a situation, and then he inserted his nitwit son into the equation and got him married!'

'So what? He didn't sneak his son in. The wedding procession went through these lanes, openly and in plain sight. He didn't conceal anything. There's no duplicity in what he did.' This was the humpbacked sweet seller. He'd been sitting in his shop, his back resting against its wall. He stood up and took a few steps forward. 'Then the purohit went and brought Harnarayan's granddaughter into the ceremony and got her married to the Diwan's son,' he continued. 'The Diwan didn't object even to this; he accepted her. What do you say to this? He could easily have demanded that he would only take Malik Mansaram's daughter as his daughter-in-law. He could have said, "I won't take the first bride home unless this condition is met." Come on, what do you have to say to this? He could have, but he didn't. He's noble. He took a poor man's daughter as his daughter-in-law.'

'It was a ploy,' Kohli, who had been actively participating in the discussion, responded. 'He duped everyone. All he wanted was to get his epileptic son married. It was to achieve this end that he created this entire charade of returning the bride and saying give us another daughter through marriage or we won't take this one with us.'

'What nonsense!' The sweet seller jumped off the platform, on to the street. 'Are you saying that if a boy has epilepsy, he can never get married? You know that's not true; he can marry into the best of families. The Diwan only wanted to teach the Maliks a lesson.'

'Mansaram is forever shamed,' Banshi commented. 'The Diwan has shut him up.'

'If you ask me, both men gained something,' said Atar Singh, who had been sitting quietly on a coir mat by the side of the street. 'The Diwan got his ill son married, and Mansaram didn't have to give up his younger daughter.'

Banshi couldn't help making a crack at this, 'Long live Purohit Ramdas! Thanks to him, both men won and both men lost.' He started laughing. Winking at his listeners, he said, 'He made a quick judgement and dragged in a different girl. There's none other like him. And what a fine little duckling he found.'

'It's a good thing,' the sweet seller said. 'Harnarayan's granddaughter is now a daughter-in-law in the mansion. Her life's definitely taken a turn for the better.'

Ramjawaya, who was sitting with his legs hanging from the platform, chipped in, 'Who's to say if Malik Mansaram's wife really fainted or if she was play-acting!'

'Why would she act? Her daughter was about to be married to an idiot. Anyone would faint! She's a mother after all.'

But Ramjawaya insisted, 'I think she fell on purpose. She did it to save her younger daughter.'

'You're omniscient, aren't you? You know what's in whose heart!'

'It was an act, nothing more.'

'After all, Diwan Dhanpat was trying to avenge an old feud,' Kohli said, supporting Ramjawaya's assertion.

'What feud?'

'The auctioning of the land adjoining the mansion, what else. Mansaram had insulted the Diwan then; now the Diwan got his chance to insult him back.'

'Come on, you're saying the purohit didn't pick Harnarayan's granddaughter by chance, but that he'd schemed this all along?'

Kohli had an answer to this as well. 'I've heard the purohit went to meet Harnarayan at his home a few days ago. Only God knows what transpired between them, but it's said two sacks of grain were sent to Harnarayan's house after that.'

Banshi howled with laughter. 'That's great! You actually think the purohit had arranged for Harnarayan's granddaughter to be playing right next to where the ceremony was going to be performed, in the middle of the night, so that he could pick her up suddenly and have her marry the Diwan's son!' He joined his hands, raised them to his forehead, bent before Kohli in a show of mock respect and said, 'I bow to thee, oh Kohli! You are great.'

And the arguments went on for a long time.

Even after it was long over, the wedding continued to gather excitement and intrigue. Some people sided with Malik Mansaram. They critiqued Diwan Dhanpat's attitude and found fault in how he'd acted. Others sided with Diwan Dhanpat, and applauded his nobility, praised him for his panache. No one said if what had happened was bad or not; the discussions always only circled around the ways of the affluent. What had happened may have been a game, but it was a game only the well-off could play.

Yes, Mausi Bhagsuddhi openly condemned Diwan Dhanpat. She screamed and shouted that, blinded by wealth, Dhanpat wasn't thinking straight any more, that his heart was drained of emotions. 'God sees all,' she cursed. 'His wrath will fall on Dhanpat soon and his progeny will suffer the consequences of his actions. He has no shame; he thinks nothing of insulting another's daughter . . .'

She could sit on her cot and scream and rant all she wanted, but it didn't matter. People pretended not to hear her. They shut out her voice and carried on with their ways.

∾

Harnarayan closed his pocket-sized prayer book. He was about to get up and go back inside the house when he saw a shadow on the ground moving towards him. He looked up—it was the purohit. Harnarayan fell back on the stool. Like a man stung, he said, 'What more do you want from me after doing what you've done?' The hand he was holding his prayer book in trembled.

'Diwanji,' the purohit addressed him respectfully, in the same manner as he addressed all the Diwans, 'we are all playthings in the hands of fate. Had Ishradeyi not fainted, her daughter would've been the one who got married. But the constellation of stars favoured Rukmo. She was blessed by fate. Her fortunes have turned, Diwanji.'

Harnarayan hadn't been able to come to terms with the way his granddaughter had been married to Kalle. He had tried consoling his aching heart with the thought that perhaps a divine power had guided the purohit's actions. But his young granddaughter had been married to an ill man; it was nothing short of coercion. His heart was in turmoil.

'And is this how you wanted to get my granddaughter married?' His voice quivered.

The purohit stayed silent, his eyes watching Harnarayan with a quiet stillness. He would wait for Harnarayan to vent his emotions, as was his way. The other person is bound to exhaust his anger at some point—let him boil over; it hardly matters. What's happened has already happened.

'The illusion of wealth has stoned Dhanpat's heart. But, Purohit, where is your kindness?'

The purohit nodded his head slowly. His eyes, set deep inside the web of age lines that richly criss-crossed his face, watched Harnarayan intently, never leaving his face for even a moment.

'May the body of the one who pushed my daughter into the fire of hell be infested with worms! May he die a painful death!' Veeranwali cursed loudly from inside the house. 'The sigh of the poor is powerful. No one in his family will remain unscathed. Constellation of stars be damned! God will take care of the one who has butchered my daughter.'

Harnarayan lowered his gaze. When Veeranwali's heart is burning with rage, how can she remain quiet? No one can stop her from speaking her mind. His own heart was tormented, but he had no words. His realization of his own helplessness had drained him of the courage to speak. On the one hand, he felt relief at having had a big responsibility taken care of without him having to lift a finger. And at the same time, he felt deeply affronted that his granddaughter should be married so suddenly, without discussion, and that too to a man who was unwell. But there was nothing to be done now.

At the same time, another line of reasoning was slowly taking hold of his mind. It went somewhat like this: Mansaram had agreed to marry his daughter to Kalle, hadn't he? And if Ishradeyi hadn't fainted, then surely their daughter would have been Kalle's bride. Seeing that the auspicious hour was passing, the purohit got hold of Rukmo. What if there was no ill will in this? What if all that the purohit thought was that my granddaughter can be married to the man that Malik Mansaram's daughter can be married to?

Harnarayan became like a patient whose body turns hot and cold by turn. His way of life had emerged over time and, like the twisting and turning lanes of this town, had its own rules and logic.

Veeranwali continued shouting curses. 'Tell him to go away. Tell him to keep his shadow away from our house. May the one who has pushed my daughter into a dark well die a slow, painful death! May mad dogs feast on his living flesh! May he be bitten by poisonous snakes . . . !'

Harnarayan's heart filled with doubt. *What if the Brahmin becomes enraged? He could curse us; he could ensure our afterlife is spent in hell.*

'That's enough, Veeran,' he stopped his daughter. 'No one can turn what fate ordains. My fate is to be blamed. It's my blighted fate that's caused all this pain. It's the reason . . .' He stopped with a catch in his throat.

A small, one-room house with a tiny loft on its roof, as dark and dank as the rest of the building, a yard in front that ended even before it began, and on which Harnarayan would set up his wicker stool and spend all his time reading from a prayer book—the house screamed of desolation. The purohit discerned and understood this. But he wasn't a sentimental man. He never let his own body pulsate with another person's pain, joy or distress; it was as if he had become immune.

Veeranwali stopped cursing. Her father's self-berating had made her break down and cry.

'Don't cry, Veeran,' Harnarayan said. 'One mustn't cry after evening falls. That's the time to remember God.' As he said this, Harnarayan felt overwhelmed. 'Please forgive me,' he joined his hands before the purohit and pleaded. 'I'm guilty of so many misdeeds. I hope you can forgive a sinner like me. It is I who has pushed that sweet, innocent child into a well . . .'

Veeran became absolutely silent. Why torment my father with my unhappiness, she thought.

When both Harnarayan and Veeranwali had been quiet for some time, the purohit said, 'Diwanji, you are related to the mansion through marriage now. I am, therefore, at your command.'

Harnarayan sat with his eyes lowered. He sensed sarcasm in the purohit's words. And yet, his words also seemed innately realistic. It was true; he was related to the elder Diwan now.

'The elder Diwan has sent you an invitation,' the purohit continued, his voice slightly louder than before so Veeranwali could hear him clearly.

'The elder Diwan has invited his in-laws and a handful of people from the clan for lunch in the mansion. You are among the invited guests.'

Another tremor ran through Harnarayan's body. After the wedding, he'd decided he wouldn't so much as look at Dhanpat's face again, that he would never set foot in the mansion. But refusing this invitation would be seen as an open insult. He shut his eyes and silently cursed his fate. He struggled to come to a decision.

How crooked the ways of life are, he thought to himself. *The past can't be relived, and the future reveals itself slowly with every passing moment, each day. Rukmo's life is tied to a man who is ill; it will unfold on the other side of the mansion's high walls. But she lives; her life lies ahead of her. May she live a*

*long life; may the years I have remaining on this earth be added
to hers . . .*

Harnarayan opened his eyes and raised his head. His
mind was in a quandary. *Is Dhanpat inviting me to the
mansion to insult me? Or is he merely following custom? Or is he
patronizing me? Is the lunch going to be an occasion for him to
make a show of what a huge favour he has done me by taking me
for an in-law?*

The purohit stood quietly in front of Harnarayan, his
hands respectfully joined before him.

Berating himself about how insufficient and helpless he
was had become Harnarayan's way. *With Dhanpat, one can
never be sure. If I refuse his invitation, it will anger him. He'll
make Rukmo's life hell. He'll demand that she insult me, make
me fall at his feet, and that only then will she be accepted as a
daughter-in-law of the mansion.*

Every situation was a source of humiliation, and would
plunge him into deep self-loathing. Suffering made him feel
stoic and find within himself the reserves of energy with
which to deal with life.

'Diwanji, the auspicious hour was waning. We were
running out of time. It so happened that Rukmo caught
my eye. It was her fate that brought her in front of me,' the
purohit broke his silence. Harnarayan listened.

The purohit realized the time was right to let loose the
strongest weapon he had in his armoury. 'Rukmini will rule
the mansion,' he said. 'Kalle may be physically weak, but he
is the older son. He is the heir apparent, the apple of the
Diwan's eye. He is being treated by a hakim from Lahore. He
will be in the pink of health in no time.'

Bending forward slightly, he whispered, 'Try and see it
for what it is—Rukmo took Malik Mansaram's daughter's

place. Had that girl's mother not fainted, this wouldn't have happened. It's an indisputable fact. For, Diwanji, do you think the mansion lacks people who want their daughters married into it? So many people came to me afterwards and said, "Purohit, keep us in mind too." It was Rukmo's luck that brought her in front of me at the exact moment. It could've been any girl from a good family in her place. The elder Diwan has lifted the weight of a big responsibility off your shoulders.'

The purohit's words were hitting their mark. Harnarayan was beginning to see things his way. *We are merely pawns in the hands of fate. Fate decides all. Who knows, maybe the purohit acted with the best of intentions. Now Rukmo has a roof over her head; she will not suffer for want of food. We're too insignificant; we could never have got her married into a well-off family.*

'The Diwan sends his invitation,' the purohit returned to the point. 'Yours is the first stop I'm making. Lunch is at the mansion next Thursday.'

The purohit could see that the invitation had been accepted. He could also tell that Harnarayan was as delighted to be invited as he had been tremulous that Rukmini had been married to Kalle.

'I should be on my way now, Diwanji. I have to go to the other in-laws' place as well.' The purohit turned and disappeared into the lane.

Harnarayan was still agitated. He didn't seem to be able to make up his mind on whether he wanted to keep sitting where he was or to get up and go inside.

Veeranwali came up to him. 'What are you thinking?' she asked.

But then, without waiting for an answer, she said, 'Since the invitation has been sent, you must go. If nothing else, at least we'll get news about Rukmo.'

Veeran seemed to have cleared her mind. The welfare of her daughter was paramount.

'I'll ready your clothes today itself. You should dress well and go. I'll starch your turban . . .' Her eyes welled up, and she quickly turned away from Harnarayan and went back inside the house.

∽

Ishradeyi held her daughter to her breast for a long moment and led her into the house. She had been able to make a quick assessment from a brief glance—the necklace her daughter was wearing was not from her dowry. The red scarf she had around her shoulders, too, was a gift from her in-laws. Her body radiated the soft scent of coitus. Everything seemed to be as it should be. The slightly lost look the girl had on her face was natural for one who was newly married.

Somewhat reassured, Ishradeyi now started searching her daughter's face for clues into the doubts that she'd been racked by since the night of the wedding. For all she knew, the Diwan was still irked and, by extension, the people of the mansion didn't give her daughter the respect that was her due. The groom had shown such impatience during the wedding feast; who knew what his temper was like and if he raised his hand to her. Not that there would be anything out of the ordinary in that, for men are given to hitting women. Often, over time, the same men become as pliable as wet clay in the hands of the same women. A woman only needs to know how to work her man.

The real concern Ishradeyi had was with regard to Kalle. Did the Diwan favour Kalle and his bride over his younger son and her daughter? It had taken Ishradeyi some time, but she had come to see how the Diwan had raised the stakes only in order to get Kalle married. What would happen if Kalle got well, if he begot a son? It would mean two able sons would stake their claim to the Diwan's inheritance. And then there was a third son too, who was in England at the moment, but would surely return for his share. When the marriage proposal had first come, Ishradeyi had carefully considered how the second son would, for all intents and purposes, be the sole inheritor. He'd be the one to manage the property; her daughter would rule over everything they owned. But the wedding had been a disaster and it filled Ishradeyi's heart with doubt. It was not that she hadn't heard stories about the boy's youthful capriciousness. But they didn't bother her. Sons of affluent families can afford to have fun, and straight arrows don't make for good husbands anyway. They are sheepish and cautious. Men who are audacious with the world also speak up for their wives. They may seem domineering, but they are lionhearted. However, she felt her daughter needed to be prepared. Her naivety could cost her dearly; Rukmini could take over the reins of the household. The Diwan's wife was still alive, no doubt. But she didn't matter. The women of the household would do what the Diwan asked of them.

The mother and daughter sat down on a cot. Ishradeyi let some time pass before she started asking her probing questions.

'How many servants and attendants are there in the house, Pushpa?'

The girl smiled. 'There's Misarji. He is a tall, tall man. So tall, Ma, that you won't believe it. He washes the kitchen day and night, and doesn't let anyone enter. Every day, five dishes are cooked, no less. We eat from petite, shiny bowls.'

She carried on, 'There's an attendant who serves only Diwanji. He refills his hookah, massages his feet, and he sits behind Diwanji and fans him.'

Ishradeyi was listening carefully. 'You should serve Diwanji his meals,' she said.

Pushpa's face turned crimson at this suggestion. 'I feel shy.'

'Shy? What's there to be shy about?'

Ishradeyi, who, just a few days ago, had been fervently praying for the well-being of her daughter, knew it was time to train her. She bent towards her daughter and whispered into her ear, 'If you don't, then that witch will.'

Pushpa strained her eyes to bring her mother's face into focus. Her mother was talking to her in the manner in which she'd seen her talk to other grown women of the neighbourhood—sitting close, whispering, lips curling, eyes enlarging, hands moving rapidly, finger pressed on chin, eyeballs rolling.

'Who keeps the keys in the mansion? Diwanji?'

'How should I know, Ma!'

'You should try to have them handed to you soon. You're the elder daughter-in-law.'

'What am I going to do with the keys, Ma?'

'If you don't get them, that witch will.'

Ishradeyi held her daughter's wrist and whispered, 'Look around the house and become well versed with what's kept where. You're not a little girl any more; you're the daughter-in-law of the mansion. You should claim what's rightfully yours.'

Pushpa noticed that her mother curled her lips whenever she spoke about Rukmini, whispered whenever she talked about the elder Diwan, and wrinkled her nose and made emphatic gestures with her hands when she talked about her brother-in-law, Kalle.

She had given her ample advice while preparing her for her wedding as well: Keep your eyes lowered to the ground, women shouldn't be bold. Keep your head covered and never answer back. Make it a habit to go to both your father-in-law's and mother-in-law's rooms every morning with your head covered, and take their blessings. But the advice she was receiving from her mother now felt different and of a kind that Pushpa couldn't quite follow.

The wedding had already changed so much. Pushpa had had to deal with new sensations and experiences. Misarji, the mansion's incredibly tall cook, was enchanting. But there were so many attendants and servants that it was confusing. And the house itself was entirely new and unfamiliar. It seemed to her that there were an infinite number of rooms in the mansion, each one more enormous than the last, and all of them unoccupied. And once the wedding celebrations ended and the relatives left, a deep silence pervaded the mansion. Her thoughts felt muddled. It was a feeling she still hadn't been able to shake off.

The palanquins carrying the brides had arrived at the mansion together with great fanfare. But once they reached the mansion, they were led into separate rooms. Pushpa found herself surrounded by lots of women when she stepped out of her palanquin. She wanted to shrink into herself and disappear. Almost immediately, the women started showering her with coins. Amidst everything else that had only confused her, she found the sound of coins falling into her lap, and on to one another, pleasing. One by one, the women stepped forward and lifted the veil that covered her face. Each woman had a comment.

'She's pretty, but Rukmo's prettier. One hesitates to touch Rukmo's creamy white skin, lest one's fingers stain it.'

'Well, at least Kalle got married on account of this one. Diwanji was only worried for Kalle.'

'What audacity—they said they wouldn't marry their daughters into this house. They swallowed their words, didn't they?'

'They had to. Diwanji would've made them drink water out of his shoes.'

'Your father put up such airs. That didn't last, did it?'

A stream of faces, the movement of lips, fingers touching her chin, the breath of many women on her face and the odour of many bodies together in one room—that's how Pushpa's first day at the mansion began and ended.

Leaping to gather coins that were being showered to celebrate the brides' homecoming, children had followed the wedding procession right up to the gate of the mansion.

It was a small procession. At the head, Kalle walked alongside the palanquin that carried his bride. The ends of his and Rukmini's dupattas had been tied together. His face was pale and drenched in sweat. His eyes were almost half closed with the exertion of the walk, and his turban had slipped down from his head on to his forehead and come undone. But he was clearly delighted. Balmukund was carrying the bag of coins. After every few steps, he would dip into the bag, extract a fistful of coins and throw them over the palanquins, into the air. He walked beside Kalle, so he could support him at all times.

The palanquin carrying the other bride followed closely. But no one seemed to pay it—or the younger son—any attention. Everyone's attention was focused on Kalle.

The Diwan's open palanquin was at the other end of the procession. The Diwan was dressed grandly and lost in some deep thought. There was no way of knowing what he was thinking, but surely, when an important man knits his brows, it means he's thinking over something significant. A rich man's thoughts are never ordinary. Every twitch on his face is a reflection of his importance. Ordinary people can never understand the richness of a rich man's mind.

Once the procession reached the mansion's gate, the baraatis took their leave. The palanquins were led into the mansion under the purohit's able guidance.

As soon as they entered the mansion, the brides were taken to meet and be introduced to the women of the family and the neighbourhood. The women showered the brides with coins as a blessing in exchange for a glimpse of their faces. They also made observations and passed comments.

When someone said the elder Diwan's wife was coming by, the women were surprised. Conversations turned to a murmur; a muffled silence took over the immense room. It was as if everyone thought it odd that the lady Diwan should come this way. Pushpa sensed the tension and became curious. She lifted her veil and looked in the direction from which the Diwanee's entrance was anticipated. She saw an old, bent-over woman come in. She walked slowly, with the support of a stick. She had a dark, broad face. A tuft of white hair hung over her forehead. She seemed to be muttering silently to herself.

Women continued to talk in hushed tones even after she had come near.

'We're blessed that you've come here. Welcome, Diwaneeji; come meet your brides.' The old woman's face remained expressionless; only her lips moved. Pushpa felt frightened at the sight of her. She didn't seem at all like the lady of the mansion. In fact, it seemed as if she had emerged from a dark, dark room after a long, long time.

'Who was she, Ma?' Pushpa asked Ishradeyi.

'Your mother-in-law. Who else would it be? The elder Diwaneeji.'

'She neither spoke, nor smiled. I thought she was a mad woman.'

'You don't know about her. She's the wife of the elder Diwan. But the Diwan never settled with her.'

Pushpa didn't follow.

'He's had nothing to do with her for a long time now. He had a wall constructed in the mansion and separated himself from her. She lives on one side and he lives on the other side of the wall.' But Ishradeyi felt this wasn't the right time to be talking about such things. Changing the tone of the conversation, she said, 'She must've come over to this side of the mansion because it had been blessed by your arrival. What did she give you?'

'She did drop something in my lap, but I can't remember what it was.'

'That's not right, Pushpa. You're a householder now. You must stay attentive in the mansion.'

'She was really very old, Ma!'

'The Diwan left her a long time ago. Raising a wall in the mansion to separate himself from her was almost the first thing he did after being granted land by the administration and taking over the mansion.'

Ishradeyi hesitated again. Now may not have been the time to be talking about such things, but Ishradeyi couldn't help herself. 'Listen, Pushpa, my child,' she added quickly, 'if you act wisely, you'll be the lady of the mansion one day. But if you don't proceed intelligently, the mansion will swallow you up.'

Her mother's cryptic words made Pushpa anxious.

'Maintain distance from Rukmini!' Ishradeyi gave her daughter her first instruction as a married woman. 'You must—slowly, but with sure steps—exercise your control over the mansion. Look out for yourself. Rukmini is merely the granddaughter of that halfpenny of a man, Harnarayan. He's a low-caste. Rukmini ended up getting married into the mansion only because the Diwanji was desperate for a bride for Kalle.'

Placing her hand on her daughter's back she asked, 'Do you spend time with Rukmo?'

Pushpa was in a dilemma. She wasn't sure if she should tell her mother the truth. What if her mother didn't like it? Then she said softly, 'Yes. She comes to my room, and we play together.'

'Do you also go to her room?'

'Sometimes, Ma.'

'Your days of playing childhood games are over!' Ishradeyi scolded her daughter. 'Now you have to manage your home. That's a big responsibility.' Then, placing her hand on her daughter's knee, she tried explaining, 'It's not a bad thing that you go to Rukmo's room. Do that sometimes. If you spend time with her, you'll know what's going on with her. You don't even have to probe; generally people open up and start talking about themselves if you spend time with them.'

Pushpa felt a weight lift from her heart.

'Is it also all right if I play with her a little?'

'Why not. But don't tell your husband that you're spending time with her.' Then gripped by another doubt she asked, 'Has Rukmo ever come to your room when your husband is around?'

'Yes, Ma! She comes whenever I call her.' Pushpa laughed a merry laugh. 'Yesterday, the two of us were playing when "he" teasingly pulled Rukmo's dupatta off her head.'

Ishradeyi's hand froze on Pushpa's back. Pushpa looked up. Her mother's lips were in a grimace, her eyes seemed to have become double their size and she was biting her tongue.

'You're going to ruin yourself!'

All kinds of new doubts had planted themselves in Ishradeyi's mind. The signs boded terrible things. She had to caution her daughter.

Once again, Pushpa couldn't understand what her mother was saying. Her mother was angry with her, and this frightened her. But she couldn't understand what she was doing wrong. The image she had of marriage was one that began and ended with the wedding, in which there was bridal finery and sparkling jewellery. She was at a loss to understand the instructions her mother seemed bent upon giving her.

'Tend to your husband carefully; look after him. Men are simple-minded; they are fools. They have to be trained. You must throw tantrums and make demands of him. A woman can get a lot out of a man that way. And be sure to look after your father-in-law as well.'

Listening to her mother's words, a girl was turning into a woman, a wife. Pushpa was getting a sense of her new role. Her mother's words were guiding her.

Watching her mother intently, Pushpa felt that she must also behave as her mother does. She watched how her mother pressed and curled her lips when she spoke, how she lowered her voice when she was saying something in confidence. She felt her eyes should spread wide when she talked about something important, just like her mother's did. Pushpa was too young to discern the good from the bad herself; her mother's instructions were the ultimate truth for her.

Pushpa felt more self-assured as the sense of her new role slowly seeped into her. She offered information, without being probed. 'He has lots of friends,' she said. 'They all come over in the afternoons. They get together and play all kinds of pranks. One of them is Mukund; he's very fat.' She laughed. 'They duck behind a wall and throw pebbles into Rukmini's courtyard. Mukund starts it, but everyone joins in.'

Once again, Ishradeyi felt alarmed.

'Your husband as well?'

'They all do it. But, Ma, it's not right, is it?'

Her mother surprised her again. 'Let them do what they want,' she said. 'Let's not waste time talking about that pauper.'

By the time Pushpa left her mother's house late that afternoon, she was filled with a nervous energy. She was married; she had responsibilities. She was a woman now, with a household to run, like her mother. She had things she must do, openly and obliquely. She had to take charge of the servants. She would keep the mansion's keys tied to the end of her dupatta. She must stay alert at all times. She would meet Rukmo so she'd know things about her, and yet maintain a distance from her. She had to take control of the reins of the house. She had to win over and tame her husband. She had to find out which people the Diwan trusted and listened to most, and who came to meet him. She had so many responsibilities, there was going to be no time to play games. She was not a child any more; she was becoming a woman.

~

Rukmini walked from corridor to corridor, from one room into another. The mansion was enormous, there were so many passages to walk about in, and the things its rooms contained! It was like a city, every street opening into another. She had walked and walked and still she couldn't keep track of where she'd started from and how she'd reached where she was. She wanted to explore all of the mansion's nooks and crannies, but its expanse seemed to have no end. She missed her mother, but the mansion enchanted her.

Today Rukmo was climbing the stairs to explore the mansion's upper storey. Her own place was on the ground floor—two huge rooms, with a large courtyard in front. There was a neem tree in the courtyard. It amazed her that a house could have a tree growing within it. That she had been married to someone who was unwell, or that the wedding had been staged—these thoughts never crossed her mind. Once she overcame her alarm at the suddenness of what had happened, her heart craved distractions. The neem tree called her to climb up its branches. That there be a tree and Rukmo not climb it—impossible! Her friend's mother didn't call her a kitten for nothing, after all. She was also called a doe, because for as long as anyone could remember, they'd only seen Rukmo dart about like one. Not only in the lanes, Rukmo was never still even when she was at home. 'Find me, Ma!' She'd hide behind the door or one of the trunks that also served as furniture, or duck under the cot, and call out to her mother. It was a small house with few things, but her mother always pretended she couldn't find her. Rukmo would laugh and run out from wherever she had been hiding.

It was chance that had brought her to Malik Mansaram's house the night of the wedding. She was playing with other girls her age, busy being mischievous. When the groom had reached the entrance to the house, a group of girls stopped him, 'You can't go in. Entry not allowed.' Little Rukmo was among them, chanting, 'Don't let him in! Don't let him in! He has to take his shoes off first.' In her excitement she was able to handle neither the betel leaf she was chewing, nor her green dupatta—her chin had become stained with the juice of the betel leaf and the dupatta kept slipping off her head.

Flaming torches had been set up along the walls to light the house. Their flickering light danced on the faces of the girls and reflected off the stars their dupattas were studded with. The girls were in no mood to relent. 'Take off your shoes; take off your shoes,' they chanted. Rukmo participated with gusto; she almost looked like she was leading the gang.

And then, when the groom took his shoes off, it was little Rukmo who leapt at them and ran off to hide them. 'Did you bring a ring for me? Only a silver ring will do if you want your shoes back,' the bride's younger sister stretched out the palm of her hand and asked the groom. Rukmo had returned by now. 'Did you bring a ring for me? Give me a ring if you want your shoes,' she repeated what she heard, not one to be left out. When the bride arrived, led by three of her close friends, and was sat down by the groom, Rukmo slid up behind them and tied the red thread braided through the bride's hair with the loose end of the groom's turban.

Rukmo was climbing the stairs to explore the mansion's upper storey. It was a long climb; she stopped to catch her breath when she reached the top.

The corridor that stretched out from the staircase was long and chock-full of furniture. What an endless, soundless corridor. Rukmo peered into it, tense. She thought about turning around and going back. A few tall, stained glass windows shone with the bright daylight outside. *What place is this, as dark as an evening?* She took a few slow footsteps forward.

Huge wooden chests, a settee, a broken bedstead, a heap of clothes—it was a haphazard place, overflowing with old things.

She saw a tall door to her right; it was slightly ajar. She stopped, hesitated, but then slowly pushed the door open. *What place is this; what am I doing here?*

She took a step forward, into the room. A thick layer of dust, settled over years, covered the floor. The door was behind her; she turned around to face it. The skylight was thick with cobwebs. They had taken over the walls and the ceiling.

She turned again towards the room. *Who is that?* Blood dried in her veins; her heart pounded. There was a man in the room, just a few steps away from her. And despite the darkness, she could tell he was a very tall man.

Who is he? Why did I come here? She took a step back, and turned to run. But then she stopped and turned for a last glance. The man was standing in the exact same place, in exactly the same position as when she'd first set eyes on him. The man was old, and as still as a statue. A white turban was wrapped around his head, and the embroidery at the edges of his angrakha was exquisite. He was watching Rukmini with unblinking eyes.

She was surprised at how still he was. But now she could make out the four golden lines that framed him, and she realized her mistake. *This is no man; it's a painting. A life-sized portrait.* But it looked real; *he* seemed real. Rukmini felt arrested by his gaze; she couldn't move.

Her eyes had begun adjusting to the darkness of the room. Encouraged, she took a few steps forward towards the painting. It was a lovely portrait. The man had large eyes and a thick moustache, the ends of which were turned up. Was it the elder Diwan? *But the Diwan has a beard and it's stained red with henna. And the Diwan's a thin man, and not as tall as the man in the painting. Maybe the painting was made some time ago, when the Diwan looked like that. But if it's his portrait, why should it be lying here? Why leave it in a room, among old things?*

Rukmini wanted to examine the painting from up close, but she was still hesitant to go too near it. The terror she'd felt just a few moments ago hadn't entirely left her body.

It must be the portrait of some ancestor. Rukmini mustered up the courage to take another few steps forward. She realized that whichever position she had seen the painting from until now, it always seemed like the man's eyes were upon her. She took three steps to the right. The man was still looking directly at her. She took five steps to the left. It was the same—the man looked at her constantly.

Rukmo's face broke into a smile. Fear had slowly been ebbing from her body. *I'd become needlessly frightened.*

She turned her attention to the rest of the room.

She saw a large chest on the right. The lid was closed and a few pairs of footwear lay on top of it. They were embroidered with gold thread, but the gold had turned black with time. *Whose joote are these?* The man in the painting had gold-embroidered joote on his feet. *Could they belong to him?*

An old carpet was spread out beneath the painting. *It's become worn from how much the man in the painting has walked on it.*

There was another chest in the room. A horse's saddle lay on top of it. *This is what the man in the painting saddled his horse with each time he went riding.* A red muslin saddlecloth was spread underneath it. A deep green gown lay next to the saddle, one arm hanging down over the chest. The gown too was beautifully embroidered with gold thread.

Pile upon pile of account books lay by a wall, and a long sword hung in its sheath. Elsewhere, there was a huge heap of clothes on the floor. And by it stood a small, low stool made of ivory. A cup, a container for water from the Ganga and a rosary made of *rudraksh* beads lay on it. The rosary hung down over the edge of the stool. A number of wooden settees, bolster cushions and old-style beds with carved legs lay here and there. It was as if things from an entire household had been hurriedly dumped here. They belonged to another time. They seemed lifeless now, but they would've witnessed the vitality of a time that had passed. Rukmini was engrossed.

She heard a noise in the room and turned around. The Diwan's attendant, his shoulders bent with age, was standing by the door. He was smiling a gentle smile. 'I see, so this is where our little bride has come exploring,' he said with great warmth. Rukmini was unused to hearing an elderly person speak so freely and warmly. Her grandfather never spoke with her this way. He usually kept to himself, always busy with his prayer books. And when he spoke, it was mostly to her mother, and he always took a preachy tone with her.

'I've been looking for you everywhere. I just couldn't find you. I knew you had to be in the mansion somewhere. I kept thinking, she's so little. She couldn't have scaled the mansion's high walls and gone off somewhere. And she's not a bird! She couldn't have flown off.' His lips widened into a smile. His eyes twinkling, he walked into the room.

'Who is that?' Rukmo asked, pointing towards the man in the painting.

The attendant came and stood next to her and looked at her with great warmth. 'It's the late Diwanji. He was the elder Diwanji's father's older brother.'

'But why is his painting here, like this? There are just old things in this room,' Rukmo asked.

The old attendant shook his head for a long time before he spoke. 'Time, young lady, moves in mysterious ways. He was the lord of this mansion at one time. It was his father who had got the mansion constructed. Do you see his fur coat? It's from Kabul. They wear coats like this there. He was a high official in Kabul for a long time. The high offices of the Lahore Durbar had deputed him there. I had come to the mansion to serve him. I was very young then, younger even than you are today.' He started laughing at the memory. His eyes laughed with him. 'Come, let me show you all the things here that are from Kabul,' he said, happy at a chance to reminisce. It was as if the occasion had presented itself after a long, long time.

He led her to the other side of the painting. 'This is a samovar; it's made of brass,' he showed her. 'It's used for making *kahwa*. And this one's made of iron.' Then he started explaining what kahwa is and how it's prepared. It was as if he was the one who used to make and serve this special tea to the late Diwan. He unrolled a small rug that was lying near one of the samovars. It was worn, even threadbare in places. 'The late Diwan used to sit on this and drink his kahwa. No one had ever tasted kahwa before he brought it here. He was the first person here ever to have had kahwa. All the things here belong to him,' he said, the sweep of his arm gesturing he meant everything on this floor. 'But they've all been lying here for years now. Time moves in mysterious ways. There was a time when we used to carefully dust and clean every single object. Not a speck of dust. The late Diwan used to bring things from his travels as gifts for his wife, the lady of the mansion.'

Rukmo felt a tinge of excitement at the mention of the lady of the mansion. She knew of her; her grandfather had told her stories about her, and now she was standing inside one of those stories. All these things, buried under layers of dust, were stirring to life right in front of her. It was as if all those voices that had been so distant from her in time and place had come close.

'Time moves in mysterious ways,' the old man repeated. 'There was such plenitude. On every festival, the lady of the mansion would distribute clothes and things among the poor. Long queues would form at the mansion's gate. She was a kind and God-fearing woman.'

The old man let the stories flow.

'She was getting a pond constructed when the war started. If it were not for the war, the people of this town would have had a pond today to bathe in. Let me show you the pond.'

He led Rukmo to one of the windows whose glass panes were broken. 'Look from here,' he said. 'Can you see it?'

Rukmo couldn't see any pond. All there was, was a small, uneven portion of land with a huge pit in the middle. 'There's nothing here,' she said, still peeping out through the broken glass. 'It's just land.'

'That's where the pond was being constructed. Do you see the pit? And do you see those cuts along the edges? Those were to be the steps that would lead into the pond. Had it been completed, it would have been as big as a lake. But the lady's desire remained unfulfilled.'

Rukmo was finding it difficult to imagine a pond where all she could see was dug-up earth.

'Work was in full swing when drums announced the start of war. I was helping out as well that day, loading baskets full of earth on to a donkey and dumping it on that mound. But war was declared, and work stopped. The pond never got made.'

'Why?'

'Because the war started. I can still see in my mind's eye how the late Diwan rushed towards the Palace of Mirrors. It was such a difficult night, the entire town stayed awake. It was just like when robbers used to attack, beating their drums and clanging the plates, driving their mules on, robbing homes, causing mayhem. People ran here and there. I remember everything . . .'

Rukmo had heard about that time from her grandfather. He too would have joined the war, but her grandmother hadn't let him. Rukmo knew many names from his stories—Manohar, Pishauri, Dayaram, Lekhraj. They were her grandfather's friends, and none of them had returned from the war. Her grandfather said Lekhraj was still alive, but he had never come back. For Rukmini, all these people had been nothing more than shadows in the twilight of the past. Coming to this room and being surrounded by things that were from that time tugged at her in a strange way.

'Time moves in mysterious ways,' the Diwan's old attendant intoned again.

So then this is what past looks like! Broken furniture, a pile of old clothes, a sword suspended on a wall, threadbare carpets, a cover of dust over everything, cobwebs dangling from ceilings, broken windowpanes in which pigeons perch and coo and cover the floor with excrement, its smell saturating the air so breathing feels laboured. Is this what's called the past?

'These clothes belonged to the lady of the mansion.' The old man had opened a long, narrow chest. Rukmini peered inside. She saw a light yellow kurta. It had a string of small silver buttons attached to it. A richly embroidered shawl lay next to it. The kurta and the shawl were both neatly folded. *It's as if they'd been readied for a journey, but then left behind.* For some reason, Rukmini was convinced the lady had gone on a journey. She also seemed to have left her prayer beads on the teapoy, by the chest. *Why would she leave for her journey without her prayer beads? And her footwear too!* There was a pair of joote right beside the trunk. Rukmini felt curious about the people whose things she was seeing. In her mind's eye, she pictured the late Diwan rushing towards the Palace of Mirrors, a walking stick in hand, and his wife seated on a low stool, her head covered, counting her prayer beads . . .

'The Diwanji,' the old attendant whispered secretively, 'the current Diwan, I mean. The late Diwan kicked him out of the mansion one day. This happened a long time ago.'

'Why?' Rukmo asked, her eyes widening with disbelief.

'Big people have big secrets,' the old man said. 'He had all his things thrown out of the mansion. I saw it with my own eyes.'

Rukmo couldn't imagine how anyone could treat the Diwanji that way.

'Diwanji was his younger brother's son. Now God only knows what the story was, but I saw what I saw. All his things were lying on the street. And he—he was a lean, young man then—he was standing on the street and shouting, "I will return to the mansion one day. I'm not a Diwan if I don't."'

Rukmini felt a tremor run through her body.

'And he did return to the mansion, little bride, but only after many years,' the old man continued, unaware that the story was frightening her. 'And the day he returned, he started throwing all of his uncle's things out on to the street. It was only because the elders of the clan pleaded with him and cajoled him that he stopped. But he had all of the Diwan's possessions shifted to this floor.'

Rukmini could hardly make sense of the things she was hearing. All she felt was sadness.

It was as if some broken remnants of the past were getting washed up with the currents of time. They were neither cohering into a whole, nor were they complete in and of themselves. Some pieces could be made sensible by attaching them to a name, a person or an incident. But most of them simply flowed past, or drowned in the vortex of time before they could make it ashore.

What significance, what meaning could these pieces, these residual fragments possibly hold for Rukmo?

Standing with her in this dusty, forgotten room, the Diwan's old attendant was trying to join a few pieces here and there, to weave a context. But they weren't joining into any precise form. There were moments when a faint image would flicker to life before Rukmo, but it would quickly vanish from her view again, to go back into hiding amidst all the other shadows that inhabited the space she knew of as the past.

'Who knows, maybe if Lekhraj had returned, he would have been the lord of the mansion today.' The old attendant was a sentimental and talkative man. Rukmo was trying to make out what he may have looked like in his younger years, but his white hair and toothless mouth made it difficult for her to conjure up that image. He seemed bent upon telling Rukmo stories, like one who'd kept himself bottled up for a long time and had now finally found an occasion to let his heart sing.

'War drums were beating. The *firangi* army was approaching. People crowded outside the Palace of Mirrors. They huddled in groups outside Grain Market all night. All eyes searched the western horizon expectantly for the arrival of a messenger with news from the battlefield. The town stayed in turmoil the entire night. People told each other the things they'd heard. I too heard and saw so much, little bride.'

And then, out of the blue, the old attendant broke into song. His voice was shaky and unsteady; the song he sang was an old one. Quite possibly, it was a song that every tongue sang in those difficult days. Rukmo was taken by surprise. But slowly, she became engrossed. It was as if the old man was singing not from his mouth, but with his entire body.

> *A true warrior is he*
> *A true warrior is he*
> *He who fights to defend the faith*
> *A true warrior is he . . .*

His feet danced to the beat of the tune he was singing. He spun about and he acted out the song—he was a warrior wielding a sword one moment, a spear the next moment.

> *He may get cut into pieces*
> *He may get cut into pieces*
> *But he doesn't leave the battlefield*
> *A true warrior is he . . .*

His feeble chest swelling, he threw his arms up in the air and his singing reached a crescendo.

> *When the sky resounds with battle drums*
> *When the sky resounds with battle drums*
> *He takes aim and hits his mark*
> *A true warrior is he . . .*

He was breathless by the time he reached the last verse of the song, and drops of perspiration gathered on his forehead.

> *Know him to be a true warrior*
> *Know him to be a true warrior*
> *Who fights to defend the faith*
> *A true warrior is he . . .*

The old man's voice was hoarse by the time the song ended. He struggled to catch his breath, yet his gaze on Rukmo was steady, and he was smiling.

'Little bride,' he said, 'we used to sing this song all the time. In those days, everyone did. Manohar, Lekhraj, Ramsingh, Pishauri—they roamed the streets all day, singing. They were singing this same song when they left for Lahore. You know where the railway station is today? There were no trains then. There was a road there, which led to Lahore. They took that road and left for Lahore . . .'

Rukmo looked at the old attendant, her eyes filled with curiosity and excitement. She had grown up in a house where silence reigned, and she had never ever seen a man such as him in her entire life. The mansion too was always quiet. But this man! He sang and danced. What an unusual man!

Rukmo realized someone was standing at the door. She looked, and saw it was her husband, Kalle. Taken by surprise, she started towards him immediately. His clothes were dishevelled, his mouth was half open and his breathing was uneven. He must have been searching for her for long. Rukmo felt bad.

Kalle stood at the door, a slight smile playing on his lips. His face was pale and he was sweating. Saliva dribbled to his shoulder. But his eyes had lit up with the joy of having found Rukmo.

BOOK TWO

BOOK TWO

The town, emerging through the ages since medieval times, gathered innumerable relics of history, becoming resplendent with memories, tales and legends. The mansion was at least a hundred years old. Its history has dissolved into the mist of the past, but the stories continue to circulate in town to this day.

The mansion's appearance changed with changes in who ruled the land. The high gate through which one enters it, the narrow balcony over it, and the majestic canopy over its upper storey go back to the times when the Sikhs ruled. Quite possibly, they draw inspiration from even further back, from the Mughal times. The stained glass on its windows and skylights—green, yellow, red and blue—signal the time when the British ruled. Some of its doors still have traces of medieval carving, but most were replaced with plain, flat doors during the British rule, in keeping with prevalent tastes.

Tracing the lives of the people who inhabited the mansion too is like making a journey through time—every person played his or her part, each in his or her own way and according to the times in which they lived, before the chapter of time turned and someone new entered the stage.

In the beginning, the mansion was a simple, single-storeyed house. It is said a man named Mathraadas built it. He was a *kardar*, a revenue official of the Sikh Empire. He came to be a well-respected man. As kardar, he was responsible for settling property disputes, and earned a reputation for being fair and just. This was long before the Sikh wars. Once, during his tenure, there was a severe drought, and a famine was portended. To avert the looming disaster, Diwan Mathraadas went all out to raise money, and put in a lot of his own money as well, to buy grain for the town. His wife prayed for the famine to not break out, and vowed that if her prayers were answered, she would have a pond constructed on part of the family land. But an epidemic broke out, and Diwan Mathraadas passed away.

Diwan Mathraadas was succeeded by his son Mayyadas. With due consideration for the services rendered by his father, the Khalsa Durbar appointed Mayyadas as the new kardar. Mayyadas had inherited many of his father's praiseworthy qualities, and proved himself to be a capable officer. In recognition of his services, and as a reward for his honesty, diligence and amicable nature, the Lahore Durbar sent for him and appointed him as an officer in the treasury of Lahore. He soon found further favour with the administration, and was promoted further and sent to Kabul as a high-ranking official. His fame spread. He gained prestige not only in his own town, but also in the entire region. The mansion was transformed by the riches that flowed into it during Diwan Mayyadas's time in Kabul.

The Diwan's abode began to reflect the prosperity of its inhabitants. Another floor was added. Ornamental merlons—the kind one sees in the havelis of nawabs—were built all along its roof. A sandstone canopy was constructed on the roof, right in its centre, in line with the mansion's gate. The mansion also became a bearer of signs that signified the majesty of the Khalsa rule. That's why an elephant was always stationed in front of the mansion. Whenever Diwan Mayyadas returned from Kabul, he would ride on the elephant to the Palace of Mirrors, to meet the regional king.

Diwan Mayyadas was a polite, unassuming man. He had accepted his appointment in Kabul with humility. He was grateful, and his gratitude strengthened his loyalty to the Khalsa court. But he was also aware of the high post he now occupied, and it showed in little ways, like how he started curling up his moustache, in the tone of authority he adopted in his voice, and in how he walked—his back erect, his shoulders pulled back. He also stopped moving about town on foot, and started riding a horse instead. However, he maintained certain continuities as well, such as in his family occupation, moneylending. He also continued looking after his ancestral property. Over time, the town acknowledged his position as the main Diwan, and he began to be called the elder Diwan. Soon, he outshone even the local king.

Mayyadas's wife, Devki, was a pious woman. Her hands always seemed to be either joined in prayer or busy giving away charity. She went to gurdwaras as well as to temples. Every time Mayyadas was promoted, she embarked on a pilgrimage; it would be Katasraj on one occasion and Amarnath on another. She kept the mansion gates open for roaming mendicants. Whenever holy men stopped on the hillock to meditate, Devki would get into a palanquin to go pay her respects.

When Mayyadas was appointed officer in the treasury of Lahore, Devki wanted to do a good deed that would match the scale of this new transformation in their lives. The work that her mother-in-law had conceived—getting the pond made—could be it. However, Mayyadas got busy with his responsibilities in Lahore, spending more and more time there, and the construction work couldn't be started. But when Mayyadas was further promoted and sent to Kabul, she became worried. She believed there was such a thing as too much fame. Afraid that it would attract the wrath of God, she decided to take charge of getting the pond constructed herself. And so, while Diwan Mayyadas left for Kabul, she stayed behind.

Under her supervision, the land adjoining the mansion began to be hollowed out for the pond. Walls lining the edges of the pond had begun to be built and work on stairs that would lead into the pond from all four sides had started. But then, news—both good and bad—started trickling in from the faraway Khalsa Durbar. Construction work was suspended yet again; the pond stayed in its unfinished state for decades. Though it was unfinished, the town had already given the pond a name. It had begun to be referred to as Mother Devki's Pond, and it lingered in the town's imagination for years—even up until when the land was auctioned during the British rule.

Seen from the perspective of history, during this time, the town was like an island in a calm sea, where life unfolded at an even, rhythmic pace. It wasn't a prosperous town, but neither was it in need. Then, without warning, the tides turned and storms raged, and life was thrown into turbulence. It's possible this view is one borne of hindsight—and that we only *think* a pocket of life enjoyed a serene harmony before it was struck by a storm. Or maybe our eyes perceive the past sentimentally, and this makes it seem attractive. For, when is life not incongruous? Forces always exist, and they exert their power, making the wheels of change turn. Sometimes though, forces—large, powerful forces—lash a place, overwhelming individual attachments and despairs, superseding them. They grip life, and steer it.

The evenness of life in this town wasn't only because of the relations people created with one another, but was also based on the values and ideals of the Sikh administration. People are people, and their attachments and despairs do determine the contours of life. But they also inhabit a milieu. The values and ideals of the milieu pervade the air; they affect life; lives draw inspiration from them. The establishment of the Khalsa rule had been animated by certain values and ideals. Power had not corroded them; they had not disintegrated or diminished through repetition. They still guided the acts of people—they evoked generosity, goodwill and sacrifice in the hearts of ordinary people, inspired extraordinary behaviour, and restrained the rule that attachment and despair can exert over life.

Kabul was hit by turbulence. It was the beginning of Mayyadas's misfortunes. It wasn't that the turbulence diminished his influence, but the very ground on which the Khalsa Durbar stood shifted. People fled from Kabul. Mayyadas too had to leave. He returned to Lahore, from where he left to visit his family for a few days. The day he reached home, his son, by now a young man, died. It was monsoon; the river had surged, broken its banks and spilled into town. This happened sometimes. The river would recede after a few days, but it would leave the lanes filled with water, causing an outbreak of malaria. Mayyadas's young son had died after a fever of just three days.

Mayyadas, followed by his retinue, had ridden on his horse through Grain Market, crossed Kabuli Darwaza and entered Sethi Street when a grief-stricken howl reached him. It came from the mansion.

Mayyadas had only one grown-up son, and he'd recently begun overseeing the family's moneylending business. His death was a bolt of lightning. Mayyadas bore the blow, but his heart was broken. People say his hair turned grey in a month, his back became bent and his face was covered with wrinkles. Compared to him, his wife, who'd done all she could to save her son, maintained equanimity. She'd nestled her son's head in her lap during his last moments. When he died, she didn't cry. She simply continued to softly recite the Sat Guru's name. Even in the days that followed, she never shed a tear. Women from the neighbourhood would gather in the mansion and express their grief. Whether they cried or beat their chest, Devki sat quietly, her hands folded before her in acknowledgement and thanks. Only her lips moved, remembering the Sat Guru. She maintained a calm veneer. The death and the grief of the family were discussed all across town for a long time. Over the years, it became part of shared memory. In it, the boy's mother sometimes appeared as a demoness, sometimes as a goddess. But there was no denying that in the days following her son's death, her face had a glow, her eyes seemed always bowed before an immense power, and her lips moved without rest, in prayer.

Mayyadas had a younger brother, Gokuldas, who helped him with the moneylending business. When Mayyadas's influence increased with his promotions, Gokuldas got appointed as kardar of the town, and thus followed in his brother's footsteps, playing the role of a revenue officer and taking care of the family business. He set up his offices where he conducted hearings as kardar on one side, and oversaw the moneylending business from a cushioned seat and table on the other side of the mansion's courtyard.

Gokuldas had three daughters. A son was eventually born to him, but that was much later and amidst a huge uproar.

Anyway, at first, the lack of an heir didn't affect his relationship with his brother and neither did it affect his work. But when luck began to favour Mayyadas, and as the mansion started filling with the wealth that came from his high administrative posts, Gokuldas started wishing he too had a son. Soon, he became possessed by this desire; his demeanour changed. Like his brother, he'd always been a calm and polite man. So much so that people would say the brothers were like Ram and Lakshman. But after a third daughter was born to him, Gokuldas became distraught. He sent his wife and daughters away to his in-laws' and didn't ask after them for years.

Gokuldas and Mayyadas's mother was still alive then. The old woman would press upon Gokuldas that she would get him a second wife if a son wasn't born to him. This was the same woman who would gather together children in the neighbourhood and tell them grandmothers' tales, for she knew innumerable stories, and her voice was melodious. She even made inquiries in the neighbourhood for her son, but Gokuldas never paid heed to the marriage proposals she brought for him. And then, he did something unexpected after his brother left for Lahore: he left for a tour for revenue collection and came back with a mistress. The town was stunned. Some speculated she was from Lahore; others thought he had picked her up from somewhere in Jhelum. The Diwans prided themselves in always behaving honourably. When Mayyadas heard about his brother's doing, he was ashamed. It also occurred to him that complications were now bound to arise around the mansion, their land and their inheritance. But with the rise in his stature and responsibilities, the problems around his family receded from his mind. He thought, whatever happens, we'll deal with it. He was immersed in his own world. This was a time when he hadn't yet been posted to Kabul and had been recently appointed to the treasury in Lahore.

Once the woman arrived in the mansion, she stayed. The town continued to speculate. No one even knew if she was mistress or wife.

Then, just as she had arrived, she left. She'd stayed in the mansion for some two and a half or three years. She was pregnant when she left. Mayyadas's son was young then. That was a time when many relatives and their families lived in the mansion. There were umpteen children, and they played and ran about in the mansion with him. The children were curious about this 'new mother'. They would lie in wait for her bedroom door to open, so they could catch a glimpse of her. Even years later, the children remembered how, after the mistress arrived, Uncle Gokuldas used to stay in his room a lot, and always with the door closed. This 'new mother' had a voluptuous body, large eyes and full, set lips. She never covered her shoulders demurely and walked in a slow, languorous way, swaying her hips. She would step out from the room muttering *'phoo phoo'* to ward off the evil eye. She would wash her face, sprinkle water on her hair—the children always wondered why—and splash several palmfuls of water on her eyes. The latter fascinated them no end, and not only the children of the mansion, but also the neighbours' children tucked into corners and waited for her to emerge from the room, fill the small pitcher with water and wash herself several times a day.

Diwan Gokuldas continued work as usual. He held his daily court as the revenue official and rode through the fields to keep an eye on the family land, as before. But he made fewer social calls. There was one more pronounced change: he had started speaking with and exercising far more authority.

He had never shied from scolding the servants before, but now he sometimes also whipped them. Once, when an attendant didn't carry out his mistress's orders with the desired promptness, Gokuldas flogged him so severely, right there in the courtyard, that the skin peeled off from his back. Whenever Gokuldas became angry, a strange glint would descend into his eyes; they would become like the eyes of an eagle that had spotted its prey. He would lock his eyes on the object of his attention, as if piercing through it, and slowly the colour of his pupils would change. Anyone who saw him at such moments would say it was as if the younger Diwan's eyes were made of glass.

But in no time, his personality began to disintegrate. Irritability began to replace authority, and everyone saw it happening.

Around this time, one day, everyone heard loud shrieks from Gokuldas's room. It was a woman's voice. 'Help me. Someone help me. He's killing me.' It was the mistress.

It so happened that Diwan Mayyadas had returned from Lahore that day. He was sitting with his family in the courtyard that fronted his room, and was getting his luggage unpacked.

He wasn't the only one who heard the screams. Others in the mansion heard them too, and ran towards Gokuldas's room. But no one had the courage to ask that the door be opened.

Diwan Mayyadas had been stunned by the screams. But, not wanting to compromise his brother's position in the eyes of the servants, he kept a straight face and didn't rush to his brother's room in panic. He stood quietly for a bit, then picked up his stick and walked down to his brother's bedroom. The children trailed behind him.

Mayyadas first hit the end of his stick against the door and waited. 'Gokuldas, Gokuldas,' he called out. 'Open the door. It's me, Mayyadas!' But when the door still didn't open and the shrieking continued, he struck the door hard with his foot and forced it open. What he saw made his hair stand on end.

The mistress was lying spreadeagled on the floor, her arms and legs flailing desperately. Gokuldas was sitting on her chest. He had her brass pitcher in his hand and he was hitting her with it, on her head, again and again. The mistress's thick, black hair had come untied, her clothes were dishevelled and she was screaming, 'Help me, help me!'

Surprised that someone had entered the room, Gokuldas turned to look. His beady eyes locked the intruder's face in their gaze, like a target. For a moment it seemed he was about to throw the pitcher at whoever had entered his room. But he became confused. He couldn't understand where his brother had materialized from and how he could be here, in his room. But he realized the situation had become fragile. Slowly, the cruel glint left his eyes and he stood up, still holding the pitcher.

The elder Diwan stood in the centre of the room. The mistress gathered herself up, adjusting her clothes, wailing, her head in her hands.

With great dexterity, Diwan Mayyadas took control of the situation. He touched his brother's shoulder gently and said, 'Gokuldas, this is bound to happen if you bring someone as treacherous as her into your home. It's good that you now see the error of your ways. It's not too late. There's no need to feel ashamed.'

The younger Diwan was cut to the quick. This was clearly an insult, but he wasn't able to say or do anything. He simply put the pitcher on the floor, walked up to the wall where his turban was hanging, took it off the peg and put it on his head. It was as if he was saying that by placing his turban on his head, his dignity had been restored.

Meanwhile, the 'new mother' stood up. Diwan Mayyadas saw that her belly was swollen. The significance was not lost on him. The future that would follow from that which was as yet unborn flashed before his eyes. The mistress had covered her head and her face, as would be expected of a bride in front of an elder male of the household. Her hands still on her head, she walked slowly out of the room into the adjoining one.

She left the mansion that day. No one in the entire mansion knew where she'd gone and with whom. She didn't tell anyone, nor did she create a scene about leaving. The people of the mansion said the witch went back to where she'd come from after smearing the mansion's name.

The next day Gokuldas demanded that Mayyadas partition the mansion and give him his share. Mayyadas was taken aback and deeply saddened, but he didn't have a response. He did what his brother had demanded; he partitioned the mansion into two. It was true that the mansion had grown to its present form owing to the money Mayyadas had earned, but the mansion was ancestral property and both brothers had an equal claim to it. That is how a wall came to be erected inside the mansion for the first time.

One day, twenty years after this episode—by which time Mayyadas had returned from Kabul, the Sikh administration was dealing with one crisis after another, and Mayyadas had lost his young son—the son of this mistress, Chandra, appeared out of nowhere and demanded his share in the property.

Gokuldas had died ten years before this happened. He was returning from an official tour when he lost control of his horse. It's possible the horse knew the way home and started racing towards it. Gokuldas fell off the horse and died instantaneously.

The son of his mistress, Diwan Dhanpat, is the same man now known as the elder Diwan of the mansion.

The day Dhanpat first appeared before Mayyadas, it was in a strange, gaudy manner. He was wearing a yellow angrakha, and he had a saffron turban on his head and joote with gold embroidery on his feet. He was astride a mule, and followed by a handcart loaded with two chests full of his luggage and drawn along by two men. He halted in front of the mansion's gate. He had taken the long route through town so that everyone in town could take his personality in—via Grain Market and Oil Pressers' Neighbourhood. And sure enough, he attracted attention. The kids helped him along no doubt. At Grain Market, a few kids, taking him to be a miracle man, started trailing him. By the time he reached Kabuli Darwaza, he had a crowd of children behind him, all of them excited and making a ruckus, and they followed him all the way to the mansion.

No one had any idea who this man was, or where he'd come from.

Upon reaching the mansion gate, he asked for an audience with his stepmother. It would seem the mistress had tutored him well. Sometime after she had left the mansion, Mayyadas had convinced Gokuldas to send for his wife and call her back. She had returned to the mansion with her daughters. Who can know what fate ordains, for she gave birth to a son a few years later. Soon enough, her three daughters were married, and she and her youngest son, Lekhraj—who was born about five years after the mistress left and was now almost a young man—lived in the mansion. She was still resolving the dilemma of whether or not to meet the guest, when Dhanpat ordered his men to shift his luggage into the mansion.

'I'm Diwan Dhanpat,' he announced and alighted from his mule. He handed the reins of the horse to the watchman at the mansion's gate and entered.

Diwan Mayyadas was away doing a round of his estates. Devki had long ago lost interest in keeping track of who came into or went out of the mansion. Ever since her son's death, she spent all her time praying. Even if she had crossed paths with Dhanpat that day, even if she had come to realize who he was, even if she had discerned his intentions, she wouldn't have refused to let him in. It wasn't only after her son's death, but a long time before that, that the meaning and significance of human relations had changed for her.

Dhanpat set up his things in the meeting room—not on his father's, but on Diwan Mayyadas's side of the wall—and announced himself as the heir of Diwan Gokuldas, and also started behaving as that. He would do a round of the town every day, and spend time with agents of Grain Market. Within two to three days, he had intimated many people of his new address. He had become the most discussed man in town.

He must have been around twenty years old then. He was a lean man with a pale face and a thin moustache. He was a sight in his disproportionately large saffron turban and bright yellow angrakha. And the half-dead mule he rode was the icing on the cake. Within a couple of days, he became the brunt of people's jokes. In no time at all, he began to be known as 'Pretender Dhanpat'.

When Diwan Mayyadas returned and learnt that the mistress's son was in the mansion, he knew there was going to be big trouble around inheritance. Mayyadas had served as a revenue official; he understood crookedness in matters of property only too well. When Dhanpat came to meet

Mayyadas, he was wearing his signature turban and angrakha, and held in his hand the whip with which he guided his mule.

Mayyadas looked him up and down. To him, he looked like a joke.

'So young man, you're Chandra's son?'

'I'm Gokuldas's son.'

Mayyadas nodded his head and looked him up and down once more.

'What brings you here? Do you have some work here?'

'I've come to my house. I'm Diwan Dhanpat, son of Gokuldas.'

Mayyadas smiled a slight smile, nodded, and looked him up and down again.

'Did you bring any papers?'

'I don't need papers. I'm myself the evidence that demonstrates the truth.'

'Where's your mother?'

'Right here. She lives on the other side of the wall.'

'Your own mother. The one who sent you here.'

Dhanpat swung the end of his angrakha a little as he took a step forward. Tapping the whip he was holding on his left palm, he said, 'Diwanji, I'll take what's mine, whether you give it to me straightaway, or in a roundabout way. I'm a Diwan too, after all.'

Mayyadas didn't say anything; he just nodded his head for some time. The conversation had reached a point where neither had anything further to say to the other. 'My respects, Tauji,' Dhanpat said, and left.

Dhanpat's presence was no more than a small inconvenience for the mansion. Mayyadas did feel that it could create complications, but since Dhanpat had neither any documentation proof of his relation with the mansion, nor any witnesses who would vouch for him, he didn't worry too much. One nagging doubt he had, however, was if his brother had given his mistress something in writing which Dhanpat might present at the opportune moment. But he had no way of knowing, and he kept silent on the matter.

Diwan Dhanpat's ways were odd even in those days.

When he served as revenue officer, Diwan Mayyadas had a clerk named Pohraam. He lived in his ancestral home, which was behind Oil Pressers' Neighbourhood, at the end of Butchers' Lane. He had worked for the Diwan for almost twenty years. But when Mayyadas was sent to Lahore, and then to Kabul, he was left without work. By the time Mayyadas returned to town because of the turbulence in Kabul, Pohraam had died. His wife lived with their young daughter, and was struggling to make ends meet. Mayyadas's wife did help them out sometimes, but Munshi Pohraam had left them nothing at all. Had his wife sold the house and left town after his death, their daughter could have had a better life and, who knows, maybe she too would have found a new life for herself. But she stayed glued to the ancestral house. The result was that by the time Mayyadas returned, she was living off her daughter Motiya's earnings.

Dhanpat started visiting Motiya. And Motiya's mother encouraged him. So what if he was born from the womb of a mistress, he was Diwan Gokuldas's son, after all. Who knew, maybe Motiya would live in the mansion one day, she reasoned to herself.

It started one day when Motiya entered Butchers' Lane via Oil Pressers' Neighbourhood. The lane wasn't far from the neighbourhood: once you crossed the lane, you reached that part of the neighbourhood where labourers, oil pressers and weavers lived. Dhanpat, riding his mule, had entered the lane from the other end. When they crossed paths, Motiya saw him and laughed. Who is to say if she was mocking him or flirting with him? Whatever it was, her laughter got Dhanpat excited. He turned his mule around and started following her. He could feel her pink dupatta call out to him; he was smitten. When Motiya heard the mule's hooves behind her, she turned to look and broke into another merry laugh. Dhanpat's heart had never felt such restlessness.

Motiya had reached the butchers' shops. Some young men had gathered there, and on seeing Motiya they started calling out to her, to draw her attention towards them. Motiya laughed at them, 'Get lost, you loser!' She strutted past them.

But thinking himself Majnu, one of the men started following her.

'Come back, Nooray!' One of his friends called out to him. 'This item's not for you. Come back.'

Seeing Noora follow Motiya, Dhanpat felt as if someone had seared his body with hot iron. He seethed.

When she reached the turn of the lane, Motiya turned around to look. Noora had caught up with her and was almost beside her. His friends continued to pass comments.

For a second, a worry line appeared on Motiya's forehead, as if Noora wasn't whom she had expected to find when she turned around. 'Get lost, loser,' she said. 'Go, your mother's calling you!' Then she turned her gaze towards the hero astride the mule, laughed and went on her way.

Two days later Dhanpat brought Motiya to the mansion to live with him.

The news spread through town at lightning speed. Diwan Mayyadas was, once again, away on work in Lahore. Everyone speculated about how he would react when he returned.

But the gossiping and speculating were short-lived. It was to get legal advice regarding Dhanpat that Diwan Mayyadas had gone to Lahore. When, on returning, he learnt that Dhanpat had brought Pohraam's daughter to the mansion as his keep, he sent for four porters and had them throw all of Dhanpat's things out, and locked up the doors of his rooms with huge locks.

Another man would have packed up and left town after such a turn of events, but not Dhanpat. He was cast from a different mould. He stood and watched his things been thrown into the street, and kept saying, 'No worries, Tauji. Go on and throw my things out. But I too am a Diwan; I'll take what's rightfully mine.'

He had the same porters who'd thrown his things out from the mansion carry them for him to Grain Market. He rented a room there and moved in. Motiya's mother took her daughter back to her house.

Dhanpat didn't stop wearing his loose angrakha, nor did he feel any embarrassment about what had happened. He continued to roam the lanes as if he owned them, and didn't stop prefixing 'Diwan' to his name.

No one knew if he continued to visit Motiya at her house. But one day, Noora's body was found outside her door. How had he died, who had killed him and why should he have been murdered in front of Motiya's house? These questions troubled the town, but the incident was forgotten after a while, and Motiya and her mother left town soon after, anyway.

There was many an evening that Lekhraj spent engrossed in the vivid tales his grandmother told, but one evening left a deep imprint on his mind. He'd been playing five stones in the maidan that fronted Kabuli Darwaza. Late afternoon had turned to evening, and the scent of roasted corncobs filled the air. Shadows had lengthened and the slight, blue haze of winters was descending by the time he started for home, when he saw a horse rider coming into town through Kabuli Darwaza. Lekhraj felt something stir in his heart, as if he had a previous memory of this man. He stood where he was, mesmerized, watching. The rider wore a blue silken robe. He had a saffron courtiers' turban on his head, a green scabbard dangled from his waist, and he was wearing pearl necklaces around his neck. Lekhraj stood transfixed, and then started following him. He trailed him from lane to lane, moving further away from home. The rider turned right from the neighbourhood of the Sethis, into the broad street that led to the Palace of Mirrors. The street swerved to the right after some distance. It was narrower from this point on, and it was darker here than it was elsewhere. Lekhraj stopped at the turning and watched the rider ride on, followed by two more men on horseback. These men held long lances and wore round army caps on their heads. Lekhraj thought the man in front must be the chief commander and the two men following him, his deputies. The chief and his blue robe were slowly blurring into the thickening darkness, and now only his bright saffron turban was slightly visible. Lekhraj could still clearly hear the clip-clop of the horses, but slowly those too dissolved into the envelope of darkness.

Lekhraj stood there for some more time, and then sprinted towards the other street that led to the Palace of Mirrors. This street was just as wide as the last one, and led to the palace's courtyard. He reached the spot from where he could observe the place that the dark and narrow street opened into. The chief and his deputies would no doubt be visible very soon, and he wanted one last glance.

When the rider appeared, the slanting rays of the setting sun fell directly on his turban's plume. Lekhraj's eyes remained riveted on the rider's bright face, taut chest, flowing robe and shining pearls.

Lekhraj remembered this image until way past his childhood, and for many years after that. When he was injured in battle, almost faint from all the blood he'd lost, with all kinds of meaningful and meaningless images flashing through his mind, this image had appeared, and stayed. Even in that state, the image of the commander had seemed enchanting to him, and he lay in a trance contemplating it in his mind's eye.

Some figures and images seep into us, becoming part of us and making us who we are. The plume, that chest, those eyes, that face and that flowing robe—it was as if for Lekhraj these had merged with the stories he heard from his grandmother, giving a form to the heroes that peopled those stories, and an image to their valour.

That evening when he went to his grandmother's room, he narrated to her what he'd seen. She said that, indeed it must have been a commander he'd seen, who'd come from Lahore to meet with the king. Lekhraj, though he watched her enraptured, was convinced that the man he'd seen was a character who'd emerged in real life from one of her stories. To him, the man looked like a royal rider, just like the ones whose stories she told him.

Lekhraj was only a child then. To him, what he'd seen blurred in with his grandmother's stories in a way that soon he found it impossible to be certain if he had in fact seen the rider, or if the entire episode had been a figment of his imagination. The chapters of the past that he heard in his grandma's tales traversed such enormous distances in time and space that whenever Lekhraj tried to recall a story, he found slivers from another story appear within it. To him, reality always merged with his imagination, and stories invariably spilled into reality.

Often in the evenings, after the earthen lamps were lit, lots of little children would gather in Grandma's room. They would watch with rapt attention how her lips moved, and the children soaked in every word of every story, growing more spirited by the minute. Each word from Grandma's mouth was like a lively image. Her stories appeared like a string of dancing images before Lekhraj's eyes, each of which his active imagination would further enliven. But it wasn't just the images, there was something else in those stories—something that wasn't visible and which always made his heart feel a fullness.

This evening Grandma was narrating:

'And then, in the dark of the night, three men entered Mai Gujjari's house. One of them was carrying a silver plate covered with a white cloth. He walked slowly with the plate, towards the flame torch that had been lit by the wall.

Emerging in this way from the darkness, he went and stood in front of Mai Gujjari. The three men remained silent. Their eyes were downcast. Guru Maharaj's wife too didn't say anything. It was as if they all knew, without anyone saying anything, what it was that they'd brought with them on that plate. Then the man lifted the cloth. It was Guru Maharaj's severed head . . .'

The children listened with bated breath. Filled with suspense, Lekhraj sat unblinking, his eyes not leaving his grandmother's face for even a second. *Any moment now she'll tell us how Guru Maharaj's head reached here and who these men who've brought it are. And where they've come from. And why have they brought just his head? Where's the rest of his body?*

'Then? Then what happened, Dadima?'

'The tyrants first killed the Guru Maharaj's three companions, then they beheaded him and threw his body and his head in the street.'

'Then?' The children were impatient to know.

'What then? Guru Maharaj's head and body lay there, in the dirt and mud. No one had the courage to go near them . . . But God has his own ways, and by evening a terrible dust storm rose. It was so bad that your right hand wouldn't know where your left hand was. Do you know what happened then?'

The children felt her voice was emerging from inside the dust storm.

'A man named Jaita was standing there. He was a follower of the Guru Maharaj. He jumped into the whirling wind, gathered up Guru Maharaj's head and hid it by wrapping a sheet around it. No one seemed to have seen him. He sneaked away and started on a journey towards Anandpur Sahib . . .'

Lekhraj was in two places at once. He was in his grandmother's room, watching her lips move and tell them this tale. And at the same time, he was elsewhere, watching a dark man in worn-out clothes, a Jat, walking on a long road towards Anandpur Sahib after having leapt into a storm and retrieved Guru Maharaj's head with great alacrity.

'But, Dadima, was Guru Maharaj's body still lying there on the street?'

'Jaita had taken the head,' Dadima continued her story. 'Now listen to what happened to the torso. Jaita had already left with Guru Maharaj's head, but the torso was still lying there. A trader lived nearby. His name was Lakheedas. He was watching this entire scene from his balcony. He too was a brave man. So what did he do? He loaded his handcart with some things and, pushing it, he walked into the storm. He went on until he reached the place where Guru Maharaj's torso was. He picked up Guru Maharaj's torso and put it on his cart, in the middle of the things he had loaded on to it. Then he pushed his cart back to his house. The storm was so intense that no one noticed him. The guards thought it was just someone who sold things from a cart who was passing by.'

'Then? Then, Dadima?' Lekhraj was on edge.

'Lakheedas took the cart back to his house. But now what was he to do? He couldn't keep Guru Maharaj's torso in his house—it needed to be cremated; it had to be passed along. So what Lakheedas did was he took Guru Maharaj's torso into his house and set fire to his house.'

The children could see tongues of flames rising from the house.

'And that's how he cremated Guru Maharaj,' Grandma concluded the story.

The children started insisting that she tell them yet another story. She agreed, and started the story of Banda Veer Bairagi:

'Banda Veer Bairagi was arrested and taken to Delhi. Do you know how they took him? Like he was some animal. They put him in a cage. Two thousand soldiers, in neat rows and with lances in their hands, marched ahead of him. Each lance had a head on it. These were heads of Veer Bairagi's brave companions. Two thousand heads . . . And seven hundred and forty more of Veer Bairagi's companions walked behind the cage. Their feet were bound and they were being herded . . .'

The curtain rose again and another scene with vivid images started before Lekhraj's eyes.

Dadima would hum, she would sing in her hoarse voice, or start reciting a poem. And Lekhraj, who must have been around seven years old then, would shift closer towards her. A sweet fragrance, like the smell of rain on dry earth, full of affection, always seemed to emanate from Dadima's old, worn-out dupatta. He often remembered her during the days of the war; when he remembered her, he could smell that same scent. He liked sitting close to his grandmother. She was like the fibre that connected his young consciousness with the past—a delicate, resplendent fibre. It was as if she had emerged from the mist of the past herself. Listening to her stories, this mist would get animated, and horses would start dancing with the wind and battalions of brave soldiers would begin their onward march. The past came alive with her stories, infused with the breath of life. Sometimes she would break into song, and clap her hands to its beat softly. When she sang, the children knew she would definitely tell them another story that day.

'Then Guru Maharaj said to the congregation, "I need a man's head." Now who was going to sacrifice himself? Maharaj repeated, "Listen, my brave friends, I need a man's head. Which one of you is a true son of his mother? Who

will offer me his head?"' Dadima used to say 'true son of his
mother' quite often during her storytelling. 'No one spoke
up. A hush had fallen over the congregation. Everyone was
dumbfounded by his demand. All of them were his devotees
and his trusted companions. But who was going to give up
his life like this? But then Guru Maharaj asked for a third
time, "My sword needs a Sikh today. Is there any true son
of his mother here who will give me what I want?" Pin-drop
silence. But then the Maharaj saw one man weaving his way
through the crowd towards him. He came and stood with his
hands folded before Maharaj. He said, "Maharaj, my head is
at your disposal."'

The children were deeply moved.

'Maharaj looked him up and down. "Who are you? What
is your name?" he asked.

'"Maharaj, my name is Dayaram," the man said.

'"Where do you hail from?"

'"Maharaj, I'm from Lahore. I belong to the Khatri caste.
My head is at your disposal."

'Maharaj looked at him for a long moment. Then what?
Maharaj drew his sword out of its sheath. The sword in
one hand, he held Dayaram's wrist with the other and took
him with him. A tent had been pitched some distance from
where they were, on top of a hillock. Maharaj took the man
into the tent. Everyone saw them go in. They were looking
towards the tent, bewildered, wondering what would happen
next. The entire congregation held its breath. Was Maharaj
going to take the life of one of his own disciples? What has
happened to Maharaj? He has never done anything like this
before, ever!

'Maharaj emerged from the tent after some time. He
was still holding the sword, and it was dripping with blood.

What's this! What has Maharaj done? He has beheaded one of his own! They were shaken to the core. Everyone looked at Maharaj, their eyes wide. Maharaj, his sword dripping with blood, walked back to the congregation . . .'

Of all the stories his grandmother had narrated, this one had moved Lekhraj the most. His throat choked up with emotion. He watched his grandmother with rapt attention.

'Guru Maharaj walked up to the congregation and said, "I want another head."'

'Everyone was dumbstruck. Now that he's got one, he wants another! Who was going to offer his life, knowing fully well that within moments his blood would be dripping from Maharaj's sword? What has happened to Guru Maharaj today? He is someone who loves his people more than his own life.'

'Then?'

'Everyone was looking at Maharaj. They were completely astonished. No one said a word. Then there was a movement. A man was making his way through the crowd towards Maharaj. He walked up to Maharaj and stood before him with his hands folded. "I am at your disposal, Maharaj. My head is yours to take."'

'"Who are you? What's your name?"'

'"Maharaj, my name is Dharamdas. I am from Hastinapur. I'm Jat by caste, Maharaj." And he bowed his head before Maharaj.'

'Then?' The children were sitting with their hearts in their mouths.

'Maharaj, still holding his blood-drenched sword, led him by his wrist towards the tent.'

'Then? Then, Dadima, then?' Lekhraj's heart skipped a beat.

'This time too it was the same. Maharaj emerged from the tent. His sword was dripping with blood. The moment he reached the congregation, he made his demand again, "I want yet another head."

'Everyone was deeply stunned. How many heads was Maharaj going to ask for? What has happened to him? How many of his own disciples' lives is he going to take like this?'

The dark of evening deepened. The children watched Dadima's twinkling eyes and moving lips as she continued to narrate the tale.

'Another man emerged from within the crowd.' The children's breathing grew as rapid as if their lungs were bellows.

'"Maharaj, my head is at your disposal."'

'Who was it, Dadima?'

'His name was Mohkamchand. He was from Dwarka. Maharaj led him into the tent, like the others. Once more, when he returned, he asked for a head. And as before, his sword was covered in blood.'

The children were agog, much like the congregation Guru Maharaj was addressing. The men were at a loss to understand what crime Guru Maharaj was punishing them for. Why was he doing this? They were his own people!

'The name of the fourth man was Himmat. He was from Jagannathpuri. And after him, the fifth man was Sahibchand, and he hailed from Bidar . . .'

Dadima's voice was wavering. Her eyelids were moist with tears; she wiped them with her dupatta. Many children began to snivel and sob.

'He killed all five men?' Lekhraj asked anxiously.

When Dadima replied, she had regained her composure, and her voice was even. 'Maharaj held the fifth man by his wrist and took him into the tent. But after some time, Guru

Maharaj . . .' The trembling in her voice returned as she continued, 'Guru Maharaj lifted the front flap of the tent, stepped out and walked slowly towards the congregation. Behind him . . . behind him walked five men. They were all dressed alike—in a long saffron shirt and with a saffron courtiers' turban on their heads. They followed the Maharaj, their heads bowed . . .'

'Who were they, Dadima?'

'When they came close, people recognized them. Oh, these are the same five men Maharaj had taken into the tent with him! Dayaram Khatri, Dharamdas Jat, Mohkamchand, Himmat and Sahibchand. They were alive, and they were walking behind Maharaj, their heads bowed reverentially. Their faces were resplendent, aglow with an inner light.'

So then Maharaj hadn't killed anyone! The children breathed a sigh of relief. They looked at each other and smiled. What a full-flavoured story this was getting to be!

'So none of them had died, Dadima?'

'So then the Maharaj hadn't killed them?'

'But then why was there blood on Maharaj's sword?'

'The Maharaj was only pretending to have killed them?'

The children all asked their questions together. Dadima said, 'Maharaj wanted to assess the depth of their conviction. He was only testing them.'

Lekhraj felt a flood tide of emotion rise within him. *Had Maharaj put me to the test, I would have done the same thing. I would have offered him my life, my head.* The story had touched him deeply, stirring a fibre in his being that was inaccessible to him.

'And then, Dadima? What happened after that?'

'Guru Maharaj walked up to the congregation and said, "These are my *panj pyare*, my five beloved ones. They're my true followers. They didn't care about their lives. They are the true Khalsa. They are the true devotees . . .'"

It was around this time that Lekhraj had seen, and been mesmerized by, the horse rider who had entered into town through Kabuli Darwaza, a saffron turban on his head, pearl necklaces around his neck, a sword hanging from his waist. Lekhraj felt he knew this man, and that he had seen him before. The man had emerged from Dadima's story on to the streets of the town.

A quiet and mellow sunlight had settled over everything when the sound of drums broke the late-afternoon slumber. People passing through Grain Market halted. The town crier was making an announcement. His voice travelled far and drew everyone towards him. The announcer was the town ballad singer's younger brother, Jalal. He was wearing a striped kurta and a red-cockaded turban which he always wore when making important announcements.

'Attention, all creatures of God who live by the commandments of the king! Each one of you, distinguished and ordinary, are hereby informed that foreign armies are advancing towards the Khalsa Sultanate. Recruitment will begin tomorrow, at the Palace of Mirrors.'

Jalal walked on along the high wall that skirted Grain Market. He was headed towards Kabuli Darwaza, beating the drum loudly. Children trailed him.

People streamed out of their houses. The maidan next to Grain Market filled up within minutes. People huddled in groups and talked. *What has happened? What will happen next?* The air was charged with a mix of curiosity and apprehension.

The atmosphere of the town had changed within seconds. *The British army has attacked. The Lahore Durbar has called upon everyone to pitch in. Recruitments will begin tomorrow.* A fog of uncertainty had descended and muddled the clear afternoon sunlight.

'I've heard the army is advancing from the Sutlej,' a man added to the discussions in a group near Grain Market's gate.

'There'll be so much looting and burning now,' a Maliar woman said to her companions. They were returning home from the market with baskets of vegetables on their heads when they heard the town crier's announcement. They quickened their pace towards their neighbourhood.

Jalal beat the drum and made an announcement at Kabuli Darwaza. Then he crossed from under the high arch of the Darwaza and disappeared into the labyrinth of lanes, the sound of his drum receding.

Apprehensions were mounting. Everyone was anxious for news. People stood in small circles, listless. Feet shuffling, carrying them from group to group; eyes expectantly searching the road that led into town from Lahore, so they may perhaps spot the arrival of a runner, or a band of soldiers on horseback, a cloud of dust trailing behind them and intimating their approach. Not long after Jalal had done his rounds, a horseback rider had in fact come into town. He was covered with dust from head to toe. 'War has started! War has started,' he had raised his hand high into the air and yelled out as he rode past the crowd of people. He didn't stop, and headed straight for the palace.

A crowd of murmurs swept through the troubled town. Someone had heard that the palace gates had been thrown open, and moneylenders, landlords, Diwans and Raizadas from all over town were on their way to confer with the king. When it comes, the declaration of war infects life with uncertainty and fear, no doubt, but it also unlatches the locks and bolts that hem in the present. The ties that regulate daily life slacken. One begins to feel something like freedom. War had started; people roamed in the maidan all day. But shades of other emotions were present too; there was a deep excitation of war. In some, it stirred the desire to put their lives at stake for the Khalsa Durbar and prove their masculinity and fearlessness on the battlefield. In others, it harvested doubt about what the future portended. The twine had snapped; now the only certainty was that something enormous was about to happen. The feeling, intangible and unexpressed, saturated the air. The town grew uneasy and tense.

Diwan Mayyadas, his walking stick in hand, emerged from Kabuli Darwaza. Everyone's attention slowly turned towards him. The eyes of the entire town followed him as he walked along the wall, towards Grain Market. He was on his way to meet the king. It made everyone realize how close to the brink the situation was. They watched him— his straight back, his serious gait, the dignified, determined expression on his face. He appeared to the town like the bearer of their honour. The life of the town was faced with a decisive moment and Diwan Mayyadas was forging ahead to play his role in it.

At about the same time as Diwan Mayyadas set out for the palace, many other eminent people of the town— Diwans, Maliks, Raizadas—stepped out of their homes and establishments and made their way to the palace as well.

Overcome by emotion, some of them were wearing their courtly attire, which included a sword at the waist. Each one threaded his way through the lanes of the town, towards the Palace of Mirrors. The king, Amirchand, may have been a minor king, but he symbolized the Khalsa kingdom. And so, he was the pivot on which emotions turned. It was through him that they could express that they understood that the breaching of the Lahore Durbar meant the entire kingdom was in peril.

Suddenly, a fountain of laughter erupted from one end of the maidan. The ornate Diwan, Dhanpat Rai, bouncing on his mule, had entered the maidan through Grain Market. He seemed to be headed towards Orchard of the Sheikhs, from where the path led caravans on their journeys. Dhanpat's arrival brought a respite. Everyone's attention had shifted to him.

Many young men were among those who had gathered at the maidan. They stood in small groups, with friends. Banshi, Harnarayan and Ramjawaya were there as well, and Diwan Dhanpat's trajectory was leading him straight towards their group.

'He's on his way to negotiate peace,' a young man said loudly.

This elicited still more laughter. Diwan Dhanpat had given the anxious gathering something to amuse itself with.

'Why peace? He'll demonstrate his valour in war,' another chipped in.

'How ably he's going to wield his lance astride this mule!' yet another young lad remarked.

'He'll fight the war dressed in his angrakha.'

Dhanpat was wearing his court dress. His sword was in a pale-green sheath that hung from his waist. It bounced with the mule's trot. Diwan Dhanpat had to keep spurring

the mule on to make it move. The flashy young man made a
perfect sight for banter.

As he crossed the group in which Banshi, Harnarayan and
Ramjawaya were standing, Banshi started running alongside
him. The mule was only a little bigger than a donkey. Banshi
jumped up and seated himself behind Dhanpat on the mule.
Everyone was in splits. Banshi put his arms around Dhanpat's
waist. It was clear Banshi's tomfoolery was for everyone's
benefit and their continued amusement.

'Get down, Banshi! Diwanji is in a hurry. He has been
summoned,' someone called from behind.

'Get down! Get down! Diwanji is getting late. The war
cannot proceed without him!'

Banshi rode with the Diwan till where the maidan ended,
then jumped off and returned to his group. He was still
laughing.

'But, where is the Diwan going? Why is he headed out of
the town?'

Dhanpat had by now disappeared from view. Only a faint
cloud of dust was visible in the direction in which he had
gone.

And this was how Diwan Dhanpat left town that day. Some
moments leave a deep imprint on the heart. This was one such
instance. The town remembered it till long after and, with the
passage of time, it attained the significance of a historic moment.

Evening had fallen; no one went home. Life had changed.
The king had dispatched his agents to recruit soldiers from
neighbouring villages. News of all kinds circulated—*Diwan
Mayyadas has donated one lakh ashrafis towards the war efforts,*

Raizada Mohanlala has donated twenty thousand, and many others have made donations as well . . .

Lekhraj had been restless ever since he'd heard the town crier's announcement. He had been at the moneylending table when he'd heard Jalal's drum. He'd left for Grain Market immediately, but then he also followed Jalal and heard him make the announcement at different places, over and over again. His heart grew agitated. He sought out his friend Manoharlal, and ever since then the two had been roaming without rest through the lanes of the town.

The next day, the two friends went to the Palace of Mirrors and admitted themselves to the army. No one knew; they had asked nobody for advice.

It wasn't as if Lekhraj had a clear picture of what war was, or what being on a battlefield meant. He was a quiet boy—polite, obedient, someone who kept to himself. He had started helping out with the moneylending business a few years earlier. But after he heard the announcement of war, his heart burnt with the desire to do something. It was an untameable feeling, an incandescent instinct.

When Diwan Mayyadas got word that his nephew had enlisted, he was surprised. The boy hadn't struck him as one interested in questions of war. He was both impressed and annoyed. The boy had shown courage, no doubt, but he'd acted on impulse, without thinking. He tried to dissuade him.

'You're not ready for war. You're not even of an age when you can shave.'

Lekhraj stood quietly, his eyes lowered respectfully. He thought answering back would be audacious. Mayyadas felt his heart melt. Stroking his nephew's back, he tried to explain to him that he was too young. He promised to talk to the king and have Lekhraj sent on an assignment outside town. But then Lekhraj suddenly found his speech and said there was no way he wasn't going to war. He had got his name enlisted and there was no going back.

'Think about your mother. She'll die crying for you. Think about what you're saying.'

But the boy didn't relent. His stubbornness annoyed Mayyadas. But hadn't he donated one lakh ashrafis himself to the Khalsa Durbar? There was a limit to how much he could argue with the boy about the war. In a way, he also felt proud. His family was supporting the war not only with money, but also by sending a young lad to the battlefront.

Lekhraj's mother wept. She pleaded with her son not to go, implored him to consider how old she was, how long she'd been a widow, and how wrong it would be for him to leave her alone and go like this. But Lekhraj was possessed by his passion; nothing could make him change his mind. How could she succeed where the Diwan had failed? In the end, she gave in to the inevitable.

There was one person who didn't try to stop Lekhraj. She was the one who had narrated to him innumerable stories about self-sacrifice—his grandmother.

The room was dark. She was sitting on her cot. Lekhraj sat down beside her, and she felt his face with her fingers. She couldn't see very much any more. Cupping her bony hands around Lekhraj's face, she drew his forehead towards her and kissed it. Her clothes smelled of the same sweet fragrance that they did when Lekhraj was a little boy.

'May God bless you! Go my child, go. Add lustre to the name of your forefathers. Bring lustre to the name of this town. Return a true warrior.'

To Lekhraj, her words felt as if they were from a story, uttered in blessing by a mother to her brave son as he left for battle.

Much of what was transpiring was driven by youthful passions. Lekhraj had enlisted, inspired by amorphous ideals, and Manohar had enlisted driven by his friendship with, and his desire to abide by, Lekhraj.

'Wherever we go, we'll go together. What will I do here when you're gone? I'm going with you,' Manohar had declared.

Was this the exuberance of youth, or its stupidity? Was it naivety, or was it sincerity? Whatever it was, it consumed the young friends.

The two were poles apart. Lekhraj was a serious young man. Manohar was an effervescent, vivacious lad—carefree, full of laughter and chatter. It was much later, when they were in the thick of war, enduring its crookedness and turmoil, that it struck Lekhraj how odd it was that Manohar should be on a battlefield. Manohar, his fair and handsome friend, who liked to wear bright and flowing clothes, and who'd say, 'I like my pocket filled with coins. They jingle when I walk, and I can take out fistfuls of them when I want.' He was quite devoted to his world of whims and fancies. What was someone like him doing in the battlefield? *Why did he come with me? Why didn't I stop him?*

They'd left for battle the day after enlisting; they were among the first batch of twenty. The entire town had gathered at the maidan. There was such fervour; everyone's hands were raised, bidding them farewell. In the midst of all this, Manohar had pointed to a group of girls standing beneath a shisham tree and said, 'Girls look so pretty, don't they? I love looking at them and listening to them! When a girl's dupatta flutters in the breeze, I can feel my heart fluttering with it. Does that happen to you too, Lekhu?'

Lekhraj laughed to himself. 'You're a madcap,' he said. 'Be quiet and look ahead.'

What a sleazebag, Lekhraj thought to himself on such occasions. *Why does he have to say everything that passes through his stupid head?*

But things changed once they reached Lahore. The war became real. Manohar looked besieged: the blood drained from his face, his eyes turned red and his lips turned dry. He was like a thirsty bird in a land without water. They went through hard training. And then, soon, the skirmishes began. The two friends were part of the same detachment, and they would go together from camp to camp, rifles on their shoulders. Manohar turned completely silent.

With time, there was going to be a whole lot that the war would show Lekhraj. But how was he to know that this friend of his, who chattered relentlessly as he walked beside him at the start of war, would have to, in time, be carried on his shoulders, a dead man whom he'd have to throw into a ravine?

But even during the terrifying days of war, something of Manohar's carefree, playful disposition stayed. It peeped out that day, for instance, when they were hiding in the forest. There were about five or six detachments, and they were all waiting for their commander's orders to descend the hillock and attack the enemy in the low-lying battlefield. Manohar had suddenly got up. Leaving the tree he was hiding behind, he moved quietly towards another tree. He'd spotted a mynah's nest. He stood there on tiptoe for a long time, looking into the nest. 'I thought, let me check if there are eggs in the nest. A mynah's eggs are very tiny. Have you ever seen them?' He'd just said this, when the war drums were sounded, and the soldiers, their battle cries filling the air, their swords raised, began their descent down the hillock.

The morning of the day he was to set out for battle, Lekhraj had snuck out of the mansion to do a last round of the town. Without willing them to, his feet had turned towards Moran's lane. Their families had been discussing their betrothal. They'd grown up in these same lanes. When Moran was still a chubby little girl who would laugh at the smallest of things, she'd come to the mansion to listen to Lekhraj's grandmother's stories. They'd grown shy of each other ever since their marriage began to be discussed. Now Lekhraj must have been eighteen, and Moran was twelve. He wanted to see her once before leaving. In his own way, he was saying his goodbyes to everyone he knew.

Moran was standing on the terrace. When she saw Lekhraj coming in through the gate, she darted into the house. By the time Lekhraj reached her house, she'd come down and was hiding behind the front door. But her giggling made it impossible for her to remain hidden.

Lekhraj had come to say farewell. He thought it would be a solemn occasion; he hadn't expected to meet a giggling Moran.

'You're going to fight in the war?' Moran chirped. 'Have you seen your face in the mirror? You're not even going to be able to lift a rifle; how in the world do you plan to fight?' she laughed.

Lekhraj felt crushed. Moran looked at him intently. After they'd stood silently before each other for some time, she said softly, 'When do you leave? Will you go straight to Lahore from here? Are you really going to go?'

'Yes, I'll be going to Lahore. We're all going to Lahore. They'll train us in the cantonment. They'll give us guns. And they'll send us on from there.'

'Why are you going, Lekhraj? What do you need to go for?' Moran's voice had changed; it was very soft. 'I'll pray for you,' she said and, tucking the end of her dupatta into her mouth in embarrassment, ran into the house.

∽

The battlefield was a different world. When Lekhraj saw the army of thousands, his heart sang. He'd never imagined such an immense gathering of soldiers was possible. Lances and spears seemed to roll out all the way to the horizon. The sky was resplendent with flags and banners of every hue and colour. Horse riders, dressed in bright colours, had green-and-red waistbands from which they hung their swords. Drumbeats filled the air. There were so many foot soldiers that it looked like the sea itself had risen. They looked unstoppable. That he was part of this enormous rising made Lekhraj's heart swell. His ardour to be a soldier reached its crescendo. He was ready to face the enemy. He would defeat the enemy, or die trying.

He fought in three battles in quick succession. The war ended in a matter of a few months. How distant this world had been from the stories his grandmother had told him.

The army crossed the River Sutlej under the command of Sardar Lal Singh. They walked for days to reach the battleground. Lekhraj saw the commander only once—he was riding a white horse; the span of his chest and the glow of his visage were inspiring. Lekhraj was moved. That this man was commanding an army of this scale, that he was steering the war, filled him with awe. And so, even though Lekhraj was deputed a distance away from the commander, his eyes continually turned to where the commander was, seeking him out. Just looking at him filled Lekhraj with courage, belief and perseverance.

They arrived at the battlefield at midday. It was a sprawling ground, almost flat and utterly bare. There were a few shrubs, fewer trees, and some sand dunes. How was one going to take a defensive position on it? How was the contingent to be stationed, and where? But this is not for the soldier to work out; the commander takes these decisions.

They were told the firangi army had camped on the other side of this flat land, almost a mile away. Lekhraj had seen many encampments by now—row upon row of pink tents flanking a wide path. The firangis' flag, with its criss-crossing blue, red and white lines, fluttered at the mouth of the encampment. Beneath the flag, there was always a glistening cannon, and next to it, an armed sentry.

But this encampment wasn't visible from where they were. There was no movement on the other side of the ground. Everything seemed undecipherable, mysterious. There was dense silence all around. Soldiers were taking position; cannon were being mounted behind sand dunes. Lekhraj's platoon had been ordered to take position behind a few shrubs. Lekhraj was on the ground, behind a shrub, and some others of his platoon had climbed up trees. Everyone took position where they found the shade of a shrub, a tree or a dune. Even though Lekhraj had experienced some skirmishes by now, this was all new to him.

They'd heard that the entire army hadn't been sent here. A part of the army had been ordered to stay behind—as a reserve for a front that was being readied under another commander.

Lekhraj focused his eyes on the other side of the grounds. But there was no movement. Then, suddenly, the

Khalsa army started firing their cannon. Cannonballs tore through the air, exploding near the horizon. The enemy must've been advancing, because of which the commander had ordered the cannon to be fired. But after some time, the firing stopped, and a dense silence enveloped them once again.

The soldiers were puzzled. *What is the next step? After cannon fire, the army should advance into the battlefield. After cannon fire, it's time to launch a full attack on the enemy. Instead, why this deafening silence?* The soldiers were ready for battle. But the war drums hadn't been sounded. They turned to look where the commander was, awaiting instructions. They were restless to leave their cover and head into the battlefield. They were ready to strike.

But whom should they attack? There was nothing but a sea of silence in front of them. Was the enemy even there?

Afternoon was turning into evening. It was as still as a painting. *What's the commander waiting for? Is it for the reserve army to show up? Is he planning another front, another line of attack? Why are the war drums not resounding?*

And then, the thunder of a hundred cannon reached their ears. It was the enemy; the enemy was firing its cannon. The soldiers ducked once more behind their cover. Their chance to attack had been lost. The horizon was ablaze with cannonballs. The cannon of the Khalsa army resumed their firing in response, but fell silent in some time. *Why has the firing stopped? Have the firangis succeeded in silencing our cannon? How is that even possible?*

The sound of war drums from the other side of the grounds filled the air. Hundreds of horse-mounted soldiers began to advance. There were so many of them, it looked like they were sprouting from the ground. The enemy had launched their attack. The cavalry of the Khalsa army too began to advance, their swords shining.

The battlefield turned bloody in no time. Horses neighed, soldiers called out battle cries and screamed in pain.

Evening descended. The fighting still showed no signs of ending. Flame torches were lit. The soldiers of the firangi army scaled the dunes and reached the Khalsa side with their lances, bayonets, spears and swords. Hand-to-hand combat continued in the shifting light cast by the torches. Soldiers screamed, guns blazed, battle cries pierced the air and wounded horses neighed. The dark of evening had deepened into night by the time the firangis' bugles were sounded, announcing the end of the day. Fighting ceased; the armies extricated themselves from the battlefield. Noise abated and a restless silence took over, broken from time to time by the groans of the wounded. The inevitable night that follows the day of battle had started. It was going to stretch out endlessly, like a terrifying nightmare. Groups of Mehtars had accompanied the army and they fanned out into the battlefield, searching for injured soldiers, to carry them back to safety.

At the crack of dawn the following day, Lekhraj found himself standing at the edge of the battleground. He'd walked into the enclosure where the injured soldiers were; from there his feet had led him here. The ground was strewn with the bodies of dead soldiers and horses, remnants of flags and banners and weapons that had been left behind. He was not alone. Through the early-morning fog that still hovered over everything, he could see that, like him, many others had come here. They were moving through the bodies, turning them over, trying to identify their own among them. His eyes travelled through this scene, and came upon a firangi officer. He too was searching for someone. He walked among the corpses, bending down for a closer look, stopping from time to time whenever he came upon a dead firangi soldier, to turn the body over. He was a heavyset, balding man. He'd come quite close to where Lekhraj was standing, when he found the one he was looking for. 'My son, my son,' he cried out and fell down on his knees beside the body. Lekhraj watched him. The man groped and grasped his son's hands, arms, legs and chest, unwilling to believe he was dead. The young man still held a trumpet in his hand. Lekhraj understood at once: the firangi army had a band, which always came deep into the battlefield with the soldiers, playing tunes to inspire them; the young man must have been a trumpeter with the band. The balding officer bent his head and muttered a prayer. He stroked the dead trumpeter's hand, ran his fingers through his hair and cried desperate tears. Lekhraj stood there for a long time, silently watching a father mourn his dead son.

Men arrived to carry the dead bodies away. The young firangi trumpeter's corpse was loaded on to a cart. His father, his head bent, his gait slow, followed the cart to the other side of the battlefield.

Despite the cold and the fog, the morning air was pleasing. But it was heavy with sadness. Lekhraj felt overwhelmed by the melancholy that pervaded the atmosphere. The transactions of the days hadn't yet begun. The bugle hadn't been sounded, and the trumpets and battle cries were quiet.

One couldn't see far through the fog, but everyone sensed the firangi army on the other side of the battlefield—poised for battle in a semicircular formation, with their cannon aimed towards this side of the battlefield. Everyone speculated about what would happen next. *Will the day's battle begin with cannon fire? Or will the firangi army attack our formation directly, like they did yesterday?*

But then word began to travel in whispers among the soldiers that the commander was nowhere to be found. He wasn't on the battlefield. He hadn't been seen since the previous evening. In fact, he hadn't been at his post even when the hand-to-hand combat had started. Everyone had assumed that he was commanding some part of the front, and couldn't be seen simply because it had become quite dark by the time the combat had started. But no, he hadn't been with his unit even when it had come under the direst attack of all. And now his white horse wasn't tethered to the banyan tree like it had been earlier. Doubt riddled every heart. Had he been killed in battle? If so, his army would be disheartened. Who would take over the command after him? Every corner of the battlefield had been scoured for him the previous evening. He was nowhere. But even though their hearts were filled with fear and doubt, the soldiers' resolve to beat back the enemy was unshaken. If anything, it was further strengthened.

Speculations were still raging when the firangis' cannon started spewing fire. Gigantic orbs of fire flashed through the fog. Retaliatory firing started. The moment the fog lifted, the vast semicircular formation on the other side of the battlefield came into view. The cannon had barely fallen silent when the bugles resounded. The firangi army began its advance. They attacked, wave upon wave of soldiers in red uniform, bearing rifles with bayonets that glared in the sun.

Something within the Khalsa army must have snapped, for their formation began to crumble. It wasn't their spirit, for the soldiers fought valiantly. But one among the three fronts was crumbling—the front that operated directly under the commander.

The soldiers fought as if possessed. They were going to win or die fighting. But they were being felled. A pitched battle raged on. There was no dune, no shrub, no patch of flat land that wasn't a site of combat. But even then, wave upon wave of firangi soldiers continued to emerge from the other side of the battlefield.

Another wave of restlessness ran through the soldiers as word travelled: The commander still can't be located. He still hasn't returned. Where could he have gone?

'Run! Run!' There was a stampede.

Lekhraj ran too, stumbling over dead bodies, tripping over banners and chain shots.

'Run! Run!' The artillerymen deserted their posts. Heaps of gunpowder were being left behind. Wounded soldiers lay on the ground, clutching their guns, convulsing with pain. Horses had been injured; their frightened neighing mixed with the sound of terror that filled the battlefield. Amidst this chaos, only one word made sense to the soldiers: 'Run!'

This was not the only scene of battle that haunted Lekhraj as a recurring nightmare even years later. They had reached a pontoon bridge, and the platoons were crossing over, one by one. It was early morning. It was cold, and there was a dense fog. The river had risen. Someone said it had been raining heavily on the other side of the hills. Lekhraj looked out at the river. His feet froze. Not one, not two, but countless corpses flowed with the water. They were corpses of Khalsa soldiers. In the river, the men's turbans had come undone and gathered around their necks. Lekhraj looked closely at a body; water had washed out its wounds. The river had washed the wounds of all the bodies. Hair covered some faces. Other faces looked clean, while some bodies had turned over and were face down. The hands of so many of the soldiers were still gripped around their swords. They had died, but hadn't let go of their swords.

Most of the corpses were bloated. One corpse was taut, as if having stubbornly resolved to be a soldier standing at attention even when floating down the river. His hand too was fastened around the green grip of his sword. Wearing yellow turbans, bearing sheaths of diverse colours, in death, they flowed down the river as they had been at the moment in which they'd been felled.

Lekhraj wasn't the only one who stood frozen in his tracks. The other soldiers who'd already started crossing the pontoon bridge were glued to their spots. But there were still others behind them, and their bodies, restless to reach the bridge and cross it, pressed on. The first batch crossed over the bridge.

Who were these soldiers in the river? No one had to look far to find an answer. No doubt, these were bodies of the soldiers beside whom they'd all fought the last battle. Once they were felled, their bodies had been discarded into the river. But there was no time to linger and contemplate. Drums announcing yet another round of fighting were being sounded in the distance, and the soldiers turned, eager to fight.

But the following day, they found themselves fleeing from the battlefield yet again. 'Reassemble at the bridge,' they called out to each other. 'Just make it to the bridge somehow. Once we cross the river, we'll be back in the safety of the Khalsa territory.'

But they weren't fated to cross the river. The bridge was broken. One of the pontoons had floated away. The gap was too wide to jump over. The soldiers were stranded. More and more were still running for their lives from the battlefield towards the river. Panicked, they thrust their weight forward. The crowd kept on swelling. There was pandemonium. It was impossible to move ahead and impossible to turn around. The soldiers were trapped. Disoriented and out of options, the soldiers flung themselves into the river. Its strong current carried them away instantaneously. The soldiers of the firangi army had been chasing after them, firing incessantly. The river turned red with blood. Terrifying screams filled the air. Lekhraj felt a push, fell and landed on a corpse. The very next moment, someone fell on top of him. That soldier was killed, but Lekhraj survived.

A few days later, Lekhraj participated in what would be his last encounter in the war. It was by a well. A firangi flag was hoisted on the roof of a small house, signalling that their camp was nearby. There was a field adjoining the well. It was lined with boulders, and Khalsa soldiers spread themselves out and created a front behind them. Here too, the ceaseless waves of firangi soldiers advanced towards them. It was a terrifying sight. They were emerging from the forest, where they must have been camping. Here too, the first attack had been with cannon fire. Then the foot soldiers attacked. Manohar was positioned behind the wellhead and Lekhraj was behind a boulder. The well was in plain view from where Lekhraj was. Manohar wasn't alone; there were three or four more soldiers with him. The foot soldiers of the firangi army advanced rapidly and with loud battle cries. They were upon the well. Fighting began. Soldiers cut and slashed at one another. The last time Lekhraj looked towards the well, he saw Manohar swinging his sword. His chest was bleeding heavily; a bayonet had pierced it. And yet, his hand kept moving.

That's all that Lekhraj could see. The bugles had been sounded somewhere. The Khalsa soldiers began to lay down their arms. Lekhraj felt the jab of a rifle butt on his back. The scattered Sikh soldiers were being taken prisoner. Lekhraj too was taken. He caught a glimpse of the firangi soldier who had taken him and was walking behind him; he was a thin-moustached man with blue, agile eyes. He was the one who had attacked Lekhraj with the butt of his rifle.

The same day, under coercion of rifle butts, he and the others who'd been taken prisoner had lifted the dead bodies of their fallen comrades and thrown them into the ravine. He lifted corpses one by one, as if in a delirium, carried them to the brink, and threw them over the edge into the river far below. He came upon Manohar's body near the well. He picked it up, threw it over his shoulder and turned towards the ravine. Manohar's arm was swinging and it hit against Lekhraj's body, as if knocking at his heart. Lekhraj kept walking towards the ravine, in a deep trance. No sharp emotion arose in his heart. All he knew was that it was Manohar's body, that it was heavy, that its arm kept hitting against his body, that the ravine was just a little ahead and that, once he reached it, he would throw the body into it, just like all the others from his platoon, who were ahead of him and behind him, were doing—they were all carrying the bodies of their dead comrades to throw them into the ravine.

Lekhraj's legs buckled once because of the weight of Manohar's body. The firangi soldier hit him on his back with the butt of his rifle.

'Look straight,' he screamed.

Lekhraj regained his balance and looked ahead. He was out of breath by the time he reached the edge of the hillock. He stood still for some time. His eyelids felt heavy and kept shutting. He was aware that he could be struck on his back any second. He bent forward, placed both his hands on his knees and thrust his right shoulder forward. The corpse hurtled down the ravine like a heavy bundle. Lekhraj's body felt light again. He looked down into the ravine. Countless vultures circled over it. Lekhraj was stunned at the sight. They were everywhere—not just in the sky, but on rocks, on boulders, on the branches of the leafless acacia trees, where they sat with their yellow beaks wide open. Whenever one vulture spread out its wings and took flight, another would settle down on a tree or a boulder. Involuntarily, Lekhraj's eyes travelled further down, to where the bodies lay in a heap. He tried to spot his friend's corpse, but he couldn't see it. He felt nauseated. A sharp stench rose from the ravine—perhaps that's what made him feel nauseated, or it could have been because he had seen scattered body parts and twisted, blood-drenched uniforms. But just at that moment, the firangi jabbed his rifle butt into his back and ordered him to head back for another corpse. Lekhraj turned around, stumbling and falling, forgetting all about his nausea.

Despite his half-conscious state, Lekhraj was taking in the surroundings—on the other side is a dried-up stream, and behind that there's that run-down building on which the firangi flag has been hoisted. His half-closed eyes had also seen that the firangis had brought their shiny cannon out of the forest. He saw soldiers in red uniform pushing it like one would push a buffalo, and taking it towards the building.

And he saw Diwan Dhanpat. He emerged from behind the building and entered it. Even here he was in his yellow angrakha and saffron turban. It really was Diwan Dhanpat. *But what's he doing here?* Lekhraj had recognized him despite his encumbered senses and half-seeing eyes. It was definitely Dhanpat. His yellow angrakha fluttered in the breeze. Lekhraj found it really odd to see that dress in the middle of battle.

Five or six porters walked behind him, heavy sacks on their backs. It really was Dhanpat at their head.

Involuntarily, Lekhraj's eyes went towards that hill which was now quiet, but from where he had descended into the battlefield along with his platoon, daring the enemy with fierce battle cries. And it dawned upon him now that Manohar had been killed. He felt an unbearable stab in his heart. He felt Manohar's hand hit against his left knee, and his heart felt as if it was slowly emptying out.

That night the sky was studded with countless stars. Lying beneath its infinite spread, Lekhraj broke down and cried.

Three big battles had been fought and that had broken the Khalsa kingdom's back. The commanders had surrendered their arms. The enemy had won. Punjab had been taken by Englishmen.

Two fingers of his left hand gone, and a deep wound in his right leg, Lekhraj wandered from one place to the other without purpose. He was no longer a boy; he was a grown man. His gaze grew distant, and something inside him had broken and couldn't be put together again. Even though they'd lost, the world seemed to carry on like before. Was he disheartened because Manohar was gone? Lekhraj's eyes had seen not just Manohar, but countless others die. *They had died fighting*. Then what was making him so restless? Was it because his grandmother's stories, which had inspired him to get enlisted, were not able to hold? Or was it because something wasn't measuring up to the standards he held dear? He was unable to return home, and unable to settle down in Lahore, where a new Sikh administration had been set up under the patronage of the firangis. He wandered from place to place.

The stories his grandmother told him hadn't been belied; he had seen outstanding instances of valour, gallantry and sacrifice in the war—he'd seen his dear Manohar too wield his sword bravely in the moment of death. Having experienced war, Lekhraj had accepted and now believed that no war is merely about victory or defeat. Neither is every war a show of strength. War, he had come to believe, was a struggle run through with self-interest, ideas about the good of others and idealism.

In the months following the war, as he wandered from place to place, town to town, city to city, some secrets had begun to unravel. But his heart was unwilling to accept what he was learning. *Can this be true? Is what I'm hearing actually what happened?* It wasn't the secrets but his wounds that were unravelling. *Can it be true that both the commanders of the Sikh army, Lal Singh and Tej Singh, had secretly joined hands with the firangis?* He had been hearing over and over that Sardar Lal Singh had deserted his army during the battle at Mudki. He hadn't left to man another front, nor fled for fear of his life. He had slunk away because he'd already done what he had set out to do: he had fulfilled the promise he'd made to the firangi governor general; he had ensured the Sikh army's defeat.

He heard a baker repeat this theory some years later. Lekhraj, exhausted by the long journey he had undertaken, sat down in the baker's shop to rest his feet. The baker, a middle-aged man, was mocking the soldiers who'd fought in the war. Lekhraj felt incensed and wanted to punch the man and break his jaw. It's not easy to dent a soldier's faith; it's faith that makes a soldier stake his life on the battlefield. But he stayed quiet. What the baker was saying was condensing in his mind everything he had heard about the war in the last few years.

During his wandering, he'd heard one thing in one place and another somewhere else. Once, he'd heard that the commander of the other front, Sardar Tej Singh, had made the forces under his command stand idle for six days when they were just minutes away from the firangis' encampment. He hadn't attacked the enemy camp because he was part of the enemy camp! Scenes of war loomed before Lekhraj's eyes under a new light. He saw once more how the commander of his front hadn't let his men attack the enemy after the round of cannon fire had stopped. He saw again how restless, how eager they'd all been to launch an offensive, and how they stayed where they were because the commander had ordered them to stay put. There is a facet of war in which the soldier stakes his life; he evokes the name of his country and his king and launches into battle with loud battle cries. And then there is another facet, of crooked moves and devious strategizing, which turn soldiers into mere pawns in a game of chess. This remains hidden from the soldiers' view. In fact, it remains hidden from the view of the entire country. And sometimes it gets buried under layers of time. Not just two, there are many facets, multiple layers. The palimpsest of history keeps so many of them hidden. Many never see the light of day.

Lekhraj had limped through the dust-laden streets of city after city under a different impression: *We lost because the enemy had more cannon power. We lost because mistakes were made in how the fronts were created.* But now he was slowly coming to the conclusion that he would never learn the truth during his lifetime. The secrets, and the reasons for their defeat, would unfold decades later, by which time firangi rule will have become established, and he and others playing their roles in this time would be long gone. The secrets will be revealed when everything will already have crumbled to dust. That's when it will come to light that the Khalsa army lost because it was stabbed in the back. The soldiers had been raring to go into battle, putting their lives at stake, but the order they'd received had been to the contrary. The army was ordered to withdraw at the exact moment when it should've been ordered to attack. This wasn't a mistake. The corpses of the Khalsa soldiers were proof of their commitment to the kingdom. How were they to know that elaborate conspiracies had been woven to have them decimated?

Sometimes, as Lekhraj lay in the shade of a tree or walked along a street, an image would emerge sharply in his mind— of the magnificent horse rider in a silken, blue robe, pearl necklaces around his neck and a courtier's turban on his head, whom he had seen in the streets of his town as a child—the true warrior who had emerged from his grandmother's stories on to the streets, who'd come to meet the king and whom Lekhraj had been mesmerized by.

Could it be that it was this same horse rider who was commanding our army?

New secrets were being revealed at every step—secrets of the war front and mysterious transgressions.

There were so many layers, and each layer concealed secrets. Why was the army brought to that flat plain where there was no hill, nor elevation to offer relief or advantage? There was nothing there, save a few shrubs and dunes. That must've been part of the conspiracy. 'This will be the weakest segment in our front, governor general. You'll be able to attack and break this front with absolute ease.' The plan was becoming clear—break the back of your own army, weaken it, waste its cannon fire so that you may be appointed minister in the new government that will be set up under the patronage of the firangis.

For, hadn't the firangis attacked that part of the front most brutally? Hadn't the commander slunk away from his post?

Hadn't the enemy, as a result, managed to decimate the Khalsa army, even as its soldiers fought them with all they had? The battle had raged until midnight. There had been no commander; no one guided the army. All that the soldiers had had were the swords they were wielding and the name of the Guru in their hearts and on their lips. Lekhraj couldn't remember how or when the stampede had started; all he remembered was that there had been one and, caught in its midst, he had run, stumbling over dead horses and chased by flaming cannonballs. It was only much later that it was learnt that eight thousand soldiers of the Khalsa army had lost their lives in that battle.

While the soldiers were fighting a battle in which they staked their lives, their commanders were setting into motion a different manoeuvre.

Khalsa soldiers were restive at being made to sit idle when the other front was being demolished and its soldiers were being decimated. The following day, a brave Nihang, his sword raised in readiness for battle, had run to the commander to ask that they be ordered to go and aid them. But when it appeared that the Sikh army had begun to tip the battle in its favour and might defeat the firangis, the commander ordered the soldiers to withdraw from the frontal attack and waste precious time circuiting around the enemy and attacking from the back.

A move had been made on the chessboard of war, and it had succeeded. While Lekhraj had to flee the battlefield like a wounded animal, the firangi army unfurled its flag and declared victory.

Broken fragments of experience and information started joining with each other. A faint image began to form in front of Lekhraj's eyes, but its contours stayed unfinished—because Lekhraj still had faith. It was unimaginable for him that a chasm of this magnitude could exist between the interests of the soldiers and commanders of the Khalsa army. By the time history pronounces its verdict, the participants of this time won't be there to hear it; they'll be long gone.

'Do you know how many Sikh soldiers died on that bridge? Four thousand! Dead soldiers fell in heaps there. And do you know who had broken that bridge? Who ordered that the pontoon be removed? The fleeing commander!'

Would Lekhraj ever let himself believe this? 'I'm going to crack your skull with a stick. Who do you think you are?' he responded, anger getting the better of him.

What had happened was not war. It was a nightmare—a terrible nightmare. But not for the commander who sent the promised secret message to the firangi general: 'I've kept my word. The Sikh army won't be able to rally together and reorganize after returning to its kingdom. Rest assured.'

As he wandered from village to village, one image surfaced over and over again in Lekhraj's mind—how Manohar's chest had been soaked with blood and pierced through by a bayonet, and yet his hands had worked the sword, fulfilling the duties of a soldier till the very end. How was Manohar to know that even as he fought the enemy in his dying moments, the commander was sitting in the firangi governor general's camp, his hands outstretched for a reward for being an ally?

'The regime has changed. Speak softly; the regime has changed. A treaty has been signed with the firangis, on their terms. A new government has been formed, and Lal Singh is the prime minister and Tej Singh is the commander-in-chief of the army. The administration has changed.'

Lekhraj got up to leave. As he continued on his journey, the words rang in his mind, 'The regime has changed. Speak softly; the regime has changed.'

A change in regime means that those who were enemies until yesterday become friends today; deserters become commanders-in-chief; the dark becomes resplendent. And what about the soldier? A soldier never changes. He fights, and he dies; he stakes his life on the battlefield, and he demonstrates his valour—because the soldier has taken a vow that he will always put his commander's word before his own life.

It was night. Exhausted by his journey, Lekhraj slept under a tree. He had a dream. Manohar is standing, leaning against a boulder. He has lifted his shirt to bare his chest and is saying, 'Look how fair I am.' Suddenly his chest becomes bloodied. Lekhraj is on his way to the commander, with some other soldiers, to tell him that Manohar has been killed, that a bullet has pierced his chest. Upon crossing the boulder and reaching the clearing, he finds the commander is gone. There's a firangi there instead. He has a thin moustache and he's holding a narrow cane, and is gently tapping the end of the cane against his thigh. Lekhraj woke up with a start. He stared into the darkness for a long time, restless, uneasy. After some time, he drifted back into a dream. The sky is blue. He is excited. He hears the trot of a horse's hooves. His pulse is racing; he is filled with anticipation. The horse rider is turning the corner and has come into view. He's wearing a blue robe. He has a courtier's turban on his head and pearl necklaces around his neck. Lekhraj is impatient and excited. The trot has become louder; the horse has come closer. Oh! He's wearing a crumpled angrakha. It's not the turbaned rider; it's Dhanpat. He's saying to the people on the street, 'I told you, didn't I? I told you the regime would change, that I would win. Didn't I say I would?'

Dhanpat entered town through Grain Market astride his mule. He was dressed as he usually was, and yet there was a difference. A black waistband was tied over his yellow angrakha; a sword in a green, silk-covered scabbard hung from it. He was wearing the traditional saffron turban of the Diwans. And the expression he wore on his face was that of a king returning to his capital, victorious in war.

Banshi and his friends had gathered as usual by a street side, a game of dice spread out between them. Banshi was rolling the die in his hands when he saw Dhanpat. He stopped.

'Look who's here,' he chirruped. 'The prince of pearls has returned!' All eyes turned towards Dhanpat. And then, for a brief moment, Banshi felt confused. Should Dhanpat be welcomed respectfully, or should he be ridiculed? Stories about him had trickled into town during the war. But the tables had turned now, and Dhanpat was no longer the Dussehra clown.

'Welcome, Diwanji, welcome back. You succeeded in settling all matters, I hope?'

This evoked some sniggering from the sprightlier among the bystanders.

Dhanpat had already sighted this gathering of troublemakers from afar. He was prepared. He didn't turn his head to look at them, and fixed his gaze on a distant point. He'd decided this was the best way to steer clear of people below his stature.

'Good morning, good morning, Diwan Sahib.' Banshi stood up when Dhanpat's mule drew near. He'd bowed and said 'Good morning' in English.

The tables may have turned and the regime may have changed, but Dhanpat's mule was the same old starveling that moved only if constantly egged on by Dhanpat's heel. It twitched its ears and flung its tail about to chase away the flies that were bothering it. The effort sent shivers through its entire body.

'Did you win the fortress?'

Diwan Dhanpat found this question to his liking. His lips spread in a smile beneath his moustache.

'You've returned to the capital after so long . . . What expedition have you embarked on today?'

The Diwan liked this question as well. Clearly, stories about his exploits and expeditions had reached town.

'Are you out on a tour of your principality?'

At this, two men, who had been sitting with their legs dangling from a raised platform, laughed.

'Perhaps it's work at the king's court that beckons?'

Diwan Dhanpat pulled the reins of his mule and halted.

'Have you lost use of your brain? Where's the court any more?'

'That's exactly what I was thinking. Why would Diwan Sahib go to the Palace of Mirrors when it's no longer the seat of the court?'

Someone objected, 'So what if it's not the seat of the court? The king still lives there. You could be on your way to see him.'

'Who wants to meet him any more? Who calls him "king" any longer? The governor general wouldn't recruit him even for his mule brigade.'

The gathering turned silent. The old regime may have dissolved, but the courtesies and etiquettes associated with it hadn't. His lustre may have dimmed, but Raja Amirchand hadn't yet become a subject of ridicule.

'Then to where does His Excellency's procession proceed?' Banshi's voice contained a subdued note of satire.

'I've said already, I'm simply taking a round.'

'Indeed,' Banshi said, then added, 'but shouldn't a sola topi adorn your head now that you've subjugated the fortress?'

Diwan Dhanpat's lips broke into a big smile. He raised his right hand and twirled his moustache. His straw-like neck became taut. His tiny eyes lit up.

'We'll take that into consideration,' he said.

A roar of laughter filled the air.

Having given his first audience to his subjects, Diwan Dhanpat spurred his mule. The mule didn't budge.

Dhanpat had been busy during the war. At first he'd disappeared and wasn't heard about for almost a year. But then stories started trickling in. Someone heard he had started trading in camels, which he bought from here and there and sold in one or another military encampment. This news was enough for people to start spinning jokes about him. But then the overseer of an estate returned to town and said he'd seen Dhanpat going towards a firangi camp with two donkeys that had huge sacks loaded on their backs. He said the sacks were filled with camels' tails. This tickled people no end. And then they heard that the Diwan had taken to cutting off the tails of dead camels, which he sold for one ashrafi a piece. This was so absurd that it caught everyone's imagination and long before he even returned to town he was nicknamed 'Trim-Tail Diwan'.

Banshi took a jibe at him: 'You've been supplying the firangi camp with camels' tails. Why, you should've kept a camel for yourself too!'

The gathering around the game of dice laughed.

Dhanpat's cheeks trembled, but he didn't respond and kept trying to spur the mule into movement. It would be foolish to argue with these good-for-nothing wretches.

'Mind your place, Banshi,' one of Banshi's friends remarked. 'That's no way to talk to those above your stature.'

Dhanpat pretended not to have heard and continued to hit his heel against the mule. The starveling still wouldn't move forward; he shifted slightly to the middle of the street. Now the Diwan struck his heel hard, and directly on its ribs. The mule shook all over, even jerked its head, but didn't move. The Diwan felt he was being embarrassed in front of people whom he considered himself to be better than. He hit the mule once more with his heel. The mule spread its rear legs and shat.

'You're great, Diwanji. You've trained your mule so well,' Ramjawaya said. Then he turned towards Banshi and said, 'Be content now, Banshi. The Diwan has answered your question.'

Feigning oblivion to what his mule was doing, the Diwan kept his gaze fixed on some invisible place in mid-air. Or perhaps he was inspecting the roofs of houses that stood in front of him.

After a brief pause, he spurred his mule again. This time, it started moving, and the Diwan had crossed the length of the street and turned with the lane, entering the wider street of Kohlis' Neighbourhood, when he heard a sing-song voice call out after him—

He's the one who stole the black hen!

He heard laughter. Then the voice started again—

He's the one who stole the black hen
No, that's not him; he's someone else

When he'd gone some distance, Dhanpat turned around to look. Many half-naked children were trailing him. They were chatting animatedly with one another and giggling. Soon some young lads joined them.

Dhanpat could easily have been of the opinion that now that the regime had changed, now that neither the Sikhs nor the Lahore Durbar held any sway, and therefore the puny king Amirchand, the one of the Palace of Mirrors, had been rendered redundant, he—and only he—remained. And while it was true that he had returned to town a frailer man—his chest had sunk and his angrakha looked like a tent billowing on a pole—he had an air of authority about him, more than he'd ever had before. As far as he was concerned, his measly mule was a majestic elephant. And what about this band of kids trailing behind him? To Dhanpat, that was his grand procession through town.

A group of hijras entered the lane. They saw Diwanji's procession and, clapping and blessing him with a long life, they too joined in. The town stirred from its slumber. A fun opportunity had presented itself after a long time. Mahmood, the town's wrestler, had just emerged from the wrestling akhara. His body was still plastered with mud, and he had only a red loincloth on. He saw the procession and stopped.

'Yaa Ali,' he called out at the top of his voice when it had come close to him, and jumped in. Patting his biceps with his palms, performing all kinds of wrestling manoeuvres, he started walking at the head of the procession.

Weavers, haberdashers, cloth sellers, goldsmiths, grocers, artisans—everyone emerged from their shops to better appreciate this spectacle. They stood on either side of the street, on the sitting platforms that fronted their shops. The Diwan's procession rode on. He could hear laughter behind him, and he saw people raise their hands to their mouths to make loud 'pi pi' sounds. But all his face showed was a deep satisfaction, as if the catcalls were hosannas to him.

'The Diwan has lost his marbles,' a man said to another. 'He really thinks this is his cortège.'

The procession had crossed the long and wide street that ran through the neighbourhood of the Kohlis. The Diwan twisted the reins of his mule and turned it in the direction of the mansion.

Seeing an opportunity to earn a little, Jalal, the ballad singer's brother, joined the procession, beating at his drum.

Silence enveloped the mansion. Diwan Mayyadas was taking his daily stroll on the terrace. In the days following the firangis' victory, shadows of uncertainty loomed over the entire town. But the mansion seemed as if plunged into utter darkness. The war had brought Mayyadas to the verge of bankruptcy. He had loaned his entire wealth to the Lahore Durbar towards the war efforts. After its defeat in the first round of fighting, when the Lahore Durbar seemed to be in peril, he sent it all the gold and silver he had. The army continued to suffer one reversal after another. By the end of the war, Diwan Mayyadas had lost everything he owned, except for the mansion and the land adjoining it. Six difficult months, during which the war consumed all he had, turned him into an old man. His shoulders became bent; his body lost its tautness. But even now, when he stepped into town, people stood up to greet him respectfully. In their eyes, he was no less wise and dignified than he'd been before the war; his nobility, his eminence were not diminished. Diwan Mayyadas didn't let his worries be seen by the world.

The clamour on the street reached his ears. He took it to be yet another parade related to the war. But then, Mahmood the wrestler came into full view, performing his wrestling manoeuvres, followed by clapping and dancing hijras. Jalal accompanied them, beating on his drum.

Diwan Mayyadas looked at the advancing procession, bewildered.

Diwan Dhanpat, astride his miserable mule, crossed the yard and came to a halt before the mansion's gate. The procession stayed close behind him. No one knew what to expect, or what would happen next.

Diwan Mayyadas saw Dhanpat, and recognized him immediately. It didn't take him long to read the triumph in his demeanour. He looked into Dhanpat's small, cunning eyes, which seemed to be contemplating him like a hunter studying its prey.

On Dhanpat's instruction, Jalal was beating at the drum as loudly as he could. The hijras had broken into wild dancing. Dhanpat drew the children into frenzy by pulling out a fistful of coins from under his angrakha and flinging them into the air. He was pleased with the result. He flung another fistful of coins in the air.

Diwan Mayyadas stood quietly on the terrace, watching this spectacle. Then he turned around and went into the mansion.

To Dhanpat, this was a sign that the enemy had conceded defeat, that he had emerged victorious in this duel. He demanded that the drums be beaten even louder than before.

But Mahmood and Jalal had begun to feel that there was something inappropriate about the entire situation, and that getting drums beaten and having hijras dance outside the mansion without any occasion having warranted it may be aimed at embarrassing the elder Diwan. They left.

'Beat the drums!' Diwan Dhanpat demanded, and flung another fistful of coins into the air. But there was no drum. Hijras continued to dance and clap.

Afternoon was ending by the time Diwan Dhanpat's show ended. By then the hijras, who had danced with gusto for him and blessed him, were cursing him and making lewd gestures at him. Dhanpat had refused to give them the tip that was their due. They eventually left for their homes, and Dhanpat turned towards Oil Pressers' Neighbourhood.

Years later, it was said that this peculiar procession marked the moment after which the town, which had prospered on the banks of the River Jhelum, began to fall to ruin. The river changed course, and receded away. River-based commerce ended. Land became saturated with saltpetre; it covered everything, even fields and homes. Yields declined.

The dice players heard about the procession Dhanpat had led to the mansion.

'Time moves in mysterious ways,' one of them said. 'Earlier, no one would have dared to behave this way with Diwan Mayyadas.'

'He went there to embarrass Diwan Mayyadas. He wanted to humiliate him.'

'What a lowlife. Who knows what he'll do next.'

'But truth be told, it's not like Diwan Mayyadas acted fairly with him. He had all his things thrown out of the mansion.'

So then, the war *had* changed perceptions. Diwan Mayyadas's image *had* faded in the eyes of people.

'In his conceit, he gave his entire wealth to the Khalsa Durbar. He was so eager to prove his loyalty. Didn't he see that fortune was favouring the firangis and that crown after crown was falling at their feet?'

Diwan Mayyadas no longer held sway in events that would constitute the future. He, and his significance, belonged with the shadows of the past. He was disconnected from the present, out of joint with the future. The war had come as a deluge that had cast Diwan Mayyadas aside. The war had changed everything.

And now, the new regime was advancing towards the town. It would bring with it its own disposition, its own people, and its own mores and codes. It would make new demands and exert novel pressures. The old order hadn't entirely passed, but it was no longer the touchstone by which the new would be evaluated. There was no denying that there was a new charge in the air. There was anticipation and curiosity about which way the new regime would sit and about what would happen next. After all, isn't it one of the ironies of life that power produces the gradient along which its subjects' perceptions and beliefs flow? Only a few manage to stay steadfast to their conscience and maintain their equanimity.

Discussions soon shifted away from Mayyadas towards the new administration that had been constituted in Lahore after the war, and in which the commanders who had betrayed their soldiers during war were given high posts. People's attitude towards them had started changing as well. Time was rescripting perceptions about their conduct during the war; they began to be talked of as far-sighted, intelligent and astute readers of time.

'Had it not been for them, the entire kingdom would have had to be ceded to the firangis,' Ramjawaya said. 'People say they joined hands with the British, but I say they did the right thing. They showed foresight. It's called strategizing. The wise have said, "Save the entire world from slipping out of your hands; give away half." If it weren't for them, the entire kingdom would have ended up under the control of the firangis.' From the way he said it, it was clear he felt strongly about the matter.

The firangis began to be spoken of as the ruler. It's convention to think of the ruler as the master, as the one before whom you must bow your head, and the one to whom you must remain loyal. There were still a few who faulted the commanders or argued that betrayal shouldn't be confused for or praised as intelligence. But they were usually silenced in arguments. 'This is what strategizing is about, my friend. How can I explain this to you? This is the way of the world; it has been since time immemorial,' Ramjawaya would say.

'This isn't about strategy; it was betrayal. Commanders aren't supposed to desert their armies!'

'Oh, that's enough,' Ramjawaya shushed. 'What does a pipsqueak like you know about such matters?' Then, turning to the gathering, he said, 'Who knows what actually happened! No one knows what must have really transpired.'

Banshi had his own unique approach to arguments. 'All I know is they're the rulers now,' he said, stretching his body lazily. He had mastered the art of eluding serious discussions. 'If tomorrow our Trim-Tail Diwan Dhanpat turns out to be the chosen one, I'll be the first to salute him.'

'Time moves in mysterious ways,' someone said, nodding in agreement.

'Time moves in mysterious ways,' Ramjawaya agreed. Then he remembered a fragment of history. 'It was against our town that Mahmud of Ghazni had launched his ninth attack. It's said there was so much wealth here that it took him months to carry it away.'

Kohli laughed. 'And the brave men of this town didn't lift a finger.' He stretched his legs and continued, 'So this town has had the honour of being licked clean by Mahmud of Ghazni.' And he made an obscene remark under his breath.

Ramjawaya was incensed. 'Don't use foul language,' he said. 'You know so little about the history and the greatness of this town. So many great warriors have been born here.'

'Brave warrior Dhanpat and brave warrior King Amirchand. Who else? You?'

'You're weak in the head. Our ancestors fought against Parashuram. Now, has there ever been a warrior more impressive than Parashuram?'

The humpbacked sweet seller who was standing on the raised platform outside the shop chipped in: 'He's right. The Khatris fought against him.'

'And your ancestors saw the whole thing,' Kohli retorted.

'Not only Parashuram, they also fought Alexander the Great,' Ramjawaya said excitedly. 'Porus ruled from here, from this very place.'

'Porus must also have been a Diwan. What do you say, Ramjawaya? You must be related to him,' Banshi laughed. 'I don't understand why you drag your sorry arse around; you should have a crown on your head.'

Kohli said, 'Yesterday he was claiming Porus belonged to the Sabharwal caste. Today he's bringing up Mahmud of Ghazni.'

'Porus was absolutely a Sabharwal. And Alexander was so impressed by the valour of the Khatris that he took five Diwans back with him to Greece.'

'He would definitely have taken you with him, Ramjawaya,' Banshi remarked. 'He would have kept you in a zoo. You'd have sat on a branch of some tree, swinging your legs in the air. The people of Greece would've looked at you and exclaimed, "Ah see, that's a Diwan."'

'There's no fire in your blood, Banshi,' Karamchand contributed. 'Ramjawaya is a Chandrawanshi, a scion of the lunar race.'

'The Kohlis are the oldest inhabitants of this region. They were here much before the Diwans.' Banshi pulled Ramjawaya's leg.

Ramjawaya was enraged. 'The Kohlis were marauders,' he said. 'They were a clan, not a caste. They never settled.'

'The Diwans had no standing; they were dirt,' Kohli retorted.

'Have you seen your face in the mirror?' Ramjawaya said, his hand dancing near Kohli's chin in irritation. 'They're good-for-nothings. They'd have no home if it weren't for the Diwans. We let them live here.'

'Go see your own face in the mirror. Neither mouth, nor forehead, you're like a djinn that's come down from a mountain. You go to weddings uninvited wearing that saffron turban of yours to feed off leftovers.'

'And who are you, huh? Your own mothers don't recognize you and you people call yourselves Khatris!'

The sweet seller took a step forward to intervene. He didn't want two men from established families to be seen fighting in front of his shop. Placing a hand on Ramjawaya's shoulder, he said, 'The Diwans are significant in their own way, and the Kohlis in their own. Diwanji, it doesn't become you to fight like this.'

But Kohli was still glaring at Ramjawaya. 'Successors of Porus, my foot. Alexander took the Diwans to Greece. Blah! Not five Diwans, he took five baboons with him, and left Ramjawaya behind to live off leftovers from wedding parties.'

'Dacoits! Robbers! You Kohlis have these catlike eyes. God knows whose offspring you are and from where you came and settled here.'

'Be careful, Ramjawaya.'

'What can you do? Huh? What are you going to do?'

Things were spiralling out of control. Banshi and the sweet seller realized it was time to break up the fight. Banshi pulled Ramjawaya away, and the sweet seller dragged Kohli towards the rug on which the dice game was laid out.

ꙮ

Uncertainty reigned over Punjab for some years following the war. Things, people hoped, might turn; the Khalsa regime might return; the British might still be overthrown. Skirmishes broke out from time to time. But the British only got stronger; their control kept tightening. Slowly, their rule over Punjab became uncontested.

The new regime began to express itself. A 'Yellow Quarter' was constructed in the area between Orchard of the Sheikhs and the hillock. It was a construction in a new vein—the rooms were large, the ceilings high, and a veranda skirted it. This was to be the revenue official's headquarters, and whenever the deputy commissioner visited town, it would be here that he would hold his court. New rules and covenants were put in place.

The first Englishman arrived in town. He was a short and plump man with a red face and he wore a white sola topi on his head. The young and old alike rushed out for a glimpse of him. But Dhanpat was the only man in the entire town who'd been called for an audience with him. Many people saw Dhanpat outside his tent, and watched him pay obeisance to the foreigner by bending down, touching the ground and then his forehead with his fingers, over and over, before entering the tent. Witnesses reported to the rest of town that Dhanpat had taken gifts along—a basket of dry fruits, two bottles of sandalwood sherbet, a length of Mushaddi cloth woven by local weavers, and *pateesa*, the savoury sweetmeat, a speciality of this town. The foreigner had laughed and accepted all the gifts, but not the cloth. People said he'd inspected it for some time before throwing it out of the tent with a, *Yeh nahi maangtaa'—This-not-want*. They said his face had turned from red to crimson.

Until now Dhanpat only rode around town on his mule. To this routine he now added something new: He started holding 'court' in an open space in Grain Market. Every evening, he'd have the ground sprayed with water, set up a couple of wicker stools and a charpoy, keep a pitcher of fresh sherbet sweetened with jaggery at hand, and urge anyone who happened to be passing by to come and sit with him. He was building contact. Slowly, people started to come by to meet him of their own accord, and soon Dhanpat's court started looking busy. But Dhanpat didn't stop here. If there was a child's tonsure ceremony anywhere in town, or if someone died, or if there was a religious discourse somewhere, Dhanpat made sure he attended it.

'He didn't make a sound when Diwan Mayyadas had all his things thrown out of the mansion,' murmurs of support for Dhanpat, though they were faint and they were few, began to travel through town. 'He quietly gathered up his things and left. Anyone else would have created a scene.'

'So what if he was born of a keep's womb? He is, after all, Mayyadas's brother's son. He has a right to the mansion.' Indeed it could be said that Dhanpat was managing to work up—at least from a few people—sympathy.

One day, as Diwan Mayyadas was walking slowly, his walking stick in hand, towards Goldsmiths' Street, he saw Dhanpat in the distance. Dhanpat was on his mule as usual, and had entered the lane from the opposite direction. Diwan Mayyadas pretended not to have noticed him, and walked quietly on. But Dhanpat stopped when they were crossing each other.

'My humble salutations to you, Tauji,' he said, without alighting from the mule. His voice was more haughty than humble.

Diwan Mayyadas looked up.

'Hope things are well with you and at your house, Dhanpat,' he said.

'Tauji, let me know if I can be of some service to you. You know, if you need something done at any government office.'

Mayyadas didn't respond. He just looked quietly at Dhanpat's face, at his smirking lips, at his moustache that had begun to turn grey, and at his cold eyes—the eyes of a scheming, compassionless man.

'There are quite a few opportunities right now. The new administration is giving out big contracts. Should I put in a word for you? The officer heeds my opinion.'

Dhanpat's sarcasm pierced straight through Mayyadas's heart. He gestured goodbye, and walked on.

'The rope is burnt, but the twists have stayed,' Dhanpat muttered under his breath as he spurred his mule.

∽

The war was beginning to fade from public memory. Platoons of the old army had scattered long ago. Thousands of soldiers had been rendered helpless. They had lost a war that was theirs to win, and now they roamed about, rudderless. And yet, their spirit had not been entirely extinguished. Their hearts were still unwilling to admit defeat and surrender to the enemy.

Clashes began, and continued to break out, in one place, then another and yet another, for three years. Lekhraj participated in several of these. He was in Multan when the firangis won there. He was in the battlefield in Gujarat when the Sikh soldiers were defeated. It was in this war that he lost two fingers of his right hand.

Then silence descended. Earlier, news about skirmishes used to trickle in, but now there was no news about explosions, fights or rebellions. The only news that came was about the new administration and its new rules.

One day Lekhraj was at an eatery with some other homeless soldiers, eating stale bread, when all of a sudden people started running out on to the road. Nawab Sahib's cavalcade was passing through. His decorated palanquin followed a procession of horses and footmen—Nawab Sahib was on his way to the Lahore Durbar, where he would pledge his allegiance to the new regime. It was in everyone's interests now to make friendly gestures towards the new rulers. Processions like these were being seen everywhere, en route to Lahore, their pomp and splendour in full display. It was only Lekhraj and some others impassioned like he was, who were refusing to accept this new reality. Lekhraj did think about returning home and asking after his people. Moran's memory still breathed in his heart. An image of her would flash before his eyes now and then—Moran standing at the threshold of her house and saying to him, 'I'll pray for you . . . come back soon,' then growing shy and dashing back into the house. It made him start towards town, and he even reached Miani. But there he ran into a few people from town and heard Moran had been married a while ago—married, and widowed. His mother was already dead. Lekhraj turned back.

People made all kinds of conjectures about Lekhraj. The dice players often thought about and discussed him. One speculated he'd enrolled himself into the firangi army. Another opined he had become a Ramdasi Faqir, because he had been seen visiting Chak Ramdas a few times. And yet another was of the opinion that he had become an ascetic, joined the Udasi Akhara and now roamed from place to place as a member.

Time passed, and his memory blurred.

New rules and ordinances were being passed every day. Commissionaries, districts and sub-districts were formed. A *kanoongo* was appointed for revenue collection in every sub-district. A deep restlessness took hold of the town the day the new revenue collection law was announced. The head revenue officer was away that day, and many people—from those who ran moneylending establishments to those who played dice on the street side—made their way to the mansion to consult Diwan Mayyadas on the meanings and implications of this new law. Diwan Mayyadas also found this new law strange. How could a way that had been followed for generations, and had become tradition, be done away with in this manner? He was of the opinion the legislation would fail in a matter of days.

'The village has a *patwari*, right? Now, what does he do? He maintains land records, right? And he keeps account of crop yields and how much revenue has to be paid by the village. Correct?' Diwan Mayyadas spoke slowly, going over details as if explaining them to everyone.

'Now, the patwari would deposit the revenue that had been collected, into the treasury twice a year. Correct?

'Until now this collection was done in kind, right? From now on, revenue can't be paid in kind. Only in cash. So this is one thing.

'Next. Until now, revenue was calculated by making estimates of how much crop the land would yield that year. From now on, the amount will be set, and revenue will have to be paid accordingly. You see? Earlier, revenue was paid as grain, after the crop was harvested. No more. From now on, revenue must be paid before harvest. Earlier the entire village used to get together and pay the revenue. Now each tiller will pay revenue for his land.

'So then. One, land will be divided. It will no longer be village land. Every tiller will have his own plot of land. Second, every tiller will have to pay land revenue in cash. Third, this revenue will be fixed. The amount that has been fixed will have to be paid. It won't change. You can't say that the yield wasn't good this year, so revenue should be less.'

'What if a farmer isn't able to pay?'

'Then he can take a loan from the moneylender. Take a loan on interest, and pay the revenue.'

'And if the yield is poor the next year as well?'

'Then take a loan again and pay the revenue.'

'What's the interest rate going to be?'

'Now who can know that in advance? The moneylender will decide how much interest he wants to give you a loan on.'

'What if there's a dispute? What if the farmer feels the interest should be less and the moneylender says it should be more? Then?'

'The court will decide. The government has set up courts as well.'

Farmers flocked to Yellow Quarter; the new building became busy. The patwari drew up papers for individual farmers and appraised their land and, in Yellow Quarter, the deputy revenue officer calculated the revenue due from each parcel of land and made entries in his account books.

The moneylenders liked this new law. When does a tiller ever have cash? Tillers only have grain. Innumerable moneylending establishments opened in Grain Market. Farmers started taking loans from them towards payment of revenue. Diwan Dhanpat too set up shop here. He first took one room, then another one adjacent to it, on rent in the market. He didn't sit here himself, preferring instead to be about town on his mule as before, and hired an accountant for the job.

What with the new legislation, Grain Market was perpetually buzzing with activity. The moneylending business boomed. Paying revenue in cash was beyond the means of a tiller. On top of that, there were the usual wedding expenses and festivals, for which additional loans had to be taken. Another law was passed, and tillers were now allowed to mortgage land to raise a loan. This only increased the moneylenders' profits. They hiked up the rate of interest further. And moneylenders who managed friendships with the deputy revenue officer and the kanoongo soon realized how easy it was to evict a tiller from his land if they took him to court for not being able to pay back his loan. Under the new administration, a low-level revenue collector like the kanoongo soon acquired higher social standing than the Sikh administration's high-ranking kardar had ever had. People had never been scared of the kardar; they trembled before the new administration's revenue collector.

Lala Gobindram set up a merchant's shop along with his moneylending establishment. His agent Malik Mansaram would bring all kinds of foreign merchandise from Jhelum. Gobindram not only offered loans, he also offered merchandise on credit. His strategy was simple—when a farmer lifts a loan and you place some of this merchandise in front of him, his eyes are sure to pop out with greed and he's bound to take something or other on credit. This was a perfect outlet for the foreign merchandise he was bringing in, while keeping his money in circulation, and growing, through loans. In this way, Lala Gobindram soon managed to have five bighas of land seized for non-payment of loans, and added to his own property.

The firangi administration also gave some facilities to the moneylenders. One was that they were free to fix interest at any rate they chose. This really helped them. The original sum is never returned too quickly, and interest only keeps mounting. This was an assurance that, when it comes back, the recovered amount will always be more than the original sum. The second was that if the loan and the interest on it are not recovered from the tiller, then the moneylender could seize his land. Farmers and moneylenders learnt of these rules much after they were written into existence, and this delay also helped the moneylenders—all they had to do was go to court, present the papers, offer a little something to the official, and have the land transferred in their name.

Where was the farmer to buy salt now? How was he to get oil? Earlier, he would go to the weaver and barter grain for cloth. But he didn't have grain to give any more. Now all transactions needed money. Money had come to rule. He needed cash for everything. But why should he pay with cash? Wasn't it better to just get some cloth from the moneylender and pay for it later, by and by? Lala Gobindram's fortune smiled at him. He had innovated and showed such enterprise with his moneylending business, that he'd found countless ways to make money. He bought grain from the tiller at a low price, and sold him foreign merchandise at inflated rates.

Diwan Mayyadas happened to be visiting Gobindram's establishment one day, when a farmer came by. She had brought a bag with twenty *sers* of grain as payment of a loan. Gobindram refused to accept payment in kind. He said, 'Sell it to me, and in return you'll have to buy something from me.' He bought the grain at the rate of eight annas for five sers—the market rate was much higher—and he sold her foreign chintz cloth at twice the market rate and sent her on her way.

'Seth, this is cheating,' Diwan Mayyadas said, unable to hold himself back.

'This isn't cheating, Diwanji; this is business.' And then he added with deep feeling, 'When do I refuse? Let her come with money, and I'll sell her things at the going market rate. I won't refuse. But they bring grain. Now what if the rate falls? Money doesn't grow on trees. I can't let them take things for free from me. Let them pay in cash, and I'll sell to them at the going market rate.'

Diwan Mayyadas didn't say anything further, but he thought of Gobindram's behaviour as rather cheap. He still lived with the glow of the respect and honour he had until so recently—where he held a high post in the Lahore Durbar, where his peer were the well-heeled and the endowed. The stature and gravitas that was his while he served the Lahore Durbar hadn't faded and become spent. Should he now set up shop where he'd have to count every penny? Should he stoop so low as to buy from farmers for less and sell to them at exorbitant rates? Should one who has lived lavishly now sell lentils and flour, and fleece others and spend his time cooking up ways to profiteer? *I've dealt with money before*, he thought to himself—*but with kings, not small change*.

But a voice inside him also told him that times had changed; what was in the past wasn't going to return. It sometimes wrenched his heart to think he may be losing touch with the world; everyone else seemed so set upon feathering their nests. But another voice would rise inside him and say, 'I'll die as honourably as I have lived.'

Here Dhanpat's life was becoming more and more mysterious. He would set out on his mule daily, do a round of the town and then duck and disappear for days, and no one would know where he could've gone. Someone would say he'd gone to Lalamusa, and another would say he'd gone to visit one of his mistresses. No one really knew what his business and dealings were.

Around this time, a strange incident occurred. It was unlike anything that had happened in the town before. And it was over something quite trivial. Two cousins—their fathers were brothers—owned land adjacent to each other. Two buffaloes of one cousin meandered into the farm of the other. This started an argument, which escalated into a full-blown fight. The bedlam stunned onlookers. Bhagsuddhi's husband, Balram, was wounded in eight places. Many others were beaten up badly. The town had never seen a dispute this vicious, a clash in which the count of the injured was so high.

The cousins had let out their land to tenants for cultivation. Grazing land lay between the two parcels of cultivable land. The fight started for a simple reason. The Baisakhi festival was around the corner and the time to harvest the crop was approaching. Two of Lala Gobindram's buffaloes crossed over into his cousin's field and started grazing on standing crop. They didn't do much damage—they only trampled a few plants and grazed on another few to quell their hunger. And they hadn't even been on the field for too long when Rampyara's tenant spotted them. He saw them, picked up a stick and rushed at them hollering threateningly, and rained down a beating on their backs. There was no doubt the buffaloes had crossed over to this side from Gobindram's fields. Now only God knows if Gobindram's tenant had let them into the other field on purpose or if they had meandered there all on their own. Whatever the case, the two tenants stood at the boundaries of their respective fields daring each other. Gobindram's agent, Bhagsuddhi's young husband, happened to be in the fields at that time. And as chance would have it, Rampyara's elder son, who'd been sauntering about the fields with his friends, wasn't too far. On seeing Rampyara's tenant beat up the buffaloes, Bhagsuddhi's husband lost all restraint, and he charged into their field, snatched the stick from the tenant and started beating him with it. He went even a step further—he swung the stick at the crops, damaging them.

The commotion caught Rampyara's son's attention, and he rushed to the scene with his friends. His young blood came to a boil quickly. Without trying to figure out what the matter was, he jumped right into the fray. His friends joined in as well. The ordinary scrap turned into a royal riot.

'First you steal and then act like you're a cop!' Rampyara's son tried to snatch the stick from Bhagsuddhi's husband Balram's hand. Balram too seethed fire.

Lala Gobindram's deputy's son ran into town screaming, 'They're beating up Balram chacha! They've beaten up Balram chacha!' People came out of their houses. Some of them picked up sticks and rushed towards the fields. All hell broke loose. If Balram's friends joined his side, then just as many of Rampyara's friends joined that side. Gobindram and Rampyara too had arrived on the scene by now. They saw Balram poised at the boundary of the field, swinging his stick at Rampyara's son's friends, all of them brandishing sticks too. The tenants were trying to break up the fight. Once word about the fight spread into town, people—without giving a second thought to what was going on and whose fault it was— fell in on the side of their friends and relatives. The town had never seen such bloodlust, such a fierce fight, before. The elders were at their wits' end and blamed time—what else, after all, could explain why people seemed bent upon killing each other over a few ears of wheat? Who could have thought such disaffection was possible between members of the same family over a small, trivial matter?

It was evening by the time the fracas ended and the valiant fighters—wielding sickles, sticks and shovels—retired into town in something akin to a procession. Eight cots, one after the other in a row, were part of this procession—each one bearing a brave soldier wounded in battle. Balram too lay on one of these cots. Small in height, with a thick moustache, Balram's forehead was bandaged, his kurta was torn in many places and his body was covered with blue welts. He was a novel version of the warrior.

The town buzzed with chatter for days—the encounter had earned Balram the status of a true warrior.

'Come on! I dare you to attack me! I'll beat you until you remember your days as an infant suckling at his mother's breast,' he'd stood at the boundary of the field and challenged everyone.

The short Balram, with his protruding belly, a moustache that hung on either side of his lips like flags, a bald head with a long knot of hair at its centre, stood at the boundary wall of his master's land, doing different wrestling manoeuvres. 'If there's a true son of his mother here, step forward!'

Balram stayed bandaged and in bed for two whole months. Bhagsuddhi tended to his wounds daily with turmeric and oil.

When Balram finally got out of bed after two months—he'd been struck on his head with a lance, and a deep gash ran across his face, from his ear to his chin—and limped through the street, showing everyone his scars, he was as triumphant as a soldier returning from the battlefield.

'We let them go this time. We thought, whatever one says, it is after all the same family. But if they get embroiled with us again, then only God can save them.'

Rampyara's son too bandied about in much the same way. 'We let them go this time, but let them release their buffaloes into our fields. We'll show them!'

The make of life in the town had indeed started to change. Nothing was the same as before.

Sahib Bahadur stepped out of the veranda, crossed the courtyard and stopped by the road. Shading his eyes from the sun with his hand, he looked into the distance. There was sign of neither horse nor palanquin.

The seriousness on his face turned a shade deeper. Clearly, a mistake had been made in wording the town crier's announcement. It should have been quite sufficient if the announcement had said only this much—'Loyal subjects of the English government, make yourself present at the sahib's court with your documents'. *Evidently, people have been unable to understand why we are here, and what the significance of the certificates we are handing out is.*

These Indians can't be trusted; anyone can mislead them. Sahib Bahadur laughed as this thought surfaced in his mind. *Mislead them . . . It's to do exactly that that I'm here—to mislead them. That's what we have been doing for the past twenty years—misleading them. First you have to mislead their rulers, have them think of you as their well-wishers; then mislead their commanders; then mislead their property owners and moneylenders . . . Mislead . . . Mislead . . . Mislead as much as you can.*

Arrangements had been made near the old Waterway of the Sardars, just one mile from town, to meet with petitioners. A provisional office had been set up here for Sahib Bahadur, and all levels of the local bureaucracy—from the revenue officials and deputy revenue officials to land record keepers, and even sub-inspectors—had been hovering here since morning. Inside the room, on a large table, was kept a smallish bundle of certificates. Next to it were a stamp, red ribbons, lac, etc. A small earthen pot, filled to the brim with khus-khus sherbet, had been kept in the veranda, near the door.

The commissioner must have been between forty-five and fifty years old. His small, blue eyes never kept still. His entire body expressed agility, certainty and self-confidence, as if he had taken on the entire responsibility of ensuring the roots of the new regime got planted firmly. His pursed lips communicated indifference and distance. It wasn't a cheerful and open face, the kind that radiates goodwill. Rather, it was a kind of face that exemplifies diligence, steadfastness, tact and disregard.

Three wicker stools had been set up in the veranda. This is where visitors would be seated before being called inside. At first, the sahib had ordered that five wicker stools be placed in the veranda. But then he changed his mind. *It might be better to have some visitors stand and wait. In fact, it would be more suitable. It will keep them in competition with each other.*

A detachment of soldiers had been stationed under a giant shisham tree to the right of the huge veranda. Eight to ten native soldiers—in red uniform, and under the command of the firangi sergeant—sat on a raised platform. A few rifles were kept near the trunk of the tree, and the firangi flag with blue, red and white stripes rested against it.

The hot sphere of the sun had by now risen above the treetops. The breeze had grown warmer. And there was no sign that any petitioner was going to arrive. *Could it be that an obstacle has been placed in their path; that some conspiracy is afoot? Could it be that the town's king has barred them from coming here? How is it that not one person has arrived? Who knows, maybe here people are inwardly hostile to the English regime, and they are refusing to cooperate?*

All kinds of speculations had circulated in town ever since the announcement about the certificates had been made: What are these certificates? Why will they be distributed? Are these certificates land deeds? Why should those be distributed? Everyone had her or his own ideas and conjectures. It also seemed mysterious to everyone that the sahib's office should be set up so far from town. Why not in Yellow Quarter? Perhaps the firangi wants that anyone who comes desiring a certificate should first cover a long distance and come like a petitioner, so they understand that they are going into the service of the sahib.

The sun was growing hotter. Seeing the sahib come into the veranda, the English sergeant and the soldiers of his detachment stood up. They had just returned after doing a round of the town. Seeing the sergeant took the sahib back to the days of war. He too had been a sergeant in the beginning, with a similar detachment of soldiers under him—bugle players, drummers, a flag bearer and so on.

Sahib Bahadur walked towards the detachment of soldiers.

The sergeant stood to attention.

'Did you do a round of the town? What did you see?'

The sergeant looked straight ahead and replied, 'We took a round of the entire town. We didn't see anything suspicious.'

Sahib Bahadur turned back towards the veranda. As soon as he stepped into the veranda, he ordered the clerk to have another five to seven wicker stools placed there so that no property owner would have to remain standing. Then he moved the curtain and went back into the room.

On the other side, in the Palace of Mirrors, the considerable as well as modest rich of town—Diwans, Raizadas, Maliks and so on—had in fact gathered and were huddled around Raja Amirchand, discussing the sahib's court and the certificates that were to be issued. The rich had all come dressed in their courtly attire—long angrakhas that hung until below their knees, turbans of different colours on each one's head, and gold-embroidered joote on their feet. Some were also wearing cummerbunds, from which they had hung swords with glinting hilts.

Seeing this gathering of the local rich, dressed in their flamboyant, old-style attire, one felt as if Raja Amirchand, his noblemen and courtiers around him for deliberation, wielded authority once more.

'I'm not going to go anywhere!' the short Raja Amirchand was saying petulantly, over and over again. 'I won't go. Why should I go? I am the king of this principality. Go to that man who has eyes like a cat? Who is he to distribute land in my kingdom? That malicious cat! How can he distribute . . .' The thin and frail Raja Amirchand, his legs dangling from his high chair, went on in this vein.

Raja Amirchand's 'kingdom' was confined to the town and the hundred or so villages that adjoined it. It was much larger once; its spread had shrunk generation after generation. It was its fortune that it was a little off the route taken by invading armies—that's why the little bit that remained did. Otherwise it would have been absorbed into the kingdom of some hakim or nawab by now. The Khalsa Durbar had granted him the status of a feudatory king.

When the war between the Sikhs and the firangis had started, the short raja was confident the firangis would be repulsed, and that the Sikh Raj, which had planted its flag from Multan to Kashmir and Kabul, would never succumb before these cat-eyed ones, and the firangis would bite the dust. *The Sikhs might have changed, but the flame of Sikh honour still burns incandescently.* Raja Amirchand believed that the Khalsa Durbar would raise its head again one day, the forces that had scattered would reunite under one flag, and route the firangis. His entire life had been spent under the patronage of the Lahore Durbar, and it was difficult for him to accept the patronage of another. He was also indignant that while his 'kingdom' had not been intervened in by the grandest of kings, this cat-eyed one had had the audacity of turning up to parcel out land! This was outright victimization, and he writhed in agony.

'We will see. No one is going to be given the permission of going to the cat-eyed one. Does the land belong to his father? How could he dare to enter without seeking my permission?'

Diwan Moolraj cast a glance towards Raizada Aftab from the corner of his eye. A couple of other Diwans too looked at each other and smiled, as if they were saying to each other, 'Look, an ant is demanding to know how an elephant has dared to enter.'

The noblemen looked at Raja Amirchand. Diwan Moolraj contemplated the walls of the Assembly Hall, which had not been whitewashed for years now. The plaster had peeled off from a couple of places. The chandeliers hanging from the ceiling were missing a number of crystals, and those that remained were layered over with dust and cobwebs. The raja's own situation had weakened since the war. He had taken to getting the grain that he received from his 'kingdom' weighed in front of him. He only wore his king's attire once a year now—on Dussehra, when he did the rounds of the town in his palanquin, and for his customary audience that evening with a few chosen traders, moneylenders and courtiers. For the sake of custom, each one still put a silver coin for the king into the tray that was passed between them.

Conflicting thoughts raced through the heads of the rich who had gathered around their king. Diwan Mayyadas felt the raja was right, and that self-respect and honour also count. *When yesterday we offered everything we had to the Khalsa Durbar, then should we go begging to the firangi today? We staked our life for the Durbar, gave it our heart, sacrificed our wealth for its sake—then should we ally with its enemy today?* Diwan Matiram's line of thinking was at variance. The Kukas were still rebelling. What if the Sikh commanders were to regroup and decide to fight the firangis as well? There had been a countrywide revolt just a few years before. The firangis had been routed in so many places. *If the tables turn, and the fortunes of the Sikhs shine once more, then? Imagine if I went out for wool and came back shorn.* Raizada Aftab Rai too was in two minds, for there was no way of predicting the firangi commissioner's attitude towards Raja Amirchand. *We have to live in this town, after all, under the authority of this king. The firangis will do their work and leave. Why should I do something that singles me out from the lot?* He decided to stay quiet. *Let's first see which direction the wind is blowing in. If these people decide they should go to the firangi ruler, then I will too.* While he thought these thoughts, he also kept nodding his head to show his agreement with whatever the raja was saying.

Diwan Gobindram was thinking otherwise. Standing to the right of the throne, he rued his decision to come here. He now felt he should have gone straight to the firangi's office.

There's still time. All I need to do is slip out of here without being noticed. How does it matter how much ruckus this raja creates? He's hardly a raja now, even in name. Who cares for him, and what standing does he have now? His survival has been incumbent on the kindness of the Lahore administration. Now that the administration itself has changed, what remains of him? He's here today, will be gone tomorrow. Now the power of the English sarkar is getting confirmed, and it is they who can be vouched for. Rajas and nawabs all across India have started bowing their heads before them, one after the other. I've made a mistake. I should make a move. And so Diwan Gobindram, still nodding his head to show his agreement with whatever the raja was saying, started to slink towards the edge of the gathering.

Many of the rich and endowed who had gathered were of this same disposition. *The administration of the Sikhs has fallen. Intelligence is in latching on to the firangis' apron strings as quickly as possible. This isn't the time to procrastinate; the English have planted their feet firmly on the ground.*

Just then, everyone heard a strange, unfamiliar sound. One by one, everyone quietened down.

'What's this noise?'

It was as if drums were being played somewhere in the distance. *What kind of sound is this? How strange. Dhum dhum*, in a regular beat. Like a band of drummers that precedes a battalion of soldiers. Those had been quite frequent. Armies used to pass near the town, on their way from here to there, and if they were on their way to war, drummers would accompany them. These drums sounded different from other familiar ones—like during a sport event or a kabaddi match, or before the town crier's announcement.

'It seems to be the drum that accompanies the firangis' army,' a nobleman said.

Everyone's ears had perked up from the moment they had first heard the drumbeats. Was the firangi attacking the town? The drums were quite near now, and they were getting closer, and closer.

'Who knows, maybe it's the Khalsa army!' Raja Amirchand said in his thin, high-pitched voice. Some of the rich found this comment absurd and laughable. What would the Khalsa army be doing here? But some started wondering. Raja Amirchand became excited, and his face turned paler than it already was.

'It does sound like the drumbeat of the firangis,' a Diwan said.

'Why would the firangis' army come here?' Raja Amirchand asked agitatedly, and got up from his throne. The sound really was quite close now, as if it had turned towards the Palace of Mirrors. The louder it got, the more it pounded on his heart and terrorized him. Could it be that armies are gathering somewhere else, and that another war has been declared? Battalions of firangi soldiers had been seen moving around in several places. The rich were all quiet. They held their breath and listened to the approaching sound. Who knows, maybe a battalion had been sent to arrest the raja? It was no secret that the raja hadn't shown allegiance towards the British—not even during the rebellion.

Around this very moment, to the south, a small battalion of firangi soldiers turned with the turn of the broad street, and appeared where the boundary wall had broken and fallen off from one place, making it a thoroughfare from and into town. It was headed by a dark-complexioned soldier in red uniform, who was hoisting up the firangi flag—a large flag with blue, red and white stripes. The flag flapped when there was breeze, and folded down when the air was still. People had begun to recognize this flag. It was being said that it is this flag which announces, by its appearance, the places where the administration has changed.

Raja Amirchand and the rich and noble had, by now, left the Assembly Hall and were standing on the raised platform that looked out from the Palace of Mirrors. The thin, short Raja Amirchand, a sequined cap on his head, stood amidst his courtiers.

A couple of steps behind the flag bearer marched a tall firangi sergeant. He held a thin baton in his hand, and he was marching with his chest taut and his eyes focused on a point in the air ahead of him. He seemed to be the officer in charge of the battalion. A few—perhaps five—steps behind him, was another firangi. A bugle hung from his shoulder. He must've been the bugler of the battalion. Behind him were five to seven rifle-bearing soldiers, all dark-skinned, and clearly Indian. They were all wearing the red uniform of the firangi army.

Raja Amirchand kept his eyes on the battalion. His heart was aflutter. He thought that once the battalion reached the palace, it would stop and salute him. He was confident that it had been sent to meet him, and that the firangi bearing the baton had been sent by the sahib-in-charge with a message for him. To ensure that the firangi with the baton, whose gaze was fixed at some point in front of him, didn't pass by him by mistake, and to draw his attention towards himself, and also thinking that it was possible he didn't know the raja himself was standing here, he took a couple of steps forward. The Diwans and the rich of the town stood flanking him, all kinds of thoughts jostling in each of their heads.

Suddenly, a tremor ran through Raja Amirchand's body. *What if these people are here to arrest me? What if they place me under arrest for being faithful to the Khalsa Durbar?* These *firangis can't be trusted. The white officer could salute me and invite me to come along with him to meet the sahib, and then throw me in a jail.* Raja Amirchand felt terror, but he stayed put where he was standing.

The firangi officer didn't cast a glance at the raja. He continued to look ahead and march on, and his battalion followed him without as much as turning their heads. The drum continued to be beaten, and the battalion marched to its beat. After they'd moved a little ahead, the bugler blew into the bugle. Raja Amirchand thought this was a signal for the battalion to come to a halt, that the officer with the baton would turn and march back towards the palace, and come and stand before him and salute him.

The raja was in a strange state of mind. He wanted the officer to pay him his respects, and at the same time, he didn't want the officer to recognize him. Excitement and disbelief were stirring up inside him simultaneously, making him restive. He wanted to take a few more steps forward so that he would be standing apart from his courtiers and then perhaps his status, which was superior to those who stood near him, could be recognized. And at the same time, his heart was tremulous with the uncertainty of what might happen next— at the thought that this battalion of rifle-bearing soldiers might approach him and seize him.

But the battalion had marched on even after the bugle had been sounded. In fact, it had already reached the end of the street and was at the turn that would lead it away from here, and towards Shah Hussains' Lane. It turned the corner, and left behind a small cloud of dust.

The raja felt slighted. He felt the firangis had intentionally insulted him. He felt the representatives of the firangi government had mocked him. As if crazed, he clenched his fists and screamed in a trembling voice, 'To think that I should go to that sly cat-eyed one! Never! Not only I, but also no nobleman from my kingdom will visit him. Come on, let's go inside, everyone. Inside!' And he went into the palace stomping his feet.

Realizing that no better opportunity would present itself than this one, Diwan Gobindram stepped a little away from the gathering, and slithered towards its edge. While the raja and the other courtiers went back into the Assembly Hall, he lingered at the threshold. When the distance between the others and him increased, he quickly turned around and leapt across the platform they had all stood on just a few moments earlier and, keeping close to the outer wall of the palace, he walked briskly until he had left the palace's perimeter.

This wasn't a question of love for or loyalty towards one's country. Nor was it a question of betraying the salt or staying true to it. It was a question, simply, of looking out for oneself. How should one proceed so that one may both escape the emergent conundrum and gain something while doing so? The status of the raja of this town was next to nothing. There were people in town far richer than him—people who had had direct contact and dealings with the Sikh Durbar. The courtesy shown by this town towards the raja was merely because that's what was warranted by convention and tradition. All it was tantamount to was a ride by the raja through the town in a palanquin or on an elephant once a year, and a tribute of merely one ashrafi that was made to him on certain occasions. That's all. He didn't count for anything; he wasn't part of any count. He was nothing more than a symbol left over from a time that had long passed.

'Go to that cat-eyed one? I?' the raja was screaming. 'Smear the good name of my ancestors? No one will go to him. None of you will go. Let that cat-eyed man learn that he is dealing with people from high families, not people who can be herded around like cattle.'

Raizada Aftab Rai had seen Diwan Gobindram slinking away and jumping over the platform. He was losing his patience. He started sliding out from the gathering. *If I keep waiting to see which direction the wind blows in, others will pounce on all the opportunities.* Having successfully slipped away from the gathering of courtiers, he stood quietly by the wall of the Assembly Hall, and inched towards the door. He cast a quick glance back at the courtiers—they were all standing with their back to him. He crossed the platform in one smooth jump, and then—hop, skip and jump—he was out of the Palace of Mirrors.

Whispering had started in the gathering. Diwan Mangalsen was whispering to Matiram, 'How can I go to the firangi sahib? I can't, even if I wanted to. If he gets to know that I had contributed to the war efforts of the Sikh Durbar, I'll have a new enemy. I don't think I should ever appear before him. No?'

Matiram nodded his head in agreement and whispered back, 'To take the certificates from the firangi government will mean pledging allegiance to it. The uprising has ended just recently. What if it starts again? What if the Sikh administration comes to wield power once more?'

The two men analysed the situation for some time. But when Matiram looked around after a while, he saw that Diwan Mangalsen was gone. He had disappeared into thin air. This startled, and troubled, him. *What if I'm making a mistake? If even the Raizada has left, then what do I think I'm going to gain by staying here? Forget it. We'll see what happens when it happens.* And he slunk away from the gathering and vanished from the scene.

One by one, everyone was slipping out. Everybody had caught on that everybody else was thinking this and doing it. The wall of loyalty hadn't taken long to crumble and collapse. A commotion gripped them all. They excused themselves from the raja's court one after the other. Each one vowed to him that he'd never go to the firangi sahib, assured him that he was devoted to the kingdom and promised he would do his utmost for the sake of its honour. But the moment they were beyond the boundary wall of the palace, they ran.

Only Mayyadas and a few other noblemen remained. Diwan Mayyadas was a man of few words, but seeing how agitated the raja was, he said, 'If the firangi wants to distribute land, then convention demands that he should come to the king. It's at the palace that he should meet people. To expect the noblemen of this kingdom to drag themselves all the way to where he is and beg for some parcels of land is an insult to their honour.'

There were some precepts that Diwan Mayyadas held in high regard. To him, even the smallest of things held import. He was strong in his belief that each thing must be given the respect and dignity that is its due. Once he pledged his loyalty, there was no question of turning back. In his eyes, tradition, the glory of one's ancestors and the dignity of one's own self were not things that could be elided or taken lightly. He could never do anything that would belittle him in his own eyes. This was also something he sought and demanded of others.

Malik Makkhanlal, though, was losing his patience. The thin-framed Makkhanlal had lost his balance the moment he'd seen Diwan Matiram leap over the standing pedestal and flee the palace. *I've delayed things; I'm losing the race. I won't get anything. That's just what I deserve. Why in the world did I even come here? To stare at this senile raja's face? The firangi battalion passed him by; they didn't even turn to look at him! And still he won't go to the cat-eyed one? He's lost his marbles.*

Even so, he wasn't able to slink away from there. His limbs felt numb. He'd tell himself over and over again that he should leave, but he was scared that the remaining courtiers would see him, and worried about what would happen if they did. He kept repeating to himself, 'I've delayed things; there's nothing I can do now; others have already made their moves; I'm going to be left out; this is all I'm good for.'

But there was a commotion again. Even the noblemen who'd vacillated until now began to slip out. Malik Sevaram Saraaf, the goldsmith—who'd been agreeing with everything that the raja was saying even as he'd been urging him to meet the firangi, that there was nothing wrong in meeting him once, that at least this way they could all get to know what it was that the firangi wanted—even he became silent and started inching away.

Whether to leave or not was no longer a question. The same thought was racing through every nobleman's head— *Get there as fast as you can!*

Most had left, now a handful remained. Some had slithered out without saying a word, while some had asked the raja's permission to return home. Of course, they weren't leaving to go back home. Everyone had dashed off in the direction of the firangi sahib's office. A few, however, did take a detour via their homes, for they had to collect their documents without which there was no point in going there. The officer wasn't about to give away certificates by seeing their faces, after all. But a detour meant those who'd carried their documents with them to the palace would reach before them. And so, after collecting their documents from home, these noblemen got on their horses and rode swiftly to the firangi officer. Diwan Matiram hurried towards Grain Market so he could hire a palanquin. It would be more possible to impress the officer of his nobility if he stepped out of a palanquin after all.

The noblemen of the town were descending on the road that led to the firangi's court astride their horses. They were worried they'd be too late, and all those who had reached before them would have already skimmed the cream off the milk, and they'd get nothing.

Clouds of dust rose on the road. Moolraj hadn't been able to find a horse, so he had scrambled on to Aftab's horse. Aftab Rai tried very hard to get him off the horse, and they'd nearly resorted to fisticuffs. But Moolraj held the bridle with all his might, and didn't budge. The Diwans who'd chosen palanquins as their mode of transport were getting left behind. Show of nobility is all right, but here the question was of speed. The noblemen had started abandoning their palanquins and were begging those on horses to take them along. Some succeeded, and the others realized there was no option but to run, and so they ran towards the office.

The sun was very bright now. It had risen high up in the sky. Sahib Bahadur had crossed the courtyard for a third time, and was standing by the unpaved road, his eyes searching the road for signs of movement. But the road, which stretched on and could be seen in the distance, was empty. Utterly empty and deserted. *A mistake has to have been made somewhere,* he thought to himself. *Or then, such elements exist in this town, and whom we don't know about, who wish to spread disquiet.* He knew that it would be an insult to the British administration if no one turned up. He resolved to look into the area properly if, indeed, no one came by the end of the day.

He stood by the road for a long time. Just as he was turning to go back to his office, he saw a cloud of dust in the distance. It was a very faint cloud of dust. But surely, it signalled someone was approaching. The cloud kept growing. There was definitely some movement there. He peered into the distance. It had to be a man on a horse; that would explain the rising dust.

It was definitely a man on a horse. Sahib Bahadur was relieved. *Looks like having the company play its bugle and drums around town did make a difference after all.* Assured, he returned to his room.

The man on the horse was Dhanpat. The Trim-Tail Diwan, Dhanpat. It wasn't a horse he was riding, but his mule. It looked like his eccentricity had got the better of him, and he'd got up and headed here just as he was, and in whatever he was wearing.

He got off his mule when he reached the courtyard. He started tethering the mule to a tree, but then thought otherwise and, pulling at the mule's rein, he dragged it with him into the courtyard and left it there. Good for the mule, for green grass grew in the courtyard and it started to graze immediately. Dhanpat, drenched in sweat, took the bridle off the mule's back and rested it against the outer wall of the courtyard.

Sahib Bahadur watched this curious guest and his odd behaviour from behind the curtain.

Dhanpat had brought a small bundle with him, which he carried pressed under his arm. His angrakha was crumpled and hung loosely on his body as if it belonged to someone else. His pyjamas were dirty, and also crumpled. His footwear had gold embroidery on it, but the threads were unravelling, and the shoes were caked with mud. In contrast, the saffron turban on his head had the shine of newness.

'Huzoor, good morning!' Dhanpat called out loudly. He was standing in the middle of the courtyard, a few steps from his mule, and with the bundle pressed under his arm.

No one emerged into the courtyard. Dhanpat looked left and right. He saw a curtain hanging at the door of a room; an orderly was stationed in front of it. To the left, a company of soldiers sat limply under a tree, watching him.

The presence of the orderly at the door indicated to Dhanpat that Sahib Bahadur, and his seat, must be inside that room. He took a couple of steps forward, until he was in line with the door and called out again, 'May Sahib Bahadur's fortunes reach the skies!' He bowed and touched the ground with his hand and then his forehead—once, twice, thrice.

The firangi continued to watch him from behind the curtain. Dhanpat took another two steps forward and said to the orderly, 'Go tell the sahib that the Diwan who deals in camels is here.'

The orderly watched Dhanpat, confused. This wasn't the sort of person who called upon the sahib. He hadn't been able to decide what to do when he heard the sahib's voice: 'Let him in.'

The orderly saluted Dhanpat and raised the curtain, gesturing to him to enter.

The bundle pressed under his arm, swinging his angrakha, Dhanpat walked up to the door. Before stepping into the room, he halted, bowed, touched the floor with his hand and then his forehead. Then he went in and sat at the sahib's feet and placed the bundle he'd been carrying between them, on the floor.

'I've seen you somewhere. Who are you?' the sahib asked.

Dhanpat smiled from ear to ear.

'Huzoor, you must have seen me at one cantonment or another. This humble servant has shuffled his feet through so many.' And saying this, he untied the knot of the bundle. 'These are what I have as documents, Huzoor. They are proof of my loyalty.'

The firangi was staring at the contents of the bundle, utterly astonished. But then, in a flash, he remembered something and burst out laughing. They were camels' tails. Small tails, with a tiny tuft of black hair at one end and their other end dry; all of them hard as batons and brownish grey in colour.

So then this is the man who used to supply the British with camels during the war, and who used to cut up and present tails of dead camels to secure new orders. The sahib had heard about him first when a man had been arrested in the cantonment late one night. This man was trying to cut off the tail of a living camel. The camel had been sleeping on the ground, but let out a cry and stood up when this man started sawing off its tail. The culprit had tried to escape, but had been caught. When it was discovered that he supplied camels to the army, he was released. So this man here was that man.

Soon, the sahib found himself listening to Dhanpat sing paeans to his ancestors. He was sitting behind his desk on his chair, while Diwan Dhanpat Rai now sat on a wicker stool, with his hands on the desk. 'Raja Porus was our ancestor; I'm from the same family, Huzoor. Alexander the Great suffered such a defeat at his hands. He and I belong to the same caste. He was a Sabharwal. That's the same caste as mine. What a valiant man Porus Sabharwal was!'

The firangi nodded his head slowly.

'Well, our ancestors have even fought Parashuram. Huzoor, have you heard of Parashuram?'

The sahib stayed quiet and studied his face.

'He too was a great warrior, Sahib. His swordsmanship was remarkable. When his sword moved, it was as if lightning was striking. Our ancestors fought him too. He was very happy with us.'

While Dhanpat couldn't present any documentary proof for his land and property, he could definitely convince the officer of his caste stature. He had not one, but several pieces of evidence for that.

'Mahmud of Ghazni also attacked this town, Huzoor! But that happened much later. You've surely heard of him?'

Then, all of a sudden, overcome with emotion, he started expounding on his loyalty. 'We are Khatris, Sahib. Khatris never betray their salt. Loyalty courses through their blood, my lord. They consider the ruler of the hour as their God.' And then he started counting the names of the Diwans who had held positions of power in different places—in Kabul, Multan, Lahore.

'The Diwan of Kabul was my chacha, Huzoor.'

The firangi's ears perked up. 'Who was he?'

Dhanpat realized his mistake. To bring up the Diwan of Kabul in front of the officer was like hacking off your own leg with an axe. Stammering, he said, 'There are Diwans, and then there are Diwans. There are all sorts of Diwans. Huzoor, not all fingers on our hand are the same size, after all. That one was a traitor.'

'Was he your uncle?'

'He was from the same caste as me. By that token, sure he was my uncle.'

The firangi smiled.

'We are Khatris, Huzoor. We are the oldest inhabitants of this area. May your fortunes reach the skies, Huzoor.

You will soon see how we stake our lives to strengthen this administration. Khatris may not stay true to their own people, but they are loyal to their master for sure.'

The firangi kept listening to the chatter of the man seated before him, quite unable to make up his mind about him. Only one man had come in from town until now, and he too turned out to be an eccentric. *He doesn't even own any land. That's evident from his clothes. His crumpled shirt, those dirty pyjamas, and those colourless, mud-caked shoes. One man! And just look at him!* But then his eyes fell on the bundle that he had brought along. The cut-up tails sticking out from it begged consideration. *These are his certificates of loyalty. If I grant him something, it will be like a slap on the face of all those noblemen who haven't come seeking my audience.*

Dhanpat had opened his mouth to start speaking again when the firangi sahib cut him short and asked, 'How many villages do you ask for?'

'Sorry, Huzoor?'

When the sahib had stopped him, Dhanpat was about to say that if he could be granted a small plot of land, just enough to see him through when he's old, he will sing a million praises of the sahib his entire life. He didn't understand the question.

'How many villages?'

'Not want villages, Huzoor; want land.'

'How many villages you want?'

'Not want villages, Huzoor; want land,' Dhanpat repeated. He simply couldn't follow what the sahib had suddenly started on. What were these villages he was asking about?

'May Huzoor's fortunes reach the skies! If for my sustenance I could be . . .'

At this the sahib lifted his forefinger and said, 'One?'

'Huzoor!'

Another finger, 'Two?'

'Huzoor!'

Yet another finger, 'Three villages? I'll give you three villages.'

Dhanpat still couldn't follow, but this time he decided it was better to keep quiet.

The firangi reached for the certificates on his table and called out to his accountant.

Dhanpat's puzzlement continued even when he, certificates for three villages under one arm and the bundle with camels' tails under the other, walked out of the sahib's office. Nevertheless he was chuffed. He may not have grasped the full import of the certificates yet, but this much he'd registered—that he'd gained something. And when he stepped into the courtyard and was about to reach for his mule's lead, he stopped, puffed out his chest and turned towards the orderly. 'Aye, orderly,' he said crisply. 'Come here.'

The orderly had, meanwhile, seen the certificates the Diwan Sahib was carrying, pressed under his arm. He also knew this man had sat in Sahib Bahadur's office for long, and that the two had chatted the entire time. He'd even heard Sahib Bahadur laugh out loud a number of times. He rushed forward, picked up the mule's lead and, pulling at it, walked the mule to the gate.

Dhanpat strapped the bundle with camels' tails to the mule's harness and tucked the certificates under his angrakha. He mounted the mule with the orderly's help, turned his head towards where the town was, and gazed in that direction for a long time. Then he twirled his moustache, puffed his chest out and gave the mule a forceful kick.

The mule started moving in the direction of the town.

In the distance, clouds of dust were rising. There was restless movement inside them. Traders, moneylenders, Diwans, Maliks and Raizadas were riding their horses towards the sahib's office. Such haste! They lashed their horses to make them move faster, and faster.

They wouldn't have covered even half the distance to the sahib's office when they saw Diwan Dhanpat astride his mule advancing from the opposite direction. The mule was trotting a merry trot, and Diwan Dhanpat, his chest more puffed up than usual, looked like he was jumping up and down and seemed to be waving some papers like a flag. As the distance between them and the Diwan closed, they saw that the papers had red ribbons hanging from them. Their hearts sank.

Each one spurred and lashed his horse to make it move faster, faster than the others.

Faraway from here, the firangi officer stood in the veranda, shielding his eyes from the sun with his right hand, inspecting the road. He saw eddies of rising dust in the distance, and knew: *The petitioners are arriving.* He turned sharply towards his orderly and ordered, 'Remove all the wicker stools. There's no need for them. Everyone can stand and wait.'

That day, after his afternoon siesta, Raja Amirchand was strolling on the roof of his palace when he noticed small whirlwinds of dust rising on the road that led into town through Waterway of the Sardars. A lot of people seemed to be making their way towards the Palace of Mirrors. The raja was surprised. *Who are these people? Has the firangi sent yet another detachment of soldiers? Is it a gang of marauders?*

But just a few moments later the angrakhas and flamboyant turbans of the riders became visible. The raja's astonishment grew. *Who could these people be? Why are they headed here? Are they my subjects?*

The raja had not yet fully emerged from the incident earlier that day. The firangi company had passed him by without saluting him. His princely pride had been slighted. He knew he'd done the right thing by forbidding his noblemen from going to meet the firangi.

But his heart grew restive. These approaching horses didn't bode well. He hurried down the stairs. *When they arrive, they should find me seated on my throne.*

It was his noblemen and the rich of town who walked in through the palace gates. One look at them and the raja knew they had submitted to the firangi. *Betrayers of their own salt! They went behind their raja's back to grovel before the firangi!* But then his heart plucked up at the thought that the firangi must have spurned them and sent them packing, and so they'd returned to their king. *One who can't be true to his king can never be true to the firangi. The firangi would have told them, 'Go and first get a letter of authority from your king. I don't know you people.' That's exactly what he must've said to them. That's why they've come running back. What were they thinking, going the way they went, begging for land! They have no shame, no pride! They don't know that a ruler will only listen to another ruler. Who are they, that they'll be heard? Look at the long faces they're pulling; look how they're returning.*

'Come in, come in,' the raja called out, beckoning with his hand. The men, who had all gathered outside, on the platform, streamed in.

'Come in, come in. I'm not going to reprimand you. Had you asked me, I would've explained things to you. A ruler will never do anything without first consulting the other ruler.'

The toadies regarded each other out of the corner of their eyes. They hesitated for a moment, but then they started pulling out the rolls of white sheets tied up with red ribbon from under their angrakhas.

'What are these?' the raja asked in a hollow voice.

'They are certificates, my lord.'

'Certificates for what?'

'Sahib Bahadur has granted me two villages.'

'Two villages? You've received two villages? Which ones?'

'Sayedpur and Noorpur, my lord.'

'But these villages are part of my kingdom. Who does that bastard think he is, parcelling out pieces of my kingdom?' the raja was screaming.

His eyes took in the certificates in the hands of each of his noblemen.

'What? This?'

That's all he said. His head slumped, and his raised arm went limp and fell.

∽

For three days after he received deeds for three villages, Diwan Dhanpat rode through the lanes of the town on his mule, showing every passer-by the certificates of his property. People were genuinely stunned. In what way should they adjust their behaviour towards Diwan Dhanpat now? If for the town, the death of their raja was enormous, then the fact that the Trim-Tail Diwan now owned three villages was seismic. Even though they'd attended the raja's funeral, no thoughts about their departed raja lingered in the minds of the noblemen. It was Diwan Dhanpat, and Diwan Dhanpat alone, who filled their thoughts. The village clown had transformed into a king overnight. Even Diwan Mayyadas was at a loss as to how he should behave towards Dhanpat.

On hearing the news that Dhanpat had received land grants, his first thought was that it would be better if he offered Dhanpat half the mansion. He knew that staking his claim to the mansion would be the first thing Dhanpat would do. In fact, had Dhanpat known that Diwan Mayyadas hadn't received anything from the firangi rulers, and moreover that he hadn't even gone to meet the firangi officer, he would probably have charged at the mansion on the very day he was emboldened with a land grant.

Diwan Mayyadas sorely missed Lekhraj. Had he been here, he'd have handed over the responsibility of the mansion and the rest of the property to him, and retired. Lekhraj would have dealt with this con man; he'd have had the energy and the wherewithal to do so. But Lekhraj hadn't come back. No one knew where he was. The handful of people who'd been returning only brought vague news. Someone has seen him in Ferozepur, and someone had seen him near Jhelum. At one time it was rumoured he'd joined the Kukas and was participating in the various clashes that were erupting everywhere against the firangis.

Instead of going to the mansion to meet Diwan Mayyadas, Dhanpat came to his station in Grain Market. Diwan Mayyadas hadn't expected this. Dhanpat arrived, halted his mule, tethered it to the trunk of the neem tree and, his angrakha swinging, his horsewhip in his hand, climbed up the steps to Diwan Mayyadas.

'My respects, Tauji,' he said without sitting down. 'I need some money.'

'Come, Dhanpat, sit.'

'I don't have time for that, Tauji. I have to go do a round of my estate. I need some money.'

Diwan Mayyadas asked with a level voice, 'What do you need the money for, young man?'

'To buy the mansion. Diwan Mayyadas's mansion,' pat came Dhanpat's reply.

Diwan Mayyadas's face turned ashen. He was at a loss as to what to say next.

'That's a very worthy thing, Dhanpat. Of course, buy the mansion. But am I the one from whom you'll take money to buy the mansion?'

'Why? Who else if not you?' And then he dug into his angrakha, pulled out the certificates he'd received from the firangi administration and, flashing them in front of Mayyadas's eyes, said, 'I'll return the sum with interest. I'm willing to mortgage one of the three lands if that's what you'd like.'

Mayyadas trained his eyes on Dhanpat for a long time, then shook his head slowly and said, 'Moneylending business is very slow these days, young man. I would've given you the money if I had it.'

'I came here to demand that which is rightfully mine,' Dhanpat said, striking the lash's hilt against the palm of his left hand. 'But it looks like you're not going to hand it to me in a straightforward way; I'll just have to extract it from you.'

Oh, for this Dhanpat to behave this way with me; for him to come to my door and threaten me! Mayyadas was crestfallen. *That I had to live to see this day.* For the first time, the thought that the world had changed and he'd been left behind, settled heavily in his heart. *People have leapt forward: They've leapt and grabbed those land certificates. And I've remained stuck: Stuck with the glue of staying true to my salt. What salt, what truth, considering the administration itself has vanished? Now this same Dhanpat is going to go to another moneylender and brandish his certificates and get the loan he wants. And then he'll file a case against me; he will make his claim for the mansion. Who knows what ruckus he'll create.*

Diwan Mayyadas's heart grew restless. His condition was like a man frozen before a poisonous snake—unable to command his feet so he could flee from it, and unable to muster the strength to injure it. All he could do was to watch the snake raise its head from inside the anthill, even as he knew that it was emerging only to strike him.

Dhanpat had come here with the sole intent of humiliating me. He must be with another moneylender now. He'll negotiate a loan with his land certificate. He'll dishonour me in the market. And then he'll come to the mansion to negotiate and make his demands.

It struck Mayyadas that not the mansion, but the land adjoining it, could be given to Dhanpat. *I won't even ask him for a price for it.* He asked his bookkeeper to run after Dhanpat and bring him back. But he returned only to say that Dhanpat was no longer in the market and that he couldn't tell which direction he should go in his pursuit.

It was in Dhanpat's character that he'd become beside himself if something he wanted couldn't be immediately fulfilled. He'd do all kinds of strange things then. He'd even go so far as to stir up trouble with the very people he'd set out to impress in the first place. It was as if some animal would rise from the depths of his being and make him do crazy things.

He'd left Diwan Mayyadas with a storm in his head. *These people still haven't recalibrated their behaviour to my new status. They still don't know who I am.*

That evening the town's inhabitants learnt that upon leaving Grain Market Dhanpat had made a sudden decision to do a round of his estate. The story of what transpired whirled across town, eliciting endless rounds of laughter.

Upon leaving Grain Market, Dhanpat went to Oil Pressers' Neighbourhood, from where he picked up a drummer. They made a long journey in the hot sun, and entered one of the villages of Dhanpat's estate with the sound of drumbeat and this announcement: 'The new master of these lands, Diwan Dhanpat Rai has entered.' The drummer walked ahead, with Diwan Dhanpat making his appearance after the announcement was made. But the results were worse than disappointing—Dhanpat turned into a spectacle. His entire life, he had wanted to be regarded with respect, and as a man of stature. He would daydream that he was seated on an elephant, heading a procession that announced his honour. But now that an opportunity had presented itself, he had let himself be swept up by his eagerness to get public acknowledgement of his newly acquired stature. Things would have turned out differently if he had prepared and come on this round of his lands with appropriate accoutrements, like on a horse instead of a mule, and in proper dress instead of the crumpled angrakha that he was wearing. And he should have planned a small procession too. He could have been accompanied by a group of his agents—well, if not agents then he could've just brought along the group of men who were always by the roadside, playing a game of dice. Right now his procession looked like a farce. It didn't inspire anyone to bow before him or salute him or run to him and touch his feet reverentially. Sure, as always, a few half-naked children started trailing him. A handful of women followed him as well—their heads covered with dupattas, they chatted among themselves and laughed. No one else paid him any attention at all. His timing was off, for the tillers hadn't returned from the fields, and there was no one in the village at this hour who should think of Diwan Dhanpat as their master.

Dhanpat eventually lost his cool. He pulled out his lash and flailed it in the air. The effect this produced was the opposite of his intent. Seeing the lash beating at the air, the children who were trailing him ran out of harm's way, but concluded that this man on the mule, accompanied by a drummer, was a performer of some kind. They clapped. When the man lowered the lash, they slowly inched back towards him. When he raised it again, they ran helter-skelter once more, giggling and clapping.

The morning light hadn't entirely broken through, and the residual darkness of the night hadn't yet dissolved into the yellow glow of the morning. Only a handful of people had stepped out of their houses for the fields; a few women, carrying earthen pots, were making their way to the town wells. It was at this hour that the sound of a whistle pierced through the air, unsettling the quiet calmness of early morning. It was a whistle like no one in this town had heard before. Hearts trembled. Birds flew out of trees and circled the sky. The long, shrill whistle that had emerged from where Orchard of the Sheikhs was, seemed to be issuing forth a challenge to the history of the town.

It was the whistle of the train. The train was passing through this town for the first time. It wasn't as if it had come out of the blue either. A railway track leading in from Lalamusa was being laid for a long time. It had been approaching the town slowly, and had reached the long platform behind Orchard of the Sheikhs a few days ago. Excitement, hope, enthusiasm, doubt—a flurry of emotions had arisen in relation to it. Speculations and conjectures built up excitement around the train.

The elderly were the most filled with doubt—

'Wherever the train passed from, land will burn to ashes,' Lakhmidas didn't tire of saying. 'A train carries a furnace in its mouth. In it, fire rages all the time. The heat burns trees and plants.'

Some people were fearful that it was to take over land that the firangis were laying train tracks.

'The iron tracks create a boundary. Once a track is laid, the firangis own the land it encircles. No one will be able to say anything. They won't even have to bring their armies to take our land.'

Tillers worried and zamindars fretted.

'In Lahore and Lyallpur, wherever the train runs, milk has begun to dry up in cows. What milk will our animals yield, after all, if all they have to feed on is burnt fodder? Wait and see what happens to the next generation of animals.'

'Not just animals, I've heard crop yields will fall by half in these places. What will burnt-up land yield, after all? Farmers, big and small, will turn into paupers.'

But there were those too who sang praises. Ramjawaya worked as a salesman now, and travelled to Lahore often to bring foreign supplies. He always talked very spiritedly about trains. He had even travelled a small distance in a train, from Lahore to Amritsar.

'It's exquisite! When you sit in a train and look out of the window,' he'd say, 'you feel like the trees are running in the opposite direction. It's as if you're sitting in a carousel. Riding a camel makes ribs hurt. A train ride is a completely different experience. There are no jerks; there's no unevenness. You can fold your legs and sit comfortably.'

Then, when people would get excited and ask him more about the train, he'd say, 'When the train moves, you can hear its wheels—chhik chacha, chhuk, chacha! Khut-khut khutakhat . . . khut-khut khutakhat!'

He would underline the intelligence of the firangis—

'The track on which a train moves is narrow, but the train never slips off, never goes off the track!'

Everyone had a comment to make. Some evoked caravans to contest trains. People undertook long journeys in caravans, some on foot, others on camels, horses and donkeys, with routes that meandered through different places. These cheerful gatherings would halt at caravanserais at night, before resuming their journey the next morning.

'There will be caravans now too, wait and see,' someone would say. 'No one's going to take the train, wait and see. Who knows, the train might catch fire, its furnace might burst. The train's wheels may slip off the tracks for all you know. What will happen then? No one's going to take the train, wait and see.'

Someone would chime in support—

'I don't mind if it takes five days to reach Lalamusa riding on a donkey's back. I'll never take the train.'

Someone else would comment—

'I met a man from Jhelum. He said people are finding it difficult to breathe ever since trains have started plying. Everyone's suffering from asthma. Many have terrible coughs.'

The elderly had another complaint—

'Sweepers and scavengers will travel by these trains. And the high-caste people will also travel by these same trains. Do our beliefs and mores not account for anything? The moneylender and the debtor in the same train! Are the noble expected to travel alongside the cobbler and the barber? What respect will remain for the noble and the wealthy if they are to ride in the train with an oilseed presser sitting opposite them!'

Some found it strange that trains would move at the same speed for landlords and for sweepers. Would the world make sense any more if a man who rides a horse reaches Sargodha in the same time as one who doesn't? 'The world would lose all sense of propriety, of high and low this way,' they said.

Some would try to console these gatherings—

'Wait and see, the noblemen will send their servants by train, but won't take the train themselves. They'll only travel with their caravans, in a palanquin or on a horse. They'll never set foot in these good-for-nothing trains.'

And now the train had entered this town, its whistle announcing its arrival, stirring up excitement.

Once the alarm that everyone felt on hearing an unfamiliar sound gave way to the realization that it was the whistle of the train, that a train had entered their town, their terror turned into intrigue and curiosity. Women forgot their pots and pitchers at the wellhead, gathered up their skirts and rushed towards the outskirts of town. People returning home from the fields changed direction, and bounded towards the hillock.

The train blew its whistle again. Excitement rose; people ran faster. They were climbing up the hillock so they could see the train better. They hurried across the maidan beyond Grain Market, from where caravans embarked on their journeys. They rushed towards the platform where, they'd heard, the train would halt.

The sky grew a shade brighter, as if a spot of silver had been mixed into it. Those who had climbed up the hillock took everything in—the endless green expanse of fields; the liveliness of bright dupattas of young girls; the deep black of the ghaghras and wraparounds of older women; the anticipation in the bodies of groups of people, huddled close together, watchful, waiting. They were also the first to spot a cloud of smoke in the distance, near Orchard of the Sheikhs. The smoke was dense and dark, and something stirred under it. And then it appeared—a black and strangely powerful locomotive. It looked as if it was sliding forward through the landscape. It had a chimney on its back, and it was from here that the smoke was coming out. Every now and then, sparks burst out through the smoke, and sometimes even a tongue of fire. They held their breath, stunned by the sight, filled with disbelief. The last dredges of darkness had lifted; the morning was at its brightest. In that resplendent shine of the morning, the beast with the chimney on its back, spewing out dark, dense smoke, came fully into view.

People huddled closer. They watched with wide eyes and bated breath. The marvel of the human mind, the miracle that moved without being drawn by horses, without being pushed, was moving forward, making its way towards them. Yes, it deepened their terror of the firangi, made them feel more fully the firangi's might. The firangi can do anything; he is capable of accomplishing any feat. No one can withstand his power. A new era was taking shape and settling into the town—the era of the firangi, with its Yellow Quarter, and its novel, foreign wares that tumbled out of Ramjawaya's bundle of things, and its 'pleasure park', and now this train—the newest manoeuvre to come out of the firangi brain. Every manoeuvre, each new marvel, generated surprise and terror, simultaneously. The tanks that decimated all that came in their way in 1857 were also born of the genius of the firangi brain. The beast, dark as ink, the front of its engine bearing what looked like a shield that covers a soldier's chest, kept moving closer.

From the hillock, people saw that the train, which had been moving in a straight line, was now turning. The engine moved, and seven bogies followed. It didn't seem like a frightening beast any more; it looked like rhythmical lace, moving sinuously, unaided by an external force. It was a mesmerizing sight. No one had ever seen anything like it, not even in a dream. It was uncanny, and wonderful.

The train crossed Orchard of the Sheikhs and past its curtain of trees. People felt it was moving faster now, and that it had straightened up again. It looked unstoppable, like it ruled the landscape, like nothing could stand in its way. Round and flat, unspeaking and listening to nothing and no one, thrusting its way through the landscape, undistracted by what it moved through—from Lalamusa, then on to Malakwal, and after a few years reaching into Miani, here it was now, in their town, the train of the firangis.

When the train crossed from in front of the hillock, people saw its circular wheels. They were like the wheels of a bullock cart, but they were made of iron! How strange that they shouldn't skid off, or stop suddenly; that they know somehow how to stay in a perfect rhythm with the iron rails.

The train was so close now, its chhuk-chhuk, chhuk-chhuk, chhuk-chhuk sound so much louder. Suddenly, from somewhere beneath its engine, where the wheels were, clouds of white smoke started to rise.

When the train passed close to them, the inhabitants of the town saw a fair, white man sitting in the engine. The glow of fire from the furnace lit up his visage and his black clothes. His face was shining; it was crimson. His elbows resting on the railing, he raised his head and looked up at the crowd that had gathered on the hillock, and smiled. He took off his cap and waved it in the air.

This delighted everyone and they waved back at him. The air filled with the sound of their joyful exclamation, 'Hoy!' Fear and doubt evaporated. Boys raised their arms and started singing, 'Ho ho'. Overcome with enthusiasm, some danced, and some picked up tiny pebbles and threw them in the direction of the train.

People stood on the hillock and stared at the train for a long time. When the engine had passed by, they saw another man in the train, in the last bogie, at the door. He too wore black clothes, and he was holding a red flag in his hand, which he kept waving. He was a firangi too; his skin was fair. He had a black cap on his head, but he didn't take it off. He didn't even smile at the gathering. Instead, he kept his eyes focused on the engine, and kept waving the red flag.

The train had come to a halt a little distance from Grain Market, on the other side of the old wall that skirted the town, by the platform that had been constructed for it.

People leapt towards the train.

For several months preceding the train's arrival into town, many people had been engaged in breaking down rocks into smaller stones to make the base for the train track. Countless people had been engaged in this work, but none knew this is what it was going to be like when the work finished.

'The engine pulls the train,' the town ballad singer said to his troupe as they descended the hillock. 'When the engine stops pulling, the train comes to a halt.'

'No,' an elderly man said in disagreement. 'The man who was waving the red flag pulls some lever, and that's what makes the train stop.'

Thoughts about the train began to be voiced.

'I've heard the train will stay here for three days, then return.'

'But how will it turn around?'

This was a difficult question indeed, one that no one had an answer to.

'It's the engine that pulls the train, but how is it going to attach itself to the other end?'

'What's so difficult about that? Twenty people will get together and lift it.'

'And who's going to turn the bogies around? Your father?'

Let alone a train, many had seen a firangi for the first time in their lives. Curiosity and excitement drew them closer to the train.

Forgetting their mischief, children had stood to one side for long and gazed at the train, frightened and with their fingers between their teeth. Now they inched towards it, and peeped inside. The barber's son was the first to climb on to the footboard of one of the bogies. He felt bolder than the others, for his father had worked for the laying of this railroad, breaking stone into gravel. It had required him to stay away from home for days. The young boy was wearing the red chintz kurta that his father had sent for him while he'd been away. He thought of the train as his own, and felt he had a special right to it. His father hadn't returned; he was engaged in breaking stones in yet another place, for the laying of newer tracks.

People stood in groups all along the train. The town's well-off stood together in a group under the neem tree. They were old, and they had all come wearing their angrakhas. They had prior intimation of the train's arrival but, like everyone, they too had no idea about how trains worked. The questions running through their heads were no different from the naive questions being discussed by the ballad singer and his troupe, but they stood quietly, looking distinguished and important. After all, no one should come to know that they were baffled like everyone else, and that something had come into town that they couldn't make sense of, nor explain.

The fair engine driver, his cap tilted to the side, his coat thrown over one shoulder, got out of the train and started walking along it, towards the last compartment. He acknowledged the people who had gathered, smiling and winking at them, raising his thumb in the air. Young lads watched his blue, restless eyes, and wondered about them.

Boxes began to be offloaded from one of the rear compartments, with Ramjawaya checking each box against a list he was holding.

Then something strange happened.

The crowd of people saw a man walking across the dusty maidan, making his way towards the train from Grain Market. At first no one recognized him. He was wearing a long coat that reached till below his knees, had a saffron turban on his head, and shining, gold-embroidered joote on his feet.

When they did recognize him, people were surprised. It was Diwan Mayyadas, and he was walking in their direction, holding a bundle in one hand. He had become thinner, his moustache was almost entirely grey now, and his back was slightly bent. *Why has Diwanji come here? When the firangi commissioner had come into town a few years ago, Diwanji had refused to meet him. He had refused to bow before the firangi ruler and ask for favours.* Diwan Mayyadas had stoically held on to a sense of dignity and honour, and people's respect for him had only deepened. Even though he had become very weak financially, everyone always met him respectfully whenever he walked—slowly, and with a stick—through the streets of the town.

Diwan Mayyadas crossed the dusty maidan and reached the long platform by which the train had halted.

All eyes watched him, puzzled. He walked past the neem tree without a nod of acknowledgement to the rich and the eminent, and headed straight towards the train. He stopped

before a bogie—the one in which the side-whiskered firangi
who'd been waving the red flag was sitting.

As soon as the sahib turned to look at him and their eyes
met, Diwan Mayyadas bowed. He bowed low and touched
the ground—as if he was doing his penance. He touched the
ground with the fingers of his right hand, then raised them
to his knees, his chest and then his forehead. The firangi
watched this curious behaviour from behind the window.
His lips had started curling with a slight smile of amusement.
He watched Diwan Sahib's face as he bent to the floor yet
again. Diwanji was bending so low that his sword, which was
hanging from his cummerbund, was knocking against the
platform floor.

'Obeisance to Huzoor. May Huzoor's fame reach the
sky.' Diwan Mayyadas did his salaam five times, repeating
this each time. Then he straightened his back, took two
steps forward, and pulled out the bundle from under his
left arm.

'May Huzoor's fame reach the sky! This humble man
who stands before you is one from among the old nobility of
this town. Huzoor, I have come to you today to seek justice.'

The firangi with sideburns had interlocked his fingers and
sat with his hands resting on his stomach. He was smiling and
nodding his head slowly. It was clear to him this man before
him was senile.

There was a movement underneath the neem tree.

Diwan Mayyadas was about to bow again to touch the
floor when a hand touched him on his shoulder. He turned
around, surprised.

It was Dhanpat.

'Tauji,' he said, 'he isn't a firangi officer; he's the train
guard. I'll take you to a real officer.'

Diwan Mayyadas turned his head to look up, and felt his heart sink.

∾

That afternoon, the dice players had gathered as usual outside the sweetmeat seller's shop. The hullabaloo around the train had quietened down, and now only a few kids were playing hide-and-seek and running around in the empty bogies. Everyone else had returned to town, as if from a fair. There was a charge in the air, and people gathered in small groups to exchange notes and stories.

But it was different with the gathering of dice players. They were talking about Diwan Mayyadas. The amazement people felt at the marvel that was the firangis' locomotive was unequal to the astonishment the dice players felt at how Diwan Mayyadas had acted in front of the firangi in the train.

'What was Diwanji thinking?' Banshi was among those people who had immense faith in Diwan Mayyadas, and was most in shock. 'He did today that which he didn't do even when he was losing everything he had. He held his head high even when he was losing everything he had earned in his entire life.'

'But the worst is that the man he was bowing so low for, whom he was doing salaam for, was but the train's guard.'

'The Diwan must not have known that. He must have assumed from his fair skin that he was an important officer.'

'When it was time to bow and bend, he stood straight,' Ramjawaya said with a note of sarcasm. 'He won't gain by bending low now.'

Banshi felt sorrowful. 'His heart didn't let him, before,' he said philosophically, very gently. 'It's difficult for a man to stray from his principles. It wasn't just about loyalty; it was a matter of principles. How could he have sucked up to the firangis in the same town where he represented the Lahore Durbar as a revenue official?'

This discussion was still continuing when a lad came running from the goldsmiths' market, shouting, 'Diwan Mayyadas has passed away! Diwan Mayyadas is no more!'

A dense silence descended over the gathering of dice players. They would have liked to stop the lad and ask him what happened; to learn from him when, where and how Diwan Mayyadas had died. But the lad ran on, repeating over and over that which he had already said.

Another of the loud Diwan's processions set out towards the mansion. But things bode differently now. The fanfare was similar, the mule was the same, Dhanpat's angrakha was just as crumpled as it had always been, and *surma* still lined his eyes, but how people viewed him had changed. He wasn't a spectacle now; he was a Diwan. His mule was as gorgeous as an Arabic horse, and Dhanpat's frail body exuded pomp and stature. Eunuchs and half-naked children who had been roaming about the streets had constituted the procession last time, but now many genteel people of town had joined it. They were participating in the homecoming of the lord of three villages. Some looked after his luggage; others tended to the needs of his family—for Dhanpat's wife and three young sons, who had been living in Sargodha until now, accompanied him. People stood along the lanes, on raised platforms, to look, and peered out from their balconies. They weren't watching a village clown clamouring for attention; this was the procession of Diwan Dhanpat, a landlord. There was no contest, no friction; the mansion gates opened and welcomed the procession in.

The first thing Diwan Dhanpat did on setting foot inside the mansion was to have all of Diwan Mayyadas and his forefathers' things thrown out into the street. He stood and watched from the same place that Diwan Mayyadas had, when he was having the same thing done to Dhanpat. Except, the purohit arrived and, 'May success always be yours, but,' he advised the new Diwan, 'don't have Diwan Mayyadas's things thrown out until you have the mansion in your complete possession, documents and all, or this move could backfire. And so Dhanpat held back and all of Diwan Mayyadas's possessions were moved to the upper storey of the mansion— in the long gallery and a spacious hall—so that at least they'd remain out of sight.

Soon afterwards, Diwan Dhanpat started setting up his courthouse. Lines of petitioners and tillers began to snake out along the lane that led to the mansion's gate. The court was run from inside the mansion. Rugs were spread, a red-and-golden seat with a high back and a footrest was installed, beside which a *chowry* bearer was stationed whenever the court was in session. On the wall, behind the high seat, hung a portrait of the firangi empress, Queen Victoria—wearing a shimmering, white dress and blue cloak, and with a crown on her head. Dhanpat altered his own attire in keeping with his current stature—the turban remained saffron, but he had a peacock feather stitched on to it. Strings of pearl necklaces adorned his neck, and, like icing on the cake, also a necktie. He wore new, gold-embroidered joote on his feet. And so it was that when he sat in his courthouse, on the seat, under the portrait of the queen, he felt like he had been enthroned. He'd started smoking the hookah a while ago, but now, sitting with his legs folded under him on his throne, giving audience to petitioners, he smoked it with panache.

He had tightened his walk ever since he'd been granted the estates. He walked as someone eminent would, with his shoulders bent forward, stopping often to look left and right, as though gazing upon his subjects. He'd grown a goatee, which he tinted with henna. Whenever anyone spoke with him, he listened as if the speaker was petitioning him for something. And yet, his eyes were shot through with scepticism and doubt, as if not only towards everyone else but also towards his own situation. He was like an actor who gesticulates more than he needs to, in order to be appreciated as an actor. If earlier his worry had been that people should recognize him to be a Diwan by pedigree, now it was that they should acknowledge his position as landlord. And even as he continued to think of the late Diwan Mayyadas as his arch-enemy, he struggled to mould himself after his image. He carried a cane and threw a scarf around his shoulders, like Diwan Mayyadas used to. He bent his shoulders and stared at the ground while he walked—slowly—like Diwan Mayyadas. A feeling worked away inside him, that he was falling short, that people weren't recognizing his splendour, that they laughed at him behind his back. He worried that he wasn't able to achieve the quiet, well-rounded majesty of Diwan Mayyadas's demeanour. His heart would beat unevenly whenever this thought rose in his mind. But over time, the palpitations lessened, for there remained no doubt that Dhanpat was the uncontested Diwan, lord of the mansion.

Now years have passed. A personality quite his own has emerged. He has his own flair, his distinctive style. Memories fade with time. Who remembers his measly mule, his crumpled angrakha or the clownishness of his ways any more? He's counted among the rich of the town now. The raised platform outside the mansion, where Diwan Mayyadas once used to stroll, is now his. He's the one who strolls there—has for years now—and people bow and greet him as they pass by. They stir into action at the slightest movement of his brow. He wields power and influence over the entire town.

Owning three villages is no small thing: Huzoor goes to meet
the deputy commissioner in his phaeton once a week, holds
his court in the mansion and rules from there. The Diwan of
the mansion comes up in every conversation in town—and
it's Dhanpat, no other, that they are talking about. Everyone
fears him. Even Banshi—who never cared for anyone and
openly poked fun at everyone—works for him, collecting
revenue, and is always at his beck and call. There's no one in
town who hasn't yielded to him—well, except perhaps Mausi
Bhagsuddhi, who sits in her dark, sunless room and makes a
face whenever she talks about him.

Dhanpat's heart, however, continues to agonize over
whether people hold him in the same regard as they did
Diwan Mayyadas. He wonders if they still laugh at him
behind his back. Maybe that's why he demonstrates his power
and dominance by doing the strange things that he does.
Inwardly, the thought gnaws at him that he has not mastered
the image, that something is still amiss.

The day had dawned, but a thick fog hung over everything.
Only a few people had stepped out of their houses, their heads
and faces covered. Then, suddenly, the sound of drums filled
the air. It was confusing, for it couldn't have been the town
crier at that hour; he always made his announcements in the
afternoon, when people were about town. It also didn't sound
like the drumbeat to which a battalion might march. And
why would it—Lahore had already been captured; Delhi too
was already theirs.

Bhagsuddhi was sitting on her cot, counting her rosary
beads and praying. The drums startled her. 'May God be

merciful, what are these drums about?' She strained her ears. The sound seemed to be coming from the direction of Sethis' Neighbourhood.

She bit her lip and shook her head. 'These have to be about an auction. It's only for an auction that drums are beaten this early in the day. The sound seems to be coming from towards the mansion,' she muttered to herself.

She got up from the cot, opened the door and looked around for a passer-by.

A hazy outline of a man appeared on the street. He was headed her way, and she strained her eyes to make out who it was. When the man came closer, and she saw that it was Ramjawaya, her suspicion was confirmed. It's impossible that misfortune should befall on someone, and Ramjawaya would stay home.

'Ramjawaya, what are these drums about?'

Ramjawaya was walking swiftly, purposefully.

'Is the mansion being auctioned?' Bhagsuddhi asked, worried.

'Not the mansion,' Ramjawaya replied, 'the land.'

Bhagsuddhi's heart sank.

'What is this about?' Bhagsuddhi called out after him as he walked on.

'The elder Diwan is bankrupt, what else! The administration is auctioning off the land. Orders have been received from beyond town.' He turned with the lane.

Bhagsuddhi returned to her room, muttering under her breath, 'Mayyadas's mother had planned a pond on this land. May she remain restful in heaven! She only ever ate after having fed a hundred guests every day. And this same land is going to be auctioned today!'

The sound of the drums echoed through every neighbourhood. Drums announcing an auction bode ill; they signalled the ruin of a family.

Bhagsuddhi remembered the day the envoy had arrived in town from Lahore, after which work on the pond had been discontinued. Land was still being dug up for the pond then, and the steps that would lead into it were almost ready. 'We'll begin again once the war ends,' Diwan Mayyadas assured his disheartened wife. 'God willing, your wish will be fulfilled; don't lose heart.' But the storm that broke out threw everything asunder, laid all plans to waste—just as much for Mayyadas's wife as for Diwan Mayyadas and for Lahore.

The auction was being discussed in every home. Those who had received land from the British—Diwan Moolraj, Raizada Tekchand, Malik Deenanath and a handful of others—were in a dilemma. Should they, or should they not, participate in the auction? They wanted to, for an auction meant they stood a chance of getting the land at a good price. But they were scared that this would mean getting into an unnecessary—and potentially harmful—tussle with Diwan Dhanpat. That shrewd man was sure to make a bid, wanting to buy the land at any cost, so he may continue with his project of insulting Diwan Mayyadas, even posthumously. Bidding against him would, they knew, hurt them in the long run. But still, they were trying to muster up the courage to participate. Saving face is important, but the fear of being publicly shamed shouldn't mean you forego a chance to profiteer, after all.

'You can't fight fate!' Harnarayan said, adopting a Vaishnavite tone. 'Who could have imagined this land would be auctioned one day!' He opened his little book of prayers and started to read a chapter from the Gita Sahasranama. To

him, the beating of drums in front of the land adjoining the
mansion was akin to the falling of a crown from a king's head
into the mud.

The boundary wall around the land, about five to six feet
high, was broken in places. Small arches of red sandstone all
along its length made it look delicate. It had been beautiful
once, like a boundary wall of a royal garden. There was
also a time when the Diwans' stables were housed here,
and horses with shining saddles, plumes adorning their
foreheads, used to emerge from its gate. But now it was
overrun with thorny bushes, trees like acacia and flame of
the forest, and donkeys.

A dark, half-asleep man was sitting in front of the
ramshackle gate of this land, beating the drum. A tall man
stood near him, a bundle of papers pressed under his arm. And
a government official sat on a wicker stool by the wall, looking
left and right, awaiting the arrival of potential buyers—people
who would make a bid for the land.

Ramjawaya was the first to arrive, and he'd brought
Banshi along. Both men were here as spectators—they
weren't of the calibre that would allow them to bid for this
land. But Ramjawaya was, after all, a well-wisher of Diwan
Dhanpat, and one of the most outspoken critics of the late
Diwan Mayyadas—though there was a time when all he
wanted was for Diwan Mayyadas to look favourably upon
him, and hovered about the mansion in case he could be of
some service. And Banshi, though he'd come along, wasn't
too happy that he had—for he believed that to watch the
land being auctioned was to revel in another's misfortune. He
thought about leaving, but his curiosity got the better of him;
he wanted to witness first-hand the game Diwan Dhanpat
would play this time.

Three more people arrived. One of them was Raizada Tekchand. He'd brought his two grown-up sons along. The attendance slowly grew. Curiosity pulled many to the auction.

People turned to look when they heard the sound of tinkling bells from the dark lane that led out of the mansion. Diwan Dhanpat's florid palanquin turned with the lane and came into view. The town's most eminent landlord was arriving.

Two palanquin bearers in front and two at the back carried the palanquin on their shoulders. They were wearing ankle bells, and bells were also tied around their foreheads. The ones around their foreheads were tiny, brass bells, sewn on to a band. Dhanpat was sitting inside the palanquin, wearing a silk angrakha with a tie—a yellow angrakha, with a gaudy saffron turban. There were strings of pearl necklaces around his neck. He'd dressed up as well as he could, for the auction of the land was a historic moment, a moment in which he was about to pulverize his biggest enemy. Never mind that this enemy had already left for his heavenly abode.

The palanquin stopped, and a little boy who had been running behind it with a shiny wicker stool—the kind whose base is smaller than the seat—leapt forward and set the stool down by the boundary wall. Diwan Dhanpat stepped out of the palanquin, cast a glance in the direction of the mansion— of which only the stone canopy was visible from here—and walked slowly towards his seat.

The palanquin bearers found a spot along the boundary wall and sat down, their backs resting against it. They were breathless. The boys who had gathered around the man beating the drums now moved towards the palanquin bearers, curious to see them—and, especially, the red bands with tiny, brass bells that they wore around their foreheads—from up close.

Having his palanquin bearers wear the bells had a special meaning for Diwan Dhanpat, for the bells not only announced to the people who lived in the town that their Diwan had emerged from the mansion and was moving through the lanes, their sound also reached Diwan Mayyadas, up there in heaven, letting him know that Dhanpat's palanquin, borne by four attendants, was making a tour of the town. There were days when Diwan Dhanpat would take two rounds of the land adjoining the mansion. It made him feel he was a tiger circling around his prey.

The moment he was seated on the stool, Diwan Dhanpat gestured to the government official to approach him.

'What's the delay?'

'We'll start very, very soon, Huzoor. It's winter, and I thought it would be good to wait a while longer, as more people may be on their way.'

'I'm here. Start the auction.'

'But we need a quorum of at least three people, so at least some bids are made.'

Dhanpat scanned the gathering. His eyes met Raizada Tekchand's, and they exchanged mild greetings. Dhanpat made a mental note that this man had come to fight him on what was rightfully his.

'Pay attention,' he said to the official. 'If no one else comes to make a bid, I'll pay five hundred rupees over the starting amount and the land is mine.'

'No one stands a chance before you, Diwanji. You should consider the land already added to your wealth. But I have to follow due process.'

A man emerged in the lane, in the distance. He must have been forty, or forty-five, and was wearing a starched salwar, a knee-length coat and a loose turban. His shoulders bent forward slightly, and he walked slowly, with his gaze fixed on the ground. It took everyone some time to recognize him, because he usually stayed away from matters concerning the town. He worked as a commissioning agent for foreign goods, and had a shop in Grain Market. He was the one who had employed Ramjawaya as his broker, responsible for the sale of goods in different neighbourhoods. It was said that Malik Mansaram—for that was his name—had been running a shop in Jhelum before he became a commissioning agent and started appointing brokers and middlemen for foreign goods in different towns.

Seeing that they didn't have a quorum to begin the auction, the official sent for a government-appointed agent who would participate, not as a buyer, but only so that there would be another person making a bid. As soon as he arrived, the official ordered the drummer to stop beating the drum, and stepped forward, a piece of paper in his hand.

'By order of the distinguished officer-in-charge, Huzoor Deputy Commissioner Sahib Bahadur, this land, located in Mangatram Street, measuring four kanal and eighteen *marla*,[1] property of the bankrupt Diwan Mayyadas, son of Diwan Mathraadas, is being publicly auctioned on this day, Friday. The individual to whom it will be sold will be required to pay one fourth of the total amount immediately, in cash, and submit the remainder within the next ten days to the treasury.' The drum was beaten loudly.

'For the haveli of the Diwans,' the government-appointed agent stepped forward and called out loudly, 'Three thousand! Three thousand rupees . . .'

At this the official in-charge of the auction, his voice steady and devoid of any trace of emotion—like the voice

---

[1] One kanal is approximately 605 square yards; twenty marla is one kanal.

of the priest who stands before a dead body and chants mantras in order to perform the funeral rituals—repeated the figure—

'Three thousand—once, three thousand—twice . . . For the haveli of the Diwans, three thousand once, three thousand twice . . .'

'Three thousand and five hundred.' Diwan Dhanpat made his bid from where he was sitting, bending his body forward a notch.

'Three thousand five hundred . . .' the official repeated, 'Three thousand five hundred—once, three thousand five hundred—twice!'

The official looked towards the agent; the agent took a step forward and was about to make his bid, when Raizada Tekchand raised his hand and called out from the other side of the lane—

'Four thousand!'

'Four thousand! Four thousand—once, four thousand—twice!'

'Four thousand five hundred!' Diwan Dhanpat called out.

The official became alert. The stakes were rising.

'Four thousand five hundred! Four thousand five hundred—once, four thousand five hundred—twice!'

He turned to look at Diwan Dhanpat, who was watching him with his sharp eyes, waiting for the official to announce the auction closed.

The gathering of people, meanwhile, looked at Raizada Tekchand.

Dhanpat turned his head in the direction of the mansion. He could have sworn he saw Diwan Mayyadas standing on the roof, watching him and smiling.

'Five thousand!' Diwan Dhanpat called out, his voice booming.

The official looked at him, perplexed. 'Diwanji,' he said, 'but the last bid, of four thousand five hundred, was yours!'

'Well, now it's five thousand,' Diwan Dhanpat said, and turned again to look at the mansion.

Diwan Mayyadas's ghost was gone.

'Five thousand!' he screamed again, as loudly as he could so that the sound would reach Diwan Mayyadas, wherever he was.

'Five thousand—once, five thousand—twice!' The official looked around and was about to wind up the auction with a 'five thousand—thrice', when a thin voice emerged out of nowhere—

'Seven thousand!'

By now, a lot more people had arrived to witness the auctioning of the land. The last bid hit them like a jolt. The auction official looked around, surprised; his eyes searched for the person who'd made the bid.

It was Malik Mansaram, who had, until now, been standing quietly to one side. There he was, his body slightly bent over a cane, his eyes steady under his bushy eyebrows, waiting.

Diwan Dhanpat stood up.

'This man is an outsider. He doesn't belong to this town.'

'Everyone has a right to make a bid, Diwanji!' the official said. 'Anyone who can fulfil the terms of payment can make a bid.'

It wasn't that people didn't know Malik Mansaram. He was of this town, but he had lived away for many years, working as a contractor, before returning to this town a year ago and setting up a shop in Grain Market, as a commissioning agent.

He lived above this shop, in a room on its roof. He was also known as Contractor Mansaram, but he'd never worked as a contractor in this town. Here, he was a commissioning agent. That he would raise a bid of seven thousand against Diwan Dhanpat was not something anyone had anticipated.

Malik Mansaram didn't stir, didn't say another word. He waited patiently for the next bid to be made.

Dhanpat felt cut up. To be insulted by a stranger, an outsider, and that too right in front of his mansion! He was burning up inside.

'Seven thousand five hundred!' he rasped, his voice sharp as a blade.

'Seven thousand five hundred,' the official repeated. 'Seven thousand five hundred—once, seven thousand five hundred—twice!'

'Nine thousand!'

What a scandal! Mansaram stood calmly, unmindful.

Dhanpat was in a dilemma. *I'm sparring with a gambler. What if I raise the bid to ten thousand and he raises it further, by another two? He's either trying to frighten me, or he really does have this kind of money. But giving up will bring me dishonour in front of the entire town.*

'Ten thousand!' He made another bid, but his voice had lost its aggression. He looked at the mansion's roof. Diwan Mayyadas had appeared again.

'Twelve thousand!'

Even Ramjawaya was shocked. But in his heart he had already shifted loyalties. There was clearly no point in kowtowing to Dhanpat any more; it was another who was emerging with a crown on his head—Agent Mansaram, Contractor Mansaram! The crowd watched, mesmerized. Mansaram's posture was as unchanging as a mannequin's.

Dhanpat had broken into a sweat. This auction was going to be his chance to demonstrate to people that he was the lord and master not only of the mansion but also of the land adjoining it. The humiliation he felt when Diwan Mayyadas had his things thrown out of the mansion was as piercing today as it had been years ago. Today was supposed to be the day the town would see the tables had turned, the game had definitively changed. He had nurtured his feelings of revenge like a snake nurtures its poison. But things had backfired. *Where the hell had this agent come into the picture from? This agent of foreign goods, this small-time player challenging the well-endowed landlords of this town . . .*

Stories about Malik Mansaram had been floating around town ever since his return. He was in Jhelum, from where he went to Rawalpindi when the commissioner's office was being constructed. He worked as a contractor when the railway line was being laid there. After that he went to Sargodha, where he'd been given the contract for making the road and two barracks for the upcoming firangi cantonment. He'd earned his wealth as a contractor, and then he became a representative for a couple of vendors of foreign goods.

Dhanpat had come to the auction dressed in an opulent angrakha. He'd dreamt of opulence for years, of being regarded as a rich man. But his angrakha, his being wealthy, his stature and his influence over this town were not helping him today. Troubled, he started pacing up and down the lane, his hands locked behind his back. He felt the eyes of the entire town upon him. He had come here to evict Diwan Mayyadas from the image of the elder Diwan and place himself there. Instead, he was stuck in a maze, unable to find his way out. His face was turning pale; sweat made his angrakha stick to his body.

In a way, the crowd was pleased. The one who, in his arrogance, wanted to fell the late Diwan had become ensnared in his own trap. But the contractor troubled them too—for his thirst seemed to be of an intensity that could outdo, and surpass, the arrogance of the wealthiest of this town.

Dhanpat's situation in life had changed only because of the firangis. But he wasn't looking to reinvent himself; his utmost desire was to attain the same stature as the Diwan before him—he wanted the same grandeur; he wanted the same pomp and splendour; he wanted the same oneness with the mansion. He'd sided with the firangis because that was the direction in which the wind was blowing. He hadn't considered that under the rule of the firangis, older mores would begin to unravel, that others would emerge unannounced—people without pedigree, without old money or inheritances, and with the gumption to challenge everyone and anyone.

News that an uncomfortable knot had formed in the auction travelled through town at lightning speed. Everyone who heard it came to witness the spectacle. This included a few wealthy moneylenders.

Diwan Moolraj knew Contractor Mansaram well. He tapped Ramjawaya for information about what had happened until now, and then went and stood beside Mansaram.

'That's enough, Lalaji,' he whispered to Mansaram. 'Don't raise the bid any higher. The prestige of the Diwans is at stake.'

Mansaram, who had been as still as if he was sculpted out of stone, raised his eyebrows.

'Why?'

'This is ancestral property of the Diwans. What is it worth to you? And in terms of price, even five thousand is more than it is worth. It's got nothing going for it. And you've raised the bid for it to twelve thousand already.'

'So what if it's broken and looks like it's in ruins at the moment, my dear lord? I'm going to transform it into something so beautiful, it will astound the world. I'm going to bring life back to this run-down piece of land; I'm going to make a pleasure park here, and it'll have people visiting it all year round.'

Diwan Moolraj couldn't believe his ears.

'You'll make a pleasure park on the Diwan's land? In this place where that saintly woman wanted to construct a pond?'

'She may have wanted anything. I'm making a pleasure park here, and what I'm willing to pay isn't that much for a pleasure park.' Then he spoke animatedly, 'There'll be swings and merry-go-rounds, and shops selling foreign goods. There'll be a bioscope and magic shows. Just wait and watch! People will forget Lahore!'

'It's the ancestral land of the Diwans,' Diwan Moolraj said softly. 'You can easily set up a pleasure park elsewhere. This is a question of the Diwan family's honour.'

'What's honour got to do with this, Diwanji? This is an auction. He is here to buy, as am I. What does family have to do with this? This has got nothing to do with a question of honour at all.'

The official called out again—

'Twelve thousand—once, twelve thousand—twice!'

Diwan Moolraj turned to look at Dhanpat, who was still pacing. One look at him and Moolraj's heart was soured. *The scoundrel, he's here to show his late uncle down. He could've easily bought the land without making a show of it. Instead, he's come to the auction to bid. He wanted the world to see. Look at his tasteless angrakha! Look at his ways!*

'Fifteen thousand!'

There was stunned silence. An ordinary auction was turning into a decisive moment in the life of the town. A crack was forming in the centuries-old way of living. If it was the land today, it could be the mansion tomorrow. Any contractor could make a bid for it.

Mansaram's bid of fifteen thousand tore up the Diwans and the wealthy of the town. They started leaving; they turned their backs and walked away. They removed themselves from the situation. Even Diwan Dhanpat was nowhere to be seen. His palanquin bearers were still sitting by the boundary wall. The palanquin was empty; the velvet-covered wicker stool was unoccupied.

'Fifteen thousand—once, fifteen thousand—twice!'

The official paused and looked around.

'Fifteen thousand—gone!'

Drumbeats resounded in the air; the auction had reached its conclusion.

⌁

The train had won people's hearts. It had been plying for some years now, but even so, whenever the 'chhuk-chhuk' of a train pulling into town reached people's ears, they'd make their way towards the 'astation'—since that's how 'station' had come to be pronounced in town. And when a train would be leaving the station, its platform would become as crowded as a fairground. The station had become something of a place of entertainment. Even though the hustle and bustle lasted for a short while, it had its own, unique flavour. When the train would stand idle at the station, boys would play hide-and-seek in its compartments. Just climbing in and out of the compartments was fun. When a train would leave, some sprightly young lads would take a ticketless ride to the next station. Girls loved sitting by the windows and watching the landscape go by. Songs had begun to be sung in praise of trains.

The train started pulling out of the station and sent a ripple of excitement through the girls who'd decided to take a joyride. Girls especially hadn't become accustomed to the train—that you get into a compartment and the train starts to move and the trees that were a short distance ahead soon get left behind, and then the train picks up speed.

A row of trees passed them by, like a screen to look through, and then Orchard of the Sheikhs arrived.

'There it is, the waterway! Can you see it?'

It was as if all the girls were stuck to the windows.

'Where? Where is it?'

'It's hidden by the trees now.'

Sumitra's eyes were glued to the ground. She was fascinated by how the earth kept running in the opposite direction, while she moved forward.

'Don't look down, Sumitra. You'll feel queasy.'

The 'khut-khut' of the train was rhythmic.

'Digg-digg, thukk-thukk, dig-digg, thukk-thukk . . .'

You could keep looking out, but your heart would still ask for more. The girls pushed each other to get closer to the windows.

Some distance away, a caravan wound its way through open ground. A cloud of dust, the same shape as the caravan, rose around it. They were many people—men, and women— and with them there were donkeys, and dogs that kept running around, and there were camels loaded with luggage.

The girls laughed.

'They'll reach Miani after two days, and we'll have been to Miani and back today itself.'

The train moved as if it had wings.

It had been moving along a straight path, but now there was a turn and a girl spotted the engine and the green-and-yellow compartments that turned with the engine, like a meandering river. It filled her with delight. 'Oh, it looks lovely.' All the girls turned to see, and watched the train turn along the track, mesmerized.

The engine spewed smoke. Beneath the engine, the long, iron spoke attached to the wheels moved up and down. All of it was so unfamiliar. Their eyes met each new thing they saw with a tinge of nervousness, but every time, they soon exploded into excited chatter.

The train had picked up speed. The girls moved away from the windows and sat down on the benches in the middle of the compartment. Sumitra started singing a ditty.

Look, look
The train hurtles down from Mangowal
Sets the old man's beard on fire

They laughed at the image, then someone started singing a song—one that had become very popular in town—and everyone joined in.

O firangi, bravo, bravo
Your rule endures!
O firangi, bravo, bravo
Your rule endures!
Bravo, bravo, you are a doer
You are the pinnacle

You reign over all
Bravo, bravo!
Bravo, bravo!

Seven seas away, in London's India House, a meeting was underway about the railways. The corridors of India House were abuzz; all who had gathered were excited.

The shareholders—people who had put in money for the laying of railroads in India—expected huge gains. Those who hadn't bought shares, who'd hesitated or been unable to buy, were repenting. Those who had staked their money were beaming at their intelligence. Now they wanted their share of the profits to reach them as soon as possible.

India House had become the epicentre of activities related to India ever since the British government had taken over from the East India Company. Its grandeur was increasing. Its rich decoration bespoke the majesty and prestige of the Empire. Its walls were panelled with oak wood, up to six feet from the ground. Above them, the shining white walls were replete with portraits of those diplomats and army officials who had played a role in unfurling the British flag in faraway places of the world. The pride of place was given to the portrait of Queen Victoria.

Things had become extremely organized since the British government had taken over. Accounts were being maintained meticulously; all affairs were conducted under the supervision of officers; and meetings, which used to be unruly earlier, had begun to be conducted systematically. All decisions made during shareholder meetings were documented, and matters were handled constitutionally.

Shareholders had arrived in black suits with stiff, pleated white shirts, as was the custom. They exuded the confidence of people gathered to take big decisions. A shareholders' meeting carried weight, had significance.

Everyone sat down on heavy chairs made of oak wood. Many were worried that India was too vast a country to be covered with railway lines, that it would need millions, and that their money would sink or, at the very least, returns would take too long. *The government is merely making promises. What about the present? When will we receive our share of the profits? Will we even get them?*

The minister, immaculately dressed in a black suit and with a wig on his head, stood up to present the report. His glasses, strung into a black thread, hung on his chest. He'd wear them when he was reading, and they would slip down to his chest on their own after he'd finish reading something. His face shone with self-confidence. He was smiling, as if he was here to fulfil a responsibility that was very dear to him. He stuck his thumbs into the pockets of his waistcoat and started speaking in a gentle voice:

'Before I present the statistics, I'd like to say a few words to my citizens and shareholders in the Indian Railways . . .'

Everyone craned their necks forward and listened attentively.

'India is a vast country. And as you are all aware, the expenses in laying railway lines from one end of the country to the other have been substantial. More expenditure is expected. But considering the scale of operations, this isn't news to anyone . . .'

Listening to his words, some shareholders became alarmed that the minister was going to inform them that there are no profits, and that things were exactly as they had feared.

'There are bound to be expenses, and there will be some wastage as well—there will be certain unproductive expenses.

We all know very well that the Hindustanis are a lazy people, and they don't work with agility and honesty. But, at the same time, the cost of labour in India is less than it is even in Africa. As long as the Hindustani labourer gets a meal a day, he is willing to work even for twelve hours . . .'

Some nodded their heads, but murmuring had begun. 'This long preamble means something is wrong.'

Speculations had started, and one agitated shareholder shot up from his chair, 'I would urge the minister that, considering how little time is available to us, it would be better to share statistics instead of a lengthy exegesis.'

The minister's body arched with attention, but he looked at his listeners with kindness in his eyes, and smiled, 'I would like to remind our shareholders that India is no longer under the East India Company. It is under the rule of Her Majesty and her government. Therefore, proceedings will be systematic and will have a method. The days of the Company's messy manners are over.'

He relaxed again. A slight smile returned to his lips and he tucked his thumbs into his pockets, took a step forward and said, 'The shareholders should not feel worried. Trains will soon be running from every part of that country to the ports. From areas where cotton is grown, from the south, where spices are grown, from tea estates, from every such place that can provide raw materials for our industries . . .'

The minister grew animated as he spoke.

'Think about it, the railways will benefit India, but will also bring Britain fabulous wealth. Cotton and coffee and tea and spices—we will have them sown and harvested, we will buy them, and we will export them . . .'

The minister paused to study the effect his words had had on his listeners. Then he craned his neck forward, raised his index finger and said, 'And let me tell you a secret. The capital you have invested in Indian Railways is a loan to India. This means your money will return to you with interest. This is separate from the profits that you earn as shareholders.'

He spoke slowly, emphasizing each word: 'The expenditure for railways is being set down in the accounts as expenditure by India. We may be the ones putting in the money, but it is our loan to India. India will pay us back this investment that we are making, with interest. If we are to really reap economic benefit, we will not only need to lay an extensive railway network, we must also take over the administration of the country. We will lay railway lines and roads; we will dig streams for irrigation; we will develop communication networks—we have to do all this.' The minister spoke as loudly as a political propagandist would.

A rich merchant from Manchester stood up.

'All this is yet to be; it's in the future. You have been promising us such green pastures for a long time now. Come to the point. What is the status of our investment, which we have put into the construction of the Indian railroads?'

The expression on the minister's face turned serious again.

'You are not the only one to have made an investment. The British government has invested at a scale much larger than all the private investors.'

'That doesn't concern us. Tell us about our investments—what is the status as of today?'

'One who frets only over his own investment can never have perspective . . . What Lord Dalhousie had predicted fifty years ago is coming true today. He had said, "We cannot imagine the gains India will make—both from an economic and from a social perspective—once railroads are laid." He had said the industrialists of England are screaming for cotton. India grows cotton, but has no mode of transporting it. If the right means of transportation are made possible, so that raw material from far-flung places can be brought to the ports, from where it can be loaded on to ships and transported to England then . . .' He stopped and smiled. 'Lord Dalhousie's prediction has proven correct.' And then, before someone could stand up and ask another question, he put on his spectacles, picked up the papers from his desk and read out loud, 'In 1813, only ninety lakh pounds worth of cotton was sent for, from India. But twenty years later, in 1833 . . .' The minister paused to build some suspense. 'In 1833, this had increased to three crore and twenty lakh pounds worth of cotton!'

He peeped out from behind his glasses at his listeners.

'Eleven years later, that is in 1844 . . .' Another pause. He looked up dramatically at his listeners, then continued while emphasizing every word, 'In 1844, cotton worth eight crores and eighty lakhs was exported from India.'

A wave of satisfaction swept through the hall. Many nodded their heads and smiled. They looked at each other, reassured. Those who had been worried that they had made a mistake investing in the shares praised themselves for their far-sightedness, for their intelligence in knowing this would be a profitable investment.

The minister put the papers back on the table and clasped his hands with satisfaction. He was smiling as if he was single-handedly responsible for these magical figures.

'Every ship loaded with cotton that reaches the British shores, believe me, is as if loaded with gold. This is not cotton; it is white gold.'

Then he lifted his index finger. He was going to let everyone in on another secret. He weighed every word as he spoke: 'The British policy is to make India our agricultural land. For this, it is not sufficient that Indian farmers send us everything they grow on their soils, it is also imperative that our countrymen travel to India and farm the land themselves— set up tea, coffee and rubber plantations . . .'

He paused dramatically and smiled. He spread his hands like the wings of an eagle and said, 'The investment being made in India must not be seen as investment. We are not spending money in India. We are loaning India money . . .'

He lowered his voice and spoke softly, as if sharing a secret, 'Like I said, the money being put into railways in India is being reflected in our account books as expenses being made by India. The money will be returned to us. We will also be paid interest. And in a way, it is India that will be paying us our profits. And this is how it should be.' Then he lowered his voice even more, as if taking everyone deeper into the secret, 'This is for India's benefit. It is on India's land that the railway network is being established. In a way, we are laying the path to India's progress.'

His voice deepened further.

'Wherever money is being spent on India's development, it is being attributed to India. For instance, expenditure during the wars in Afghanistan and China is under the heading of India's expenses. This should assure you that the money you have invested is safe; no harm will come to it. So friends, the nature of our relationship with India has changed. Now that the British government is at the helm of things, every aspect of the relationship stands transformed. India will definitely be made into our farmland.'

He elaborated:

'The more the import of cotton from India, the bigger the market for our cloth in India becomes. Do you understand what I'm saying? This is called opening up newer markets.'

And, like a teacher, he explained to the traders sitting before him as if they were children in his classroom: 'Bettering the communication and transportation infrastructure of India will not only help augment our production, it will also increase the demand for our goods in India. The Indian market will keep opening up to our goods.'

At this, a man, who looked more like a teacher than a trader—he was tall and thin, and his hair was dishevelled—raised his hand and stood up. He was in fact a teacher who had bought some shares in Indian Railways at the insistence of a relative.

'If I'm not mistaken,' he said, 'cloth was already being produced in India—and very good-quality cloth. Where is the sense in selling our cloth there?'

The minister looked at him, smiling and nodding, just like a father listens to his son's childish questions and keeps smiling until he finishes his babble so that he can then wrap up things with a couple of sentences in response. 'Yes,' he said, 'they do make cloth. On hand-operated looms. That's an outmoded way. Centuries old.'

Raising his index finger like a schoolteacher, he continued, 'We have a responsibility, over and above the demands of trade. That tradition-bound country has to be pulled into the modern era. Just like a father catches hold of his son's hand and helps him cross a deep crevice, we have taken India's hand and are pulling her out of the Middle Ages into the modern era. Otherwise why would we set up such an extensive network of railways there? Otherwise why would we send machine-produced cloth to that country? Why would we dig streams and canals? And do not forget, India is an undeveloped, agricultural country. They have been farming—only farming—for centuries. We are supporting them by purchasing their cotton and the other things that they grow.'

The teacher raised his hand again.

'It's not true that India is primarily a nation of farmers. It is industrial as well. Things produced in India are sold the world over. That you want it to become entirely a land for farming is unjust.'

A wave of discomfort spread through the hall. *Who is this madman mouthing all these stupid things? From where has an India-lover landed here, in our midst?*

The teacher continued, 'I would urge the minister that he share with us the board of directors' thoughts on this matter. You have the report.'

The minister was in a dilemma, but he thought it would be best to handle this line of questioning with a straightforward answer.

'It is correct that in the report of the Board of Directors, Lord William Bentinck says that this trade has meant a big change, and caused a lot of hardship for many classes of people in India. However . . .' The minister had regained his sense of assurance as he spoke. 'Wherever there is a change, the situation always worsens a little before it begins to get better.'

The teacher stood up again.

'Is it true that thumbs of the weavers of Murshidabad were chopped off so they wouldn't be able to make their fine, handspun cloth any more, because if they continue to weave their cloth, the cloth from Manchester won't find a market?'

A brief spell of silence preceded the screaming and shouting that soon started.

'Who is this traitor? He's so bothered about Indians.'

Another got up and said, 'He's a snake in the grass.' He turned to the minister and said, 'I would suggest we don't engage in such debates. We have come here to listen to the report, not to debate it.'

The minister's face had a certainty—the kind of certainty one found in any resolute person who is participating in the establishment of the Empire, a task of immense national significance for which no sacrifice was too great. It was his resolve towards this responsibility that had, over time, made his jaw clenched and brought a hint of glassiness in the blue of his eyes. It said, *the establishment of the Empire is a Herculean task and I must fulfil my responsibilities; I am a pillar of the immense hall of the Empire.*

'Britannia rules the waves,' he muttered to himself. For a moment he felt like he was a commander of a huge army that was advancing steadily through islands, deserts and oceans, and flags were being lowered at his feet, announcing his victory. This image gave him a sense of equanimity.

A gentleman, a factory owner from Macksfield, stood up. 'I have full sympathy for the Indian worker,' he said, 'but compared to his family, I have more empathy with my own. There's no intelligence in thinking I should sacrifice the interests and comforts of my family because the weavers of India are having a bad time.'

The merchant from Manchester raised his hand and said gently, 'India is a vast country. The main question concerning commerce with India is if the people of India can pay for the goods that we produce with what they grow on their soil.'

Expressing his appreciation for the question, the minister spread his hands again and said, 'You didn't let me finish. But I have only praise for the enthusiasm of the members. I would like to turn your attention again to the statistics. I've already talked about cotton.'

The disturbance that had arisen moments ago seemed to be quietening. People were silent again, though some were still eyeing the teacher, who was sitting at the far end of the second row.

'I've presented some statistics related to cotton. Now I'd like you to listen to some statistics related to other kinds of raw materials.'

He smiled, picked up his papers from the table, put on his glasses and, looking at his audience, said, 'I know that some are more interested in learning about dividends, but I have to fulfil my obligations.' Replacing his glasses, he read from the sheets, 'Here are some statistics for sheep wool—In 1833, only three thousand and seven hundred pounds worth of wool was exported by India. But eleven years on, that is, in 1844 . . .' and the minister paused once more for dramatic effect, 'in 1844,' he continued, 'wool worth twenty lakh and seventy thousand pounds was exported.'

The hall resounded with loud applause. A wave of happiness swept through everyone. These statistics really did signal progress and development.

The enthusiasm pleased the minister and he laughed. He raised a finger to quieten everyone and said, 'How many statistics should I present? In 1833, only one thousand and one hundred bushels of cotton were produced. Eleven years later, in 1844 . . .' he paused, smiled, then continued, 'eleven years later, in 1844, it has reached thirty-seven thousand bushels.'

The hall again echoed with applause. There was loud clapping after every statistic now. Each time, the clapping would continue for quite long.

'Is it true that wheat and rice are also imported from India?' The teacher got up from his seat once more.

'What are you implying?'

'I'm merely asking a question so I may become informed.'

'What do you want to know?'

'Just if food grain is also being exported by India. And if yes, then how much? As a shareholder, I am well within my rights to ask this question.'

The minister was quiet for some time. He was thinking about what this questioner might ask next. On the basis of this, he would decide if he should give him an answer or end this conversation right here. He cast a piercing look at the teacher, then smiled and said, 'You're a British citizen, as am I. Both of us have the interest of Britain in mind— its progress and development—and that's exactly how it should be.'

The teacher replied, 'Besides having love for my country, I also have love for justice and values. Our country swears by these too.'

The minister said gently, in a placatory voice, 'Our relations with India are not based only on ideas of our economic benefit, but are also inspired by values. Like I just said, we want to modernize India and its economy.'

'Will the minister answer my question? What quantity of grain is being brought here from India?'

Seeing that the minister looked startled, some people asked the teacher to sit down. 'Sit down!' they started calling out. 'Sit down!'

'This is utter nonsense!'

'Our time's being wasted.'

'Who is this?'

The minister said in a calm voice, 'You'll get these statistics from any report.'

'Why don't you tell me?' the teacher said.

'Just tell him. Let's just get done with him,' some people called out.

The minister picked up the report from the table. He flipped pages, then collected himself and read, 'We mostly bring wheat and rice from India. The figures are as follows:

'1849—Eight lakh and fifty-eight thousand pounds' worth
'1858—Three crore and eighty lakh pounds' worth
'1877—Seven crore and ninety lakh pounds' worth
'1901—Nine crore and thirty lakh pounds' worth expected.'

The minister had barely finished reading these figures out when the eccentric teacher said, 'So the imports have increased, and will have increased by one hundred times in fifty years. They'll reach nine crore pounds from eight lakh pounds . . . I have another, small question. Can the minister present the statistics related to famines in India in this same period?'

But someone screamed, 'Why are these questions being asked?'

Another screamed, 'This is a traitor in our midst. He's a snake in the grass!'

'Sit down! Sit down! This is no shareholder; he's a political agitator.'

'I'm waiting for the minister's answer.'

The minister was trembling with rage. He was very close to losing his composure. If he weren't a minister, he would have ordered this man to be picked up by the scruff of his neck and thrown out. But he kept quiet. He turned the page with trembling hands and read out, 'In the first fifty years of the century, there were seven famines in India.' He paused before continuing, 'And in the last fifty years, there have been twenty-four famines.'

'Seven earlier, and now twenty-four!'

There was stunned silence in the hall. Famine—what an ill-omened, terrifying word. Some were irritated with the minister—this eccentric teacher should have been scolded and silenced right at the beginning. Where was the need of knowing these statistics?

'Now kindly also tell us the death toll resulting from these famines.'

The minister, his face crimson with anger, his hands trembling with rage, read out, 'In the first fifty years of the last century, fifteen lakh. In the last fifty years, two crores . . .'

'I've nothing more to say.'

He got up from his seat.

The pall of silence that had descended in the gathering was refusing to lift. Two crores was merely a statistic, but still, it jarred the mind. The minister stood behind his desk, perplexed about how to proceed. A few members exchanged glances.

'What does this have to do with this meeting?' a factory owner from Manchester asked from his seat. 'Have we come here to discuss commerce or famines?'

The minister knew it would be a mistake to let the meeting end on this note. People will leave from here filled with guilt. The teacher had turned his back to the gathering and was walking out of the hall. The moment he was out of the door, the atmosphere felt a little less oppressive. The minister clasped his hands together, took a step forward and, trying to evoke the same enthusiasm in his voice as he'd had when he spoke earlier, said, 'I want to remind you all that the dinner being hosted by Her Majesty—for which you are all invited to Birmingham Palace—in honour of the progress being made by this country, begins in an hour.'

And filled with the feeling that he too had a hand and was playing a significant role in this progress, each man present there got up from his seat and everyone clapped together. They clapped for a long time.

ↄ

Miles away, across seven seas, the girls of a small town on their first railway journey, were clapping and dancing with delight as they sang:

> *O firangi, bravo, bravo*
> *Your rule endures!*
> *Bravo, bravo, you are a doer*
> *You are the pinnacle*
> *You reign over all*
> *Bravo, bravo!*
> *Bravo, bravo!*

BOOK THREE

Lekhraj moved through the lanes of the town like a restless shadow. The people he knew had grown old, or were dead. The lanes seemed narrower than he remembered them; the town's colours had faded.

His feet took him from lane to lane; he halted in one place, then the next, looking, searching.

A 'Yellow Quarter' had come up outside Grain Market. The firangi deputy commissioner held his court here, and it was always crowded. So the administration really had changed. He went to the Palace of Mirrors. The doors had lost their colour and were broken; there were pigeon nests everywhere and bats flew about in the dark rooms; the palace was a ruin. The king used to walk up and down this very platform, wearing a long robe and with a glittering cap, studded with stars and sequins, on his head. He was always surrounded by the rich and eminent people of the town, who would wear their traditional clothes when they came to meet him.

Many houses had come up in the area around the palace. It almost seemed to Lekhraj as if people had taken bricks and stones out of the palace and used them for the construction of their homes. Need a stone slab? Let's just get it from the palace. Need to get the wall plastered? Why bother, just carve

the wall out from the palace's outer pavilion and use it. While
he walked around the palace, a group of boys arrived and
walked straight into the meeting hall, where one of the boys
started shouting out, 'The seat of the raja! Raja . . . raja . . .
raja . . . Palace of Mirrors! Mirrors . . . mirrors . . . mirrors . . .'
His words echoed, multiplying by three before fading away.
'Raja Amirchand . . . Amirchand . . . Amirchand . . .' It was as
if Raja Amirchand himself was vanishing.

The game unsettled Lekhraj so much that he left
immediately.

The streets were busy with new kinds of people—lawyers
in their black coats and white salwar kameez, and their
bookkeepers with bundles of papers tucked under their arms.

Everything was the same—the streets, the houses, the
faces—but they seemed to be missing something. Something
that, in having left, had rendered them lifeless. Was his youth
the missing link? Or had the town changed and become
unrecognizable? It had been two days since Lekhraj had
returned to his home town, and his feelings of being homeless
seemed to already be catching up with him.

It wasn't that he hadn't come into town before then.
He had come back before as well. Each time, something
heartbreaking happened, and made him leave. The first time
was when he was exhausted and downcast by the war, and
impatient to be back home, his heart filling with expectation
of a reunion with Moran. But on reaching Miani he learnt
his fiancée was no longer his—she'd already been married,
and widowed. His heart had sunk, and he had turned back.
He made another attempt to return, some years later. He got
on the train—it was the first time a train was going to enter
his town—and he felt the same excitement and elation about
returning as he had the first time. But what he witnessed was

so unexpected that it soured his heart—as he looked out of
the window of his compartment, he saw Diwan Mayyadas
bowing low before the train's firangi guard. Mayyadas, the
symbol of the pride and dignity of the town, the man who,
even when he'd lost everything, had not let go of his self-
respect. Lekhraj's heart filled with sadness, and he left at once.
This was when he joined the Kukas and fought alongside
them against the British. The heart has its own reasons; what
is one to do if one loses control of it? And then, each person
acts according to his own nature. Lekhraj had now, finally,
returned to town after crossing the threshold of old age, but
even so his eyes searched for the familiar. He sought refuge
in the familiar, but all he found was change that made him
feel displaced.

On leaving Sethis' Neighbourhood—from where he'd
been looking upon the mansion—he came into a lane that
ended near a well. He crossed paths with an old woman whom
he didn't pay much attention to at first, but after she'd crossed
the lane, they both turned to look at each other.

The old woman seemed to have recognized him already.
Strands of grey hair danced on her wrinkle-laden face. 'Moran!'
Lekhraj exclaimed, and felt immense joy and unbearable pain
rise up inside him. The memory he had preserved of Moran
all these years was of a young girl with a round, dark face and
a sparkling smile.

'Lekhraj!' The old woman walked back towards him.
'You're Lekhraj, aren't you? You've come back? Where were
you all this time?' Then she continued in the same tone,
'Veeranwali's daughter got married into the Diwan's. It's the
old purohit's doing. You've heard, right?'

This last sentence tore through the web of the past that
Lekhraj had tended to with so much care all these years.

'She'll be looked after in the mansion, sure . . . But she has to spend her entire life with an epileptic husband.' And then she asked, in the same unsentimental voice, 'Are you going to stay, or will you leave again?'

She turned around and started crossing the road without waiting for his answer. Lekhraj was left wondering if she had forgotten who he had been to her once upon a time. In the twenty years he'd spent away from here, he hadn't let go of the memories he had of this town. But he had slipped out of lives, become irrelevant.

The old woman turned around again. She was laughing. Her laughter had the same ring as it did when she was younger, the same ring that had helped Lekhraj through many a terrifying night during the wars.

'Lekhraj, do you remember how we used to go looking for pebbles on the hillock?' It was as if his memories held her feet and kept them from walking away.

'I remember,' he replied. *She does remember me,* he thought to himself, and this feeling gave him happiness. But he also understood that the thread of her memories was fragile, and could snap any time. He watched her walk away. They weren't co-travellers in their present.

Lekhraj was finding it hard to keep his heart from breaking. *What was the sense in coming back? Why did I come back? For another look at this old town? Moran isn't a young girl, and Shivraj doesn't go wrestling every morning—he's deaf in one ear and he sits in his room on the roof like a wooden doll, staring into space. The people I carry around with me in my head don't exist. What did I hope to find here? Whom was I hoping I'd meet? At least while they lived in my head, all those people had an existence for me. I'm losing them all here, one by one. The more I seek them out and want to make them real, the more they disappear. But why do I need to preserve these memories anyway? What more are they than shadows that emerge from time to time to please or torment me? I've been carrying Moran in my mind for so long, but that Moran doesn't exist, and I don't exist for Moran.*

The humpbacked sweet seller's shop was exactly where it used to be. So, some things hadn't changed after all. The shop had its frying pans and stoves like he remembered them, and the sweet seller was wearing clothes dirtied by cooking, like he always had. Just that he'd grown old. He was sitting at the back of the shop, wrapped up inside a blanket.

'Lekhraj! My goodness, Lekhraj! Oh look who's here!'

The dice players who had been sitting nearby turned to look. The oldest among them recognized Lekhraj at once. Two of the players were young, and looked confused, but they'd heard of a Lekhraj who had gone to fight in the war.

Banshi stood up immediately and walked up to Lekhraj and embraced him. Banshi's body had aged. His stomach was protruding and the rest of his body wobbled, jelly-like.

'So you're alive? You're not Lekhraj's ghost, are you? Come, sit!'

Lekhraj felt his throat tighten with emotion. This was the first time he got a feeling of homecoming.

Everyone had aged. Kesar Singh's beard and moustache had greyed and he had bags under his eyes. What hadn't changed was his love for the game of dice and he continued to play as before—his eyes lowered like a ceremonial reader of the Sri Guru Granth Sahib in a gurdwara, his expression no different from a sadhu's. With his grey hair, he fit the image even more than before.

Ramjawaya sat on the other side of the lane, his legs dangling from the raised platform in front of a shop. Even years ago, he'd sit like this for hours and comment on things.

The shop he was sitting in front of now had a painted door, and Lekhraj saw firangi objects inside—kerosene lamps, umbrellas, satin kerchiefs, ribbons. It appeared to be Ramjawaya's shop.

The dice players abandoned their game and gathered around Lekhraj.

'You've ruined our game. Now tell us where you've been roving all this time,' Banshi said.

'It's been decades since the war. Even the administration's changed. But Lekhraj's battles have continued,' Kesar Singh added.

'If you've come back for your share in the mansion, then don't bother. You won't get anything there.'

News that Lekhraj was back in town had been circulating for some time. People had heard he was staying with Mausi Bhagsuddhi, who was a distant cousin of his mother's.

Lekhraj gauged from the conversations that unfolded that these old friends regarded him with pity. To them, he'd been unable to make anything out of his life. He'd come back to town the same way that he'd left—empty-handed, rudderless. The Khalsa Durbar that he'd waged the war on behalf of didn't have any place or meaning in their lives. Now the firangis were all-important, and Lekhraj had failed to make a place for himself in their administration. As far as they were concerned, Lekhraj had come back defeated.

'You should go to Diwan Dhanpat and ask him to keep you as an accountant. He'll definitely give you some work.'

'Forget the years you've lost. If you get in Diwan Dhanpat's good graces, you can spend the rest of your life peacefully under his roof.'

'Make sure you gauge his mood from his eyes before you speak with him. He's a crooked one.'

Banshi repeated his suggestion: 'It'll be best if you can get an attendant's job with the Diwan. If that works out, you'll be able to earn a little on the side. And you'll wield some influence as well. Diwanji owns three villages!'

Lekhraj looked at their faces, completely perplexed.

'You're not getting it. Dhanpat moves around in a palanquin now. He's become a big-shot landlord. He's the most important Diwan in this town.'

Lekhraj hadn't witnessed the ascent of Dhanpat. He still remembered Dhanpat as the character who roamed the lanes on his mule.

Banshi was repeating, 'Go to Diwan Dhanpat. He's sure to give you some work. You're no longer at an age where you should be running around.'

Then he started talking about how just Diwan Dhanpat was. There was a tiller who hadn't paid his dues for three years. The Diwan summoned him to his courtroom. He had him lashed ten times and warned him that if he didn't pay the revenue next year, with interest, he'd be evicted from that land. But then he also gave him two sacks of grain: one sack as seeds, and the other to feed his family.

This started a debate. One young lad with pointy moustaches said, 'Where's the justice in this? Considering how dire his situation is, what's he going to plant, and what's he going to eat?'

'But at least the Diwan showed compassion. The question was of extracting his dues; he didn't have to give that man anything at all.'

'Time moves in mysterious ways.' The sweet seller spoke up. He had come out of his shop. 'Land couldn't be taken away from the tiller earlier. Now it can be. If you don't pay revenue for two years, your land can be confiscated from you the following year.'

'If you don't pay your dues, then of course your land will be confiscated. What else is there to do?' Ramjawaya said.

The conversation steered towards how good this administration was at record-keeping, because of which anyone could go to court and demand a hearing. That's not how it used to be earlier. Earlier things used to weigh heavily on the revenue official—whether he was merciful, what he was thinking—but now things happen according to law. Law dictated things now.

But the sweet seller was still talking about the Diwan. He said, 'It was the elder Diwan who stayed loyal to Raja Amirchand. He lost everything. And those who betrayed? Their stars shone.'

'Listen, oh humpbacked,' Ramjawaya spoke in a loud voice, 'loyalty and betrayal are meaningless things. All of us pay obeisance to whoever rules; that's the way of the world.'

'I hear they're setting up a pleasure park on the land of the Diwans. Isn't it so, Ramjawaya?'

'The Diwans no longer own that land. It belongs to Malik Mansaram now,' Ramjawaya replied.

Banshi didn't let the chance to poke some fun slip by. 'Request Malik Mansaram to gift you a voluptuous woman.'

Everyone laughed; Ramjawaya felt bad.

'What's he going to do with a voluptuous woman at this age?' Kesar Singh quipped. 'Anyway, let the pleasure park get made and then, why one, twenty women will appear out of nowhere.'

'Here comes the Kuka,' Banshi said in a subdued voice. 'Kuka Hari Singh.'

'Ram Ram, Bhagatji. Ram Ram, sirs.' Hari Singh greeted everyone as he walked past.

'The father swats a fly, and the son claims to have become an archer,' Ramjawaya mocked softly.

No one paid any attention. Ramjawaya commented again, 'They were shooting in the dark, these Kukas. The firangis can't be defeated so easily. Now he's hiding here.'

Banshi turned to Lekhraj and said, 'We heard you had joined up with the Kukas as well.'

Lekhraj didn't respond. His face darkened with the shadow of unbearable pain.

'Were they really tied to the mouth of cannon and shot?'

'Yes.'

'Why?'

'They'd attacked the fortress of the nawab of Malerkotla.'

'Why?'

'What do you mean by "why"? When the rebellion broke out, the nawab allied with the firangis.'

'Then?'

'What then! The firangi tied the Kukas—more than sixty of them—to the mouths of cannon and fired the cannon. Many others were ordered to leave the country.'

Ramjawaya said in a mocking tone, 'And then one Kuka ran to this town!'

'What did the Kukas want?' Banshi asked.

'They wanted the firangis to leave the country. They wanted everyone to fight the firangis. They wanted people to not attend the courts and sessions of the firangis. And for people to not buy firangi goods, not wear firangi cloth.'

Ramjawaya continued to mock the Kukas. 'The Kukas cooed and cooed, and then fell silent. No one can get the better of the firangis.'

'They were also incensed that the firangis converted Maharaja Ranjit Singh's son and had him sent to their country.'

This started another debate. Lekhraj realized that the people of this town had a very essentialist view of history. They believed that because something happened, therefore it should have happened, and that human beings should accept things as they happen and mould themselves accordingly.

As the debate carried on, it touched upon the Poorabiyas. Ramjawaya, who until now had been hiding behind mockery, now started openly taking the firangis' side. 'These are the same people who helped the firangis win Punjab. Now if they decide to take on the same firangis during the mutiny, are we supposed to help them?'

Banshi laughed. 'What is this "we", Ramjawaya? War or rebellion, you never moved your arse. So who's this "we" now?'

Kesar Singh added, 'Ramjawaya's mouth has got diarrhoea ever since he became an agent for firangi goods. He's turned into quite the firangi well-wisher.'

'The "we" is great!' Banshi continued joking.

'This isn't Ramjawaya speaking. It's his agent-ness speaking,' the sweet seller said.

'I don't have to take lessons from you,' Ramjawaya said heatedly. 'Guru Teg Bahadur Maharaj had himself prophesized that a cap-wearing Sikh would come from across the seas and avenge his death. Did he predict this or not? The firangi is that cap-wearing Sikh.'

'Ramjawaya, you're such a sympathizer, but the firangi didn't give you even a tiny patch of land in return,' Banshi continued joking.

Kesar Singh laughed. 'That's because he's going to be gifted a buxom woman. And because he's become an agent. And look at his shop—it's decked up like a new bride!'

Everyone turned to look at the raised platform on which Ramjawaya's shop was.

Lekhraj had already witnessed the town's fascination for foreign goods the day before, when he'd sat down to rest his back against a wall in Sethis' Neighbourhood. Ramjawaya had walked into the lane, a foot ruler in his hand for measuring cloth, followed by a porter who was carrying a basket on his head and another enormous bundle on his back, both filled with foreign knick-knacks. Within seconds, girls flocked around him, chirping with excitement. Ramjawaya removed the cover from over the basket and brought out items one by one—vibrant ribbons, laces, clips, shiny knives with golden and green handles, brass locks and so on. All the things were really quite lovely. The girls snatched them from each other's hands for a look.

'What's this?' a girl asked, picking up a small, green thing from the basket.

'It's for hair; it's a "kilip".'

'Sorry, what is it called?'

'Your head!' Ramjawaya got miffed.

Lekhraj realized Ramjawaya didn't know the names of things himself.

There was a pair of such clips on a piece of cardboard. A girl picked them up and shyly clipped them on to her hair.

'Who's going to see those when your head's covered with a dupatta?'

'I'll move the dupatta back a little bit.'

One of the elder girls bit her lower lip at this and said, 'You're shameless! You'll walk around with your head uncovered? Won't you feel ashamed?'

'You'll wear flowers in your hair and walk about showing them to strangers?' an older woman, who was sitting nearby working on a spinning wheel, added.

Ramjawaya untied the bundle his porter was carrying. Rolls upon rolls of cloth emerged from within it. Each roll had a picture on it—some had the laughing face of a woman, and others had a faithful-looking dog. Ramjawaya pulled out dupattas of fine muslin cloth from under the bundles of cloth. The girls leapt towards them and started trying them on. The older women sitting nearby turned up their noses— the girls' hair was visible from under these dupattas. This was unacceptable.

Banshi was joking again when another man passed by. He was an older man, and he was holding a short cane. He joined his hands in greeting and walked past the group. He was wearing pyjamas with broad sleeves and a knee-length coat; he had a thick, thorny moustache and his back was slightly bent. Lekhraj didn't know him; he didn't seem to be of this town. His attire wasn't like that of the people of this town either.

'He doesn't seem to be from here.' Lekhraj turned to Banshi.

'He's not. He's come from Sargodha,' Banshi said. 'He's a teacher, and calls himself Vaanprasthi. He's going to start a girls' school here.'

Lekhraj was surprised. 'How come a school?'

'That's going to be the second school. One was started recently by the missionaries.'

Ramjawaya piped in irritated, 'The old fool! He's lost his mind. He's come here to take our girls' dupattas off.' Then he kept grumbling, 'His brain has gone for a walk. Girls' school! Let him try.'

Lekhraj found Ramjawaya's annoyance strange, but he stayed quiet. Just yesterday, when he was selling dupattas to young girls, the older women had been annoyed with him for bringing such sheer dupattas into the market. He spent so much time entreating the girls to buy them. And now he was saying girls' heads would get uncovered because of Vaanprasthi's school!

The dice players had started debating the school when Lekhraj left them.

✍

For now, the pleasure park had been set up under a tent in the maidan outside town, behind Oil Pressers' Neighbourhood. It would soon be shifted to the land that Malik Mansaram had bought at the auction. This is what Lekhraj had gathered. He walked towards it.

A man was posted outside, on a stone pedestal, with a megaphone that he screamed through continuously, extolling the attractions of the pleasure park. There was a thin film of dust in the air and many lads, young and old, were walking around.

'Come see Krishna's games with his gopis on the big screen! Come witness the magic of the bioscope! See scenes from Bombay! See the crown of the Empress of England! See the buxom woman!'

Children were coming out from the maidan. Some were whistling; some held toys in their hands. These toys weren't made of clay but of some other material, and they were very beautiful. One child held a cow and a lion in his hands. Both looked weightless.

Propelled by his curiosity, Lekhraj walked on into the maidan.

There were carousels, as well as a scattering of shops. But the main attraction was the decorated tent. There was a crowd of people outside it trying to go in.

It was dark inside the tent. Black curtains hung everywhere, and images were being shown on one of the curtains at the back of the tent. This was new even for Lekhraj. There was a table right at the centre of the tent, and it had some kind of instrument on it. A beam of light emerged from this instrument and fell directly on the curtain. This was what was making the images. A man sat by the instrument, and he moved one of its parts from time to time. Each time he did this, the image on the curtain would change. Another man stood by the curtain, holding a stick. He'd tap the ground with the stick and that seemed to be the cue for the man by the instrument to move the part, so the image would change.

'This is Bal Gopal. He's stolen butter and is eating it.'

Bal Gopal was wearing blue clothes. He had jet-black, curly hair, with a peacock feather tucked into it. He wore a pearl necklace. His right hand covered his mouth, and there were white smears on his cheek from the butter he was eating. An earthen pot lay next to him. A viewer could immediately tell the young Krishna was taking butter out of this pot. He was smiling and winking mischievously.

There was a look of surprise on the onlookers' faces, as if they hadn't expected to encounter this image here. They joined their hands reverentially. One man was overcome with emotion. 'Jai to Bal Krishna Baldev,' he cried out.

'Jai!' many repeated after him.

The image changed. The next image too was of Krishna Maharaj. He was dancing with gopis, who encircled him, holding hands. The gopis wore striking long skirts, and Krishna held a flute to his lips. He was standing with one foot behind the other and smiling gently. He had a sheer dupatta over his shoulders, a long tilak on his forehead, a peacock feather in his hair and a pearl necklace around his neck.

'Say "Jai" to Krishna Baldev!'

The sound of 'Jai' filled the tent as everyone cheered. The bosoms of the dancing gopis seemed to be escaping their tight blouses. People watched, fascinated. An excited lad who was sitting right in front of Lekhraj thrust his elbow into his friend who was sitting right next to him. The lad laughed coyly.

The tent filled with the cheer for the lord again: 'Repeat after me, Jai to Krishna Baldev!'

People laughed.

Then the much-awaited image of the voluptuous woman, called 'the washerwoman who weighs twelve maunds', appeared on the screen. A half-naked woman, heavyset, lay sprawled on the bed, her back propped up by pillows. People watched with bated breath. Her skin was pink, thighs were thick, breasts were enormous, and hair was black and curly and fell over her shoulders. She was holding a fan. A slight smile played on her lips.

People watched with hungry eyes, their breathing tense. The image stayed on the screen for a long time.

There were just a couple of images after this—Queen Victoria's palace in London and then an image of Bombay. And that was that; game over.

People had been cajoled in with promises and entreaties, but now they were made to leave in haste so another round of visitors could be brought in.

Lekhraj was outside again.

A short distance away, there was another, smaller tent.

A long banner outside this tent had this written on it in Urdu:

'Unhappy people of this world, come to me; I'll give you comfort.'

Lekhraj really felt like he'd landed on an alien planet. This was not how this town used to be! His town never had pleasure parks and bioscopes.

The tent had been set up by missionaries. Lekhraj had heard about them, but he hadn't encountered any. A thin man, dressed in a white robe, black shoes and with a thin, white towel thrown over his shoulder, stood outside the pleasure park. Young kids had gathered around him, and he was chatting with them. Some of the children stood with their palms stretched out. The man would smile, ruffle a kid's hair, talk with his forefinger sticking in the air. Lekhraj noticed that another long banner hung here, and it said, 'You, who have lost your way in the world, trust in me and I will grant you the gift of life.'

The priest produced a glass jar from under his arm, opened its lid, pulled out a few sugar cakes and put one in each of the children's palms. The kids were thrilled, and ran off happily.

The priest spotted Lekhraj and walked towards him. He pulled out a small booklet from his bag and offered it to him.

'We hold prayer meetings every morning and evening. Please do come.'

Lekhraj peeped into the tent—there were two or three more priests inside. They were standing in front of a fair man, nodding their heads. This man was a firangi, and he was dressed differently from the rest. He wore a black skullcap with a pointy top, and a black robe, but with a white collar that was separate from the robe. He wore a pair of glasses and his beard was golden brown. He saw Lekhraj, smiled and gestured to him to come inside. Lekhraj stood where he was, momentarily surprised, but then he walked away.

He'd walked a short distance from the pleasure park when he saw yet another tent, open on one side. There was quite a crowd here as well. Lekhraj wondered if there was yet another show going on inside. Many young men were standing in a row along a table facing away from where he was.

He was about to enter the tent, when someone approached him and handed him a small box. It had something inscribed on it in English.

'What is this?'

'Cigarette. The English bidi. There are five in the box.'

Lekhraj turned the box over in his hands, then said, irritably, 'I don't have money.'

'Who's asking for money! Smoke them, brother. Enjoy yourself.' The man's lips parted in a smile beneath his thick, black moustache. Then he pointed towards the tent and said, 'Go on in, try your luck.'

Lekhraj went in. A game was being played inside. Lots of figurines of different colours, each with a number on it—5, 9, 7, 3 and so on—had been set up on a long, low table. Young men had lined up behind the table. Lekhraj saw one pick up a wooden ball from a basket that had been placed at one end of the table, and aim it at a figurine that had the number '7' written on it. He missed by a hair's breadth. He aimed again, this time at a figurine further away, and which had the number '2' written on it. He succeeded; the figurine fell. One of the men running the show picked up two packs of cigarettes from among a large number kept on a long bench, and gave them to him.

'Here you go, your reward.'

The lad looked happy. He gave another two paise as fee and picked up two more balls to try his luck again, but failed.

'I'll come again tomorrow,' he said to his companion, 'and win four packets.'

'The game ends today. No more free cigarettes from tomorrow.'

'Why?'

'It was the same in Lalamusa. A pleasure park had been set up there as well. They dole out free cigarettes for a few days, but then they stop.'

Seeing a crowd around the peepul tree, Lekhraj paused. People had gathered around a half-naked man. He was playing a wooden clapper and singing:

> *Oh, there's a craze for watches and spectacles today*
> *Fashion has made me bankrupt, oh my darling*
> *Fashion is squeezing the life out of me*
> *Fashion . . .*

His audience laughed. Every couplet produced fresh guffaws of laughter. Someone called out, 'Surdas, have you ever seen a watch?'

Another asked, 'Surdas, have you ever seen glasses?'

The man joined his hands before them all and said, 'No, my esteemed sirs, I haven't seen spectacles. No, sirs, I haven't seen a watch.'

'So you haven't seen either, and you're going around town saying people are going bankrupt?'

'Surdas, have you seen a train?'

'No, my sirs, but I've heard its whistle.'

'Surdas, have you seen a firangi?'

'No, my sirs, but I've heard he looks like a monkey.'

There was a loud burst of laughter all around him.

But then someone emerged from the tent, and Lekhraj recognized him immediately—it was Ramjawaya. He held the man by his arm and pushed him towards the road that led into town. 'Get lost.'

Someone called out, 'Surdas, have you seen a monkey?'

The blind man was in a mood for jest. 'One's holding me by my arm right now,' he said.

He was blinking rapidly and he flashed a big smile at his audience. Ramjawaya pushed him. 'That's enough of your rubbish. Get lost.'

'As you say, sir. Forgive my trespasses,' he said, his hands folded. Then he turned around and, tapping his cane on the ground, walked away.

∾

The next day, Lekhraj stood at the threshold of the mansion.

The mansion looked grand. The green gate beneath the arched gateway at its entrance had been recently touched up; it glistened. Quite possibly, the entire mansion had been painted recently because of the weddings. Strings of flowers hung from places, though they'd dried long ago; there were colourful flags everywhere. There was a crowd of people and Lekhraj immediately understood these were petitioners—villagers and farmers who'd come in groups. A gatekeeper stood guard at the gate. Beyond the gate, two horses were tethered to one side, and the palanquin that Lekhraj had seen Diwan Dhanpat ride through town in was parked nearby. There was a raised platform on the left of the gate; it stretched for quite a distance. Lekhraj remembered how his uncle, the elder Diwan, strolled on it. He used to be a serious, tall and very impressive-looking man. He'd walk up and down this pedestal alone, in silence. A door opened on to this platform.

There were two windows, with coloured glass panes, on either side of the door. Lekhraj saw many servants and attendants walking around. The Diwan lived in great luxury.

Lekhraj's eyes roved to the right of the gate. In the old times, a huge peg used to be fastened into the ground here, to which an elephant always stood tethered. The peg was still there, but instead of the elephant, two horses—one white, the other brown—were tethered to it.

Lekhraj walked towards the gate, and the gatekeeper stopped him. 'The court is not in session yet. Diwan Sahib will be arriving shortly.'

Lekhraj felt his heart twinge: the gatekeeper didn't know he'd been born in this house and had grown up running around in its enormous rooms. His gaze stayed fixed on the gatekeeper's face for some time, then he took a few steps back.

'When will Diwan Sahib come?'

'Any moment now.'

The gatekeeper sensed that the man he was talking to wasn't a petitioner from a village; he looked more like someone from the Diwan's caste or clan who happened to be travelling through town. He softened a little bit. 'If you're here to meet Diwanji, you can go sit in the courtroom. The session hasn't started yet.' And he moved his spear out of Lekhraj's way.

Lekhraj couldn't decide if he should wait outside or go in. Then thinking that it would be better to meet Diwan Dhanpat in a crowded courtroom than an empty one, he left.

He walked around purposelessly in the lanes around the mansion for some time. His heart was in turmoil again. That the gatekeeper had stopped him hadn't hurt him, but it had woken him up to the distance that stretched between him and the Diwan. He began to feel the dominance this Diwan had over the town, the terror he evoked. When he returned to the mansion gate after roaming around for some time, everyone was gone. The petitioners had all gone into the courtroom.

Lekhraj stepped in through the gate, walked across the porch and entered the courtyard. Diwan Dhanpat held his court sessions here, every Wednesday. He was sitting on a chair with a high back on the raised platform to the right. The petitioners were sitting on the floor before him.

Lekhraj stood motionless and looked. Diwan Dhanpat was sitting with his feet tucked under him, as he usually did, puffing at the hookah. His clothes were the same as they had been all those years ago. But looking at them carefully, it struck Lekhraj that Dhanpat's attempt was to dress up like a king—or at least like he thought kings dressed. His turban was saffron, but it had a peacock feather on it; his angrakha was yellow, but he'd embellished his look with a tie and pearl necklaces. He looked like a farce. A chowry bearer was swinging a huge chowry behind him and an attendant holding a parchment stood to attention next to him, like a seneschal in a king's court. Lekhraj knew the attendant—it was Banshi. That Banshi worked for the Diwan shocked him, and he looked at him closely, at his body that had loosened with age, and his hair that had lost its blackness. Lekhraj decided it was best to stand to one side, behind the crowd, and that he'd look for an opportunity to speak with the Diwan after the court session ended.

On two benches on either side of the raised platform sat two accountants, each with an immense account book opened up before him. They had their backs to the petitioners. A petitioner stood before the Diwan, his hands folded in deference. 'No, my lordship, no, Huzoor,' he pleaded.

A picture of the queen of England hung on the wall behind the Diwan's chair. Lekhraj's eyes settled on the high seat which looked so much like a throne. A footrest had been placed in front of it, covered with a red cloth. Lekhraj smiled. Diwan Dhanpat had had a high seat made, but he wasn't tall enough to reach it. Why, his feet didn't even reach the high footrest from the seat! That's why he kept his legs folded under him. His gold-embroidered joote lay on the footrest.

The Diwan took the tip of the hookah out of his mouth. 'When will you pay your dues?' Then, suddenly, he started speaking in a vulgar voice, 'Give this son of a pig a good thrashing. Bastard! I ask him something, and he replies to some other question.' The Diwan's harsh voice sent a shiver through the petitioners.

Lekhraj had a blanket wrapped around him. When he'd entered the courtyard, he felt Diwan Dhanpat had looked in his direction and that his eyes had lingered on his face as if trying to recognize him. But then the Diwan had got busy with his hookah and the business of the court.

Four strongmen emerged from nowhere. The farmer was grovelling, 'Have mercy, have mercy, my lord.'

Diwan Dhanpat was puffing at his hookah again, and looked unbothered.

The petitioner was sitting on the floor, his hands folded before him. One of the strongmen bent forward and pulled him up by the scruff of his kurta until he was standing upright, and another punched him in the face and then slapped him a few times. All this happened so quickly that the Jat didn't have time to respond. He didn't stand a chance. The first punch had knocked the daylights out of him; his face had turned ashen. He let out a terrible scream, fell on the floor and crawled towards the Diwan, sobbing.

Lekhraj looked at the Diwan, who was still puffing at his hookah. It seemed to him the Diwan was looking right at him.

Lekhraj left the mansion and walked listlessly from lane to lane, his mind in a tumult. There is a form of rule, he thought to himself, which encourages and intensifies the good in humans—their compassion, desire to serve, generosity, tolerance and empathy towards one another. And then there is another form of rule that emphasizes snatching–hurting, hatred–resentment and greed–gluttony. The former nourishes that which is noble in people, feeds the goodwill people feel for one another. Sure, the fingers in our hand are not equal; there are always people who look after their self-interest before the interest of others. But at least the poison of selfishness doesn't saturate the air—the majority sentiment puts a restraint on ill will. Lekhraj had, of course, seen a time when the wellspring of kindness in people's hearts hadn't dried up, when sharing whatever you had with others was the norm, when people were God-fearing and stopped themselves from thinking poorly of others and doing something bad unto others.

Lekhraj had been postponing meeting Harnarayan. *It will only increase the clamour in my head.* Bhagsuddhi had already narrated to him the story of Rukmo's wedding. He knew that no one except Bhagsuddhi had raised an objection to it. *He'll assume I've come to watch the spectacle of his misery.* But then, one day, he couldn't hold back any longer and he went towards the hillock, which is where, he'd heard, Harnarayan was spending his days.

Harnarayan was sitting under a banyan tree, writing. Lekhraj recognized him at once. He'd always been a man of small build, but now he looked like a bag of bones. White kurta, white pyjamas, pinched cheeks, a grey, drooping moustache.

Lekhraj went and stood in front of him.

Harnarayan looked up, startled. He worried that Diwan Dhanpat may have sent another emissary of death to further torture him, but his eyes began to focus slowly, and Lekhraj's features emerged in their clarity. Harnarayan recognized Lekhraj, but that didn't produce any reaction in him. The excitement and affection we have for people ends with our childhood; after that it is with ourselves that our involvement becomes most intense, and we start becoming melancholic towards others.

'Come, Lekhraj, sit. I'd heard you were back in town.'

Lekhraj sat down next to him, and his eyes fell on the thick sheet of paper on a wooden board, on to which Harnarayan had been writing what appeared to be a sacred hymn. He noticed there were a number of sheets below the one on top, and inkpots with blue and red ink lay next to Harnarayan. He was scribbling with a thick-nibbed pen.

'What are you writing, Harnarayan?' Lekhraj asked, bending slightly towards the sheet.

'You're welcome to read it.'

Lekhraj picked up the wooden board. The words on top of the page were in red ink, and in Sanskrit: 'I bow to you, oh Vasudeva, form of the absolute.' And underneath it, the page was filled with what appeared to be mantras. Lekhraj knew nothing of the scriptures, but he could tell that Harnarayan was writing out slokas that he—probably vaguely—remembered from childhood. For Harnarayan didn't have any knowledge of the shastras either.

'What is this that you're writing, Harnarayan?'

'I'm remembering God, chanting his name. This is where happiness lies. After I finish with these, I've decided, I'll copy out the Gita Sahasranama. I remember that by heart as well.' And he began to hum.

'I remember a whole lot of them,' he said.

Then, placing a hand on Lekhraj's knee, he continued, 'Supreme joy can be found, Lekhraj, if one surrenders to Lord Krishna. When I sit here, the Lord appears before me . . . the one who wears a crown made of a peacock feather, the one who's always dressed in yellow, the one who plays the flute . . .' He was overcome with emotion. He lowered his legs from the raised platform, and sang softly, clicking his fingers to give beat, his head moving from side to side.

I bow to you, oh Vasudeva, form of the absolute!
I bow to you, oh Vasudeva, form of the absolute!

His eyes became moist. He was becoming immersed, and he repeated the sacred line over and over, his lips quivering, his voice laden with emotion. It was as if he was standing before Krishna's idol and paying tribute to him.

Lekhraj sat quietly, looking at him. Harnarayan re-emerged from this deep, heartfelt delirium after several minutes. He then folded his hands and mumbled softly, 'Forgive me my trespasses, Maharaj. Keep this servant of yours within your merciful sight.' He repeated this several times, became quiet and stared into nothingness. Lekhraj felt Harnarayan was no longer aware that he was sitting next to him.

'Where is Ramlal?' he asked to start a conversation. 'Ramlal, your cousin. I didn't see him.'

Harnarayan was startled, as if assailed by Lekhraj's voice.

'Ramlal is no more,' he answered. 'He was returning from court one day, when he stopped by the well for a rest, and died there. It's been ten, maybe twelve years.'

'And Tarachand?'

'He left town and went and settled somewhere else,' Harnarayan replied, still staring into space.

Lekhraj felt that each time he asked a question, the haze that surrounded Harnarayan cleared a little, but that it resettled as soon as he finished answering the question. Trying to draw his attention, he said, 'Let me tell you a story, Harnarayan!' And he started laughing. 'Before I left for the war, Ramlal and I used to go walking around in the fields. We were really thick.'

Harnarayan turned his head and looked at Lekhraj.

'One day, we were chatting about what the world would be like when we grew old. Ramlal said to me, "Come, let's make a pact that when you and I are sixty, we'll meet on the hillock, on Baisakhi day." And . . .' Lekhraj's voice fell. 'Who knew then where I'd be on that Baisakhi day, forty years on, and where he would be. Or that he'd be gone a long time by then.'

Lekhraj realized Harnarayan was looking at him with unblinking eyes, as if the mist of time was finally clearing, and Lekhraj was emerging before him. *Does he not know who I am? Is it possible that he didn't recognize me all this time?* 'This Dhanpat is a terribly cruel man!' The words came out of Lekhraj's mouth suddenly, unexpectedly.

The expression on Harnarayan's face changed. He looked horror-stricken. But then he bowed his head slightly and said philosophically, 'Fate determines all; nothing is in our hands . . .'

Lekhraj and Harnarayan weren't able to sync; the threads of their conversation weren't joining. Harnarayan hadn't even asked Lekhraj when he'd returned, where he'd been all these years, what he would do now that he was back. He was utterly lost in himself.

From where they were sitting on the hillock, they could see the town as well as its edges: The railway line, where it left the town; the fields stretching out beyond Orchard of the Sheikhs; the row of broken arches, which must have been built over a nawab's resting lodge at some point. Below them, to the left, was Grain Market, and right next to it, Kabuli Darwaza—two of its minarets had fallen. And further away, almost at the centre of the town, the Palace of Mirrors, which was now turning into a ruin.

Lekhraj said, 'Remember when the caravans used to leave from here?'

'Of course. I travelled with them several times, to Jhelum.'

'Times have really changed.'

Harnarayan was quiet for some time, then mumbled, 'Time moves in mysterious ways.' Then he started staring into space again.

'How's Rukmini? You do ask after her from time to time, don't you?' Lekhraj asked, out of the blue.

'Everyone's destiny is their own, Lekhraj. She isn't fated to be happy.'

'She comes home sometimes, I'm sure?'

'Where she lives now is her home. Whether good or bad, it's her home. No one can fight their fate, Lekhraj.'

And Harnarayan started speaking in verses again.

> *Mothers give birth to their sons, but cannot alter*
> *what's destined for them*
> *One son might attain knighthood, while the*
> *other roves begging for morsels*

It was as if this restive verse had lain tucked away somewhere in the recesses of his mind, forgotten but gestating.

'My mother used to recite this,' he said. 'It must have been with me in mind, I suppose—the younger son who begs for scraps to live on . . .' His eyes welled up and his chin quivered, but his heart felt soothed by its own modesty, as if he believed he was receiving what fate ordained for him, that he should receive it humbly as that is what the Lord wants, that if you know this, your restlessness recedes and calmness takes over, that acceptance brings serenity.

'I'm the lowest of the lowly,' he muttered.

Self-derision gave Harnarayan pleasure. Every time he felt emotional, he let himself sink deeper and deeper into this feeling—it gave him great satisfaction to remind himself of his own insignificance. He was reciting a verse again.

> *The rich moneylender deals in money*
> *While people like me*
> *Beg for scraps*

Sometimes Harnarayan felt he was tumbling downhill, and this feeling gave him joy.

> *Help a senseless creature like me cross the ocean,*
> *oh Lord*
> *Help a senseless creature like me cross the ocean . . .*

As Lekhraj studied Harnarayan's face, a storm of questions rose in his mind. Is asceticism a way of those who are unable to achieve anything in life? Is it failure that makes one renounce the world and its ways? Or does it come from a capacity to see and think differently? Or is it that a person becomes an ascetic when he feels terrorized by forces more powerful than him?

Lekhraj brought up Rukmini once more. 'I'm sure you get news of her from time to time?'

'What news?' Harnarayan said in a tired voice. 'Louts from across town gather in the mansion day in and day out. I've heard they pass comments at her, throw pebbles at her. Poor thing. They sit around in front of her kitchen, in the gallery on the upper floor and make lewd gestures at her.'

'And Diwan Dhanpat? He doesn't intervene?'

'They don't do this when he's around. It's only when he's away touring his estates—he's gone for days sometimes—that the gathering of no-gooders materializes.'

'Harnarayan, you must let Diwan Dhanpat know of this at once. He should at least be made aware that this happens.'

'What's to be gained in that? If he had any compassion at all in his heart, would he have done what he's done to me?' Then he lowered his voice and said, 'Dhanpat did all that he did to get Kalle married, and now his middle son is hell-bent on getting the property divided even while his father's alive.'

'Isn't there a third son? He has three sons, right?'

'The third one isn't here. He's studying to be a barrister, in England.' Then he mumbled, 'Dhanpat will reap what he has sown.'

And, though his anger had given him the force to utter this, he bit his tongue the very next moment and joined his hands in prayer. 'Forgive me, oh Lord, for having spoken ill of another.' Then he spoke in a more steady tone, 'He thought he'd get Kalle settled this way, but it's resulted in the exact opposite.'

Lekhraj had become agitated. 'I don't care if you don't say anything, but I will.'

Harnarayan trembled. 'What will you say? Whom will you say it to?'

'I'll talk to Dhanpat himself . . .'

Harnarayan watched Lekhraj. Could any man really have courage enough to stand in front of Dhanpat?

'Everyone's fate is preordained, Lekhraj. No one can do anything. My daughter is ill-fated. I am ill-fated. Why would this happen to my granddaughter otherwise?'

But Lekhraj said resolutely, 'Are we to sit doing nothing while our little girl suffers?'

'You've been away, Lekhraj. You don't know Dhanpat.'

'And what of your granddaughter? Little Rukmini! Doesn't she ever come to meet you?'

'She came once, but I told her to stay away. I said to her that the mansion is her home now. Good or bad, that is where her life is, that is where she now lives, and that is where she will die. She didn't visit me after that.' He paused before continuing philosophically, 'All things in this world have a cure, Lekhraj. All things but one—the widowhood of your daughter. That's a fact, and that's how it's been since time immemorial.'

'Her mother doesn't go to visit her either?'

'Veeran? Veeran gets news of her from Bhagsuddhi sometimes, when she attends weddings and death ceremonies.'

'If Dhanpat is one butcher, the other one is you,' Lekhraj mumbled angrily.

These words made Harnarayan tremble; a deep sadness overcame him.

'I'm here today, gone tomorrow, Lekhraj. But my widowed daughter has to live for some more time after me, doesn't she? You don't make an enemy out of the crocodile when you live in a river. No one can turn fate. What is one to do if your fate works against you!'

Lekhraj looked at Harnarayan for a long moment. His hollowed-out cheeks were still trembling, his eyes were pale and frightened, his face ashen. His turban was very dirty in places, but had been tied in a way that would hide the dirt to the extent possible.

Harnarayan sat shaking his head and saying over and over, 'No one can do anything. No one can fight fate.'

Lekhraj wondered: *Is this the same Harnarayan I knew as a child? That Harnarayan would walk boldly through the lanes of town, picking up arguments with people. That Harnarayan, despite his short height, would take risks, step up to challenges. He would walk around with a cane thrown across his shoulders. Who is to know when something inside him broke and made him become what he is today.* And then, for a moment Harnarayan looked to him like someone who'd been sitting here, under the banyan tree, his entire life, passively accepting everything that fate doled out to him. He saw him sitting, head bowed, eyes closed, hands folded before him, his hair turning grey. *And now, this is all he knows how to do—he lives it like a religion—and he searches for the grain of his happiness within it, his self-confidence destroyed by the termites of reclusion.* Lekhraj thought of Harnarayan's propensity to surrender so completely before another as disdainful. *It's all right if a person has no pride, but Harnarayan seems to have lost all sense of dignity.*

Harnarayan's cheeks had stopped trembling. But he was still staring into space dismally. It bothered Lekhraj. 'I don't agree with you, Harnarayan. We must do something. We can't stand by and watch our girl being tormented. Even a dying man shows restlessness for life; a drowning man flails his arms, attempting to stay afloat. He does everything in his power; he fights to keep his nose above water.'

'All a man can do is pray. He can beg to God. That's all one can do.'

Harnarayan would sing devotional songs, hoping to make his way out of stretches of darkness, only to stumble into another dark cloud. God was his only anchor, his sense of security.

'It's up to one's fate, Lekhraj. Everything depends on one's fate.' Harnarayan repeated these lines like the refrain of some song. He thought being philosophical was a balm that would soothe his wounds. He broke into another devotional song, and Lekhraj got up and left without saying a word.

Lamps had been extinguished in almost the entire lane. Footsteps in the street were few and far between, and those that were heard resounded in the dense silence of the night.

A clamour rose from the direction of the mansion. Everyone's ears perked up. There was no doubt this sound came from the far end of the lane, where the mansion was.

Most doors were shut. Where lamps were still lit, their soft light streamed out of cracks in the doors. People had tucked into quilts, and conversations were in quiet tones, the kind one has just before drifting off to sleep. When night descended, stoves and lamps would be put out almost simultaneously in the entire town.

A man was shouting. Then he also started pounding on a door.

This clamour was definitely coming from the direction of the mansion. People began to step out of their houses, their quilts and blankets wrapped around them.

The old woman Bhagsuddhi, who had been sitting on her cot wrapped in her quilt and praying, heard the noise. She listened for some time, then shook her head and concluded, 'Clearly, Manjhle will relent only after he kills his brother.

He's creating a ruckus again.' She had recognized the voice; it was Diwan Dhanpat's middle son.

Ramjawaya too had almost the same reaction to the noise. His shop was four houses away from Bhagsuddhi's house, and he had settled for the night on the raised platform outside it. 'He'll pull down the mansion's walls. Manjhle won't let the old Diwan live in peace.'

Rumours had been circulating for a few days now: Manjhle had rebelled. It seemed that, since his wedding, he was always in a bad mood, and always badly behaved—especially with his father. It was also being said that Diwan Dhanpat had raised a wall in the mansion once again, and his sons now lived separately. It had also been heard that Manjhle and his good-for-nothing friends had made Rukmini's life hell—that they climbed up the dividing wall and made strange sounds at her, teased Kalle, threw pebbles into their courtyard and made lewd gestures.

The first thought that came to everyone's minds when they heard the noise that night was that Diwan Dhanpat may have passed away. But in that case, someone would have been weeping and there would have been a different sort of commotion. This sounded more like a quarrel, more like the issuing of threats. Quarrels around property were not unknown to this town; this noise didn't have that ring.

'Until now, differences were at least contained within the walls of the mansion. Now that which should remain within is spilling out on to the street.' Ramjawaya mumbled to himself as he pulled his shoes out from under his cot. It was impossible that there be a fight in town and he should stay away.

The noise cascaded through the streets and reached Harnarayan as well. His heart started pounding and he snuggled deeper into his quilt and turned over on his side.

People walked towards the mansion in ones and twos.

Manjhle was standing at the turn in the lane into which one of the doors of the mansion opened, screaming at the top of his lungs. Across the lane, the tiny flame of an earthen lamp flickered in the Sufi saint's shrine, and the branches of the *kikar* tree that stretched out above stirred in the breeze, casting deep shadows on each other. The lamp was the only source of light in the lane.

Manjhle held an axe in his hand. Two men were standing next to him, and though the dark made it difficult to tell who they were, everyone could guess they must be his friends.

'I'm going to chop the legs off anyone who steps out of this house!' Manjhle screamed. He seemed to be talking to the door—on the other side of which Kalle and Rukmini lived.

'We're not dead, after all. This shamelessness won't be tolerated. We're not going to let the good name of this family be dragged through mud. Be warned—I'm going to chop your legs off.'

The onlookers weren't quite sure whom Manjhle was threatening. *Whose legs is he going to chop off? What shamelessness is he not going to tolerate? Is he calling out to Kalle? Why does he have to scream at night about chopping off Kalle's legs?*

Manjhle sensed people had gathered behind him. He turned his voice up a few notches and threw a blow at the door with the axe.

'I'm not going to let anyone smear the name of my ancestors. I dare you, if you step out of this house, I'm going to chop you into tiny pieces.'

Carried away by the thought of chopping something into tiny pieces, he started hacking the door with the axe.

By now, people's eyes had adjusted to the dark. The shadowy figures standing beside Manjhle were his friends

Balmukund and Chamanlal. Balmukund's misdemeanours were no secret. This was the same fellow who'd jumped on to his neighbour's roof late one night and tried to force himself on the neighbour's daughter. That's how bold he was. The girl's family would have disembowelled him, but he was let go because he was one of the closest friends of the Diwan's son. And the fact was that he was the one who, encouraged by Manjhle, would climb up the wall that divided the mansion on the pretext of chatting with Kalle, and throw pebbles at Rukmini and make snide remarks at her.

'Oh Kalle, are you listening?' Manjhle screamed even louder than before. He kicked the door and continued, 'Keep your wife under control. She'll know my wrath if she dares to step out of the house.'

The crowd had thickened, but everyone stayed beyond the shrine, outside the faint glow that the clay lamp was casting on the lane. Ramjawaya, shielded from the cold by a monkey cap and a thick sheet that he'd wrapped around himself, walked up to the mansion's door.

'What's the matter, Diwanji? What has made you so upset?'

Manjhle was like a man possessed. Seeing Ramjawaya, he huffed even more.

'Kalle! Oh Kalle! Have you poured oil in your ears? Your wife will see the worst of me if she steps out of this house.'

He struck the axe once more at the door.

Now that he had Ramjawaya as audience, Balmukund too became excited. Poking the air with his finger he said, 'We're not going to let the women of our house be de-veiled. Our sister-in-law isn't some woman of the street.'

It was now that he realized he actually had more audience, and there were more people watching him from the dark, just a few steps away. 'Listen, everyone,' he yelled, 'listen carefully. Our sister-in-law isn't some woman of the street.'

Balmukund was a little drunk; his voice had a drunken lilt. But Manjhle wasn't drunk; he was behaving the way he was out of anger and unbridled emotion.

'Where is that oldie? That man from Sargodha?' Manjhle screamed. 'Let him try talking to me! Always spinning schemes behind everyone's back! Bastard! Motherfu . . . I'm going to break his legs if I see him anywhere near the mansion. They land up from nowhere to waylay our girls.'

Everyone stood quietly, shielded by the dark. The hullabaloo at the mansion produced both curiosity and horror. Eminent people always have such eminent matters and concerns.

'But what is the matter, Diwanji?' Ramjawaya touched Manjhle's elbow and asked sincerely.

'The matter? You're asking me what the matter is?' Manjhle continued in his aggravated tone. 'Why me? Ask Kalle!' Then, his voice dripping with hurt and injury, he said, 'Kalle's wife has gone and enrolled at the school. She has smeared black grease on our faces!'

After Manjhle's words, the silence of the onlookers deepened even more. For a few days now, ever since the man from Sargodha had had the room for the school constructed, he had been going door to door to collect funds. The school had come into everyone's conversation, and no two people felt the same way about a school for girls in their town.

'Is the daughter-in-law of the Diwans now going to bare her face and go to school?' Balmukund screamed emphatically. 'We won't allow such shamelessness. We're not dead. How dare someone cast an eye on our daughters and daughters-in-law! I'm going to pull their eyes out!'

Balmukund's voice was stumbling again, and his spittle was frothing.

Ramjawaya had already guessed that this ruckus had something to do with Rukmini. Manjhle was known all over town for his errant ways, and his gang of friends as well was made up of out-of-control and uncouth lads. Ramjawaya had also heard that Manjhle had been throwing tantrums, demanding his share of the property be given to him, while his friends had taken to tormenting Rukmini. But the matter at hand was entirely different—Rukmini had gone and got her name enrolled in school! Ramjawaya was troubled. He began to see the logic in all this screaming and shouting.

'Are girls of respectable families supposed to walk around without covering their faces?' Balmukund shouted again, this time as if he was addressing Ramjawaya directly.

Not just Ramjawaya but many of those who had gathered in the lane were in a dilemma. Manjhle was standing with an axe in his hand and attacking his brother's door. This was terrible, horrifying behaviour. But now that they knew why he was behaving this way, their sadness and anger abated somewhat. The tension they had been feeling began to ease.

'Let it be, Diwanji. Go inside. It doesn't befit you to stand outside the mansion and raise your voice like this.'

'Let it be? What should I let be? I'm going to break Kalle's legs. I'm going to break that shameless woman's legs.'

The crowd began to murmur. 'What's going on, Mausi Bhagsuddhi?' An elderly man asked Bhagsuddhi, who was witnessing this deplorable, unfortunate incident with everyone else.

'They will know when the sigh of the weak consumes them. Right now it looks like they've forgotten the existence of God and man.'

'But Harnarayan's daughter too hasn't done a good thing—going and getting her name enrolled in school.'

At this, an elderly man remarked, 'So now this is what the daughters and daughters-in-law of good families have come to.' He jerked his head and turned to leave.

'What does she want to study for? Is she going to get a job?'

Mausi Bhagsuddhi muttered, 'That, or she's going to die in that mansion.'

Her answer surprised many people.

'It's strange that you should say this, Mausi. After all, don't women marry men who are crippled? Does that mean they should abandon their veils?'

While everyone had felt bad that Rukmini had been married to Kalle, there seemed to be a general consensus that her having decided to attend school was a far worse thing. They were sure that someone had misled her; she could never have taken such a step on her own.

The crowd started to disperse. People knew Balmukund and his ways well. They also knew Manjhle's rights and wrongs. But whatever their behaviour now, Rukmini's was deemed worse. *Balmukund may be a bum and a terrible person, but Rukmini should have behaved better than she had.*

Mausi Bhagsuddhi's temper soared. She called out to Manjhle and his cohort, 'Ghanshyam! Balmukund! Oh, you cruel people! You've brought someone else's daughter into your home; why are you tormenting her?'

Manjhle turned around and peered into the dark. He'd recognized Mausi Bhagsuddhi's voice. 'Who is it? Aunty Bhagsuddhi? What are you doing here? Why have you come? Go home. Go and sleep. Go, go away from here.'

At this others turned to her and advised, 'Don't get involved, Mausi. You know these people well. Why pick a fight with them?'

'Manjhle is right, Mausi. Is it a good thing that the Diwan's daughter-in-law should walk in the streets without her veil?'

Mausi Bhagsuddhi shook her head and muttered, 'The innocent child! She's landed up in the hands of butchers.'

She contemplated the high walls of the mansion with her weak eyes. In the darkness, they looked to her like the walls of a fortress. *A bird can never escape its cage*, she thought to herself. *It tries, but only ends up wounded. This, it seems, is to be Rukmini's fate.*

'What had to happen has happened, Mausi. If pain and sorrow is what destiny has in store for Rukmini, then that is what she will get, whether she stays within the confines of her house or steps out.'

Manjhle sensed that his neighbourhood agreed with him. He started extolling the moral boundaries upheld by the mansion.

'We can't accept this irresponsible, wayward behaviour. Our family has a name, a standing and respect in this town. We can't let all that be dragged through mud.'

Mausi Bhagsuddhi couldn't bear to hear this. 'A thief is sermonizing. Wow! How incredible! What an amazing time has come upon us. Oh Ghanshyam! Why don't you say outright that you want the entire mansion for yourself? That you want to throw them out? You can do anything you want right now. Why play games?'

Manjhle screamed back, 'Mausi, don't talk nonsense. Who called you here? This is a family matter. Who are you to interfere?'

Mausi Bhagsuddhi with her pale face and chiselled features stood facing Manjhle directly. She was among the handful whose hearts weren't governed by the mansion's terror, who—even though they were mere commoners— could talk back to the people of the mansion. She wasn't scared of anyone.

What Mausi Bhagsuddhi saw forming before her was the dense knot of a situation that would unfurl over time to untold ramifications, and the axe-wielding Ghanshyam, the impoverished Balmukund and the red-eyed old creature called the 'elder Diwan' were all playing their terrible parts in it.

'What you are doing is wrong, Ghanshyam. You haven't a grain of shame left in you,' she said, then spat on the ground and walked away.

Manjhle was still screaming. He had moved away from the door and was standing in the middle of the lane. 'I'm going to pull out the intestines of anyone who does something to tarnish the name of this family. I'm not going to let the honour of my forefathers be dented.'

Dawn was breaking. The clay lamp in the saint's shrine was still lit, but its flame had dimmed. Darkness was withering and letting go of walls slowly. People started to return to their homes. Seeing everyone leave, Manjhle screamed even more—as if he thought they were leaving because his voice didn't impress them like the elder Diwan's did.

He turned once more towards the door, and was about to strike it with the axe when a slab of stone fell on the ground from a height. Manjhle was still a few steps away from the door. He quickly moved further away and looked up. The mansion was old, and bricks and stone slabs had become loose in places, and sometimes did fall from its old walls, especially off the merlons. There wasn't enough light yet to be able to tell where this slab may have come loose from, but then he saw a shadow on the roof, and froze.

Another slab fell. No, it wasn't a slab this time, but a brick. And then he saw Kalle, bent over the wall and with a large slab of stone in his hands.

Manjhle moved back immediately. Balmukund had seen Kalle too, and he took two steps back as well.

The crazy one dropped the stone slab and bent over the top of the gate, his hands resting on the crest, breathing hard. To Manjhle, he looked like an ape.

'Come down, Kalle. Come down and let me see how brave you are. If you're your father's son, come down,' Balmukund screamed.

Manjhle changed tack. He raised his left hand in the air and said, as if hurt by what Kalle was doing, 'Throw another. Go on. Throw a brick at me and break my head. Go bring a bigger stone slab than the one in your hand and throw that at me. How will people know otherwise that you are my brother! Go ahead.'

People had begun to gather again.

Manjhle felt that it wouldn't serve his interest to threaten Kalle or beat down the door. *He's mad, and people will only see his actions as those of a madman. I, however, will be blamed if I react. No one's going to think much of his actions, but they'll think badly of me for calling him names.*

He turned around and addressed the crowd, which seemed to be thickening again, 'You can see what's going on. You are my witness. All I have been saying is that daughters of respectable houses shouldn't cast off their veils, and he has started raining bricks down on me. Strike me, go on, throw a brick on my head and crack my skull. If it takes my blood to cool you down, then so be it.'

By now there was enough light for the half-crazy one's pale, sweat-laden face and unfocused eyes to become visible to all.

People started dispersing again. It was one thing to stand around in the dark of the night and watch the strange misbehaviour of the mansion dwellers, but it was becoming bright now. Watching what was unfolding before them felt strange, and besides, it wasn't without its dangers. Ramjawaya was the first to slink away.

ॐ

Rukmini stood silently on the other side of the mansion's wall. She was so young, what sense would she be making of all this? It must all be a haze for her—a haze filled with screams, threats and terror, in which the faint ray of light emanating out of her own mind was her only guide.

The half-crazy one sat on the cot and watched her with unblinking eyes. She had sat on the floor across from him, having turned completely silent after the first blows had rained down on their door. She hadn't even looked up from the floor since then.

Rukmini had been listening to every screaming voice, every strike on the door, unable to find clarity. She kept thinking of Mausi Bhagsuddhi—the one person in this town who had stood by her—when she felt her husband's eyes on her. She looked up. She'd often find him staring at her, but whenever she returned his look, all she encountered was a vacant nothingness. This time, however, she glimpsed an emotion in his eyes—a mute but restless emotion that she'd never noticed before.

She found it difficult to look away. There was a deep empathy in his eyes, and a deep pain. It was as if he was trying to say something to her. His eyes were moist, his mouth half-open, and his head tilted to one side. Spittle flowed out of the corner of his mouth and fell on his shoulder.

Rukmini felt his eyes caressing her, her entire being, and she felt a deep affection rise up inside her. Infinite affection. She felt for the first time that she wasn't alone, that she had found a support in life, and she felt soothed and excited.

She felt her eyes lock into his, and felt he was both looking at her, and looking away, as if he wanted to say: This is happening because of me. It's because of me that our door is being struck with an axe. It's because of me that my brother is standing outside, shouting insane things. I'm the one who's brought you this suffering.

But what Rukmini was feeling at this moment was something entirely different. To her, his caressing gaze was like a soft glow of light in the darkness she felt surrounded by. It dispelled her intense loneliness, filled her with a feeling she couldn't describe, but which every cell of her body was pulsating with.

She smiled. It was a soft smile, full of affection. She didn't know when she had walked up to the cot and settled down with her back resting against its frame, right by him, and taken his hand in hers.

Kalle's eyes welled up. When his tears fell on Rukmini's hands, she looked up, startled. What should she say to assure him? She couldn't think of what to say, but she turned around and, propping herself up on her knees, wiped his tears with the edge of her dupatta.

'Don't cry, ji, don't cry. Why should you cry?'

Rukmini felt as if she had discovered her shield—that with which she could guard herself, her life. She was no longer alone, no longer helpless.

Manjhle and his friends had finished screaming and banging at the door and they left. Kalle too had climbed back down from the gate. Now he and Rukmini sat in their house, overcome with emotion. They were laughing, and they were crying. Rukmini kept wiping his tears, and Kalle kept saying, 'Lukman is ayne, Lukman is ayne!' *Rukmin is mine, Rukmin is mine.*

When Diwan Dhanpat had got Kalle married, it was with the thought that this would get Kalle settled down, that he would have his own household and, after Dhanpat's death, he wouldn't remain dependent on his brothers. But Kalle's wedding had affected Manjhle differently than he had hoped. For one, Manjhle seemed angry all the time. In his mind, his father had used him as a pawn; he was convinced that his own wedding was nothing more than a pretext to get Kalle married. Not only that, he was certain that he and his friends had been incited on purpose so that they would misbehave during the wedding feast. He'd learnt from somewhere that it was on Ramjawaya's encouragement that his friend had provoked him by saying, 'It's your wedding and no one's even looking after you. You don't have a papadam in your plate, and no one cares.' Then he'd said, 'The world only pays attention to those who know how to impress and apply pressure. Even a mother doesn't feed her infant unless it cries!' And that's why Manjhle had screamed, 'Papadam! Papadam!' There was also no denying that Kalle's, and not his wedding, had been the talk of the town. And wasn't it true that the Diwan, even now, always spoke gruffly with Manjhle, while his tone with Kalle was always gentle and he always smiled on seeing him? Kalle's wife was better looking too, and though his own wife was fair, he didn't like how she looked. These were some of the things that seemed to preoccupy him, and he felt burnt up inside. Plus, his friends had taken to inciting him about familial property—they'd say he wasn't the only contender for inheritance any longer, and that Kalle would be the one who'd be called the elder Diwan one day, because he is the elder son after all, and the seriousness with which his treatment is being done probably means he will get well one day, and then he'll have children. This last was perhaps troubling Manjhle the most. And then, there was also every possibility that the third son, who was in England, could return at any time and demand his share in the property.

Things had deteriorated after the wedding, or perhaps we should say weddings. Visitors to the mansion would ask after Kalle a lot more than they did about Manjhle. They also praised Kalle's wife more. Soon, Manjhle himself started disregarding his own wife. He said to her one day, 'We'd returned your palanquin. Are you shameless that you came back?' Pushpa had felt very hurt. He used to get irritated with her over every small thing anyway.

Manjhle was severely affected by what his friends said with regard to inheritance, and he said to his father one day, 'I want to live apart. Give me my share, so I can be on my way.'

The Diwan had looked sharply at him for a very long moment and then said in a stern voice, 'How about I disinherit you? Why don't I just throw you out of the house? I'm cautioning you, if you roll off your tongue like this again, I'll have your bedding thrown out on the street.'

Manjhle hadn't retorted, but he'd continued to smoulder inside. The result was that he beat up Kalle one day, and that too right before his father's eyes. The matter had been trivial—Kalle was sitting on the cot in the courtyard, looking at his wife, who was sitting a little distance away, stitching up some cloth that she'd stretched over her knees. When Kalle was happy, he'd keep laughing and spittle would flow out of his mouth; when he was incensed, he'd jerk his head about and hit his cane on the ground. But that day, he was sitting quietly, and looking at his wife. This was enough to make Manjhle lose his mind—*Just look at how he's sitting there like a harmless young lover, when in fact he's going to gobble up a giant share of the property really soon, while I've been tied for life to a woman whom I find too unbearable to even speak with.*

Her fate must have been displeased with her, for exactly at this moment Rukmini's mother walked into the house. The sight of her sent Manjhle's temper soaring. She rarely came to the mansion to visit her daughter, for coming to the mansion to meet her daughter made her nervous; the elder Diwan made her nervous; and truth be told, the mansion itself made her nervous. The high walls of the mansion seemed to her to be the walls of a prison. But she worried about her daughter and thought about her night and day. She had avoided coming to the mansion for the longest time, but then one day she mustered up the courage and made her way to it. As luck would have it, she'd just entered the courtyard when she ran into the elder Diwan. He not only welcomed her, he also spoke courteously with her. He said, 'You're Rukmini's mother Veeranwali, aren't you? Come in, come in . . . You can go in from here. Your darling daughter is inside.' He even told her she must come and meet her more often. This reassured her, and she started visiting the mansion from time to time, like she did today. And because you can't go to your daughter's house empty-handed, she saved money all month and cooked savoury *panjiri*, which she'd brought with her in a plate. But, unknown to her, a strange situation had been brewing in the mansion that day. And besides, whatever the elder Diwan thought, Manjhle never liked that she visited the mansion. He thought her visits were part of yet another conspiracy against him, one in which Kalle's wife and mother-in-law were increasing their influence in the mansion. The elder Diwan talked gently with Rukmini and he even ate rotis that she made, but he felt differently about Pushpa. He'd succeeded in getting Pushpa's family to give in to his demands, but his ill will towards them never went away. He stayed annoyed at them for having considered that they'd never marry another daughter into the Diwans' family. But the truth was that he'd never let go of the insult he felt when Malik Mansaram had outbid him at the auction in front of the entire town; and he had waited for years to exact his revenge. The wedding had been his perfect plan—not only would he show Malik Mansaram his place, but the wedding would also mean that the land might return to him, and if he played his cards well perhaps he could get his elder son married as well. But the die had not rolled in his favour; he had been unable to rub Mansaram's nose in dust. This irked him no end. That's why, even now, he kept cooking up plans, stopped all business transactions with him, and never uttered a nice word to his daughter. Rather, he always found something nasty to say to her.

That day Diwan Dhanpat was out touring his estates. It was a perfect opportunity for Manjhle and his friends to have their way in the mansion. The widow Veeranwali entered the mansion with a plate of panjiri, which she had covered with her dupatta. Manjhle was the first person she saw and instead of turning in the direction of her daughter's room, she went to him, uncovered the panjiri, and offered him some. 'Here, younger Diwan Sahibji, something to sweeten the day.'

Manjhle replied brusquely, 'You covered the plate with your dirty dupatta? Not even the low-caste eat food touched by such filth. I don't want any.'

The widow was stunned out of her wits and started trembling, so much so that it was impossible for her to remain standing there. She turned to leave, but then became confused about what to do with the plate—should she take it with her or leave it here? She was pacing the courtyard, her mind in a muddle, when Rukmini, who had heard her voice, rushed out to meet her and hugged her. But her mother was still terrified, and she broke into tears, put the plate down and left the mansion without saying a word.

It so happened that Diwan Dhanpat had just returned from his tour and was sitting on the raised pedestal on the other side of the courtyard, smoking his hookah. His attendant had just taken his shoes off and started massaging his toes.

The Diwan had seen Rukmini's mother enter the mansion, and wished she'd see him and come this way. He couldn't hear what Manjhle had said to her, but when he saw her emerge into the courtyard again, the end of her dupatta stuffed in her mouth, he knew it must have been something obnoxious.

Then he saw Kalle come into the courtyard and call out, 'Bebeji, Lukmo's mother . . . Bebeji.' He bent down to pick up his cane when Manjhle blocked his path and pushed him.

'Oh, you son of a pig,' the Diwan yelled, 'what do you think you're doing! How dare you raise your hand to your brother!'

Manjhle was surprised to hear Diwan Dhanpat's voice, for he hadn't realized his father had returned from his tour. But to Diwan Dhanpat's surprise, he reacted in the exact opposite way to what would be expected. Maybe if Manjhle hadn't heard his father's voice, he would have stopped after pushing his brother; but he got even more incensed on hearing his father's voice and started raining down blows and slaps on his brother. 'Oh, please let him go. What are you doing, let him go,' Rukmini screamed and inserted herself between the two brothers.

The Diwan stood up, trembling with rage. 'Bastard! What do you think you're doing?' He marched towards his sons.

By the time he reached where they were, Kalle was face down on the cot. His right cheek bore an imprint of his brother's hand, and Rukmini was bending over him, supporting herself with the edge of the cot and screaming, 'Help, help!'

Manjhle saw his father approaching and took a few steps back. His breath had quickened. He cast a sideways glance at his father and jerked his hands as he said, 'I'm letting you go today, but see how I mash you up like baked aubergine next time.' Without turning around to look at his father, he walked away, into the mansion.

'Bastard! Wait! Where do you think you're going?' the Diwan screamed, calling up his most forceful voice.

Manjhle turned around on reaching the end of the courtyard and muttered, 'I'll deal with everyone,' before walking into the mansion.

The first thought that came to the Diwan's mind was that he should disinherit Manjhle that very moment, that he should announce Manjhle was no longer his son and that he was giving all his property to Kalle and his youngest son. But he let go of this thought the moment he returned to the raised platform. The chowry bearer and a couple of other servants of the house had by now rushed out to aid and take care of Kalle. Rukmini was still moaning in pain.

Diwan Dhanpat had thought his worries would be over once he got his sons married. He had seen all his desires fulfilled one by one; and having got his sons married he felt there was nothing more he wanted, that now he could just enjoy being a Diwan, overseeing his little empire from his throne, smoking his hookah. A feeling of satiation had been spreading through his body. Getting what was rightfully his, ruling over land, obtaining the highest stature possible in this town, lording over a hundred servants—he had achieved all this on his own.

It was a splendid full moon that night and, as always, the Diwan went up to the roof to sleep. The roof was bathed in moonlight and awash with the river air. The outside seemed to reflect what the Diwan was feeling within.

His bed had been readied in the centre of the roof and a white sheet was spread over it. Next to it, on the side where the pillow was, a silver tumbler and carafe filled with water were placed on a teapoy. It was a beautiful carafe, with delicate carving on it. Dhanpat had bought it in Lahore. The attendant had left after preparing the bed, and he would come back in some time, when the Diwan would already be in bed, to massage his legs until the Diwan started to snore.

Diwan Dhanpat didn't feel like getting into bed immediately. He felt captivated by the beauty of the night and wanted to look out into the distance. He especially wanted to behold the mansion tonight. *This isn't just a mansion; it's a fortress—the seat of my power.* He looked at the sandstone canopy that stood majestically on the coping towards the main street. Stone canopies like these were usually only made for fortresses and palaces. Dhanpat liked that it was there on his mansion. He walked slowly towards it until he was standing right under it. A small, two-foot long extension had been made on the roof as a base for it. If you stood on this extension, the entire town looked like it was rolling out under your feet. Standing under this beautiful canopy made people passing by the lane below look up at you and automatically join their hands reverentially. *I should have used this spot, and often. I should have stood here and given audience to my subjects. People would have looked at me and said, 'That's Diwan Dhanpat, standing beneath that stone canopy, wearing a yellow angrakha. He is the most eminent man in this town.' They would have sung my praises, 'He was thrown out of this mansion once, but look at him now—look at his stature! He is the master of this mansion; he is the most important Diwan of this town.'* The riverbank was far away, to the west. The river shone in the moonlight. Looking towards it he imagined himself standing under the canopy in his court attire—a saffron turban on his head, a necktie, a yellow angrakha, pearl necklaces. Perhaps he could also have held, by way of a symbol of authority, a baton sheathed in silver like he had seen in the hands of Her Majesty, the Queen of England, in pictures. He hadn't done this until then. He always seemed surrounded by troubles. And in a flash he realized that he had begun to see himself differently—as Diwan Dhanpat, separate from the man Dhanpat. He'd spent so many years working towards becoming Diwan Dhanpat that he'd never really got a chance to look at himself as the elder Diwan. He'd remained entangled in other hassles all his life.

The silence of the lane accentuated the eminence of the mansion, made it seem more intimidating. There was a time when vegetable sellers used to sit all along this lane, along the mansion's boundary, selling vegetables. There used to be so much noise the entire day—of buying and selling, of people haggling. But the day the mansion came under his control, all he had had to do was growl with displeasure, and the lane emptied at once.

Diwan Dhanpat stood under the canopy and looked out at the town for a long time. All his contenders were gone— they'd died, or become bankrupt, or their businesses had folded. *Moneylenders are the only ones who've survived. Even among them Malik Mansaram is the only one who has been able to create some wealth for himself, and that too only because he's a commissioning agent for foreign goods. But even he won't dare lock horns with me any more. Where is Diwan Mayyadas now? How I wish he was alive and could see me today! Where is Raja Amirchand? Where are Gokuldas and Hargobind? I wish I'd reached this position in life before they'd died, for they too would have had to bow before me.*

The Diwan locked his hands behind him and walked slowly towards the low wall on the right. Oh, he'd forgotten—a big achievement of his life had been right here. Years ago, if one were to stand here and look down into the mansion, all he'd see was a maze of walls. Not just cousins and nephews, but distant relatives—men and women spanning three generations—had settled down right here. It was always so noisy here as well. He'd cleaned it all up. He had all the walls pulled down. He had all those trespassers thrown out. Dhanpat smiled as he remembered. This was the same mansion he'd been thrown out of once. *My trunk and bundle of clothes and the small bedding I owned were all thrown out.* The scene flashed before his eyes. *Diwan Mayyadas—the elder Diwan of that time, like I am of this time—once got my things thrown out as he stood on this very roof, just like I am standing here today, dressed in a white muslin kurta. Where is he now, and where is his authority?*

Enraptured by his achievements, going over them in his mind one by one, he strolled about the roof and then came back to the stone canopy. He wanted to bend and catch a glimpse of that exact spot outside the main gate where his things had been cast on that fateful day.

The street looked deserted. Moonlight fell in places, and a long shadow of a wall covered a part of the lane, lending it a deep air of mystery.

Dhanpat's gaze spilled over to the land that had once been part of the property of the mansion dwellers, and he felt a tug of disappointment in his heart. Mansaram had won the tussle for the land in an auction. Dhanpat felt deep regret at how clever the city trader had proved to be, not only winning the land but also publicly showing Dhanpat up. He just wouldn't stop raising the bid. But then, suddenly, a wave of triumph rose inside him. *I showed him too, didn't I? I made him grovel, and only then did I let his daughter into my house. And once his daughter's in the mansion, the land returns to the mansion.* It was the condition of the wedding after all—that the land Malik Mansaram had bought would be given back as dowry.

Diwan Dhanpat thought he saw a man come into the lane from the darkness and linger in the moonlit part of the lane before merging again into the shadows.

Dhanpat felt alarmed. *Who could it be at this hour?* But then he thought anyone could have stepped out of the mansion, possibly an attendant or a servant, or even one of Manjhle's friends. The next moment he thought that couldn't be the case, because no one would go out of the mansion so late at night. *This man was walking slowly, which means he isn't young.* From how he was dressed and walking, he didn't look like an attendant or servant. *Who was he? Could it have been Lekhraj?* Dhanpat trembled at the thought. *Why would Lekhraj come here?*

He'd been hearing things about Lekhraj the last few days. That Lekhraj had returned to town was something he'd known for long. He'd heard from Ramjawaya, the purohit and several other people that they'd seen Lekhraj about town.

It was true that Dhanpat had been a little antsy since he'd learnt of Lekhraj's return. There had been a couple of occasions when he'd grown worried, and he'd had to calm his heart by saying, 'Relax, Dhanpat. Lekhraj can't do a thing. He's penniless; he has no means to start a confrontation with you. It's not like he can file a suit. At the most, he'll come and appeal to you.' But then, another thought sometimes pricked him—*He does have a right over the mansion; he's the son of Diwan Mayyadas's younger brother after all. Blood makes him the true inheritor of the mansion. What will be left of me in this town if he takes the line that his is the legitimate claim? People know him by name. Everyone knows he fought bravely and risked his life in the Sikh wars. It was a different matter until he wasn't here, but now that he's returned everyone's probably thinking he's the rightful heir to the mansion. But why hasn't he made this demand yet? Does he even have the wherewithal to make such a demand? Does he have it in him to fight a case against me? I can shut him down in two hearings!*

That day when he'd had the tiller Karim Khan whipped in his courtroom, he'd sensed someone's presence behind the crowd of farmers—cloaked by a blanket, the man was following the court proceedings intently. Dhanpat scanned him for clues by which to recognize him, when the thought struck him that it might be Lekhraj, and he felt shaken up. When Karim Khan's case came up, he had him whipped mercilessly so that Lekhraj would realize how things would end were he to take up the cudgels against Diwan Dhanpat.

But why in the world has he returned? There's no knowing whom he has been complaining to about me, how many houses he visits each night to hatch a conspiracy against me. But what can he do that can possibly harm me? I'm the one the estates have been granted to. They aren't family inheritance; no one can claim them. That leaves the mansion—yes, he could claim his share in the mansion—or the land adjoining it—but the land was auctioned off. So then, the maximum he can do is stake a claim in the mansion. But how much can he claim for? And he won't get anything until he files a suit, and how is he going to muster up the resources to file a suit? Dhanpat had succeeded in calming his heart again.

His eyes drifted to the street once more, and again he sensed a presence—a man cloaked in a sheet appeared from the darkness, and walked through a moonlit patch before disappearing once more into the shadows.

Dhanpat scanned the street for a long time, his eyes moving between the square and triangular patches of shadows being cast by different houses. He waited for the man to appear again, to cross the street once more, so he could make out if it was Lekhraj. But the man didn't return. Dhanpat gave up his vigil and decided to retire for the night.

I should get Purohit Ramdas to prepare a chart so he can read the stars and tell me if Lekhraj's return will hurt me and if Lekhraj will succeed in his plans. The purohit, meanwhile, had updated him on whom Lekhraj had been meeting.

'He'd been roaming about in the pleasure park pavilion a few days ago. Your in-law's pleasure park. The other day he came out from there and sat under a tree for a really long time. Absolutely alone. And one day he went to the hillock, Generous One, and talked with Harnarayan for long. Harnarayan is also your in-law.' The purohit spoke as if he was illuminating some deep conspiracy.

Sudden long shadows in the stairwell startled Dhanpat. It was only his attendant—he'd come to the roof, a hurricane lamp in his hand. But Dhanpat had been lost in his thoughts and had become frightened by the shadows.

'What is it?' he asked his attendant gruffly.

'Nothing at all, my lord. I came to massage your feet.' The attendant was surprised he should be questioned this way, since massaging his master's feet at night was part of his daily routine.

'No, there's no need tonight. Leave.'

'As you command,' the attendant said. Picking up the hurricane lamp, he lowered its wick to lessen the light, set it down near the stairwell wall and returned the same way that he'd come.

But just as he entered the stairwell, his legs cast long shadows on the wall, and Diwan Dhanpat thought a shadow had emerged from the darkness and followed the attendant in.

'I'm imagining things,' he mumbled as he lowered himself into the bed. Seeds of doubt had planted themselves in his heart, but as he had been thinking about his glory just moments ago, he brushed them aside and said to himself, 'What's one Lekhraj? Twenty like him can't harm me.'

'Ey, attendant! Ramrakha!' he screamed. His voice echoed in the stillness of the roof.

Ramrakha came back running.

'Who was it that followed you inside?'

Ramrakha looked at his master, confused. 'Who, my lord? No one went in with me!'

'Bastard, I'm going to skin you alive. I saw with my own eyes. He had hidden behind the wall, and he followed you down the stairs.'

'No, sir, no one went in with me.'

Diwan Dhanpat felt slightly reassured. *It must have been my imagination.*

'I'll break your legs if someone sneaks into the mansion when I'm not looking . . .'

'Yes, my lord.'

'Now stay here. Sleep here tonight. Stay alert when you work.'

Diwan Dhanpat turned to look at the stairwell a number of times. It seemed unfamiliar and mysterious in the moonlight.

Dhanpat lay down on the spotless white sheet, and the attendant stayed up massaging his legs. His troubled heart took a long time calming down; sleep didn't come to him easily. The thrall he had felt running his achievements through his mind on this beautiful, moonlit night had been disrupted by a shadow.

This morning when Vaanprasthi stepped out of the school compound and into Haberdashers' Market, Ramjawaya had already opened his shop and was sitting on the raised platform in front of it. Vaanprasthi spotted him from behind his thick glasses and felt ill at ease about having to deal with him first thing in the morning. He almost thought it inauspicious. But when you have wisdom that comes with age, as Vaanprasthi did, things don't bog you down so easily. *We'll see*, he thought to himself.

It had been six months since Vaanprasthi had come to this town, and since then there hadn't been a day when this elderly man wasn't seen walking through the lanes, a big spinning top in his hand.

'How nice to see you so early in the morning, Masterji! I hope it doesn't mean you didn't sleep last night.' Ramjawaya lifted the front of his kurta and scratched his stomach.

Oh Lord, grant me endurance! Vaanprasthi thought to himself and continued on his way. 'Namaste, Ramjawaya,' he greeted Ramjawaya as he crossed him.

'What's this "namaste", Master? Can't you say "Ram Ram" or "Jai Sita Ram"? What's "namaste"?' Then he turned to the grocer in the adjoining shop and said, 'Lala, you should also say "namaste". Forget your "Ram Ram". It's going to be "namaste" around here from now on.' Then he called out to Vaanprasthi, 'Is the construction of the school done? The roof's been laid? I want to study as well, Masterji. Will you teach me, or are you only going to teach girls?'

It gladdened Vaanprasthi to hear the school being mentioned. *Ramjawaya knows the roof's been laid—he's seen it. Let him speak in jest if he wants to. He'll have no choice but to stop once the school opens.* Vaanprasthi felt infinitely satisfied. He paused. A gentle smile flickered on his lips.

'Yes, thanks to the lord above, the roof has been laid.'

The room really had got readied last night. Four walls and a roof. It had become dark by the time the masons and the head mason had climbed down from the roof. Vaanprasthi's own hands were caked with cement mixture, and his pyjama legs, though he'd rolled them up, had a spattering of the mixture on them. His legs shivered and back ached from the strain of repeatedly bending and lifting up the tub of mixture and loading it on to the labourer's head. He'd sat down on the cot in front of the room, his hands still unwashed, and gazed at the room for a long time. *I'll whitewash the walls tomorrow. I can do that myself. It's OK even if I don't do it very soon; it can wait. I'll go out tomorrow—it'll be great if I can find someone to give me sackcloth, and I'll try and collect some money as well, for books. I can start teaching even if I can't get books immediately. I'll teach the alphabet first. The room's ready—that's the most important thing.* Even in the dark of night, Vaanprasthi couldn't take his eyes off the room. He got up, opened his small trunk, took out a piece of chalk and wrote in big letters on the wall: *Putri Patshala.* A school for daughters. Girls' school.

He read the words and felt deep pride and a sense of satisfaction.

He sat down on the cot again, his legs still quivering. The cement mixture on his hands was drying. 'My insignificant self has done at least this much.' Vaanprasthi joined his hands in gratitude.

The flame of the hurricane lamp flickered. He used to light the lamp only for some time each night. In this town, people still lit clay lamps with wicks dipped in linseed oil after sunset. They'd douse them and get into bed before it got too dark. Before turning out the lamp, Vaanprasthi crossed the courtyard for a look at the room from the lane. It really was a room. A room meant there was now a school. The most difficult of the tasks had been accomplished.

But the night didn't pass well for him—despite his feeling of satisfaction, despite his belief that the most arduous stretch of the journey was now behind him.

He lived in a hut with a thatched roof, in the same courtyard as the room that was to be the school. An earthen pitcher was kept outside it. He poured water from it and washed his hands. He splattered his eyes with some of that cool water, drank a few sips and picked up his cane and headed out. His feet were taking him towards the sweet seller's shop. He felt like saccharine-sweet, hot, crispy-fried jalebi dipped in a cupful of hot milk. His hand even started towards his pocket, but then he suppressed his desire. *Every penny counts, and it's a mistake anyway to get so excited about your achievement. It's arrogance. I'm merely the medium; He is the one who does everything. If He stays benevolent, the school will succeed.* And thinking this, he steered his mind away from the plate of jalebis, towards God.

'The roof is laid,' he said to the sweet seller. 'It's by the grace of God, and because of the support all of you have given that this first step has been achieved.'

The humpbacked sweet seller's shop had been a site of raging debates and discussions around the school, and he heard things of all sorts. But this wasn't the occasion to pass those along to this old man. And anyway, the sweet seller was the kind of man who listened to everyone, but kept his own opinion to himself. It was not his way to get embroiled in an argument. After all, one of the rules of running a shop is listen to the customer and hold your tongue. The customer is no less than God for a shopkeeper. But the sweet seller didn't have much faith in this thing that the old teacher had set out to do.

Vaanprasthi wanted to tell the humpbacked sweet seller that now that the room was constructed, he was going to host night-long prayer meetings every Sunday. There would be havans, and devotional songs would be sung. 'I'm going to conduct the prayer meetings myself,' he wanted to tell the sweet seller, 'I know all the hymns and prayers by heart.' But he didn't say anything. His mother had told him when he was a child that if you utter before everyone the thing you want most, your wish won't come true. Wishes can catch a cold too.

The humpbacked sweet seller watched the teacher drink a glass of milk. The teacher seemed to him to be a decent man. *His forehead has the shine of a decent man.* The humpback used to say that he could tell what a man was like by the way he drank milk. 'The way a man drinks his milk,' he'd say, 'speaks volumes about his heart.' The teacher's sips were discreet, as if he was praying.

'You didn't eat today, Teacher. Only milk for you today?' Vaanprasthi's eyes lit up.

'There was no time. There was too much work. The mason left but a while ago. Look at my hands; they're still covered in mud.' And, like a child, Vaanprasthi extended his right hand forward for the sweet seller to see.

'Should I pour you some water so you can wash them?'

'I'll wash them, I'll wash them. I washed them at home too, but the mud still sticks. At least it's dried now.'

That his hands were still dirty pleased him somewhat. It was the dust of the school. It indicated that he'd played a part in the physical construction of the school, that he too had made his oblations in the holy yajna.

He ended up missing dinner often. And when he was going door to door for donations for the school, this happened frequently. Wherever he would go and ask for money, arguments would invariably ensue. Someone would start about idol worship, someone about fasting, and Vaanprasthi would get involved. His temper too would start to rise, and pull him deeper into the debate. By the time he'd get up to leave, it would be night, his forehead would be hot and his throat would feel as if pricked by thorns. On nights such as these, he would drink some cool water and go to bed.

There was an oven a short distance from the sweet seller's shop. Vaanprasthi would eat two rotis and curry in the day and two rotis and a cupful of lentil soup at night there. And if ever the teacher didn't turn up for his meal until late at night, the owner of the oven would send his son with a meal on a plate to his hut.

When you take up a task in your old age, stability comes to it automatically. Vaanprasthi had worked out a monthly arrangement for his meals. He'd also bought a cot from Haberdashers' Market and set it up under the thatched roof that he'd installed in the school's courtyard. Wake up in the morning, go to the fields to freshen up, take a bath in Orchard of the Sheikhs on the way back, sit under a tree there and offer your prayers, and return chanting the Gayatri Mantra. This routine neither had room for hot rotis prepared by his wife, nor did it hop and skip with the laughter of little children. But once Vaanprasthi had adopted a certain life, there was no question of turning back. Yes, in the beginning, his heart did play games with him. Even if he somehow succeeded in keeping his wife and daughter out of his thoughts during the day, at night, just before he'd fall asleep or, suddenly, as he would turn on his side, they would appear, sometimes both, sometimes one or the other—his daughter and her mother. Before letting go of his life as a householder and acquiring Vaanprastha, when he worked as a bookkeeper, his wife used to pack him lunch. Every day, when he'd return from work, he'd see her from a distance at the door, waiting for him. The joys and pleasures of living are not from having a house and courtyard, they are not contained in the things you decorate your house with—they linger in the cooling shade of the woman who runs the household; they come from her affectionate presence.

Desires and wishes still bubbled under Vaanprasthi's hard exterior—the enchantment of a home and a family, of living under the same roof with grandsons and granddaughters, of a warm hearth, of the delicious smell of food being prepared in the kitchen, of sitting a while and chatting. There was a lot that had been crushed under the armour of duty and devotion. He had almost forgotten the taste of rotis prepared by his wife. Sometimes as he walked through the lanes at night, he'd hear little children laughing, and his feet would stop where they were and his heart would well up. If the smell of rotis reached him, he'd hear the gentle cling of his wife's bangles with it. This would happen when he'd be returning at night, after collecting donations the entire day, not having eaten a morsel, his feet hurting from all the walking. He'd silently cross the sweet seller who, at that hour, would be ending his day by washing his large frying pan.

He no longer found it difficult to overcome his pangs of hunger. What was still difficult was that moment when— whether asleep or awake—his daughter's face would appear before his eyes at night. She'd appear, her hand on the door chain, wearing her dark kurta, her eyes beseeching him. It sent waves of restlessness through Vaanprasthi. He'd feel as if she stayed standing there for a long time, and his heart would feel perturbed, filled with guilt. He'd turn on his side to face the other way, so that she may disappear. But she would just walk over to that side and stand in front of him again. When this would go on for a long time, and she wouldn't leave even when he'd turned over on his side several times, he'd sit up. He'd join his hands and plead to God for forgiveness; he'd utter the Gayatri Mantra over and over; he'd get up from the cot and pace the courtyard.

'Oh Omniscient One,' he'd pray, 'please free me of these attachments. Oh Lord, may everyone find happiness in their homes. Please give me the strength, the capacity that I may be able to fulfil my duties. Oh Merciful One . . .' And the irony! Sometimes even as he prayed, the silent, beseeching face of his daughter would float up before his eyes. Vaanprasthi would open his eyes restlessly. He'd feel embarrassed that he was so weak. He'd splash cool water on his eyes. They'd start closing on their own, and he'd go back and fall on his bed. And there it would be again—the forlorn face of his young daughter, Sumitra, pale with the sadness of widowhood, her mute eyes looking out at her father.

His daughter had been married into a house in Sargodha itself. This was during the days when the railway lines were being laid. His son-in-law, Sumitra's husband, would leave for work and travel even as far as Wazirabad. Once during those days, he too had to leave home for some work. His son-in-law fell ill in Wazirabad, and wrote letter after letter telling them he was unwell, that they should come and take him home. The postman delivered the letters, but there was no one at home who could read them. Sumitra thought the letters were for her father, and that he'd read them once he returned home. She kept the letters safe on the shelf. Three letters arrived. Then there was silence; no more letters came. Vaanprasthi read the letters when he returned home, and left for Wazirabad the same day. But by then, his son-in-law was dead; his young daughter had been widowed.

There was no one at her in-laws to look after her, so she stayed back. But soon, she caught tuberculosis. Every evening, she'd stand at the door and wait for her father's return. Her youth slowly wilted. It was during those days that she once said that she wished she'd learnt to read. *Maybe then my husband would have lived*. During her days of illness, this thought gripped her heart, and she'd often say one thing or another that echoed it.

It didn't take his daughter long to submerge into the vortex of time, but her words didn't drown with her. They reverberated in the teacher's head, got etched in his mind as if someone had marked him with a branding iron.

With time, while he did get restless each time Sumitra's face floated up in front of him, it also cemented his belief that even though his daughter wouldn't benefit from the work he had come to do here, it would help some girl, even if another, and at least his hard work would be of use to someone.

'So Teacher, did you ensnare any hen yet?' Ramjawaya asked and cast a sidelong glance at the grocer. He was laughing, his hand under his kurta, scratching his stomach.

'Why don't you get some low-caste girl to join? That can't be difficult for you. It's not like you avoid them; you're an Arya Samaji after all.'

Vaanprasthi stood where he was, his eyes downcast.

'May I leave now?' he said, and started walking.

'Listen carefully, old man, we're not going to allow you to open a whorehouse here.'

Vaanprasthi turned around and walked back.

'How does a place where girls learn a few letters of the alphabet become a whorehouse?' Vaanprasthi was shaking with anger. 'If our daughters get an education, we'll end up with a whorehouse?' He was screaming now. There was a tremor in his voice. He had screamed so loudly that passers-by had stopped.

Ramjawaya was dumbfounded. He hadn't expected that Vaanprasthi would become so enraged and he looked at Vaanprasthi, aghast. But he regained his composure soon enough and, with an annoying laugh, he said, 'Go, go, do what you want to do. Aren't you the greatest man of faith there ever was! Who knows what your lineage is, from where you've been bestowed upon this world!' He looked away and stared at the street.

Two men had heard Vaanprasthi scream, and stopped. The grocer turned in his seat, towards the sweet seller's raised platform, and said to Vaanprasthi, 'Come, come, sir. This one's a loudmouth. Why engage with him so early in the morning? Please, you should carry on with your day.'

Then he turned to Ramjawaya and said, 'That's enough, Ramjawaya. You should consider whom you're speaking with before you open your mouth and blabber away.'

Ramjawaya continued in the same vein as before. 'The old man's crazy. Pour cold water on his head, for he's going to start spewing fire any moment now.'

The grocer turned to Vaanprasthi. 'There is one thing, Masterji,' he advised. 'You should stop saying "namaste". "Ram Ram" is more suitable. You're a Hindu, as am I. This "namaste" won't do.'

Vaanprasthi had somewhat recovered his balance by now, even though his cheeks still trembled. He said to the two men who'd stopped on the street, 'Is education a bad thing? If girls learn how to read and write, they'll be able to read letters, they'll be able to read books.'

One of the men nodded his head and said, 'Indeed, there's nothing wrong with becoming literate. I've heard the Queen of England is educated. There's nothing wrong in that.'

Ramjawaya again spoke in the same manner as before, 'Go, go. Do your thing. I'll see how you open a school here. You've come here to take veils off the daughters of respectable families.' He scratched his stomach again. 'Go get your own daughters and daughters-in-law first, then talk to us.'

Ramjawaya was feeling encouraged by the audience that was slowly gathering in the street. 'There's a Christian missionary as well who roams around here. He distributes sugar cakes to little children. You should also tuck a jar of sugar cakes under your arm! That's a good way to lure people to Arya Samaj!' And amused by his own words, he started laughing.

'You should mind whom you're speaking with, Ramjawaya,' the grocer said in a superior tone again. 'Have you entirely lost your sense of shame?'

'What untoward thing have I said? All I've said is that we won't let a whorehouse be set up here.'

Vaanprasthi's temper was rising once more.

'Come to think of it, Masterji,' the grocer said as if trying to arbitrate, when he was in fact only adding fuel to the fire, 'Ramjawaya's words do have a ring of truth to them. Won't you be de-veiling girls if you're going to be teaching them? They'll roam about on the streets with their heads uncovered. Are they going to go get jobs after they're educated?'

Just last night, when the roof had been laid, Vaanprasthi's heart had leapt with joy that the battle had been won. That the room was ready meant the school could start in a few days. But now he realized that he was up against an impenetrable wall. It had stayed invisible; now it seemed insurmountable. He had been hearing minor critiques about the girls' school everywhere he'd gone to ask for donations. But he had no idea that so much malice had been brewing inside people's hearts about this school.

He was standing in the middle of the street. His eyelids felt heavy. His back bent, his body supported by his cane, he was receiving Ramjawaya's and the grocer's comments like lashes. Never before had he felt so lonely in this unfamiliar town. How unexpected all this was, how concealed by layers. Just last night he'd been full of cheer at the thought that in a few days, a few girls from the town would bless the school with their presence, enlivening it like a garden in spring. He'd even been thinking of distributing laddus—he'd thought he would scrape up some money and buy a plateful of the sweets from the sweet seller. It would have made for a lovely inauguration treat.

He looked up. Ramjawaya and the grocer were gesturing to each other, jeering and laughing at him. Crestfallen and overwhelmed, he joined his hands to say goodbye to them and the other men on the street, and turned towards his lane.

He had walked but a few steps when he heard a catcall behind him. Then someone said, 'When their mothers don't care for them, they come and hide in this town.'

Vaanprasthi turned around. Ramjawaya looked away and the grocer quickly turned to look into his shop. A small knot of people had formed in the middle of the street; everyone was looking at Vaanprasthi and laughing.

All day that day, Vaanprasthi went from door to door, telling people that the school was now open. All he got were vague responses—no one promised they'd send their daughter, and no one refused outright. The shadows had lengthened by the time he returned home, tapping his cane on the ground, his legs weighing a ton, uncertainty looming over his heart.

How dark this night is, he thought to himself as he lowered himself into his cot. *Even anguish isn't being merciful; tonight it rises inside me with the force of a tidal wave; it slashes my insides like a catling.* He sat with his hands on the shaft of the cot, his eyes roving over the room from behind his thick glasses, his heart full of anguish and dismay.

But it didn't last. Not even an hour had passed when he was sitting cross-legged on the cot, gently clapping to the beat of the devotional song he was singing:

> *The mountain peak is lofty*
> *Can an ant climb up to it?*
> *A blind man wants to see the moon*
> *A mosquito becomes an elephant*
> *In Your infinite magnificence*
> *The improbable becomes probable*
> *Keep our eyes open to Your boundless glory—*
> *That's what we lesser beings must do*

Then it was the same as it was every evening—he felt slowly unburdened. As his immersion increased, his heart recovered its place. He felt as if he was bathing in an enormous, blue lake, whose water was washing away all his heartache, all the insult, the exhaustion and the disappointment that had gathered up inside him through the day, and strength flowed back into his body.

His head moved as he sang, his eyes became moist and his back bent further in prayer. The song ended; he joined his hands and placed them in his lap, closed his eyes and prayed.

'Oh Lord, oh Merciful One, those who bear malice towards us, or whom we bear malice towards, oh Lord, we all turn to you for justice, oh Father . . .'

Just as a tree standing alone on barren land nourishes itself from that very soil, Vaanprasthi drew strength, courage and peace from around him. He got up, walked into his hut, brought his *ektara* with him, and started singing one of his favourite devotional verses:

> *Don't keep in mind my failings, oh Lord*
> *Whether a piece of iron was used in a holy ritual,*
> *Or if it was sharpened as a butcher's tool*
> *The philosopher's stone doesn't wonder—*
> *It turns every base metal into gold*
> *Don't keep in mind my failings, oh Lord*

As he sang 'Whether a piece of iron was used in a holy ritual', his throat caught, and he stopped. After a brief pause, he repeated the line in a more composed voice.

Stars had appeared in the sky. They twinkled. Down below, on earth, the darkness grew denser. By the time Vaanprasthi emerged from his singing, bathed in the songs, his heart felt quiet—calm and still—and he felt like he was an offering in the holy fire of life. Merely an offering, but it was as if supreme joy lay in being that—supreme joy, supreme calmness and capability.

He was ready once more for the running around, the annoyances and the commotion that the routine of the next day would bring.

That's when he raised his eyes and looked in front of him. It was a young girl. Vaanprasthi was taken by surprise. *Who is she, and when did she come here? I didn't see her until now.* He hadn't noticed her walk across the courtyard and come and stand right in front of him. *Am I dreaming?* But he wasn't. She was wearing a white kurta-salwar, and a radiant white dupatta was wrapped around her shoulders. She was here, right in front of him.

'Who are you, child? Where have you come from?'

'Ji, I'm here to have my name included in the school.'

Vaanprasthi still couldn't believe that a girl had come of her own accord to enrol in the school. A flood tide of hope rose up inside him. He looked at her for a long time with disbelief in his eyes.

'Where are you from, child? Who are you?'

'Ji, I've come from the Diwan's mansion. I'm his daughter-in-law.'

Vaanprasthi was stumped. He wasn't unaware of the events that had marked this town. *Could this be the same girl who had been married to the Diwan's lunatic son? Or is it another girl?*

Vaanprasthi felt overwhelmed. His heart filled with untold compassion, sympathy and goodwill towards the girl, as if it was to teach *her* that he had come to this town. But then doubt and dilemma cast their shadows.

He asked, 'Child, have you taken permission from your family members?'

Rukmini didn't say anything. She stared at the ground, her eyes downcast. Vaanprasthi repeated his question, and she said, 'Ji, whom should I ask?'

This jolted Vaanprasthi and he studied the girl. There was such innocence in her dark face. Rukmini was still staring at the floor. Her answer had pierced Vaanprasthi's heart; in a single sentence she had laid bare the acuteness of her situation. Another tide of emotion rose in his heart—it was clear the girl had slipped out of the house; there's no way the daughter-in-law of the Diwans would be allowed to step out of the house, alone, in the dark, dressed in such simple clothes.

'Child, what if your family objects?'

Rukmini raised her eyes and looked directly at Vaanprasthi's face. It was as if doubt had begun to creep up inside her that the deep hope she had come here with was going to go unanswered. But she answered in a steady voice, 'I want to study.'

Rukmini's eyelids were becoming heavy; they were half closed. Her face was burning and beads of perspiration had formed all over it. She seemed to be withdrawing into herself. Whenever she was inattentive and didn't hide her emotions, her gentleness would become writ on her face, in her hesitating eyes, her thin, trembling lips, her round, dark-complexioned face.

It struck Vaanprasthi that the girl's decision to study came from the depths of her being, from having ridden and overcome the unruly waves of sadness and tribulations. Who's to know how long her heart had twisted and turned, what it had considered and discarded before this decision manifested itself clearly, in all its brilliance, boldness and straightforwardness.

'You will study, child. Yes, you will.' And Vaanprasthi placed his hand on Rukmini's back.

In the market that rolled out along the length of the lane, only a few shops had opened at this early hour. At one end of it, the sweet seller's son was rinsing out the pan that was used to boil milk, when he heard a commotion. The noise brought people out of their houses; all eyes were pointed in the same direction. A girl was walking down the narrow lane that opened into this one. It didn't take the sweet seller's son long to recognize her. His first response was of surprise, but then it was as if blood drained from his face. He propped the pan against the wall and stood up.

'It's Rukmini! It's the Diwan's daughter-in-law! Look how she's walking out in the open without her veil!'

The other night, Manjhle had stood outside his elder brother's house with an axe, screaming and threatening him, and trying to break the door down. The entire town had talked about it.

The humpbacked sweet seller also stood and watched. 'Look, Bishan,' he said to his son, 'if the daughter-in-law of the Diwans has stepped into the street in this shameless manner, then things really have gone too far. The mansion won't survive this.'

Bishan already had his eyes glued to the lane. It really was Rukmini walking down the lane, a white dupatta draped around her. His response was rather different from that of his father.

'It's not as if Manjhle did a good thing. Who comes out into the lane and shouts abuses at his own people! He was letting out a stream of invective at his brother, shouting at him, and in doing that, he ruined his family's honour. Who is he to say anything any more?'

'Yes, but it's different when it comes to women. When they forsake their veils, family honour crumbles into dust.'

The sweet seller held the mansion in great esteem. What went on inside the mansion was none of his business, but for the mansion's daughter-in-law to be walking out into the streets this way was a mistake. *The mansion has a social standing; its stature goes back in time, through generations.* Rukmini may be Harnarayan's granddaughter, but she was the mansion's daughter-in-law now. There was a time when a hundred people ate at the mansion every day. The humpbacked sweet seller had seen those days. Cauldrons of sweetmeats used to be sent to the mansion. If anyone from Diwan Mayyadas's extended family or caste happened to visit, he would never be allowed to leave the mansion without sharing a meal. And today, the daughter-in-law of this same mansion had stepped out in this way—and despite her younger brother-in-law having forbidden her!

'It's not like they've done her any good, getting her married to that madman,' Bishan said.

'Don't speak such nonsense, Bishan. Mind your own business.' The father and son became quiet.

Rukmini was quite close now. The crowd that had gathered outside the shops looked on. People were apprehensive. *What in the world is this girl up to! Her behaviour is going to cause such a furore.*

It was Rukmini all right. She walked in the middle of the lane, shrinking within herself. She was wearing a white kurta-salwar and a white dupatta covered her head. She kept her eyes focused in front of her. A knot formed in the humpbacked sweet seller's heart. He always sought the shadow of destiny in everything. She had been wedded barely a year ago and she was draped in a white dupatta. Did anyone ever see a newly married woman dressed this way!

'What's going on?' Ramjawaya arrived, ready to open his shop.

'It's Rukmini, the Diwan's elder daughter-in-law. She's headed this way.'

Ramjawaya looked out at where the lanes met and jerked his head. 'This girl and her histrionics. She's going to bring infamy to the Diwans. She's shameless.' He spat on the ground.

Rukmini was very close now. She walked quietly, her eyes still focused in front of her, away from the crowd of people growing on either side of the lane. Her face glowed with brilliance.

And then the humpbacked sweet seller noticed the Diwan's mad son, who had emerged at the far end of the lane, where the mansion's back door was, a fat cane thrown over his shoulders, behind his head. He was moving into the lane, swinging from side to side.

Even an old woman who was walking past, unmindful of the scene that was brewing, stopped to look.

'Oh my goodness, look at him! He looks stark raving mad!'

He looked like he was dancing more than walking. He'd raised the cane, which had two red tufts attached to one end, high up in the air. The old woman covered her mouth with the end of her dupatta and burst out laughing. 'Look at him! He looks like a joke!' She said this, but then bit her lip and said, 'Goodness, he's gone completely mad.' Then the word 'bechara' escaped her lips: 'poor thing!' Her eyes welled up. It was as if in the mockery that this man presented, she had inadvertently glimpsed Rukmini's misfortune.

Prancing, swaying, dancing, he had covered the length of the narrow lane and reached the street.

The sweet seller turned to look behind him. Many people—men and women—had gathered at the mouth of the lane.

Kalle was still moving forward, his cane swinging in the air. From time to time he'd stop—his legs parted, his chest puffed out, the cane raised in the air. Then he'd change his manoeuvres and move forward again.

He was amusing to the onlookers. The way he'd carried the cane on his shoulders and jumped on to the street barefooted had reminded them of the theatrical entrance reserved for Hanuman during performances. The sweet seller's young grandson had run out into the street to look, and was laughing. It was the laugh of the innocent, for he thought the crazy man was copying someone, and he was trying to guess who it could be. A wrestler before he enters the akhara? A soldier wielding a sword? A tightrope walker?

Kalle had almost caught up with Rukmini.

'Oh dear, what's he going to do?' the old woman said out loud. 'What if he hits her with his cane?'

'Someone stop him. He's going to hurt somebody,' one of the onlookers standing on the side of the street said.

'He can't. He doesn't have any idea what he's doing.'

'He thinks he's Bheem, out for a walk with his club.'

Kalle crossed the street and reached the humpbacked sweet seller's shop. His eyes were only half open, his face was pale and covered with sweat, his cheeks were shining.

Two sprightly young lads stepped out of the crowd and blocked his path.

'Diwanji, why not hand me your cane? It's of no use to you.'

'Diwanji, respectable people like you shouldn't come out of their house barefoot. Come, let's go back home. Come with me.'

The sweet seller's grandson got excited. He stepped forward and caught hold of the crazy man's cane. Kalle didn't turn to look at him, but he held on to the cane.

'Let go of that cane! What do you think you're doing?'
When the young boy heard his grandfather's stern voice, he
let go of the cane immediately.

People stepped forward, closing in around the madman.
The crowd near the sweet seller's shop too grew denser.

That's when Bhagsuddhi appeared. She was returning
from the temple and had walked into the street. A widow's
dupatta covered her head, and she held a leaf-cup with prasad
from the temple in her hand. She saw the crowd and wondered
what it was about, but then she spotted the Diwan's eldest
son. Her eyes searched for, and found, Rukmini. She read
the situation immediately—Rukmini had taken the lead, and
her husband had followed her, barefoot and with a cane in
his hands. She felt a lump in her throat—who knew what lay
ahead for this couple.

'Oh good people, let him be. Why torment the
unfortunate? Let him go where he will.'

'Mausi, what if he hits someone with that cane of his?'

'Why would someone who can barely guard his own life
hurt another? Go home, all of you.' Then she saw Ramjawaya.

'And you're just standing by, enjoying the show?'

Ramjawaya replied angrily, 'If you want to lecture
someone, there's Rukmini. What are you pointing fingers at
me for? That darling has discarded her veil and is on her way
to school.'

'Her life's at stake. Poor thing. What's she to do?'

'That doesn't mean she should walk around the market
without her veil!'

Bhagsuddhi turned to look at Rukmini's husband—the
halfwit with his sweat-drenched, pale face, uneven breathing,
skeletal frame, face unshaven for days—and at his eyes, which
only watched Rukmini.

Without saying another word, Bhagsuddhi stepped forward to where he stood. 'Have mercy; let him go where he will.' She pushed aside the lad who had stood gripping his cane. Then she walked to the side, muttering under her breath.

Meanwhile Rukmini kept walking on. She was lost in her own thoughts; she had no idea what was going on behind her. She hadn't turned to look even after the voices behind her had grown excited, which they had because of the mad one's arrival. Some people stood up and a few even started making loud comments. She still hadn't turned around to see what all the noise was about.

'Arre, Rukmo! Wait!' Bhagsuddhi called out.

But Rukmo didn't hear her voice. She kept moving forward.

People wouldn't have dared to raise the cane on Kalle, but they wouldn't have hesitated to do the same to Rukmini. A madman couldn't be trusted; he could react unexpectedly. Bhagsuddhi felt nervous. She called out again, 'Rukmo, my child, move to the side!'

The humpbacked sweet seller turned to his son, 'Go, Bishan, and take the cane from him. Go, quick.'

Bishan wiped his hands on his shorts and ran, but he was still some distance away when the mad one had already shortened the gap between himself and Rukmini. Once he was close, he slowed down his pace. He continued to walk his crooked walk—as if he was dancing not walking—behind her.

Rukmo heard a movement and stopped. She turned around to find her husband just a few steps behind her. Her eyes widened, she stepped to one side and waited silently for him to catch up with her. She saw how many people had gathered, and she thought it odd how far the crowd stretched out. Kalle, panting, his half-open eyes focused on her face, and a slight smile dancing on his lips, stopped by her side, as if asking something of her. All Rukmini wanted to do in this moment was to shut everyone out and wipe the sweat off his brow and forehead, but she stood quietly, her eyes lowered. Then, after a few moments, she turned around and started walking as before, and her husband—the one variously called mad, crazy, halfwit, fully crazed, raving mad, lunatic—resumed walking behind her, like a baton-bearing foot soldier follows the cavalryman.

People stood all along the street—some had taken their place on raised platforms, others on the side of the street. Bishan had caught up with Rukmini a long time ago, but he'd had no choice but to hold back.

The sweet seller became annoyed. 'Say anything you want, but she's the daughter-in-law of a respected family; she's the daughter-in-law of the Diwans; she's newly married—is this the way to act? Is this how daughters of established households behave? So they can be jeered at by everyone? So they become a spectacle?'

He heard Ramjawaya's voice: 'Just look how stubborn she is, my god! Manjhle tried so hard to hammer some sense into her. But no! If a girl from my family acted this way, I'd break her legs.'

The humpbacked sweet seller kept quiet. His heart had become restless, but Ramjawaya's seemed deadened. All Ramjawaya could see in the girl was shamelessness, and how what she was doing was a defiance of tradition.

'See if I don't get Vaanprasthi's school closed. I'll change my name if I don't. He's come here to spread filth in our town—making our girls discard their veils!' Ramjawaya was burning up.

Rukmini, meanwhile, was moving further and further away, and the crowd of people was slowly scattering.

But when it was time for Rukmini to return from school, some people had already gathered at the school's gate. Word had spread like wildfire through town that the mansion's daughter-in-law had bared her face and gone to school. Some people had reached the school out of curiosity, some out of disbelief, and some just to see the show that was inevitably going to result. For there was no doubt in anyone's mind that Manjhle was going to create a furore. There was no way he was going to sit back.

Manjhle didn't go to the school himself, but sent his friends—Balmukund, Chamanlal and Lachhman—instead. They had started bad-mouthing Vaanprasthi the moment they arrived. A crowd gathered slowly, and the mood was turning rather electric.

The school day ended. Now calling it a school was a stretch really, because three girls had come to study in it. One was Rukmini, the second was from Sethis' Neighbourhood, and the third was from Oil Pressers' Lane—she was the daughter of a lawyer's accountant. Rukmini was much older than the other two.

The school day had lasted about two or two and a half hours. Those who had gathered at the gate watched Vaanprasthi emerge with the three girls from the lone room in the compound. They were crossing the courtyard and coming towards the street.

Vaanprasthi saw the crowd and stopped. He knew immediately that something was wrong. Why would people have gathered at the gate otherwise? He didn't want trouble while the girls were there. He felt nervous, and at a loss about what to do next. The three girls were from different parts of town—it was impractical to take them together through the lanes of the town and drop them one by one.

His heart filled with doubt. *I've rushed things. I should have asked Rukmini to join later. I should have stopped her for a few days at least. She should have started after the school was already functioning. What should I do now? Where should I take these girls?* He didn't know where to turn.

Then Bhagsuddhi emerged, cutting through the crowd. She walked right up to where Vaanprasthi stood with the girls and embraced Rukmini. Lekhraj walked in too, right behind her.

Mausi Bhagsuddhi patted Rukmini's head. 'Come, my child, come with me,' she said. 'We've come to escort you home.' She took Rukmini's hand, stepped out of the gate, and walked with her through the crowd. The three of them—Mausi Bhagsuddhi, Lekhraj and Rukmini—walked together towards the mansion.

The other two girls were free to leave now, and they left school smiling and chatting with each other, and went towards their own homes.

Vaanprasthi stood in the school's courtyard for some time, then turned and went back inside. Balmukund was left standing in the middle of the street, growling and muttering. He and his companions lingered for a while, glaring at Vaanprasthi, but then they left. The crowd had already scattered.

৩

She was known as Mausi Bhagsuddhi. But only a rare few knew whose mother's sister she was, and if she even was! All people knew about her was that she was a bag of bones, and that she lived in a dingy room with crumbling walls in Sethis' Neighbourhood. Most had only known her as someone who had developed this incredible capacity to reach someone's house when they'd be happy to have an extra helping hand, whether for a festive occasion or when there was a bereavement. If there were a ceremony in a house, she'd help out with a hundred chores; if there were a wedding, she'd be found singing wedding songs. She knew how to make things festive. And when there was no such occasion, she'd keep to her room, strike up conversations with passers-by, ask after their well-being and bless them, stay abreast of the major and minor events that shape the life of a community, pray and make predictions and tell fortunes. She lived all alone in her dingy one-room house, but she made room for the entire world in her life. But everyone also knew that she was given to speaking bluntly—she never dressed what she said. Her words were always piercing, never mind if they hurt. She neither knew fear, nor showed consideration.

That night, another minaret of Kabuli Darwaza fell. It had been drizzling and people had stayed indoors. The sound of the minaret falling reached many houses and all those who recognized the '*dhumm*' sound were troubled, for it meant the town had stumbled into yet another twist in its destiny. Knowing glances were exchanged in the unsteady light cast by earthen lamps, but it was as if words were unnecessary. This was, after all, the sound of the footsteps of time—for time inhabited the hollow remains of these age-old minarets, just like it inhabited the worn-down wall that encircled the town. It inhabited Raja Amirchand's Palace of Mirrors too, which now had more owls and pigeons living in it than it had bricks in its walls.

'Another minaret has fallen!' Bhagsuddhi muttered to herself. 'This is definitely the sound of a minaret falling.' She became quiet for some time, but then, overcome with emotion, she said, 'Who knows what enthusiasm drove which ruler to have this gate made!'

There was no one else in the room with her. She joined her hands under her dupatta and sang softly:

> *Whither do the thrones go,*
> *From which kings wield their authority*
> *Whither does your world go, mighty emperor,*
> *Bulleshah the poet is curious to know*

Bhagsuddhi had herself waded through the shadows of time to reach here. In what now seemed to be aeons ago, she had married into this town from Jhelum. She had arrived here by barge, as a new bride. Boats, large or small, no longer docked in this town, but there had been a time when the river was immense and its water used to rush up against its banks. People would carry flaming torches to see the barges that would come to dock at night, and there would be excitement all night long. The barge would leave again at daybreak— the oarsmen singing, rowing energetically with the current, towards their next destination. The life these docks had once known had ceased to be. The robust singing of the oarsmen had become distant and faint—it now reached town only if an errant fragment of a song managed to ride the wind.

Bhagsuddhi clearly remembered the day she had first set foot in this town. She had come by river, with her husband, and it was night by the time they were approaching the docks. The water was shallow towards the docks, and their barge had run aground. All the other people—there must have been sixty on board—got off and waded through the water to the bank. Only the shy, young bride, Bhagsuddhi, her veil drawn over her face, dressed in her bridal finery, and her husband, remained. Then, suddenly, he jumped into the water, reached out towards her, lifted her up and carried her to shore. How embarrassed she had felt, and how utterly in love she fell.

That was the last barge that ever came to this town. Barges never turned this way again.

For years afterwards, as long as her husband lived, Bhagsuddhi would narrate the anecdote of that night: 'The moon shone in the sky. The docks were lit with flaming torches. They were so full of life. The river reflected the silver of the night. The barge was dark and heavy, and it kept floating away from the riverbank. The oarsmen were growing tired and their singing had turned mellow.'

She could still hear the echoes of their songs in her room. She'd clap her hands gently to give their song a beat and she'd sing along:

> *From where do the boats come, oh Merchant*
> *Ranjha?*
> *From where do the oarsmen come, oh Heer?*
> *The boats come from the east, oh Merchant Ranjha*
> *The boatsmen come from the west, oh Heer*

Her eyes would brim over with tears as she sang, making passers-by wonder what about this song made her cry and why her lips trembled as she sang. The boats come from the east and the oarsmen from the west—there's nothing to cry about in this! Someone would say she reminisces about old days and thinks about how alone she is today. Someone would say she grew up playing on these docks and memories of those days knock at her. Some people even said that all the melancholy of the town, and the lives that are led in it, has seeped into her, and it makes her yearn for love in the divine.

Her husband Balram had a playful nature. He loved kabaddi and wrestling, loved spending time with friends and roaming around the streets with them. His liveliness and whimsicality had rubbed off on Bhagsuddhi too. She would sneak into the akhara and secretly watch him wrestle. She'd cheerfully joined in whenever he and his friends gathered at home and discussed sports. She was always abreast of news—who the wrestlers were, who in town had challenged the big-moustached wrestlers of Wazirabad and Sialkot to a bout, and who had mercilessly defeated whom. Balram used to go to the akhara every morning, which was in Orchard of the Sheikhs. By the time he would return home, walking through the streets like a warrior, sometimes alone, sometimes accompanied by a friend or two, his clothes thrown over his shoulders, his face and bare body smeared with mud, with only the loincloth he wore for wrestling on him, the sun would be high up in the sky. Bhagsuddhi would receive him with laughter. 'You look like a ghost,' she'd say. 'And also like Roshan Lal gave you a good beating today!'

This was the same Balram who'd jumped into the terrible fight that had broken out in the neighbourhood between cousins over grazing animals after the British administration had enforced new laws.

He had worked as a moneylender's broker, responsible for collecting dues every Tuesday. It was into this moneylender's land that buffaloes from the adjoining land, which belonged to his cousin, had strayed. Balram had jumped into the fray out of loyalty for his employer, and had had to be carried back home on a cot at the end of the day.

Then something unexpected happened. The cousins patched up their differences, and Balram became the bad one.

This was because—though Balram had beaten up many men in that fight—the one whose skull he'd fractured was related to both the cousins. Balram began to be looked upon as a loafer and a criminal.

He lost his job, and soon after that, though no one quite knew why, he also lost his house. The husband and wife—they didn't have any children—shifted to a tiny house at the end of a blind alley in Sethis' Neighbourhood.

Despite all that happened, Balram's spirit was not squashed and he soon resumed wrestling and exercising. He was quite young, probably no more than twenty-five or twenty-six years old then.

Bhagsuddhi stayed on in this house even after Balram's death. Over time, the house came to be closest to the lane from which this blind alley branched out—because the other two houses in front of it collapsed. Their rubble was never cleared out.

Bhagsuddhi's husband had died of snakebite on the same cot on which she now spent her days. The snake had been lurking in the cross-strings at the foot of the cot. Balram had just returned from the akhara, where he'd been wrestling with his friends. He was bare-chested and covered all over with red mud. He'd only just sat down on the cot and was setting his bundle of clothes down with one hand and lifting his other arm to take the bowl of cooling lassi from Bhagsuddhi when he heard the snake hiss. Such little sunlight ever reached the room; it was always quite dark inside. The cobra had raised its hood and taken a striking position. Bhagsuddhi even remembers she saw its half-open mouth—it was all red inside. She remembers how its fangs turned on her husband's thigh, and how he screamed, 'Oh Mother!' He clutched his thigh with both hands, and tossed his head to the left and to the right as if possessed. She saw the long, black snake slither down along the cot's leg and then along the floor until it disappeared somewhere in the back of the room. She had never felt such fear; she couldn't move; she was shivering. She was very young then, and so terrified that she stood in front of her husband and moaned. Balram was turning blue, he was frothing at the mouth, his eyes widening in agony.

By evening, Bhagsuddhi was sitting in Diwan Ram Labhaya's courtyard, surrounded by the women of her husband's family, having the hair on her head pulled.

> *You wretched Mangali*
> *You swallowed your husband*
> *You wretched Mangali*

They beat their chests and chanted these lines of lament and accusation, pausing from time to time to bend forward and grab hold of Bhagsuddhi's hair and pull at it. Word spread through town—the stars Bhagsuddhi was born under had caused Balram's death.

A rug had been spread out in the lane for the men to gather and sit on and offer their condolence. They sat discussing this same thing.

'He used to say he'd had her horoscope read.'

'Really? Then the purohit has played a dirty trick.'

Women's voices streamed outside:

> *You wretched Mangali*
> *You swallowed your husband*
> *You wretched Mangali*

Elderly women stood in the middle of the room in a circle and beat their chests. The circle had formed on its own, to the rhythm of the chest-beating. Their hollow faces were filled with wrinkles; sweat made strands of their grey hair stick to their foreheads and necks. Women were still coming in. They'd start beating their chests and chanting laments the moment they turned into the lane. And as soon as they'd join the group inside, the chanting would get more fervent:

> *Dust rises in the lane*
> *Dust rises*

Bhagsuddhi sat in the centre of this circle. She'd been in a daze ever since she'd seen the snake bite her husband, its mouth fiery-red. But the horror she felt in this moment was different. She knew all these women—she had been hugged and blessed by each one of them, one time or another. But at this moment—as she sat surrounded by them and they beat their chests and howled and filled the room with their displeased exhalation—these women felt more like shadows than people. It was like being in a nightmare.

> *This wretched Mangali*
> *She swallowed her husband!*
> *She swallowed our darling son!*
> *Swallowed him, swallowed him!*
> *Dust rises in the lane!*
> *Dust rises, dust rises!*

Blood flows into a wound and coagulates to stop its own flow. Bhagsuddhi felt nothing. Another hand reached for her hair. She shut her eyes.

She was at her mother's; she was sent back; she was in her own house once again; she was covered with a widow's white and worn-out dupatta; she was going from house to house to wash utensils and eke out her sustenance. Years of her life passed this way; her spirit remained unbroken.

Thirty years went by. The walls of her one-room house aged, as did she.

Another snake appeared in her house—a black, hooded snake, two feet long. It crept out of the house and into the lane. Bhagsuddhi was lying on the cot and she sat up with a start. But then, the very next moment, she joined her hands in prayer and thanks. It was the Snake God, giving her an audience after thirty years. For who could miss how gently it had moved past its devotee's cot, without raising its hood or hissing threateningly at her. Bhagsuddhi sat on her cot with folded hands and chanted a prayer. The snake had crossed the lane and the narrow drain, and was now moving along the mud wall. Bhagsuddhi got up, poured milk in a cup and set the cup down by the threshold of her house.

'Divine Cobra, please purify my house with your presence.'

Not immediately, but the snake did return—for when Bhagsuddhi returned home after telling her friends about how he had made an appearance, the cup was empty. The divine creature must have drunk his fill of milk before going back into the house.

From that day on, Bhagsuddhi and the Divine Cobra started living in the same house. Well, the Divine Cobra had lived until then in the rubble adjoining the house, and had come into Bhagsuddhi's house that day through a hole in the wall. But now that his devotee started placing a cupful of milk at the threshold of her house, he started appearing in her house every day. The room was always cool, and sometimes

he'd linger for long hours along the wall of the room, behind
the small trunk or the utensils. Bhagsuddhi was never afraid—
perhaps because she felt he had come to relieve her of this life,
just like he had done for her husband, or maybe because in her
infinite devotion she believed that, just like her widowhood,
the divine creature too had been sent to her by fate and so
it was her duty to accept its presence. Word spread in the
neighbourhood that there was a cobra in Bhagsuddhi's house,
and people changed their route a little bit so they wouldn't
have to walk past the house, but no one thought of killing
the venomous snake. And soon, like Bhagsuddhi, everyone
else's fear melted away. After all, this wasn't the only snake
in the neighbourhood—half the neighbourhood was in ruins,
and there were snakes everywhere. Not only snakes, but also
mongooses and many other creatures. It wouldn't do to be
scared, and was best to accept fate and what it brought. One
day, a snake bit a weaver not far from where Bhagsuddhi lived.
His body turned blue in minutes and he died before Baba
Roda, a healer who lived at the other end of town, could reach
him. People only blamed the weaver. *Why did he need to tap
his cane on the ground as he walked? Had his cane not struck the
snake, it would never have bitten him. Doesn't Bhagsuddhi live
in a house which a snake visits every day? She hasn't been bitten!*

Bhagsuddhi had a strange dream one night. This was
when Diwan Dhanpat had become the unquestioned lord and
master of the mansion, and was scheming about how he could
acquire Diwan Mayyadas's land. She dreamt of a bird. The
bird, which had shining wings, had flown over a vast distance
to reach this town. It was a large bird, and once it reached
the town, it started circling above it. Its tail was long, like a
peacock's. Even in her dream, Bhagsuddhi was enraptured.
She'd never seen a bird such as this. The bird seemed to be

looking down at the houses—it saw the mansion, the markets, all the houses; it scanned the town from the sky, searching for a place to alight. It was as if the bird thought of the town as a board game and was contemplating its move.

The bird delighted Bhagsuddhi; her heart raced.

'Come, Maharaj, come rest in my hut,' Bhagsuddhi mumbled in her sleep. 'You are the divine Garuda, aren't you? Come, Maharaj!'

The bird stretched its immense wings and hovered over Bhagsuddhi's house. It was so close, Bhagsuddhi could see its white, soft down fluttering in the breeze. *Oh! Maharaj's body is so immense and awe-inspiring, his wings brown, black and red and studded with shining gems. But from beneath, his body is so tender.* Bhagsuddhi felt that if she stretched out her hand, she would be able to touch him. And she felt that she had in fact touched him. Her heart overflowed with emotion.

Suddenly, the bird swooped down, faster than lightning, its wings contracting until it became a sharp line. Bhagsuddhi's heart beat faster. *Maharaj is really entering my hut; he has heard my prayer.* Bhagsuddhi heard a sharp rustle of wind, and the next moment she saw the divine bird ascending towards the sky, a long, wriggling, black snake in its beak. The bird continued its ascent; the snake was helpless. It rose, higher and higher, until it was no more than a speck in the sky, and the snake a frail thread.

Bhagsuddhi didn't realize when her dream ended. She wasn't sure if she had seen a dream, or if it had been real. She sat up, panting, and joined her hands in prayer. *Did Garuda Maharaj really come into my humble home? Did he really carry the black cobra away in his beak?*

When Bhagsuddhi woke up the next morning, she felt a sense of lightness. It was as if a heavy burden had been lifted off her. When she went into town, she told many women she met that Garuda Maharaj had visited her house the previous night and carried the cobra away. 'I saw with my own eyes,' she told them. Some women thought she had lost her mind, and some dismissed what she had seen as a dream. But a few women told her Garuda was a bird that could see into the past, present and the future. They said it was a kind of bird that, according to the sacred books, flies into this world once every hundred or two hundred years, and then disappears again.

Garuda Maharaj had plucked the cobra out of her life. Bhagsuddhi changed. She felt elated, free of worries. She had kept to herself for years, but now she started speaking her mind. She began to assume a new role in town, as if a shadow had lifted off her. It could be that one stops fearing misfortune as old age approaches. Maybe when one has suffered one's entire life, there comes a time when one realizes it's futile to live in fear of suffering that the future may yet have in store. But Bhagsuddhi thought otherwise; she believed that Garuda Maharaj had visited her and granted her the boon of fearlessness.

The school had picked up. Four more girls joined after Rukmini. Vaanprasthi drew the letters of the alphabet on each girl's slate, teaching them a few in the first three days. But when Rukmini reached school on the fourth day, there was no sign of him. The girls hung around in the courtyard and, as usual, Rukmini's husband stood with a stick outside the school, in the street.

Someone screamed in the lane that Vaanprasthi had been found badly wounded near Orchard of the Sheikhs. The other girls were too young to understand, but Rukmini was terrified. Soon, two men carrying a cot came towards the school. Lekhraj was walking ahead of them, and Bhagsuddhi walked behind them. She was holding Vaanprasthi's spectacles in her hand and screaming, 'You people are butchers. How could you hurt a man who came to your town from elsewhere? You will die a painful death. You will be scathed by the sighs of the poor. Ramjawaya, you should die of shame. Diwan Dhanpat, that you let such terrible wrongs be committed in front of your eyes can only mean you have no conscience, no shame. That you sit back and watch such terrible things happening can only mean the tears in your eyes have completely dried . . .'

A wave of horror swept through town. It was one thing to oppose a school for girls, and quite another to have an elderly stranger, a guest, beaten up. People rushed out in support. Everyone felt bad about what had happened. Everyone was aware whose handiwork this was, but no one had the courage to apportion blame.

Vaanprasthi's face was bloodied; his pyjamas were torn in different places and covered in mud. As soon as they reached the school, Bhagsuddhi began tending to his wounds, while Lekhraj took the girls home.

The school stayed open. Lekhraj took over Vaanprasthi's role and started teaching the girls the alphabet. Vaanprasthi was immobilized and confined to his thatched hut, but Lekhraj and Bhagsuddhi turned up at school daily; the girls' education continued.

After a few days, Lekhraj turned up in Diwan Dhanpat's court. It was a Sunday morning. Petitions had just begun to be heard, and Diwan Dhanpat was sitting on his throne, his feet tucked under him, puffing at his hookah. Lekhraj jumped over the boundary wall and walked right into the courtyard.

Diwan Dhanpat recognized him immediately. Seeing Lekhraj walk into his court surprised and alarmed him. He was well aware of what had happened, but hadn't made up his mind yet about what stance he should adopt. When the school hadn't yet opened, Vaanprasthi had gone door to door all over town, collecting donations. He'd come to Diwan Dhanpat as well for a donation, but the Diwan had shown no interest in the school, and Vaanprasthi had never knocked at his door again. The Diwan had felt slighted. And then, Rukmini—his daughter-in-law, the wife of his eldest son— had started attending this same school. She'd taken this step at Vaanprasthi's encouragement, without even discussing it with him. To top it all, Lekhraj had gone and joined hands with Vaanprasthi. Dhanpat read this as Lekhraj's attempt at strengthening ties in the neighbourhood. In his mind, the school was only a pretext, and Lekhraj was gathering allies and preparing the ground to spring an attack on him and demand his share in the property.

On the other hand, he wasn't oblivious of his middle son's and his mates' actions—they had got Vaanprasthi beaten up. That boy was becoming insolent; it was essential, Dhanpat realized, to rein him in. But equally importantly, the attitude of the British had to be kept in mind. Schools were being set up everywhere. A missionary school for boys had recently started in town. If the administration hadn't objected to Vaanprasthi's school, it meant that he, Diwan Dhanpat, must support it too.

These were the thoughts that swirled in Diwan Dhanpat's head when he found Lekhraj standing before him.

'I'm Lekhraj, Diwanji. I've come to request you that . . .'

Dhanpat was staring at him, unable to decide—considering so many eyes were watching him—whether he should show or refuse recognition.

'All I'm here to say is that if anyone from this household does this kind of terrible deed again, and if it leads to violence, he will have no one but himself to blame. Don't say later that you weren't warned.'

Diwan Dhanpat hadn't stirred this entire time. But listening to Lekhraj, his cunning mind decided its move and, his voice laced with deep affection, he said, 'Lekhraj, you returned to town so long ago, and you didn't come to meet me even once. You should be ashamed. And now that you have come to me, it's to threaten me!' He turned to his servants and said, 'Oye, bring him a chair!'

Two attendants ran to fetch a chair. But Lekhraj didn't stay. He only said, 'Far from helping the school, you had that old man's legs broken.' And he left.

Lekhraj came, said his piece and left. But Dhanpat was thrown into deep thought. *What should be made of Lekhraj's threat? With whose backing had he come here? He's using that old teacher to issue me threats. He's doing this only to plant his feet deeper into this town . . . so that one day he can make a court case against me. I'd had an inkling from the beginning that this was going on. So I wasn't wrong then.* And Dhanpat started planning and scheming again.

Word spread all over town that Lekhraj had intercepted the Diwan's court and glowered at him, threatened him. Whatever their stand on the girls' school may be, people were impressed and they praised Lekhraj for his gumption and for openly challenging the Diwan.

Vaanprasthi was in walking condition within a month, and resumed teaching. Lekhraj started going door to door to gather funds for the school, and Bhagsuddhi stayed at the school every day—she kept the courtyard clean, swept and mopped the classroom, and escorted the girls back home after school.

The situation was returning to normal when a sub-inspector from the Sargodha Police Station came to town with a few constables to conduct an enquiry into the attack on Vaanprasthi. The Diwan's son wasn't summoned, but two of his friends—Balmukund and Chamanlal—were handcuffed and taken to Sargodha. The two were back in town within a couple of days, and they carried on with their ways as usual, but the conclusion people drew from the entire episode was that the days of Manjhle and his friends' dominion over town were now over.

A few days later they saw—and the surprise they felt wasn't small—that Rukmini was going to school in a palanquin. It wasn't any plain palanquin either; it was florid and it had bells attached to it. It was Diwan Dhanpat's palanquin! This was sensational. What an utterly unexpected step, especially considering how dead against the school his middle son was and how much he had opposed Rukmini's decision to study. This started a whole new round of chitter-chatter in town. This step is in line with the British stance, someone conjectured. He's doing this to teach his son a lesson, another quipped. Diwan Dhanpat, meanwhile, became as busy as a bee—he kept himself abreast of the nitty-gritty of the inquiry, and even visited Sargodha twice to meet the deputy commissioner.

It was dawning upon Dhanpat that there was no sure way of knowing the administration's stance on matters, and that the administration's disposition could change without signal or warning. When Dhanpat had had Karim Khan beaten up, he'd been worried an inquiry might be set up to look into it, but nothing happened. When Manjhle had had but two sacks of grain, product of their own land, unloaded from the train, an inspector had arrived from Jhelum to investigate the matter. He'd even recorded a statement from Dhanpat.

Then one night, the same sub-inspector who had taken Manjhle's friends to Sargodha came once more to town and arrested Lekhraj. He said Lekhraj was required for the inquiry, and that he'd be back in town as early as the next evening. Bhagsuddhi kicked up a big fuss. It woke people and they poured into the street. Bhagsuddhi wasn't letting the sub-inspector leave. People intervened and reasoned that Lekhraj was being taken away for a routine inquiry, and that he'd surely be back in no time at all. But Bhagsuddhi was inconsolable. Her fear was that a 'routine inquiry' wasn't the reason Lekhraj was being taken way. She followed the sub-inspector and Lekhraj all the way to the railway station, screaming and howling.

What she feared turned out to be true. Lekhraj didn't return. Two days passed. Then two weeks went by. The two weeks turned into two months, which turned into two years. He'd been whisked away; he wasn't coming back. Bhagsuddhi went to Sargodha, and she went to Jhelum. She even went all the way to Lahore. There was no trace of Lekhraj. She couldn't find out anything about him. He had vanished into thin air.

'This is Dhanpat's doing,' she kept screaming. 'He's had Lekhraj arrested.'

It really was Dhanpat's doing. It was probably the darkest among all the things he had done in his lifetime. 'Sahib Bahadur,' he told the deputy commissioner during one of their meetings, 'Lekhraj is someone who's fought the British for years. During the days of the war, when your humble servant was getting supplies to your army, that man was enlisted in the Sikh army. And he didn't stop there, Sahib; he later joined the Kukas and was with them for years. Now he's come back and is spreading disquiet in town.'

This testimony by Dhanpat proved sufficient. Lekhraj was never seen in town again. All he had managed was a month in town, maybe a little more. People were troubled, but no one said anything. That could be because they were hopeful of his return—the administration could go about its inquiry for a few days, but then he'd be released because, after all, he hadn't done anything wrong. He'd only helped Vaanprasthi. But Lekhraj never came back. It was like before, when he had vanished for years—except this time, it was forever.

Some years later, when Rukmini asked Bhagsuddhi about him, she said, 'He was a godlike man. He was overjoyed when

you started school. He said to me, "Mausi . . ." He called me
Mausi like everybody else. "Mausi, a lamp has been lit. Its flame
will light up this dark town." He had thrown himself behind
Vaanprasthi from day one. He'd say to me, "Bhagsuddhi, I've
found my home. This is the work I'll do: I'm going to run the
master's school." Sometimes he'd get excited like a child. He'd
say to Vaanprasthi, "I'll go door to door and gather funds for
you." I asked him one day, "Lekhraj, are you doing this for the
sake of the school?" And he replied, "No, Mausi, this is about
our darling girl, Rukmini." When you crossed through the
school gates the first time, he'd run all the way to the hillock to
tell your grandfather what a feat you had accomplished.'

What irony. When Lekhraj had finally decided to settle
in the town, they'd whisked him away. There was something
inside him that had always tormented him. Mausi Bhagsuddhi
was saying, 'I asked him one day, "Lekhraj, why do you wander
about so? Why have you wandered about all your life?" He
didn't answer for the longest time, and then he said, "I don't
know, Mausi!" One time he said, "My life would've been very
different if I hadn't enlisted for the war." When I argued that
others too fought in that war, he said, "Yes, Mausi, they did.
And they fought valiantly. Manohar died fighting."

'"Was it Manohar's death that made you restless?"

'"I don't know, Mausi," he said, and became quiet. It
was always this way with him—he'd say a few words, then
turn silent. He always seemed to be in some inner dialogue
with himself. He said after some moments, "Maybe I'd never
have enlisted if I hadn't heard all those stories from my
grandmother."

'"But, Lekhraj," I argued again, "stories are part of
everyone's lives. Is there anyone in the world who doesn't
listen to stories?" He stayed silent, didn't say anything.

'He used to go meet your grandfather sometimes. They'd sit on the hillock for hours, but on returning he'd say, "Bhagsuddhi, you won't find a man more frightened than him in this entire town." I used to say to him, over and over again, "Lekhraj, you should claim your rights from the Diwan. Why don't you claim what's yours?" He'd laugh and say, "Should I go and live in the mansion, Mausi? At this age? I, who have no past nor future?" Then he'd softly say, "The town is my home. I'm happy being in its lanes."'

Listening to Mausi, it would seem to Rukmini that, before disappearing from this world, every person becomes an image of himself. In fact, even when a person is alive, skin, bones and all, it is this image that gives him his reality. The image pulls from the person's past, from his entire life—it's an image of how he has lived in this world. An image such as this had also formed around Lekhraj; it had distilled out of the aura that had surrounded him over the years, and was born from stories that people heard about him. The same was true for Diwan Dhanpat and Diwan Mayyadas as well. The man who held court and travelled in a palanquin with bells wasn't Diwan Dhanpat; rather, the entirety of his life, as condensed into an image, is what reflected the person he had been. All the misdeeds a person has done in his lifetime come together to constitute this image. The image, and not the physical form of a person, reflects the reality of his being.

Lekhraj had an intense response when Rukmini joined school. He ran all the way to and up the hillock. 'Harnarayan, your granddaughter has enrolled herself in school!' He had looked out at the town from the hillock emotionally and said, 'Life has returned to town, Harnarayan. The town has come alive. A lamp has been lit. It's no longer dark.'

'What's to be happy about in this, Lekhraj? If you ask me, Rukmo has sowed thorns for herself. For herself, and for us all.'

Lekhraj stared at Harnarayan's face, stumped. He was speechless. He'd never imagined such cowardice, especially not in a man who believed in God and spent all his time praying.

'I'm here today but will be gone tomorrow. Where is she going to seek refuge when I'm gone?' Harnarayan continued. Then he said something really strange. 'She's giving me so much trouble at my age. I can barely look after myself anyway. Is it right that she should sadden her grandfather so? Doesn't she have any duties towards me?'

'Do you really think what she's done is wrong?'

'Of course it's wrong. Lekhraj, that girl will drown and she'll drag me down with her. Can we possibly win against the mansion dwellers?'

Lekhraj had started back irritated. But as he walked down the hillock, he was taken over once more by thoughts about Rukmini's daring. He was convinced that nothing was going to remain the same now, that something had been stirred awake, that things were going to begin turning.

What happened next was there for the entire town to see.

§

Only a few days had passed since Lekhraj had been arrested. Like every day, Dhanpat wrapped up work at his court and returned to his room. His attendant helped him out of his angrakha, put his turban away, removed his joote and sat down to press his feet and pull the weariness of the day out from his toes. Diwan Dhanpat said, 'Bring me water.'

The attendant got up and brought him a silver tumbler filled with water cooled in the slender-necked goglet.

Dhanpat had barely taken the tumbler to his lips when he felt there was a strange smell coming from it.

'It's stinking! Where did you bring it from?'

'Master?' The attendant was surprised, and a little frightened. 'From the goglet. I filled it with fresh water just this evening.'

'Then it must be your hands, you shirker!'

'I washed my hands, my lord. And I rinsed the tumbler as well.'

'Stop my-lording me! When I'm saying there's a smell!' Dhanpat said sternly. And then he did a strange thing.

'Come here, bring your hands close,' he screamed. The attendant was trembling by now.

Dhanpat drew his attendant's hands towards his nose.

'Keep them steady. Stop shaking them so!'

The attendant controlled his trembling with great difficulty.

'Please, Master, I washed my hands before pouring water for you.'

'What did you wash them with?'

'With clay, my lord.'

'Rascal! Haven't I said that you should wash them with firangi soap!'

'My master, my lord!'

The attendant took the tumbler from Dhanpat's hand and ran out to refill it. He washed his hands again—this time with English soap. He washed the tumbler again. He sniffed at the mouth of the goglet a few times. Only when he was convinced that there was no smell anywhere did he fill the tumbler.

Dhanpat could still smell something, but he drank the water.

The attendant was about to leave when the Diwan said in his deep voice, 'Refill the hookah and bring it.'

The attendant ran out and returned with the hookah. The Diwan sat on his bed and puffed at it for a long time, and the attendant stood behind him, fanning him.

The Diwan sat on the white bedspread in his milky-white pyjamas and muslin kurta that fluttered in the gentle breeze of the hand fan, puffing hard at the hookah, and slowly forgot about that rotten smell that had troubled him so just a while before.

It was his habit to sleep on his left side. This night, as he lay down on his bed on the roof, and when he'd just rested his head on the pillow, a strong whiff of that smell rose again. It was stronger than it had been in the evening. Diwan Dhanpat sat up. So it wasn't from the water; it was coming from somewhere else. But there was no doubt it was there. *My nose can't be playing tricks on me.* He was looking at the low wall that skirted the roof when he realized the smell was coming from the gutter outside. *Bastards, no one does what they're supposed to. This, when I have explicitly told them to pour a few buckets of water into the drain every evening. These shirkers turn a deaf ear to everything unless you kick them.*

The smell, however, disappeared after some time. Possibly, the direction of the wind had changed. Dhanpat lay down, set his head back on the pillow, and turned over to his left side.

There was no doubt that things had been a bit nerve-racking recently. Manjhle had taken to insolently staring back at him. It's not that the Diwan had been blind to this earlier. Youth is reckless, he'd tell himself. But there was no denying that Manjhle was proving to be more insolent than was acceptable. *He's misbehaving with his elder brother—what's it going to be like once I'm gone? I'd wanted to make sure Kalle was settled while I'm still alive, that's why I got him married. How was I to know that this would sow in his heart seeds of anger towards me and of jealousy towards Kalle? And my third son, that good-for-nothing! He'd gone to study law and become a barrister, but it's as if he's settled down there. He's completely mum about when he'll return.* Dhanpat felt weighed down. And then, he'd had Karim Khan whipped. *No, but that was the right thing to do. If you show tenants leniency once, they'll never pay their dues.* But there was so much blood—a pool of blood had formed on the floor. *I hadn't expected that.* The other petitioners had got up and walked out of the court, one by one. There was such gloom on their faces. *Some didn't even bow their salutations to me before leaving.* This incident too had been gnawing at him.

During this same time, one day, the Diwan was returning in his palanquin from a tour of his estates. He had covered a long distance and was very close to the town when a stench ballooned up from somewhere and engulfed him. It left him shaken. It was so strong that it was unbearable.

'Where is this loathsome stink coming from?' he asked, gasping for breath.

Four palanquin bearers—two in front, and two at the back—were carrying the palanquin. Even though Banshi was his friend, as his employee he was not riding with the Diwan; he was on foot, ahead of the palanquin.

For a moment the Diwan thought the smell might be from the rotting carcass of an animal, hidden behind the bushes. His head started to spin.

'Move faster!' he growled.

The palanquin bearers quickened their pace; the palanquin moved faster. *The rotting carcass will soon be behind us; these gusts of smell will be gone.* But when the smell didn't lessen even after they'd covered quite some distance, the Diwan began to suspect that it was emanating from one of the palanquin bearers. The two in front were bare-chested; they wore only red loincloths, and had wrapped their thin cotton towels around their heads.

'Stop, bastards, stop,' Dhanpat screamed and lashed his whip at the air.

The palanquin stopped.

The bodies of the palanquin bearers, darkened by the sun, were soaked in sweat and emitted a pungent smell.

'Oh Banshi, you fool!' Dhanpat screamed.

But Banshi didn't know the palanquin had stopped. He'd walked on, lost in his own thoughts.

'Oh Banshi, you son of a pig! Can't you hear me?'

Banshi heard a voice in the distance, behind him. He turned around. He was roughly the same age as Dhanpat. But he was fat. It was torturous for him to go from village to village with Dhanpat, walking long distances ahead of the palanquin. Sometimes Dhanpat even used to hand him an umbrella to hold up over his head. But truth be told, this wasn't so unbearable for Banshi, for it gave him the opportunity to chat with Dhanpat. The real torture was in having to walk ahead of the palanquin. It made his feet blister and his mouth dry. How he wanted to stop and laze under a tree, to rest his back. But who was going to allow him that! This thought always made him very angry. He was serving the man whom he had spent his youth playing and joking with. He was accompanying his palanquin like some mace bearer, dragging himself about everywhere in the heat.

He started back towards the palanquin.

'What is your order, Diwanji? Why have you asked the palanquin to be stopped?'

'Stopped, my foot! What sorry excuse of palanquin bearers have you burdened my existence with—unwashed, unbathed! They stink!'

Banshi could make neither head nor tail of what was going on.

'Come here, Banshi, you idiot! Smell his body! Smell it! Smell it! What are you staring at my face for! Smell him!'

Banshi was duty-bound, and had no choice. He stepped forward, towards the palanquin bearer, stuck out his nose and sniffed his back.

'Does that answer your question? It's him! Stink is bursting out from his body. Smell it, smell it! Bastard! They come here unbathed.'

The bewildered Banshi, already exhausted and irritated, took a step forward and slapped the palanquin bearer.

'Why didn't you bathe?' he yelled.

'Tell me why I shouldn't be slapping you, Banshi, you idiot! Is slapping going to make the stink go away?' Diwan Dhanpat growled. But the smell was gone. *The direction of the wind must have changed*, thought Dhanpat, *and the animal carcass must have finally got left behind*.

'Lift up the palanquin. What are you standing and staring at my face for?' he screamed.

Diwan Dhanpat felt unsteady. This wasn't how things generally were with him. Usually, once he dug his nails into something, he didn't let go. In his single-mindedness and bottomless concentration he was comparable to a raptor stalking its prey. Just like an eagle tightens its claws around a pigeon and pulls out its feathers, one by one, so too Diwan Dhanpat, once his mind focused on something, would pull it apart until every possible way of looking at it had been exhausted. But something had changed. His mind was easily distracted. Instead of staying focused on the thing at hand, it would begin to wander.

Diwan Dhanpat was entering a new phase of his life. The outside world was shrinking; things were becoming distant; his grip on them was loosening. But even now, sometimes, something would boil up inside him, a bugle would sound within like it used to before, and his body would feel charged. A while ago, emulating the deputy commissioner of Sargodha, he'd got a phaeton made. Just like the deputy commissioner, he would ride through town in it, to catch some fresh air. His whip lashing, he'd race the horses that pulled his phaeton towards Orchard of the Sheikhs. But this was only on evenings when that old fire would blaze and something would surge inside him.

He'd been governed by such surges his entire life. They drove all his actions, his wilfulness, his arbitrariness. But now, all of a sudden, these surges had slackened. Not only that, they'd become touched by sadness. Sometimes, he felt a wave was gathering momentum and advancing towards him, that it was rising higher and higher, and that it would engulf him one day, that he would drown.

One night, Diwan Dhanpat was lying on his bed, unable to sleep. He tossed and turned for a long time before his eyelids finally felt heavy, and he started drifting into the ocean of sleep. But then, a face floated up before him, and a stink ballooned up and engulfed him and left him tormented. The face was Karim Khan's. Blood streamed from his nose, and his shivering hands were joined in supplication. His turban had loosened and slipped off his head. An unbearable smell rose up around Dhanpat at the same time. He woke up, rattled, disconsolate. Even though he was now awake, the smell persisted and the image of a badly wounded Karim Khan—

faint, faded, incomplete—floated in front of his eyes. In this image, Karim Khan's mouth was open, and clots of blood covered his moustache and days-old stubble. The clots were shining. One moment, Karim Khan's blood-covered stubble would come into focus, and another moment the face would blur and the unfurled turban hanging loosely around his neck would come into focus. Then slowly, the image faded and disappeared.

Dhanpat's breathing had become laboured; a pool of sweat gathered on his chest. *Karim Khan returned to his village a long time ago. Why would the smell of his blood reach me here? Am I losing my mind? What's happening to me?*

He got off the bed and started pacing. Karim Khan's face had dissolved away, but the smell lingered. Dhanpat walked up and down his room, alone and desperate. He returned to his bed after hours of pacing about the room, but all he could do was lie with his face down. Sleep didn't return to his eyes even then, but his legs felt exhausted, his shins hurt.

He lay on his side and curled up. His hands clenched into fists and tucked under his red, well-trimmed beard, he looked like a child lying in bed begging for sleep to engulf him and carry him away.

'Lord, please, grant me some sleep. Sleep, even if for a little while, even if for a few moments.'

He looked so insubstantial curled up on that immense bed with ivory-inlaid legs, whimpering, praying for sleep. The prayers gave way to a sound, *'oonh-oonh'*. He felt shielded by it. 'Oonh-oonh.' It diverted his attention. It was like a lullaby. It soothed him. Sleep flickered in his tired eyes; he was dozing. The 'oonh-oonh' had stopped. Sleep—further— almost. But then he sensed a stench in his breath. It was mild; it wasn't so strong that it should startle him awake, make him sit up in anguish. In his slumberous state, he felt the breath he was inhaling was mixing in with this foul smell, and also that, somewhere, this smell was germinating inside him. His descent into sleep continued, his body stirred, he turned over on his side. 'Oonh-oonh.' But he didn't wake up. The smell didn't change. In his sleep he thought the smell was rising out from his attendant's body, who was sitting at the foot of his bed, pressing his feet. But he didn't have the strength to make him leave. The attendant had, in fact, come to the room earlier, to ask the Diwan if he would like his feet pressed, but Dhanpat had gestured and sent him away. But now in his state of slumber he felt the attendant was sitting by his feet, and the smell was coming from his body.

But then, even as he slept, Dhanpat felt once more that it was from his own body that the smell—that slight, mild stink—was emerging. But he was so tired that he couldn't concentrate. His body stirred again, a couple of times. Then he turned over on his side, made the 'oonh-oonh' sound a few times more, and fell into deep sleep.

Some days later, one morning when the attendant brought the Diwan his hookah, he found the Diwan sitting up in his resting chair, stroking his beard.

He took the hookah and, like always, asked after the attendant's family and inquired about other news, his heart free from anxiety, and then—after he had smoked to his heart's content and handed the hookah back to his attendant, and as he was about to rise from his chair and his right hand went near his nose—he smelt an odour. It was a smell of something rotting. It came from his fingers. He stretched out his hands before him. He looked at them, palm up, palm down. They looked clean. And still, when he raised his fingers to his nose, there it was again—the smell of decay.

A soft moan escaped his lips. He raised his fingertips once more up to his nostrils. There was a stink. It was undeniable. His nose could smell it. He examined his fingers again. He cleaned out his nails with the needles that he used for cleaning his nails and ears, and which he kept hanging around his neck. He took his time; he picked out all the dirt. Then he yelled for the attendant to bring him soap and water, washed his hands, scrubbed them with a towel and sniffed again. The stink! It was still there!

His body was numb. *What in the world is going on? Is it my body that this smell is coming from?*

After this, Diwan Dhanpat went into a loop, as if crazed. He'd take his fingertips to his nose, hold them there for a long time, and then, troubled, raise them to his eyes and stare at them. He washed his hands over and over, compulsively. There were moments when he thought he could clearly sense that it was his breath, not other things, that stank. *But then*, he would think, *if it's my breath, the smell should be constant—I should be able to smell it all the time. But that's not how it is.*

One morning, the attendant came into his room just before daybreak. He found the Diwan sitting on his haunches on his bed, like a monkey. He was cleaning his nails over and over again, and taking his fingertips to his nose again and again. He didn't look up even when the attendant came and stood right next to him, and when he finally did look up, the attendant saw that the Diwan's eyes had developed a squint.

∽

No doubt, it had taken Dhanpat years to attain the status and glory he now enjoyed. His star had ascended, gradually and with certainty. But when the time came for it to be extinguished, the extinguishing was sudden.

Many things had been wearing him down. It was fine that the teacher, Vaanprasthi, had been beaten—what had happened had happened. But that a sub-inspector had arrived from out of town and taken his middle son's friends for an inquiry, and that too openly through the lanes of town, for everyone to see, had caused him intense anguish. *The administration has insulted me. They've dragged my prestige through mud. The police official could have just taken the boys into a room and scolded them; he could easily have ended things right there. But what they did was like a slap on my face, and that too in front of the entire town. This will only make Manjhle worse. He'll think the police action was taken on my provocation. As it is, he's burnt up that I send Rukmini to school in my palanquin.*

He couldn't sleep a wink that night. Blasts of smell rose up and gathered about him. Earlier he smelt it only when he lay on his right side, but he was lying on his left that night, and here it was, on this side as well. He started making 'oonh-oonh' sounds again.

'Master!' The attendant, who was lying on the floor not far from the bed, got up immediately.

Dhanpat felt an ache in his head, slightly above his forehead. The moment he'd try to go to sleep, he'd feel a boil had really risen there—right above his forehead, in the centre—and that it was getting heavier and heavier.

'My lord, should I press your feet? Are you unable to sleep? Would you like a drink of water, Master?'

The attendant's voice felt good. The desolation in the room had been too horrible. When it's day, one doesn't mind even troubling entanglements; but tussling with one's loneliness at night is frightening. He felt supported by the fact that he wasn't alone in the room.

Dhanpat knew that all he had to do was call out, and someone would come running. But he didn't want people to come running to his room and find it stinking.

'Where is this stink coming from?' he screamed.

'There's no smell here, sir,' the attendant replied.

'You are lying! The room is stinking!'

His nose was near bursting with all the smell it had to sense. He tossed and turned in bed.

'Would you like a drink of water, my lord?'

'Oonh!'

Since the Diwan made no other reply, the attendant sat down on the cot's edge and started pressing his master's feet with his strong hands.

By and by, Dhanpat fell asleep. The attendant continued pressing his feet until daybreak. *It doesn't lessen me; it brings him some relief.*

But when it was dawn, and sunlight began to filter into the room, and the attendant was just about to get up from the bed, he saw something that startled him. The Diwan's legs were folded and his knees were raised, while his upper body was turned to the right as if he was sleeping on his side. His mouth was open and he was inhaling and exhaling like a bellows. Two ants had crawled on to the bed sheet. The attendant felt his heart tightening. He bent forward, picked up the ants one by one, and threw them away. The Diwan woke up, opened his eyes and closed his mouth—but only for a tiny moment. Then he fell back into a deep sleep. He'd pulled up his left knee, and the attendant saw three more ants on the bed. He shook the sheet a little, bent forward, picked up the ants and threw them on the floor.

⟋

The Diwan entered his court. He was in one of his moods—the kind where he was like a being that has risen after a whipping and now nothing can rein in its ruthlessness. A number of tenants were going to be presented for a hearing, and there was a crowd of petitioners too, outside the Diwan's court.

But fate had different plans. The Diwan had barely entered the court when Manjhle blocked his way. His face bore an expression that said he didn't care that he was blocking the path of the master of three estates, Diwan Dhanpat, in his own court.

'You send Rukmini to school in your palanquin? Is she your mother?' Manjhle glowered at the Diwan, his lips contorted.

'I'm going to bring this mansion down! Give me my share! Partition the mansion, and do it now!' He was utterly beside himself.

The Diwan's eyes were red with rage. His body was becoming taut with an agitation he'd never felt before. But he didn't say anything. He was dressed in his court attire; he started walking slowly, with studied steps, towards his red seat. He was going to pardon his son's demented behaviour; he was going to enter his court, climb up the three steps to his throne and sit down.

But his son caught his sleeve from behind, stood in front of him and said, 'Did you hear what I said? Did you hear me?' And his lips contorted even more. 'The entire town is spitting on my face. You've gone out of your way to have this happen to me. I'm going to see to you. I'm going to see to it all . . .'

Some of the petitioners had by now walked into the court. Some had even seen Manjhle pull his father's sleeve disrespectfully. They'd heard him scream.

Diwan Dhanpat didn't say anything to his son even then. He walked resolutely towards the three steps that he was going to climb, which were going to lead him to his throne.

'I'm going to see to every bastard. I'm going to throw that Kalle out of the house today. I swear, otherwise I'll change my name!' He jerked his father's sleeve loose and stormed out of the court, screaming.

This much is common in all the narratives about what happened next—the Diwan climbed up the steps and sat down on his throne. He took his shoes off and folded up his legs under him. He gestured to his court seneschal to come near, and when he did, the Diwan raised the index finger of his right hand—the finger was shaking—and said something to him. But then his voice floundered. His booming voice came out as a whisper, and blood started to drip out of his nose. What had he said? What was he going to say? This is where narratives changed. According to some, the Diwan said, 'I declare this son of mine . . .' and then his voice drowned. Others said they'd also heard him say, 'disinherited'.

At first, no one noticed the drip-drop of blood from the Diwan's nose. Not even the Diwan. He felt something scraping the inside of his nose, so he raised his handkerchief to it. That's when he saw the blood. Before he could even register anything, more drops of blood fell on his kerchief, and then blood poured out in a continuous trickle.

The Diwan was confounded. Holding the handkerchief to his nostrils, he lowered his feet and slipped his shoes on. He'd even descended a step, but his legs gave way. He slumped to the floor, right by his throne.

About a month later, late one afternoon—when the sunlight still glowed golden but had lost its harshness, and there was a nip in the air—Diwan Dhanpat sat on a chair that had been set out in the sun for him by the new wall that stretched across the mansion, dividing it, and his attendant, Ramrakha, sat by him on the floor, pressing his legs. Because a lot of blood had flowed out, the stroke had been less severe than it could have been and the Diwan was spared being completely paralysed. But his body more or less lost its ability to move. He could walk, but only if supported by his attendant, and even then he'd drag his leg. He had lost sensation in that leg. When he spoke, his tongue didn't move as he wanted it to—it just rolled in his mouth—and all he could do was produce a *'baih-baih'* sound. When he got agitated, his right cheek would tremble. Sometimes, while sitting, he'd start making 'baih-baih' sounds and tears would roll from the corners of his eyes.

He had felt a sense of wellness that day after a long time and smoked the hookah, aided by Ramrakha. His mind felt clearer, more focused than it had felt in weeks. Like they had started doing every day now, the Diwan sat on a chair in the sun and Ramrakha pressed his legs for a while before shifting him back into the room. While one leg felt as stiff and lifeless as wood, the mild massage always brought relief to the leg that had been spared by the stroke. The doctor had advised that the Diwan be given pigeon soup for strength, and that the affected leg be massaged regularly and that the Diwan practise walking a little every day. The responsibility for this had come to Ramrakha.

Ramrakha's sturdy hands expunged all the tiredness from the Diwan's legs. He felt relaxed today, after so many days. Of course, Manjhle's gathering of no-gooders had to turn up today! They entered the mansion, chatting and giggling like morons at everything. Balmukund was walking ahead of everyone. He saw the Diwan, but that didn't seem to change anything. He didn't stop in confusion, didn't touch his feet in respect or fold his hands in greeting. He kept laughing his *'khee-khee'* laugh, climbed right up the wall that separated Manjhle's portion of the mansion from the crazy one's, threw one leg on the other side to balance himself, and started singing songs of romance:

> *Your teeth shine like pearls*
> *When you laugh, lads swoon and fall*

He was singing, tapping his hands on his thighs to the cadence of the song, his head nodding to the tune, his eyes dancing.

Two cots had been spread by the wall. Manjhle sat on one, and Bishan and Chamanlal on the other. Tumblers of cold *bhaang sardai* streamed in from the kitchen. The friends drank with pleasure, smacking their lips.

Balmukund continued singing. He'd take two sips of the sardai, stretch out his arms, turn his head towards the crazy one's courtyard, put his hand on his chest, as if on his heart— as if he was soaked in the colour of love—and resume the stanza from where he'd left off:

> *Your teeth are like a diamond necklace*
> *Oh my girl, Jamalo*

He sat on the wall, his hands raised in the air, giving a beat to his singing with his fingers dancing on his waist, and his friends sat underneath, on cots, clapping to the tune.

He started sending flying kisses towards the courtyard and crossed his arms over his chest as if he was embracing his beloved.

'Oh Kalle, I hope you're listening,' Balmukund called out.

His friends jeered, 'Well, as long as his wife can hear us!'

'Oh Kalle!' Balmukund called out again, and picked up tiny stones from the top of the wall and aimed them at Rukmini's room.

The Diwan's attendant, who had been pressing his legs, shuddered. He looked up at the Diwan—the Diwan's right cheek was trembling uncontrollably, his eyes were red and a thread of spittle dangled from his mouth to his shoulder. Suddenly, his lips fluttered, and he broke into 'Baih-baih-baih . . .' His hands were trembling; the hookah fell on the floor.

'Let's take you inside, Master,' the attendant said. 'It's turning cold.' He picked up the hookah, put it on the side table and stood up.

One hand under his knees, the other under his neck, the attendant lifted the Diwan and carried him across the yard, into the room.

∽

One afternoon some days later, the Diwan was sitting on his bed, his eyes looking vacantly at the world, when Manjhle's wife drifted into his field of vision. Fair-complexioned, dressed in gaudy colours, she lingered at the threshold for a moment, and looked left and right into the corridor before quickly stepping into the room. Then she swiftly turned, shut the door and bolted it.

Dhanpat looked at her. It was as if he was straining to recognize her.

Ever since word had spread in town that the Diwan was bedridden, everyone had been speculating about what would happen next. Like vultures and jackals drawn to carrion, relatives had started pouring into the mansion. Elderly women only distantly related to the family would sit by the Diwan's bed and ask after his health, offering prayers for his health—but their eyes would search the Diwan's face for signs to the contrary. Manjhle's mother-in-law, Pushpa's mother, had shifted into the mansion, and had even taken over its day-to-day running.

Pushpa had walked into the middle of the room. And though she knew that Diwan Dhanpat, her father-in-law, was nothing more than a mass of meat, and that he couldn't shout even if he wanted to, she was avoiding his gaze. She kept her veil drawn over her head, and didn't look in his direction.

She stood where she was for some time, confused about how to proceed. But her mother had prepared her. 'Today is the day. Take what you can. You won't get this opportunity again.' Remembering her mother's words, she felt capable again and darted towards Dhanpat's bedstead, slid her hand beneath his pillow, and searched.

It's tough to know if Dhanpat understood what Pushpa was up to, but he started making a 'baih-baih' sound. His voice echoed in the room. It frightened her.

There was an iron cupboard behind the bed. The last few days, Dhanpat's gaze had been shifting towards it again and again.

Pushpa leapt to the other side of the bed. She continued her search under the mattress, but to no avail.

Finally, it struck her that the bunch of keys must be in the pocket of the Diwan's waistcoat. She stood where she was for a few seconds, hesitating. Diwan Dhanpat was still making 'baih-baih' sounds. His palms were turned up, and he looked like he was complaining. To Pushpa, the helpless Diwan

seemed both frightening and contemptible. In her heart of
hearts, she was glad she was tormenting him—this man had,
after all, humiliated her father.

She drew courage from this rush of emotion that she'd
suddenly felt, and went and stood near his head. Without
saying a word, she frisked his waistcoat with both her hands.
Diwan Dhanpat whimpered helplessly.

She found the bunch of keys. And despite the risk—
for someone could have heard the Diwan's baying—she
unlocked the cupboard. The Diwan stared at her; he was still
whimpering. Pushpa pulled out a heavy iron safe from the
cupboard and opened it—right in front of the Diwan's eyes.
Jewellery in all its fullness sparkled before her—beautifully
carved twenty-*tola* bracelets, seven-stringed necklaces,
necklaces inset with ashrafis and Nadirshahi coins! Pushpa's
eyes widened.

She turned to the cupboard again and pulled out all
the documents; her husband had specially asked for them.
Then she locked the cupboard calmly, replaced the keys in
the Diwan's waistcoat, bundled up the jewellery and the
documents, and walked out of the room. She left the Diwan
whimpering on the bed.

When his attendant returned with the doctor, he found
the Diwan on his enormous bed—face down, alone and dead.

Around twenty years would have passed since these last events.

There was a terrible flood a few days after Diwan Dhanpat's death. The rage of the river wasn't new to this town; it was witnessed every five to seven years. It would rain, the river would swell, its water would flood the town, lanes would fill with water and mud houses would collapse. When it finally receded a few days later, the river would leave behind slush everywhere. The slush would take days to dry, in which time malarial fever would grip every home. Bodies would shiver with cold and tremble with high fever. And when the fever finally subsided, it would leave the body half dead.

But that year, the river seemed more enraged than ever before. It started, as always, with the first spell of rain, when children rushed out laughing into the streets. The old purohit had meandered through the lanes, saying, 'This isn't rain, it's a cataclysm. Look at the colour of the sky. Gather up your belongings and head to the hillock.' No one heeded his warnings, not even when the drizzle turned into an incessant downpour and water started gushing through lanes, puddles joined to become small ponds, and garbage surfaced everywhere. It was old garbage, like leftovers from wedding feasts that had accumulated in courtyards of dilapidated, broken-down houses. In their youthful ignorance, young lads joked from the safety of sitting platforms that it was a good thing the town was getting a much-needed wash. The purohit knew better, and got busy going from shop to shop, gathering up all the *harmala* seeds and *giloy* herbs he could find. There was no doubt there would be an outbreak of malaria after the river receded, and these herbs were the only known cure.

Houses started collapsing; roofs caved in; people felt besieged. One of the walls of old Bhagsuddhi's house crumbled and fell, burying her while she lay on her cot. Another minaret of Kabuli Darwaza fell. This frightened people—not only because it was a bad omen, but also because they wondered what would happen to their houses if a construction as strong as Kabuli Darwaza was falling apart. Bhagsuddhi's body was retrieved from the rubble with much difficulty.

The river surged and overflowed its banks, flooding houses, spreading panic. People somehow escaped from their houses, carrying small bundles of their belongings on their heads. They waded through waist-high water towards the safety of the hillock and the railway station. To stay in town meant offering yourself up to one or another collapsing roof. The rain was laying to waste stores of grain and oil. There was no time to check on others, and no one knew what became of the purohit. But some said they'd seen him leaving town when water had risen only to knee-level. They said he led his cow by its reins, and a bag hung from his shoulder. His wife followed him with great difficulty, as she had a canister on her head and a number of bundles hung from her shoulders.

The deluge felled many houses. It was a torturous time for people, and many left town. But slowly, life started returning to its usual rhythm. Broken houses were repaired, parapets were constructed, thatched roofs were erected on poles, and embankments were fortified. The town slowly returned to its usual routine, and gatherings of dice players returned to their sitting platforms on street intersections.

So much had changed in these twenty years. The train had started arriving in town daily, instead of once a week. A railway station was constructed where there had only been a platform before. Its walls had the same kind of holes that are made in forts, so that if the need arose, it could be used like a fort.

Where there was just one district office earlier, now there were a number of other government offices as well. Houses were constructed for officers near Waterway of the Sardars, where the land certificates had been distributed. It was a colony, in fact, with paved roads on which soldiers of the firangi army moved about. An army recruitment office was set up in town. The missionary middle school became a high school, with classes till tenth grade. Rukmini's school was now a brick-and-cement building with a high boundary wall. Rukmini was now a senior teacher in this school. Vaanprasthi had taught her till class four, and then taken her to Sargodha with him for the primary school exam.

The important players of town had changed. Ramjawaya had left. It was heard that he'd set up a cloth shop in Wazirabad a while ago. But truth be told, as the years passed, the town's inhabitants gradually lost interest in keeping track of who among these old players lived, who died, when they died, and where. People simply kept growing old and slowly disappeared from view. And as they fell out of the flow of life, new people and new lives took their place. People had started to forget Diwan Dhanpat. His third—the youngest—son had taken his place in the mansion. He'd been away, studying law in England, and had returned after almost fourteen years. Just a few months after coming back, he had packed his elder brother Manjhle's bags, and sent him off to oversee farming on their estate.

'That's a more suitable place for someone uneducated like you,' he'd said. 'Go and attend to farming.'

The barrister son had turned the mansion into a mini-England very soon after returning. In keeping with his foreign ways, he employed bearers and orderlies, and redecorated the mansion according to his foreign tastes. Pots with flowering creepers were set up in the veranda, and curtains were hung over windows and doors. Emulating the deputy commissioner, he got a phaeton constructed for himself. He would use it both to roam about town in his free time, and also when he would go to the district court on work. Sometimes he'd put on a turban, and sometimes a white sola topi, but he'd always wear a black suit.

A few days after Diwan Dhanpat's death, Rukmini and her husband left the mansion and started living in a two-room construction above the grocery shop that was right opposite the school. Kalle was much better now than he'd ever been— he'd even started talking—but his entire life wove around Rukmini. Every afternoon, at the hour the school would end for the day, he would be lingering at the school gate, stick in hand. He always followed all of Rukmini's instructions, except for the one that he shouldn't be at the school gate at closing time. Now that Rukmini's life had become more settled and stable, the school was becoming the centre of her attention and her worries.

She often remembered and missed Vaanprasthiji and Chacha Lekhraj and Mausi Bhagsuddhi. She sometimes wondered how it was possible that someone could be attacked and his legs broken for something as simple as opening a school. She would think about all the insults Vaanprasthiji had had to bear, how much he was made to suffer. And Chacha Lekhraj? For years, she asked everyone who came to town from Lahore about him. But no one had any news. They didn't even know his name. Rukmini had never come to know fully the thing that Lekhraj had sacrificed his life for.

Once she left the mansion, Rukmini never looked back.

The old players had disappeared from the scene, and new ones had emerged. Her mother had died of malaria, and her grandfather had breathed his last on the hillock. It made no sense to make calculations about life with them in mind. Life hadn't changed its pace; only the players had changed. Only the setting had changed, the scenario had changed.

Malik Mansaram's pleasure park had opened right behind the mansion, on the Diwans' land. Apart from the carousels and bioscope shows, a Meena Bazaar had also opened there. Ramjawaya's son acquired the country-liquor store across the street from the pleasure park. If the queue for entering the pleasure park was long, the line that would form at the liquor store was even longer. Fights would break out every other day.

Moneylenders' houses grew stronger and higher. Many of them now had two-storeyed, brick-and-cement houses. This was the scenario in almost every lane—among the mostly broken-down houses, there would be two or three that looked new and were constructed with brick and cement. Totems—round mounds of mud crafted into faces with fiery-red tongues sticking out from between their lips—hung on the outer walls of these houses, to ward off the evil eye.

Officers roamed the streets—low-ranking as well as high-ranking officials, and officials wearing elaborate turbans, and

police officers and revenue administrative officers. All of
them vied for the British deputy commissioner's attention,
and prayed that his benevolent gaze would fall upon them.

∽

The sky had finally cleared after two days and two nights of
storm. The group had reached this halt in their journey three
days ago. The one who walked with the support of a staff had
told the others that the Sheshnag's Lake was here. But no
one had had the chance to see it yet. All they'd heard was the
thundering sound of many waterfalls, and they had walked
down narrow, precarious routes through the mountains and
reached here in the dark of night. At that hour, they were only
able to make out the mountains that surrounded them, and
the clouds that covered the sky. Exhausted by the journey,
they lay down and spent the night in the long hall that had
been constructed as a guest house for travellers.

But the skies were calm this morning. Rukmini came out
even though the night had not yet lifted. Waterfalls thundered
in the distance, but there was stillness all around. A handful
of stars twinkled above a high mountain peak, and Rukmini
sat down on the steps of the guest house and gazed out at
the magnificence of the mountains in the slowly dissolving
darkness.

The cold draught made her shiver, but even this delighted
her. Somewhere, a waterfall was cascading into a lake with a
deep, incessant roar. The silence of the mountains absorbed
its relentless thunder within it, making it a part of itself.
Rukmini's heart welled up, as if inveigling her to open the
floodgates and allow it to flow into this profound silence, and
merge with this immensity.

Another layer of the cover of darkness lifted from over the mountaintop; brightness increased by another notch. One by one, the layers of darkness crumbled, and the mountain was bathed in light. The stars that had been crowning it began to fade away. The landscape grew more still, more vivid. So quiet, so clear, so serene. She had never imagined she'd find herself before such an immense landscape one day. Silver had mixed into the darkness and brought out the sky. And then, slowly, a blush of pink dissolved in it, and the mountain draped itself in this pink cover. How resplendent it all was— her eyes, her skin, every pore of her body felt caressed.

Right beside Rukmini, a small plant danced gently in the breeze, as if welcoming her. Its branches were bending with the cold breeze. Not far from where she sat, branches of the deodar trees too bent with every gust of wind. Rukmini felt as if everything around her was dancing to a rhythm. The roar of the distant waterfall had mixed in with this rhythm, and fused with it. *Isn't this what Vaanprasthiji used to say, that trees and plants bow and do namaskar to the gods, sing paeans to them?* Birds chirruped and flitted from branch to branch, tree to tree; it was as if they too were singing paeans to the wonder that surrounded them.

Rukmini wanted to wander off, to walk until she found the lake that she still hadn't been able to see. She peeped into the guest house. Old Lachhmi had woken up and, like she did every morning, she was sitting with her back against the wall, her head and face covered, and reciting the Sukhmani. Bhanga and Parmeshwari were still asleep; it'd be some time before they woke up. Parmeshwari liked her sleep—she'd get horizontal the moment they halted their journey somewhere, and she slept so deeply that you could beat a drum loudly next to her ear and she wouldn't stir.

Rukmini stepped out again. She suddenly remembered the sadhus and was about to turn towards the neighbouring log house to check on them when she remembered they had left. There were two sadhus, and they'd decided to accompany them on this pilgrimage out of the blue. They'd reached the town from somewhere, and once there, they had changed their minds completely; instead of carrying on with their own journey, they had decided to join the group from town that was embarking on a pilgrimage to Amarnath.

The day before the previous day when, in the morning, she'd gone to their room, the sadhus were sitting with their backs resting against the wall. One of them was tall. He was reticent and polite, but he was very troubled by the cold. He was a timid man. If someone gave him something, he'd accept it, but if he wasn't offered something, he'd hover about instead of asking for it. On seeing him, Lachhmi had said, 'Sadhu Maharaj, you've chosen the wrong guise. You have to show some gumption if you want to be considered a sadhu.'

The tall sadhu hadn't understood what she meant and looked back at her blankly before raising his hands to bless her. Lachhmi found it difficult to hold back any more, and she'd uncovered the basket and put a fistful of *choorma* on the palm of his hand.

'Now I can't possibly bear to have you look so forlorn, can I? Here, eat.'

Then she'd turned to her companion and laughed, 'He should've been part of a herd of camels. Then he could've lain around without food and water for days. Or he should've been born in some rich man's house. How did he land up in the company of sadhus? He doesn't know how to ask for anything.'

The other sadhu was a short and stout man and though he could stay silent for long stretches, when he'd open his mouth, he'd say the bitterest things that crushed the listener. It was his nature to scold and reprimand. But it was as if he was made of iron. He'd walked without rest, or food, ever since they'd left Srinagar. If he got a drink of milk, he'd drink it; if he didn't get anything, he stayed quiet. Mile after mile, he stayed within himself. Rukmini only ever glimpsed him ahead of everyone, walking in an even pace on to the next mountain, disappearing at the turn of the road, on a hillock in the distance, or going over the bridge of a river that the rest of the group had yet to reach. She'd catch sight of his ochre robes—never in clear view, always disappearing around a bend. And she had seriously begun to wonder if he was in fact a person or a shadow that had stumbled on to these mountains by mistake, and which appeared and disappeared between places. Only a shadow, after all, can keep walking without eating—a person made of flesh and bones would surely faint and fall. This sadhu without a home or resting place, who felt neither hunger nor thirst, who thought of no one as his own and felt estranged from everyone . . .. Or was it that to him everyone was his own, and no one was a stranger? What flame burns inside him that he journeys from city to city, valley to valley? What is it like being a sadhu? Is he a renouncer? Sadhus don't give up cities. They sever ties with the world and yet they keep its people close; they distance themselves from material desires, but realize it's impossible to be entirely rid of those. Is he made of *ashtdhatu*, the alloy of eight metals? The sadhu would both surprise her, and make her restless.

On the morning of the day before yesterday, it had been drizzling. Rukmini had peeped into their room, and pulled back. Who knew, maybe they were meditating. Who knew, maybe they'd be offended if a woman walked into their room.

'Ey, Rukmini! Come here!'

The sharp voice of the short, stout sadhu had summoned her. Rukmini was startled.

'A terrible storm will rage today. All of you must stay put here.'

'What storm, Maharaj? The sun should be out any moment now. The rainfall's almost over. Come out and see for yourself,' Rukmini had laughed and said.

'If you find sheep's milk, bring some for us too. We'll be setting out soon now. But all of you should stay. Heed my words.'

'Step out of the room and look, Maharaj. The cloud cover is broken.'

But no sound of response came to her from the room. She went out in search of sheep's milk, but didn't find any.

She saw that a pilgrims' procession had set up a camp in the valley below, but she was only still thinking of making her way there when the clouds thickened and started thundering. She was still some distance away from her own room when a heavy downpour started. By the time she returned, the sadhus had left.

The sadhus had left before the storm had started. The frightening thunderclap and rumbling of clouds made Rukmini and her co-travellers wonder about the safety of the sadhus all day. Who knew where they'd be now. Who knew, maybe they had merged with nature. Who knew, maybe this was the desire that had driven them to this journey. Who knew, maybe they'd found shelter behind a rock. But how will they protect themselves from the cold? All that the tall sadhu had was a blanket, which he hung around his shoulders; but the other sadhu didn't even have anything warm with him.

What is it that holds a person together from within, that doesn't let him scatter, which gives him strength to walk the path of life undeterred, which gives him the strength to take his next, and then the next, step?

Rukmini thought about this as she sat in the forlorn log house amidst her co-travellers on that day of the storm. *Vaanprasthiji too was cast from this same mould. He stayed steadfast on the path he had chosen. He too held together, drawing strength to do so from within himself.* She had thought about Vaanprasthi often during this journey. Where had he gone? He'd got left behind, somewhere. It had been at least twenty years since he'd departed. But even now, whenever she thought of him, Rukmini's throat would choke with emotion, and his memory would only give her strength.

Sitting with her back resting against the wall, Rukmini— now thirty-five years old—the same Rukmo who'd gone to Vaanprasthi to get her name enrolled in school—was now Rukmini Devi, a teacher in the school. Class four was the highest one could study in that school then, and Vaanprasthi had taught her till class four. He didn't consider it necessary for girls to study any more than that. He thought it was sufficient for a girl to study as much as would help her read and write her own letters, and not depend on anyone else for it. Was it the memory of his daughter, Sumitra, that kept his personality together? It was her untimely death, after all, which had given direction to his life—the direction he stayed steadfastly on.

The rain and storm continued for two more days. Stepping out was out of the question. Far from it, Rukmini and her co-travellers were worried that the roof of the log house might collapse in the storm, or a wall might crumble under the force of the winds. Rukmini spent this time singing devotional songs with her co-travellers. When they weren't singing, the three would chat about town, about their families and about people they knew. And when they would tire even of this, they would each cover their heads with their blankets and lie down.

The storm made them melancholic. They started thinking they'd made a mistake setting out on such a long journey. *If something were to happen to us while we're here, who'll come to help us? At least there was some support while the sadhus were with us.*

Rukmini was overcome with gloom. And once sadness descends, the mind travels towards things—bad things, regrets. This was a mistake, and that was a mistake. However much she tried to make herself think otherwise, no matter what she said, a worry lurked in her heart—what condition must her husband be in? Different images of him would appear before her eyes. Because of her insistence, he'd stopped dancing around with his cane. Otherwise, earlier, he would raise the cane high above his head and swirl about making a 'ho-ho' sound at the slightest provocation. His mannerisms had changed significantly since she'd become a teacher, and also after Vaanprasthi had died, after which she'd been appointed headmistress of the school. But still, once the bell announcing the end of the school day would be sounded, he couldn't get himself to stay inside the house. However much she asked him not to, he always came out of the house. They had been staying in the two-room construction above the grocer's shop opposite the school for many years now. If you stood on the balcony, you could see the school's courtyard. He could see Rukmini come in and go out of the rooms of the school all day. But when the last bell rang, and even if he was standing in the balcony at that time, he would rush down to the school's gate. At that time, a lot of other people used to be there—people who'd come to take girls back home, like someone's grandfather, or a servant from someone's house, someone's uncle or aunt. He would come and stand among them. The husband and wife had become so used to this that Rukmini's eyes would involuntarily start searching for him the moment she crossed the courtyard. When she'd see him, she'd feel irritated and, at the same time, a sense of immense joy would rise up inside her. The two may have remained physically incompatible, but their souls had intertwined. It may be a still and quiet love, but it was deep, like a lake. It had brought meaning to their lives, given life a definition. It's not our bodies, but our spirits that hunger.

That is why right now, miles away from him, Rukmini felt alone, and her heart writhed with agony. Warm tears trickled down from the corners of her eyes and an image kept surfacing in her mind's eye—She's sitting in their small house and making chapattis on the stove, and her husband is sitting on the edge of the cot across from her and gazing at her lovingly. She missed his stories, which he told her in his stammering speech, laughing and always looking for ways to joke with her and amuse her. Rukmini knew this was his way of trying to entertain her after her day at work, to help her unwind.

With time, his health was better, his heart seemed more settled, and his epileptic fits too had reduced. But he still seemed unhinged. And he still stammered. Earlier, whenever he got excited, he would start dancing, tear his clothes off his body and run around in the streets, completely out of control. But now this was unusual. If it did happen, it was only about once or twice a year. Somewhere, he was becoming cognizant

of his situation. He knew, this is Rukmini, my everything;
this is Rukmini's wish, my obligation. This is Rukmini's time
for going to bed, this is time for her to wake up, and this is
time for her to go to school.

Years upon years passed this way. A brick wall now stood
around the school, and there were four rooms in the school
instead of just one big hall. As she was the headmistress,
Rukmini had a small room all to herself. This room had been
constructed on the same spot where Vaanprasthi's room with
the thatched roof had once stood, under which he used to sit
on a cot and sing devotional songs. That same 'room' was now
the headmistress's room. The school's courtyard was always
filled with girls—so many came to school now. Vaanprasthi
had planted a couple of trees on the edge of the courtyard;
they were big now. To Rukmini, the school was like a temple,
because the sacred memory of Vaanprasthi was tied to it.
That's why Rukmini, full of feeling, her hands folded and in
her lap, used to say, 'I've received so much from life. God has
filled my lap.' And waves of immeasurable gratitude would
rise in her heart.

And now, this far from home, the more she surrounded
herself with memories of her situation, the more agony she
felt when she emerged from them—and the desire to run back
home would seize her, to run to where he was, to find out how
he was.

'Rukmo,' an elder had advised her just before the summer
break started, 'a new hospital has opened in Lahore, where
they treat madness. Your husband will become well. Have him
admitted there. It's only a question of two or three months
after all. He will be healed.'

Rukmini was in a dilemma. She struggled for a month
with the thought of whether or not to have Kalle admitted

there. Her heart would say, *it'll be a good thing, it'll be so good if this can make him healthy; his illness will be gone for good; I'll have a man in my house who is well; his troubles will cease; he won't roam around on the streets in this sorry way.* The elderly man had said that the hospital was government-run, you don't have to pay a fee and, after all, your husband's ailment is so mild. It's a minor disorder, and even that will pass if he stays in the hospital. Many people had the same opinion. His heart gets plucked if a young boy throws a stone at him; he becomes agitated if someone pulls at his stick. If he loses his balance on such occasions, his condition invariably worsens. If a treatment is available, then why not avail of it?

On the other hand, she would think, *when he's here I'm within his reach all the time, I'm there for him, looking at me brings him succour, he follows me, listens to everything I say. He'll become more restless than ever in a place that's unknown to him, where his eyes don't find me when they seek me. What will happen to him then? At least here, I'm with him. His life may not find its complete dimensions, but he at least has me for support, at least he doesn't lose heart.*

As she sat in the log house, the scene with them standing before the gates of the asylum in Lahore tormented her. She kept repeating to him, and gesturing, that she'd brought him here for treatment, that she wasn't going anywhere, that he was going to emerge healed from here, and that she would take him back home with her.

A person who knew his ailment would have understood, but how could someone understand if he didn't know he was ill? He looked at her—at her face—with his mouth open.

She'd almost changed her mind once they were inside. It was only when the doctor examined him, and said, while he checked under his eyelids, that he would get well, that he could be completely healthy, that she managed to persuade her heart that this was the right thing, and would be for the best. She got him admitted to the asylum. It was a question of a couple of months, after all. *I'll be back in no time, before the summer vacations end, and take him back with me.* She felt calmer and surer.

She stayed while her husband changed into hospital clothes, with a white cloth cap on his head. Seeing him in that uniform crushed her heart. But she never got a chance to say a final goodbye. The moment they put him in hospital clothes, they took him through a door into another room and he disappeared from view. Rukmini was left where she was, alone.

And now, Rukmini felt tormented and hopeful by turn. She clung to the thought of how she would head straight for Lahore once the pilgrimage to Amarnath was over and she would find him at the same door that he had disappeared through, but now he would be smiling, his face would be resplendent, and he would come out and meet her. His eyes wouldn't roll back any more, strands of spittle would no longer hang out of his mouth, and his face wouldn't look lost and senseless. *He will come to me, walk right towards me and we'll return to our town, hand in hand.*

It was the old Lachhmi who had suggested they go on a pilgrimage to Amarnath. Lachhmi used to work at the school running some errands and cleaning. 'Trust in God and come along,' she said to Rukmini. 'If you stay here, you'll dissolve within yourself. Your heart will remain restless. Let's go there. You'll get His blessings and there'll be so much else besides to keep you distracted. Leave it to God; he makes sure every boat reaches the shore.'

And so Rukmini had set out on this pilgrimage. *When my eyes no longer anchor his gaze, how does it matter if I stay in town or tour through the valleys of Kashmir? The pilgrimage might earn me some virtue. May the holy blessings I earn go to him, may he become well. And I'll return in a month, after all. He's in the hospital, with doctors keeping an eye on him; it's not like he's alone, and not like he's wandering through the streets.*

The human heart is capable of providing boundless protection and shelter, and also of producing the most unbearable misery and distress.

As long as the pilgrims moved from place to place, Rukmini's heart was able to hold her husband's image in abeyance. It would emerge in her mind's eye at night, making her toss and turn, but she'd be so exhausted by the day's journey that she would soon be in deep sleep. And the days were full of such wonders to behold all around. Even the pilgrims intrigued her. There were so many kinds of people—people whose existence she'd never conceived. Like that old woman, bent over so much with age that her eyes were always fixed to the ground, who walked slowly with the support of her walking stick, her feet barely lifting off the ground, and who hoped at every place they stopped that it would be the place from where she'd depart this world. But she didn't, and the next morning she'd be up again, chanting mantras under her breath, walking stick in hand, onward to the next place. She was all skin and bones, and her mouth was hollow. Her turbid eyes couldn't even make out shapes around her, but she'd been making the pilgrimage to Amarnath every year for the last three years, having decided that it would be on this journey that she would have her life end. She'd come from faraway Bengal. Rukmini even asked her once, 'Maji, why are you so impatient to lose your worldly guise? Its time will come; it'll be discarded one day, no doubt.' But this question held no meaning for the old woman. As far as she was concerned, she had returned disappointed from these pilgrimages for the last three years now. To her, she hadn't been able to earn the virtue that she'd set out to earn.

If only the storm hadn't forced Rukmini to remain enclosed in the room, her days had been passing very well. But the storm outside had turned her inward. There was even a moment when her throat had choked up with emotion and she had sat up, tormented. *How can this pilgrimage to Amarnath possibly bring peace to a sinner like me? No, I will die a slow, painful death, for I have committed a sin for which there is no penance.*

Then she had lain down again, closed her eyes, joined her hands and prayed softly under her breath, 'Please keep him safe, my Lord, I will be forever in your debt, please let nothing untoward happen to him. Please keep him in your protective shade until I'm with him again, my Lord, your slave begs of you . . . What have I done, my Lord, please forgive me!'

Parmeshwari, Lachhmi and Bhanga were asleep, and snoring softly.

But then, once the three days of tempestuousness had passed, the world was as if transformed completely. When Rukmini first came and sat on the stairs that led into the log house, she'd felt so weary that she hadn't raised her eyelids to look around. But now, perhaps because of the cool breeze, or maybe because she had finally woken up, she opened her eyes. She had never seen anything like what she saw before her. Day was beginning between the mountains. When she stepped out, black shadows still covered the mountain peak on her left, and the stars were still shining over it, and to the right, where the mountains gave way to a valley, silver had begun to mix into the sky and the atmosphere was becoming brighter. The sound of the waterfall filled the air, and the deodar and *chir* trees on the base of the mountains rustled in the wind.

Rukmini watched the vista before her, spellbound. She had seen the scene change at every turn ever since she started her journey through the mountains, walking along narrow paths with a walking stick. Even the mountain stream changed from moment to moment—sometimes it collided against the cliffs and rose towards the sky, its spray refracting sunlight into a resplendent rainbow, and sometimes its milky, blue water would flow evenly and you could see whirlpools spinning within it. Rukmini would climb on to rocks for a clearer view and watch, mesmerized, until she felt the water had started flowing in the opposite direction and her head would start to spin. Sometimes after a turn, the path would open unexpectedly into a meadow run over with wild flowers gently dancing in the breeze, or filled with grazing sheep while shepherds—sometimes a father and a young son, sometimes a bearded old man—sat on one side, under an overhang. Her heart filling with delight, Rukmini would tie her dupatta around her waist and walk with her head uncovered, ready to run, to jump, to dance.

But nothing compared with the scene that stretched out before her at this moment. Rukmini had left the steps that led into the log house and followed one mountain trail, then another, until she reached a giant cliff that overlooked Sheshnag's Lake. The mountain range rolled on into the distance on the right, and she marvelled at how many mountains had been crossed to reach here. The one—that dear madman—with whom the threads of her being were intertwined, was beyond these mountains, thousands of miles away. This sudden realization surprised her. *Given how immense the universe is*, she thought, *it's strange that these invisible threads should keep two people*

*firmly tied to each other even when a vast distance separates them.
What's stopping me from letting go of him in my mind? Why am I
unable to lose myself in the magnificence that surrounds me? Can
one person mean so much to me that it makes the entire universe
insignificant?* Her pain subsided by a notch as these questions
found expression inside her.

Rukmini wasn't very educated; she'd only studied till class
four, after all. But like a parched bird that never stops looking
for drops of water, she gathered knowledge everywhere—
even by striking up a conversation with a passing sadhu.
She'd hang on to every word he'd say, watch him wide-eyed
and think, 'These people know so much. I know nothing.'
It was with these same eyes, filled with curiosity, belief,
faith and enthusiasm, that she was looking out today at the
enormity of the universe before her, with its inviting cover of
unsolvable mysteries, so proud, so clear, so beautiful, and yet,
so mysterious. She felt she was witnessing grandeur, and that
it was calling out to her, tugging at the strings of her heart,
making her forget, dissolving itself within her.

The more Rukmini looked, the more she took in, the larger
everything seemed to grow. Before her, beyond the lake, was a
mountain, its immense forehead covered by a sheet of snow.
Around her, trees and plants danced to an unknown rhythm
and innumerable waterfalls tumbled into the white expanse of
the lake. And yet, everything was steeped in an unfathomable
silence. A small blue fruit peeped out from under the cliff,
swinging in the breeze; the bush it was attached to was invisible.
The fruit would come into view one moment and disappear the
next. It seemed to be playing hide-and-seek with Rukmini.

Something would surge up inside Rukmini, over and
over again—a feeling of joy that would turn into unbearable
anguish all on its own and pound at her heart.

The sun had become hot now, but Rukmini continued sitting on the cliff. Old Lachhmi came looking for her. 'The pilgrims will set out later than usual today,' she told her, and advised Rukmini not to sit in the sun. 'Sit in the shade of a boulder or a cliff or a tree,' she said. But Rukmo was lost in her own thoughts, and Lachhmi left her alone.

Rukmo hadn't averted her gaze from the lake. She'd been looking at it for a long time now, losing herself in its waters. And then she felt she saw something more—someone had appeared on the surface of the lake. She looked with half-closed eyes—it was someone dancing, a captivating, attractive figure. Every inch of his body seemed to be dancing. Rukmini's eyes were arrested. Then, for a moment, it disappeared from view. But the moment she averted her gaze, there it was again—the dancing figure had appeared again.

It was Krishna. A peacock's feather in his crown, blue complexioned, he was dancing on the waves that had formed on the lake, and was playing his flute. He looked exactly as her grandfather had described him. A thin waist, a godly smile on his lips—it was as if he was looking straight at her and smiling, as if he had appeared only to enchant her with his splendour. 'Come along, Rukmini, I've come to take you with me,' he seemed to be saying. Rukmini sensed that the booming waterfall, the flowing wind, the dancing trees and the plants had all succumbed to the rhythm of his flute. And she felt herself in the same rapture as them. She found herself in the throes of immense joy and boundless pain. She wanted to get up and start dancing, to dance towards Him and become one with Him. She wanted to immerse herself in the dance of the universe.

She felt she had stood up, but that only her shadow was walking towards the lake. The shadow reached the mountain track that would lead to the lake, turned around and looked at Rukmini, and smiled; her nose ring glistened as it caught the sun and then she turned again and walked around a boulder and disappeared. Rukmini felt her dupatta flutter in the wind. A tremor ran through her body; her shadow jumped into the lake.

Rukmini raised her eyes and looked. But who was that, dancing on the surface of the lake? Krishna? No, someone was dancing, but it wasn't Krishna. That's not a flute he's holding in his hand, but a cane with small red tufts and bells hanging from one end. He isn't dancing to the rhythm of divine melody but in order to express human pain.

Who is this, here? What an odd dance, full of torment. He has been looking for me; his search has brought him here. And hadn't I been calling out for him every moment? God has heard my prayers. He must be so tired. He's come from so far. Look how parched his lips are, how his feet are faltering in their steps. Oh, I fear he might fall . . .

Rukmini tried once more to get up. *Let me tell him I'm here. His eyes are searching for me. I'm here, look, on this cliff. Can you see me?* Rukmini felt her right arm rise in the air, and she felt it waving to her husband, calling him.

But why isn't he looking in my direction? Why can he not hear me? Listen, please, I'm here. She became anxious. *Why don't you look at me? I'm waving at you. What are you looking at? Here, I'm here, look here . . .*

When Lachhmi, Bhanga and Parmeshwari came to the cliff looking for Rukmini, calling out her name, she was no longer sitting on the cliff. Her body was down below, in the deep pit at the bottom of the cliff.

ॐ

That same evening—when dust hadn't yet settled after the lathi charge, and batons had only just retreated into the belts of policemen, and while the sub-inspector dusted his shoes against the cuffs of his pants and ordered his men to line up once more even as demonstrators carried their five injured men on cots and on their shoulders—the deputy commissioner, Henry Sahib, emerged into the lane, waving his right hand in front of his face, as if slapping dust for misbehaving.

The Diwan was standing on the raised platform outside the mansion. When the police charged at them, some of the demonstrators had rushed into the lane that fronted the mansion, and the police chased them there. Even now, three policemen on horseback were riding up and down the lane, keeping watch. Stones were pelted at the mansion, breaking several windows and skylights.

And now Henry Sahib—the lord and master of the entire district—had himself arrived at the scene. The Diwan was troubled. *What if he's here to express his displeasure at how things turned out? What if he starts screaming and yelling?*

The demonstration had been a first in this town. The deputy commissioner had been recently posted here, and Diwan Hukumat Rai's advice to him on how to contain the situation had been in line with British strategies of ruling. 'Sometimes direct action—force—is what's needed, Henry. What's bad and wrong should be muzzled right at its inception,' he had said to the deputy commissioner that very afternoon. It had to be a result of his advice that policemen had been ordered to charge at the demonstrators with batons, throwing their disciplined procession into disarray. After the batons had rained down for a while, the demonstrators had had no choice but to run—some climbed up trees, others disappeared into narrow lanes or hid under sitting platforms or whichever corner they could find. *But who's to know what the officer thinks? I'll be blamed for whatever didn't go well.*

It appeared to the Diwan that the officer was headed straight towards him. This sent a slight shiver down his legs. But he braced himself and decided to continue to engage as an equal. After all, as a Hindustani who had spent a number of years in England, he was allowed to.

'Hello, Henry,' the Diwan said as he climbed down from the raised platform, and continued in English, 'seen a bit of the Indian mob, haven't you? They have no guts, I tell you. You had only to wield your baton and they were running for their lives.' He laughed as he said this, then added, 'Didn't I tell you?'

He kept his trepidation to himself. *I've said what I should have; now let's see. The English are far-sighted; they always take the long-term view. It's entirely possible he thinks things went out of control because of my advice, and people were injured so badly that they had to be carried out of here. Who knows what kind of mood there is in the city? Maybe his reading is that my advice has caused more fuel to be added to the fire. If the deputy commissioner says something along these lines, I'll admit to him I made a mistake. I'll say I gave advice that I thought was best for the Empire, and that I couldn't have known the lathi charge was going to be so aggressive.*

The deputy commissioner smiled when their eyes met, and continued to smile as he came closer to the Diwan. He tapped the end of his cane on the Diwan's shoulder and said, 'You have a head over your shoulders, Diwan, I must say.'

The Diwan felt shaken up, but in a sweet, pleasing sort of way. 'Anything for the Empire, Henry,' he said emotionally. 'We both worship at the same altar!' He felt awash with self-confidence, ready to rise up to whatever the future might throw at him. He would support the Empire through everything.

As the two men walked together slowly along the lane, the Diwan's eyes roved over the houses on either side. He could feel hundreds of pairs of eyes upon him from behind windows, latticed walls and half-open doors. *How in awe they must be of me at this moment, seeing me chat so comfortably with this man—the lord and master of the district.*

They walked until they reached Kabuli Darwaza. This was where the lathi charge had started. The deputy commissioner smiled. He tapped the Diwan's shoulder once again with the end of his cane and said, 'You will soon be a Rai Bahadur, you know. I shall recommend your name.' Then he tapped the Diwan's shoulder with his cane yet again, to underline his approval of him. 'See you,' he said, turned and started walking across the maidan.

The Diwan watched him with total surrender. 'My last drop of blood for the Empire, Henry, and you know that!' he called out. But Henry was too far away by then.

Joga still has a memory of that day, however faded. He must have been five or six years old then. What a big demonstration it was! After it had been dispersed, he and his friends were walking around town and had reached the mansion. They spent a long time looking at the stones and broken pieces of glass that lay scattered everywhere. Many children had participated in the demonstration. Tilak Raj 'Azad' and his comrades had gathered boys and girls from schools, and they had all stood in a long line—the grown-ups had been at the front of the demonstration, and the children had walked behind them. But then the demonstration had been disrupted. The lathi charge had started somewhere at the head of the demonstration, and Azad Chacha had come running towards the children and taken them quickly towards Orchard of the Sheikhs, from where they were all sent to their respective homes. But by afternoon, the children started trickling out of their houses. At first they lingered around Diwan Hukumat Rai's mansion, and then they got busy playing gilli-danda.

One of them struck the short billet of wood too hard, and it landed on the overhang of the mansion's first floor. Joga looked up, and saw an owl sitting under the canopy on the roof. The kids forgot their game and watched the owl.

The slanting rays of the setting sun lit up the canopy, and the owl's wings looked yellow and its eyes sparkled. Even though the billet had fallen so close to it, the owl hadn't stirred. It didn't even flutter its wings. It just sat where it was, unbothered. Joga felt captivated by its large and beady yellow eyes.

The boys tried to make it fly away. A couple threw pebbles in its direction. It had been Joga's turn to strike the billet, so he was holding the stick. He tried to shoo the owl away by waving the stick in its general direction. Some boys jumped and flailed their arms. The owl just sat there, motionless. The boys wondered if it was a wooden toy, not a real owl. Its large eyes were wide open, and it hadn't blinked once until now—as if it saw everything, but heeded nothing.

After some time, realizing that the chances of retrieving the billet were remote, the boys began to disperse. A frail-looking servant of the mansion was sitting at the edge of the raised platform, near the mansion's gate, smoking a chillum. A small group of boys approached him for help, but he didn't even look at them. The lower part of his chillum wrapped in a dirty rag, he kept his face tilted, puffing away at the chillum and blowing out little clouds of smoke. The boys watched him, enraptured. They watched how his eyes turned red after the fourth puff. He pulled at the chillum a couple of times more, then turned the clay pipe over and tapped it against the platform to empty it before putting it into the pocket of his waistcoat.

'Our billet's landed on the roof. May we go up and get it?' Joga asked. But the red-eyed servant didn't respond.

The boys watched him nervously. Then, realizing that he was buzzed, and scared that he might just leap up and slap them, they shifted away.

Joga slid towards the gate, which the servant was sitting with his back towards, and went noiselessly into the mansion. He felt scared, but he was drawn on by the desire to see the mansion from inside.

He crossed the yard and entered a long veranda, which was really like a broad corridor. There was pin-drop silence all around. He strained his ears, but couldn't hear a sound. Not just the veranda, the entire mansion seemed steeped in silence. Countless rooms were attached to the veranda—all of them soundless. Everything seemed so inward, lost in itself. A huge head of a large animal hung from a wall. Its enormous, unblinking eyes stared out at the world.

'Ey, boy! What are you doing here?' It was a sharp voice; it made Joga tremble. It had come from one of the rooms. Joga ran as fast as he could, and stopped only after he was outside the mansion gates.

Joga had seen the Barrister Diwan innumerable times. Barrister Diwan's face was broad and dark, and he had a big moustache. He always wore an English cap over his heavy head, a black coat, black tie, white trousers and superbly polished black shoes. A gold chain hung across his chest, between the pockets of his waistcoat. Barrister Diwan always smoked an English pipe. His hands tucked into his trouser pockets, the pipe between his teeth, he'd stroll up and down the mansion's raised platform, blowing smoke. Joga had seen him like this often.

That night, as Joga sat down for dinner with his family, he told them about the owl he'd seen perched on the mansion's roof.

His mother was sitting by the stove. 'Be quiet,' she said, troubled. 'It couldn't have been an owl. Barrister Diwan is blessed with fortune; he owns so much land. Why would an owl sit on the roof of his house?'

Joga couldn't understand his mother's response.

His father was sitting near him, his back resting against the wall. He didn't say anything. Joga's two sisters were sitting to his left, eating their food.

'But Ma, I really did see an owl. The other boys saw it too.'

His mother stuck her tongue between her teeth, then said, 'You must've seen something else. Barrister Diwan is such a well-to-do man. You should say auspicious things at night.'

Seeing that the owl wouldn't be discussed any further, Joga started talking about the demonstration. That night, it would have been the topic of discussion in every home.

Anyone who saw the demonstration from afar would have seen how waves of energy seemed to travel through the row of demonstrators. Years later, when he was much older, that's how Joga remembered the demonstration—as waves, as energy. Not just once, the wave rose again and again, electrifying, exciting, charging up the crowd of demonstrators every time it rose. It travelled from Grain Market, all the way to Orchard of the Sheikhs. Joga was there, among the young boys who were part of the demonstration. He too was rocked by the wave. Only when you stepped out of the demonstration and looked did you realize how long a procession it was, how far it extended on either side. Everyone was holding up cloth banners. Joga was at one end of the procession, and the other end . . . It was far away, so far that you couldn't see it. It dissolved into a whirl. He'd stepped out of the flow once, to look. He climbed on to a high pedestal by the street and looked in the direction of Orchard of the Sheikhs. But he wasn't able to see where the demonstration ended. As he looked around, he saw Azad Chacha walking briskly towards where he was. Azad Chacha was so tall. He was wearing a white kurta-pyjamas, and his cheeks looked flushed. To Joga it seemed he was walking right towards him. He thought about how, once Azad Chacha reached him, he would lift him up on his shoulders and all his friends would know then that he was Joga's Azad Chacha, that Azad Chacha was his own and loved him dearly. But he didn't slow down; he didn't pay Joga any attention, and walked right past him.

When the demonstration had started moving, Azad Chacha and his friends had run up and down, shouting and calling out to everyone that they must continue in single file. Their faces had turned red with the effort. Even so, Azad Chacha had lifted Joga up and hoisted him on to his shoulders. It was then, looking at the demonstration from a height, from over everyone's heads, that Joga had seen the wave rise—a wave that started from one end and travelled to the other, through everyone who was part of the demonstration.

But suddenly, people had started to run. Horse riders had appeared from somewhere, and people were running helter-skelter to avoid being in their path. They were running into streets and lanes, away from the demonstration. Azad Chacha had looked in that direction for a long time, then set Joga down on the ground, gathered up all the children and led them towards Orchard of the Sheikhs.

Even now, sitting in the kitchen, Joga kept turning to look at his Azad Chacha, who was sitting behind his sisters, by the wall, eating his food.

'Of course owls will prowl on the mansion's roof now. What else is to be expected?' Azad Chacha said in his heavy voice.

Joga's father turned his head sharply towards him and asked, 'And you think demonstrations will chase the British away?'

Azad Chacha didn't reply. He shifted forward a little and pushed his plate away, towards Joga's mother. Joga was trying, but he couldn't decode his father's words.

What he had gathered from the day's exchanges was that a man had died. It is to this that Azad Chacha now turned.

'He was imprisoned for six years. Why was he thrown in jail?' Azad Chacha's chin quivered as he said this; his lips lost their shape. Joga thought Azad Chacha was going to burst into tears. Ma looked at him with unblinking eyes. She seemed to be at a loss for words. He was breathing rapidly. It was as if his lungs were trying, but they'd lost the power to exhale. Joga's heart melted for his Azad Chacha; he sensed his restlessness. Then he heard him breathe in sharply, gulp in a tear and say, 'They killed him. I wish ruin upon them.'

Another muffled cry escaped his throat. He got up, put his plate near the drain in the kitchen and, wiping his eyes with his sleeve, left the room.

Joga looked up at his brother, who was sitting across from him. His eyes were moist. His sisters' faces were ashen. His mother stared gloomily at the floor, the fingers of her hands locked into each other. 'What was the need to say anything? His heart is heavy,' she said to her husband.

Joga's father stayed quiet. He kept his lips pursed and stared at his plate. Then he said, 'So what if I said what I said? One man's death is no reason to create a ruckus. What was their relation, anyway?'

'They may not have been related, but he was an impressive man. He gave up his life for others.'

Joga's father became quiet for a while. He didn't have an answer to what his wife had said but then, as if unaffected by Azad Chacha's tears, he said, 'Are the British going to leave because of all this? Is it that simple? Does he think making the British leave is as simple as visiting a relative's house for the weekend?'

Joga was unable to follow the conversation. But he could read faces. Azad Chacha's face—his trembling chin, his words drowning in sadness, the catch in his throat, his curly, black hair; his mother—her confused look, as if she didn't care for anything except for Azad Chacha's pain. It was as if she felt it was her fault this tiny crisis had precipitated in the kitchen, and that she wished she'd never asked Azad Chacha where he'd been roaming with the kids. She'd been worried from the beginning, ever since Azad Chacha had started preparing for the demonstration by buying a drum and roaming in the lanes with it, making announcements.

Even years later, when Joga would recall this day of the demonstration, images of crowds shouting slogans, and of Azad Chacha and his friends running from here to there would flash before his eyes. He would recall how the town reverberated with the sound of drums in the days leading up to the demonstration, how the maidan near Kabuli Darwaza bustled with activity, and how Azad Chacha's group roamed through the lanes of town, singing. Joga was always asleep when the singing started, and he would be woken up by it:

> *Let our efforts bear fruit, oh Lord*
> *Let this bondage end; let our country be free!*

Those days it seemed everyone was singing this song.

Suddenly, Joga's father said to him, 'If you saw the owl, why didn't you throw a pebble and make it fly away?'

'I didn't know it was an owl. But I did throw stones at it. The other boys did as well.'

His mother said, 'What good can pebbles do?' Then after a pause she added, 'Owls come when they want to, and they leave of their own will.'

After that, as far as Joga could make out, his parents started talking about the Barrister Diwan.

'As he does, so shall he reap,' his mother muttered under her breath.

These words annoyed Joga's father. 'You should think before you speak. Who knows what your son saw on that roof and what he didn't see! And you're making pronouncements!'

'What have I said that's wrong? You know—the entire city knows—everything.'

Joga's father was quiet. But his mother said agitatedly, 'Like father like son. Did his father ever do anything good that his son will now emulate it?'

Joga felt his mother wasn't wrong, otherwise his father would surely have countered her. He would have said something sharply just once, and she would have become quiet.

Suddenly, she was laughing. It was a full, open laugh. Everyone turned to look at her. What's happened to her that she's laughing like this? But her laughter lightened the mood in the room.

'His father had become rich by cutting tails off camels' backs,' she said.

Joga's father smiled.

The children looked at each other. They had heard the story of the Trim-Tail Diwan from their mother several times. They knew he used to go around collecting camels' tails during the days the Sikhs fought the British. She had told them so many stories.

Suddenly, Joga's elder sister asked, 'Ma, what happened to that madman whom Rukmini had left at the mental asylum in Lahore?'

'Oh poor thing!' Joga's mother said. 'Rukmini went on a pilgrimage to Amarnath and died there.'

'Ma, did you know Rukmini?'

'Of course I did. She was the headmistress of the school then. She came to our house one day. She'd placed her hand on my head and said to my mother, 'I'm going to take this child into my school.' And she hugged me affectionately and patted my cheeks for a long time.'

The thought of his mother as a child confused Joga.

She was saying, 'Rukmini was really beautiful. She had such a lovely face.' Remembering Rukmini always brought tears to her eyes.

'And what became of the madman?'

'He returned to town completely treated. Really, he didn't do any strange things when he came back. The doctors had cured him. But when he saw that Rukmini wasn't in town, his mind slipped again. He started talking weirdly again. He'd roam about in the lanes and suddenly start dancing, waving that cane of his about, or stand outside the school for hours waiting for Rukmini. And when she wouldn't appear, he'd say:

> *Rukmini is a liar*
> *I swear by the Lord*
> *Rukmini is a liar!*

'He'd keep composing and reciting many such poems. He really thought Rukmini had betrayed him, and that she'd left him.

> *If only Rukmini were to laugh and talk to me one*
> *more time*
> *It would untangle the knots that riddle in my heart*
> *Without her, my good-for-nothing heart shatters*

'He'd gather small, colourful rags and hang them on his cane and dance and run through the lanes, do all kinds of antics—and when the school day ended, he'd come stand at the gate. It was as if his wait for Rukmini was renewed every day. And when she wouldn't emerge from the school, he'd start screaming again:

> *Rukmini is a liar*
> *I swear by the Lord*
> *Rukmini is a liar!*

'One day he disappeared. No one knows where he went. Someone said he'd gone to Miani, someone said something else, and yet another said something entirely different.' She shook her head. 'They're all dead now,' she said, 'why are we thinking about them?' And she turned her thoughts towards the mansion. 'If not an owl, then are lovebirds going to sit on the mansion's roof?' She brought up the owl herself, though she'd scolded Joga for talking about inauspicious things just minutes ago!

'Listen, why do you think the owl chose that house?' From her manner of speaking, it was clear her question was addressed to her husband. 'Why would it fly through forests and the wilderness to sit there, and there alone? That house has everything. The Barrister Diwan is well respected. But the house must be decaying from within. No? Owls visit ruins. They can see ruins, even when we can't. An owl can perceive ruins even where we see palaces. An owl is an emissary of time. It can sense misdeeds. That's what it is. An owl is no ordinary bird; it roams between the ages. Because it can see *trikaal*— the past, the present and the future—it can read between the layers of time. When it flies, it travels through the past and into the future. It doesn't fly to look for food; it flies because it's an emissary of time . . .'

Joga's mother talked in this vein, long into the night.

The owl sat on the roof, and Barrister Hukumat Rai, the current master of the mansion, third son of Diwan Dhanpat, sat beneath the roof, taking a pause from the flurry of the day. He needed a rest.

He'd just returned from the deputy commissioner's bungalow, where he'd been invited that evening to discuss the situation in the city, over drinks. In fact, he'd got off the phaeton and entered the mansion just moments ago. He felt quite smug, for achievements are afoot for the one who socializes with the British deputy commissioner.

His being a barrister gave him power in town. And this wasn't the town of yesteryears; today it housed the district headquarters, and it had even begun to be called a city.

Word in the city was that if you're about to murder someone, make sure to put aside one thousand rupees for Diwan Hukumat Rai, and then you can carry on and commit the murder, that too in broad daylight if you so please. No harm will come to you; your situation will be as smooth as that of a hair in a slab of butter on a warm day. Hukumat Rai wielded the same power, commanded the same veneration as his father had, before him.

Where Diwan Dhanpat used to move about in a palanquin, Barrister Hukumat Rai used a phaeton, wore black suits, smoked pipes and groomed a pointy moustache. An attendant in white uniform with a green belt always stood at the back of his phaeton.

Diwan Hukumat Rai had created a mini-England on the ground floor of the mansion. The rooms were decorated in the British style, and he lived in them in the English way. The cook would wake him up with a cup of piping hot English tea in the morning, and part the curtains at the window, just as he had been instructed to. The moment he'd get out of bed, he'd put on the dressing gown he'd bought many years ago at Oxford Street, and light his pipe. Fireplaces were made in the bedrooms and the living room, and they were lit daily during the winters. That, and a glass of whisky, kept him warm on winter evenings. It's something he'd picked up from his British friends during his student years. There were other things he'd learnt during his student years that he continued with even now. Among them were eating at a table with a fork and a knife, evening tea with cake and biscuits, and well-polished shoes.

Flowering plants lined the veranda, and a red coir mat ran between them along the entire length of the corridor. Heads of stags, and also of a cheetah, adorned the walls, accompanied by a few framed photographs showing the Diwan Sahib hunting with the British. Thick curtains hung in every room, come summer or winter. A black, round table here, a dark-brown low stool and table there, teapoys and different kinds of chairs—all the furniture was made of the best-quality oak wood. Yet a fine haze of dust hung in the rooms. You could wipe the windowsill clean with a duster, and a new layer of dust would settle on it the very next moment. At sundown, when lanterns were lit and their bright light filled the rooms, darkness seemed merely to withdraw and wait behind doors, curtains and the expensive furniture. Each night when the flames were extinguished, the mansion was cloaked in absolute darkness.

The barrister played records on the gramophone, which he had brought with him from abroad, to dispel the silence in the mansion. The gramophone would play during and after meals. Once it was turned off, silence would assert its rule over the mansion again.

The Diwan walked towards the gramophone. He was tipsy. He'd been drinking with the deputy commissioner, but on returning he'd felt like drinking some more. He was exultant—no one from this town had ever been appointed 'Rai Bahadur', and now *he* was about to be. He tottered from room to room, his drink in his hand.

Suddenly, he was laughing. He set his glass down on the teapoy and started undressing. He loosened his tie and flung it across the room; he took off the collar of his starched shirt and threw it in the opposite direction. *The servants can clean up in the morning.*

He sat down on his high bed and unbuttoned his trousers. He'd seen, when he was abroad, that it was possible to take your pants off without removing your shoes. That's how many of his English classmates took their pants off. But one leg got stuck and wouldn't come out. Because he was drunk, he wasn't quite managing the best angle. If he'd just pulled at the end of the trouser leg and slid his foot up through it, he would've managed. But he'd dropped his pants down, turned them inside out over his shoes, and was utterly stuck. He could still just untie his shoelace and take off the shoe that had got stuck in the pant leg, but he kept pulling instead. And the more he pulled, the more he failed, and the more his masculinity felt threatened. He was becoming angry.

'How dare you! How dare you not come off! I'll see about you! You . . .' He panted with the exertion of it all.

His eyes fell on the full-length mirror on the wall at the foot of the bed. He saw his reflection and his hands froze. What he saw in the mirror was a man with a bare head and one bare leg, pulling at his trousers to get them off the other leg. He had a hard time coming to terms with the fact that this was his own reflection. The man in the mirror wasn't the man he thought himself to be. He'd never imagined he'd see himself this way—pants down and head bare. How small the head looks when there's no turban on it.

'You look like one of Shah Daula's mouse children!' he mumbled to himself and reached for his turban, which was hanging from a peg on the wall, its shape intact, placed it over his head and went and stood in front of the mirror. His trousers were still pulled down, and the right trouser leg was still stuck in the heel of his shoe.

Pointing his index finger at his reflection, he said, 'Rai Bahadur! Prince Honourable! Prince Brave! Rai Bahadur Diwan Hukumat Rai! Now you look like you should. I never want to see you without a turban again, not even at home, understand?' Then he softened his gaze and said affectionately, 'Rai Bahadur!' He stumbled back towards his bed, dragging his trousers behind him.

Who knows what got into him suddenly, for he started dancing.

'You're happy, Rai Bahadur! You're happy today! These demonstrators, these . . .' He swore. Then he got busy with his trousers again.

The stout Diwan Hukumat Rai now hopped towards the window. He parted the curtain slightly, and screamed, 'Maliks! Masters of the godowns! Where are you now? Your next six generations could try and you still wouldn't become Rai Bahadurs!

'Rascals, they think so highly of themselves . . .'

And he stumbled again, and laughed again. But he stayed at the window and, changing his tune, he called out, 'Oh Henry, darling!' and sent a flying kiss into the night air.

One may be aware of one's conscious self, but each person is constituted by countless layers and there's no way of knowing when any one of these layers may get scratched, releasing a troubling memory. As he sat back down on his bed, Hukumat Rai felt the soft scent of Lajo's body mingling with his breath. 'Oh, there's no doubt this is the scent of her body,' he mumbled.

When she had come to the mansion after their wedding, Hukumat Rai had found her carefree ways very appealing. She'd comb her hair, but it would still stay entangled; when she walked, her arms and legs danced everywhere; when she spoke, she lingered on words. He found everything about her intoxicating. Whenever he set eyes on her, he felt eager to enfold her into his arms and soak in her scent. But after a few years her scent smelt stale to him and he deemed her carefree ways unrefined. When he'd just returned from England, he'd found this local girl lovely and endearing, but seven years later he shunned her as a native and started reminiscing about his dalliances in England. Something wilted inside Lajwanti, and timidity replaced the curiosity and enthusiasm that used to shine through her eyes.

But he missed her tonight—*She wasn't so bad!* Her scent had risen up from some layer of the drunk Diwan's subconscious. It had the same freshness as when he had first smelt it, and it left him restless. *She wasn't bad!* An unquenchable desire rose in him and he wanted to entwine his body with hers. He wanted to gather her slim body, her small frame into his arms—no other woman had ever fit as perfectly in his arms as she did. And her bashful smile! It always danced tantalizingly at the corners of her lips. He would kiss her and she would embrace him like a creeper entwines itself around a tree. 'She was so delicate,' he said out loud, and remembered how he'd said to her once, 'I'll embrace you so completely, it will crush your bones.' Lajo had lifted her eyes and said softly, 'Why don't you? Crush me, break my bones.' And she had nestled further into his arms, curled up around him more than she ever had. Held in his embrace, she repeated over and over again, 'Go on, crush my bones, why don't you? Go on, crush them.' He felt the warmth of her body against him and heard her voice whispering to him, 'Crush me. Go on, break my bones.'

Hukumat Rai staggered out of bed, reached for the bottle of alcohol that was lying on the table and took a gulp. *That's not how you drink in England, Hukumat Rai. You pour your alcohol in a glass and then you drink it.* But right now, he wasn't himself. And, besides, it's not like anyone was watching.

He returned to the bed. 'She was lovely. Lovely. Motherfu...' he muttered.

With a fresh round of alcohol coursing through his veins, he felt his body's restlessness subside a notch. Lajo was not in his arms, neither could she ever be. She'd been dead for twenty years now. She had burnt to death. Be that as it may, she was the one the future Rai Bahadur was desirous of today. Though, truth be told, it wasn't Lajo he was missing; it was her nubile body and its scent that he craved.

He'd begun to feel weighed down by Lajo ever since he started visiting the wealthy widow. It annoyed him that whenever he returned after meeting her, he'd find Lajo sitting on the windowsill, waiting for him. It could be late into the night, and it could be at daybreak, but he had to knock at the door just once, and it would open immediately.

The widow was clever; she had her ways and knew so many moves. She was broad-framed, had large hips and wore make-up. One look from her, and Hukumat Rai's body would light up with desire. He'd dress up well when he had to go meet her. He'd reach her house, and she would shut the door in his face. Then she'd stand on the other side of the latticed wall and watch his mounting desperation. His ardour rising, he would beg her to let him in. She'd let him beg and beseech her, and would let him in only when she felt he'd been tormented enough. Once he was inside the house, she'd often make him press her legs, and once she even made him lick the soles of her feet. Once a man gets a taste of me, he'll dance to any tune I play, she'd say. She made him get on all fours and climbed on to his back once, then made him take her all around the room. She'd laughed the entire time, and kicked him with her heels.

After all this, when he'd walk through the dark streets of the town and return home, he'd see his room—and only his room in the entire town—was still lit up by the flickering flame of a lamp. He knew Lajo would be sitting on the windowsill, waiting for him. That damn woman, he'd curse under his breath, is keeping tabs on me.

To exist, one must bite hard at insults. Eclipsed, Lajo turned into a shadow and dissolved wordlessly into the darkness. Shadows are poor proxies for existence.

She burnt to death.

Hukumat Rai heard her scream. The screams surprised and disconcerted him. But as they got louder, they annoyed him. *Can't she die without screaming so much! She's not screaming with pain; she's screaming so that the world may hear her. She's screaming to malign me, to make me the laughing stock of town . . .*

And yet, he felt tormented by her memory today. 'Motherfu . . . She was lovely.' A person like Hukumat Rai has no place for the softer emotions of life. If he had to crush someone or lick someone's feet to get ahead, or if it served his purpose to make someone trip and fall, he would. It was all the same to him. But with intoxication, even piercing desires sometimes acquire gentleness. Yearning for Lajo in this moment, he was struck anew by her innocence and sensuality. These feelings had arisen from his yearning for her body, and there they would end. But for all that, at this moment, right now, Hukumat Rai missed Lajo, and not Bitty, or Lisa, or Rosa. *Had Lajo been here, she'd have untied the knots in my heart with her nimble fingers.* And he felt Lajo's fingers unfettering the knots in his heart. He really felt them working away at him.

He heard a sound. He thought he saw the curtain move. The lamp too seemed to have flickered. *Maybe it's the wind.*

His eyes narrowed to a slit as he tried to focus. He heard the sound again; it was as if a cat had jumped into the balcony, or as if a mouse had emerged from its hole and was scampering about.

He sensed footsteps. They were approaching him. *Who can it be? Someone's come to meet me. It must be a client. The idiots—they don't let me be even at night.*

Hukumat Rai was pulling up his pants when he saw someone was standing at the door.

'Who is it? Who are you? How did you get inside?'

That someone should appear at his balcony door like this at this hour filled Hukumat Rai with terror. *Who? Who is that? What is he doing here?* He narrowed and widened his eyes by turn to focus them. He saw a tall man before him. The man's head was bare, he was fair, and he wore a white kurta-pyjamas.

'Are you a client? Have you come here to discuss a case? What's the meaning of coming to see the Barrister Sahib at this hour? Didn't anyone stop you?'

The man just stood there. *Who is this! Why isn't he saying anything?*

Hukumat Rai stood where he was. He shut his left eye and peered at the intruder through his right eye. Then he opened both his eyes.

'Who are you, you low life? Why have you come here? Why don't you answer me?'

'Don't you recognize me, Hukumat Rai?'

'Who are you?'

'I'm Tilak Raj. Tilak Raj "Azad".'

Hukumat Rai recoiled. *What is he doing here? Who let him in? I must speak with Henry Sahib and have him arrested.* He looked carefully at the face before him: fair, with a sharp moustache and residual marks from small pox. *I know him. He was the ringleader; he was the one leading the demonstration.*

'Why have you come here? What's the purpose of your visit?'

'I've come to tell you there will be another demonstration tomorrow.'

'Demonstration? What kind of demonstration?'

'The kind you got lathi-charged.'

'I? Why would I? It was the rulers who ordered the lathi charge.'

'Tirathram is dead. He just died. I came to tell you.'

'Tirathram who?'

'He was among those who were injured in the lathi charge.'

'Why did you come here? Get out of here.'

'I've come to tell you there's going to be another demonstration tomorrow. Tirathram's bier will head this demonstration. The others who were injured in today's lathi charge will follow it. And the entire town will follow them.'

Hukumat Rai looked carefully at the man. He wasn't showing any signs of leaving.

'Have this demonstration lathi-charged as well. But why stop at batons? Go after us with bullets. Today some people got confused and ran. But not tomorrow! No one will run . . . We hear you're going to be a Rai Bahadur?'

'Get out of here!'

Hukumat Rai thought he saw the curtain at the window move. Could it be that even more people had gathered outside? *I know him. He was the leader of the demonstration. He's the one who goes about town with the drummer and gets those announcements made. I should've got him arrested when the announcements started. It was a mistake not to have. Now he's in my house. He's brought others with him. Are they going to come in as well?*

Hukumat Rai heard another sound and turned to look. There was definitely some movement outside that he couldn't see from where he was. Movement: beyond the mansion's walls, in the streets, inside houses, and in houses behind those houses. Something had started to stir, and it wasn't going to stop any time soon.

Hukumat Rai turned towards the door again, but Tilak Raj was gone. He had disappeared into the deep darkness on the other side of the door.

The flame in the room continued to flicker.

Diwan Hukumat Rai finally succeeded in taking his trousers off. He threw them on the floor and sprawled on the bed, his turban still on his head. His head in the clouds, he mumbled, 'Rai Bahadur . . . Brave Prince.' Then he turned on his side and fell into deep slumber.

The sun had risen. Despite the heavy curtains, sunlight streamed into the bedroom. It woke Barrister Hukumat Rai. He lay on his bed, trying to recall the events of the previous night. Outside, a new day had dawned and he heard voices rising in the air. People were stepping out of their houses and pouring into the streets. They had been gathering to demonstrate. The town was astir. Many marched together, their voices singing in unison. The sound of their song ricocheted from the old walls of the town. They sang:

> *Let our efforts bear fruit, oh Lord*
> *Let this bondage end, let our country be free!*

PRAISE FOR THE BOOK

'Clarity of vision, evocative language, an enthralling narrative, all combine to make *Mansion* an unforgettable book . . . It is history come alive'—*Nayi Kahaniyan*

'The story relates to the transitional period between the collapse of the Khalsa Raj and the emergence of British rule in the Punjab. Breaking free from the constraints of dates and events, the author, with rare subtlety and insight, recreates a highly imaginative and authentic portrayal of men and events of the time'—*Sameeksha*

'The author has handled with rare deftness and versatility the numerous strands of the story. Not one page is redundant. What transpires in one small town epitomizes what is happening all over India. An outstanding work of fiction'—*Sheeraza*

'It is a tremendous task to trace the progress of civilization during a transitional period. The author has brilliantly succeeded in doing so'—*Alochana*

PENGUIN MODERN CLASSICS
Mansion

BHISHAM SAHNI (1915–2003) was an iconic writer who transformed the landscape of Hindi literature. Sahni was fluent in several languages—Punjabi, Hindi, Sanskrit, Urdu and English—and his oeuvre encompassed a wide range of literary forms: novels, short stories, plays, essays. *Tamas*, his best known novel, won the Sahitya Akademi Award in 1975 and was subsequently adapted into a National Award–winning film by Govind Nihalani. His other well-known novels include, among others, *Jharokhe* (published in Penguin Classics as *Boyhood*), *Basanti* and *Mayyadas Ki Marhi* (published in Penguin Classics as *Mansion*). Sahni also wrote numerous short stories (a selection of which has been published in Penguin Classics as *Middle India*), six plays and a biography of his brother, the eminent film and stage actor Balraj Sahni. His autobiography, *Aaj Ke Ateet*, is published in Penguin Classics as *Today's Pasts*.

Born in Rawalpindi, Sahni later went to college in Lahore. In his youth he became involved with the Indian People's Theatre Association as well as the Indian National Congress. After Partition, he settled down in Delhi and began to teach at Delhi University. From 1957–63, he was in the USSR to work as a translator at the Foreign Languages Publishing House, before returning to Delhi. He edited the literary journal *Nayi Kahaniyan* from 1965–67, and was the general secretary of the All-India Progressive Writers' Association from 1975–85.

Sahni was awarded the Padma Bhushan in 1998, and the Shalaka Samman, the Delhi government's highest literary prize, in 1999.

SHVETA SARDA is the translator of *Trickster City* (*Bahurupiya Shehr*) by Azra Tabassum et al. (Penguin Books India, New Delhi, 2010), co-editor of *Cybermohalla Hub* (Sternberg Press, Berlin, 2012), and editor of *With an Untimely Calendar* (National Gallery of Modern Art, New Delhi, 2014). Between 2001 and 2013, during her time at Delhi's creative adventure called Sarai, she worked with writers and practitioners in working-class neighbourhoods across the city.